IN STEP WITH THE TIMES

If you do not have time to read every issue of every science fiction magazine and anthology, you can still reap the crop of the best of those stories. Because the editors of this annual selection have done the work for you.

Every year there are fine stories by the established masters and surprising tales by newcomers. Science fiction is a flourishing and self-renewing field of literature in step with a world that is going ahead in scientific development and the working out of the world's future.

In this, the 1980 collection, you will find such familiar names as George R. R. Martin, John Varley, Larry Niven, and others.

You will also encounter brilliant new writers including Connie Willis, Tanith Lee, Somtow Sucharitkul, Orson Scott Card, and more.

We've picked the ten best—and added a special bonus story too!

Anthologies from DAW

THE 1975 ANNUAL WORLD'S BEST SF
THE 1976 ANNUAL WORLD'S BEST SF
THE 1977 ANNUAL WORLD'S BEST SF
THE 1978 ANNUAL WORLD'S BEST SF
THE 1979 ANNUAL WORLD'S BEST SF

WOLLHEIM'S WORLD'S BEST SF: Vol. 1
WOLLHEIM'S WORLD'S BEST SF: Vol. 2
WOLLHEIM'S WORLD'S BEST SF: Vol. 3

THE YEAR'S BEST HORROR STORIES: I
THE YEAR'S BEST HORROR STORIES: II
THE YEAR'S BEST HORROR STORIES: III
THE YEAR'S BEST HORROR STORIES: IV
THE YEAR'S BEST HORROR STORIES: V
THE YEAR'S BEST HORROR STORIES: VI
THE YEAR'S BEST HORROR STORIES: VII

THE YEAR'S BEST FANTASY STORIES: 1
THE YEAR'S BEST FANTASY STORIES: 2
THE YEAR'S BEST FANTASY STORIES: 3
THE YEAR'S BEST FANTASY STORIES: 4
THE YEAR'S BEST FANTASY STORIES: 5

AMAZONS!

HEROIC FANTASY

ASIMOV PRESENTS THE GREAT SF STORIES: 1
ASIMOV PRESENTS THE GREAT SF STORIES: 2
ASIMOV PRESENTS THE GREAT SF STORIES: 3

THE 1980 ANNUAL WORLD'S BEST SF

Edited by

DONALD A. WOLLHEIM

with Arthur W. Saha

DAW BOOKS, INC.

DONALD A. WOLLHEIM, PUBLISHER

1633 Broadway, New York, N.Y. 10019

Cover art by Jack Gaughan.

FIRST PRINTING, MAY 1980

1 2 3 4 5 6 7 8 9

PRINTED IN U.S.A.

Table of Contents

INTRODUCTION

Recently we spent an evening with a well-known science fiction writer and his wife whose hobby is world travel. Present also were another couple with the same itching foot, and the evening was spent listening to reminiscences of their visits to the most remote and exotic places on the surface of this planet, including some rarely visited clusters of islands in the Indian Ocean. At one point we ventured to ask why, having seen dozens of primitive communities, they still wanted to see more.

We were pounced upon with the assertion that, while these communities may be poor and primitive, each had its own quaint customs and unique forms of art. Well, we have given this a lot of thought, inquiring of ourselves why we lacked the compulsion to visit with wide eyes communities of semi-paupers in no-plumbing comfortless homes, lacking vision of the world beyond their village boundaries, condemned to relatively short lives, scant medicine (if any), illiteracy, monotonous diets, and unchanging futures.

Yes, we accept that the superstructures of these societies are different. After all, these people are *homo sapiens*, with brains as good as any, and they have imaginations, and each community has created a mental, religious and social superstructure to its own concepts, limited though their horizons may be. But the basics, the elemental facts of life that put food into their stomachs and clothes (if any) on their backs, are the same essentially the world over.

You could pluck a family from any of thousands of small illiterate villages in Asia, Africa, Oceanica, or Latin America, and switch it with a similar family half a world away, and in a few weeks, once the family mastered the few hundred words that constitute the effective working language of these communities, and got the hang of the changed date for market day, and the nature of the crop that would have to be scratched out of the small plot of ground, they would soon be right at home, indistinguishable from the rest of the village. Because the basics of primitive day-to-day existence are all the same: simple, hard, poorly rewarded, stultifying to the imagination and to ambition, ignorant, and sufficient only for subsistence and a life expectancy of about thirty-five years.

This is the way it was for all humanity for hundreds of generations in the past. Things were even simpler and rougher when humanity was back in the hunter-gatherer stage which preceded agriculture. There must have been thousands of virtually unchanging generations in which our ancestors thought that was all there could be to life. Just about two jumps above the beasts and that was it. The superstructures which made the difference were the by-products of an oversized brain which imagined that which it could not explain.

But everything changed in the past five thousand years for some communities. In the past one thousand years things changed even more. And during the past hundred and fifty years life for some changed to a startling degree. What happened was the creation and the flowering of the high technology, high energy society that has become the way of life today in some parts of the world—North America, Western Europe, Japan, and here and there in large urban centers elsewhere.

Now we are at a crisis point, a transitional phase of human society. To maintain this high technology culture we need energy, we need education, we need a maximum display of human ingenuity. To fail is to drop slowly backward to the level of our primitive ancestors. Our horizons today are infinite, stretching to the unseen boundaries of the entire cosmos. Our imagination, based on the progress of scientific investigation and technological innovation can logically conjecture lives of luxury, health, and happiness such as could never have been projected before—and these visions are capable of achievement for future generations if . . .

. . . if the sources of energy do not run out too soon . . . if research in science does not dry up . . . if young people do not become entrapped by the apologetics for poverty which emanate from the old ignorant writings and the primitive heritage we all still share.

Energy, if it is not to be limited to the finite supplies of oil and coal (and they are *finite*), must be solar and nuclear. The problem of how to harness these forces must be solved within the limited time bounded by the existing reserves of the old fuels—or else it is back to the mud huts for all time to come.

Nothing in nature—or the universe—stands still. If you do not go forward, you must go backward.

The safest means of obtaining both forms of energy is via the solar power accumulator satellite. Research and development have been done on these but thus far they have not been brought to the public's attention nor received the political backing necessary. Oil is occupying the world too much. But these power-source satellites will come—they are inevitable and will include the use of the lunar surface for nuclear plants—and they represent the guarantee of high technology living for all humanity for the indefinite future. They also mean that space flight is an absolute necessity if this is to be achieved.

So science fiction readers have a stake in space flight (as they have always had) that means more than just adventures on exotic planets or sightseeing among the stars. It is either space or back to the jungle.

A lecture of this sort may seem out of place in an anthology of the year's best science fiction but it is not. Because science fiction does reflect the advanced conjectures of the superstructure of a high technology society. This previous year's stories reflect very much the deep controversy that is beginning to sink into the consciousness of civilized people everywhere.

No, these stories do not deal with oil prices and allotments of energy. That is not the function of science fiction. One of the aspects of this high technology derived literature is concern with humanity as it may develop in that new era, with humanity as it confronts space and the infinite, with humanity as it adjusts, sometimes painfully, to a future that is not limited to the cabbage patch and the village shaman.

Utopianism is a strong part of science fiction's heritage, but utopias must be tempered with understanding of human nature—and human nature is violent, argumentative, fallible, and given to endless fantasizing.

Going over the novelettes and short stories of the year we were struck with this transition-period philosophical concern. Will we break away from the deeply entrenched heritage of our millions-years ancestry? If so, how? How will men reconcile the philosophies of today with the conditions of a vast tomorrow?

It was a fertile year for assessments of what is likely to come. There are some very provocative stories here, calculated to make you weigh the values of today. So here they are, our pick of the ten best and most memorable stories of the previous year—plus one extra for a very special reason that you will learn when you come to it.

—DONALD A. WOLLHEIM

THE WAY OF CROSS AND DRAGON

by George R. R. Martin

The orthodoxies of all established churches have two contradictory things in common. First, at any specific time they believe that they represent the final and absolute word on the Creator and the Duties of Man. Second, they invariably keep shifting their interpretation of their doctrines to conform with the constantly altering conditions and politics of men. George R. R. Martin, who has shown a very perceptive understanding of anthropology and its permutations, projects this paradox onto the screen of a populated galaxy.

"Heresy," he told me. The brackish waters of his pool sloshed gently.

"Another one?" I said wearily. "There are so many these days."

My Lord Commander was displeased by that comment. He shifted position heavily, sending ripples up and down the pool. One broke over the side, and a sheet of water slid across the tiles of the receiving chamber. My boots were soaked yet again. I accepted that philosophically. I had worn my worst boots, well aware that wet feet were among the inescapable consequences of paying call on Torgathon Nine-

Klariis Tûn, elder of the ka-Thane people, and also Archbishop of Vess, Most Holy Father of the Four Vows, Grand Inquisitor of the Order Militant of the Knights of Jesus Christ, and counselor to His Holiness Pope Daryn XXI of New Rome.

"Be there as many heresies as stars in the sky, each single one is no less dangerous, Father," the archbishop said solemnly. "As Knights of Christ, it is our ordained task to fight them one and all. And I must add that this new heresy is particularly foul."

"Yes, my Lord Commander," I replied. "I did not intend to make light of it. You have my apologies. The mission to Finnegan was most taxing. I had hoped to ask you for a leave of absence from my duties. I need rest, a time for thought and restoration."

"Rest?" The archbishop moved again in his pool, only a slight shift of his immense bulk, but it was enough to send a fresh sheet of water across the floor. His black, pupilless eyes blinked at me. "No, Father, I am afraid that is out of the question. Your skills and your experience are vital for this new mission." His bass tones seemed to soften somewhat then. "I have not had time to go over your reports on Finnegan," he said. "How did your work go?"

"Badly," I told him, "though ultimately I think we will prevail. The Church is strong on Finnegan. When our attempts at reconciliation were rebuffed, I put some standards into the right hands, and we were able to shut down the heretics' newspaper and broadcasting facilities. Our friends also made certain that their legal actions came to nothing."

"That is not *badly*," the archbishop said. "You won a considerable victory for the Lord and the Church."

"There were riots, my Lord Commander," I said. "More than a hundred of the heretics were killed, and a dozen of our own people. I fear there will be more violence before the matter is finished. Our priests are attacked if they so much as enter the city where the heresy has taken root. Their leaders risk their lives if they leave that city. I had hoped to avoid such hatreds, such bloodshed."

"Commendable, but not realistic," said Archbishop Torgathon. He blinked at me again, and I remembered that among people of his race blinking is a sign of impatience. "The blood of martyrs must sometimes be spilled, and the blood of heretics as well. What matters it if a being surrenders his life, so long as his soul is saved?"

"Indeed," I agreed. Despite his impatience, Torgathon would lecture me for another hour if given a chance. That prospect dismayed me. The receiving chamber was not designed for human comfort, and I did not wish to remain any longer than necessary. The walls were damp and moldy, the air hot and humid and thick with the rancid-butter smell characteristic of the ka-Thane. My collar was chafing my neck raw. I was sweating beneath my cassock, my feet were thoroughly soaked, and my stomach was beginning to churn.

I pushed ahead to the business at hand. "You say this new heresy is unusually foul, my Lord Commander?"

"It is," he said.

"Where has it started?"

"On Arion, a world some three weeks' distance from Vess. A human world entirely. I cannot understand why you humans are so easily corrupted. Once a ka-Thane has found the faith, he would scarcely abandon it."

"That is well known," I replied politely. I did not mention that the number of ka-Thane to find the faith was vanishingly small. They were a slow, ponderous people, and most of their vast millions showed no interest in learning any ways other than their own, or following any creed but their own ancient religion. Torgathon Nine-Klariis Tûn was an anomaly. He had been among the first converts almost two centuries ago, when Pope Vidas L had ruled that nonhumans might serve as clergy. Given his great life span and the iron certainty of his belief, it was no wonder that Torgathon had risen as far as he had, despite the fact that fewer than a thousand of his race had followed him into the Church. He had at least a century of life remaining to him. No doubt he would someday be Torgathon Cardinal Tûn, should he squelch enough heresies. The times are like that.

"We have little influence on Arion," the archbishop was saying. His arms moved as he spoke, four ponderous clubs of mottled green-gray flesh churning the water, and the dirty white cilia around his breathing hole trembled with each word. "A few priests, a few churches, some believers, but no power to speak of. The heretics already outnumber us on this world. I rely on your intellect, your shrewdness. Turn this calamity into an opportunity. This heresy is so palpable that you can easily disprove it. Perhaps some of the deluded will turn to the true way."

"Certainly," I said. "And the nature of this heresy? What must I disprove?" It is a sad indication of my own troubled faith to add that I did not really care. I have dealt with too many heresies. Their beliefs and their questionings echo in my head and trouble my dreams at night. How can I be sure of my own faith? The very edict that had admitted Torgathon into the clergy had caused a half-dozen worlds to repudiate the Bishop of New Rome, and those who had followed that path would find a particularly ugly heresy in the massive naked (save for a damp Roman collar) alien who floated before me and wielded the authority of the Church in four great webbed hands. Christianity is the greatest single human religion, but that means little. The non-Christians outnumber us five to one, and there are well over seven hundred Christian sects, some almost as large as the One True Interstellar Catholic Church of Earth and the Thousand Worlds. Even Daryn XXI, powerful as he is, is only one of seven to claim the title of Pope. My own belief was strong once, but I have moved too long among heretics and nonbelievers, and even my prayers do not make the doubts go away now. So it was that I felt no horror—only a sudden intellectual interest—when the archbishop told me the nature of the heresy on Arion.

"They have made a saint," he said, "out of Judas Iscariot."

As a senior in the Knights Inquisitor, I command my own starship, which it pleases me to call *Truth of Christ*. Before the craft was assigned to me, it was named the *St. Thomas*, after the apostle, but I did not feel a saint notorious for doubting was an appropriate patron for a ship enlisted in the fight against heresy. I have no duties aboard the *Truth*, which is crewed by six brothers and sisters of the Order of St. Christopher the Far-Traveling and captained by a young woman I hired away from a merchant trader.

I was therefore able to devote the entire three-week voyage from Vess to Arion to a study of the heretical Bible, a copy of which had been given to me by the archbishop's administrative assistant. It was a thick, heavy, handsome book, bound in dark leather, its pages edged with gold leaf, with many splendid interior illustrations in full color with holographic enhancement. Remarkable work, clearly done by someone who loved the all-but-forgotten art of bookmaking. The paintings reproduced inside—the originals were to be found on the walls of the House of St. Judas on Arion, I gathered—were masterful, if blasphemous, as much high art as the Tammerwens and RoHallidays that adorn the Great Cathedral of St. John on New Rome.

Inside, the book bore an imprimatur indicating that it had been approved by Lukyan Judasson, First Scholar of the order of St. Judas Iscariot.

It was called *The Way of Cross and Dragon.*

I read it as the *Truth of Christ* slid between the stars, at first taking copious notes to better understand the heresy that I must fight, but later simply absorbed by the strange, convoluted, grotesque story it told. The words of the text had passion and power and poetry.

Thus it was that I first encountered the striking figure of St. Judas Iscariot, a complex, ambitious, contradictory, and altogether extraordinary human being.

He was born of a whore in the fabled ancient city-state of Babylon on the same day that the Savior was born in Bethlehem, and he spent his childhood in alleys and gutters, selling his own body when he had to, pimping when he became older. As a youth, he began to experiment with the dark arts, and before the age of twenty he was a skilled necromancer. That was when he became Judas the Dragon-Tamer, the first and only man to bend to his will the most fearsome of God's creatures, the great winged fire lizards of Old Earth. The book held a marvelous painting of Judas in some great dank cavern, his eyes aflame as he wielded a glowing lash to keep at bay a mountainous green-gold dragon. Beneath his arm is a woven basket, its lid slightly ajar, and the tiny scaled heads of three dragon chicks are peering from within. A fourth infant dragon is crawling up his sleeve. That was in the first chapter of his life.

In the second, he was Judas the Conqueror, Judas the Dragon-King, Judas of Babylon, the Great Usurper. Astride the greatest of his dragons, with an iron crown on his head and a sword in his hand, he made Babylon the capital of the greatest empire Old Earth had ever known, a realm that stretched from Spain to India. He reigned from a dragon throne amid the Hanging Gardens he had caused to be constructed, and it was there he sat when he tried Jesus of Nazareth, the troublemaking prophet who had been dragged before him bound and bleeding. Judas was not a patient man, and he made Christ bleed still more before he was through with Him. And when Jesus would not answer his questions, Judas—contemptuous—had Him cast back out into the streets. But first Judas ordered his guards to cut off Christ's legs. "Healer," he said, "heal thyself."

Then came the Repentance, the vision in the night, and Judas Iscariot gave up his crown and his dark arts and his riches, to follow the man he had crippled. Despised and taunted by those he had tyrannized, Judas became the Legs of the Lord, and for a year he carried Jesus on his back to the far corners of the realm he had once ruled. When Jesus did finally heal Himself, then Judas walked at His side, and from that time forth he was Jesus' trusted friend and counselor, the first and foremost of the Twelve. Finally, Jesus gave Judas the gift of tongues, recalled and sanctified the dragons that Judas had sent away, and sent his disciple forth on a solitary ministry across the oceans, "to spread My Word where I cannot go."

There came a day when the sun went dark at noon and the ground trembled, and Judas swung his dragon around on ponderous wings and flew back across the raging seas. But when he reached the city of Jerusalem, he found Christ dead on the cross.

In that moment his faith faltered, and for the next three days the Great Wrath of Judas was like a storm across the ancient world. His dragons razed the Temple in Jerusalem and drove the people from the city and struck as well at the great seats of power in Rome and Babylon. And when he found the others of the Twelve and questioned them and learned of how the one named Simon-called-Peter had three times betrayed the Lord, he strangled Peter with his own hands and fed the corpse to his dragons. Then he sent those dragons forth to start fires throughout the world, funeral pyres for Jesus of Nazareth.

And Jesus rose on the third day, and Judas wept, but his tears could not turn Christ's anger, for in his wrath he had betrayed all of Christ's teachings.

So Jesus called back the dragons, and they came, and everywhere the fires went out. And from their bellies he called forth Peter and made him whole again, and gave him dominion over the Church.

Then the dragons died, and so, too, did all dragons everywhere, for they were the living sigil of the power and wisdom of Judas Iscariot, who had sinned greatly. And He took from Judas the gift of tongues and the power of healing He had given, and even his eyesight, for Judas had acted as a man blind (there was a fine painting of the blinded Judas weeping over the bodies of his dragons). And He told Judas that for long ages he would be remembered only as Betrayer, and people would curse his name, and all that he had been and done would be forgotten.

But then, because Judas had loved Him so, Christ gave him a boon, an extended life, during which he might travel and think on his sins and finally come to forgiveness, and only then die.

And that was the beginning of the last chapter in the life of Judas Iscariot, but it was a very long chapter indeed. Once Dragon-King, once the friend of Christ, now he became only a blind traveler, outcast and friendless, wandering all the cold roads of the earth, living even when all the cities and people and things he had known were dead. And Peter, the first Pope and ever his enemy, spread far and wide the tale of how Judas had sold Christ for thirty pieces of silver, until Judas dared not even use his true name. For a time he called himself just Wandering Ju', and afterward many other names.

He lived more than a thousand years, and became a preacher, and a healer, and a lover of animals, and was hunted and persecuted when the Church that Peter had founded became bloated and corrupt. But he had a great deal of time, and at last he found wisdom and a sense of peace, and finally Jesus came to him on a long-postponed deathbed, and they were reconciled, and Judas wept once again. And before he died, Christ promised that He would permit a few to remember who and what Judas had been, and that with the passage of centuries the news would spread, until finally Peter's Lie was displaced and forgotten.

Such was the life of St. Judas Iscariot, as related in *The Way of Cross and Dragon.* His teachings were there as well, and the apocryphal books that he had allegedly written.

When I had finished the volume, I lent it to Arla-k-Bau, the captain of the *Truth of Christ.* Arla was a gaunt, pragmatic woman of no particular faith, but I valued her opinion. The others of my crew, the good sisters and brothers of St. Christopher, would only have echoed the archbishop's religious horror.

"Interesting," Arla said when she returned the book to me.

I chuckled. "Is that all?"

She shrugged. "It makes a nice story. An easier read than your Bible, Damien, and more dramatic as well."

"True," I admitted. "But it's absurd. An unbelievable tangle of doctrine, apocrypha, mythology, and superstition.

Entertaining, yes, certainly. Imaginative, even daring. But ridiculous, don't you think? How can you credit dragons? A legless Christ? Peter being pieced together after being devoured by four monsters?"

Arla's grin was taunting. "Is that any sillier than water changing into wine, or Christ walking on the waves, or a man living in the belly of a fish?" Arla-k-Bau liked to jab at me. It had been a scandal when I selected a nonbeliever as my captain, but she was very good at her job, and I liked her around to keep me sharp. She had a good mind, Arla did, and I valued that more than blind obedience. Perhaps that was a sin in me.

"There is a difference," I said.

"Is there?" she snapped back. Her eyes saw through my masks. "Ah, Damien, admit it. You rather liked this book."

I cleared my throat. "It piqued my interest," I acknowledged. I had to justify myself. "You know the kind of matter I deal with ordinarily. Dreary little doctrinal deviations, obscure quibblings on theology somehow blown all out of proportion, bald-faced political maneuverings designed to set some ambitious planetary bishop up as a new pope, or to wring some concession or other from New Rome or Vess. The war is endless, but the battles are dull and dirty. They exhaust me, spiritually, emotionally, physically. Afterward I feel drained and guilty." I tapped the book's leather cover. "This is different. The heresy must be crushed, of course, but I admit that I am anxious to meet this Lukyan Judasson."

"The artwork is lovely as well," Arla said, flipping through the pages of *The Way of Cross and Dragon* and stopping to study one especially striking plate. Judas weeping over his dragons, I think. I smiled to see that it had affected her as much as me. Then I frowned.

That was the first inkling I had of the difficulties ahead.

So it was that the *Truth of Christ* came to the porcelain city Ammadon on the world of Arion, where the Order of St. Judas Iscariot kept its House.

Arion was a pleasant, gentle world, inhabited for these past three centuries. Its population was under nine million; Ammadon, the only real city, was home to two of those millions. The technological level was medium high, but chiefly imported. Arion had little industry and was not an innovative world, except perhaps artistically. The arts were quite important here, flourishing and vital. Religious freedom was a basic tenet of the society, but Arion was not a religious world either, and the majority of the populace lived devoutly secular lives. The most popular religion was Aestheticism, which hardly counts as a religion at all. There were also Taoists, Erikaners, Old True Christers, and Children of the Dreamer, along with a dozen lesser sects.

And finally there were nine churches of the One True Interstellar Catholic faith. There had been twelve.

The three others were now houses of Arion's fastest-growing faith, the Order of St. Judas Iscariot, which also had a dozen newly built churches of its own.

The bishop of Arion was a dark, severe man with close-cropped black hair who was not at all happy to see me. "Damien Har Veris!" he exclaimed in some wonder when I called on him at his residence. "We have heard of you, of course, but I never thought to meet or host you. Our numbers are small here—"

"And growing smaller," I said. "A matter of some concern to my Lord Commander, Archbishop Torgathon. Apparently you are less troubled, Excellency, since you did not see fit to report the activities of this sect of Judas worshipers."

He looked briefly angry at the rebuke, but quickly he swallowed his temper. Even a bishop can fear a Knight Inquisitor. "We are concerned, of course," he said. "We do all we can to combat the heresy. If you have advice that will help us, I will be more than glad to listen."

"I am an Inquisitor of the Order Militant of the Knights of Jesus Christ," I said bluntly. "I do not give advice, Excellency. I take action. To that end I was sent to Arion, and that is what I shall do. Now tell me what you know about this heresy and this First Scholar, this Lukyan Judasson."

"Of course, Father Damien," the bishop began. He signaled for a servant to bring us a tray of wine and cheese, and began to summarize the short, but explosive, history of the Judas cult. I listened, polishing my nails on the crimson lapel of my jacket, until the black paint gleamed brilliantly, interrupting from time to time with a question. Before he had half-finished, I was determined to visit Lukyan personally. It seemed the best course of action.

And I had wanted to do it all along.

Appearances were important on Arion, I gathered, and I deemed it necessary to impress Lukyan with my self and my station. I wore my best boots, sleek dark handmade boots of

Roman leather that had never seen the inside of Torgathon's receiving chamber, and a severe black suit with deep burgundy lapels and stiff collar. From around my neck hung a splendid crucifix of pure gold; my collar pin was a matching golden sword, the sigil of the Knights Inquisitor. Brother Denis painted my nails carefully, all black as ebony, and darkened my eyes as well, and used a fine white powder on my face. When I glanced in the mirror, I frightened even myself. I smiled, but only briefly. It ruined the effect.

I walked to the House of St. Judas Iscariot. The streets of Ammadon were wide and spacious and golden, lined by scarlet trees called whisperwinds, whose long, drooping tendrils did indeed seem to whisper secrets to the gentle breeze. Sister Judith came with me. She is a small woman, slight of build even in the cowled coveralls of the Order of St. Christopher. Her face is meek and kind, her eyes wide and youthful and innocent. I find her useful. Four times now she has killed those who attempted to assault me.

The House itself was newly built. Rambling and stately, it rose from amid gardens of small bright flowers and seas of golden grass, and the gardens were surrounded by a high wall. Murals covered both the outer wall around the property and the exterior of the building itself. I recognized a few of them from *The Way of Cross and Dragon* and stopped briefly to admire them before walking on through the main gate. No one tried to stop us. There were no guards, not even a receptionist. Within the walls, men and women strolled languidly through the flowers, or sat on benches beneath silverwoods and whisperwinds.

Sister Judith and I paused, then made our way directly to the House itself.

We had just started up the steps when a man appeared from within; he stood waiting in the doorway. He was blond and fat, with a great wiry beard that framed a slow smile, and he wore a flimsy robe that fell to his sandaled feet, and on the robe were dragons bearing the silhouette of a man holding a cross.

When I reached the top of the steps, the man bowed to me. "Father Damien Har Veris of the Knights Inquisitor," he said. His smile widened. "I greet you in the name of Jesus, and St. Judas. I am Lukyan."

I made a note to myself to find out which of the bishop's staff was feeding information to the Judas cult, but my composure did not break. I have been a Knight Inquisitor for a long, long time. "Father Lukyan Mo," I said, taking his hand, "I have questions to ask of you." I did not smile.

He did. "I thought you might," he said.

Lukyan's office was large but spartan. Heretics often have a simplicity that the officers of the true Church seem to have lost. He did have one indulgence, however.

Dominating the wall behind his desk/console was the painting I had already fallen in love with, the blinded Judas weeping over his dragons.

Lukyan sat down heavily and motioned me to a second chair. We had left Sister Judith outside, in the waiting chamber. "I prefer to stand, Father Lukyan," I said, knowing it gave me an advantage.

"Just Lukyan," he said. "Or Luke, if you prefer. We have little use for titles here."

"You are Father Lukyan Mo, born here on Arion, educated in the seminary on Cathaday, a former priest of the One True Interstellar Catholic Church of Earth and the Thousand Worlds," I said. "I will address you as befits your station, Father. I expect you to reciprocate. Is that understood?"

"Oh, yes," he said amiably.

"I am empowered to strip you of your right to administer the sacraments, to order you shunned and excommunicated for this heresy you have formulated. On certain worlds I could even order your death."

"But not on Arion," Lukyan said quickly. "We're very tolerant here. Besides, we outnumber you." He smiled. "As for the rest, well, I don't perform those sacraments much anyway, you know. Not for years. I'm First Scholar now. A teacher, a thinker. I show others the way, help them find the faith. Excommunicate me if it will make you happy, Father Damien. Happiness is what all of us seek."

"You have given up the faith then, Father Lukyan?" I said. I deposited my copy of *The Way of Cross and Dragon* on his desk. "But I see you have found a new one." Now I did smile, but it was all ice, all menace, all mockery. "A more ridiculous creed I have yet to encounter. I suppose you will tell me that you have spoken to God, that He trusted you with this new revelation, so that you might clear the good name, such that it is, of Holy Judas?"

Now Lukyan's smile was very broad indeed. He picked up the book and beamed at me.

"Oh, no," he said. "No, I made it all up."

That stopped me. "What?"

"I made it all up," he repeated. He hefted the book fondly. "I drew on many sources, of course, especially the Bible, but I do think of *Cross and Dragon* mostly as my own work. It's rather good, don't you agree? Of course, I could hardly put my name on it, proud as I am of it, but I did include my imprimatur. Did you notice that? It was the closest I dared come to a by-line."

I was speechless only for a moment. Then I grimaced. "You startle me," I admitted. "I expected to find an inventive madman, some poor self-deluded fool firm in his belief that he had spoken to God. I've dealt with such fanatics before. Instead I find a cheerful cynic who has invented a religion for his own profit. I think I prefer the fanatics. You are beneath contempt, Father Lukyan. You will burn in hell for eternity."

"I doubt it," Lukyan said, "but you do mistake me, Father Damien. I am no cynic, nor do I profit from my dear St. Judas. Truthfully, I lived more comfortably as a priest of your own Church. I do this because it is my vocation."

I sat down. "You confuse me," I said. "Explain."

"Now I am going to tell you the truth," he said. He said it in an odd way, almost as a cant. "I am a Liar," he added.

"You want to confuse me with child's paradoxes," I snapped.

"No, no," he smiled. "A *Liar*. With a capital. It is an organization, Father Damien. A religion, you might call it. A great and powerful faith. And I am the smallest part of it."

"I know of no such church," I said.

"Oh, no, you wouldn't. It's secret. It has to be. You can understand that, can't you? People don't like being lied to."

"I do not like being lied to," I said.

Lukyan looked wounded. "I told you this would be the truth, didn't I? When a Liar says that, you can believe him. How else could we trust each other?"

"There are many of you," I said. I was starting to think that Lukyan was a madman after all, as fanatic as any heretic, but in a more complex way. Here was a heresy within a heresy, but I recognized my duty—to find the truth of things and set them right.

"Many of us," Lukyan said, smiling. "You would be surprised, Father Damien, really you would. But there are some things I dare not tell you."

"Tell me what you dare, then."

"Happily," said Lukyan Judasson. "We Liars, like all other religions, have several truths we take on faith. Faith is always required. There are some things that cannot be proved. We believe that life is worth living. That is an article of faith. The purpose of life is to live, to resist death, perhaps to defy entropy."

"Go on," I said, growing even more interested despite myself.

"We also believe that happiness is a good, something to be sought after."

"The Church does not oppose happiness," I said dryly.

"I wonder," Lukyan said. "But let us not quibble. Whatever the Church's position on happiness, it does preach belief in an afterlife, in a supreme being, and a complex moral code."

"True."

"The Liars believe in no afterlife, no God. We see the universe as it *is*, Father Damien, and these naked truths are cruel ones. We who believe in life, and treasure it, will die. Afterward there will be nothing, eternal emptiness, blackness, nonexistence. In our living there has been no purpose, no poetry, no meaning. Nor do our deaths possess these qualities. When we are gone, the universe will not long remember us, and shortly it will be as if we had never lived at all. Our worlds and our universe will not long outlive us. Ultimately entropy will consume all, and our puny efforts cannot stay that awful end. It will be gone. It has never been. It has never mattered. The universe itself is doomed, transitory, and certainly it is uncaring."

I slid back in my chair, and a shiver went through me as I listened to poor Lukyan's dark words. I found myself fingering my crucifix. "A bleak philosophy," I said, "as well as a false one. I have had that fearful vision myself. I think all of us do, at some point. But it is not so, Father. My faith sustains me against such nihilism. Faith is a shield against despair."

"Oh, I know that, my friend, my Knight Inquisitor," Lukyan said. "I'm glad to see you understand so well. You are almost one of us already."

I frowned.

"You've touched the heart of it," Lukyan continued. "The truths, the great truths—and most of the lesser ones as well—they are unbearable for most men. We find our shield in faith. Your faith, my faith, any faith. It doesn't matter, so long as we *believe*, really and truly believe, in whatever lie we cling to." He fingered the ragged edges of his great blond beard. "Our psychs have always told us that believers are the happy ones, you know. They may believe in Christ or Buddha or Erika Stormjones, in reincarnation or immortality or nature, in the power of love or the platform of a political faction, but it all comes to the same thing. They believe. They are happy. It is the ones who have seen truth who despair, and kill themselves. The truths are so vast, the faiths so little, so poorly made, so riddled with errors and contradictions. We see around them and through them, and then we feel the weight of darkness on us, and we can no longer be happy."

I am not a slow man. I knew, by then, where Lukyan Judasson was going. "Your Liars invent faiths."

He smiled. "Of all sorts. Not only religious. Think of it. We know truth for the cruel instrument it is. Beauty is infinitely preferable to truth. We invent beauty. Faiths, political movements, high ideals, belief in love and fellowship. All of them are lies. We tell those lies, and others, endless others. We improve on history and myth and religion, make each more beautiful, better, easier to believe in. Our lies are not perfect, of course. The truths are too big. But perhaps someday we will find one great lie that all humanity can use. Until then, a thousand small lies will do."

"I think I do not care for you Liars very much," I said with a cold, even fervor. "My whole life has been a quest for truth."

Lukyan was indulgent. "Father Damien Har Veris, Knight Inquisitor, I know you better than that. You are a Liar yourself. You do good work. You ship from world to world, and on each you destroy the foolish, the rebels, the questioners who would bring down the edifice of the vast lie that you serve."

"If my lie is so admirable," I said, "then why have you abandoned it?"

"A religion must fit its culture and society, work with them, not against them. If there is conflict, contradiction, then the lie breaks down, and the faith falters. Your Church is good for many worlds, Father, but not for Arion. Life is too kind here, and your faith is stern. Here we love beauty, and your faith offers too little. So we have improved it. We studied this world for a long time. We know its psychological profile. St. Judas will thrive here. He offers drama, and color, and much beauty—the aesthetics are admirable. His is a tragedy with a happy ending, and Arion dotes on such stories. And the dragons are a nice touch. I think your own Church ought to find a way to work in dragons. They are marvelous creatures."

"Mythical," I said.

"Hardly," he replied. "Look it up." He grinned at me. "You see, really, it all comes back to faith. Can you really know what happened three thousand years ago? You have one Judas, I have another. Both of us have books. Is yours true? Can you really believe that? I have been admitted only to the first circle of the order of Liars. So I do not know all our secrets, but I know that we are very old. It would not surprise me to learn that the gospels were written by men very much like me. Perhaps there never was a Judas at all. Or a Jesus."

"I have faith that that is not so," I said.

"There are a hundred people in this building who have a deep and very real faith in St. Judas and the Way of Cross and Dragon," Lukyan said. "Faith is a very good thing. Do you know that the suicide rate on Arion has decreased by almost a third since the Order of St. Judas was founded?"

I remember rising slowly from my chair. "You are as fanatical as any heretic I have ever met, Lukyan Judasson," I told him. "I pity you the loss of your faith."

Lukyan rose with me. "Pity yourself, Damien Har Veris," he said. "I have found a new faith and a new cause, and I am a happy man. You, my dear friend, are tortured and miserable."

"That is a lie!" I am afraid I screamed.

"Come with me," Lukyan said. He touched a panel on his wall, and the great painting of Judas weeping over his dragons slid up out of sight, and there was a stairway leading down into the ground. "Follow me," he said.

In the cellar was a great glass vat full of pale green fluid, and in it a *thing* was floating—a thing very like an ancient embryo, aged and infantile at the same time, naked, with a huge head and a tiny atrophied body. Tubes ran from its arms and legs and genitals, connecting it to the machinery that kept it alive.

When Lukyan turned on the lights, it opened its eyes. They were large and dark, and they looked into my soul.

"This is my colleague," Lukyan said, patting the side of the vat. "Jon Azure Cross, a Liar of the fourth circle."

"And a telepath," I said with a sick certainty. I had led pogroms against other telepaths, children mostly, on other worlds. The Church teaches that the psionic powers are a trap of Satan's. They are not mentioned in the Bible. I have never felt good about those killings.

"Jon read you the moment you entered the compound," Lukyan said, "and notified me. Only a few of us know that he is here. He helps us lie most efficiently. He knows when faith is true and when it is feigned. I have an implant in my skull. Jon can talk to me at all times. It was he who initially recruited me into the Liars. He knew my faith was hollow. He felt the depth of my despair."

Then the thing in the tank spoke, its metallic voice coming from a speaker-grill in the base of the machine that nurtured it. *"And I feel yours, Damien Hars Veris, empty priest. Inquisitor, you have asked too many questions. You are sick at heart, and tired, and you do not believe. Join us, Damien. You have been a Liar for a long, long time!"*

For a moment I hesitated, looking deep into myself, wondering what it was I did believe. I searched for my faith, the fire that had once sustained me, the certainty in the teachings of the Church, the presence of Christ within me. I found none of it, none. I was empty inside, burned out, full of questions and pain. But as I was about to answer Jon Azure Cross and the smiling Lukyan Judasson, I found something else, something I *did* believe in, something I had always believed in.

Truth.

I believed in truth, even when it hurt. *"He is lost to us,"* said the telepath with the mocking name of Cross.

Lukyan's smile faded. "Oh, really? I had hoped you would be one of us, Damien. You seemed ready."

I was suddenly afraid, and I considered sprinting up the stairs to Sister Judith. Lukyan had told me so very much, and now I had rejected them.

The telepath felt my fear. *"You cannot hurt us, Damien,"* it said. *"Go in peace. Lukyan told you nothing."*

Lukyan was frowning. "I told him a good deal, Jon," he said.

"Yes. But can he trust the words of such a Liar as you?" The small misshapen mouth of the thing in the vat twitched

in a smile, and its great eyes closed, and Lukyan Judasson sighed and led me up the stairs.

It was not until some years later that I realized it was Jon Azure Cross who was lying, and the victim of his lie was Lukyan. I *could* hurt them. I did.

It was almost simple. The bishop had friends in government and the media. With some money in the right places, I made some friends of my own. Then I exposed Cross in his cellar, charging that he had used his psionic powers to tamper with the minds of Lukyan's followers. My friends were receptive to the charges. The guardians conducted a raid, took the telepath Cross into custody, and later tried him.

He was innocent, of course. My charge was nonsense; human telepaths can read minds in close proximity, but seldom anything more. But they are rare, and much feared, and Cross was hideous enough so that it was easy to make him a victim of superstition. In the end, he was acquitted, and he left the city of Ammadon and perhaps Arion itself, bound for regions unknown.

But it had never been my intention to convict him. The charge was enough. The cracks began to show in the lie that he and Lukyan had built together. Faith is hard to come by, and easy to lose, and the merest doubt can begin to erode even the strongest foundation of belief.

The bishop and I labored together to sow further doubts. It was not as easy as I might have thought. The Liars had done their work well. Ammadon, like most civilized cities, had a great pool of knowledge, a computer system that linked the schools and universities and libraries together, and made their combined wisdom available to any who needed it.

But, when I checked, I soon discovered that the histories of Rome and Babylon had been subtly reshaped, and there were three listings for Judas Iscariot—one for the betrayer, one for the saint, and one of the conqueror-king of Babylon. His name was also mentioned in connection with the Hanging Gardens, and there is an entry for a so-called Codex Judas.

And according to the Ammadon library, dragons became extinct on Old Earth around the time of Christ.

We purged all those lies finally, wiped them from the memories of the computers, though we had to cite authorities on a half-dozen non-Christian worlds before the librarians and academics would credit that the differences were anything more than a question of religious preference.

By then the Order of St. Judas had withered in the glare of exposure. Lukyan Judasson had grown gaunt and angry, and at least half of his churches had closed.

The heresy never died completely, of course. There are always those who believe, no matter what. And so to this day *The Way of Cross and Dragon* is read on Arion, in the porcelain city Ammadon, amid murmuring whisperwinds.

Arla-k-Bau and the *Truth of Christ* carried me back to Vess a year after my departure, and Archbishop Torgathon finally gave me the leave of absence I had asked for, before sending me out to fight still other heresies. So I had my victory, and the Church continued on much as before, and the Order of St. Judas Iscariot was thoroughly crushed. The telepath Jon Azure Cross had been wrong, I thought then. He had sadly underestimated the power of a Knight Inquisitor.

Later, though, I remembered his words.

You cannot hurt us, Damien.

Us?

The Order of St. Judas? Or the Liars?

He lied, I think, deliberately, knowing I would go forth and destroy the Way of Cross and Dragon, knowing, too, that I could not touch the Liars, would not even dare mention them. How could I? Who would credit it? A grand star-spanning conspiracy as old as history? It reeks of paranoia, and I had no proof at all.

The telepath lied for Lukyan's benefit so he would let me go. I am certain of that now. Cross risked much to ensnare me. Failing, he was willing to sacrifice Lukyan Judasson and his lie, pawns in some greater game.

So I left, and I carried within me the knowledge that I was empty of faith, but for a blind faith in truth—truth I could no longer find in my Church.

I grew certain of that in my year of rest, which I spent reading and studying on Vess and Cathaday and Celia's World. Finally I returned to the archbishop's receiving room, and stood again before Torgathon Nine-Klariis Tûn in my very worst pair of boots. "My Lord Commander," I said to him, "I can accept no further assignments. I ask that I be retired from active service."

"For what cause?" Torgathon rumbled, splashing feebly.

"I have lost the faith," I said to him, simply.

He regarded me for a long time, his pupilless eyes blinking. At last he said, "Your faith is a matter between you and your confessor. I care only about your results. You have done good work, Damien. You may not retire, and we will not allow you to resign."

The truth will set us free.

But freedom is cold, and empty, and frightening, and lies can often be warm and beautiful.

Last year the Church granted me a new ship. I named this one *Dragon.*

THE THIRTEENTH UTOPIA

by Somtow Sucharitkul

Contrasting this story with that of George R. R. Martin shows that both start from much the same premise: a galactic inquisitor whose task is to puncture heresies. In this case, the claim to have created utopia is a heresy because—as we are told even in 20th Century philosophies—utopias are contrary to human nature and hence any such claim must contain a flaw. Here's a situation that seemed to be the exception to that rule. Or was it?

He came to Shtoma in the cadent lightfall, his tachyon bubble breaching the gilt-fringed incandescent clouds like a dark meteor.

Some feelings are never unlearned. Some wonders never fade with experience. So he reflected, Ton Davaryush, master iconoclast, purger of planets, transformer of societies. Especially one: the thrill of power, of potentiality . . . of a virgin utopia, ripe for the unmasking of its purifying flaw.

Every utopia has its flaw. Ton Davaryush wished it were not so. He was sad—but only for a moment—that he must wreak havoc on this planet, even though it lay at the very limits of the Dispersal of Man; but he had learned not to compromise. With the destruction of twelve deceptive utopias, experience had at least banished misgivings. For

Davaryush was two hundred and thirteen years old, and at the height of his analytic powers.

He closed his curiously heavy-lidded eyes to the shimmering of the cloud-banks and the extravagance of the alien landscape that grew constantly as he fell, with its strange sharp-angled trees like gigantic pink spiders, their photosynthesizing pigment having a ferric, not a magnesium base, and its whimsical spiral dwellings of transparent plastic, jutting up at irregular intervals from the blanket of dense vegetation, crimsons and vermilions. He ignored them, and the savage thrashings of the wind as his translucent sphere automatically adjusted to the gravity, softening his fall for landing on Shtoma.

And thought of the covenant: *for the breaking of joy is the beginning of wisdom.* And thought, pathetically: I, Ton Davaryush, expelled from the mainstream of human society by time dilations and the gulfs of space, am too alone. He tried to bury himself—eyes still closed to the atmospheric turmoil—in analyses of what he had been told about this world. How they had fallen into a pattern, an ecological stasis, from which he must release them, whatever the cost. And this was no backward, back-to-nature primitivistic planet, exulting in its own self-conscous apartness and ignorance, but a world whose technical sophistication rivalled his own; exceeded it, in at least one respect, for Shtoma alone, in the entire Dispersal of Man, knew the secret of gravity control. For which they had no use, except for the manufacture of toys. And which they guarded with such miserliness and irrational fervor as to belie their much-vaunted saintliness, their notorious lack of greed and every other human quality. And the rumor that Shtoma was a utopia was more than could be tolerated.

If it was a utopia it could be destroyed. This he knew. He understood every facet of the utopian heresy. He was a master iconoclast, dedicated to the perpetuation of change. *Every utopia has its flaw.* He clutched this knowledge to him like a secret prayer.

I may be a saviour.

He opened his eyes finally. And saw the incredible wildness, the intractable angularity of the landscape, the lurid carmines and scarlets of the trees that lurched toward him with their arachnoid arms outstretched. His bubble slowed itself, gradually, to bring him to the field of rust-colored grass. Alien buzzings and high-pitched song-snatches assailed his ears.

He deactivated his tachyon bubble with a flick of his mind—the keys were cybernetically brain-implanted—and was now at the mercy of the alien environment. At some indeterminate future, he would be rescued—when the computer on homeworld decided.

I may be a saviour. This was more important to him than why they had jealously hidden their secret from a galaxy where knowledge was not for concealing, why they had not used their secret for conquest, as was their right. But this would come. *I am bringing them their human nature,* he thought. The thrill of it lived in his heart. (For this thrill he had joined the Inquest.)

He drew his shimmercloak over his shoulder. It absorbed the fresh air and began to radiate in the safe range, as he knew it would: he stroked it softly as it blushed, pink against the aquamarine fur; wishing, as always, that it was not a dumb semi-sentient. For he was alone.

Turning in the direction of the nearest habitation, he reviewed once more all he had been told about Shtoma.

A planet unaccountably close to its primary, a white dwarf, yet environmentally anomalous: Earth-sized, temperate, with the wrong atmosphere. With incredible potential for economic power, yet with no armed forces, which ignored the rest of the Dispersal of Man, the galactic authority—leading inexorably to the heretic suspicion of utopia! He began walking. It was not the Inquest's way to arrive conspicuously, gaudy with the trappings of salvation.

But then a stranger stood in his path, unmoving. An oldish man, clad severely in a brown tunic; clearly a peasant or slave. He was looking at the ground, and Davaryush had come quite close to him.

The stranger looked up at Davaryush and sang, in a clear tenor, the first alien words he had heard since his arrival, words he was to hear so many times on Shtoma:

qithe qithembara
udres a kilima shtoisti.

Davaryush signalled to his polyglot implant, then closed his eyes to see, as though inscribed on a white page before him, the words

"soul, renounce suffering;
you have danced on the face of the sun."

It appeared to be a form of greeting. But the strange words, with their opaque and patently sinful meaning, strengthened his suspicions; and he approached the stranger diffidently. There was one other thing experience never banished: fear.

Activating his implant so that it would intervene in his speech functions, he said: "I am from another world. Who may I address?"

The alien's gaze chilled him, though it contained no malice. "You are Inquestor Davaryush, of the Clan of Ton. Welcome." Abruptly the stranger beamed and stretched out his arms to embrace Davaryush. The Inquestor yielded ungracefully. He had misjudged; this was no peasant. "We were expecting you."

"Yes. I come to investigate Shtoma's utopian possibilities, so that it may be considered for the honour of being named a Human Sanctuary." Davaryush did not blush at the lie, for it came easily to him by now.

"So! How delightful." His eyes laughed themselves into a hatchwork of wrinkles. "I am your host, Ernad. You must be weary; come."

Who was this man, poorly dressed and without a single attendant, who dared to address a Master Inquestor by name and who knew his mission? Again the alienness of the world unnerved him. The clouds had parted to reveal the white dwarf sun, unnaturally close. The rough wind tousled the grass, blood-red and tall. He started to answer Ernad, but the old man had turned, expecting Davaryush to follow him.

A stony path, pebbled with shiny stones, led to the first recognizably human artifact: a displacement plate, metallic and incongruous in the middle of the field. He was unprepared for this. He was forced to remind himself that this was no primitive world—in spite of the absence of war or, apparently, slavery. "When can I begin my investigation? The Inquest must know soon, in time for the Grand Convocation," he said.

Ernad beckoned Davaryush onto the plate. "Frankly, we have so little involvement with the worlds outside—" he began, then stopped himself. "Well, as you wish; whenever you wish." Davaryush was suspicious of the warmth in his voice, but it appeared convincing. Clearly he was dealing with a master of ambiguity. But the impropriety and unashamedness of "little involvement" compounded his bewilderment.

They materialized in what appeared to be one of the structures he had glimpsed during the landing.

He reeled with the vertigo of it—the crazy swirlings and spirallings of transparent walls, the cacophony of chimings and chirpings that bombarded his senses. How could they live amid such a wilderness of sensual stimuli? Where was their discipline, their culture? A woman nearly ran into him, then trotted away, laughing, children and young people sauntered by, gaily calling out "*qithe qithembara; udres a kilima shtoisti*!" completely without respect. "You must forgive them," said Ernad, interrupting his dismay. "You are an off-worlder, and . . . well, it is especially exciting for them now. It is almost time for the festival of Initiation, and anything can spark their enthusiasm." He said this matter-of-factly, with no trace of criticism in his voice, again pointing up his alienness.

"They are your attendants?" Surely someone important enough to be his host would have servants of a kind.

"No; neighbours, relatives, friends. My house is theirs."

But Davaryush was thinking: what of the initiation ceremony? Perhaps that was the flaw. Perhaps there was some unspeakable rite, some trauma they were all forced to go through . . . perhaps this would be the handle he could use to save this misguided people.

"Ernad, I must rest," he said. "But after, I would see everything on your world: your games, your pleasures, your prisons, your criminals, your asylums, your places of execution."

"Ah. Yes, I have heard of madmen and criminals. I am not uneducated, Inquestor Ton," replied Ernad mysteriously. They turned down a corridor of glass that swerved upwards into the air, and Davaryush felt a sudden dislocation, as though he had changed weight or *down* had become sideways, and he found they were walking upside down, on the ceiling. "What is happening?"

Ernad laughed mildly. "It is the same principle, you know, as the varigrav coasters. You must have seen them, our principal export—"

"But why fool around with gravity inside your dwellings?"

"Why not? Would you not be bored, if all directions remained constantly the same . . . ?"

Up became *down* again. They reached a large chamber that seemed to be perched, precariously, on the point of a translucent pyramid in the sky. "Your resting place. It is my own chamber, Inquestor; I trust you will find it comfortable."

Davaryush's eye alighted on the only adornment of the room, apart from the resting-pad. It was a huge, capelike sheet of some sheer material that hung on one wall, like a rainbow sail, rippling softly in the ventilating breeze. It was beautiful, he conceded, but bewilderingly complex, uncivilized. "This cape? What is it for?"

"Oh. My wings," Ernad said.

Davaryush knew then how addicted they must be to the varigrav coasters, those toys they had inflicted on the rest of the galaxy. And he looked at the old man, who seemed utterly ingenuous, and wondered if it were possible that this sincerity were not, after all, the product of a trained deviousness, but merely a product of his lower mentality.

For here was a toy, hanging on the wall as though it were a god.

"Leave me, Ernad," he said brusquely.

He was trying to establish authority, the distancing proper for an Inquestor. He needed to preserve his mask of sternness, for he was already sad. He was vulnerable, he realized, even after twelve successful missions.

For he was nothing if not compassionate.

You have compassion, Davaryush.

"Yes, Father." He was twelve years old, veteran of three wars, and now an initiate. And alone, in the small room, with the Inquestor, whose eyes glared fire and millennial wisdom. Now after more than two centuries, the scene returned, vivid.

When you came to kill the condemned criminal, you did not torture him or play with him, as was your right, an essential part of the initiation. You killed him cleanly, in a matter of seconds, slicing him into two congruent parts with your energizer. It was artistically done. But why?

"Father, it was necessary to show skill, not cruelty. I have already killed many people." He feigned an assurance that was far from his true feelings.

Very well. I name you to the Clan of Ton.

Davaryush started, gasped audibly despite his knowledge of proper conduct . . . he had come expecting to fail, to be returned to homeworld. The Clan of Ton . . . that would mean seminary, long lonely years on harsh, inhospitable planets, unwelcome, thankless labour for the sake of pure altruism. "Father—"

You are unworthy. I know. Nevertheless, the Inquest takes what it can get.

His first mission was the planet Gom, a hot planet of a blue-white star. The people lived in tall buildings, thousands to a building, fifteen billion to the planet. But they were happy. They were quite ignorant of their responsibilities as a fallen race; reliant on automata, they pursued their hedonistic existence without regard for their true natures. They suffered from the heresy of utopia.

He remembered how he found the flaw to that utopia. Every year, in a special ceremony marked by compulsive gratifications of the senses, all those over the age of fifty intoxicated themselves and then committed suicide, leaping by thousands into the volcanic lava lakes that boiled ubiquitously on every continent.

He had saved them. Whispering to only one or two: *and what if you did not die?* he had created civil wars, revolutions, unhappiness. People ran mad, setting fire to the machines that had succored them. Then the ships of the Inquest came, bringing comfort with them, comfort and truth.

But the happiness had tempted him. *Remember, man is a fallen creature, Davaryush. Utopias exist only in the mind, a state to which it is given us to aspire. But to imagine we have attained that state—that is to deny life. The breaking of joy is the beginning of wisdom.*

Now he was no longer tempted. For he had seen such as the planet Eldereldad, where the happy ones feasted on their own children, which they produced in great litters, by hormonal stimulation; and the planet Xurdeg, his most recent mission, where the people smiled constantly, irritatingly, showing no face except the face of rapt ecstasy, until he finally learned that the penalty for grief was dismemberment, to feed the hungry demands of the degenerating bodies of five-thousand-year-old patriarchs . . . yet when he had asked one of these ancients, what he most desired, he had replied: *To feel grief. But I am afraid to die for it.*

Ton Alakamathdes, Grand Inquestor of his Sector, who had watched his initiation and had chosen him out for the Clan of Ton, had said to him that day when he was a young boy facing his new destiny: *Never forget the lie. This lie is the sacrifice that you must make, the little sin that you must commit, for the sake of saving countless millions. The lie is this: the Inquest is seeking a perfect utopia, a planet that will be designated a Human Sanctuary, for the edification and glory of the Dispersal of Man. You will tell them that always, and always you will understand in your heart that there will exist one tragic flaw.*

And always, the ships of the Inquest would follow him. And after, in a year or two, or perhaps a few decades, they would awake to their true natures, and they would fight wars and exhibit avarice and pitilessness, like all the other worlds. Man is a fallen being.

Remember: you are a guardian of the human condition. He felt the eyes of Ton Alkamathdes on him, even two centuries away and countless parsecs, boring into his soul, purifying him; and in their sternness he drew a kind of comfort. But then he awoke, long before dawn, and was on Shtoma and frighteningly alone, exposed to the alien sky under the structures of glass and clear plastics. He found a young girl singing to him, "qithe qithembara, Lord Inquestor."

He sat up abruptly, reaching for a nonexistent weapon. "Who are you?"

"I am Alk, daughter of Ernad." (The voice haunted his thoughts for many days, reminding him of the whispering sea on homeworld.) "Will you be pleased with me? Of all the children who saw you, I was most taken by you, Inquestor."

They were depraved, shockingly amoral! They sent their own children to sleep with strangers! "No!" he cried out, and the severity of his own emotion startled them both. "On our worlds we do not do things like this."

"But father said to show you our love, the love of *udara.*"

Udara? (Their name for the dwarf star, their sun, whispered his polyglot implant. Again he was puzzled.)

"Leave me, please." He tried to exclude the pain from his voice. Shame flooded him. In the starlight he saw disappointment on her face, and thought: they do not even hide their emotions! what savages, what innocents! And without a further word she rose and left him, noiseless as a breeze.

Quickly he ran through what he had learnt in those few hours. They dressed severely, denying all rank and pomp and selfimportance; they made curious fetish of their wings, they were morally loose, they did not make any effort to conceal their feelings, but were like children, wholly innocent of the need for tact and diplomacy—and this last thing, the love of *udara.* That could mean anything. Every perversion, every practice of perversion was possible, because of the human condition.

And, under the strange constellations, knowing that he had no weapons and that he could not know when he would be rescued, he began to recite the first prayer he had ever learnt. Its meaning, for its language was no longer spoken, was a sublime mystery to the Inquest, but all who went through the seminary could repeat it, as a solace, in times of emotional turmoil. The nonsense words—perhaps little more than gibberish distorted by man's long history—were a kind of bond between the members of the Inquest, all solitary men: "pater noster, qui es in inferno . . ."

"But—what is *in* these black boxes? I have seen several during my stay here," Davaryush demanded of the heretic priest.

The white-bearded old man—a magnificent mottlement of wrinkles and discolorations, without the common decency of cosmetics—smiled beneficently at him. "*Udara,*" he said. "*Udara* is in them.

"Will you not touch it?" the priest said, beckoning to him. The temple's black box—it was perhaps a meter square—stood in the center of the transparent hall which could have held ten thousand people without any trouble. It was the only object in the chamber. "Come, touch; you will feel *udara.*"

Hesitantly, Davaryush went up to it with his hand outstretched. He felt wobbly-kneed, as though his weight were constantly shifting, as though he were losing control of his limbs. Gingerly, he brushed the cool metal with his fingertips.

Overwhelming joy coursed through his thoughts for a moment. He saw homeworld fleetingly, and ached for it; heard the music of the sea, saw vividly the faces of his parents, whom his own time dilation had stranded in an unreachable past . . . they smiled at him, he was a child half their height, reaching up to touch their faces, laughing . . .

And snatched away his hand as though he had been burnt. This was dangerous, clearly some powerful hallucinogenic device. He stared at his hand in terror.

The happiness he had just felt echoed in his mind. He was tempted to reach out again, and he controlled himself with tremendous difficulty, and knew he had stumbled upon one of the key clues to what was wrong with Shtoma.

They were selfdeluders, obviously, intoxicating themselves with false memories and artificially induced joys.

"Did you not feel the love of *udara*, stranger?"

"No, priest. I felt—I remembered something I thought I had lost forever." He turned to leave.

"You do not wish for more? Ah, but you have not danced on the face of the sun."

He turned again, saw the look of pity in the priest's face, the expression of *ah, but you are incapable of understanding.*

So he walked hurriedly out, not bothering to acknowledge the priest's hearty "qithe qithembara."

Ernad was waiting for him, and the girl Alk, who was—by daylight—a creature of striking beauty, not in her facial features but in the way she moved and spoke; and another of Ernad's children, Eshly, a little boy of about six, who prattled and asked questions as though he were much younger, and was quite devoid of discipline. They walked on to the next displacement plate: Ernad smiling, the girl and her brother running excitedly, then lagging behind, Davaryush moody. Ernad told him more about the Shtoikitha, the people of the dance (and they called their planet Shtoma, *Danceworld.*)

"Yes, we're a very thinly populated planet, only half a million souls . . . what do we eat? There is fruit in the forests, small animals too, crustacea of fantastical shapes in the rivers; we don't have agriculture here. The fruit of the *gruyesh* falls to the ground and ripens, and when it turns mauve we tap it for the *zul*, that mildly fermented sweet juice that you drank this morning . . ."

"Crime?"

"Why should anyone commit it?" Ernad laughed gently. "We have *udara*, you see, so it isn't necessary."

"I don't understand. My polyglot implant translates that word simply as "sun"; but I have heard it in at least a dozen meanings since I came to Shtoma. I know that semantics aren't perfect, but could I be missing something? You can't tell me that your people, in all their evident complexity, attribute all your fortunes to some mythical property of your sun!"

Davaryush was exasperated now. It was becoming a strain to maintain his investigator's pose. Clearly the problem on this planet had to do with some fundamental misunderstanding of the workings of the universe.

They had come to a small clearing, having vanished and rematerialized several times: it was level, dotted with pink shrubs . . . the two children, or rather the young woman and the boy, had run forward, breathless, and had collapsed, exhausted, on the grass . . . *by now, they would both be warriors, in the real world,* he thought. How sad, that they were trapped in a permanent preadolescence.

The boy he felt compassion for: he was like a retarded child who is nevertheless extremely beautiful. But Ernad was talking again.

"Still you don't see, you don't comprehend the elegant simplicity of it. Relax! Feel the singing in the sky: one cannot commit evil here."

He tried to feel, sensing, in the absurdity of the old man's beliefs, some core of faith that he would never be able to alter . . . the soft sussurant rustlings of the red forests sang to him, but in their singing was mingled, chillingly, an image of homeworld . . . he tensed, instinctively, knowing he was playing with fire.

"Have you ever ridden a varigrav coaster?"

"No!" The thought horrified him. Abandonment to the senses, to utter helplessness! Never would he . . .

"It is a pity. What *did* you feel, when I asked you to listen to the music of *udara*?"

(Again, some obscure semantic twist.) "I don't know. A memory. It doesn't matter."

"On the contrary; it probably *does* matter. But you will learn at the initiation ceremony, perhaps."

"I am to take part?" Nothing would induce him to take part in any barbarian rite! Why, he might be mutilated, he might have to watch some unspeakable evil . . . but Ernad smiled the smile that excluded him from those who understood, frustrating him even more. "*Udara* is the key to what you are searching for, you know. Without it, this world would surely not be the paradise it has become."

"Why, that's ridiculous."

The two children of his host had come up and were watching him intently. "Father," said the boy Eshly, "don't be hard on the poor man."

He was so naive, so tactless, so ignorant! But Alk only looked at him, knowing what had passed between them in the night. (He knew now that no stigma was attached to sexual promiscuity; an expression of affection, nothing more. Finally, he had had to concede that this in itself was no flaw.)

"I must show you—" Ernad began.

"Take him to the nearest varigrav coaster, *please*, Father," Eshly cried urgently. He clasped Davaryush's hand—such presumption in a stripling, such undeserved trust—and propelled him towards the nearest displacement plate.

And in an instant they were at the edge of a cliff, sheer and blindingly white, that stretched perhaps half a kilometer down to a cleared and endless plain, without the pink of vegetation. The plate where they had arrived stood in the shadow of a tremendously tall column of the transparent building material they used. It was slender—the width of a few men, and it reached up to vanish somewhere in the vague loftiness of the clouds that hid *Udara* from view then. This was nothing like the varigrav coasters he had seen, children's pleasure things. This was overpoweringly stark, and huge; a quasi-religious luminousness emanated from it. Its vastness distorted the scale of everything, so he felt a crazy disorientation, while the two children, in nonchalant irreverance, were pushing him to the other side, shouting at him to hurry.

"Quick, come, Inquestor!" shouted Eshly. A lift platform was descending for them. Turning to watch the sky beyond the cliff, Davaryush saw black dots and smudges, microscopic in the expanse of sky and white plain, and he knew what they were. An ancient fear petrified him, he was like a robot as they buckled him in to the elevator. Suddenly, with a wild jerk, they were aloft, racing up to the starting point in the clouds, and the rushing blood in his brain crashed against the rushing of the mad winds. He was nauseous; he closed his eyes and muttered his ancient prayer, longing for an end.

At the top there was a sort of control room, diving platforms of various sizes, racks where sets of wings were set out, not the rainbow-colored type that adorned his resting-room, but plain ones, black or gray. Alk and Eshly each seized a set of wings and had run to the platforms and leapt off the edge while Davaryush fought a wild impulse to go to their rescue.

He saw them in the air, falling, falling with dizzying speed, and soon they had vanished—and then he saw them again, flung violently upward by the interplay of differing gravity fields, screeching with delight as the varigravs hurled them into turbulent whirlpools, and the wind, which was pulled in so many different directions that it was a distended, distorted tornado blasting his ears. He found himself clutching the railings in terror, he who had seen nine wars.

But the squeals of pleasure became fainter. The two became black dots, joining the rapidly shifting patterns of swirling specks in the distance. It was more tolerable to look at, pretty patterns against the sky, but when he thought about what was happening to them (gravity fields wrenching them in different directions, stretching their bodies' tolerance to its very limits, how could anyone find it pleasurable?) he—

"Please, take me out of this."

"As you wish."

They went into the control room. They shut out the roaring of the winds and the silence shocked him for a moment, before he gathered his analytic senses enough to look around him . . . it was an empty room, like all the others he had seen on Shtoma, domed in the standard material, so that *udara* shone relentlessly inside, with a half-dozen of the black boxes predictably scattered, haphazardly, across the floor.

"I'm impressed." Davaryush tried to sound sincere. "How does it all work, incidentally?" He laboured a little over the casual tone of this question, since finding out the secret would make a great difference to the other civilized worlds.

"The scientific principle, or the technical aspects?" Davaryush was startled for a moment by the man's willingness to reveal.

"Both."

"Well, you know as well as I do that gravity control works by selective graviton exchange . . . the coaster also manufactures antigravitons, which exist of course only with some difficulty under normal conditions."

"But how *do* you manufacture antigravitons?" Davaryush was excited; uncautiously he let it slip through, was not devious enough in asking the question. Ernad seemed not to be aware of such things.

"I'm simply not a scientist," he said—he did not sound at all as if he was trying to put Davaryush off—"and in any case *udara* controls details like that." He pointed happily to the boxes.

Again the evasive tactics, the semantic deceptions! If the people of Shtoma were able to lie with such easy naturalness, perhaps Shtoma had never been a logical candidate for utopiahood. Perhaps his journey had been wasted.

But the Grand Inquestor had entrusted him, and the Inquest was wise.

He saw the children returning, swung upwards in a golden arc that transsected *udara* through the shimmering cloud banks . . .

"Time to go home. It will be night." Ernad motioned to his guest. "I hope you will feel more comfortable this time, and not be so afraid of the height."

The black boxes glinted in the *udara*-light. They attributed everything to those boxes, Davaryush thought. Was there something in it? Of course not. They were lying to him, creating some enormous joke at his expense.

Walking home through the ruddy terrain, Ernad told him how everybody on Shtoma participated in the initiation ceremonies every five years, almost to a man, because those who had been through it once could be renewed, purified. "You will understand everything, you know, once you have taken part—the black boxes, the *udara*-concepts. I know that you find us strange." He chuckled to himself, then added earnestly, "You will take part, won't you?"

Slowly, with the realization that he might well be falling into a trap, a trap cleverly constructed upon his own curiosity and on the necessities of his mission, he said: "I have no choice." For his mission was to understand, and after understanding to control. Even now, compassion touched him, more than ever before.

The accident happened.

Eshly, the boy, had run on ahead to the next displacement plate. He tripped and stumbled, face down, and the power surged. They were upon him, the resounding clang echoing in the woods. The three of them knelt down by the plate.

He lay like a discarded toy. The displacement field had aborted—it was an accident that practically never occurred, was almost unthinkable—and had wrenched half his body away and then slung it back in a nanosecond, so that he was in one piece, but impossibly bent.

Davaryush waited for the tears, for the signs of grief. But the only sighing was the breeze and the voices of the alien forest. Lightfall was ending.

"Go on, Alk," Ernad whispered to his daughter, "the others will want to know." His voice was icy calm.

Davaryush stood to follow as he lifted up the corpse, which seemed merely asleep until one saw the inhuman angle of the arms, and carried it into the encroaching forest, and returned without it, with the red shadows darkening him. There seemed to be no sadness in his face. Indeed, he almost smiled. Was this some incredible fortitude, even in the face of an impossible tragedy? Davaryush devoured the man with his eyes, seeking some clue to his emotions. And he thought: *I have found the flaw.*

And now it was time to plant the doubt, because the lowest point in a man's being is also the beginning of his ascent. Davaryush thought bitterly: here is a people that blithely throws the bodies of its sons into the forests to rot, that has forgotten grief, that does not value human life at all. Here was the flaw.

Davaryush tried to put a lot of anger into his voice, to exclude compassion while not striving too much for an oracular effect: "You don't care about your child," he said. "Love is not part of your utopia, is it? Humanity is what you have abandoned, isn't it?" *Now you are going to break down. Now your repressed humanity will come rushing to the surface.* It had happened twelve times before, and countless other times with our Inquestors.

Ernad did not collapse. He stared at Ernad with unmitigated pity.

"Of course I grieve for him. I am desolate, Davaryush. But you do not understand our perspectives, or our overview of life. With renewal my grief will be cleansed. And I grieve for him most, that he did not live to dance on the face of the sun."

And Davaryush knew that he had understood nothing at all, nothing. Never had he felt so palpably the alienness of this world, the total incommunicableness of it. His mind whirled in a wild kaleidoscope of images: strange winds, blood-crimson forests with spider arms, flagrantly immodest buildings open to the elements, a dead child unmourned, a dead child who had been playing games amidst the incomprehensible forces of black boxes that manipulated gravity fields . . . and this strange man's face, which should be racked with sorrow, yet insulted him with an unwanted pity. *I wish I could kill him.*

The death-impulse rose in him, a monster of the subconscious, and he suppressed it with a superhuman effort. *He is a product of his misguided culture, not to be blamed,* he reminded himself. *I have come to save him; I must never forget that: even if I cause his death, I come as a saviour.*

He had miscalculated again. Thinking to elicit from the stranger his hidden guilt, his dormant human responses, he had instead forced his own desire to kill to the surface. This desire should long have been dead, since he had renounced it for the sake of the salvation of the Dispersal of Man; yet it haunted him still, a specter from the buried past. Perhaps the will of the man was stronger than his . . .

At last he found he could feel a bond between himself and the alien, in this moment of deepest misunderstanding. For they were both men, both fallen beings.

"Ernad," said Davaryush, "I pity you." The two of them walked, through the miscoloured landscape, up to the twisted house.

Asleep that night, he was nine years old, celebrating the end of his first war.

And they came to Alykh, the pleasure planet. He and Tymyon and Ayulla and Kyg and the other companions, lost themselves in the cacophony of the crowds.

"Wait till you see *this*!" Kyg shouted, and she leapt on to the plate like a cat. They disappeared—

And Davaryush saw it, a topless tower of brick and stone and concrete and plastic and sparkling amethysts, studding the walls like jewelled knuckle-dusters . . .

"What *is* it?"

"Daavye, don't you know *anything*?" Tymyon cackled offensively.

Kyg said, with mock primness: "It's a . . . VARIGRAV COASTER!"

The tower glinted oddly, catching the sunset. "Look," said Kyg impatiently, "you dive off the top, you see, and it sets into action a series of random gravity-field interferences, and you plummet like a hawk and you float upward and you swing dangerously and you curve and then you land where you started, like a feather."

("It's beautiful," whispered Ayulla the silent.)

"Well, let's GO!" Tymyon and Kyg raced each other to the tower, and the crowds were everywhere, aliens, child-warriors brandishing their weapons, pimps, crusader-flagellants, Inquestors and their retinues, slave-hunters, veiled Whisper-shadows from the borders of the Dispersal, dirty children strumming on dreamharps, dissonant alien musics, and an itinerant space opera howling full-blast through amplification jewels, and Davaryush was spellbound, unmoving.

He had never . . .

The tower held him.

And the little specks that were people, dust-motes in the violet sunset.

"Aren't you coming?" Ayulla's voice was almost lost in the confusion.

"No." He was petrified.

"Come *on*! They're all the rage now, all the way from Shtoma you know, from the limits of the Dispersal . . ."

"No! No!" (It was said that the greatest thrill, when you fell, was the very certainty of death, suddenly averted by a twist of the field. At the moment of inevitable doom, it was said, you felt so *alive*.)

Ayulla was laughing at him. "How many people have you killed, Daavye? How can you be so scared of *life*?"

(He was ashamed. He resolved, then, to change his circle of friends.)

Now wake up. Face the hostile planet.

He moved, murmuring "Homeworld."

Shrill cries of children awakened him. And then Alk was at the entrance to his room: "Initiation, Inquestor; hurry."

He threw on his shimmercloak. It tightened around him, sensing his need for warmth, though it was not cold.

The wings on the walls had gone.

The whole family, a dozen or more of them, trooped without ceremony into his room, heady exhilaration in their faces. Quickly he followed them outside, struggling to keep up with them. His heart had sunk when he saw that the wings had vanished. For he had an inking, now, of what this rite must involve, and it terrified him.

Many displacements later, they were on a mountain top overlooking a vast plain that glittered silver-gray with a thousand spaceships. The ships littered the fields, end to end so that the red grass was quite covered, all the way to the horizon . . . he could not imagine what they were for. Shtoma had hardly any commerce with other worlds.

"Isn't it breathtaking?" Alk grasped his arm, and he felt himself shivering . . .

"How many of them *are* there, Ernad?" he said, wonderingly. This ceremony involved a journey, it seemed; perhaps on some satellite, some other planet.

The children were dancing and tugging at him and hollering in circles round him, and Ernad did not seem disposed to answer his questions. "Come," he said, and after another displacement they were at the entrance to a ship. (It was much as he knew them; ships did not differ much, having been perfected many millennia ago, before the Dispersal.) But the number of them! And the mobs of people, their wings tucked under their arms, giggling, chattering away as they climbed into them!

In the mid-distance, some of them had already risen. They rose at even intervals, in perfect order, and he could see a long chain of them stretching into the sky, where they glittered like a jewelled necklace in the early lightfall. Quickly (almost shamefacedly) he stifled his wonder, for he knew he must analyze *everything*, if he was to solve the most taxing problem of his life, the enigma of Shtoma.

So he climbed the steep steps into the belly of the ship.

It was only a small cruiser, built for perhaps five hundred; there must be a thousand of them, then, to hold the whole population of Shtoma. It was impersonal, gray-walled like every ship; and it appeared to be a short-hauler, so Davaryush knew they were not going off-system. People were filing into their chambers, seeming to know exactly where they belonged; Davaryush stood stupidly for a few moments before Alk came for him, and took him to the family's cabin.

After a while, he felt the noiseless lifting of the ship.

Some time later Ernad led him to the viewroom, whose screens afforded an unobstructed three hundred and sixty degree view of space; and he saw how the line of ships trailed behind and before, each an exact distance from the other, links in a metal serpent of space . . . he asked Ernad where they were going.

"To *udara*, of course!" The old man looked blankly at him.

"Not seriously."

"Are there any other planets in this system? Any moons? We are not a mendacious people, Davaryush; perhaps that has not occurred to you yet." He spoke patiently, as though reproving a favorite child, and the attitude stung Davaryush.

He turned to see, on the other side of the room, that *udara* had swollen and was a blindingly white flameball against the blackness. He knew by now that when the word *udara* came up he would get nowhere; so he tried something else. The ubiquitous black boxes were everywhere; in the viewroom they were stacked neatly in the middle of the floor.

"Those *udara*-boxes: they power the ship perhaps?" he said, only half-skeptical.

Ernad laughed again, enjoying his guest's ignorance. (Again Davaryush felt a bitter hate, a death-lust, for his host). "Not at all; they are quite empty, and our spaceships work in the normal way."

After a moment he said: "Now look, Inquestor: they are darkening the screen, or else *udara* would become unbearable."

"How can you say we are going there!"

"Just look at the face of the sun. There, look."

Udara was growing rapidly, and Davaryush saw: "There's a black spot on the sun's surface!"

"*That's* where we are going."

The black dot was perfectly round. This was impossible. "It must be artificial!" he gasped. These people, far from being simple utopians, were capable of galaxy-dominating technological feats!

"Artificial? In a manner of speaking." Then he explained, "The dot of course is only black by comparison, obviously; when we get there it will appear white and incandescent."

The screen was cut in half! One side was completely black, the other painfully bright, and there were white flame-tongues that shot up, a hundred kilometers high. They were approaching the sun's atmosphere; in its heart, Davaryush knew, matter was packed into inconceivable density.

"And now . . . there are tablets you must take, since you will not be able to breathe for a few hours; they will release oxygen into your bloodstream."

"What do you mean?"

"You're going to jump into the sun."

Davaryush understood now. They had led him on, and all the time were preparing this elaborate fiery execution. "I'll vaporize instantly!" he said.

"You don't understand, do you?" Ernad countered with surprising vehemence. "Gravity is under control, heat is under control! This is no ordinary star, this is *udara*. Every five years, we all ride on the gravity-fields here, and become clean . . ."

Davaryush's mind reeled under the impact of this relevation. The sun filled the screen completely now, unbelievably white . . . "You mean that you *built* this star? You built a *varigrav coaster* on the surface of a *sun*?"

"If only we had the technology!" Ernad smiled a little. "Why, the mind boggles. You are so close to the answer, and yet so far, so incredibly far! Well, we are all bound by the limits of our experience. It is time to live; explanations will follow."

They were in the airlock, then; waves of nausea crashed in his head, and he stood stock-still like a martyr waiting for death (which he felt himself to be) while they put the wings on him and the tittering of the children pelted his brain like painful hailpellets—

The airlock opened!

There was whiteness, such whiteness. He shut his eyes and fell.

Fell. Fell.

His blood was burning. He was burning, he was falling into hell, plummeting helplessly into the scorchswift firebreath of the sunwind. He screamed, he thrashed his body uselessly against emptiness, he opened his eyes and the whiteness shattered his vision, the featureless whiteness, so he screamed and screamed, until he was no longer aware of his screaming.

He heard voices out of the past (Kill the criminal Daavye no I can't I can't you have compassion my son compassion man is a fallen being).

He reached the limit of his falling. And soared! And was flying upwards, upwards, on an antigraviton tide! And swerved, and fell headlong again, and swooped in tandem with a tongue of flame, and his scream was a whisper in the thunder of the wind (come on Daavye you fool it's the latest craze *no!* are you afraid of life or something Daavye Daavye?) and fell and fell (pater noster qui es in inferno) and fell . . .

And soared! And caromed into the roaring flame! And fell. And saw death, suddenly, and came face to face with himself, and knew death intimately . . . and fell (Kill the criminal Daavye compassion compassion) and fell . . .

Trust me.

Falling, the voice embraced him. The voice sang through him. The voice made him tingle like a perfect harp-string, dispelling his terror in a moment. He was a nothing touched by love.

(Memories came like endless printouts but there was one memory on the verge of crystallizing, and he was waiting for it, waiting for it to come, clear as a presence—)

The voice was like homeworld. The roaring was the whisper of the sea. He could almost see his parents again: and fell and fell and was touched by love and fell and lost consciousness, becoming one with an ineffable serenity.

"Answers! I want answers!" He woke, sweating, in the room in the twisted house. Ernad was there, and the whole family; he felt their concern, and then he broke down and sobbed violently, hopelessly.

"I think we deserve some answers too, Ton Davaryush," Ernad said softly; there was iron in his gentleness. (He heard the others whispering among themselves: "When he came back to the ship, he was in a trance, unconscious." "He's been like this for weeks.")

"Now understand this, Davaryush," said Ernad, "you are not the first Inquestor to visit our planet. And will not be the last either."

Davaryush did what he never dreamed he would do: between fits of weeping, he told them the whole story, how he had come to Shtoma to save its people from themselves, how he had been defeated, how he understood nothing now, nothing at all.

(They fed him with sweet *zul* and were so kind to him. This, too, evoked a strange wonder and respect in him; for he had wanted to betray them.)

"Well, you were promised an explanation. Listen, then: *Udara* is no ordinary star. Of course we didn't build him; that's ridiculous. But—do you know anything about the origins of sentience? Well, you know how life evolves: how certain arrangements of atoms, certain paradigms, created purely by chance interactions, you understand, becoming living beings, self-aware, sometimes . . . white dwarfs are created by incredible cataclysms, by a star going nova, dying . . . somehow, a spark of life was made, after the nova, and *udara* became self-aware. *Udara* is alive, Davaryush! and we have acquired a symbiotic relationship with him that permits us to exist in this scientifically anomalous state . . . do you follow? In the black boxes, Davaryush: pieces of the sun."

Davaryush lay back, stupefied, his thoughts fired by the incredible imagery of it.

"Did you imagine that mere people like we could create and uncreate gravitons and anti-gravitons? How much power is available, without the resources of a star? Could we make and unmake gravitational fields? Could we dim the sunlight on one area of the sun, so as to be unharmed by its heat? *Udara* does all this, by his own will; his knowledge of physical laws is several orders beyond our understanding. We think that he is aware of himself, not only in this four-dimensional continuum, but also in other continua."

"But with this power," Davaryush said, "with this sun to do your bidding, can't you conquer the galaxy, win wars?"

"You still don't understand! The sun does not do our bidding; the sun does all this because he *loves* us." (Davaryush remembered, suddenly, how love had touched him when he was plummeting towards death.) "You felt it in the sunlight. You would always have felt it, but you were so full of confusion and contradiction, and so many people had lied to you . . . but when you fell into the sun, when you danced on the sun's face, then you understood. You see, we can't commit evil, because, in the act of dancing—what the rest of humanity thinks of as our little children's game—we have partaken of a tiny fragment of his nature . . .

"But let me plant a doubt in your *mind*. That is what you came to do to us, isn't it? Well: what if the Inquest existed, not for salvation, but for destruction? What if its sole purpose were to perpetrate its leaders' desire for conquest, and its mouthpieces, the "Inquestors," were simply indoctrinated with pseudoreligiousness to make them more fanatical, more serviceable? . . ."

And Davaryush knew that he had lost his faith. (He wondered what answer he would give them about Shtoma. It would probably be unsatisfactory; they would undoubtedly have to send another Inquestor. But he no longer cared what the Inquest thought.)

Finally there came a day when Alk came running in to him, breathlessly: "Your tachyon bubble, it's hovering above the house!"

He stepped outside. The sun shone on him, bathing him with inexpressible joy.

Suddenly the memory came to him, the memory that was just beginning to come to him, before he became unconscious—

He was six years old. The ship was waiting to take him to the war. He was standing there with his father, by the sea shore, and his father seized him, on impulse, and threw him into the air, and he screamed for help, half-laughing, and fell for an eternity, into the arms that were for him, for protecting him, for loving him.

At last he understood the love of *udara*.

. . . But the children of the house had come and were clustered around him, making much of him, and Ernad stood at the entrance, waving to him.

"*Qithe qithembara*!" he yelled frantically, forcing back his tears—

He took one more step towards the bubble.

You have danced on the face of the sun.

OPTIONS

by John Varley

There have been many books lately about sex change and many by changelings themselves about their lives as men and then as women . . . and occasionally the other way around. In every instance it would appear that the operation takes many painful months and sometimes years, that it is never truly complete, producing at best a reasonable "passing" facsimile of the new sex. This is not said in derogation of the "change"—quite clearly it is accepted in psychology as the best solution to a personal conflict with one's assigned gender role. But suppose that sex change is perfected, is made quick, total, and painless. What would be the effect on the society in which that could be a commonplace decision to any citizen? John Varley picks up the options. . . .

Cleo hated breakfast.

Her energy level was lowest in the morning, but not so the children's. There was always some school crisis, something that had to be located at the last minute, some argument that had to be settled.

This morning it was a bowl of cereal spilled in Lilli's lap. Cleo hadn't seen it happen; her attention had been diverted momentarily by Feather, her youngest.

And of course it had to happen *after* Lilli was dressed.

"Mom, this was the *last* outfit I *had*."

"Well, if you wouldn't use them so hard they might last more than three days, and if you didn't . . ." She stopped before she lost her temper. "Just take it off and go as you are."

"But Mom, nobody goes to school naked. *No*body. Give me some money and I'll stop at the store on—"

Cleo raised her voice, something she tried never to do. "Child, I know there are kids in your class whose parents can't afford to buy clothes at all."

"All right, so the poor kids don't—"

"That's enough. You're late already. Get going."

Lilli stalked from the room. Cleo heard the door slam.

Through it all Jules was an island of calm at the other end of the table, his nose in his newspad, sipping his second cup of coffee. Cleo glanced at her own bacon and eggs cooling on the plate, poured herself a first cup of coffee, then had to get up and help Paul find his other shoe.

By then Feather was wet again, so she put her on the table and peeled off the sopping diaper.

"Hey, listen to this," Jules said. " 'The City Council today passed without objection an ordinance requiring—' "

"Jules, aren't you a little behind schedule?"

He glanced at his thumbnail. "You're right. Thanks." He finished his coffee, folded his newspad and tucked it under his arm, bent over to kiss her, then frowned.

"You really ought to eat more, honey," he said, indicating the untouched eggs. "Eating for two, you know. 'By, now."

"Good-by," Cleo said, through clenched teeth. "And if I hear that 'eating for two' business again, I'll . . ." But he was gone.

She had time to scorch her lip on the coffee, then was out the door, hurrying to catch the train.

There were seats on the sun car, but of course Feather was with her and the UV wasn't good for her tender skin. After a longing look at the passengers reclining with the dark cups strapped over their eyes—and a rueful glance down at her own pale skin—Cleo boarded the next car and found a seat by a large man wearing a hardhat. She settled down in the cushions, adjusted the straps on the carrier slung in front of her, and let Feather have a nipple. She unfolded her newspad and spread it out in her lap.

"Cute," the man said. "How old is he?"

"She," Cleo said, without looking up. "Eleven days." And five hours and thirty-six minutes. . . .

She shifted in the seat, pointedly turning her shoulder to him, and made a show of activating her newspad and scanning the day's contents. She did not glance up as the train left the underground tunnel and emerged on the gently rolling, airless plain of Mendeleev. There was little enough out there to interest her, considering she made the forty-minute commute run to Hartman crater twice a day. They had discussed moving to Hartman, but Jules liked living in King City near his work, and of course the kids would have missed all their school friends.

There wasn't much in the news storage that morning. She queried when the red light flashed for an update. The pad printed some routine city business. Three sentences into the story she punched the reject key.

There was an Invasion Centennial parade listed for 1900 hours that evening. Parades bored her, and so did the Centennial. If you've heard one speech about how liberation of Earth is just around the corner if we all pull together, you've heard them all. Semantic content zero, nonsense quotient high.

She glanced wistfully at sports, noting that the J Sector jumpball team was doing poorly in the intracity tournament without her. Cleo's small stature and powerful legs had served her well as a starting sprint-wing in her playing days, but it just didn't seem possible to make practices anymore.

As a last resort, she called up the articles, digests, and analysis listings, the newspad's *Sunday Supplement* and Op-Ed department. A title caught her eye, and she punched it up.

Changing: The Revolution in Sex Roles
(Or, Who's on Top?)

Twenty years ago, when cheap and easy sex changes first became available to the general public, it was seen as the beginning of the revolution that would change the shape of human society in ways impossible to foresee. Sexual equality is one thing, the sociologists pointed out, but certain residual inequities—based on biological imperatives or on upbringing, depending on your politics—have proved impossible to weed out. Changing was going to end all that. Men and women would be able to see what it was like from the other side of the barrier that divides humanity. How could sex roles survive that?

Ten years later the answer was obvious. Changing had appealed to only a tiny minority. It was soon seen as a harmless aberration, practiced by only 1 per cent of the population. Everyone promptly forgot about the tumbling of barriers.

But in the intervening ten years a quieter revolution has been building. Almost unnoticed on the broad scale because it is an invisible phenomenon (how do you know the next woman you meet was not a man last week?), changing has been gaining growing, matter-of-fact acceptance among the children of the generation that rejected it. The chances are now better than even that you know someone who has had at least one sex change. The chances are better that one out of fifteen that you yourself have changed; if you are under twenty, the chance is one in three.

The article went on to describe the underground society which was springing up around changing. Changers tended to band together, frequenting their own taprooms, staging their own social events, remaining aloof from the larger society which many of them saw as outmoded and irrelevant. Changers tended to marry other changers. They divided the childbearing equally, each preferring to mother only one child. The author viewed this tendency with alarm, since it went against the socially approved custom of large families. Changers retorted that the time for that was past, pointing out that Luna had been tamed long ago. They quoted statistics proving that at present rates of expansion, Luna's population would be in the billions in an amazingly short time.

There were interviews with changers, and psychological profiles. Cleo read that the males had originally been the heaviest users of the new technology, stating sexual reasons for their decision, and the change had often been permanent. Today, the changer was slightly more likely to have been born female, and to give social reasons, the most common of which was pressure to bear children. But the modern changer committed him/herself to neither role. The average time between changes in an individual was two years, and declining.

Cleo read the whole article, then thought about using some of the reading references at the end. Not that much of it was really new to her. She had been aware of changing, without thinking about it much. The idea had never attracted her, and Jules was against it. But for some reason it had struck a chord this morning.

Feather had gone to sleep. Cleo carefully pulled the blanket down around the child's face, then wiped milk from her nipple. She folded her newspad and stowed it in her purse, then rested her chin on her palm and looked out the window for the rest of the trip.

Cleo was chief on-site architect for the new Food Systems, Inc., plantation that was going down in Hartman. As such, she was in charge of three junior architects, five construction bosses, and an army of drafters and workers. It was a big project, the biggest Cleo had ever handled.

She liked her work, but the best part had always been being there on the site when things were happening, actually supervising construction instead of running a desk. That had been difficult in the last months of carrying Feather, but at least there were maternity pressure suits. It was even harder now.

She had been through it all before, with Lilli and Paul. Everybody works. That had been the rule for a century, since the Invasion. There was no labor to spare for baby-sitters, so having children meant the mother or father must do the same job they had been doing before, but do it while taking care of the child. In practice, it was usually the mother, since she had the milk.

Cleo had tried leaving Feather with one of the women in the office, but each had her own work to do, and not unreasonably felt Cleo should bear the burden of her own offspring. And Feather never seemed to respond well to another person. Cleo would return from her visit to the site to find the child had been crying the whole time, disrupting everyone's work. She had taken Feather in a crawler a few times, but it wasn't the same.

That morning was taken up with a meeting. Cleo and the other section chiefs sat around the big table for three hours, discussing ways of dealing with the cost overrun, then broke for lunch only to return to the problem in the afternoon. Cleo's back was aching and she had a headache she couldn't shake, so Feather chose that day to be cranky. After ten minutes of increasingly hostile looks, Cleo had to retire to the booth with Leah Farnham, the accountant, and her three-year-old son, Eddie. The two of them followed the proceedings through earphones while trying to cope with their children and make their remarks through throat mikes. Half the people at the conference table either had to turn around when she spoke, or ignore her, and Cleo was hesitant to force them to that choice. As a result, she chose her remarks with extreme care. More often, she said nothing.

There was something at the core of the world of business that refused to adjust to children in the board room, while appearing to make every effort to accommodate the working mother. Cleo brooded about it, not for the first time.

But what did she want? Honestly, she could not see what else could be done. It certainly wasn't fair to disrupt the entire meeting with a crying baby. She wished she knew the answer. Those were her friends out there, yet her feeling of alienation was intense, staring through the glass wall that Eddie was smudging with his dirty fingers.

Luckily, Feather was a perfect angel on the trip home. She gurgled and smiled toothlessly at a woman who had stopped to admire her, and Cleo warmed to the infant for the first time that day. She spent the trip playing hand games with her, surrounded by the approving smiles of other passengers.

"Jules, I read the most interesting article on the pad this morning." There, it was out, anyway. She had decided the direct approach would be best.

"Hmm?"

"It was about changing. It's getting more and more popular."

"Is that so?" He did not look up from his book.

Jules and Cleo were in the habit of sitting up in bed for a few hours after the children were asleep. They spurned the video programs that were designed to lull workers after a hard day, preferring to use the time to catch up on reading, or to talk if either of them had anything to say. Over the last few years, they had read more and talked less.

Cleo reached over Feather's crib and got a packet of dopesticks. She flicked one to light with her thumbnail, drew on it, and exhaled a cloud of lavender smoke. She drew her legs up under her and leaned back against the wall.

"I just thought we might talk about it. That's all."

Jules put his book down. "All right. But what's to talk about? We're not into that."

She shrugged and picked at a cuticle. "I know. We did talk

about it, way back. I just wondered if you still felt the same, I guess." She offered him the stick and he took a drag.

"As far as I know, I do," he said easily. "It's not something I spend a great deal of thought on. What's the matter?" He looked at her suspiciously. "You weren't having any thoughts in that direction, were you?"

"Well, no, not exactly. No. But you really ought to read the article. More people are doing it. I just thought we ought to be aware of it."

"Yeah, I've heard that," Jules conceded. He laced his hands behind his head. "No way to tell unless you've worked with them and suddenly one day they've got a new set of equipment." He laughed. "First time it was sort of hard for me to get used to. Now I hardly think about it."

"Me, either."

"They don't cause any problem," Jules said with an air of finality. "Live and let live."

"Yeah." Cleo smoked in silence for a time and let Jules get back to his reading, but she still felt uncomfortable. "Jules?"

"What is it now?"

"Don't you ever wonder what it would be like?"

He sighed and closed his book, then turned to face her.

"I don't quite understand you tonight," he said.

"Well, maybe I don't, either, but we could talk—"

"Listen. Have you thought about what it would do to the kids? I mean, even if I was willing to seriously consider it, which I'm not."

"I talked to Lilli about that. Just theoretically, you understand. She said she has two teachers who change, and one of her best friends used to be a boy. There's quite a few kids at school who've changed. She takes it in stride."

"Yes, but she's older. What about Paul? What would it do to his concept of himself as a young man? I'll tell you, Cleo, in the back of my mind I keep thinking this business is a little sick. I feel it would have a bad effect on the children."

"Not according to—"

"Cleo, Cleo. Let's not get into an argument. Number one, I have no intention of getting a change, now or in the future. Two, if only one of us was changed, it would sure play hell with our sex life, wouldn't it? And three, I like you too much as you are." He leaned over and began to kiss her.

She was more than a little annoyed, but said nothing as his kisses became more intense. It was a damnably effective way of shutting off debate. And she could not stay angry: she was responding in spite of herself, easily, naturally.

It was as good as it always was with Jules. The ceiling, so familiar, once again became a calming blankness that absorbed her thoughts.

No, she had no complaints about being female, no sexual dissatisfactions. It was nothing as simple as that.

Afterward she lay on her side with her legs drawn up, her knees together. She faced Jules, who absently stroked her leg with one hand. Her eyes were closed, but she was not sleepy. She was savoring the warmth she cherished so much after sex; the slipperiness between her legs, holding his semen inside.

She felt the bed move as he shifted his weight.

"You did make it, didn't you?"

She opened one eye enough to squint at him.

"Of course I did. I always do. You know I never have any trouble in that direction."

He relaxed back into the pillow. "I'm sorry for . . . well, for springing on you like that."

"It's okay. It was nice."

"I had just thought you might have been . . . faking it. I'm not sure why I would think that."

She opened the other eye and patted him gently on the cheek.

"Jules, I'd never be that protective of your poor ego. If you don't satisfy me, I promise you'll be the second to know."

He chuckled, then turned on his side to kiss her.

"Good night, babe."

"G'night."

She loved him. He loved her. Their sex life was good—with the slight mental reservation that he always seemed to initiate it—and she was happy with her body.

So why was she still awake three hours later?

Shopping took a few hours on the vidphone Saturday morning. Cleo bought the household necessities for delivery that afternoon, then left the house to do the shopping she fancied: going from store to store, looking at things she didn't really need.

Feather was with Jules on Saturdays. She savored a quiet lunch alone at a table in the park plaza, then found herself walking down Brazil Avenue in the heart of the medical district. On impulse, she stepped into the New Heredity Body Salon.

It was only after she was inside that she admitted to herself she had spent most of the morning arranging for the impulse.

She was on edge as she was taken down a hallway to a consulting room, and had to force a smile for the handsome young man behind the desk. She sat, put her packages on the floor, and folded her hands in her lap. He asked what he could do for her.

"I'm not actually here for any work," she said. "I wanted to look into the costs, and maybe learn a little more about the procedures involved in changing."

He nodded understandingly, and got up.

"There's no charge for the initial consultation," he said. "We're happy to answer your questions. By the way, I'm Marion, spelled with an 'O' this month." He smiled at her and motioned for her to follow him. He stood her in front of a full-length mirror mounted on the wall.

"I know it's hard to make that first step. It was hard for me, and I do it for a living. So we've arranged this demonstration that won't cost you anything, either in money or worry. It's a nonthreatening way to see some of what it's all about, but it might startle you a little, so be prepared." He touched a button in the wall beside the mirror, and Cleo saw her clothes fade away. She realized it was not really a mirror, but a holographic screen linked to a computer.

The computer introduced changes in the image. In thirty seconds she faced a male stranger. There was no doubt the face was her own, but it was more angular, perhaps a little larger in its underlying bony structure. The skin on the stranger's jaw was rough, as if it needed shaving.

The rest of the body was as she might expect, though overly muscled for her tastes. She did little more than glance at the penis; somehow that didn't seem to matter so much. She spent more time studying the hair on the chest, the tiny nipples, and the ridges that had appeared on the hands and feet. The image mimicked her every movement.

"Why all the brawn?" she asked Marion. "If you're trying to sell me on this, you've taken the wrong approach."

Marion punched some more buttons. "I didn't choose this image," he explained. "The computer takes what it sees, and extrapolates. You're more muscular than the average woman. You probably exercise. This is what a comparable amount of training would have produced with male hormones to fix nitrogen in the muscles. But we're not bound by that."

The image lost about eight kilos of mass, mostly in the shoulders and thighs. Cleo felt a little more comfortable, but still missed the smoothness she was accustomed to seeing in her mirror.

She turned from the display and went back to her chair. Marion sat across from her and folded his hands on the desk.

"Basically, what we do is produce a cloned body from one of your own cells. Through a process called Y-Recombinant Viral Substitution we remove one of your X chromosomes and replace it with a Y.

"The clone is forced to maturity in the usual way, which takes about six months. After that, it's just a simple non-rejection-hazard brain transplant. You walk in as a woman, and leave an hour later as a man. Easy as that."

Cleo said nothing, wondering again what she was doing here.

"From there we can modify the body. We can make you taller or shorter, rearrange your face, virtually anything you like." He raised his eyebrows, then smiled ruefully and spread his hands.

"All right, Ms. King," he said. "I'm not trying to pressure you. You'll need to think about it. In the meantime, there's a process that would cost you very little, and might be just the thing to let you test the waters. Am I right in thinking your husband opposes this?"

She nodded, and he looked sympathetic.

"Not uncommon, not uncommon at all," he assured her. "It brings out castration fears in men who didn't even suspect they had them. Of course, we do nothing of the sort. His male body would be kept in a tank, ready for him to move back whenever he wanted to."

Cleo shifted in her chair. "What was this process you were talking about?"

"Just a bit of minor surgery. It can be done in ten minutes, and corrected in the same time before you even leave the office if you find you don't care for it. It's a good way to get husbands thinking about changing; sort of a signal you can send him. You've heard of the androgenous look. It's in all the fashion tapes. Many women, especially if they have large breasts like you do, find it an interesting change."

"You say it's cheap? And reversible?"

"All our processes are reversible. Changing the size or shape of breasts is our most common body operation."

Cleo sat on the examining table while the attendant gave her a quick physical.

"I don't know if Marion realized you're nursing," the woman said. "Are you sure this is what you want?"

How the hell should I know? Cleo thought. She wished the feeling of confusion and uncertainty would pass.

"Just do it."

Jules hated it.

He didn't yell or slam doors or storm out of the house; that had never been his style. He voices his objections coldly and quietly at the dinner table, after saying practically nothing since she walked in the door.

"I just would like to know why you thought you should do this without even talking to me about it. I don't demand that you *ask* me, just discuss it with me."

Cleo felt miserable, but was determined not to let it show. She held Feather in her arm, the bottle in her hand, and ignored the food cooling on her plate. She was hungry but at least she was not eating for two.

"Jules, I'd ask you before I rearranged the furniture. We both own this apartment. I'd ask you before I put Lilli or Paul in another school. We share the responsibility for their upbringing. But I don't ask you when I put on lipstick or cut my hair. It's my body."

"I like it, Mom," Lilli said. "You look like me."

Cleo smiled at her, reached over and tousled her hair.

"What do you like?" Paul asked, around a mouthful of food.

"See?" said Cleo. "It's not that important."

"I don't see how you can say that. And I said you didn't have to ask me. I just would . . . you should have . . . I should have *known*."

"It was an impulse, Jules."

"An impulse. An *impulse*." For the first time, he raised his voice, and Cleo knew how upset he really was. Lilli and Paul fell silent, and even Feather squirmed.

But Cleo liked it. Oh, not forever and ever: as an interesting change. It gave her a feeling of freedom to be that much in control of her body, to be able to decide how large she wished her breasts to be. Did it have anything to do with changing? She really didn't think so. She didn't feel the least bit like a man.

And what was a breast, anyway? It was anything from a nipple sitting flush with the rib cage to a mammoth hunk of fat and milk gland. Cleo realized Jules was suffering from the more-is-better syndrome, thinking of Cleo's action as the removal of her breasts, as if they had to be large to exist at all. What she had actually done was reduce their size.

No more was said at the table, but Cleo knew it was for the children's sake. As soon as they got into bed, she could feel the tension again.

"I can't understand why you did it *now*. What about Feather?"

"What about her?"

"Well, do you expect me to nurse her?"

Cleo finally got angry. "Damn it, that's *exactly* what I expect you to do. Don't tell me you don't know what I'm talking about. You think it's all fun and games, having to carry a child around all day because she needs the milk in your breasts?"

"You never complained before."

"I . . ." She stopped. He was right, of course. It amazed even Cleo that this had all come up so suddenly, but here it was, and she had to deal with it. *They* had to deal with it.

"That's because it isn't an awful thing. It's great to nourish another human being at your breast. I loved every minute of it with Lilli. Sometimes it was a headache, having her there all the time, but it was worth it. The same with Paul." She sighed. "The same with Feather, too, most of the time. You hardly think about it."

"Then why the revolt, now? With no warning?"

"It's not a revolt, honey. Do you see it as that? I just . . . I'd like you to try it. Take Feather for a few months. Take her to work like I do. Then you'd . . . you'd see a little of what I go through." She rolled on her side and playfully punched his arm, trying to lighten it in some way. "You might even like it. It feels real good."

He snorted. "I'd feel silly."

She jumped from the bed and paced toward the living room, then turned, more angry than ever. "Silly? Nursing is silly? Breasts are silly? Then why the hell do you wonder why I did what I did?"

"Being a *man* is what makes it silly," he retorted. "It

doesn't look right. I almost laugh every time I see a man with breasts. The hormones mess up your system, I heard, and—"

"That's *not true!* Not anymore. You can lactate—"

"—and besides, it's my body, as you pointed out. I'll do with it what pleases me."

She sat on the edge of the bed with her back to him. He reached out and stroked her, but she moved away.

"All right," she said. "I was just suggesting it. I thought you might like to try it. *I'm* not going to nurse her. She goes on the bottle from now on."

"If that's the way it has to be."

"It is. I want you to start taking Feather to work with you. Since she's going to be a bottle baby, it hardly matters which of us cares for her. I think you owe it to me, since I carried the burden alone with Lilli and Paul."

"All right."

She got into bed and pulled the covers up around her, her back to him. She didn't want him to see how close she was to tears.

But the feeling passed. The tension drained from her, and she felt good. She thought she had won a victory, and it was worth the cost. Jules would not stay angry at her.

She fell asleep easily, but woke up several times during the night as Jules tossed and turned.

He did adjust to it. It was impossible for him to say so all at once, but after a week without love-making he admitted grudgingly that she looked good. He began to touch her in the mornings and when they kissed after getting home from work. Jules had always admired her slim muscularity, her athlete's arms and legs. The slim chest looked so natural on her, it fit the rest of her so well that he began to wonder what all the fuss had been about.

One night whilc they were clearing the dinner dishes, Jules touched her nipples for the first time in a week. He asked her if it felt any different.

"There is very little feeling anywhere but the nipples," she pointed out, "no matter how big a woman is. You know that."

"Yeah, I guess I do."

She knew they would make love that night and determined it would be on her terms.

She spent a long time in the bathroom, letting him get settled with his book, then came out and took it away. She got on top of him and pressed close, kissing and tickling his nipples with her fingers.

She was aggressive and insistent. At first he seemed reluctant, but soon he was responding as she pressed her lips hard against his, forcing his head back into the pillow.

"I love you," he said, and raised his head to kiss her nose. "Are you ready?"

"I'm ready." He put his arms around her and held her close, then rolled over and hovered above her.

"Jules. *Jules.* Stop it." She squirmed onto her side, her legs held firmly together.

"What's wrong?"

"I want to be on top tonight."

"Oh. All right." He turned over again and reclined passively as she repositioned herself. Her heart was pounding. There had been no reason to think he would object—they had made love in any and all positions, but basically the exotic ones were a change of pace from the "natural" one with her on her back. Tonight she had wanted to feel in control.

"Open your legs, darling," she said, with a smile. He did, but didn't return the smile. She raised herself on her hands and knees and prepared for the tricky insertion.

"Cleo."

"What is it? This will take a little effort, but I think I can make it worth your while, so if you'd just—"

"Cleo, what the hell is the purpose of this?"

She stopped dead and let her head sag between her shoulders.

"What's the matter? Are you feeling silly with your feet in the air?"

"Maybe. Is that what you wanted?"

"Jules, humiliating you was the farthest thing from my mind."

"Then what *was* on your mind? It's not like we've never done it this way before. It's—"

"Only when *you* chose to do so. It's always your decision."

"It's not degrading to be on the bottom."

"Then why were you feeling silly?"

He didn't answer, and she wearily lifted herself away from him, sitting on her knees at his feet. She waited, but he didn't seem to want to talk about it.

"I've never complained about that position," she ventured. "I don't *have* any complaints about it. It works pretty well." Still he said nothing. "All right. I wanted to see what it looked like from up there. I was tired of looking at the ceiling. I was curious."

"And *that's* why I felt *silly*. I never minded you being on top before, have I? But before . . .well, it's never been in the context of the last couple weeks. I *know* what's on your mind."

"And you feel threatened by it. By the fact that I'm curious about changing, that I want to know what it's like to take charge. You know I can't—and wouldn't if I could—force a change on you."

"But your curiosity is wrecking our marriage."

She felt like crying again, but didn't let it show except for a trembling of her lower lip. She didn't want him to try and soothe her; that was all too likely to work, and she would find herself on her back with her legs in the air. She looked down at the bed and nodded slowly, then got up. She went to the mirror and took the brush, began running it through her hair.

"What are you doing now? Can't we talk about this?"

"I don't feel much like talking right now." She leaned forward and examined her face as she brushed, then dabbed at the corners of her eyes with a tissue. "I'm going out. I'm still curious."

He said nothing as she started for the door.

"I may be a little late."

The place was called Oophyte. The capital "O" had a plus sign hanging from it, and an arrow in the upper right side. The sign was built so that the symbols revolved; one moment the plus was inside and the arrow out, the next moment the reverse.

Cleo moved in a pleasant haze across the crowded dance floor, pausing now and then to draw on her dopestick. The air in the room was thick with lavender smoke, illuminated by flashing blue lights. She danced when the mood took her. The music was so loud that she didn't have to think about it; the noise gripped her bones and animated her arms and legs. She glided through a forest of naked skin, feeling the occasional roughness of a paper suit and, rarely, expensive cotton clothing. It was like moving underwater, like wading through molasses.

She saw him across the floor and began moving in his direction. He took no notice of her for some time, though she danced right in front of him. Few of the dancers had partners in more than the transitory sense. Some were celebrating life, others were displaying themselves, but all were looking for partners, so eventually he realized she had been there an unusual length of time. He was easily as stoned as she was.

She told him what she wanted.

"Sure. Where do you want to go? Your place?"

She took him down the hall in back and touched her credit bracelet to the lock on one of the doors. The room was simple, but clean.

He looked a lot like her phantom twin in the mirror, she noted with one part of her mind. It was probably why she had chosen him. She embraced him and lowered him gently to the bed.

"Do you want to exchange names?" he asked. The grin on his face kept getting sillier as she toyed with him.

"I don't care. Mostly I think I want to use you."

"Use away. My name's Saffron."

"I'm Cleopatra. Would you get on your back, please?"

He did, and they did. It was hot in the little room, but neither of them minded it. It was healthy exertion, the physical sensations were great, and when Cleo was through she had learned nothing. She collapsed on top of him. He did not seem surprised when tears began falling on his shoulder.

"I'm sorry," she said, sitting up and getting ready to leave.

"Don't go," he said, putting his hand on her shoulder. "Now that you've got that out of your system, maybe we can make love."

She didn't want to smile, but she had to, then she was crying harder, putting her face to his chest and feeling the warmth of his arms around her and the hair tickling her nose. She realized what she was doing, and tried to pull away.

"For God's sake, don't be ashamed that you need someone to cry on."

"It's weak. I . . . I just didn't want to be weak."

"We're all weak."

She gave up struggling and nestled there until the tears stopped. She sniffed, wiped her nose, and faced him.

"What's it like? Can you tell me?" She was about to explain what she meant, but he seemed to understand.

"It's like . . . nothing special."

"You were born female, weren't you? I mean, you . . . I thought I might be able to tell."

"It's no longer important how I was born. I've been both. It's still me, on the inside. You understand?"

"I'm not sure I do."

They were quiet for a long time. Cleo thought of a thousand things to say, questions to ask, but could do nothing.

"You've been coming to a decision, haven't you?" he said, at last. "Are you any closer after tonight?"

"I'm not sure."

"It's not going to solve any problems, you know. It might even create some."

She pulled away from him and got up. She shook her hair and wished for a comb.

"Thank you, Cleopatra," he said.

"Oh. Uh, thank you . . ." She had forgotten his name. She smiled again to cover her embarrassment, and shut the door behind her.

"Hello?"

"Yes. This is Cleopatra King. I had a consultation with one of your staff. I believe it was ten days ago."

"Yes, Ms. King. I have your file. What can I do for you?"

She took a deep breath. "I want you to start the clone. I left a tissue sample."

"Very well, Ms. King. Did you have any instructions concerning the chromosome donor?"

"Do you need consent?"

"Not as long as there's a sample in the bank."

"Use my husband, Jules La Rhin. Security number 4454390."

"Very good. We'll be in contact with you."

Cleo hung up the phone and rested her forehead against the cool metal. She should never get this stoned, she realized. What had she done?

But it was not final. It would be six months before she had to decide if she would ever use the clone. Damn Jules. Why did he have to make such a big thing out of it?

Jules did *not* make a big thing of it when she told him what she had done. He took it quietly and calmly, as if he had been expecting it.

"You know I won't follow you in this?"

"I know you feel that way. I'm interested to see if you change your mind."

"Don't count on it. I want to see if you change yours."

"I haven't *made up* my mind. But I'm giving myself the option."

"All I ask is that you bear in mind what this could do to our relationship. I love you, Cleo. I don't think that will ever change. But if you walk into this house as a man, I don't think I'll be able to see you as the person I've always loved."

"You could if you were a woman."

"But I won't be."

"And I'll be the same person I always was." But would she be? What the hell was *wrong?* What had Jules ever done that he should deserve this? She made up her mind never to go through with it, and they made love that night and it was very, very good.

But somehow she never got around to calling the vivarium and telling them to abort the clone. She made the decision not to go through with it a dozen times over the next six months, and never had the clone destroyed.

Their relationship in bed became uneasy as time passed. At first, it was good. Jules made no objections when she initiated sex, and was willing to do it any way she preferred. Once that was accomplished she no longer cared whether she was on top or underneath. The important thing had been having the option of making love when she wanted to, the way she wanted to.

"That's what this is all about," she told him one night, in a moment of clarity when everything seemed to make sense except his refusal to see things from her side. "It's the option I want. I'm not unhappy being female. I don't like the feeling that there's *anything* I *can't* be. I want to know if I feel more secure being aggressive as a man, because I sure don't, most of the time, as a woman. Or do men feel the same insecurities I feel? Would Cleo the man feel free to cry? I don't know any of those things."

"But you said it yourself. You'll still be the same person."

They began to drift apart in small ways. A few weeks after her outing to the Oophyte she returned home one Sunday afternoon to find him in bed with a woman. It was not like him to do it like that; their custom had been to bring lovers home and introduce them, to keep it friendly and open. Cleo was amused, because she saw it as his way of getting back at her for her trip to the encounter bar.

So she was the perfect hostess, joining them in bed, which seemed to disconcert Jules. The woman's name was Harriet, and Cleo found herself liking her. She was a changer—something Jules had not known or he certainly would not have chosen her to make Cleo feel bad. Harriet was uncomfortable when she realized why she was there. Cleo managed to put her at ease by making love to her, something that surprised Cleo a little and Jules considerably, since she had never done it before.

Cleo enjoyed it; she found Harriet's smooth body to be a whole new world. And she felt she had neatly turned the tables on Jules, making him confront once more the idea of his wife in the man's role.

The worst part was the children. They had discussed the possible impending change with Lilli and Paul.

Lilli could not see what all the fuss was about; it was a part of her life, something that was all around her which she took for granted as something she herself would do when she was old enough. But when she began picking up the concern from her father, she drew subtly closer to her mother. Cleo was tremendously relieved. She didn't think she could have held to it in the face of Lilli's displeasure. Lilli was her first born, and though she hated to admit it and did her best not to play favorites, her darling. She had taken a year's leave from her job at appalling expense to the household budget so she could devote all her time to her infant daughter. She often wished she could somehow return to those simpler days, when motherhood had been her whole life.

Feather, of course, was not consulted. Jules had assumed the responsibility for her nurture without complaint, and seemed to be enjoying it. It was fine with Cleo, though it maddened her that he was so willing about taking over the mothering role without being willing to try it as a female. Cleo loved Feather as much as the other two, but sometimes had trouble recalling why they had decided to have her. She felt she had gotten the procreation impulse out of her system with Paul, and yet there Feather was.

Paul was the problem.

Things could get tense when Paul expressed doubts about how he would feel if his mother were to become a man. Jules's face would darken, and he might not speak for days. When he did speak, often in the middle of the night when neither of them could sleep, it would be in a verbal explosion that was as close to violence as she had ever seen him.

It frightened her, because she was by no means sure of herself when it came to Paul. Would it hurt him? Jules spoke of gender identity crises, of the need for stable role models, and finally, in naked honesty, of the fear that his son would grow up to be somehow less than a man.

Cleo didn't know, but cried herself to sleep over it many nights. They had read articles about it and found that psychologists were divided. Traditionalists made much of the importance of sex roles, while changers felt sex roles were important only to those who were trapped in them; with the breaking of the sexual barrier, the concept of roles vanished.

The day finally came when the clone body was ready. Cleo still did not know what she should do.

"Are you feeling comfortable now? Just nod if you can't talk."

"Wha . . ."

"Relax. It's all over. You'll be feeling like walking in a few minutes. We'll have someone take you home. You may feel drunk for a while, but there's no drugs in your system."

"Wha' . . . happen?"

"It's over. Just relax."

Cleo did, curling up in a ball. Eventually he began to laugh.

Drunk was not the word for it. He sprawled on the bed, trying on pronouns for size. It was all so funny. *He* was on *his* back with *his* hands in *his* lap. He giggled and rolled back and forth, over and over, fell on the floor in hysterics.

He raised his head.

"Is that you, Jules?"

"Yes, it's me." He helped Cleo back onto the bed, then sat on the edge, not too near, but not unreachably far away. "How do you feel?"

He snorted. "Drunker 'n a skunk." He narrowed his eyes, forced them to focus on Jules. "You must call me Leo now. Cleo is a woman's name. You shouldn't have called me Cleo then."

"All right. I didn't call you Cleo, though."

"You didn't? Are you *sure?*"

"I'm very sure it's something I wouldn't have said."

"Oh. Okay." He lifted his head and looked confused for a moment. "You know what? I'm gonna be sick."

Leo felt much better an hour later. He sat in the living

room with Jules, both of them on the big pillows that were the only furniture.

They spoke of inconsequential matters for a time, punctuated by long silences. Leo was no more used to the sound of his new voice than Jules was.

"Well," Jules said, finally, slapping his hands on his knees and standing up. "I really don't know what your plans are from here. Did you want to go out tonight? Find a woman, see what it's like?"

Leo shook his head. "I tried that out as soon as I got home," he said. "The male orgasm, I mean."

"What was it like?"

He laughed. "Certainly you know that by now."

"No, I meant, after being a woman—"

"I know what you mean." He shrugged. "The erection is interesting. So much larger than what I'm used to. Otherwise . . ." He frowned for a moment. "A lot the same. Some different. More localized. Messier."

"Um." Jules looked away, studying the electric fireplace as if seeing it for the first time. "Had you planned to move out? It isn't necessary, you know. We could move people around. I can go in with Paul, or we could move him in with me in . . . in our old room. You could have his." He turned away from Leo, and put his hand to his face.

Leo ached to get up and comfort him, but felt it would be exactly the wrong thing to do. He let Jules get himself under control.

"If you'll have me, I'd like to continue sleeping with you."

Jules said nothing, and didn't turn around.

"Jules, I'm perfectly willing to do whatever will make you most comfortable. There doesn't have to be any sex. Or I'd be happy to do what I used to do when I was in late pregnancy. You wouldn't have to do anything at all."

"No sex," he said.

"Fine, fine. Jules, I'm getting awfully tired. Are you ready to sleep?"

There was a long pause, then he turned and nodded.

They lay quietly, side by side, not touching. The lights were out; Leo could barely see the outline of Jules's body.

After a long time, Jules turned on his side.

"Cleo, are you in there? Do you still love me?"

"I'm here," he said. "I love you. I always will."

Jules jumped when Leo touched him, but made no objection. He began to cry, and Leo held him close. They fell asleep in each other's arms.

The Oophyte was as full and noisy as ever. It gave Leo a headache.

He did not like the place any more than Cleo had, but it was the only place he knew to find sex partners quickly and easily, with no emotional entanglements and no long process of seduction. Everyone there was available; all one needed to do was ask. They used each other for sexual calisthenics just one step removed from masturbation, cheerfully admitted the fact, and took the position that if you didn't approve, what were you doing there? There were plenty of other places for romance and relationships.

Leo didn't normally approve of it—not for himself, though he cared not at all what other people did for amusement. He preferred to know someone he bedded.

But he was here tonight to learn. He felt he needed the practice. He did not buy the argument that he would know just what to do because he had been a woman and knew what they liked. He needed to know how people reacted to him as a male.

Things went well. He approached three women and was accepted each time. The first was a mess—so *that's* what they meant by too soon!—and she was rather indignant about it until he explained his situation. After that she was helpful and supportive.

He was about to leave when he was propositioned by a woman who said her name was Lynx. He was tired, but decided to go with her.

Ten frustrating minutes later she sat up and moved away from him. "What are you here for, if that's all the interest you can muster? And don't tell me it's my fault."

"I'm sorry," he said. "I forgot. I thought I would . . . well, I didn't realize I had to be really interested before I could perform."

"Perform? That's a funny way to put it."

"I'm sorry." He told her what the problem was, how many times he had made love in the last two hours. She sat on the edge of the bed and ran her hands through her hair, frustrated and irritable.

"Well, it's not the end of the world. There's plenty more out there. But you could give a girl a warning. You didn't have to say yes back there."

"I know. It's my fault. I'll have to learn to judge my capacity, I guess. It's just that I'm used to being *able* to, even if I'm not particularly—"

Lynx laughed. "What am I saying? Listen to me. Honey, I used to have the same problem myself. *Weeks* of not getting it up. And I know it hurts."

"Well," Leo said, "I know what you're feeling like, too. It's no fun."

Lynx shrugged. "In other circumstances, yeah. But like I said, the woods are full of 'em tonight. I won't have any problem." She put her hand on his cheek and pouted at him. "Hey, I didn't hurt your poor male ego, did I?"

Leo thought about it, probed around for bruises, and found none.

"No."

She laughed. "I didn't think so. Becuase you don't have one. Enjoy it, Leo. A male ego is something that has to be grown carefully, when you're young. People have to keep pointing out what you have to do to be a man, so you can recognize failure when you can't 'perform.' How come you used that word?"

"I don't know. I guess I was just thinking of it that way."

"Trying to be a quote *man* unquote. Leo, you don't have enough emotional investment in it. And you're *lucky*. It took me over a year to shake mine. Don't be a man. Be a male human, instead. The switchover's a lot easier that way."

"I'm not sure what you mean."

She patted his knee. "Trust me. Do you see me getting all upset because I wasn't sexy enough to turn you on, or some such garbage? No. I wasn't brought up to worry that way. But reverse it. If I'd done to you what you just did to me, wouldn't something like that have occurred to you?"

"I think it would. Though I've always been pretty secure in that area."

"The most secure of us are whimpering children beneath it, at least some of the time. You understand that I got upset because you said yes when you weren't ready? And that's *all* I was upset about? It was impolite, Leo. A male human shouldn't do that to a female human. With a man and a woman, it's different. The poor fellow's got a lot of junk in his head, and so does the woman, so they shouldn't be held responsible for the tricks their egos play on them."

Leo laughed. "I don't know if you're making sense at all.

But I like the sound of it. 'Male human.' Maybe I'll see the difference one day."

Some of the expected problems never developed.

Paul barely noticed the change. Leo had prepared himself for a traumatic struggle with his son, and it never came. If it changed Paul's life at all, it was in the fact that he could now refer to his maternal parent as Leo instead of mother.

Strangely enough, it was Lilli who had the most trouble at first. Leo was hurt by it, tried not to show it, and did everything he could to let her adjust gradually. Finally she came to him one day about a week after the change. She said she had been silly, and wanted to know if she could get a change, too, since one of her best friends was getting one. Leo talked her into remaining female until after the onset of puberty. He told her he thought she might enjoy it.

Leo and Jules circled each other like two tigers in a cage, unsure if a fight was necessary but ready to start clawing out eyes if it came to it. Leo didn't like the analogy; if he had still been a female tiger, he would have felt sure of the outcome. But he had no wish to engage in a dominance struggle with Jules.

They shared an apartment, a family, and a bed. They were elaborately polite, but touched each other only rarely, and Leo always felt he should apologize when they did. Jules would not meet his eyes; their gazes would touch, then rebound like two cork balls with identical static charges.

But eventually Jules accepted Leo. He was "that guy who's always around" in Jules's mind. Leo didn't care for that, but saw it as progress. In a few more days Jules began to discover that he liked Leo. They began to share things, to talk more. The subject of their previous relationship was taboo for a while. It was as if Jules wanted to know Leo from scratch, not acknowledging there had ever been a Cleo who had once been his wife.

It wasn't that simple; Leo would not let it be. Jules sometimes sounded like he was mourning the passing of a loved one when he hesitantly began talking about the hurt inside him. He was able to talk freely to Leo, and it was in a slightly different manner from the way he had talked to Cleo. He poured out his soul. It was astonishing to Leo that there were so many bruises on it, so many defenses and insecurities. There was buried hostility which Jules had never felt free to tell a woman.

Leo let him go on, but when Jules started a sentence with, "I could never tell this to Cleo," or, "Now that she's gone," Leo would go to him, take his hand, and force him to look.

"I'm Cleo," he would say. "I'm right here, and I love you."

They started doing things together. Jules took him to places Cleo had never been. They went out drinking together and had a wonderful time getting sloshed. Before, it had always been dinner with a few drinks or dopesticks, then a show or concert. Now they might come home at 0200, harmonizing loud enough to get thrown in jail. Jules admitted he hadn't had so much fun since his college days.

Socializing was a problem. Few of their old friends were changers, and neither of them wanted to face the complications of going to a party as a couple. They couldn't make friends among changers, because Jules correctly saw he would be seen as an outsider.

So they saw a lot of men. Leo had thought he knew all of Jules's close friends, but found he had been wrong. He saw a side of Jules he had never seen before: more relaxed in ways, some of his guardedness gone, but with other defenses in place. Leo sometimes felt like a spy, looking in on a stratum of society he had always known was there, but had never been able to penetrate. If Cleo had walked into the group its structure would have changed subtly; she would have created a new milieu by her presence, like light destroying the atom it was meant to observe.

After his initial outing to the Oophyte, Leo remained celibate for a long time. He did not want to have sex casually; he wanted to love Jules. As far as he knew, Jules was abstaining, too.

But they found an acceptable alternative in double-dating. They shopped around together for a while, taking out different women and having a lot of fun without getting into sex, until each settled on a woman he could have a relationship with. Jules was with Diane, a woman he had known at work for many years. Leo went out with Harriet.

The four of them had great times together. Leo loved being a pal to Jules, but would not let it remain simply that. He took to reminding Jules that he could do this with Cleo, too. What Leo wanted to emphasize was that he could be a companion, a buddy, a confidant no matter which sex he was. He wanted to combine the best of being a woman and being a man, be both things for Jules, fulfill all his needs. But it hurt to think that Jules would not do the same for him.

"Well, hello, Leo. I didn't expect to see you today."

"Can I come in, Harriet?"

She held the door open for him.

"Can I get you anything? Oh, yeah, before you go any further, that 'Harriet' business is finished. I changed my name today. It's Joule from now on. That's spelled j-o-u-l-e."

"Okay, Joule. Nothing for me, thanks." He sat on her couch.

Leo was not surprised at the new name. Changers had a tendency to get away from "name" names. Some did as Cleo had done by choosing a gender equivalent or a similar sound. Others ignored gender connotations and used the one they had always used. But most eventually chose a neutral word, according to personal preference.

"Jules, Julia," he muttered.

"What was that?" Joule's brow wrinkled slightly. "Did you come here for mothering? Things going badly?"

Leo slumped down and contemplated his folded hands.

"I don't know. I guess I'm depressed. How long has it been now? Five months? I've learned a lot, but I'm not sure just what it is. I feel like I've grown. I see the world . . . well, I see things differently, yes. But I'm still basically the same person."

"In the sense that you're the same person at thirty-three as you were at ten?"

Leo squirmed. "Okay. Yeah, I've changed. But it's not any kind of reversal. Nothing turned topsy-turvy. It's an expansion. It's not a new viewpoint. It's like filling something up, moving out into unused spaces. Becoming . . ." His hands groped in the air, then fell back into his lap. "It's like a completion."

Joule smiled. "And you're disappointed? What more could you ask?"

Leo didn't want to get into that just yet. "Listen to this, and see if you agree. I always saw male and female—whatever that is, and I don't know if the two *really* exist other than physically and don't think it's important anyway. . . . I saw those qualities as separate. Later, I thought of them like Siamese twins in everybody's head. But the twins were usually fighting, trying to cut each other off. One would beat the other down, maim it, throw it in a cell, and never feed it, but they were always connected and the beaten-down one would make the winner pay for the victory.

"So I wanted to try and patch things up between them. I

thought I'd just introduce them to each other and try to referee, but they got along a lot better than I expected. In fact, they turned into one whole person, and found they could be very happy together. I can't tell them apart any more. Does that make any sense?"

Joule moved over to sit beside him.

"It's a good analogy, in its way. I feel something like that, but I don't think about it anymore. So what's the problem? You just told me you feel whole now."

Leo's face contorted. "Yes, I do. And if I am, what does that make Jules?" He began to cry, and Joule let him get it out, just holding his hand. She thought he'd better face it alone, this time. When he had calmed down, she began to speak quietly.

"Leo, Jules is happy as he is. I think he could be much happier, but there's no way for us to show him that without having him do something that he fears so much. It's possible that he will do it someday, after more time to get used to it. And it's possible that he'll hate it and run screaming back to his manhood. Sometimes the maimed twin can't be rehabilitated."

She sighed heavily, and got up to pace the room.

"There's going to be a lot of this in the coming years," she said. "A lot of broken hearts. We're not really very much like them, you know. We get along better. We're not angels, but we may be the most civilized, considerate group the race has yet produced. There are fools and bastards among us, just like the one-sexers, but I think we tend to be a little less foolish, and a little less cruel. I think changing is here to stay.

"And what you've got to realize is that you're lucky. And so is Jules. It could have been much worse. I know of several broken homes just among my own friends. There's going to be many more before society has assimilated this. But your love for Jules and his for you has held you together. He's made a tremendous adjustment, maybe as big as the one you made. He *likes* you. In either sex. Okay, so you don't make love to him as Leo. You may never reach that point."

"We did. Last night." Leo shifted on the couch. "I . . . I got mad. I told him if he wanted to see Cleo, he had to learn to relate to me, because I'm *me*, dammit."

"I think that might have been a mistake."

Leo looked away from her. "I'm starting to think so, too."

"But I think the two of you can patch it up, if there's any damage. You've come through a lot together."

"I didn't mean to force anything on him, I just got mad."

"And maybe you *should* have. It might have been just the thing. You'll have to wait and see."

Leo wiped his eyes and stood up.

"Thanks, Harr . . . sorry. Joule. You've helped me. I . . . uh, I may not be seeing you as often for a while."

"I understand. Let's stay friends, okay?" She kissed him, and he hurried away.

She was sitting on a pillow facing the door when he came home from work, her legs crossed, elbow resting on her knee with a dopestick in her hand. She smiled at him.

"Well, you're home early. What happened?"

"I stayed home from work." She nearly choked, trying not to laugh. He threw his coat to the closet and hurried into the kitchen. She heard something being stirred, then the sound of glass shattering. He burst through the doorway.

"Cleo!"

"Darling, you look so handsome with your mouth hanging open."

He shut it, but still seemed unable to move. She went to him, feeling tingling excitement in her loins like the return of an old friend. She put his arms around him, and he nearly crushed her. She loved it.

He drew back slightly and couldn't seem to get enough of her face, his eyes roaming every detail.

"How long will you stay this way?" he asked. "Do you have any idea?"

"I don't know. Why?"

He smiled, a little sheepishly. "I hope you won't take this wrong. I'm so *happy* to see you. Maybe I shouldn't say it . . . but no, I think I'd better. I like Leo. I think I'll miss him, a little."

She nodded. "I'm not hurt. How could I be?" She drew away and led him to a pillow. "Sit down, Jules. We have to have a talk." His knees gave way under him and he sat, looking up expectantly.

"Leo isn't gone, and don't you ever think that for a minute. He's right here." She thumped her chest and looked at him defiantly. "He'll always be here. He'll never go away."

"I'm sorry, Cleo, I—"

"No, don't talk yet. It was my own fault, but I didn't know any better. I never should have called myself Leo. It gave you an easy out. You didn't have to face Cleo being a male. I'm changing all that. My name is Nile. N-i-l-e. I won't answer to anything else."

"All right. It's a nice name."

"I thought of calling myself Lion. For Leo the lion. But I decided to be who I always was, the queen of the Nile, Cleopatra. For old time's sake."

He said nothing, but his eyes showed his appreciation.

"What you have to understand is that they're both gone, in a sense. You'll never be with Cleo again. I look like her now. I resemble her inside, too, like an adult resembles the child. I have a tremendous amount in common with what she was. But I'm not her."

He nodded. She sat beside him and took his hand.

"Jules, this isn't going to be easy. There are things I want to do, people I want to meet. We're not going to be able to share the same friends. We could drift apart because of it. I'm going to have to fight resentment because you'll be holding me back. You won't let me explore your female side like I want to. You're going to resent me because I'll be trying to force you into something you think is wrong for you. But I want to try and make it work."

He let out his breath. "God, Cl . . . Nile. I've never been so scared in my life. I thought you were leading up to leaving me."

She squeezed his hand. "Not if I can help it. I want each of us to try and accept the other as they are. For me, that includes being male whenever I feel like it. It's all the same to me, but I know it's going to be hard for *you.*"

They embraced, and Jules wiped his tears on her shoulder, then faced her again.

"I'll do anything and everything in my power, up to—"

She put her finger to her lips. "I know. I accept you that way. But I'll keep trying to convince you."

UNACCOMPANIED SONATA

by Orson Scott Card

There are utopias of hope and utopias of technology, utopias of reason and utopias of organization, but here's a future for humanity which creates a contented and perfectly functioning world by means which are not only unprecedented but positively frightening. The gooseflesh thing about this new political concept is that it might work.

Tuning Up

When Christian Haroldsen was six months old, preliminary tests showed a predisposition toward rhythm and a keen awareness of pitch. There were other tests, of course, and many possible routes still open to him. But rhythm and pitch were the governing signs of his own private zodiac, and already the reinforcement began. Mr. and Mrs. Haroldsen were provided with tapes of many kinds of sound, and instructed to play them constantly, waking or sleeping.

When Christian Haroldsen was two years old, his seventh battery of tests pinpointed the future he would inevitably follow. His creativity was exceptional, his curiosity insatiable, his understanding of music so intense that the top of all the tests said, "Prodigy."

Prodigy was the word that took him from his parents' home to a house in a deep deciduous forest where winter was savage and violent and summer a brief desperate eruption of green. He grew up cared for by unsinging servants, and the only music he was allowed to hear was birdsong, and windsong, and the cracking of winter wood; thunder, and the faint cry of golden leaves as they broke free and tumbled to the earth; rain on the roof and the drip of water from icicles; the chatter of squirrels and the deep silence of snow falling on a moonless night.

These sounds were Christian's only conscious music; he grew up with the symphonies of his early years only a distant and impossible-to-retrieve memory. And so he learned to hear music in unmusical things—for he had to find music, even when there was none to find.

He found that colors made sounds in his mind: sunlight in summer a blaring chord; moonlight in winter a thin mournful wail; new green in spring a low murmur in almost (but not quite) random rhythms; the flash of a red fox in the leaves a gasp of startlement.

And he learned to play all those sounds on his Instrument.

In the world were violins, trumpets, clarinets and crumhorns, as there had been for centuries. Christian knew nothing of that. Only his Instrument was available. It was enough.

One room in Christian's house, which he had alone most of the time, he lived in: a bed (not too soft), a chair and table, a silent machine that cleaned him and his clothing, and an electric light.

The other room contained only his Instrument. It was a console with many keys and strips and levers and bars, and when he touched any part of it, a sound came out. Every key made a different sound; every point on the strips made a different pitch; every lever modified the tone; every bar altered the structure of the sound.

When he first came to the house, Christian played (as children will) with the Instrument, making strange and funny noises. It was his only playmate; he learned it well, could produce any sound he wanted to. At first he delighted in loud, blaring tones. Later he began to learn the pleasure of silences and rhythms. Later he began to play with soft and loud, and to play two sounds at once, and to change those two sounds together to make a new sound, and to play again a sequence of sounds he had played before.

Gradually, the sounds of the forest outside his house found their way into the music he played. He learned to make winds sing through his Instrument; he learned to make summer one of the songs he could play at will; green with its infinite variations was his most subtle harmony; the birds cried out from his Instrument with all the passion of Christian's loneliness.

And the word spread to the licensed Listeners:

"There's a new sound north of here, east of here; Christian Haroldsen, and he'll tear out your heart with his songs."

The Listeners came, a few to whom variety was everything first, then those to whom novelty and vogue mattered most, and at last those who valued beauty and passion above everything else. They came, and stayed out in Christian's woods, and listened as his music was played through perfect speakers on the roof of his house. When the music stopped, and Christian came out of his house, he could see the Listeners moving away; he asked, and was told why they came; he marveled that the things he did for love on his Instrument could be of interest to other people.

He felt, strangely, even more lonely to know that he could sing to the Listeners and yet would never be able to hear their songs.

"But they have no songs," said the woman who came to bring him food every day. "They are Listeners. You are a Maker. You have songs, and they listen."

"Why?" asked Christian, innocently.

The woman looked puzzled. "Because that's what they want most to do. They've been tested, and they are happiest as Listeners. You are happiest as a Maker. Aren't you happy?"

"Yes," Christian answered, and he was telling the truth. His life was perfect, and he wouldn't change anything, not even the sweet sadness of the backs of the Listeners as they walked away at the end of his songs.

Christian was seven years old.

First Movement

For the third time the short man with glasses and a strangely inappropriate mustache dared to wait in the underbrush for Christian to come out. For the third time he was overcome by the beauty of the song that had just ended, a mournful symphony that made the short man with glasses feel the pressure of the leaves above him even though it was summer and they had months left before they would fall. The fall was still inevitable, said Christian's song, through all their life the leaves hold within them the power to die, and that must color their life. The short man with glasses wept—but when the song ended and the other Listeners moved away, he hid in the brush and waited.

This time his wait was rewarded. Christian came out of his house, and walked among the trees, and came toward where the short man with glasses waited. The short man admired the easy, unpostured way that Christian walked. The composer looked to be about thirty, yet there was something childish in the way he looked around him, the way his walk was aimless and prone to stop just so he could touch (not break) a fallen twig with his bare toes.

"Christian," said the short man with glasses.

Christian turned, startled. In all these years, no Listener had ever spoken to him. It was forbidden. Christian knew the law.

"It's forbidden," Christian said.

"Here," the short man with glasses said, holding out a small black object.

"What is it?"

The short man grimaced. "Just take it. Push the button and it plays."

"Plays?"

"Music."

Christian's eyes went wide. "But that's forbidden. I can't have my creativity polluted by hearing other musicians' work. That would make me imitative and derivative instead of original."

"Reciting," the man said. "You're just reciting that. This is Bach's music." There was reverence in his voice.

"I can't," Christian said.

And then the short man shook his head. "You don't know. You don't know what you're missing. But I heard it in your song when I came here years ago, Christian. You want this."

"It's forbidden," Christian answered, for to him the very fact that a man who knew an act was forbidden still wanted to perform it was astounding, and he couldn't get past the novelty of it to realize that some action was expected of him.

There were footsteps and words being spoken in the distance, and the short man's face became frightened. He ran at Christian, forced the recorder into his hands, then took off toward the gate of the preserve.

Christian took the recorder and held it in a spot of sunlight coming through the leaves. It gleamed dully. "Bach," Christian said. Then, "Who the hell is Bach?"

But he didn't throw the recorder down. Nor did he give the recorder to the woman who came to ask him what the short man with glasses had stayed for. "He stayed for at least ten minutes."

"I only saw him for thirty seconds," Christian answered.

"And?"

"He wanted me to hear some other music. He had a recorder."

"Did he give it to you?"

"No," Christian said. "Doesn't he still have it?"

"He must have dropped it in the woods."

"He said it was Bach."

"It's forbidden. That's all you need to know. If you should find the recorder, Christian, you know the law."

"I'll give it to you."

She looked at him carefully. "You know what would happen if you listened to such a thing."

Christian nodded.

"Very well. We'll be looking for it, too. I'll see you tomorrow, Christian. And next time somebody stays after, don't talk to him. Just come back in the house and lock the doors."

"I'll do that," Christian said.

When she left, he played his Instrument for hours. More Listeners came, and those who had heard Christian before were surprised at the confusion in his song.

There was a summer rainstorm that night, wind and rain and thunder, and Christian found that he could not sleep. Not from the music of the weather—he'd slept through a thousand such storms. It was the recorder that lay behind the Instrument against the wall. Christian had lived for nearly thirty years surrounded only by this wild, beautiful place and the music he himself made. But now.

Now he could not stop wondering. Who was Bach? Who *is* Bach? What is his music? How is it different from mine? Has he discovered things that I don't know?

What is his music?

What is his music?

What is his music?

Until at dawn, when the storm was abating and the wind had died, Christian got out of his bed, where he had not slept but only tossed back and forth all night, and took the recorder from its hiding place and played it.

At first it sounded strange, like noise, odd sounds that had nothing to do with the sounds of Christian's life. But the patterns were clear, and by the end of the recording, which was not even a half-hour long, Christian had mastered the idea of fugue and the sound of the harpsichord preyed on his mind.

Yet he knew that if he let these things show up in his music, he would be discovered. So he did not try a fugue. He did not attempt to imitate the harpsichord's sound.

And every night he listened to the recording, for many nights, learning more and more until finally the Watcher came.

The Watcher was blind, and a dog led him. He came to the door and because he was a Watcher the door opened for him without his even knocking.

"Christian Haroldsen, where is the recorder?" the Watcher asked.

"Recorder?" Christian asked, then knew it was hopeless, and took the machine and gave it to the Watcher.

"Oh, Christian," said the Watcher, and his voice was mild and sorrowful. "Why didn't you turn it in without listening to it?"

"I meant to," Christian said. "But how did you know?"

"Because suddenly there are no fugues in your work. Suddenly your songs have lost the only Bachlike thing about them. And you've stopped experimenting with new sounds. What were you trying to avoid?"

"This," Christian said, and he sat down and on his first try duplicated the sound of the harpsichord.

"Yet you've never tried to do that until now, have you?"

"I thought you'd notice."

"Fugues and harpsichord, the two things you noticed first—and the only things you didn't absorb into your music. All your other songs for these last weeks have been tinted and colored and influenced by Bach. Except that there was no fugue, and there was no harpsichord. You have broken the law. You were put here because you were a genius, creating new things with only nature for your inspiration. Now, of course, you're derivative, and truly new creation is impossible for you. You'll have to leave."

"I know," Christian said, afraid yet not really understanding what life outside his house would be like.

"We'll train you for the kinds of jobs you can pursue now.

You won't starve. You won't die of boredom. But because you broke the law, one thing is forbidden to you now."

"Music."

"Not all music. There is music of a sort, Christian, that the common people, the ones who aren't Listeners, can have. Radio and television and record music. But live music and new music—those are forbidden to you. You may not sing. You may not play an instrument. You may not tap out a rhythm."

"Why not?"

The Watcher shook his head. "The world is too perfect, too at peace, too happy for us to permit a misfit who broke the law to go about spreading discontent. The common people make casual music of a sort, knowing nothing better because they haven't the aptitude to learn it. But if you—never mind. It's the law. And if you make more music, Christian, you will be punished drastically. Drastically."

Christian nodded, and when the Watcher told him to come, he came, leaving behind the house and the woods and his Instrument. At first he took it calmly, as the inevitable punishment for his infraction; but he had little concept of punishment, or of what exile from his Instrument would mean.

Within five hours he was shouting and striking out at anyone who came near him, because his fingers craved the touch of the Instrument's keys and levers and strips and bars, and he could not have them, and now he knew that he had never been lonely before.

It took six months before he was ready for normal life. And when he left the Retraining Center (a small building, because it was so rarely used), he looked tired, and years older, and he didn't smile at anyone. He became a delivery truck driver, because the tests said that this was a job that would least grieve him, and least remind him of his loss, and most engage his few remaining aptitudes and interests.

He delivered donuts to grocery stores.

And at night he discovered the mysteries of alcohol, and the alcohol and the donuts and the truck and his dreams were enough that he was, in his way, content. He had no anger in him. He could live the rest of his life this way, without bitterness.

He delivered fresh donuts and took the stale ones away with him.

Second Movement

"With a name like Joe," Joe always said, "I had to open a bar and grill, just so I could put up a sign saying Joe's Bar and Grill." And he laughed and laughed, because after all Joe's Bar and Grill was a funny name these days.

But Joe was a good bartender, and the Watchers had put him in the right kind of place. Not in a big city, but in a smaller town; a town just off the freeway, where truck drivers often came; a town not far from a large city, so that interesting things were nearby to be talked about and worried about and bitched about and loved.

Joe's Bar and Grill was, therefore, a nice place to come, and many people came there. Not fashionable people, and not drunks, but lonely people and friendly people in just the right mixture. "My clients are like a good drink, just enough of this and that to make a new flavor that tastes better than any of the ingredients." Oh, Joe was a poet, he was a poet of alcohol and like many another person these days, he often said, "My father was a lawyer, and in the old days I would have probably ended up a lawyer, too, and I never would have known what I was missing."

Joe was right. And he was a damn good bartender, and he didn't wish he were anything else, and so he was happy.

One night, however, a new man came in, a man with a donut delivery truck and a donut brand name on his uniform. Joe noticed him because silence clung to the man like a smell—wherever he walked, people sensed it, and though they scarcely looked at him, they lowered their voices, or stopped talking at all, and they got reflective and looked at the walls and the mirror behind the bar. The donut delivery man sat in a corner and had a watered-down drink that meant he intended to stay a long time and didn't want his alcohol intake to be so rapid that he was forced to leave early.

Joe noticed things about people, and he noticed that this man kept looking off in the dark corner where the piano stood. It was an old, out-of-tune monstrosity from the old days (for this had been a bar for a long time) and Joe wondered why the man was fascinated by it. True, a lot of Joe's customers had been interested, but they had always walked over and plunked on the keys, trying to find a melody, failing with the out-of-tune keys, and finally giving up. This man, however, seemed almost afraid of the piano, and didn't go near it.

At closing time, the man was still there, and then, on a

whim, instead of making the man leave, Joe turned off the piped-in music and turned off most of the lights, and then went over and lifted the lid and exposed the grey keys.

The donut delivery man came over to the piano. *Chris*, his nametag said. He sat and touched a single key. The sound was not pretty. But the man touched all the keys one by one, and then touched them in different orders, and all the time Joe watched, wondering why the man was so intense about it.

"Chris," Joe said.

Chris looked up at him.

"Do you know any songs?"

Chris's face went funny.

"I mean, some of those old-time songs, not those fancy ass-twitchers on the radio, but *songs*. 'In a Little Spanish Town.' My Mother sang that one to me." And Joe began to sing, "In a little Spanish town, 'twas on a night like this. Stars were peek-a-booing down, 'twas on a night like this."

Chris began to play as Joe's weak and toneless baritone went on with the song. But it wasn't an accompaniment, not anything Joe could call an accompaniment. It was instead an opponent to his melody, an enemy to it, and the sounds coming out of the piano were strange and unharmonious and by God beautiful. Joe stopped singing and listened. For two hours he listened, and when it was over he soberly poured the man a drink, and poured one for himself, and clinked glasses with Chris the donut delivery man who could take that rotten old piano and make the damn thing sing.

Three nights later Chris came back, looking harried and afraid. But this time Joe knew what would happen (had to happen) and instead of waiting until closing time, Joe turned off the piped-in music ten minutes early. Chris looked up at him pleadingly. Joe misunderstood—he went over and lifted the lid to the keyboard and smiled. Chris walked stiffly, perhaps reluctantly, to the stool and sat.

"Hey, Joe," one of the last five customers shouted, "closing early?"

Joe didn't answer. Just watched as Chris began to play. No preliminaries this time; no scales and wanderings over the keys. Just power, and the piano was played as pianos aren't meant to be played; the bad notes, the out-of-tune notes were fit into the music so that they sounded right, and Chris's fingers, ignoring the strictures of the twelve-tone scale, played, it seemed to Joe, in the cracks.

None of the customers left until Chris finished an hour and

a half later. They all shared that final drink, and went home shaken by the experience.

The next night Chris came again, and the next, and the next. Whatever private battle had kept him away for the first few days after his first night of playing, he had apparently won it or lost it. None of Joe's business. What Joe cared about was the fact that when Chris played the piano, it did things to him that music had never done, and he wanted it.

The customers apparently wanted it, too. Near closing time people began showing up, apparently just to hear Chris play. Joe began starting the piano music earlier and earlier, and he had to discontinue the free drinks after the playing because there were so many people it would have put him out of business.

It went on for two long, strange months. The delivery van pulled up outside, and people stood aside for Chris to enter. No one said anything to him; no one said anything at all, but everyone waited until he began to play the piano. He drank nothing at all. Just played. And between songs the hundreds of people in Joe's Bar and Grill ate and drank.

But the merriment was gone. The laughter and the chatter and the camaraderie were missing, and after a while Joe grew tired of the music and wanted to have his bar back the way it was. He toyed with the idea of getting rid of the piano, but the customers would have been angry at him. He thought of asking Chris not to come anymore, but he could not bring himself to speak to the strange silent man.

And so finally he did what he knew he should have done in the first place. He called the Watchers.

They came in the middle of a performance, a blind Watcher with a dog on a leash, and a Watcher with no ears who walked unsteadily, holding to things for balance. They came in the middle of a song, and did not wait for it to end. They walked to the piano and closed the lid gently, and Chris withdrew his fingers and looked at the closed lid.

"Oh, Christian," said the man with the seeing-eye dog.

"I'm sorry," Christian answered. "I tried not to."

"Oh, Christian, how can I bear doing to you what must be done?"

"Do it," Christian said.

And so the man with no ears took a laser knife from his coat pocket and cut off Christian's fingers and thumbs, right where they rooted into his hands. The laser cauterized and sterilized the wound even as it cut, but still some blood spattered on Christian's uniform. And, his hands now meaningless palms and useless knuckles, Christian stood and walked out of Joe's Bar and Grill. The people made way for him again, and they listened intently as the blind Watcher said, "That was a man who broke the law and was forbidden to be a Maker. He broke the law a second time, and the law insists that he be stopped from breaking down the system that makes all of you so happy."

The people understood. It grieved them, it made them uncomfortable for a few hours, but once they had returned home to their exactly-right homes and got back to their exactly right jobs, the sheer contentment of their lives overwhelmed their momentary sorrow for Chris. After all, Chris had broken the law. And it was the law that kept them all safe and happy.

Even Joe. Even Joe soon forgot Chris and his music. He knew he had done the right thing. He couldn't figure out, though, why a man like Chris would have broken the law in the first place, or what law he would have broken. There wasn't a law in the world that wasn't designed to make people happy—and there wasn't a law Joe could think of that he was even mildly interested in breaking.

Yet. Once Joe went to the piano and lifted the lid and played every key on the piano. And when he had done that he put his head down on the piano and cried, because he knew that when Chris lost that piano, lost even his fingers so he could never play again—it was like Joe losing his bar. And if Joe ever lost his bar, his life wouldn't be worth living.

As for Chris, someone else began coming to the bar driving the same donut delivery van, and no one ever saw Chris again in that part of the world.

Third Movement

"Oh what a beautiful mornin'!" sang the road crew man who had seen *Oklahoma!* four times in his home town.

"Rock my soul in the bosom of Abraham!" sang the road crew man who had learned to sing when his family got together with guitars.

"Lead, kindly light, amid the encircling gloom!" sang the road crew man who believed.

But the road crew man without hands, who held the signs telling the traffic to Stop or go Slow, listened but never sang.

"Whyn't you never sing?" asked the road crew man who liked Rodgers and Hammerstein; asked all of them, at one time or another.

And the man they called Sugar just shrugged. "Don't feel like singin'," he'd say, when he said anything at all.

"Why they call him Sugar?" a new guy once asked. "He don't look sweet to me."

And the man who believed said, "His initals are C. H. Like the sugar. C&H, you know." And the new guy laughed. A stupid joke, but the kind of gag that makes life easier on the road building crew.

Not that life was that hard. For these men, too, had been tested, and they were in the job that made them happiest. They took pride in the pain of sunburn and pulled muscles, and the road growing long and thin behind them was the most beautiful thing in the world. And so they sang all day at their work, knowing that they could not possibly be happier than they were this day.

Except Sugar.

Then Guillermo came. A short Mexican who spoke with an accent, Guillermo told everyone who asked, "I may come from Sonora, but my heart belongs in Milano!" And when anyone asked why (and often when no one asked anything) he'd explain. "I'm an Italian tenor in a Mexican body," and he proved it by singing every note that Puccini and Verdi ever wrote. "Caruso was nothing," Guillermo boasted. "Listen to this!"

Guillermo had records, and sang along with them, and at work on the road crew he'd join in with any man's song and harmonize with it, or sing an obligatto high above the melody, a soaring tenor that took the roof off his head and filled the clouds. "I can sing," Guillermo would say, and soon the other road crew men answered, "Damn right, Guillermo! Sing it again!"

But one night Guillermo was honest, and told the truth. "Ah, my friends, I'm no singer."

"What do you mean? Of course you are!" came the unanimous answer.

"Nonsense!" Guillermo cried, his voice theatrical. "If I am this great singer, why do you never see me going off to record songs? Hey? This is a great singer? Nonsense! Great singers they raise to be great singers. I'm just a man who loves to sing, but has no talent! I'm a man who loves to work on the road crew with men like you, and sing his guts out, but in the opera I could never be! Never!"

He did not say it sadly. He said it fervently, confidently. "Here is where I belong! I can sing to you who like to hear me sing! I can harmonize with you when I feel a harmony in my heart. But don't be thinking that Guillermo is a great singer, because he's not!"

It was an evening of honesty, and every man there explained why it was he was happy on the road crew, and didn't wish to be anywhere else. Everyone, that is, except Sugar.

"Come on, Sugar. Aren't you happy here?"

Sugar smiled. "I'm happy. I like it here. This is good work for me. And I love to hear you sing."

"Then why don't you sing with us?"

Sugar shook his head. "I'm not a singer."

But Guillermo looked at him knowingly. "Not a singer, ha! Not a singer. A man without hands who refuses to sing is not a man who is not a singer. Hey?"

"What the hell did that mean?" asked the man who sang folksongs.

"It means that this man you call Sugar, he's a fraud. Not a singer! Look at his hands. All his fingers gone! Who is it who cuts off men's fingers?"

The road crew didn't try to guess. There were many ways a man could lose fingers, and none of them were anyone's business.

"He loses his fingers because he breaks the law and the Watchers cut them off! That's how a man loses fingers. What was he doing with his fingers that the Watchers wanted him to stop? He was breaking the law, wasn't he?"

"Stop," Sugar said.

"If you want," Guillermo said, but for once the others would not respect Sugar's privacy.

"Tell us," they said.

Sugar left the room.

"Tell us," and Guillermo told them. That Sugar must have been a Maker who broke the law and was forbidden to make music anymore. The very thought that a Maker was working on the road crew with them—even a lawbreaker—filled the men with awe. Makers were rare, and they were the most esteemed of men and women.

"But why his fingers?"

"Because," Guillermo said, "he must have tried to make

music again afterward. And when you break the law a second time, the power to break it a third time is taken away from you." Guillermo spoke seriously, and so to the road crew men Sugar's story sounded as majestic and terrible as an opera. They crowded into Sugar's room, and found the man staring at the wall.

"Sugar, is it true?" asked the man who loved Rodgers and Hammerstein.

"Were you a Maker?" asked the man who believed.

"Yes," Sugar said.

"But Sugar," the man who believed said, "God can't mean for a man to stop making music, even if he broke the law."

Sugar smiled. "No one asked God."

"Sugar," Guillermo finally said, "there are nine of us on the crew, nine of us, and we're miles from any human beings. You know us, Sugar. We swear on our mother's graves, every one of us, that we'll never tell a soul. Why should we? You're one of us. But sing, dammit man, sing!"

"I can't" Sugar said. "You don't understand."

"It isn't what God intended," said the man who believed. "We're all doing what we love best, and here you are, loving music and not able to sing a note. Sing for us! Sing with us! And only you and us and God will know!"

They all promised. They all pled.

And the next day as the man who loved Rodgers and Hammerstein sang "Love, Look Away," Sugar began to hum. As the man who believed sang "God of our Fathers," Sugar sang softly along. And as the man who loved folksongs sang "Swing Low, Sweet Chariot," Sugar joined in with a strange, piping voice and all the men laughed and cheered and welcomed Sugar's voice to the songs.

Inevitably Sugar began inventing. First harmonies, of course, strange harmonies that made Guillermo frown and then, after a while, grin as he joined in, sensing as best he could what Sugar was doing to the music.

And after harmonies, Sugar began singing his own melodies, with his own words. He made them repetitive, the words simple and the melodies simpler still. And yet he shaped them into odd shapes, and built them into songs that had never been heard of before, that sounded wrong and yet were absolutely right. It was not long before the man who loved Rodgers and Hammerstein and the man who sang folksongs and the man who believed were learning Sugar's songs and singing them joyously or mournfully or angrily or gaily as they worked along the road.

Even Guillermo learned the songs, and his strong tenor was changed by them until his voice, which had, after all, been ordinary, became something unusual and fine. Guillermo finally said to Sugar one day, "Hey, Sugar, your music is all wrong, man. But I like the way it feels in my nose! Hey, you know? I like the way it feels in my mouth!"

Some of the songs were hymns: "Keep me hungry, Lord," Sugar sang, and the road crew sang it too.

Some of the songs were love songs: "Put your hands in someone else's pockets," Sugar sang angrily; "I hear your voice in the morning," Sugar sang tenderly; "Is it summer yet?" Sugar sang sadly; and the road crew sang it, too.

Over the months the road crew changed, one man leaving on Wednesday and a new man taking his place on Thursday, as different skills were needed in different places. Sugar was silent when each newcomer came, until the man had given his word and the secret was sure to be kept.

What finally destroyed Sugar was the fact that his songs were so unforgettable. The men who left would sing the songs with their new crews, and those crews would learn them, and teach them to others. Crewmen taught the songs in bars and on the road; people learned them quickly, and loved them; and one day a blind Watcher heard the songs and knew, instantly, who had first sung them. They were Christian Haroldsen's music, because in those melodies, simple as they were, the wind of the north woods still whistled and the fall of leaves still hung oppressively over every note and—and the Watcher sighed. He took a specialized tool from his file of tools and boarded an airplane and flew to the city closest to where a certain road crew worked. And the blind Watcher took a company car with a company driver up the road and at the end of it, where the road was just beginning to swallow a strip of wilderness, the blind Watcher got out of the car and heard singing. Heard a piping voice singing a song that made even an eyeless man weep.

"Christian," the Watcher said, and the song stopped.

"You," said Christian.

"Christian, even after you lost your fingers?"

The other men didn't understand—all the other men, that is, except Guillermo.

"Watcher," said Guillermo. "Watcher, he done no harm."

The Watcher smiled wryly. "No one said he did. But he broke the law. You, Guillermo, how would you like to work as a servant in a rich man's house? How would you like to be a bank teller?"

"Don't take me from the road crew, man," Guillermo said.

"It's the law that finds where people will be happy. But Christian Haroldsen broke the law. And he's gone around ever since making people hear music they were never meant to hear."

Guillermo knew he had lost the battle before it began, but he couldn't stop himself. "Don't hurt him, man. I was meant to hear his music. Swear to God, it's made me happier."

The Watcher shook his head sadly. "Be honest, Guillermo. You're an honest man. His music's made you miserable, hasn't it? You've got everything you could want in life, and yet his music makes you sad. All the time, sad."

Guillermo tried to argue, but he was honest, and he looked into his own heart, and he knew that the music was full of grief. Even the happy songs mourned for something; even the angry songs wept; even the love songs seemed to say that everything dies and contentment is the most fleeting thing. Guillermo looked in his own heart and all Sugar's music stared back up at him and Guillermo wept.

"Just don't hurt him, please," Guillermo murmured as he cried.

"I won't," the blind Watcher said. Then he walked to Christian, who stood passively waiting, and he held the special tool up to Christian's throat. Christian gasped.

"No," Christian said, but the word only formed with his lips and tongue. No sound came out. Just a hiss of air. "No."

"Yes," the Watcher said.

The road crew watched silently as the Watcher led Christian away. They did not sing for days. But then Guillermo forgot his grief one day and sang an aria from *La Bohème*, and the songs went on from there. Now and then they sang one of Sugar's songs, because the songs could not be forgotten.

In the city, the blind Watcher furnished Christian with a pad of paper and a pen. Christian immediately gripped the pencil in the crease of his palm and wrote: "What do I do now?"

The blind Watcher laughed. "Have we got a job for you!

Oh, Christian, have we got a job for you!" The dog barked loudly, to hear his master laugh.

Applause

In all the world there were only two dozen Watchers. They were secretive men, who supervised a system that needed little supervision because it actually made nearly everybody happy. It was a good system, but like even the most perfect of machines, here and there it broke down. Here and there someone acted madly, and damaged himself, and to protect everyone and the person himself, a Watcher had to notice the madness and go to fix it.

For many years the best of the Watchers was a man with no fingers, a man with no voice. He would come silently, wearing the uniform that named him with the only name he needed—Authority. And he would find the kindest, easiest, yet most thorough way of solving the problem and curing the madness and preserving the system that made the world, for the first time in history, a very good place to live. For practically everyone.

For there were still a few people—one or two each year—who were caught in a circle of their own devising, who could neither adjust to the system nor bear to harm it, people who kept breaking the law despite their knowledge that it would destroy them.

Eventually, when the gentle maimings and deprivations did not cure their madness and set them back into the system, they were given uniforms and they, too, went out. Watching.

The keys of power were placed in the hands of those who had most cause to hate the system they had to preserve. Were they sorrowful?

"I am," Christian answered in the moments when he dared to ask himself that question.

In sorrow he did his duty. In sorrow he grew old. And finally the other Watchers, who reverenced the silent man (for they knew he had once sung magnificent songs), told him he was free. "You've served your time," said the Watcher with no legs, and he smiled.

Christian raised an eyebrow, as if to say, "And?"

"So wander."

Christian wandered. He took off his uniform, but lacking neither money nor time he found few doors closed to him.

He wandered where in his former lives he had once lived. A road in the mountains. A city where he had once known the loading entrance of every restaurant and coffee shop and grocery store. And at last to a place in the woods where a house was falling apart in the weather because it had not been used in forty years.

Christian was old. The thunder roared and it only made him realize that it was about to rain. All the old songs. All the old songs, he mourned inside himself, more because he couldn't remember them than because he thought his life had been particularly sad.

As he sat in a coffee shop in a nearby town to stay out of the rain, he heard four teenagers who played the guitar very badly singing a song that he knew. It was a song he had invented while the asphalt poured on a hot summer day. The teenagers were not musicians and certainly not Makers. But they sang the song from their hearts, and even though the words were happy, the song made everyone who heard it cry.

Christian wrote on the pad he always carried, and showed his question to the boys. "Where did that song come from?"

"It's a Sugar song," the leader of the group answered. "It's a song by Sugar."

Christian raised an eyebrow, making a shrugging motion.

"Sugar was a guy who worked on a road crew and made up songs. He's dead now, though," the boy answered.

"Best damn songs in the world," another boy said, and they all nodded.

Christian smiled. Then he wrote (and the boys waited impatiently for this speechless old man to go away): "Aren't you happy? Why sing sad songs?"

The boys were at a loss for an answer. The leader spoke up, though, and said, "Sure I'm happy. I've got a good job, a girl I like, and man, I couldn't ask for more. I got my guitar. I got my songs. And my friends."

And another boy said, "These songs aren't sad, mister. Sure, they make people cry, but they aren't sad."

"Yeah," said another."It's just that they were written by a man who knows."

Christian scribbled on his paper. "Knows what?"

"He just knows. Just knows, that's all. Knows it all."

And then the teenagers turned back to their clumsy guitars and their young, untrained voices, and Christian walked to the door to leave because the rain had stopped and because he knew when to leave the stage. He turned and bowed just a little toward the singers. They didn't notice him, but their voices were all the applause he needed. He left the ovation and went outside where the leaves were just turning color and would soon, with a slight inaudible sound, break free and fall to the earth.

For a moment he thought he heard himself singing. But it was just the last of the wind, coasting madly through the wires over the street. It was a frenzied song, and Christian thought he had recognized his voice.

THE STORY WRITER

by Richard Wilson

The moving hand writes and having writ moves on . . . and if you use an eraser or hire a good rewrite man what the moving hand wrote can be rewrit or even unwrit. This is contrary to Omar Khayyam, perhaps, but may not be contrary to the way things are if we are to believe the suspicions of physicists that nothing in the universe is either fixed or absolute. Dick Wilson, one of the original Futurians—a fabled club of science fiction fans whose relation to modern fandom is rather like that of Caesar's Rome to Waldheim's U.N.—having observed professionally the way things are reported shows what a story writer can achieve if he has the right backers.

A man at a flea market sat at a typewriter reading. His table was the barest of all. On it were a ream of paper, a pencil and a sign: "This Typewriter for Hire. A Story Written about You: $1 a Page." The typewriter was an old Remington office model on a stand next to the table.

Other tables were crowded with curios, knickknacks, carnival and depression glass, insulators, china, woodenware, campaign buttons, barbed wire and other collectibles and bygones. Few dealers brought valuable antiques to an outdoor flea market; there was always the threat of pilferage or breakage or rain.

The story writer was a man of 55 with a tidy mustache. He was William Wylie Ross, one of the last of the old-time pulp writers. He was smoking a pipe and reading a book of short stories by Slawomir Mrozek called *The Elephant*.

A boy of 10, who had stood watching Ross, went up to him and said: "Dzién dobry."

"I beg your pardon?" Ross said.

"I said good morning in Polish. You are reading a book by a Pole and I am of Polish descent. I thought you might be too."

"No. I read Mrozek only in translation. Good morning. What is your name?"

"Nazywam sie Henry. Jak sie pan nazywa? I said in Polish: 'My name is Henry. What is your name?' My father, who was born in Poland, says it is good to preserve the traditions. I am bilingual."

"Your father is wise," Ross said. "My name—Nazywam sie Ross. Did I say it right?"

"Very well. Is Ross your first or your last name?"

Ross gave the boy a card. It said: *William Wylie Ross, freelance writer; short paragraphs at the going rate, full-fledged autobiographies by arrangement.*

The boy read the card. "It says nothing of a story about me."

"That could be a biography; they run 300 pages up. In your case maybe 20 pages, depending on how intensely you've lived. A shorter work, as the sign says, is a dollar a page. Would you like one?"

"Can you write a ghost story?" Henry asked.

"Would you like a sample? No charge."

"Yes, please."

Ross put down his book and rolled a sheet of paper into the typewriter. He wrote. "Henry sat alone in his room. He was the last person on Earth. There was a knock at the door."

He took the sheet out and gave it to Henry. "That's the world's shortest ghost story."

"It doesn't have a title. And it doesn't say who wrote it."

"A critic, are you?" Ross put it back in the machine. He typed WORLD'S SHORTEST GHOST STORY and, below that, by *W. W. Ross*. He said to the boy: "I don't use my full name on such a short piece. Besides, it's not original except for the name of the protagonist."

"What's a protagonist?"

"You are. The main character. The boy in the room. The one who knocked at the door may be the antagonist."

"Oh. Can you write a true story about me?"

"I can."

Henry took a dollar from his pocket and put it on the table. Ross wrote a story about a ghost writer and a boy named Henry who asked him to write a ghost story. He worked quickly on the story, which was similar to what you have just read, except that he left out the Polish because he couldn't spell it. Double-spaced, it ran to two pages plus a paragraph on the third.

Henry looked embarrassed. "I have only a dollar."

Ross handed him the pages. "No extra charge. It's really a collaboration."

A man had come to watch. He said to Ross: "I am Henry's father."

"How do you do."

"I am well, thank you. I am glad Henry spent his dollar here instead of in a foolish way. You read Mrozek. Do you admire Polish writers? Korzeniowski? Later he called himself Conrad."

"I admire good writers whatever their nationality. I admire Conrad."

"Dziekuje bardzo. Thank you very much. And thank you for what you have written for Henry, moj syn. My son. I think he could be a writer one day. Dowidzenia. Good-by."

"Dowidzenia," Ross said. "Dziekuje bardzo, Henry."

Several tables away a young dealer had set up at the back of his camper. His sign read *Mad Wayne Anthony, Stony Point, N.Y.*, ANTIQUES 1870 UP. Ross supposed it meant some of his wares qualified as antiques by being at least a hundred years old and that Wayne had combined an allusion to their price; his least expensive was marked $18.70. There was a small hand-lettered card on his table which said *We haggle*.

Wayne Anthony had old 78-rpm records. He played one now and again on a Victrola. He had a ritual of wiping it with a treated cloth, holding it by its edges as he settled it over the spindle, winding the machine and carefully placing the needle. The music, not amplified except by the big old horn, was clear but unobtrusive. Ross could ignore it if he chose or he could give it his attention and savor the old melodies. At the moment, Wayne, who explained to his fellow dealers that the records were not for sale and that he was planning to go to Heuvelton where there was a barn full of real oldies, was playing *It's Like Old Times.*

Ross saw his next customer. Sometimes he could tell who it would be. She was a plump young woman who had stood within earshot until Henry and his father left. She walked sideways to Ross's table as if she were going somewhere else. Ross became engrossed in relighting his pipe until the girl was at his elbow. He picked up his book, said casually "Hello, young lady," found his place and pretended to read.

The girl said: "Excuse me. Could you write a story about me?"

He exhaled smoke and put the book down. "If I knew something about you I could try."

"There's not much to tell."

"There might be. Let's start with names. Mine's Ross. What's yours?"

"It's funny you should ask that because I've changed it."

"*Did* you? That's a beginning. Tell me about it."

Ross and the girl talked. People who had watched while he wrote Henry's story went away. She talked more freely. She said things to him, a stranger, that it was possible she'd never told another.

"Yes," he said. "I can write your story. If you don't care for it you needn't pay. But you haven't told me your name or why you changed it."

"My name is Mabel." She talked some more.

Ross wrote this story:

Once a young woman named Mabel who thought she was plain changed her name to May-Belle because she wanted something about her to be beautiful. She was not really plain. She had good features and a ripe, honest figure. But she was afraid her boy friend found her unattractive. She thought he preferred Jane, who painted her face and had a fashion-model figure. The boy, Ralph, went off to war and came back blind.

Jane went to see him once, out of duty, at his parents' house. She never went again.

May-Belle invited Ralph to a picnic and they had a fine day. After that they were together often. Inevitably they talked about Jane. Ralph said: "You know, I used to like Jane but I don't any more."

"I can't understand why," May-Belle said. "She's prettier than ever."

"Is she?" Ralph asked. "It must be skin-deep pretty because I can't see it. I can see you, though, and I see you beautiful, Mabel." The blind boy called her by her old name and she liked it.

Ralph learned Braille and got a job at a radio station and after awhile he was a popular disk jockey. And when he and the girl of his choice went to the town clerk to get a marriage license she spelled her name Mabel because he liked it that way.

A simple story for a simple girl? No, a straightforward story for a straightforward girl. Ross had felt good writing it and she'd been pleased with her dollar's worth.

Ross didn't wish the boy blindness, except to Jane's skin-deep beauty. He wished heartily for the happiness of May-Belle, by any name. He had an idea her last name would be Ralph's.

William Wylie Ross had not been as prolific as Max Brand or Lester Dent but he had done well enough in the pulp magazines after a stint in reporting. He had come to the pulp field later than the veterans but had earned his two or three cents a word when that was good money. He used a distinctive three-name byline as many had before him—Carroll John Daly, William MacLeod Raine, Joel Tinsley Rogers, Edgar Rice Burroughs.

After the paperbacks killed the pulps he wrote for them and later for television. He adapted one of his western tales as a pilot for a television series. It sold to a network, caught on with the public and was renewed year after year. Ross had a good agent and got one of the best of the early contracts. He owned a piece of the property and wrote the scripts for many seasons. Later he became story editor and executive producer. Others wrote them, hewing to his guidelines. Royalties, residuals and foreign rights made him rich and he retired before he was 50. The series still ran in prime time and reruns were syndicated around the world.

Ross had married once but he and his wife had no children. They learned that it was he who was sterile. They joked about it sometimes, referring to him as the barren one, and once he signed them into a hotel as Baron and Lady Ross. Another time he registered as W. W. Ross, Bart., and Lady and during their stay some of the staff called them Mr. and Mrs. Bart.

They were content for a while but she always resented the hours his writing demanded and his refusal to adopt a child. On the day she turned 30 she divorced him and married a widower with three children by whom she subsequently had three of her own. He remained friends with her and got to like her husband, a professor of American literature, who came to like him. The six kids knew him as Uncle Bart.

After he retired he collected. At first he sought copies of his old pulp stories in second-hand stores. He had written more than he remembered—detective, adventure, air-war, science fiction, westerns. Before long he decided he was indulging in narcissistic nonsense. He began to collect American first editions, specializing in former pulp writers who had made it big—Dashiell Hammett, Raymond Chandler, Cornell Woolrich.

He retired because his old friend Marv had told him to slow down. Doctor Marv had told him straight, not in his office but in his home after dinner in the presence of Doctor Tina—Marv's wife who'd just earned her Ph.D. with a concentration in gerontology. It was stress, high blood pressure, hypertension, whatever the current terms were, brought on by who knows what but helped along by overweight and alcohol. Smoking two packs a day wasn't helping any, either.

Marv had told him: "Quit the stress and do what you'd really like to do because if you don't—Just do it, Will. For me, if not for yourself. I want you around a bit longer." Tina told him please to keep on aging so she could study him properly now that she had her degree.

So he moved out of New York, to which he had returned after his long television stint in Hollywood, and went upstate, where he had been raised. He bought a house in Auburn, the small city which had been the home of Samuel Hopkins Adams, the writer, and before that, William Henry Seward, who had bought Alaska.

It was a fine old house. He filled it with period furniture, Adams' first editions and Seward memorabilia. He bought a few canvases by Auburn painters Barney, Rising and Sunter.

He liked a morning walk and a late breakfast at the Auburn Inn. He wore suntan pants and shirt and an old-fashioned vest which held pens, pencils, a slim notebook and paraphernalia for his pipe. He ate scrambled eggs, whole wheat toast, marmalade and coffee. Liz, the waitress, who was as old as he was, called him Will. He always tipped her a dollar.

From the inn he walked to the old brick and frame gallery on William Street to see whether Bob Muggleton had found anything of interest.

In his absence from the house Minnie Barnes let herself in once a week and cleaned. Then she visited a friend who was serving a term for armed robbery in the Auburn prison. Minnie carried a Bible in a brown paper bag and often invited Ross to attend a service at her church. He went once and sat in the back row. He was the only white person there and although he enjoyed the sermon and the singing he felt like an intruder and didn't go again. He had put a hundred-dollar bill in the collection plate and made a note to send an annual contribution.

From church he went to an auction in a barn near Skaneateles and sat in the second row while bids went by him on cast iron banks, barbed wire, a mammy bench, post-hole diggers and a cranberry scoop. His only bid was on a Little Big Book based on his western hero. It cost six-fifty to take it home.

Home was where the heart should have been. He put his acquisition on a shelf next to old stuff he'd written. A re-run of his series was on television but he didn't watch it. He had a drink and smoked a pipe and went to bed.

His collecting led him to the flea market. Jud Ransom, a dealer friend, had invited him. "You never know what you'll find," he told Ross. "Too much of it is junk but I'm often surprised."

Jud had a shop in town. It specialized in mechanical banks, old typewriters, penny movie machines and other things that people collected now. The shop had a good trade; other dealers made their way to it from many states.

They went to the flea market in Jud's Econoline van, shunpiking at an easy speed and enjoying the scenery along the older roads.

"I'm satisfied if I clear expenses," Jud said. "I bring two or three fine pieces. It's good advertising; people notice them and take my cards. Weeks later they telephone or drop in at the shop. The rest is stuff I sell cheap."

At the First Original Famous Flea Market, in the lee of a farmhouse on Route 3 north of Port Ontario, Ross helped Jud unload the big table, two camp chairs, the penny machine that showed an early Charlie Chaplin short, an Oliver typewriter, a bank that shot a coin into a tree trunk, a cherry pitter, a broken spinning wheel and other bygones. The biggest was the old Gypsy Fortune Teller. They eased her from the van to a level place near the table. "Never could have brought her without you," Jud said. "Takes two to handle her."

It was a big rectangular box whose glass top enclosed a gray-haired wax figure of a woman in faded Romany garb. Her hand hovered over playing cards fanned out in an arc. A sign said: "Gypsy Granny Tells Your Fortune—5¢."

Ross put a nickel in the slot. Hidden machinery came to reluctant life. The head turned from side to side. The hand moved back and forth above the cards, then stopped. A pasteboard fortune fell into a tray. Ross read it: "You will do a good deed and happiness will result."

"Granny always has an upbeat message," Jud said. "She attracts trade and earns me a few nickels."

They finished setting up and relaxed in the camp chairs. Jud poured coffee from a Thermos. "Don't expect a roaring trade. I enjoy the fresh air and the people."

There were few customers that early. Dealers dropped by and chatted. One said he had a gadget that might interest Jud, who went to see it. Ross finished his coffee and lit his pipe. A few cars came off the road and parked in the field down the hill. A man stopped to look at the typewriter. "Does it work?"

"Probably," Ross said. He took a page from his vest-pocket notebook and rolled it into the Oliver. He tapped out: "My name is Oliver. Oliver Twist. What the Dickens—I really write! More?"

The man nodded. "When I was a boy I had H-O Oats for breakfast. There was a picture of Oliver Twist on the box, asking for more. How much is it?"

"The tag says thirty dollars."

"I see that. What do you have to get for it?"

"I'm just minding the store. Come back when Jud Ransom's here. Maybe you can work out something better."

"I may do that." The man went to look at a set of Jerry Todd books at another table.

A young couple came by. The girl took up the cherry picker. "I saw one of these in Joel Salter's paper," she said. "See? The prongs go down and push out the pits and the prongs come up with the cherries and they fall into this thing down here."

"I suppose that means you can't live without it?" the young man said.

"Not if you want cherry pie like your grandmother made."

"We'll take it," he said. "Seven-fifty?"

"That's it, plus tax." They worked it out and Ross took the money, feeling as good as if he had sold a story.

Jud returned with an elongated wooden object that scissored open. It had grooves in unlikely places. "Nobody knows what it is but I never saw anything like it."

"Couldn't live without it?"

"You're picking up the jargon."

"A few people were here," Ross said. "I sold your cherry picker and got a feeler on the typewriter."

"Good man. The price on the Oliver is firm. It cost me twenty."

A plump blue-haired woman in sun glasses put a nickel in the Gypsy machine. It whirred as before and the wax head and hand moved. But then it clanked to a stop. No fortune dropped.

Jud said: "Sorry, ma'am. I'll refund your nickel."

"I'd rather have the fortune."

"I suppose I could open it up and get you one. No. I didn't bring the key."

Ross said: "That's all right, madam; there is a backup arrangement. In case of malfunction Granny's message is transmitted to the keys of this venerable typewriter."

"Really?" the woman said.

"Yes. You see, the patent dates of the Gypsy and the typewriter are the same. They also happen to be the year of my birth. Thus an affinity is established."

"You're putting me on. But I love charlatans. For a nickel—"

"Make yourself comfortable in Mr. Ransom's chair and I'll see what Oliver has to say. You realize I haven't the Gypsy's years of experience in this work."

"Charming. Just make up something. It doesn't have to be Romany. A cookie fortune would do."

Ross took the other chair. He poised his fingers over the keys of the old typewriter. "You realize there are professionals in that line of work? They're the people who write greeting card verses."

"Well, pretend you're a professional and write me an upbeat fortune."

Ross bit his pipestem. He said: "First your name."

"Effie Ostrander. Miss."

"Excellent. The initials E and O start us off—Each of us has hidden talents; yours will help another."

"Lovely. Go on."

"As the sun shines on you today so it will for infinite tomorrows. May all kinds of ethnic fortune smile on you. Romany, Chinese or USAmerican, your happy future is assured."

Miss Ostrander said: "It's a fine message. Please elaborate."

"For five cents Oliver can go no further," Ross said. "Like most of us he has his price."

"Thirty dollars," Jud said in the background.

"That's for Oliver, not his words," Ross said.

"I must admit I've had more than my nickel's worth," Miss Ostrander said. "What would he charge to go on?"

"It's a question that hasn't come up before. A dollar?"

"Fair enough."

They spoke a little longer and this told Ross some things about her. He filled three pages, recapitulating events of the morning from her point of view. Part of it was about him. The last paragraph read:

"Miss Ostrander spent a dollar and five cents. She had the satisfaction of passing the time pleasantly in the open air and the bonus of having been the catalyst that fed Ross's springs of invention, making him something of the story writer he had been."

She took the typed pages and went away reading them again, her blue hair reflecting the morning sunlight.

On the drive home Ross said: "I forgot. I owe you Miss Ostrander's dollar."

"Keep it. You earned it."

Back home with his recollections of the day Ross thought he might go again with Jud but with proper paper and his own typewriter. Another Sunday he could set up his own table. It was a vagrant thought but it intrigued him. People would be there, each with a story. He could draw them out and write about them. For the first time in many nights he went to sleep thinking ahead instead of back.

It was early August at the First Original Famous Flea Market and Ross had had his own table for many Sundays.

Jud, having seen him settled in, was off on a buying trip to Vermont. The weather had been wonderfully good. Not once had the dealers been forced indoors to the crowded old barn; it rained in midweek, as if the gods smiled on their Sundays.

Ross had packed a lunch. A chunk of Swiss cheese, a small box of raisins, a spiced beef stick, a raw carrot and hot coffee in a Thermos. And after the eating the reaming of the dottle from the pipe and the refilling and the luxuriant lighting-up and the first mouthful of satisfying smoke.

Savoring his pipe, Ross listened to Mad Wayne Anthony's Victrola playing *Mad Dogs and Englishmen*, an orchestral arrangement of the Noel Coward song. Ross thought: No dog shall bark—Mad Anthony Wayne's infamous but necessary order as he prepared to storm the British-held height at Stony Point.

Associating, Ross thought for the first time in months of his friend Dirk Easterly and Dirk's dog Drool, a Labrador retriever who never hurt you when he gentled your hand in his jaws but whose saliva wet you in a loving way. In the presence of slobbering, loving Drool he and Dirk had signed a youthful pact at the base of a tree in the urban-bound woods of Alley Pond Park, Queens. Dirk said in 17-year-old solemnity: "One day one of us will need the other and we vow here in our blood—get down, Drool!—that nothing will interfere with that. There may be no one else to help—wife, dog, lawyer, friend—but each will know the other will come if needed, if the blood oath is invoked. This we swear, knowing all it may mean, whether we're a continent or worlds apart. You call, I come. I call, you come. This we swear, on pain not only of death, which is bearable, but of disillusionment, which would be too much."

Dirk read a lot and his language showed it. They had not invoked the pledge but in infrequent meetings over the years they recalled it, laughed about it and then, in an adult but not denigrating way, reaffirmed it. Laughing on the surface, as if to indulge their younger selves, but meaning it underneath they reswore, sealing the other with a toast to the departed Drool, their friend and bond.

People walked past Ross's table. He had a good place, between the lady with the treen, which is what they call woodenware in the trade, and the family with new and old books and prints. Ross had bought his Mrozek paperback from them for ten cents.

Trade being slow, he refilled his pipe and read Mrozek's

story about spring in Poland, which was a season other than any he'd known. Ah, to be in Poland in such a spring! It was good to be here, too, close to the burgeoning fields, within earshot of a lowing cow and a squawking crow and a brook gurgling as heartily as if still fed by snowmelt.

Nevertheless he was marking time. There was more to be said than he had ever written. Long ago he knew he'd not write the great novel or the immortal story. Somewhere, because he was professionally good with words, he knew there was a challenge to meet that would give him satisfaction. But there weren't as many futures now as when he'd been twenty, when the horizons were infinite. Since then he had spent a lot of time learning his trade until he could write almost anything passably well. But he recognized his limitations. Not for him the Nobel or the Pulitzer. His limited talent had earned him a good living but it would not bring immortality.

He was in this frame of mind, reflective, semi-sad but satisfied with what he had, enjoying nature's sounds and his pipe and taking comfort from the presence of his typewriter, filled with untapped tales, when the cloaked stranger stopped at his table.

Ross had known weirdos and freaks, as they called themselves. He could sympathize with their dramatic ways, having been one of them himself, long ago.

(If only then he had known his potential; the freedom to do anything that could be done! But he hadn't known. He'd been limited by his needs—to make a living, bring in the extra dollar, take the higher-paying job.)

The stranger regarded him with knowing eyes. "I know you and you will know me and we needn't go on about that now."

"Possibly so," Ross said.

"It's as so as I stand here. Explanations later. William Wylie Ross, will you, for the purposes of the story you will write, accept me on faith?"

"I have no faith," Ross said. "I've lived too long."

"Hardly long enough," the stranger said. "You are on the threshold. Believe this. You have been investigated and chosen, if you will agree."

"I think I know who you are. I don't know if I will agree."

"Tell me who I am. I'll be what you say."

Ross considered him, letting his mind wander. Another customer to while away the day. "Your name is Street. First name?"

"None. Or anything you wish."

"John? There's a John Street in New York, downtown."

"If you say so."

"You're one of the street people—once called beats or beatniks, then hippies, freaks, weirdos. You're a mystery man, a local character, odd but harmless."

"I sound dull."

"You roam by night, scanning the sky and talking to it."

"That's better. Does the sky talk to me?"

"Recently it did. You encoded the message on the back of a picture postcard of the First Baptist Church of somewhere. Whilomville? You signed it 'St.' "

"What message?"

"Decoded, it meant 'Contact established.' But what you wrote was 'Nothing new but hello anyway. St.' "

" 'Hello' was the key word?"

"Probably. A postal clerk read your card and mentioned it to a friend, who told a reporter. The reporter didn't write a story but word spread that a man with long hair and a long cloak was calling himself a saint."

"Street abbreviated 'St.,' " said Street.

"And because the postcard showed the First Baptist Church there was talk that you considered yourself St. John the Baptist. There's John again."

"You do tie things together. Do I look like a saint?"

"You might pass. You're nothing like Simon Templar, of course."

"The name means nothing to me."

"I suppose not. They keep a sharper eye on you now, in case you're dangerous. A religious fanatic. A potential threat."

"Am I?"

"You may be a threat to our way of life. Because you're alien."

"My papers show I was born in Canastota, New York."

"Sure they do. And possibly your papers say you're seventh or eighth in a long line of Streets. Do you know Eighth Street? In the Village?"

"The village of Canastota?"

"Greenwich Village. Nobody'd give you a second glance there, among the street people of Eighth Street."

"It sounds more friendly than John Street. Why do you call me alien?"

"You're lonely. You wonder if you have been abandoned

by your kind but your loyalty prevents your making friends here."

"Yet I've sought you out."

"Tell me why."

"You tell me. Write a story about it."

Ross considered it. He'd already begun, in his mind, as they talked. But it would take many pages—many more than the simple stories he'd written for Henry and May-Belle and Effie Ostrander. The stranger called Street was probably no more than he seemed—a Kesey-Kerouac type who had seen his youth go by, who had rejected the establishment but had been rejected himself by the new youth. An outcast, a weirdo now not weird enough. All at once Ross felt close to the man who stood there, tall, composed but lonely in his assumed grandeur, defiantly costumed.

"I'll write your story," Ross said.

"Thank you. It may be your story as well."

"Possibly. I rarely know how a story will end."

This is what the story writer wrote:

"A man at a flea market sat at a typewriter reading. His table . . ."

He wrote that and the other words you've read so far. Though he typed steadily it took him a long time. Street was patient.

People came by. Some paused and, seeing Ross engrossed, passed by.

Ross stopped typing. "I've taken it up to now," he told Street."

"Take it further."

"It's tiring work. I've written many dollars worth but I've seen no money."

"I offer more than money. That's not your need."

"What do you offer?"

"Write," Street said. "Put it down now. Whatever you say is possible. What can you lose? An hour of your time?"

"Shall I write a fantasy?"

"Anything. Put it down and see how it comes out."

Ross stretched in his chair and relit his pipe. He drew in a great mouthful of smoke. As it trickled out he thought what he might write, half-listening to the cows and the brook and the old Victrola *Bye, Bye, Blackbird.*

"You hesitate," Street said.

"I'm a skeptic. Who can believe you?"

"Aren't you also a romantic?"

"Yes, I am. But what's better is that you've given me a deadline. I find that I want to do it and I will."

"I'll load your other pipe."

"Thank you. I'll want it." Ross rolled a clean page into the typewriter. He asked: "Anything?"

The stranger sat on the ground and stuffed the pipe with tobacco and tamped it well. "Anything," he said.

Ross began to write.

This is what he wrote:

Think of the possibilities. Ignore the likelihood that this fantastically-garbed stranger called Street is other than he hints he is. Take him at his word. As he says, what's to be lost?

Let us assume he's what he implies he is, how I imagine him to be, and let's get words on paper, in the old way, one after another, revisions later.

Let's take a 55-year-old hack writer with nothing in his future except more money than he needs and let's just imagine. What else is there to do this Sunday afternoon?

This isn't really the time or place for so large a work. Another time: late evening, when the mystery would be greater than it is here in the sunshine. Another place: home in privacy where I could bang it out in first draft with refinements and corrections to come.

But I make excuses. I'm a professional. I can do what I must.

Must I do this? No, but I want to. I can't explain. It may become clearer as I write.

Let me describe Street, my cloaked stranger, my catalyst. Not a physical description but what, for the purpose of the story, he must be. Let me pretend I am writing fiction, which is my skill or talent.

Street is a visitor here, or hereabouts, from a far-off place I'll name later. He has a specific purpose. Street needs me, or someone like me, or he'd not have sought me out.

He is a foreign service officer in his alien government; an important person not quite in the top hierarchy. I see him as the alien equivalent of a deputy assistant Secretary of State in the United States Department of State. A career man, skilled, dedicated, with limited authority in his area of expertise but with some powers of decision delegated to him.

We need a name for his government—short for easy

pronunciation and typing, with an X in it for the unknown. Lux? Good in Latin, but here it's just soap. Lex, for law? As a freelance who once ghosted a Burroughs novel I think Lex Barker, whilom screen Tarzan. Sax as in Rohmer? Bix as in Beiderbecke? Max as in Brand? Lox as with bagels? You see my problem. The name mustn't be associative or comic.

Street (obviously not his real name) is silent as I write and I flank the X with vowels—Axa, Exe, Ixi, Oxo, Uxu. One sounds like a weapon, two is a river, Ixi sounds icky, four is a bullion cube. Five will do. Uxu. Pronounced *ucks*—oo.

The Uxu had problems. (Past tense now. Shift your point of view, please.) They'd lived long on scattered planets to which they'd fled when their own world gave signs that it would be destroyed at the impact of a free-flying planet with an affinity for their world's magnetic core. Their calculations told them none could survive such a collision. So off they went in many small spacecraft to the many little worlds they'd tested and found congenial. There could be no mass migration to any other world; none within their reach was big enough for all of them.

So they migrated in different directions but kept in touch over the years.

And while they were apart they built a great ship in sections, a bit here, a bit there, which eventually was assembled in space, tested and deemed suitable for star travel. It was big enough for all, and capable of the extended journey there had been no time to prepare for when the iron planet precipitated their exodus.

Now a reunion was in order. No more diaspora. Time to put it all together again. The fatherland, the homeland, the promised land awaits, they told each other. It's reunion time, alumni, and alma mater calls. Sing the anthem, wave the flag, appeal to the ethnos. Let's regroup, gang. Everybody back in the house.

They all fitted in nicely, having reduced themselves in size, just as the separate parts of the star ship had merged into a working whole.

Now they were ready to roam the galaxies, going from sun to sun, comfortably self-contained as they sought a new world suitable for them all.

They had been on their way for many years when a great helic eruption affected their sun-powered engines. Their ship was tossed as by a tempest and they were thrown irrevocably off course.

Thus by chance they made landfall on this island in a far system, this Earth.

They had expected that they would be somewhat different when they reached their destination but they did not expect a change of such magnitude—that they would suffer a space change, though "suffer" could be less than the accurate word. Their suffering was mingled with hope; they realized that the sun storm could have destroyed them and it was possible that the change they had experienced had benefited them. After all, as Ariel told Ferdinand some hundreds of years earlier, the change was into something rich and strange.

Some changes result from suffering. But suffer has another meaning; it means let. So after the great storm they let it happen to them, whatever it was, as their journey continued on a new course. The space change they had suffered, or let happen because they had no choice, was indeed a beneficial one. It prepared them for the alien conditions they had to adapt to when they got here and came to know us as creatures not too dissimilar from themselves. Street's people had been modified to the way they needed to be to survive among us, in my world.

I tend to forget, as I write, that the truth is what I say it is in these growing pages of manuscript. I have no special interest except to write a story for him, to keep the keys clacking as honestly as possible.

The length bothers me a bit. At a dollar a page I wonder if he'll be able to afford my discursive typescript.

Street looks over my shoulder. He says nothing.

The Victrola plays *Where Is the Life That Late I Led?* A loneliness creeps in. For them? For me?

The world they found was Earth, and they began to make their home on it, in an interstitial way. But Earth was giving them a hard time because Earth was scared of them.

Who on Earth? . . .

Not the ordinary man or woman in the United States, China, Russia, Lapland or Uruguay, because the ordinary people hadn't heard about them. The frightened ones were at the highest echelons—the presidents and prime ministers, the semi-autonomous investigative agencies, the military, the foreign ministries.

All had contingency plans for alien contact but the plans were out of date. They had been drawn up first in the dark ages of modern diplomacy, when a Frenchman named Verne wrote persuasive extraplanetary stories about the moon. Suppose some day somebody actually went to the moon and found a threat there? So plans to deal with that contingency were drawn up. Later an Englishman named Wells excited people with a story about Martians invading Earth. But Wells' vision was fiction; real invaders would not necessarily succumb to the common cold. The contingency plans were updated. (They really have people doing this. You'd be surprised at their titles and salaries.)

Then a transplanted European named Gernsback upset them anew with a stream of publications from Hudson Street in which authors from around the world wrote convincingly of menaces from all the universe and beyond.

Then, in a relatively new medium, came Orson Welles, a theatrical type who borrowed from the English Wells and scared a nation one Halloween. Then came specialized periodicals whose writers told of interplanetary intrigue that threatened the wellbeing of Earth.

These visionaries made fictional but putative menaces cheap and available to the masses.

Not only was it necessary for the rulers of Earth to be aware of the extraterrestrial threat—it was necessary for them to make the masses see that they were doing something about it.

And so, just as in years past there had been appointed an atomic chief, a transportation czar, an energy boss, an inflation fighter, the great minds of Earth established a bureau to consolidate all the other bureaus that had been dealing theoretically with the possibility of extraterrestrial contact. And in their wisdom they endowed it with extralegal powers and gave it the code name Stab.

Some thought Stab was an abbreviation for Establishment but nobody knew for sure, and nobody knew who headed it. Nobody but a relative handful of higher-ups who saw to it that a public information office was set up to issue press releases that assured everybody else that everything was Under Control, that the Alien Menace, if menace there was, would be Dealt With.

In a once-popular parlor game the victim was told the others would make up a story he could reconstruct by asking questions. His questions would be answered Yes, No or Maybe. He was told the answers would give him clues.

He didn't know there was no story, that the answers were based on a formula. If the last word of his question ended in a consonant the answer was No. If it ended in a vowel the answer was Yes. If it ended in a Y the answer was Maybe. Thus the questioner made up a story of his own that sometimes looked into his subconscious.

I think I'm doing that with Street. I question him and he replies. But as in the parlor game I wonder how much of what I write is from my subconscious or my imagination.

It is decreed in their philosophy (religion?) that in a new land they will find a philosopher—a prophet?—and that although he will make great demands on them he will guarantee them security. He will protect them from potential enemies. Though his price is high it is fair because it will enable them to settle and regroup and rebuild and multiply.

They call it their future book. Maybe I'm not the philosopher-prophet their book foretold but I'm the best they have. They apparently searched far before they found me and I have to believe their faith is justified.

I'd like to quote from their future book—their *Tome of Time*, as it translates. But of course I haven't seen it. I know only what Street has told me about it; more accurately, what I've pieced together from his answers to my questions. You must bear this caveat in mind: all he has said has been filtered through my ears and into my typing fingers; my understanding may be imperfect but I must believe that what I write is true.

Street nods approval. On the Victrola George Brunis is singing *I'm Gonna Sit Right Down and Write Myself a Letter.*

I must believe what their philosophy holds: that only what is written endures. My moving fingers type, leaving a record that will not be erased. Because it exists it is so. It is so because it exists. It is true because I have said it and believed it. It stands as an addendum to the *Tome of Time*, the future book becomes present, then past and immutable.

Street nods: I have said it. It is written, as foretold, and joins other prophecies that control their lives and now guide mine.

I've suspended my disbelief to the extent that I see logic in this. It's an attractive concept for a man who's created a kind of reality from gossamer things—the idle thought, the 2 a.m. inspiration, the hope that vagrant words, inked on paper from ribbon or pen, will persuade their readers, at least during the reading, that such things can be.

It's not easy to say where the Uxu are. They're not physically among us on the Earth we know. It's a dimensional phenomenon. I can put it best in nonscientific words, the only ones I command.

Try this: Railroaders, dispatch trains in opposite directions over single-track lines. The runs are precisely scheduled and no train meets another at a wrong place. The dispatchers use sidings, bypasses, lay-bys; the terms differ around the world but the result is the same—minimum space accommodates maximum traffic.

In a more sophisticated way communications engineers find room in their undersea cables and telephone, radio and satellite circuits for more than one message at a time. What was once a single, or at best dual, circuit now carries many messages simultaneously.

There are lots of unused spaces. Dr. Dolittle used them when he wrote upside down between lines and in margins.

Factory workers used these spaces in World War II when housing was short and people on different shifts slept in the same beds at different times.

So with us and the Uxu. It's clear now that they coinhabit the Earth in a separate dimension, on a plane that they, but not we, have discovered. They coexist with us, sharing land, sea and sky, in the interstices of our being. Their heartbeats complement ours. We breathe in while they breathe out. They ecologize our waste spaces, utilize our not-yet-depleted plenty: two trains on a single track; hundreds of messages on a single beam; twice as many words on a page; twice as many people in a bed.

They're not quite here and only a few of us have had an inkling that there are aliens in our midst, interstitially. They're literally among us but invisible, as we are to them—except when they deliberately cross the dimensional border. Yet they're uneasily sensed, uncomfortably poised just beyond the threshold of perception. They're like figures in Escher's symmetry drawings—flocks of geese, schools of fish flying, swimming in opposite directions, one group light and one dark, each apparently unaware of the other and each taking up exactly as much space as the other leaves unfilled.

"Rest for a time," Street said (or I wrote that he said it, needing a few minutes away from the typewriter). "Stretch your legs."

"Good idea." I got up and headed for the old farm privy that had been reactivated for exhibitors and customers. At the cook shed I bought a root beer. Sipping it, I went round the tables, saying hello and looking at wares.

Mrs. Shearer said: "I saved something for you." It was a fine old Autofiller made by the Schaaf Foundation Pen Co. of Toledo, patented June 30, 1903. "It doesn't fill anymore," she said, "but it writes a lot with one dip and a writer should have it."

"It's a beauty," I said. "How much do you have to get for it?"

"Fifty cents?"

"That's not enough, surely."

"It was in a box from an attic in Weedsport. I couldn't ask more."

Pleased to have it, I paid with a Franklin half dollar. I knew Mrs. Shearer collected them.

Nearby was Hester Goodbout's display of tramp art—old cigar box wood intricately whittled and carved and glued to form picture frames, jewel boxes, letter holders. A vanished and little-known craft only lately appreciated. I bought two pieces from Miss Goodbout, to give her some trade, and we talked about the art of homeless men who hadn't begged but had exchanged their special talent for meals or shelter.

Back at my table I looked for Street. He was not in sight.

I finished the root beer and looked at the sheet of paper in the Remington. Refreshed, I wanted to get back to work. I was annoyed at Street's absence. The devil with him; maybe I could go on without him. Was he not a saint but a devil? Was I Faust and he come to tempt me? Undeniably I am a latter-day Faust; before me there was a pulp writer named Frederick Faust, better known as Max Brand, creator of Dr. Kildare and millions of words of westerns.

The neighborly Victrola played the Furtwangler version of a scene from Gounod's Faust.

As a former story editor I knew there were one or two things in the plotline that needed fixing. I set the bottle on the table and my fingers stroked the guide keys: a s d f, j k l ; . . . I . . .

I looked beyond the flea market to the drumlin that hid part of Lake Ontario, shimmering bright on each side. The slope of the hill seemed to move. A slow down avalanche against the green growth. But not a dirt slide. No; a procession of people. A mass of cowled figures. A multitude in monk's cloth, moving down, coming this way. Thirty, fifty, sixty of them; I couldn't count. Far enough away to be indistinguishable one from another; near enough to fear. They were coming here.

On level ground now, they came determinedly across the flat of the land between. The outer exhibitors saw them and called to others. Eyes turned, then stopped. Then everything stopped except the brown mass of cowled monks.

The other exhibitors had been immobilized in the middle of a gesture, a sale.

Only I had special dispensation, to type away, to put it all down.

The strangers came among us, faces hidden deep inside their cowls, and went from table to table, touching the goods quickly, moving on. One came to my table, bringing a chill breeze as a cloud crossed the sun. The figure stood at my side as if to know what I wrote. I strained to see past the shadow of the cowl but could find no face, only a darkness punctuated by what might have been stars, or eyes. The being touched the page in my typewriter and exchanged words in a strange musical tongue with another of its kind. All the others moved away. The visitor remained, the star-eyes as inscrutable as before, the presence as awesome.

The others moved back up the drumlin. As they topped its rise and vanished the flea market came to life. People moved, fingered goods, haggled, bought, moved to other tables. The Victrola played *When the Saints Go Marching In* and I gathered courage to look directly into the star eyes of the cowled figure who had remained at my side.

I saw the features of a woman. I stood in greeting and regarded her frankly. She wore leather sandals and her small feet were perfect. I looked from toe to head and said, "Good afternoon."

"Good afternoon," she replied. "I came as you would have wished, had you known me sooner."

"I know you now," I said, and dared to add: "You are Uxura. You must be."

"Because you've written it so?"

"Do we need a because?" I realized that she was not young, observing the sun wrinkles at her eyes and the smile lines at her mouth. I appreciated them, having creases of my own.

"Welcome to our Earth," I said.

"Thank you, if Earth this be. I'll meet you closer later, perhaps, through the barrier."

"I see no impediment between us."

"If you see that, so it must be. You are the prophet, the seer and scribe, the molder of our destiny."

"I write. I know little of prophecy."

"You know my name and I know yours, Mr. William Wylie Ross."

"You are Uxura but why do I know that? And you have most delightfully come, Uxura, but why?"

"You reply. Write it and we both will know."

"It may be known later, when the story is finished."

"It is in your hands. Let them make me a useful person. Let your fingers give me depth and purpose, to contribute to the peace and security of our peoples."

I hardly knew what I wrote, what consciousness guided my words. "My fingers write that you have already given much. Your husband, a great man, piloted an early Uxu ship. He died when it crashed in a test. You are Street's mother. Yet you are so young."

"I am proud to be all of these, except young. My son tells me you are the scribe the gods foretold, that you were always in our destiny."

"Waiting in the wings with a workable scenario? I can't really accept this god business."

"Then better for us all. Rather a doubting but well-intentioned godservant than an arrogant unfeeling one who delights in power for its own sake." She smiled. "I beg your pardon, but it is you who puts the words in my mouth—which longs to know yours . . ." She stopped in surprise.

"Really—" I said, as surprised as she at the reality of her saying the words that had been in my thoughts.

The presence of this woman who appealed to me so vitally and who said the words I'd dared not say aloud made me want to race ahead with the narrative, to reach the obligatory setback, to overcome it logically and get on to an ending, preferably happy.

There's not space here to describe Uxura. I'd have to ask many a man what kind of woman he admires. Twain's Joan? A childhood sweetheart? Doyle's Holmes' Irene Adler? Lena Horne? Margaret Sullavan? Amelia Earhart? The grandmother you ran to when your mother punished you?

Put them all together and they spell mother, wife, lover, companion, love object, sweetheart, the eternal woman. My feelings, still chaotic, about Uxura. So soon? So late?

If the women I've named are too old for you—I'm an old

party myself—how about Jenny Agutter, Becky Thatcher, Tatum O'Neal, Peter Pan's Wendy Darling?

That much I wrote and, though much must have been strange to her, she responded in an age-old feminine way. She drew my head to her breast and put her lips to my forehead.

It was more than an embrace. In that brief contact we exchanged two lifetimes of experience. I felt her life flow into mine and fill me with understanding of all she had known. I knew that at the same time she was absorbing everything that had made me whatever I was or believed myself to be.

In that moment we came to know each other in a more intimate way than I'd known any other, even—I thought of my marriage—even after living with someone for nearly a decade.

I learned from that touch between Uxura and me that the difference in our ages was far greater than the distance which had once separated us. She was not the young middle-aged woman of 50-odd years my eyes saw her to be, but three times that. Her son Street was not 30 but 90. I, a mere 55, with three years to live or a hope for twice that if I took care of myself, as Doctor Marv and I knew I probably wouldn't, could expect a lifespan of many more years on Uxu if I allowed myself to be transported there—to live not to an unfulfilled 58 or 61 but possibly to a robust 64 or 73.

This she told me in knowledge greater than words and this I believed.

Much more passed between us then; more than I can tell here; more than I could care to tell if I had all the space and time to tell it.

As we drew apart I felt we had woven a bond impossible to sever. Her warm glance said the same was true for her.

But then I wondered how many others she had shared herself with in such a way and I was saddened. She was quick to sense my thought. She touched me lightly, fingers to cheek, and I knew I was the first beyond her family to know her thus, and I was comforted. Even in that brief aftertouch, as I questioned why, she told me I was different, I was special.

I believed and was satisfied.

Thus my decision to go where she dwelt—I hoped not only for the pleasure of her company but to give her the pleasure of mine for more than a moment of time. Sweet Uxura. Selfishly I chose to go not for the wish to save our two worlds as I had begun to believe I might, not for the adventure of it and the new experiences I might translate into fiction; no—only so I could cling longer to life and in the respite cling to Uxura.

It was time to write an exit line for her, knowing I'd write her in again, and return her son Street to the stage. Mad Wayne Anthony's Victrola played *Somewhere I'll Find You.*

I delayed Street's entrance and said to Uxura: "You know we'll meet again? And that when we do there will be more time for us and for many other things?"

"Yes," she said, "but you write in question marks. There are things you must accomplish. Some do not concern me but others do, most vitally. You will say it in the writings. It is a charming quark."

Why had she used that word? I searched my memory and recalled that a physicist had invested some nuclear particles with certain wondrous qualities. He called these particles quarks, borrowing the word from Joyce.

Later other physicists spoke of refined particles they called charmed quarks that one day might help make clear to man the basic nature of matter. Then they combined a charmed quark with its negative number and produced what they called a charmonium.

Whatever the scientists postulated, their speculations ended in question marks, as most good theories should pending another Einstein.

But long before that a humbler breed of men had made quarks part of their everyday, if specialized, language. They were the telegraph operators.

When I was a cub reporter in awe of their easy professionalism they used "quark" routinely in their messages. It was an abbreviation that shortened their Morse transmissions, just as they shortened White House to WHU, Supreme Court of the United States to SCOTUS and, later, Nelson Rockefeller's recurring phrase "brotherhood of man under the Fatherhood of God" to BOMFOG. To these hamfisted realists, quark was simply the abbreviation of question mark. Play that on your charmonium.

I thought of Murray Gell-Man, James Bjorken, Theodore Kalegeropoulos and other physicists who pondered the ultimate. Uxura's amber eyes recalled me to the present.

"These things are beyond me," she said. "You among others control my destiny. I am glad we have met, Will."

Her token of farewell was a touch of her hand to my cheek. I gave her a warm symbol of my own, a kiss on that hand.

"When will you come again?" I asked.

"I'll be near when there is need," she replied.

I made that her exit line. There are needs and needs.

She was gone. Would I see her again? A charming quark whose answer I knew.

Uxura was gone and in her place was Street, somber, disturbed.

"I met your mother," I told him. "She—"

"No time for that. Is it true that your people plan to obliterate us?"

Street was casting a pall over what had been, all in all, a pretty nice day. Why was I letting him? I much preferred his mother.

He went on: "Can it be that such a plan, which we know exists, would be implemented? Are there those in your government so callous—"

Street spoke of a pre-emptive strike, a massive retaliation ordered by Earth's military chiefs. Angry, looking betrayed, he said it had been plotted by second-level people who nevertheless had the power to set it in motion.

He brandished a paper he called a secret document. I tried to get him to hold it still so I could see it but he talked with an intensity that was working into fury.

Finally I was able to take the paper from him. It was a much-Xeroxed Jack Anderson column from an unidentified newspaper, undated. What looked like a memo from one high-ranking officer to another had been copied on the same page. It said something like "Great opportunity to try out Plan P. Can we persuade K to consider?"

K might be Kronwald, a high functionary at the State Department. The names of the officers meant nothing to me.

I tried to tell Street that Anderson produced hundreds of columns a year and that not all of his informants could be believed. I tried to explain that chairborne officers in the Pentagon forever filled their time by playing war games. War was their trade, after all, but their games were just games.

"Policy is made at a much higher level," I said, and offered to seek out the facts from a friend who knew truth from talk and right from wrong and who, with his access to high places, could confirm that what alarmed Street was no more than a mongered rumor.

In fact, I offered to visit Dirk Easterly, who with his access to the highest councils, could guarantee that my interpretation was correct and that the Uxurans had nothing to fear from Earth.

"You would go?" Street asked, and I said I would, happily, to reassure him if he no longer trusted me.

He demurred, saying it was not me he distrusted but others.

How could he not trust me, I asked, if I was their prophet? This led to a philosophical discussion that ended with renewed assurances of his confidence in me—but only while I was with him, where he could keep an eye on me.

"That confidence will be immeasurably strengthened when you are resident with us on Uxu," he said. "Your high friend will then protect you and therefore us."

"It is not my wish to travel to Uxu," I told him. I don't know why I lied.

"Nevertheless it is the only solution."

"You would hold me hostage?"

"That is not a word we use."

"Captive, then?" I was indignant.

"You are our prophet and scribe," he said. "We have agreed to that; you are one of us. Therefore you belong among us."

"And if I refuse to go?" I was careful not to say I refused. The thought of Uxura was in my mind. But I'd have preferred to travel to her land of my own will.

"It is not a question of going," Street told me. "You are already on Uxu."

What he said after that made it clear that I had been transported to his land during the time-stop when the wave of cowled monklike figures descended the hill. This meant that the people of my friendly flea market were not the people they had been before. They were duplicates of the original Earthpeople, mockups created by the aliens.

My indignation returned. I told Street kidnapping was a federal offense. I said I would not be their scribe under duress. I said he had betrayed our mutual trust. I told him I could not live away from my beloved house in Auburn, where all my possessions were.

As if to placate me, Street said I would perceive no difference. All I had known would be the same. They had duplicated my house and everything in it just as they had replicated the flea market.

"Am I to be a prisoner in my own house?" I asked, feeling less annoyed. Thoughts of Uxura helped. Nevertheless I went on a bit: "Won't I be able to go to the Auburn Inn for breakfast? Can't I visit the library and museum?"

Street reassured me. Nearly a square mile of the territory around my house in Auburn had been duplicated in their interstitial way. Other requirements of mine would be met on demand.

I accepted the compromise, and told him so.

But why had I accepted? It was self-evident, now that I thought about it. It was my salvation as well as theirs. For them I was, if not a hostage, at least a guarantee that I would not let anything happen to them that I did not want to happen to me. The safety of their world depended on my well-being. My own well-being, indeed my future existence, depended on their environment offering an extended life expectancy. My days were numbered wherever I was, but the numbers were greater in the other land.

There were still other cards in my hand. I could set the terms. I could make demands. I could ask and what I asked would be granted because that was the way it was written in their book and I was the author of that book. I had only to take my fingers from the typewriter to wreck their plans. And so I asked, leaving it to them to agree gracefully, lest my reasonable requests escalate into demands which could not be denied. Mine was the pen that wrote their book of existence and it was a pen mightier than any sword they might wield. I ticked off my requests in a matter-of-fact way, as if to say These are the least of my needs, without which I cannot function, and there will be more, not needs but wants which I shall also expect from you.

Street looked troubled, and two or three times his face withdrew deep within his cowl as if he were communicating with a higher authority, but he always agreed, and I wrote it that way and it became our compact, our contract.

My reconstituted house in Ux-Auburn was not altogether to my liking. They'd fixed me up more faithfully than I'd expected, but it wasn't home. It had a desk identically like mine but it didn't have the shelves of books that sat on the back of my desk at home—the rarely consulted but comforting books where I could look up, if I wanted to, the name of George Washington's dentist, the date of the crossing of the Rubicon, the words that rhymed with sang, the number of miles between Coventry and Stonehenge, the descriptions of ships I'd traveled in.

There was my typewriter but not the folders of manuscripts I planned to finish one day. Nor was there the big box of articles I'd torn from newspapers for later reference. A bookcase I recognized was there but it was empty of the books and magazines and scripts I'd written or contributed to. There was nothing printed at all, although there were a few reams of blank paper.

This alarmed me until I found that my typewriter produced words just as it always had. I had feared that no written words of Earth could exist on Uxu. There are many of them here now but all of them are words of my own, most of them those of this work in progress.

There was a refrigerator in the kitchen and there was food in it and on the pantry shelves but it was their kind of food, wholesome I supposed but unfamiliar. They didn't replace it until I complained. Then they provided Earth-style eggs and bread and butter and milk and coffee and other goods I demanded. They were all right but not altogether satisfactory. It was like the difference between getting my copy of the *New York Times* fresh on the doorstep each morning (they couldn't manage that) versus looking at a microfilm copy in a library years later. There's something about the genuine article. The reconstruction, the duplication, the replica—none is ever as good.

And of course they reneged on the library. The building was there, an empty shell, locked, but I could see through the windows that there were no books inside. The museum was there, not locked, and pictures hung on its walls but they were not titled and there was no reference materials of any kind.

There was no radio in the house and I missed that. I'd kept mine tuned to a noncommercial station that satisfied my tastes in music and my daily need to know what was going on in the world.

I missed the voice of Terry Johnson, the morning man on Auburn's FM station, who told me the time and what the weather was like. His way of speaking sometimes amused me. He used the odd aural punctuation of Radioland—"From our bin of golden oldies we have brought you the music of (a pause, longish for radio) Tommy Dorsey and now the weather."

And I remember that once he'd said "At 7:30 I'm Terry Johnson." I wondered who he thought he had been at 7 and whether he would be someone else at 8.

There was no FM set in Ux-Auburn but something else spoke to me. I became aware of it gradually. Many days had passed before I realized that someone had been communicating subliminally. Rarely to me directly but to me among others.

The voice, if it was a voice, never identified itself but I came to know the speaker, or rather the transmitter of the words or thoughts, as Exus. The messages of Exus reached me not by transistor but inside my head. He recapitulated the important events of his world, not mine, and spoke occasionally of me.

It startled me at first to be referred to in this public way, to be singled out by this commentator as one of the important people of their world. I record in this narrative some of my impressions of him.

On one of Street's visits I asked him to tell me about Exus but he only smiled as if to say You invented him, you tell me. But I feel it's more than my invention here; there is a person whose words reflect Vox Populi, the Everyman of the Uxu people I know only dimly. I call him Exus because the name embodies the mandatory X and because from him, through him, come the thoughts and comments of the multitude of Uxurans I have been thrust among. Exus distills their feelings and gives them artistic form.

Unlike Terry Johnson, Exus knew who he was at all times and I heard him whenever he wanted me to. One of his first observations went something like this:

"Eggs he wants, and books by Dickens;
We have to evolutionize to chickens
And reproduce endless novels
At the expense of unroofed hovels."

Who is Exus and what is he telling me?

In describing Exus through his words I give you an alien scribe, not unlike me, who synopsizes, compressing to stanzas what I'd need pages to say. He's a newsman of a certain kind, transmitting facts—sometimes flawed facts—fresh to those who hear his distillations.

I never did get the Dickens, or any printed matter and I had to conclude that Exus allows himself a certain poetic license.

My alien colleague encapsulates complicated events into little space. I feel I have come to know him. I can't reach him but he reaches me. I endow him with certain freedoms of language and alien clichés. You'll grasp them in their context. Listen to Exus:

"Pens he craves and spending money
And a craft of bees he calls honey.
Halt the de-sal of a sea!
Hurry up and plan a bee."

But another verse was less harsh:

"I voice the words, the gripes, the woes
Of him who can't see past his nose;
Others see him as he's painted:
Our prophet come and partly tainted."

I sense a fraternal bond with this fellow of the alien airwaves. Both of us write. We seem to be of an approximate age, the fires of youth spent. That gives us a certain objectivity and a mordant way of looking at things. Neither is a hireling. We freelance, in the best and oldest sense of the word, defending truth and honor, telling what we believe is true. We may exaggerate, ironically, to make a point.

Still, Exus is dim, I'll have to limn him, get him out from behind the scrim of mystery and myth.

Where does he churn out his stuff? High on an alien hilltop, it may be. I like to think of him there, in a golden afternoon, far horizons broadening his viewpoint.

I use a typewriter, a relatively recent invention. His instrument is an ancient but superior device through which his thoughts roam, to be edited—much as I might X out—until in a more Uxuran way they reach me and others.

I hear what he says and believe we think alike despite our differences. One difference is obvious: my words remain on the sheets where I type them; his fly to all his world—and to my ears now that I am a part of it.

Even as I write of him, he speaks of me:

"Is it worth it, many ask,
Bending to the ordained task?
Weighing prophet against loss,
Do we need you, Mister Ross?"

Exus has a bite to him, but he softens it:

"To steal his phrase, we knock on wood;
We need him for the greater good.
So let him have his precious bees
To put him at his proper ease."

Street visited from time to time to see how I was getting on, to talk, to know what I was writing about our mutual problem.

I was sorry for their troubles that I hadn't caused them. I was sorry for Earth's troubles too, if the Earthpeople's resources were to be diminished by having to share them with uninvited visitors. If there was room for both, I wanted peace between us; if there was not enough room—I thought of Abe Burrows' parody of a popular song: You came to me from out of nowhere so why don't you go back where you came from?

But then there was Street's belief that the Earthpeople, or some villains among them, were prepared to obliterate the visitors who had been tossed on an alien shore and who hoped only for peaceful coexistence in a land with plenty for all—but could it be that its fabled wealth was limited? That its bounty was bounded by human overgrowth? That its largely empty continents would be overrun in a matter of decades by its own burgeoning billions?

If this were true it was easy to believe the "documentary" evidence Street had acquired—the widely disseminated warning that a secret group of Earthpeople had decreed doom for the Uxurans—a secret strike by paragovernmental forces of a dozen major powers that would annihilate the storm-tossed, the spacechanged involuntary immigrants. The Uxurans had asked only to share, at no loss to anyone, the interstitial wealth of a world whose surface resources were finite but whose submagma and supratropospheric treasures waited to be tapped and could be, easily, with the knowledge the new inhabitants had brought with them.

We had always welcomed refugees, up to now. With certain exceptions we had taken in the homeless, the tempest-tossed.

But now some people in the hierarchy wanted to draw the line at alien aliens. Nowhere, they claimed, was there a mandate to gather flotsam from beyond the stars. They argued that this would threaten our own kind. We had had no compunctions about wiping out the anopheles mosquito, the tse tse fly, the screw worm. If we warred on fellow creatures such as these for the greater good of the rest of us, how could we extend friendship to even greater potential threats to our well-being? So spoke the exclusionists whose words, interpreted by Jack Anderson, had so alarmed Street.

I told Street it was unthinkable that the good people of Earth, most of them mired in poverty, should be deprived of a bounty beyond their belief by the act of a handful of irregulars whose fealty was to the status quo and not to the promise the aliens—no fellow terrestrials—held out to them.

Street was only half convinced, although I hinted that the Uxurans' spacechanged engines, instead of mining the jointly-held Earth and the resources below and above it, could harness their power in another way and, with their interstitial ingenuity, blow us all to kingdom come.

Street said: "If your irregulars attack, you share our fate. If Uxuran engines can mine your land and ours exponentially, you share our bounty. If we answer Earth's attack by invading interstitially, Earth is doomed. You are with us and will share our fate, whatever it may be. That is why you are with us."

There was tension between Street and me; tension I didn't need; a sullen standoff.

Street has gained presence on his native Uxu. The verses of Exus refer to him often. I sense that Street speaks for his world virtually with full authority. He is far more representative of his people than I am of mine. If I could speak as he did we could arrange a summit meeting at this tired typewriter, manned by a tired scribe, and solve all the problems of two worlds. I acknowledge that I lack the kind of authority he has but he is content to wait, implying that as I chafe in my hostage status the solution will occur to me.

He is satisfied that as their prophet I will work out the details in a way acceptable to me and therefore to him. I am to be the Prince of Concinnity, with the burden of making gospel of a bold but unconvincing narrative. Poo-Bah's law. A dash of verisimilitude will do it if I can find the recipe, the key.

I find only the guide keys of my typewriter but am inspired to think Exus, my versifying colleague, may help. I address him directly. My words are poor compared to his but I trust him to hear the core of meaning. Exus the sweet singer of Uxu and Ross the freewheeling freelance of Earth, communicating in a transdimensional bond, seeking to avoid a stalemate, looking for a way to achieve a common good that transcends artificial boundaries. My words flow out in an Exuslike stanza:

"Are we close, my alien poet?
Is there a chance that we can go it?
I think there is; the door's ajar.
Are we friends? I think we are."

Exus does not reply. I am disappointed. I am restless. I roam the house, unable to sit at the typewriter. I wander outdoors and pace the grounds. There is a lawn chair in the dappled shade of a tree. I sit in it briefly, then am up again. Without a book to hand I cannot properly relax; and there are no books on Uxu. Nothing to read except what I write, and I am growing sick of that.

I find the little garden I have started and abandoned. It is weed-choked. A shovel is stuck in the ground. I pull it out. Garden needs spading, I think. I shove it back in the ground. Dig is what a space does.

I chop away at the weeds. Work is what a man does. Cry is what a babe does. What am I saying? Mewl is what a cat does. Bark is what a dog does. Drool is what a fool does. Drool? Stab is what a dirk does. Dirk? Heal is what a wound does. Drool? Dirk heal?

I run to the house, to the typewriter. I write the chaotic words and soon Street is there.

"I need help," I tell him. "I am only half effective without my blood brother, Dirk Easterly." I tell Street of our pact, of our mute witness, Drool the dog. "I have invoked our solemn agreement. Obviously he cannot come to me; therefore I must go to him. It is the only possible way."

Street is dubious. I can see he is torn between my persuasiveness as prophet and the possible defection of his hostage.

"Then keep me here," I say, "but send my image. It will be as real as the people at the flea market at the time I joined your cause. Yet my true self will remain to share your fate if my mission fails."

Street seems to listen to words I cannot hear. He is silent for some moments, then agrees to my plan to go to Washington across the dimensional divide.

"It will be done; with your special help, of course," Street said. "Our programmers are relieved that no major recreation is involved. It will be a simple transsubstantiation, such as brought you among us."

"You mean I have to write it that way," I said resignedly. I was tired.

"You need not write it now. You will later."

"Oh? It sounds like a loan. I have to write it to make it happen. But because I will write it you'll advance me a trip that I'll pay for with a future account of it?"

Street almost smiled. "Describe it as you will. I believe your people have been known to trade in futures?"

Within an hour of my agreement with Street, after packing a small bag, I was set down, or I materialized—I can't describe it—at the end of the Glen Echo trolley line in suburban Washington. It had been my choice.

I don't know why I had wanted this means of getting to Washington. It stood to reason that the trolley line had been long abandoned, just as the Glen Echo Amusement Park no longer existed. Yet the pleasure of both lived in my memory; that must have been enough for Street.

"It's a nickel," the trolley car conductor said in answer to my question; "same as always."

I asked no more. It was a cheap and wonderful ride through the glen beside the waterway, the trolley bucketing along, its bell clanging at intersections or whenever the motorman felt like treading on the foot pedal in the sheer pleasure of transporting his passengers on a sunny day.

At the terminal I exchanged smiles of goodby with my fellow passengers and found a cab whose driver knew the old tavern where I was to meet Dirk Easterly.

Despite the many years between I recognized Dirk easily. He knew me too and with a clap on the shoulder led me to a booth where the waiter had set out two brimming beers in sweat-beaded glasses. I had been there last in the forties, when Dirk was off in the Balkans, or maybe the Baltic. "It looks the same," I said. "A little dustier, maybe."

"Nobody's dusted since Lincoln drank here, or so they say. Here's to Drool and the high school kids." We sipped in pleasure.

Stab (short for establishment?) was the bureau the OWI, OSS and CIA had evolved into. It was a unit of the executive office of the White House and of the United Nations, sometimes written STAB as if it were an acronym. The hundred or so people who knew about Stab occupied themselves in trying to pin down its function by making up a name for the letters: Space Travel Accessibility Bureau; Substation Terra, Authenticating Branch; Search, Travel, Assess, Bomb; Seek Terrestrialoids and Beneficize; Section Two, Alien Bureau; Scientists Terrestrializing Alien Beings; Something Traumatic Always Begins.

Dirk Easterly, my childhood blood brother, was a civil servant of awesome background, respected or deplored by his colleagues, consulted by the President but little known beyond a small international circle.

Dirk and I had gone to the same high school and had traded copies of H. G. Wells and Wonder Stories magazine. We'd seen each other only rarely since that time. There had been occasional post cards to each other from odd places on our separate paths but there'd never been a call until today, when I'd sent him my message from Uxu.

We have had other bonds, he as a civil servant, I as a reporter. He'd known Tasha, who was Tito's woman in the Balkans, and I'd known Tasha. We'd both known Philip before he married his queen-to-be. We had played chess at different times against the same Russian who's been privy to the secrets of Stalin and Khrushchev and Brezhnev and we almost always lost.

He was Dirk Easterly of Stab and, as I had lately recalled, stab is what a dirk does.

His outward idiosyncracy was to affect the trappings of a Hollywood-style soldier of fortune. He habitually wore a belted and shoulder-strapped trench coat and a pulled-down hat and almost always had a cigarette going in the corner of his mouth. I must have seemed as odd to him with my deliberately Ronald Colman mustache, my Dolittle-like note-taking on insides of match covers and margins of newspapers and my flea market business card.

Our reunion was pleasant. We drank beer and ate peanuts and gabbed of intervening years. We spoke of lost friends and recalled how it had been when we were among a precious few who were convinced that man would reach another planet or that men of another planet would find us.

We recalled our youthful appreciation of prophetic comic strips. Young Dirk had pasted up the Brick Bradford daily strips. I collected them later in Big Little Book reprints at fancy prices.

We understood each other. We associated still.

"Nov shmoz ka pop," Dirk said.

"The Nuț Brothers, Ches and Wal," I replied.

"Thimble Theatre."

"Segar. Popeye and the Sea Hag."

Our oysters came, reminding me of the Potomac and the Hudson, which recalled Stony Point. "No dog shall bark," I said.

"Mad Anthony Wayne," Dirk said. "Melville; Ishmael."

"Ish Kabibble. Kay Kyser's Kollege of Musical Knowledge."

"Old-time radio. Hard times. Two chickens in every pot."

"Pot. The grass is always greener. It's better on the other side."

"The other side. We have seen the natives and they are friendly."

We paused as the waiter brought a fresh pitcher of beer. He set down two clean clamshell ashtrays and took away those we'd filled with butts and dottle.

"I smoke too much," Dirk said. "I just noticed."

"Why worry? You could be run down tonight by a Treasury truck."

"Or an interstitial alien."

"So you know." I told him what I'd been doing and he told me much I hadn't known. I said: "It seems unreal, here in Washington, but obviously I've been doing more than fooling around in a flea market."

Dirk said: "We're making policy here. What I recommend will be approved because hardly anybody else knows what it's all about. Are the Uxu a real threat? If they are you'd better tell me now."

It was hard to say, I told him. "Maybe it depends on how much I demand of them. The more I require, the greater the drain on their economy. I try not to sap their energies too much when they're recycling waste or reclaiming a desert. But what will they do if they're convinced Earth is planning a pre-emptive strike?"

"They'll invade. Territoriality makes for inevitability."

"Only if I permit it," I said. "You see, what I'm scribbling here on match covers and what I owe them in manuscript is the definitive text. There's something cabalistic about them. What I write will happen."

"You're writing their constitution?"

"I'm writing something; it's more like their Bible."

"And what you prophesy will come to pass?"

"As in our Bible? 'Now write what you see, what is and what is to take place hereafter.' Revised Standard Version.

Or, in the King James: 'He knows the future and is able to control it.' Others have said it. So it would be more exact to say that what I write is happening. Or that what I've written has happened. I'm their historian and when I say something is so, it's so. Irrevocably."

"You sound as if they've made you their god. Why would they do that?"

"I don't know that they have. Prophet, they call it. They seem to trust me."

"Is that trust deserved?" Dirk asked. "Do they know what we're talking about here?"

"They'll know what I've written. I owe them that. I consider you the guarantor of the stability of two worlds."

"You believe that."

"Once I wouldn't have," I said. "I do now. Maybe they'll include you in their prayers. The great brother god. God Brother of Stability."

"Would they offer up nubile maidens to me?"

"If I wrote it that way. Is nubile maidens what you want?"

"Not in groups. I'm your age, you know. But one at a time? That's a kind of benefit I don't get from Stab."

"Then you shouldn't expect it from the Uxu."

"Let the sacred writings show that I'm only kidding. Make me a small-g god with a sense of humor. Unless you're in upper case; then I'd expect equal billing."

"I don't want to be God or a god," I said. "I should make that clear."

"I'm glad you did because it wasn't clear to me. I'd better sort out what I'll have to tell the President. He may not want details at this point but I've got to be ready for him."

"What does he know so far?"

"He has the facts on the Uxu. Where they are—coexistent, dimensionally, with us. He isn't concerned about them now and neither is the Sec-Gen. You do know I report jointly to the White House and to N. K. Mboto, Secretary-General of the United Nations?"

"I've kept track. Then your guarantee is also that of the UN. Anything you've said, over beer and oysters here, is what Earth says. Is that right?"

"It's right enough," Dirk said. "But don't forget that if what you tell me about your prophesying is true, the Uxu are only an incantation away from being physically among us on Earth. So watch your language. They can have their interstices and we intend to keep ours. I'm depending on you not to write anything you don't want to happen."

"I give you my word, blood brother."

"Good enough. Somebody has to advise the White House and the UN on the interstitial situation. Stab does that. And for all practical purposes I'm Stab."

"With the same disclaimer, I'm Uxu," I said. "Then if you and I have a drink on it, it's as good as a treaty. Is that right?"

We shook hands and drank some beer. The stability of Uxu and of Earth was assured. There's a way of doing these things.

We went to Harvey's for a seafood dinner. Afterwards we got a cab and Dirk dropped me off at my hotel, where I wrote up what you see here, paying my debt to Street.

I finished typing my notes in the Washington hotel after leaving Dirk—fulfilling my futures contract with Street—and considered my return to Uxu. I was looking forward to getting back; anxious, in fact. I'd had my sentimental journey on the Glen Echo trolley and wanted a faster return trip.

The business atmosphere of the capitol almost made me forget that I had the means at hand—the rented typewriter I'd been pounding for an hour. I rolled a fresh sheet of paper into it to do a postscript. But I found my fingers writing:

"The threat of interstitial kill
Was lifted by our Prophet Will
In concert with unstabbing Dirk—
What a lovely piece of work!"

Unmistakably Exus. So they already knew.

Later I wrote, of my own volition, that I was tired and ready for bed. That I would prepare for sleep in Washington. That as slumber neared I would prophesy that I would wake in my house in Ux-Auburn. That I would have a reunion breakfast among friends.

It happened.

Except that there was only one friend. "I'm glad you forced us to invent the hen," Uxura said as she served eggs, whole wheat toast and coffee.

I was delighted to see her but wondered where Street was.

She said she had sent him on his way. "He has much to

do. He was glad to shed his diplomat's cloak and get back into his more comfortable laboratory jacket. His job is to halt the building of war engines and convert our economy to peace and trade with our new-found friends. There is much we can share with you."

We talked of that for a time and I said: "Then Street really is Uxu's top man. I rather suspected it."

"Yes; he's inherited his father's genius and whatever I've been able to give him. My son has done well and I'm proud of him. He has earned the right to be top man, as you call it. But he's not the boss."

"Oh?" I was confused. "Then who is? Will I meet him?"

"Not him," Uxura said. "And we have already met."

I could only look at her, wordless, as she poured more coffee.

"It was not always so," she said. "You told us of the space change we have undergone. We learned many things from our Prophet Will."

Speechless still, I lifted my cup. Then I said inanely: "You make excellent coffee."

"That too," she said, and smiled.

Then she said: "My instincts are important. I'm not just a woman—I'm Woman, from far back. And woman's instincts are more than just feminine intuition. Our whole experience shows we have age-old ways of knowing more than we are credited with."

I knew what she was talking about. I'd read in a journal that women had greater sensitivity to the character of others, a sensitivity honed by the needs of thousands of generations of silent subservience to the more powerful males of their tribe or society. The enforced silences gave them opportunity, more than their men, to be attentive to nonverbal signs, to store up knowledge thus learned and to be able to act on it in time of danger. Not only mothers protecting their children were respected by the men for their instincts, but older women with acknowledged abilities became high priestesses whose canniness and prescience were respected by all in the tribe.

And then we talked of things that need concern no one else. There was a kiss of a kind different from the one at the flea market and we made certain plans . . .

And then there was a glimmering of subliminal thought that turned to words inside my head:

"There's a later bridge to cross:
Could you share a woman boss?"

I knew she'd also heard it. She was smiling sweetly, eyes cast down, looking almost girlish.

I didn't answer the question. I said: "You're not Exus too?"

"No, no," she said, "though he is all of us, as you said his name implies." She added softly: "You didn't answer the question."

"You must know—" I began. "I think I prefer to write the answer. I will do that soon."

"That will be fitting," she said. "I am content to wait."

"It will take only a little while," I said. "I'd like to go back to the flea market to do it properly. May I?"

"Street will escort you," she said and Street appeared at the door, looking interrupted. His mother explained. "It's our prophet's sense of concinnity," she said. "Take him there one more time."

"I have missed some of the narrative, being busy elsewhere," Street said, masking annoyance.

"You will know it later, at your convenience," his mother said. "Take him there now. It is his obligatory scene. We have our ways; he has his."

Street took me there; it was the place I had known.

One asks: Was my trip to Washington an actuality or was it theatrically programmed for me by the Uxurans? The questions is academic. By their own rules what I have written is fact because I have written it. It is so. Ask Street or Exus or Uxura. Ask Dirk Easterly. Ask the President of the United States or the Secretary-General of the United Nations.

Ask ten-year-old Henry, for whom I also write.

Things happen or they don't. This happened. Has the sun risen? Does a bird sing in a tree? Can you go for a walk or kiss your beloved or pick up the phone and have a pizza delivered?

Everything is as it was, pretty near. What's good is still good and what's bad is still bad but, by and large, aren't you content?

We're coexisting with an alien race, not on our block but just around a dimensional corner, and we're still very much alive. Nothing has changed that wouldn't have changed anyway, for better or for worse.

Contrariwise, nobody is taking up cudgels against the foe. Nobody hankers today to go with pike and sword to Christianize the infidel, or to loose uncontrollable weapons to make the planets safe for our particular brand of life. Probably we've had enough crusading in foreign climes, minding other people's business when there are injustices of our own to correct.

It would be good if this were so. I hope it is.

In fact, the power of my word being what it is, I decree it.

As for them, their way is that of a peaceable people. As they borrowed my mind and familiarity with Earth to give them what they needed, so did I permeate their destiny to prevent them from harming us. And I've absorbed enough of their knowledge to benefit us all in ways that will be apparent in good time. Their space change has affected us as well.

They are as incapable of waging war on us as I am incapable of letting it happen in these writings. As Dirk Easterly cautioned me solemnly: "Don't let the moving finger write anything it couldn't cancel out."

It's my finger he was talking about. I won't let it happen.

Is that a strong enough guarantee? For me it is. Either you take me on faith, you of Uxu and you of Earth, or you gave up on me some time ago. If you're still with me you must be convinced that a common-sense arrangement had to be made to keep things from exploding. And sometimes things are arranged by concerned people of less than the highest rank who are accidentally well placed, like Dirk and me.

It may be a flimsy reed to lean on but if we lean gently and keep talking to each other, all of us may survive.

William Wylie Ross was nearly at the end of his story. The back of his neck hurt because he had sat so long. He pulled the last page from the typewriter, put the sheets together and handed them to Street, who waved them away. "I know all that you have written."

"Is that how it will happen?" Ross asked.

"It is the way it has happened," Street said.

Ross looked around. Many dealers had left and others were packing their wares, folding their tables. The Victrola Man was playing a coda: *Good Night, Ladies*. Few customers remained. The sun was low.

"It's hard to believe I'm on Uxu," Ross said. "Or have I gone and come back?"

"You are where you want to be. Call it Earth, call it Uxu,

call it simply the First Original Famous Flea Market. They're all yours, you know."

Ross looked at the familiar land and sky. Cars went by on Route 3. A man took down the roadside sign that said Flea Market Every Sunday May to Oct. Park in Field Below.

"It's quite real, isn't it?" Street said. "Can all of us be merely the product of your imagination? Be satisfied. Hasn't it been a good day?"

"We've traveled in time?" Ross asked. "After all that has happened everything is the same as it was?"

"We are here, now or again. It is a good moment in time, which is relative, anyway. Why limit it by tense? You question too much."

Ross examined the scene he was told he'd made. He looked for flaws, for the possibility that it would dissolve like a dream or the end of a movie. Nothing changed. It was as solid and simple as any warm Sunday afternoon in the field back of the old farmhouse that was the weekly summer setting of the First Original Famous Flea Market.

Mrs. Ellis, from three tables away, brought doughnuts in a paper napkin. "Last Sunday the sugar glaze didn't go well," she said. "This time it's the cinnamon sprinkles. I know you like both. Give one to our friend."

"Thank you, Mrs. Ellis," Ross said. "When will you let me write your story? On the house, of course."

"Oh, some day when we're all less busy. I'll come over; I'll be your shill."

"Do that, Mrs. Ellis. Thanks for the doughnuts." To Street he said: "Mrs. Ellis used to work carnivals. She's a pro."

Street smiled at her. "I've eaten Mrs. Ellis' doughnuts before. Thank you, ma'am."

"You're welcome, Mr. Street. I hope you enjoy them." She went to pack up.

Ross stood and stretched. "I suppose you'll tell me I wrote that dialōg in my head, on Uxu."

"Sure you did," Street told him. "Shall we go?"

"Where?"

"To your house in Ux-Auburn and all that awaits you there."

"How? As easily as we came?"

"Yes, or if you prefer, in your Volkswagen."

"Let's go, then. No, wait. Henry and his father are still here."

"The boy you wrote a story for?"

"Yes. I want to do something for him. Maybe he'd like my typewriter."

"Make it happen, then."

Ross sat and relit his pipe. Then he wrote:

"This typewriter, once for hire, is now at liberty. W. W. Ross needs it no longer. Take it and use it. Dowidzenia, Henry."

Mr. Ross had been in plain sight when Henry decided to go back and say goodbye. But when Henry got there, after walking around a truck, Mr. Ross and the other man were gone. There was only the typewriter on the table with the note in it.

Henry asked: "May I have it, father?"

"He means it to be yours. It would not be courteous to refuse."

Henry's father carried the machine to the back of their station wagon and Henry jumped up on the tailgate. Henry rolled the paper a little and, using two fingers, typed: "Dowidzenia, Mr. Ross. Goodby, sir."

"Is that the end?" somebody asked.

"That's the end," Ross said. It was written.

It was almost the end.

Henry sat in the back with the typewriter as his father drove away. Under Mr. Ross's words he typed, just for fun:

"A man at a flea market . . ."

DAISY, IN THE SUN

by Connie Willis

Here's a wholly new idea in doomsday tales. There have been some scary novels written about what would happen if a comet strikes the Earth or the sun goes nova or a meteor shower intercepts our orbit, but this is not a novel but a short story and what is even stranger—it's not scary. On the other hand, it's not exactly comfortable either.

None of the others were any help. Daisy's brother, when she knelt beside him on the kitchen floor and said, "Do you remember when we lived at Grandma's house, just the three of us, nobody else?" looked at her blankly over the pages of his book, his face closed and uninterested. "What is your book about?" she asked kindly. "Is it about the sun? You always used to read your books out loud to me at Grandma's. All about the sun."

He stood up and went to the windows of the kitchen and looked out at the snow, tracing patterns on the dry window. The book, when Daisy looked at it, was about something else altogether.

"It didn't always snow like this at home, did it?" Daisy would ask her grandmother. "It couldn't have snowed all the time, not even in Canada, could it?"

It was the train this time, not the kitchen, but her grandmother went on measuring for the curtains as if she didn't notice. "How can the trains run if it snows all the time?" Her grandmother didn't answer her. She went on measuring the wide curved train windows with her long yellow tape measure. She wrote the measurements on little slips of paper, and they drifted from her pockets like the snow outside, without sound.

Daisy waited until it was the kitchen again. The red cafe curtains hung streaked and limp across the bottom half of the square windows. "The sun faded the curtains, didn't it?" she asked slyly, but her grandmother would not be tricked. She measured and wrote and dropped the measurements like ash around her.

Daisy looked from her grandmother to the rest of them, shambling up and down the length of her grandmother's kitchen. She would not ask them. Talking to them would be like admitting they belonged here, muddling clumsily around the room, bumping into each other.

Daisy stood up. "It *was* the sun that faded them," she said. "I remember," and went into her room and shut the door.

The room was always her own room, no matter what happened outside. It stayed the same, yellow ruffled muslin on the bed, yellow priscillas at the window. She had refused to let her mother put blinds up in her room. She remembered that quite clearly. She had stayed in her room the whole day with her door barricaded. But she could not remember why her mother had wanted to put them up or what had happened afterward.

Daisy sat down cross-legged in the middle of the bed, hugging the yellow ruffled pillow from her bed against her chest. Her mother constantly reminded her that a young lady sat with her legs together. "You're fifteen, Daisy. You're a young lady whether you like it or not."

Why could she remember things like that and not how they had gotten here and where her mother was and why it snowed all the time yet was never cold? She hugged the pillow tightly against her and tried, tried to remember.

It was like pushing against something, something both yielding and unyielding. It was herself, trying to push her breasts flat against her chest after her mother had told her she was growing up, that she would need to wear a bra. She had tried to push through to the little girl she had been before, but even though she pressed them into herself with the flats of her hands, they were still there. A barrier, impossible to get through.

Daisy clutched at the yielding pillow, her eyes squeezed shut. "Grandma came in," she said out loud, reaching for the one memory she could get to, "Grandma came in and said . . ."

She was looking at one of her brother's books. She had been holding it, looking at it, one of her brother's books about the sun, and as the door opened he reached out and took it away from her. He was angry—about the book? Her grandmother came in, looking hot and excited, and he took the book away from her. Her grandmother said, "They got the material in. I bought enough for all the windows." She had a sack full of folded cloth, red-and-white gingham. "I bought almost the whole bolt," her grandmother said. She was flushed. "Isn't it pretty?" Daisy reached out to touch the thin pretty cloth. And . . . Daisy clutched at the pillow, wrinkling the ruffled edge. She had reached out to touch the thin pretty cloth and then . . .

It was no use. She could not get any farther. She had never been able to get any farther. Sometimes she sat on her bed for days. Sometimes she started at the end and worked back through the memory and it was still the same. She could not remember any more on either side. Only the book and her grandmother coming in and reaching out her hand.

Daisy opened her eyes. She put the pillow back on the bed and uncrossed her legs and took a deep breath. She was going to have to ask the others. There was nothing else to do.

She stood a minute by the door before she opened it, wondering which of the places it would be. It was her mother's living room, the walls a cool blue and the windows covered with venetian blinds. Her brother sat on the gray-blue carpet reading. Her grandmother had taken down one of the blinds. She was measuring the tall window. Outside the snow fell.

The strangers moved up and down on the blue carpet. Sometimes Daisy thought she recognized them, that they were friends of her parents or people she had seen at school, but she could not be sure. They did not speak to each other in their endless, patient wanderings. They did not even seem to see each other. Sometimes, passing down the long aisle of the train or circling her grandmother's kitchen or pacing the blue living room, they bumped into each other. They did not stop and say excuse me. They bumped into each other as if they did not know they did it, and moved on. They collided without sound or feeling, and each time they did they seemed less and less like people Daisy knew and more and more like strangers. She looked at them anxiously, trying to recognize them so she could ask them.

The young man had come in from outside. Daisy was sure of it, though there was no draft of cold air to convince her, no snow for the young man to shrug from his hair and shoulders. He moved with easy direction through the others, and they looked up at him as he passed. He sat down on the blue couch and smiled at Daisy's brother. Her brother looked up from his book and smiled back. He has come in from outside, Daisy thought. He will know.

She sat down near him, on the end of the couch, her arms crossed in front of her. "Has something happened to the sun?" she asked him in a whisper.

He looked up. His face was as young as hers, tanned and smiling. Daisy felt, far down, a little quiver of fear, a faint alien feeling like that which had signaled the coming of her first period. She stood up and backed away from him, only a step, and nearly collided with one of the strangers.

"Well, hello," the boy said. "If it isn't little Daisy!"

Her hands knotted into fists. She did not see how she could not have recognized him before—the easy confidence, the casual smile. He would not help her. He knew, of course he knew, he had always known everything, but he wouldn't tell her. He would laugh at her. She must not let him laugh at her.

"Hi, Ron," she was going to say, but the last consonant drifted away into uncertainty. She had never been sure what his name was.

He laughed. "What makes you think something's happened to the sun, Daisy-Daisy?" He had his arm over the back of the couch. "Sit down and tell me all about it." If she sat down next to him he could easily put his arm around her.

"Has something happened to the sun?" she repeated, more loudly, from where she stood. "It never shines anymore."

"Are you sure?" he said, and laughed again. He was looking at her breasts. She crossed her arms in front of her.

"Has it?" she said stubbornly, like a child.

"What do you think?"

"I think maybe everybody was wrong about the sun." She stopped, surprised at what she had said, at what she was remembering now. Then she went on, forgetting to keep her arms in front of her, listening to what she said next. "They all thought it was going to blow up. They said it would swallow the whole earth up. But maybe it didn't. Maybe it just burned out, like a match or something, and it doesn't shine anymore and that's why it snows all the time and—"

"Cold," Ron said.

"What?"

"Cold," he said. "Wouldn't it be cold if that had happened?"

"What?" she said stupidly.

"Daisy," he said, and smiled at her. She reeled a little. The tugging of fear was farther down and more definite.

"Oh," she said, and ran, veering, around the others milling up and down, up and down, into her own room. She slammed the door behind her and lay down on the bed, holding her stomach and remembering.

Her father had called them all together in the living room. Her mother perched on the edge of the blue couch, already looking frightened. Her brother had brought a book in with him, but he stared blindly at the page.

It was cold in the living room. Daisy moved into the one patch of sunlight, and waited. She had already been frightened for a year. And in a minute, she thought, I'm going to hear something that will make me more afraid.

She felt a sudden stunning hatred of her parents, able to pull her in out of the sun and into darkness, able to make her frightened just by talking to her. She had been sitting on the porch today. That other day she had been lying in the sun in her old yellow bathing suit when her mother called her in.

"You're a big girl now," her mother had said once they were in her room. She was looking at the outgrown yellow suit that was tight across the chest and pulled up on the legs. "There are things you need to know."

Daisy's heart had begun to pound. "I wanted to tell you so you wouldn't hear a lot of rumors." She had had a booklet with her, pink and white and terrifying. "I want you to read this, Daisy. You're changing, even though you may not notice it. Your breasts are developing and soon you'll be starting your period. That means . . ."

Daisy knew what it meant. The girls at school had told her. Darkness and blood. Boys wanting to touch her breasts, wanting to penetrate her darkness. And then more blood.

"No," Daisy said. "No. I don't want to."

"I know it seems frightening to you now, but someday soon you'll meet a nice boy and then you'll understand—"

No. I won't. Never. I know what boys do to you.

"Five years from now you won't feel this way, Daisy. You'll see—"

Not in five years. Not in a hundred. No.

"I won't have breasts," Daisy shouted, and threw the pillow off her bed at her mother. "I won't have a period. I won't let it happen. No!"

Her mother had looked at her pityingly. "Why, Daisy, it's already started." She had put her arms around her. "There's nothing to be afraid of, honey."

Daisy had been afraid ever since. And now she would be more afraid, as soon as her father spoke.

"I wanted to tell you all together," her father said, "so you would not hear some other way. I wanted you to know what is really happening and not just rumors." He paused and took a ragged breath. They even started their speeches alike.

"I think you should hear it from me," her father said. "The sun is going to go nova."

Her mother gasped, a long, easy intake of breath like a sigh, the last easy breath her mother would take. Her brother closed his book. "Is that all?" Daisy thought, surprised.

"The sun has used up all the hydrogen in its core. It's starting to burn itself up, and when it does, it will expand and . . ." he stumbled over the word.

"It's going to swallow us up," her brother said. "I read it in a book. The sun will just explode, all the way out to Mars. It'll swallow up Mercury and Venus and Earth and Mars and we'll all be dead."

Her father nodded. "Yes," he said, as if he was relieved that the worst was out.

"No," her mother said. And Daisy thought, "This is nothing. Nothing." Her mother's talks were worse than this. Blood and darkness.

"There have been changes in the sun," her father said. "There have been more solar storms, too many. And the sun is releasing unusual bursts of neutrinos. Those are signs that it will—"

"How long?" her mother asked.

"A year. Five years at the most. They don't know."

"We have to stop it!" Daisy's mother shrieked, and Daisy looked up from her place in the sun, amazed at her mother's fear.

"There's nothing we can do," her father said. "It's already started."

"I won't let it," her mother said. "Not my children. I won't let it happen. Not to my Daisy. She's always loved the sun."

At her mother's words, Daisy remembered something. An old photograph her mother had written on, scrawling across the bottom of the picture in white ink. The picture was herself as a toddler in a yellow sunsuit, concave little girl's chest and pooching toddler's stomach. Bucket and shovel and toes dug into the hot sand, squinting up into the sunlight. And her mother's writing across the bottom, "Daisy, in the sun."

Her father had taken her mother's hand and was holding it. He had put his arm around her brother's shoulders. Their heads were ducked, prepared for a blow, as if they thought a bomb was going to fall on them.

Daisy thought, "All of us, in a year or maybe five, surely five at the most, all of us children again, warm and happy, in the sun." She could not make herself be afraid.

It was the train again. The strangers moved up and down the long aisle of the dining car, knocking against each other randomly. Her grandmother measured the little window in the door at the end of the car. She did not look out the little window at the ashen snow. Daisy could not see her brother.

Ron was sitting at one of the tables that were covered with the heavy worn white damask of trains. The vase and dull silver on the table were heavy so they would not fall off with the movement of the train. Ron leaned back in his chair and looked out the window at the snow.

Daisy sat down across the table from him. Her heart was beating painfully in her chest. "Hi," she said. She was afraid to add his name for fear the word would trail away as it had before and he would know how frightened she was.

He turned and smiled at her. "Hello, Daisy-Daisy," he said.

She hated him with the same sudden intensity she had felt for her parents, hated him for his ability to make her afraid. "What are you doing here?" she asked.

He turned slightly in the seat and grinned at her.

"You don't belong here," she said belligerently. "I went to Canada to live with my grandmother." Her eyes widened. She had not known that before she said it. "I didn't even know you. You worked in the grocery store when we lived in California." She was suddenly overwhelmed by what she was saying. "You don't belong here," she murmured.

"Maybe it's all a dream, Daisy."

She looked at him, still angry, her chest heaving with the shock of remembering. "What?"

"I said, maybe you're just dreaming all this." He put his elbows on the table and leaned toward her. "You always had the most incredible dreams, Daisy-Daisy."

She shook her head. "Not like this. They weren't like this. I always had good dreams." The memory was coming now, faster this time, a throbbing in her side where the pink and white book said her ovaries were. She was not sure she could make it to her room. She stood up, clutching at the white tablecloth. "They weren't like this." She stumbled through the milling people toward her room.

"Oh, and Daisy," Ron said. She stopped, her hand on the door of her room, the memory almost there. "You're still cold."

"What?" she said blankly.

"Still cold. You're getting warmer, though."

She wanted to ask him what he meant, but the memory was upon her. She shut the door behind her, breathing heavily, and groped for the bed.

All her family had had nightmares. The three of them sat at breakfast with drawn, tired faces, their eyes looking bruised. The lead-backed curtains for the kitchen hadn't come yet, so they had to eat breakfast in the living room where they could close the venetian blinds. Her mother and father sat on the blue couch with their knees against the crowded coffee table. Daisy and her brother sat on the floor.

Her mother said, staring at the closed blinds, "I dreamed I was full of holes, tiny little holes, like dotted swiss."

"Now, Evelyn," her father said.

Her brother said, "I dreamed the house was on fire and the fire trucks came and put it out, but then the fire trucks caught on fire and the firemen and the trees and—"

"That's enough," her father said. "Eat your breakfast." To his wife he said gently, "Neutrinos pass through all of us all the time. They pass right through the earth. They're completely harmless. They don't make holes at all. It's nothing, Evelyn. Don't worry about the neutrinos. They can't hurt you."

"Daisy, you had a dotted swiss dress once, didn't you?" her

mother said, still looking at the blinds. "It was yellow. All those little dots, like holes."

"May I be excused?" her brother asked, holding a book with a photo of the sun on the cover.

Her father nodded and her brother went outside, already reading. "Wear your hat!" Daisy's mother said, her voice rising perilously on the last word. She watched him until he was out of the room, then she turned and looked at Daisy with her bruised eyes. "You had a nightmare too, didn't you, Daisy?"

Daisy shook her head, looking down at her bowl of cereal. She had been looking out between the venetian blinds before breakfast, looking out at the forbidden sun. The stiff plastic blinds had caught open, and now there was a little triangle of sunlight on Daisy's bowl of cereal. She and her mother were both looking at it. Daisy put her hand over the light.

"Did you have a nice dream, then, Daisy, or don't you remember?" She sounded accusing.

"I remember," Daisy said, watching the sunlight on her hand. She had dreamed of a bear. A massive golden bear with shining fur. Daisy was playing ball with the bear. She had in her two hands a little blue-green ball. The bear reached out lazily with his wide golden arm and swatted the blue ball out of Daisy's hands and away. The wide, gentle sweep of his great paw was the most beautiful thing she had ever seen. Daisy smiled to herself at the memory of it.

"Tell me your dream, Daisy," her mother said.

"All right," Daisy said angrily. "It was about a big yellow bear and a little blue ball that he swatted." She swung her arm toward her mother.

Her mother winced.

"Swatted us all to kingdom come, Mother!" she shouted and flung herself out of the dark living room into the bright morning sun.

"Wear your hat," her mother called after her, and this time the last word rose almost to a scream.

Daisy stood against the door for a long time, watching him. He was talking to her grandmother. She had put down her yellow tape measure with the black coal numbers and was nodding and smiling at what he said. After a very long time he reached out his hand and covered hers, patting it kindly.

Her grandmother stood up slowly and went to the window,

where the faded red curtains did not shut out the snow, but she did not look at the curtains. She stood and looked out at the snow, smiling faintly and without anxiety.

Daisy edged her way through the crowd in the kitchen, frowning, and sat down across from Ron. His hands still rested flat on the red linoleum-topped table. Daisy put her hands on the table, too, almost touching his. She turned them palm up, in a gesture of helplessness.

"It isn't a dream, is it?" she asked him.

His fingers were almost touching hers. "What makes you think I'd know? I don't belong here, remember? I work in a grocery store, remember?"

"You know everything," she said simply.

"Not everything."

The cramp hit her. Her hands, still palm up, shook a little and then groped for the metal edge of the red table as she tried to straighten up.

"Warmer all the time, Daisy-Daisy," he said.

She did not make it to her room. She leaned helplessly against the door and watched her grandmother, measuring and writing and dropping the little slips of paper around her. And remembered.

Her mother did not even know him. She had seen him at the grocery store. Her mother, who never went out, who wore sunglasses and long-sleeved shirts and a sunhat, even inside the darkened blue living room—her mother had met him at the grocery store and brought him home. She had taken off her hat and her ridiculous gardening gloves and gone to the grocery store to find him. It must have taken incredible courage.

"He said he'd seen you at school and wanted to ask you out himself, but he was afraid I'd say you were too young, isn't that right, Ron?" Her mother spoke in a rapid, nervous voice. Daisy was not sure whether she had said Ron or Rob or Rod. "So I said, why don't you just come on home with me right now and meet her? There's no time like the present, I say. Isn't that right, Ron?"

He was not embarrassed by her at all. "Would you like to go get a coke, Daisy? I've got my car here."

"Of course she wants to go. Don't you, Daisy?"

No. She wished the sun would reach out lazily, the great golden bear, and swat them all way. Right now.

"Daisy," her mother said, hastily brushing at her hair with

her fingers. "There's so little time left. I wanted you to have—" *Darkness and blood. You wanted me to be as frightened as you are. Well, I'm not, Mother. It's too late. We're almost there now.*

But when she went outside with him, she saw his convertible parked at the curb, and she felt the first faint flutter of fear. It had the top down. She looked up at his tanned, easily smiling face, and thought, "He isn't afraid."

"Where do you want to go, Daisy?" he asked. He had his bare arm across the back of the seat. He could easily move it from there to around her shoulders. Daisy sat against the door, her arms wrapped around her chest.

"I'd like to go for a ride. With the top down. I love the sun," she said to frighten him, to see the same expression she could see on her mother's face when Daisy told her lies about the dreams.

"Me, too," he said. "It sounds like you don't believe all that garbage they feed us about the sun, either. It's a lot of scare talk, that's all. You don't see me getting skin cancer, do you?" He moved his golden-tanned arm lazily around her shoulder to show her. "A lot of people getting hysterical for nothing. My physics teacher says the sun could emit neutrinos at the present rate for five thousand years before the sun would collapse. All this stuff about the aurora borealis. Geez, you'd think these people had never seen a solar flare before. There's nothing to be afraid of, Daisy-Daisy."

He moved his arm dangerously close to her breast.

"Do you have nightmares?" she asked him, desperate to frighten him.

"No. All my dreams are about you." His fingers traced a pattern, casually, easily on her blouse. "What do you dream about?"

She thought she would frighten him like she frightened her mother. Her dreams always seemed so beautiful, but when she began to tell them to her mother, her mother's eyes became wide and dark with fear. And then Daisy would change the dream, make it sound worse than it was, ruin its beauty to make it frighten her mother.

"I dreamed I was rolling a golden hoop. It was hot. It burned my hand whenever I touched it. I was wearing earrings, like golden hoops in my ears that spun like the hoop when I ran. And a golden bracelet." She watched his face as she told him, to see the fear. He traced the pattern aimlessly with his finger, closer and closer to the nipple of her breast.

"I rolled the hoop down a hill and it started rolling faster and faster. I couldn't keep up with it. It rolled on by itself, like a wheel, a golden wheel, rolling over everything."

She had forgotten her purpose. She had told the dream as she remembered it, with the little secret smile at the memory. His hand had closed over her breast and rested there, warm as the sun on her face.

He looked as if he didn't know it was there. "Boy, my psych teacher would have a ball with that one! Who would think a kid like you could have a sexy dream like that? Wow! Talk about Freudian! My psych teacher says—"

"You think you know everything, don't you?" Daisy said.

His fingers traced the nipple through her thin blouse, tracing a burning circle, a tiny burning hoop.

"Not quite," he said, and bent close to her face. Darkness and blood. "I don't know quite how to take you."

She wrenched free of his face, free of his arm. "You won't take me at all. Not ever. You'll be dead. We'll all be dead in the sun," she said, and flung herself out of the convertible and back into the darkened house.

Daisy lay doubled up on the bed for a long time after the memory was gone. She would not talk to him anymore. She could not remember anything without him, but she did not care. It was all a dream anyway. What did it matter? She hugged her arms to her.

It was not a dream. It was worse than a dream. She sat very straight on the edge of the bed, her head up and her arms at her side, her feet together on the floor, the way a young lady was supposed to sit. When she stood up, there was no hesitation in her manner. She walked straight to the door and opened it. She did not stop to see what room it was. She did not even glance at the strangers milling up and down. She went straight to Ron and put her hand on his shoulder.

"This is hell, isn't it?"

He turned, and there was something like hope on his face. "Why, Daisy!" he said, and took her hands and pulled her down to sit beside him. It was the train. Their folded hands rested on the white damask tablecloth. She looked at the hands. There was no use trying to pull away.

Her voice did not shake. "I was very unkind to my mother. I used to tell her my dreams just to make her frightened. I used to go out without a hat, just because it scared her so much. She—couldn't help it. She was so afraid the sun would explode." She stopped and looked at her hands. "I think it did explode and everybody died, like my father said. I think . . . I should have lied to her about the dreams. I should have told her I dreamed about boys, about growing up, about things that didn't frighten her. I could have made up nightmares like my brother did."

"Daisy," he said. "I'm afraid confessions aren't quite in my line. I don't—"

"She killed herself," Daisy said. "She sent us to my grandmother's in Canada and then she killed herself. And so I think that if we are all dead, then I went to hell. That's what hell is, isn't it? Coming face to face with what you're most afraid of."

"Or what you love. Oh, Daisy," he said, holding her fingers tightly. "Whatever made you think that this was hell?"

In her surprise, she looked straight into his eyes. "Because there isn't any sun," she said.

His eyes burned her, burned her. She felt blindly for the white-covered table, but the room had changed. She could not find it. He pulled her down beside him on the blue couch. With him still clinging to her hands, still holding onto her, she remembered.

They were being sent away, to protect them from the sun. Daisy was just as glad to go. Her mother was angry with her all the time. She forced Daisy to tell her her dreams, every morning at breakfast in the dark living room. Her mother had put blackout curtains up over the blinds so that no light got in at all, and in the blue twilight not even the little summer slants of light from the blinds fell on her mother's frightened face.

There was nobody on the beaches. Her mother would not let her go out, even to the grocery store, without a hat and sunglasses. She would not let them fly to Canada. She was afraid of magnetic storms. They sometimes interrupted the radio signals from the towers. Her mother was afraid the plane would crash.

She sent them on the train, kissing them goodbye at the train station, for the moment oblivious to the long dusty streaks of light from the vaulted train-station windows. Her brother went ahead of them out to the platform, and her mother pulled Daisy suddenly into a dark shadowed corner. "What I told you before, about your period, that won't happen now. The radiation—I called the doctor and he said not to worry. It's happening to everyone."

Again Daisy felt the faint pull of fear. Her period had started months ago, dark and bloody as she had imagined. She had not told anyone. "I won't worry," she said.

"Oh, my Daisy," her mother said suddenly. "My Daisy in the sun," and seemed to shrink back into the darkness. But as they pulled out of the station, she came out into the direct sun and waved goodbye to them.

It was wonderful on the train. The few passengers stayed in their cabins with the shades drawn. There were no shades in the dining room, no people to tell Daisy to get out of the sunlight. She sat in the deserted dining car and looked out the wide windows. The train flew through forests, then branch forests of spindly pines and aspens. The sun flickered in on Daisy—sun and then shadows and then sun, running across her face. She and her brother ordered an orgy of milkshakes and desserts and nobody said anything to them.

Her brother read his books about the sun out loud to her. "Do you know what it's like in the middle of the sun?" he asked her. *Yes. You stand with a bucket and a shovel and your bare toes digging into the sand, a child again, not afraid, squinting up into the yellow light.*

"No," she said.

"Atoms can't even hold together in the middle of the sun. It's so crowded they bump into each other all the time, bump bump bump, like that, and their electrons fly off and run around free. Sometimes when there's a collision, it lets off an X-ray that goes *whoosh*, all the way out at the speed of light, like a ball in a pinball machine. *Bing-bang-bing*, all the way to the surface."

"Why do you read those books anyway? To scare yourself?"

"No. To scare Mom." That was a daring piece of honesty, suitable not even for the freedom of Grandma's, suitable only for the train. She smiled at him.

"You're not even scared, are you?"

She felt obliged to answer him with equal honesty. "No," she said, "not at all."

"Why not?"

Because it won't hurt. Because I won't remember afterwards. Because I'll stand in the sun with my bucket and shovel and look up and not be frightened. "I don't know," Daisy said. "I'm just not."

"I am. I dream about burning all the time. I think about how much it hurts when I burn my finger and then I dream about it hurting like that all over forever." He had been lying to their mother about his dreams, too.

"It won't be like that," Daisy said. "We won't even know it's happened. We won't remember a thing."

"When the sun goes nova, it'll start using itself up. The core will start filling up with atomic ash, and that'll make the sun start using up all its own fuel. Do you know it's pitch dark in the middle of the sun? See, the radiations are X-rays, and they're too short to see. They're invisible. Pitch dark and ashes falling around you. Can you imagine that?"

"It doesn't matter." They were passing a meadow and Daisy's face was full in the sun. "We won't be there. We'll be dead. We won't remember anything."

Daisy had not realized how relieved she would be to see her grandmother, narrow face sunburned, arms bare. She was not even wearing a hat. "Daisy, dear, you're growing up," she said. She did not make it sound like a death sentence. "And David, you still have your nose in a book, I see."

It was nearly dark when they got to her little house. "What's that?" David asked, standing on the porch.

Her grandmother's voice did not rise dangerously at all. "The aurora borealis. I tell you, we've had some shows up here lately. It's like the Fourth of July."

Daisy had not realized how hungry she had been to hear someone who was not afraid. She looked up. Great red curtains of light billowed almost to the zenith, fluttering in some solar wind. "It's beautiful," Daisy whispered, but her grandmother was holding the door open for her to go in, and so happy was she to see the clear light in her grandmother's eyes, she followed her into the little kitchen with its red linoleum table and the red curtains hanging at the windows.

"It is so nice to have company," her grandmother said, climbing onto a chair. "Daisy, hold this end, will you?" She dangled the long end of a yellow plastic ribbon down to Daisy. Daisy took it, looking anxiously at her grandmother. "What are you doing?" she asked.

"Measuring for new curtains, dear," she said, reaching into her pocket for a slip of paper and a pencil. "What's the length, Daisy?"

"Why do you need new curtains?" Daisy asked. "These look fine to me."

"They don't keep the sun out," her grandmother said. Her

eyes had gone coal-black with fear. Her voice was rising with every word. "We have to have new curtains, Daisy, and there's no cloth. Not in the whole town, Daisy. Can you imagine that? We had to send to Ottawa. They bought up all the cloth in town. Can you imagine that, Daisy?"

"Yes," Daisy said, and wished she could be afraid.

Ron still held her hands tightly. She looked steadily at him.

"Warmer, Daisy," he said. "Almost here."

"Yes," she said.

He untwined her fingers and rose from the couch. He walked through the crowd in the blue living room and went out the door into the snow. She did not try to go to her room. She watched them all, the strangers in their endless, random movement, her brother walking while he read, her grandmother standing on a chair, and the memory came quite easily and without pain.

"You wanta see something?" her brother asked.

Daisy was looking out the window. All day long the lights had been flickering, even though it was calm and silent outside. Their grandmother had gone to town to see if the fabric for the curtains had come in. Daisy did not answer him.

He shoved the book in front of her face. "That's a prominence," he said. The pictures were in black and white, like old-fashioned snapshots, only under them instead of her mother's scrawled white ink it said, "High Altitude Observatory, Boulder, Colorado."

"That's an eruption of hot gas hundreds of thousands of feet high."

"No," Daisy said, taking the book into her own lap. "That's my golden hoop. I saw it in my dream."

She turned the page.

David leaned over her shoulder and pointed. "That was the big eruption in 1946 when it first started to go wrong only they didn't know it yet. It weighed a billion tons. The gas went out a million miles."

Daisy held the book like a snapshot of a loved one.

"It just went, *bash*, and knocked all this gas out into space. There were all kinds of—"

"It's my golden bear," she said. The great paw of flame reached lazily out from the sun's black surface in the picture, the wild silky paw of flaming gas.

"This is the stuff you've been dreaming?" her brother

asked. "This is the stuff you've been telling me about?" His voice went higher and higher. "I thought you said the dreams were nice."

"They were," Daisy said.

He pulled the book away from her and flipped angrily through the pages to a colored diagram on a black ground. It showed a glowing red ball with concentric circles drawn inside it. "There," he said, shoving it at Daisy. "That's what's going to happen to us." He jabbed angrily at one of the circles inside the red ball. "That's us. That's us! Inside the sun! Dream about that, why don't you?"

He slammed the book shut.

"But we'll all be dead, so it won't matter," Daisy said. "It won't hurt. We won't remember anything."

"That's what you think! You think you know everything. Well, you don't know what anything is. I read a book about it and you know what it said? They don't know what memory is. They think maybe it isn't even in the brain cells. That it's in the atoms somewhere and even if we're blown apart that memory stays. What if we do get burned by the sun and we still remember? What if we go on burning and burning and remembering and remembering forever?"

Daisy said quietly. "He wouldn't do that. He wouldn't hurt us." There had been no fear as she stood digging her toes into the sand and looking up at him, only wonder. "He—"

"You're crazy!" her brother shouted. "You know that? You're crazy. You talk about him like he's your boyfriend or something! It's the sun, the wonderful sun who's going to kill us all!" He yanked the book away from her. He was crying.

"I'm sorry," Daisy was about to say, but their grandmother came in just then, hatless, with her hair blowing around her thin sunburned face.

"They got the material in," she said jubilantly. "I bought enough for all the windows." She spilled out two sacks of red gingham. It billowed out across the table like the northern lights, red over red. "I thought it would never get here."

Daisy reached out to touch it.

She waited for him, sitting at the white-damask table of the dining car. He hesitated at the door, standing framed by the snow of ash behind him, and then came gaily in, singing.

"Daisy, Daisy, give me your theory do," he sang. He carried in his arms a bolt of red cloth. It billowed out from the bolt as he handed it to her grandmother—she standing on the chair, transfixed by joy, the pieces of paper, the yellow tape measure fallen from her forever.

Daisy came and stood in front of him.

"Daisy, Daisy," he said gaily. "Tell me—"

She put her hand on his chest. "No theory," she said. "I know."

"Everything, Daisy?" He smiled the easy, lopsided smile, and she thought sadly that even knowing, she would not be able to see him as he was, but only as the boy who had worked at the grocery store, the boy who had known everything.

"No, but I think I know." She held her hand firmly against his chest, over the flaming hoop of his breast. "I don't think we are people anymore. I don't know what we are—atoms stripped of our electrons maybe, colliding endlessly against each other in the center of the sun while it burns itself to ash in the endless snowstorm at its heart."

He gave her no clue. His smile was still confident, easy. "What about me, Daisy?" he asked.

"I think you are my golden bear, my flaming hoop, I think you are Ra, with no end to your name at all, Ra who knows everything."

"And who are you?"

"I am Daisy, who loved the sun."

He did not smile, did not change his mocking expression. But his tanned hand closed over hers, still pushing against his chest.

"What will I be now, an X-ray zigzagging all the way to the surface till I turn into light? Where will you take me after you have taken me? To Saturn, where the sun shines on the cold rings till they melt into happiness? Is that where you shine now, on Saturn? Will you take me there? Or will we stand forever like this, me with my bucket and shovel, squinting up at you?"

Slowly, he gave her hand back to her. "Where do you want to go, Daisy?"

Her grandmother still stood on the chair, holding the cloth as if it were a benediction. Daisy reached out and touched the cloth, as she had in the moment when the sun went nova. She smiled up at her grandmother. "It's beautiful," she said. "I'm so glad it's come."

She bent suddenly to the window and pulled the faded curtains aside, as if she thought because she knew she might be granted some sort of vision, might see for some small moment the little girl that was herself—with her little girl's chest and toddler's stomach—might see herself as she really was: Daisy, in the sun. But all she could see was the endless snow.

Her brother was reading on the blue couch in her mother's living room. She stood over him, watching him read. "I'm afraid now," Daisy said, but it wasn't her brother's face that looked back at her.

"All right, then," Daisy thought. "None of them are any help. It doesn't matter. I have come face to face with what I fear and what I love and they are the same thing."

"All right, then," Daisy said, and turned back to Ron. "I'd like to go for a ride. With the top down." She stopped and squinted up at him. "I love the sun," she said.

When he put his arm around her shoulder, she did not move away. His hand closed on her breast and he bent down to kiss her.

THE LOCUSTS

by Larry Niven and Steve Barnes

Once again what is the proper adjustment of humanity to its planet? Maybe our troubles are caused by having too large a brain for the environment in which we dwell. Or maybe that large brain is for the purpose of emigrating elsewhere so that the readjustment of humanity can take place under uncrowded conditions just like those at the dawn of time. Utopia, no. Not to our way of thinking. But peace and a full stomach—possibly yes. Nature's way is not necessarily all art and beauty.

There are no men on Tau Ceti IV.

Near the equator on the ridged ribbon of continent which reaches north and south to cover both poles, the evidence of Man still shows. There is the landing craft, a great thick saucer with a rounded edge, gaping doors and vast empty space inside. Ragged clumps of grass and scrub vegetation surround its base, now. There is the small town where they lived, grew old, and died: tall stone houses, a main street of rock fused with atomic fire, a good deal of machinery whose metal is still bright. There is the land itself, overgrown but still showing the traces of a square arrangement that once marked it as farmland.

And there is the forest, reaching north and south along the sprawling ribbon of continent, spreading even to the innumer-

able islands which form two-thirds of Ridgeback's land mass. Where forest cannot grow, because of insufficient water or because the carefully bred bacteria have not yet built a sufficient depth of topsoil, there is grass, an exceptionally hardy hybrid of Buffalo and Cord with an abnormal number of branding roots, developing a dense and fertile sod.

There are flocks of moas, resurrected from a lost New Zealand valley. The great flightless birds roam freely, sharing their grazing land with expanding herds of wild cattle and buffalo.

There are things in the forest. They prefer it there, but will occasionally shamble out into the grasslands and sometimes even into the town. They themselves do not understand why they go: there is no food, and they do not need building materials or other things which may be there for the scavenging. They always leave the town before nightfall arrives.

When men came the land was as barren as a tabletop.

Doc and Elise were among the last to leave the ship. He took his wife's hand and walked down the ramp, some little-boy part of him eager to feel alien loam between his toes. He kept his shoes on. They'd have to make the loam first.

The other colonists were exceptionally silent, as if each were afraid to speak. Not surprising, Doc thought. The first words spoken on Ridgeback would become history.

The robot probes had found five habitable worlds besides Ridgeback in Earth's neighborhood. Two held life in more or less primitive stages, but Ridgeback was perfect. There was one-celled life in Ridgeback's seas, enough to give the planet an oxygenating atmosphere; and no life at all on land. They would start with a clean slate.

So the biologists had chosen what they believed was a representative and balanced ecology. A world's life was stored in the cargo hold now, in frozen fertilized eggs and stored seeds and bacterial cultures, ready to go to work.

Doc looked out over his new home, the faint seabreeze stinging his eyes. He had known Ridgeback would be barren, but he had not expected the *feel* of a barren world to move him.

The sky was bright blue, clouds shrouding Tau Ceti, a sun wider and softer than the sun of Earth. The ocean was a deeper blue, flat and calm. There was no dirt. There was dust and sand and rock, but nothing a farming man would call dirt. There were no birds, no insects. The only sound was that of sand and small dust-devils dancing in the wind, a low moan almost below the threshold of human hearing.

Doc remembered his college geology class' fieldtrip to the Moon. Ridgeback wasn't dead as Luna was dead. It was more like his uncle's face, after the embalmers got through with him. It looked alive, but it wasn't.

Jase, the eldest of them and the colony leader, raised his hand and waited. When all eyes were on him he crinkled his eyes happily, saving his biggest smile for his sister Cynnie, who was training a holotape camera on him. "We're here, people," his voice boomed in the dead world's silence. "It's good, and it's ours. Let's make the most of it."

There was a ragged cheer and the colonists surged toward the cargo door of the landing craft. The lander was a flattish dome now, its heat shield burned almost through, its Dumbo-style atomic motor buried in dust. It had served its purpose and would never move again. The great door dropped and became a ramp. Crates and machinery began to emerge on little flatbed robot trucks.

Elise put her arm around her husband's waist and hugged him. She murmured, "It's so empty."

"So far." Doc unrolled a package of birth control pills, and felt her flinch.

"Two years before we can have children."

Did she mean it as a question? "Right," he said. They had talked it through too often, in couples and in groups, in training and aboard ship. "At least until Jill gets the ecology going."

"Uh huh." An impatient noise.

Doc wondered if she believed it. At twenty-four, tall and wiry and with seven years of intensive training behind him, he felt competent to handle most emergencies. But children, and babies in particular, were a problem he could postpone.

He had interned for a year at Detroit Memorial, but most of his schooling related directly to General Colonization. His medical experience was no better than Elise's, his knowledge not far superior to that of a 20th century GP. Like his shipmates, Doc was primarily a trained crewman and colonist. His courses in world settling—"funny chemistry," water purification, basic mine engineering, exotic factor recognition, etc.—were largely guesswork. There were no interstellar colonies, not yet.

And bearing children would be an act of faith, a taking possession of the land. Some had fought the delay bitterly.

The starship would have been smelling of babies shortly after takeoff if they'd had their way.

He offered Elise a pill. "Bacteria and earthworms come first. Men last," he said. "We're too high on the chain. We can't overload the ecology—"

"Uh huh."

"—before we've even got one. And look—"

She took a six-month birth control pill and swallowed it.

So Doc didn't say: suppose it doesn't work out? Suppose we have to go home? He passed out the pills and watched the women take them, crossing names off a list in his head.

The little Robot trucks were all over the place now. Their flat beds were endless belts, and they followed a limited repertoire of voiced orders. They had the lander half unloaded already. When Doc had finished his pill pushing he went to work beside Elise, unloading crates. His thirty patients, including himself, were sickeningly healthy. As an unemployed doctor he'd have to do honest work until someone got ill.

He was wrong, of course. Doc had plenty of employment. His patients were doing manual labor in 1.07 gravities. They'd gained an average of ten pounds the moment the landing craft touched down. It threw their coordination and balance off, causing them to strain muscles and gash themselves.

One of the robot trucks ran over Chris' foot. Chris didn't wince or curse as Doc manipulated the bones, but his teeth ground silently together.

"All done here, Chris." Doc smiled. The meteorologist looked at him bleakly from behind wire-rimmed glasses, eyes blinking without emotion. "Hey, you're a better man than I am. If I had a wound like that, I'd scream my head off—"

Something only vaguely like a smile crossed Chris' lips. "Thanks, Doc," he said, and limped out.

Remarkable control, Doc mused. But then again, that's Chris.

A week after landing, Ridgeback's nineteen-hour day caught up with them. Disrupted body rhythms are no joke; adding poor sleep to the weight adjustment led to chronic fatigue. Doc recognized the signs quickly.

"I'm surprised that it took this long," he said to Elise as she tossed, sleepless.

"Why couldn't we have done our adjusting on ship?" she mumbled, opening a bleary eye.

"There's more to it than just periods of light and darkness. Every planet has its own peculiarities. You just have to get used to them before your sleep cycles adjust."

"Well what am I supposed to do? Jesus, hand me the sleeping pills, wouldja please? I just want to sleep."

"Nope. Don't want anyone hooked on sleeping pills. We've got the 'russian sleep' sets. You'll have one tomorrow." The "russian sleep" headsets were much preferred over chemical sedatives. They produced unconsciousness with a tiny trickle of current through the brain.

"Good," Elise yawned. "Sunset and dawn, they both seem to come too soon."

The colony went up fast. It was all prefabs, makeshift and temporary, the streets cluttered with the tools, machinery and electric cables which nobody had put away because there was no place for them. Gradually places were made. Hydroponic tanks were assembled and stocked, and presently the colonists were back on fresh food.

Much more gradually, the stone houses began to appear.

They blasted their own rock from nearby cliffs with guncotton from the prefab chemical factory. They hauled the fractured stone on the robot trucks, and made concrete to stick it together. There was technology to spare, and endless power from the atomic motor in the landing craft. They took their time with the houses. Prefabs would weather the frequent warm rains for long enough. The stone houses were intended to last much longer. The colonists built thick walls, and left large spaces so that the houses could be expanded when later generations saw fit.

Doc squinted into the mirror, brushing his teeth with his usual precise vertical movements. He jumped when he felt a splash of hot water hit his back. "Cut that out, Elise," he laughed.

She settled back in her bathtub, wrinkling her nose at him. Three years of meagre showers on the ship had left her dying for a real bathtub, where she could waste gallons of water without guilt.

"Spoilsport," she teased. "If you were any kind of fun, you'd come over here and . . ."

"And what?" he asked, interested.

"And rub my back."

"And that's supposed to be fun?"

"I was thinking that we could rub it with you." She grinned, seeing Doc's eyes light up. "And then maybe we could rub you with me . . ."

Later, they toweled each other off, still tingling. "Look!" Doc said, pulling her in front of the mirror. He studied her, marveling. Had Elise become prettier, or was he seeing her with new eyes? He knew she laughed louder and more often than when they had met years ago in school, she the child of a wealthy family and he a scholarship student who dreamt of the stars. He knew that her body was more firm and alive than it had been in her teens. The same sun that had burnt her body nut-brown had lightened her reddish hair to strawberry blond. She grinned at him from the mirror and asked, "Do you propose to take all the credit?"

He nodded happily. He'd always been fit, but his muscles had been stringy, the kind that didn't show. Now they bulged, handsome curves filling out chest and shoulders, legs strong from lifting and moving rock. His skin had darkened under the probing of a warm, friendly sun. He was sleeping well, and so was she.

All of the colonists were darker, more muscular, with thicker calluses on hands and feet. Under open sky or high ceilings they walked straighter than the men and women of Earth's cities. They talked more boldly and seemed to fill more space. In the cities of Earth, the ultimate luxury had been building space. It was beyond the means of all but the wealthiest. Here, there was land for the taking, and twelve foot ceilings could be built. The house Doc was building for Elise—almost finished now—would be as fine as any her father could have built for her. One that would be passed on to their children, and then to their grandchildren . . .

She seemed to echo his thought. "One last step. I want a bulge, right here," and she patted her flat abdomen. "Your department."

"And Jill's. We're up to mammals already, and we're adjusting. I've got half the 'russian sleep' sets back in the infirmary already."

The Orion spacecraft was a big, obtrusive object, mace-shaped, cruising constantly across the sky. What had been a fifth of a mile of deuterium snowball, the fuel supply for the starship's battery of laser-fusion motors, was now a thin, shiny skin, still inflated by the residue of deuterium gas. It was the head of the mace. The life support system, ending in motors and shock absorbers, formed the handle.

Roy had taken the ground-to-orbit craft up and was aboard the Orion now, monitoring the relay as Cynnie beamed her holotape up. It was lonely. Once there had been too little room; now there was too much. The ship still smelled of too many people crowded too close for too long. Roy adjusted the viewscreen and grinned back at Cynnie's toothy smile.

"This is Year Day on Ridgeback," she said in her smooth announcer's voice. "It was a barren world when we came. Now, slowly, life is spreading across the land. The farming teams have spent this last year dredging mulch from the sea bed and boiling it to kill the native life. Now it grows the tame bacteria that will make our soil." The screen showed a sequence of action scenes: tractors plowing furrows in the harsh dirt; colonists glistening with sweat as they pulled boulders from the ground; and Jill supervising the spreading of the starter soil. Grass seed and earthworms were sown into the trenches, and men and machines worked together to fold them into the earth.

Cynnie had mounted a camera on one of the small flyers for an aerial view. "The soil is being spread along a ten-mile strip," she said, "and grains are being planted. Later we'll have fruit trees and shade trees, bamboo and animal feed."

It was good, Roy thought, watching. It was smooth. Getting it all had been rough enough. Before they were finished the colonists had become damn sick of Roy and Cynnie poking their cameras into their every activity. That sign above the auditorium toilet: Smile! Roy Is Watching!

He'd tried to tell them. "Don't you know who it is that builds starships? It's taxpayers, that's who! And they've got to get something for their money. Sure we're putting on a show for them. If we don't, when election time comes around they may ask for a refund."

Oh, they probably believed him. But the sign was still up.

Roy watched Cynnie interview Jase and Brew in the fields; watched Angie and Chris constructing the animal pens. Jill thawed some of the fertilized goat eggs and a tape was shown of the wriggling embryos.

"At first," Cynnie reminisced, "Ridgeback was daunting. There was no sound: no crickets, no birdsongs, but no roar of traffic either. By day, the sky is Earthlike enough, but by night the constellations are brighter. It's impossible to forget how far from home we are—we can't even see Sol, invisible somewhere in the northern hemisphere. It's hard to forget that no help of any kind could come in much less than twenty-five years. It would take five years just to refuel the ship. It takes fourteen years to make the trip, although thanks to relativity it was only three years 'ship time.'

"Yes, we are alone." The image of Cynnie's sober face segued to the town hall, a geodesic dome of metal tubing sprayed with plastic. "But it is heartening that we have found, in each other, the makings of a community. We come together for midday meal, discussions, songfests and group worship services."

Cynnie's face was calm now, comforting. "We have no crime, and no unemployment. We're much too busy for marital squabbles or political fighting." She grinned, and the sparkle of her personality brought pleasure to Roy's analytical mind. "In fact, I have work to do myself. So, until next year, this is Cynnie Mitchell on Ridgeback, signing off."

A year and a half after landing, a number of animals were out of incubation with a loss of less than two percent. The mammals drank synthetic milk now, but soon they would be milling in their pens, eating Ridgeback grass and adding their own rich wastes to the cooking compost heaps.

Friday night was community night at the town hall.

From the inside the ribs of the dome were still visible through the sprayed plastic walls, and some of the decorations were less than stylish, but it was a warm place, a friendly, relaxing place where the common bond between the Ridgebackers was strengthened.

Jill, especially, seemed to love the stage, and took every opportunity to mount it, almost vibrating with her infectious energy.

"Everything's right on schedule," she said happily. "The fruit flies are breeding like mad." (Booo!) "And if I hear that again I'm gonna break out the mosquitos. Gang, there are things we can live without, but we don't know what they are yet. Chances are we'll be raising the sharks sooner or later. We've been lucky so far. Really lucky." She cleared her throat dramatically. "And speaking of luck, we have Chris with some good news for the farmers, and bad news for the sunbathers. Chris?"

There was scattered applause, most vigorously from Chris' tiny wife Angie. He walked to the lecturn and adjusted the microphone before speaking.

"We, uh," he took off his glasses, polishing them on his shirt, then replaced them, smiling nervously. "We've been having good weather, people, but there's a storm front moving over the mountains. I think Greg can postpone the irrigation canals for a week, we're going to get plenty wet."

He coughed, and moved the microphone close to his mouth. "June and I are working to program the atmospheric model into the computer. Until we do, weather changes will keep catching us unaware. We have to break down a fairly complex set of thermo and barometric dynamics into something that can be dealt with systematically—wind speed, humidity, vertical motion, friction, pressure gradients, and a lot of other factors still have to be fed in, but we're making progress. Maybe next year we'll be able to tell you how to dress for the tenth anniversary of Landing Day."

There were derisive snorts and laughter, and Chris was applauded back into his seat.

Jase bounded onto the stage and grabbed the mike. "Any more announcements? No? Alright, then, we all voted on tonight's movie, so no groans, please. Lights?"

The auditorium dimmed. He slipped from the stage and the twin beams of the holo projector flickered onto the screen.

It was a war movie, shot in flatfilm but optically reconstructed to simulate depth. Doc found it boring. He slipped out during a barrage of cannon fire. He headed to the lab and found Jill there already, using one of the small microscopes.

"Hi hon," he called out, flipping on his desk light. "Working late?"

"Well, I'm maybe just a wee bit more bugged than I let on. Just a little."

"About what?"

"I keep thinking that one day we'll find out that we left something out of our tame ecology. It's just a feeling, but it won't go away."

"Like going on vacation," Doc said, deliberately flippant. "You know you forgot something. You'd just rather it was your toothbrush and not your passport."

She smeared a cover glass over a drop of fluid on a slide and set it to dry. "Yes, it feels like that."

"Do you really have mosquitos in storage?"

She twinkled and nodded. "Yep. Hornets too."

"Just how good is it going? You know how impatient everyone is."

"No real problems. There sure as hell might have been, but thanks to my superior planning—" she stuck out her tongue at Doc's grimace. "We'll have food for ourselves and all the children we can raise. I've been getting a little impatient myself, you know? As if there's a part of me that isn't functioning at full efficiency."

Doc laughed. "Then I think you'd better tell Greg."

"I'll do better. I'll announce it tonight and let all the fathers-to-be catch the tidings in one shot."

"Oh boy."

"What?"

"No, it has to be done that way. I know it. I'm just thinking about nine months from now. Oh boy."

So it was announced that evening. As Doc might have expected, someone had already cheated. Somehow Nat, the midwestern earthmother blond, had taken a contraceptive pill and, even with Doc watching, had avoided swallowing it. Doc was fairly sure that her husband Brew knew nothing of it, although she was already more than four months along when she confessed.

Nat had jumped the gun, and there wasn't a woman on Ridgeback who didn't envy her. A year and eleven months after Landing Day, Doc delivered Ridgeback's first baby.

Sleepy, exhausted by her hours of labor, Nat looked at her baby with a pride that was only half maternal. Her face was flushed, yellow hair tangled in mats with perspiration and fatigue. She held her baby, swaddled in blankets, at her side. "I can hear them outside. What do they want?" she asked drowsily, fighting to keep her eyelids open.

Doc breathed deeply. Ridiculous, but the scentless air of Ridgeback seemed a little sweeter. "They're waiting for a glimpse of the little crown princess."

"Well, she's staying here. Tell them she's beautiful," Ridgeback's first mother whispered, and dropped off to sleep.

Doc washed his hands and dried them on a towel. He stood above the slumbering pair, considering. Then he gently pried the baby from her mother's grip and took her in his arms. Half-conscious mother's wish or no, the infant must be shown to the colony before they could rest. Especially Brew. He could see the Swede's great broad hands knotting into nervous fists as he waited outside. And the rest of them in a half-crescent around the door; and the inevitable Cynnie and Roy with their holotape cameras.

"It's a girl," he told them. "Nat's resting comfortably." The baby was red as a tomato and looked as fragile as Venetian glass. She and Doc posed for the camera, then Doc left her with Brew to make a short speech.

Elise and Greg, Jill's husband, had both had paramedic training. Doc set up a rotating eight-hour schedule for the three of them, starting with Elise. The group outside was breaking up as he left, but he managed to catch Jase.

"I'd like to be taken off work duties for a while," he told the colony leader, when the two were alone.

Jase gripped his arm. "Something's wrong with the baby?" There was a volume of concern in the question.

"I doubt it, but she is the first, and I want to watch her and Nat. Most of the women are pregnant now. I want to keep an eye on them, too."

"You're not worried about anything specific?"

"No."

When Elise left her shift at the maternity ward, she found him staring at the stone ceiling. She asked, "Insomnia again? Shall I get a 'russian sleep' set?"

"No."

She studied his face. "The baby?"

She'd seen it too, then. "You just left the baby. She's fine, isn't she?"

"They're both fine. Sleeping. Harry?" She was the only one who called him that. "What is it?"

"No, nothing's bothering me. You know everything *I* know. It's just that . . ."

"Well?"

"It's just that I want to do everything right. This is so important. So I keep checking back on myself, because there's no one I can call in to check my work. Can you understand what I'm getting at?"

She pursed her lips. Then said, "I know that the only baby in the world could get a lot more attention than she needs. There shouldn't be too many people around her, and they should all be smiling. That's important to a baby."

Doc watched as she took off her clothes and got into bed. The slight swell of her pregnancy was just beginning to show. Within six months there would be nine more children on Ridgeback, and one would be theirs.

Predictably, Brew's and Nat's daughter became Eve.

It seemed nobody but Doc had noticed anything odd about Eve. Even laymen know better than to expect a newborn child to be pretty. A baby doesn't begin to look like a baby until it is weeks old. The cherubs of the Renaissance paintings of Foucquet or Conegliano were taken from two-year-olds. Naturally Eve looked odd, and most of the colony, who had never seen newborn children, took it in their stride. . . .

But Doc worried.

The ship's library was a world's library. It was more comprehensive, and held more microfilm and holographically encoded information than any single library on earth. Doc spent weeks running through medical tapes, and got no satisfaction thereby.

Eve wasn't sick. She was a "good baby"; she gave no more trouble than usual, and no less. Nat had no difficulty nursing her, which was good, as there were no adult cows available on Ridgeback.

Doc pulled a microfisch chip out of the viewer and yawned irritably. The last few weeks had cost him his adjustment to Ridgeback time, and gained him . . . well, a kind of general education in pediatrics. There was nothing specific to look for, no *handle* on the problem.

Bluntly put, Eve was an ugly baby.

There was nothing more to say, and nothing to do but wait.

Roy and Cynnie showed their tapes for the year. Cynnie had a good eye for detail. Until he watched the camera view trucking from the landing craft past the line of houses on Main Street, to Brew, to a closeup of Brew's house, Doc had never noticed how Brew's house reflected Brew himself. It was designed like the others: tall and squarish, with a sloped roof and small window. But the stones in Brew's house were twice the size of those in Doc's house. Brew was proud of his strength.

Roy was in orbit on Year Day, but Cynnie stayed to cover the festivities, such as they were. Earth's hypothetical eager audience still hadn't seen Year Day One. Jase spoke for the camera, comparing the celebration with the first Thanksgiving Day in New England. He was right: it was a feast, a display of the variety of foods Ridgeback was now producing, and not much more than that.

His wife June sang a nondenominational hymn, and they all followed along, each in his own key. Nat fed Eve a bit of corncake and fruit juice, and the colonists applauded Eve's gurgling smile.

The folks back on Earth might not have thought it very exciting, but to the Ridgebackers it meant everything. This was food they had grown themselves. All of them had bruises or blisters or calluses from weeding or harvesting. They were more than a community now, they were a world, and the fresh fruit and vegetables, and the hot breads, tasted better than anything they could have imagined.

Six months after the birth of Eve, Doc was sure. There was a problem.

The children of Ridgeback totaled seven. Two of the women had miscarried, fewer than he might have feared, and without complications. Jill was still carrying hers, and Doc was beginning to wonder; but it wasn't serious yet. Jill was big and strong with wide hips and a deep bust. Even now Greg was hard put to keep her from commandeering one of the little flyers and jouncing off to the coastline to check the soil, or inland to supervise the fresh water fish preserve. Give her another week . . .

The night Elise had delivered their child, it had been special. She had had a dry birth, with the water sack rupturing too early, and Doc had had to use a lubrication device. Elise was conscious during the entire delivery, eschewing painkillers for the total experience of her first birth. She delivered safely, for which Doc had given silent thanks. His nerves were scraped to supersensitivity, and he found himself just sitting and holding her hand, whispering affection and encouragement to her, while Greg did much of the work. With Elise's approval he named their son Gerald, shortened to Jerry. Jerry was three weeks old now, healthy and squalling, with a ferocious grip in his tiny hands.

But even a father's pride could not entirely hide the squarish jawline, the eyes, the . . .

All the children had it, all the six recent ones. And Eve hadn't lost it. Doc continued his research in the microlibrary, switching from pediatrics to genetics. He had a microscope and an electron microscope, worth their hundreds of thousands of dollars in transportation costs; he had scrapings of his own flesh and Eve's and Jerry's. What he lacked was a Nobel Prize geneticist to stand behind his shoulder and point out what were significant deviations as opposed to his own poor slide preparation techniques.

He caught Brew looking at him at mealtimes, as though trying to raise the nerve to speak. Soon the big man would break through his inhibitions, Doc could see it coming. Or perhaps Nat would broach the question. Her eldest brother had been retarded, and Doc knew she was sensitive about it. How long could it be before that pain rose to the surface?

And what would he say to them then?

It was not a mutation. One could hardly expect the same mutation to hit all of seven couples in the same way.

It was no disease. The children were phenomenally healthy.

So Doc worked late into the night, sometimes wearing a black scowl as he retraced dead ends. He needed advice, and advice was 11.9 light years away. Was he seeing banshees? Nobody else had noticed anything. Naturally not; the children all looked normal, for they all looked alike. Only Brew seemed disturbed. Hell, it was probably Doc that was worrying Brew, just as it was Doc that worried Elise. He ought to spend more time with Elise and Jerry.

Jill lost her baby. It was stillborn, pitiful in its frailty. Jill turned to Greg as the dirt showered down on the cloth that covered her child, biting her lip savagely, trying to stop the tears. She and her husband held each other for a long moment, then, with the rest of the colonists, they walked back to the dwellings.

The colonists had voted early, and unanimously, to give up coffins on Ridgeback. Humans who died here would give their bodies to the conquest of the planet. Doc wondered if a coffin would have made this ceremony easier, more comforting in its tradition. Probably not, he thought. Dead is dead.

Doc went home with Elise. He'd been spending more time there lately, and less time with the miscroscopes. Jerry was crawling now, and he crawled everywhere; you had to watch him like a hawk. He could pick his parents unerringly out of a crowd of adults, and he would scamper across the floor, cooing, his eyes alight . . . his deepset brown eyes.

It was a week later that Jase came to him. After eight hours of labor June had finally released her burden. For a newborn infant the body was big and strong, though in any normal context he was a fragile, precious thing. As father, Jase was entitled to see him first. He looked down at his son and said, "He's just like the others." His eyes and his voice were hollow, and at that moment Doc could no longer see the jovial colony leader who called square dances at the weekly hoedown.

"Of course he is."

"Look, don't con me, Doc. I was eight when Cynnie was born. She didn't look like any of them. And she never looked like Eve."

"Don't you think that's for me to say?"

"Yes. And damned quick!"

Doc rubbed his jaw, considering. If he was honest with himself he had to admit he ached to talk to somebody. "Let's make it tomorrow. In the ship's library."

Jase's strong hand gripped his arm. "Now."

"Tomorrow, Jase. I've got a lot to say, and there are things in the library you ought to see."

"Here," he said, dialing swiftly. A page appeared on the screen, three-quarters illustration, and one-quarter print to explain it. "Notice the head? And the hands. Eve's fingers are longer than that. Her forehead slopes more. But look at these." He conjured up a series of growth states paired with silhouettes of bone structure.

"So?"

"She's maturing much faster than normal."

"Oh."

"At first I didn't think anything about the head. Any infant's head is distorted during passage from the uterus. It goes back to normal if the birth wasn't difficult. And you can't tell much from the features; all babies look pretty much alike. But the hands and arms bothered me."

"And now?"

"See for yourself. Her face is too big and her skull is too small and too flat. And I don't like the jaw, or the thin lips." Doc rubbed his eyes wearily. "And there's the hair. That much hair isn't unheard of at that age, but taken with everything else . . . you can see why I was worried."

"And all the kids look just like her. Even Jase Junior."

"Even Jerry. And Jill's stillbirth."

In the ship's library there was a silence as of mourning.

Jase said, "We'll have to tell Earth. The colony is a failure."

Doc shook his head. "We'd better see how it develops first."

"We can't have normal children, Doc."

"I'm not ready to give up, Jase. And if it's true, we can't go back to Earth, either."

"What? Why?"

"This thing isn't a mutation. Not in us, it can't be. What it could be is a virus replacing some of the genes. A virus is a lot like a free-floating chromosome anyway. If we've got a disease that keeps us from having normal children—"

"That's stupid. A virus here, waiting for us, where there's nothing for it to live on but plankton? You—"

"No, no, no. It had to come with us. Something like the common cold could have mutated aboard ship. There was enough radiation outside the shielding. Someone sneezes in the airlock before he puts his helmet on. A year later someone else inhales the mutant."

Jase thought it through. "We can't take it back to Earth."

"Right. So what's the hurry? It'd be twenty-four years before they could answer a cry for help. Let's take our time and find out what we've really got."

"Doc, in God's name, what can we tell the others?"

"Nothing yet. When the time comes I'll tell them."

Those few months were a busy time for Ridgeback's doctor. Then they were over. The children were growing, and most of the women were pregnant, including Angie and Jill, who had both had miscarriages. Never again would all the women of Ridgeback be having children in one ear-shattering population explosion.

Now there was little work for Doc. He spoke to Jase, who put him on the labor routines. Most of the work was agricultural, with the heavy jobs handled by machines. Robot trucks, trailing plows, scored rectangular patterns across the land.

The fenced bay was rich in Earth-born plankton, and now there were larger forms to eat the plankton. Occasionally Greg opened the filter to let discolored water spread out into the world, contaminating the ocean.

At night the colonists watched news from Earth, 11.9 years in transit, and up to a year older before Roy boarded the starship to beam it down. They strung the program out over the year in hour segments to make it last longer. There were no wars in progress, to speak of; the Procyon colony project had been abandoned; Macrostructures Inc. was still trying to build an interstellar ramjet. It all seemed very distant.

Jase came whistling into Doc's lab, but backed out swiftly when he saw that he had interrupted a counselling session with Cynnie and Roy. Doc was the closest thing the colony had to a marriage therapist. Jase waited outside until the pair had left, then trotted in.

"Rough day?"

"Yeah. Jase, Roy and Cynnie don't fight, do they?"

"They never did. They're like twins. Married people do get to be like each other, but those two overdo it sometimes."

"I knew it. There's something wrong, but it's not between them." Doc rubbed his eyes on his sleeve. "They were sounding me out, trying to get me talking about the children without admitting they're scared. Anyway . . . what's up?"

Jase brought his hands from behind his back. He held two bamboo poles rigged for fishing. "What say we exercise our manly prerogatives?"

"Ye gods! In our private spawning ground?"

"Why not? It's big enough. There are enough fish. And we can't let the surplus go; they'd starve. It's a big ocean."

By now the cultivated strip of topsoil led tens of miles north and south along the continent. Jill claimed that life would spread faster that way, outward from the edges of the strip. The colony was raising its own chicken eggs and fruit and vegetables. On Landing Day they'd been the first in generations to taste moa meat, whose rich flavor had come *that* close to making the New Zealand bird extinct. Why shouldn't they catch their own fish?

They made a full weekend of it. They hauled a prefab with them on the flyer and set it up on the barren shore. For three days they fished with the springy bamboo poles. The fish were eager and trusting. They ate some of their catch, and stored the rest for later.

On the last day Jase said, "I kept waiting to see you lose some of that uptight look. You finally have, a little, I think."

"Yeah. I'm glad this happened, Jase."

"Okay. What about the children?"

He didn't need to elaborate. Doc said, "They'll never be normal."

"Then what are they?"

"I dunno. How do you tell people who came twelve light years to build a world that their heirs will be . . ." He groped for words. "Whatever. Changed. Animals."

"Christ. What a mess."

"Give me time to tell Elise . . . if she hasn't guessed by now. Maybe she has."

"How long?"

"A week, maybe. Give us time to be off with Jerry. Might make it easier if we're with him."

"Or harder."

"Yeah, there's that." He cast his line out again. "Anyway, she'll keep the secret, and she'd never forgive me if I didn't tell her first. And you'd better tell June the night before I make the big announcement." The words seemed to catch in his throat and he hung his head, miserable.

Tentatively Jase said, "It's absolutely nobody's fault."

"Oh, sure. I was just thinking about the last really big announcement I helped make. Years ago. Seems funny now, doesn't it? 'It's safe, people. You can start dreaming now. Go ahead and have those babies, folks. It's all right . . .' " His voice trailed off and he looked to Jase in guilty confusion. "What could I do, Jase? It's like thalidomide. In the beginning, it all looked so wonderful."

Jase was silent, listening to the sound of water lapping against the boat. "I just hate to tell Earth, that's all," he finally said in a low voice. "It'll be like giving up. Even if we solve this thing, they'd never risk sending another ship."

"But we've got to warn them."

"Doc, what's *happening* to us?"

"I don't know."

"How hard have you—no, never mind." Jase pulled his line in, baited it and sent it whipping out again. Long silences are in order when men talk and fish.

"Jase, I'd give anything I have to know the answer. Some of the genes look different in the electron microscope. Maybe. Hell, it's all really too fuzzy to tell, and I don't really know what it means anyway. None of my training anticipated anything like *this*. *You* try to think of something."

"Alien invasion."

Pause. "Oh, really?"

Jase's line jumped. He wrestled in a deep sea bass and freed the hook. He said, "It's the safest, most painless kind of invasion. They find a world they want, but there's an intelligent species in control. So they design a virus that will keep us from bearing intelligent children. After we're gone they move in at their leisure. If they like they can use a countervirus, so the children can bear human beings again for slaves."

The bamboo pole seemed dead in Doc's hands. He said, "That's uglier than anything I've thought of."

"Well?"

"Could be. Insufficient data. If it's true, it's all the more reason to warn Earth. But Ridgeback is doomed."

Jerry had his mother's hair, sun-bleached auburn. He had too much of it. On his narrow forehead it merged with his brows . . . his shelf of brow, and the brown eyes watching from way back. He hardly needed the shorts he was wearing; the hair would have been almost enough. He was nearly three.

He seemed to sense something wrong between his parents. He would spend some minutes scampering through the grove of sapling fruit trees, agile as a child twice his age; then suddenly return to take their hands and try to tug them both into action.

Doc thought of the frozen fertilized eggs of dogs in storage. Jerry with a dog . . . the thought was repulsive. Why? Shouldn't a child have a dog?

"Well, of course I guessed *something*," Elise said bitterly. "You were always in the library. When you were home, the way that you looked at Jerry . . . and me, come to think of it. I see now why you haven't taken me to bed much lately." She'd been avoiding his eyes, but now she looked full at him. "I *do* see. But, Harry, couldn't you have asked me for help? I have some medical knowledge, and, and I'm your wife, and Jerry's mother, damn it Harry!"

"Would you believe I didn't want you worrying?"

"Oh, really? How did it work?"

Her sarcasm cut deep. Bleeding, he said, "Nothing worked."

Jerry came out of the trees at a tottering run. Doc stood up, caught him, swung him around, chased him through the trees . . . came back puffing, smiling, holding his hand. He almost lost the smile, but Elise was smiling back, with some effort. She hugged Jerry, then pulled fried chicken from the picnic basket and offered it around.

She said, "That alien invasion idea is stupid."

"Granted. It'd be easy to think someone has 'done' it to us."

"Haven't you found anything? Isn't there anything I can help with?"

"I've found a lot. All the kids have a lower body temperature, two point seven degrees. They're healthy as horses, but hell, who would they catch measles from? Their brain capacity is too small, and not much of it is frontal lobe. They're hard to toilet train and they should have started babbling, at least, long ago. What counts is the brain, of course."

Elise took one of Jerry's small hands. Jerry crawled into her lap and she rocked him. "His hands are okay. Human. His eyes . . . are brown, like yours. His cheekbones are like yours, too. High and a little rounded."

Doc tried to smile. "His eyes look a little strange. They're not really slanted enough to suspect mongolism, but I'll bet there's a gene change. But where do I go from there? I can see differences, and they're even consistent, but there's no precedent for the analysis equipment to extrapolate from." Doc looked disgusted. Elise touched his cheek, understanding.

"Can you teach me to use an electron microscope?"

Doc sat at the computer console, watching over Jill's shoulder as she brought out the Orion vehicle's image of Ridgeback. The interstellar spacecraft doubled as a weather eye, and the picture, once drab with browns and grays, now showed strips of green beneath the fragmented cloud cover. If Ridgeback was dead, it certainly didn't show on the screen.

"Well, we've done a fair old job." Jill grinned and took off her headset. Her puffy natural had collected dust and seeds and vegetable fluff until she gave up and shaved it off. The tightly curled mat just covered her scalp now, framing her chocolate cameo features. "The cultivated strip has spread like weeds. All along the continent now I get CO_2-oxygen exchange. It jumped the ridges last year, and now I get readings on the western side."

"Are you happy?"

"No," she said slowly. "I've done my job. Is it too much to want a child too? I wouldn't care about the . . . problem. I just want . . ."

"It's nobody's fault," Doc said helplessly.

"I know, I know. But two miscarriages. Couldn't they have known back on Earth? Wasn't there any way to be sure? Why did I have come all this way . . ." She caught herself and smiled thinly. "I guess I should count my blessings. I'm better off than poor Angie."

"Poor Angie," Doc echoed sadly. How could they have known about Chris? The night Doc announced his conclusions about the children, there had been tears and harsh words, but no violence. But then there was Chris.

Chris, who had wanted a child more than any of them could have known. Who had suffered silently through Angie's first miscarriage, who hoped and prayed for the safe delivery of their second effort.

It had been an easy birth.

And the morning after Doc's speech, the three of them, Chris, Angie and the baby, were found in the quiet of their stone house, the life still ebbing from Chris' eyes and the gaps in his wrists.

"I'm sorry," he said over and over, shaking his head as if he were cold, his watery brown eyes dulling. "I just couldn't take it. I just . . . I just . . ." and he died. The three of them were buried in the cemetery outside of town, without coffins.

The town was different after the deaths, a stifling quiet hanging in the streets. Few colonists ate at the communal meals, choosing to take their suppers at home.

In an effort to bring everyone together, Jase encouraged them to come to town hall for Movie Night.

The film was "The Sound Of Music." The screen erupted with sound and color, dazzling green Alps and snow-crested mountains, happy song and the smiling faces of normal, healthy children.

Half the colonists walked out.

Most of the women took contraceptives now, except those who chose not to tamper with their estrogen balance. For these, Doc performed painless menstrual extractions bimonthly.

Nat and Elise insisted on having more children. Maybe the problem only affected the firstborn, they argued. Doc fought the idea at first. He found himself combatting Brew's sullen withdrawal, Nat's frantic insistence, and a core of hot anger in his own wife.

Earth could find a cure. It was possible. Then their grandchildren would be normal again, the heirs to a world.

He gave in.

But the children were the same. In the end, Nat alone had not given up. She had borne five children, and was carrying her sixth.

The message of failure was halfway to Earth, but any reply was still nineteen years away. Doc had adopted the habit of talking things over with Jase, hoping that he would catch some glimpse of a solution.

"I still think it's a disease," he told Jase, who had heard that before, but didn't mention it. The bay was quiet and their lines were still. They talked only during fishing trips. They didn't want the rest of the colony brooding any more than they already were. "A mutant virus. But I've been wondering, could the changes have screwed us up? A shorter day, a longer year, a little heavier gravity. Different air mixture. No common cold, no mosquito bites; even that could be the key."

On a night like this, in air this clear, you could even see starglades casting streaks across the water. A fish jumped far across the bay, and phosphorescence lit that patch of water for a moment. The Orion vehicle, mace-shaped, rose out of the west, past the blaze of the Pleiades. Roy would be rendezvousing with it now, preparing for tomorrow's Year Day celebration.

Jase seemed to need these trips even more than Doc. After the murders the life seemed to have gone out of him, only flashes of his personality coming through at tranquil times like these. He asked, "Are you going to have Jill breed mosquitos?"

". . . Yes."

"I think you're reaching. Weren't you looking at the genes in the cytoplasm?"

"Yeah. Elise's idea, and it was a good one. I'd forgotten there were genes outside the cell nucleus. They control the big things, you know: not the shape of your fingers, but how many you get, and where. But they're hard to find, Jase. And maybe we found some differences between our genes and the children's, but even the computer doesn't know what the difference *means*."

"Mosquitos." Jase shook his head. "We know there's a fish down that way. Shall we go after him?"

"We've got enough. Have to be home by morning. Year Day."

"What exactly are we celebrating *this* time?"

"Hell, you're the mayor. You think of something." Doc sulked, watching the water ripple around his float. "Jase, we can't give up—"

Jase's face was slack with horror, eyes cast up to the sky. Doc followed his gaze, to where a flaring light blossomed behind the Orion spacecraft.

"Oh my God," Jase rasped, "Roy's up there."

Throwing his bamboo pole in the water, Jase started the engine and raced for shore.

Doc studied the readouts carefully. "Mother of God," he whispered. "How many engines did he fire?"

"Six." Jill's eyes were glued to the screen, her voice flat. "If he was abroad, he . . . well, there isn't much chance he survived the acceleration. Most of the equipment up there must be junk now."

"But what if he *did* survive? Is there a chance?"

"I don't know. Roy was getting set to beam the messages down, but said that he had an alarm to handle first. He went away for a while, and . . ." She seemed to search for words. She whispered, "Boom."

"If he was outside the ship, in one of the little rocket sleds, he could get to the shuttle vehicle."

Jase walked heavily into the lab.

"What about Cynnie? What did she say?" Doc asked quickly.

Jase's face was blank of emotion. "She talked to him before the . . . accident."

"And?"

"It's all she would say. I'm afraid she took it pretty bad. This was sort of the final straw." His eyes were hollow as he reminisced. "She was always a brave kid, you know? Anything I could do, she'd be right behind me, measuring up to big brother. There's just a limit, that's all. There's just a limit."

Doc's voice was firm, only a slight edge of unease breaking through his control. "I think we had better face it. Roy is dead. The Orion's ruined, and the shuttle-craft is gone anyway."

"He could be alive . . ." Jill ventured.

Doc tried to take the sting out of his voice, and was not entirely successful. "Where? On the ship, crushed to a paste? Not on the shuttle. It's tumbling further from the Orion every second. There's no one on it. In one of the rocket sleds?" His face softened, and they could see that he was afraid to have hope. "Yes. Maybe that. Maybe on one of the sleds."

They nodded to each other, and they and the other colonists spent long hours on the telescope hoping, and praying.

But there was nothing alive up there now. Ridgeback was entirely alone.

Cynnie never recovered. She would talk only to her brother, refusing even to see her child. She was morose and ate little, spending most of her time watching the sky with something like terrified awe in her eyes.

And one day, seven months after the accident, she walked into the woods and never returned.

Doc hadn't seen Jerry for three weeks.

The children lived in a community complex which had some of the aspects of a boarding school. The colonists took turns at nursing duty. Jill spent most of her time there since she and Greg were on the outs. Lately, Elise had taken up the habit too. Not that he blamed her; he couldn't have been very good company the last few months.

Parents took their children out to the T-shaped complex whenever they felt like it, so that some of the children had more freedom than others. But by and large they all were expected to live there eventually.

Brew was coming out of the woods with a group of six children when Doc stumbled into the sunlight and saw Jerry.

He wore a rough pair of coveralls that fit him well enough, but he would have looked ludicrous if there had been anything to laugh about. Soft brown fur covered every inch of him. As Doc appeared he turned his head with a bird-quick movement, saw his father, and scampered over. Jerry bounced into him, wrapped long arms tight about his rib cage and said, eagerly, "Daddy."

There was a slight pause.

"Hello, Jerry." Doc slowly bent to the ground, looking into his son's eyes.

"Daddy Doc, Daddy Doc," he chattered, smiling up at his father. His vocabulary was about fifteen words. Jerry was six years old and much too big for his age. His fingers were very long and strong, but his thumbs were small and short and inconsequential. Doc had seem him handle silverware without much trouble. His nose pugged, jaw massive with a receding chin. There were white markings in the fur around his eyes, accentuating the heavy supraorbital ridges, making the poor child look like—

The poor child. Doc snorted with self-contempt. *Listen to me. Why not my child?*

Because I'm ashamed. Because we lock our children away to ease the pain. Because they look like—

Doc gently disengaged Jerry's fingers from his shirt, turned and half-ran back to the ship. Shivering, he curled up on one of the cots and cursed himself to sleep.

Hours later he roused himself and, woozy with fatigue, he went looking for Jase. He found him on a work detail in the north fields, picking fruit.

"I'm not sure," he told Jase. "They're not old enough for me to be sure. But I want your opinion."

"Show me," said Jase, and followed him to the library.

The picture on the tape was an artist's rendering of Pithicanthropus erectus. He stood on a grassy knoll looking warily out at the viewer, his long-fingered hand clutching a sharp-edged throwing rock.

"I'll smack your head," said Jase.

"I'm wrong, then?"

"You're calling them apes!"

"I'm not. Read the copy. Pithicanthropus was a small-brained Pleistocene primate, thought to be a transitional stage between ape and man. You got that? Pith is also called Java Man."

Jase glared at the reader. "The markings are different. And there is the fur—"

"Forget 'em. They're nothing but guesswork. All the artist had to go on were crumbling bones and some broken rocks."

"Broken rocks?"

"Pith used to break rocks in half to get an edged weapon. It was about the extent of his tool-making ability. All we know about what he looked like comes from fossilized bones—very much like the skeleton of a stoop shouldered man with foot trouble, topped with the skull of an ape with hydrocephalus."

"Very nice. Will Eve's children be fish?"

"I don't know, dammit. I don't know anything at all. Look. Pith isn't the only candidate for missing link. Homo Habilis looked a lot more like us and lived about two million years ago. Kenyapithicus Africanus resembled us less, but lived eighteen million years earlier. So I can't say what we've got here. God only knows what the next generation will be like. That depends on whether the children are moving backwards or maybe sideways. I don't know, Jase. I just don't *know*!" The last words were shrill, and Doc punctuated them by slamming his fist against a wire window screen. Then, because he could think of nothing more to say, he did it again. And again. And—

Jase caught his arm. Three knuckles were torn and bleeding. "Get some sleep," he said, eyes sad. "I'll have them send Earth a description of Eve the way she is now. She's oldest, and best developed. We'll send them all we have on her. It's all we can do."

Momentum and the thoroughness of their training had kept them going for eight years. Now the work of making a world slowed and stopped.

It didn't matter. The crops and the meat animals had no natural enemies on Ridgeback. Life spread along the continent like a green plague. Already it had touched some of the islands.

Doc was gathering fruit in the groves. It was a shady place, cool, quiet, and it made for a tranquil day's work. There was no set quota. You took home approximately a third of what you gathered. Sometimes he worked there, and sometimes he helped with the cattle, examining for health and pregnancy, or herding the animals with the nonlethal sonic stunners.

He wished that Elise were here with him, so they could laugh together, but that was growing infrequent now. She was growing more involved with the nursery, and he spent little of his time there.

Jill's voice hailed him from the bottom of the ladder. "Hey up there, Doc. How about a break?"

He grinned and climbed down, hauling a sack of oranges.

"Tired of spending the day reading, I guess," she said lightly. She offered him an apple. He polished it on his shirt and took a bite. "Just needed to talk to somebody."

"Kinda depressed?"

"Oh, I don't know. I guess it's just getting hard to cope with some of the problems."

"I guess there have been a few."

Jill gave a derisive chuckle. "I sure don't know Greg anymore. Ever since he set up the brewery and the distillery, he doesn't really want to see me at all."

"Don't take it so hard," Doc comforted. "The strain is showing on all of us. Half the town does little more than read or play tapes or drink. Personally, I'd like to know who smuggled the hemp seeds on board."

Jill laughed, which he was glad for, then her face grew serious again. "You know, there'd probably be more trouble if we didn't need someone to look after the kids." She paused, looking up at Doc. "I spend a lot of my time there," she said unnecessarily.

"Why?" It was the first time he'd asked. They had left the groves and were heading back into town along the gravel road that Greg and Brew and the others had built in better days.

"We . . . I came here for a reason. To continue the human race, to cross a new frontier, one that my children could have a part in. Now, now that we know that the colony is doomed, there's just no motive to anything. No reason. I'm surprised that there isn't more drinking, more carousing and four-somes and divorces and everything else. Nothing seems to matter a whole lot. Nothing at all."

Doc took her by the shoulders and held her. Go on and cry, he silently said to her. God, I'm tired.

The children grew fast. At nine Eve reached puberty and seemed to shoot skyward. She grew more hair. She learned more words, but not many more. She spent much of her time in the trees in the children's complex. The older girls grew almost as fast as she did, and the boys.

Every Saturday Brew and Nat took some of the children walking. Sometimes they climbed the foothills at the base of the continental range; sometimes they wandered through the woods, spending most of their efforts keeping the kids from disappearing into the trees.

One Saturday they returned early, their faces frozen in anger. Eve and Jerry were missing. At first they refused to discuss it, but when Jase began organizing a search party, they talked.

They'd been ready to turn for home when Eve suddenly scampered into the trees. Jerry gave a whoop and followed her. Nat had left the others with Brew while she followed after the refugees.

It proved easy to find them, and easier still to determine what they were doing with each other when she came upon them.

Eve looked up at Nat, innocent eyes glazed with pleasure. Nat trembled for a moment, horrified, then drove them both away with a stick, screaming filth at them.

Over Nat's vehement objections and Brew's stoney refusal to join, Jase got his search party together and set off. They met the children coming home. By that time Nat had talked to the other mothers and fathers at the children's complex.

Jase called a meeting. There was no way to avoid it now, feelings were running too deep.

"We may as well decide now," he told them that night. "There's no question of the children marrying. We could train them to mouth the words of any of our religions, but we couldn't expect them to understand what they were saying. So the question is, shall we let the children reproduce?"

He faced an embarrassed silence.

"There's no question of their being too young. In biological terms they aren't, or you could all go home. In our terms, they'll never be old enough. Anyone have anything to say?"

"Let's have Doc's opinion," a hoarse voice called. There was a trickle of supportive applause.

Doc rose, feeling very heavy. "Fellow colonists . . ." The smile he was trying on for size didn't fit his face. He let it drop. There was a desperate compassion in his voice. "This world will never be habitable to mankind until we find out what went wrong here. I say let our children breed. Someday someone on Earth may find out how to cure what we've caught. Maybe he'll know how to let our descendants breed men again. Maybe this problem will only last a generation or two, then we'll get human babies again. If not, well, what have we lost? Who else is there to inherit Ridgeback?"

"No!" The sound was a tortured meld of hatred and venom. That was Nat, sunhaired loving mother of six, with her face a strained mask of frustration. "I didn't risk my life and leave my family and, and train for years and bleed and sweat and toil so my labor could fall . . . to . . . a bunch of goddamned *monkeys*!"

Brew pulled her back to her seat, but by now the crowd was muttering and arguing to itself. The noise grew louder. There was shouting. The yelling, too, grew in intensity.

Jase shouted over the throng. "Let's talk this out peacefully!"

Brew was standing, screaming at the people who disagreed with him and Natalie. Now it was becoming a shoving match, and Brew was getting more furious.

Doc pushed his way into the crowd, hoping to reach Brew and calm him. The room was beginning to break down into tangled knots of angry, emotionally charged people.

He grabbed the big man's arm and tried to speak, but the

Swede turned bright baleful eyes on him and swung a heavy fist.

Doc felt pain explode in his jaw and tasted blood. He fell to the ground and was helped up again, Brew standing over him challengingly. "Stay out of our lives, *Doctor*," he sneered, openly now. "You've never helped anything before. Don't try to start now."

He tried to speak but felt the pain, and knew his jaw was fractured. A soft hand took his arm and he turned to see Elise, big green eyes luminous with pity and fear. Without struggling, he allowed her to take him to the ship infirmary.

As they left the auditorium he could hear the shouting and struggling, Jase on the microphone trying to calm them, and the coldly murderous voices that screamed for "no monkey Grandchildren."

He tried to turn his head towards the distant sound of argument as Elise set the bone and injected quick-healing serums. She took his face and kissed him softly, with more affection than she had shown in months, and said, "They're afraid, Harry." Then kissed him again, and led him home.

Doc raged inwardly at his jaw that week. Its pain prevented him from joining in the debate which now flared in every corner of the colony.

Light images swarm across his closed eyes as the sound of fists pounding against wood roused him from dreamless sleep. Doc threw on a robe and padded barefoot across the cool stone floor of his house, peering at the front door with distaste before opening it. Jase was there, and some of the others, sombre and implacable in the morning's cool light.

"We've decided, Doc," Jase said at last. Doc sensed what was coming. "The children are not to breed. I'm sorry, I know how you feel—" Doc grunted. How could Jase know how he felt when he wasn't sure himself? "We're going to have to ask you to perform the sterilizations . . ." Doc's hearing faded down to a low fuzz, and he barely heard the words. This is the way the world ends . . .

Jase looked at his friend, feeling the distance between them grow. "All right. We'll give you a week to change your mind. If not, Elise or Greg will have to do it." Without saying anything more they left.

Doc moped around that morning, even though Elise swore to him that she'd never do it. She fussed over him as they fixed breakfast in the kitchen. The gas stove burned methane reclaimed from waste products, the flame giving more heat control than the microwaves some of the others had. Normally Doc enjoyed scrambling eggs and wok-ing fresh slivered vegetables into crisp perfection, but nothing she said or did seemed to lift him out of his mood.

He ate lightly, then got dressed and left the house. Although she was concerned, Elise did not follow him.

He went out to the distillery, where Greg spent much of his time under the sun, drunk and playing at being happy. "Would you?" The pain still muffled Doc's words. "Would you sterilize them?"

Greg looked at him blearily, still hung over from the previous evening's alcoholic orgy. "You don't understand, man." There was a stirring sound from the sheltered bedroom behind the distillery, and a woman's waking groan. Doc knew it wasn't Jill. "You just don't understand."

Doc sat down, wishing he had the nerve to ask for a drink. "Maybe I don't. Do you?"

"No. No, I don't. So I'll follow the herd. I'm a builder. I build roads, and I build houses. I'll leave the moralizing to you big brains."

Doc tried to say something and found that no words would come. He needed something. He needed . . .

"Here, Doc. You know you want it." Greg handed him a cannister with a straw in it. "Best damn vodka in the world." He paused, and the slur dropped from his voice. "And this is the world, Doc. For us. For the rest of our lives. You've just got to learn to roll with it." He smiled again and mixed himself an evil-looking drink.

Greg's guest had evidently roused herself and dressed. Doc could hear her now, singing a snatch of song as she left. He didn't want to recognize the voice.

"Got any orange juice?" Doc mumbled, after sipping the vodka.

Greg tossed him an orange. "A real man works for his pleasures."

Doc laughed and took another sip of the burning fluid. "Good lord. What *is* that mess you're drinking?"

"It's a Black Samurai. Sake and soy sauce."

Doc choked. "How can you drink that stuff?"

"Variety, my friend. The stimulation of the bizarre."

Doc was silent for a long time. Senses swimming he watched the sun climb, feeling the warmth as morning melted into afternoon. He downed a slug of his third screwdriver and said irritably, "You can't do it, Greg. If you sterilize the children, it's over."

"So what? It's over anyway. If they wanna let a drunk slit the pee pees of their . . . shall we say atavistic progeny? Yeah, that sounds nice. Well, if they want me to do it, I guess I'll have to do it." He looked at Doc very carefully. "I do have my sense of civic duty. How about you, Doc?"

"I tried." He mumbled, feeling the liquor burning his throat, feeling the light-headedness exert its pull. "I tried. And I've failed."

"You've failed so far. What were your goals?"

"To keep—" He took a drink. Damn, that felt good. "To keep the colony healthy. That's what. It's a disaster. We're at each other's throats. We kill our babies—"

Doc lowered his head, unable to continue.

They were both silent, then Greg said, "If I've gotta do it, I will, Doc. If it's not me, it'll be someone else who reads a couple of medical texts and wants to play doctor. I'm sorry."

Doc sat, thinking. His hands were shaking. "I can't do that." He couldn't even feel the pain anymore.

"Then do what you gotta do, man," and Greg's voice was dead sober.

"Will you . . . can you help me?" Doc bit his lip. "This is *my* civic duty, you know?"

"Yea, I know." He shook his head. "I'm sorry. I wish I could help."

A few minutes passed, then Doc said drunkenly, "There's got to be a way. There just has to be."

"Wish I could help, Doc."

"I wish you could too." Doc said sincerely, then rose and staggered back to his house.

It rained the night he made his decision, one of the quick, hot rains that swept from the coast to the mountains in a thunderclap of fury. It would make a perfect cover.

He gathered his medical texts, a Bible and a few other books, regretting that most of the information available to him was electronically encoded. Doc took one of the silent stunners from the armory. The nonlethal weapons had only been used as livestock controllers. There had never been another need, until now. From the infirmary he took a portable medical kit, stocking it with extra bandages and medicine, then took it all to the big cargo flyer.

It was collapsible, with a fabric fusilage held rigid by

highly compressed air in fabric structural tubing. He put it in one of the soundless electric trucks and inflated it behind the children's complex.

There was plenty of room inside the fence for building and for a huge playground with fruit trees and all the immemorial toys of the very young. After the children had learned to operate a latch, Brew had made a lock for the gate and given everyone a key. Doc clicked it open and moved in.

He stayed in the shadows, creeping close to the main desk where Elise worked.

You can't follow where I must go, he thought regretfully. *You and I are the only fully trained medical personnel. You must stay with the others. I'm sorry, darling.*

And he stunned her to sleep silently, moving up to catch her head as it slumped to the table. For the last time, he gently kissed her mouth and her closed eyes.

The children were in the left wing—one room for each sex, with floors all mattress and no covers, because they could not be taught to use a bed. He sprayed the sound waves up and down the sleeping forms. The parabolic reflector leaked a little, so that his arm was numb to the elbow when he was finished. He shook his hand, trying to get some feeling back into it, then gave up and settled into the hard work of carrying the children to the flyer.

He hustled them through the warm rain, bending under their weight but still working swiftly. Doc arranged them on the fabric floor in positions that looked comfortable—the positions of sleeping men rather than sleeping animals. For some time he stood looking down at Jerry his son and at Lori his daughter, thinking things he could not afterwards remember.

He flew North. The flyer was slow and not soundless; it must have awakened people, but he'd have some time before anyone realized what had happened.

Where the forest had almost petered out he hovered down and landed gently enough that only a slumbering moan rose from the children. Good. He took half of them, including Jerry and Lori, and spread them out under the trees. After he had made sure that they had cover from the air he took the other packages, the books and the medical kit, and hid them under a bush a few yards away from the children.

He stole one last look at them, his heirs, small and defenseless, asleep. He could see Elise in them, in the color of their hair, as Elise could see him in their eyes and cheeks.

Kneading his shoulder, he hurried back to the ship. There was more for him to do.

Skipping the ship off again, he cruised thirty miles west, near the stark ridge of mountains, their sombre grey still broken only sparsely by patches of green. There he left the other seven children. Let the two groups develop separately, he thought. They wouldn't starve, and they wouldn't die of exposure, not with the pelts they had grown. Many would remain alive, and free. He hoped Jerry and Lori would be among them.

Doc lifted the flyer off and swept it out to the ocean. Only a quarter mile offshore were the first of the islands, lush now with primitive foliage. They spun beneath him, floating brownish-green upon a still blue sea.

Now he could feel his heartbeat, taste his fear. But there was resolve, too, more certain and calm than any he had known in his life.

He cut speed and locked the controls, setting the craft on a gradual decline. Shivering already, he pulled on his life jacket and walked to the emergency hatch, screwing it open quickly.

The wind whipped his face, the cutting edge of salt narrowing his eyes. Peering against the wall of air pressure he was able to see the island coming up on him now, looming close. The water was only a hundred feet below him, now eighty, sixty . . .

The rumbling of the shallow breakers joined with the tearing wind, and, fighting his fear, he waited until the last possible moment before hurling himself from the doorway.

He remembered falling.

He remembered hitting the water at awful speed, the spray ripping into him, the physical impact like the blow of a great hand. When his head broke surface Doc wheezed for air, swallowed salty liquid and thrashed for balance.

In the distance, he saw the flash of light, and a moment later the shattering roar as the flyer spent itself on the rocky shore.

Jase was tired. He was often tired lately, although he still managed to get his work done.

The fields had only recently become unkempt, as Marlow and Billie and Jill and the others grew more and more inclined to pick their vegetables from their backyard gardens.

So just he and a few more still rode out to the fields on the tractors, still kept close watch on the herds, still did the hand-pruning so necessary to keep the fruit trees healthy.

The children were of some help. Ten years ago a few of them had been captured around the foothill area. They had been sterilized, of course, and taught to weed, and carry firewood, and a few other simple tasks.

Jase leaned on his staff and watched the shaggy figures moving along the street, sweeping and cleaning.

He had grown old on this world, their Ridgeback. He regretted much that had happened here, especially that night thirty-some years before when Doc had taken the children.

Taken them—where? Some argued for the islands, some for the West side of the mountain range. Some believed that the children had died in the crash of the flyer. Jase had believed that, until the adult Piths were captured. Now, it was hard to say what happened.

It was growing chill now, the streetlights winking on to brighten the long shadows a setting Tau Ceti cast upon the ground. He drew his coat tighter across his shoulders and walked back to his house. It was a lonelier place to be since June had died, but it was still home.

Fumbling with the latch, he pushed the door open and reached around for the lightswitch. As it flicked on, he froze.

My God.

"Hello, Jase." The figure was tall and spare, clothes ragged, but greying hair and beard cut squarely. Three of the children were with him.

After all this time . . .

"Doc . . ." Jase said, still unbelieving. "It is you, isn't it?"

The bearded man smiled uncertainly, showing teeth that were white but chipped. "It's been a long time, Jase. A very long time."

The three Piths were quiet and alert, sniffing the air of this strange place.

"Are these—?"

"Yes. Jerry and Lori. And Eve. And a small addition." One of the three—God, could it be Eve? sniffed up to Jase. The soft golden fur on her face was tinged with grey, but she carried a young child at her breast.

Jerry stood tall for a preman, eyeing Jase warily. He carried a sharpened stick in one knobby hand.

Jase sat down, speechless. He looked up into the burning eyes of the man he had known thirty years before. "You're still officially under a death sentence, you know."

Doc nodded his head. "For kidnapping?"

"Murder. No one was sure what had happened to you, whether you or any of the children had survived."

Doc, too, sat down. For the first time the light in his eyes dimmed. "Yes. We survived. I swam to shore after crashing the flyer, and found the place where I had left the children." He thought for a moment, then asked quietly. "How is Elise? And all the others?"

Jase said nothing, unable to raise his eyes from the floor. At last he beckoned a small voice. "She died three years ago, Doc. She was never the same after you left. She thought you were dead. That the children were dead. Couldn't you have at least told her about your plan? Or gotten her a message?"

Doc's fingers played absently with his beard as he shook his head. "I couldn't involve her. I couldn't. Could you . . . show me where she's buried, Jase?"

"Of course."

"What about the others?"

"Well, none of the people were the same after the children left. Some just seemed to lose purpose. Brew's dead. Greg drank himself under. Four of the others have died." Jase paused, thinking. "Do any of the others know you're here?"

"No. I slipped in just at dusk. I wasn't sure what kind of a reception I'd get."

"I'm still not sure." Jase hesitated. "Why did you do it?"

The room was quiet, save for a scratching sound as Jerry fingered an ear. Fleas? Absurd. Jill had never uncrated them.

"I had to know, Jase," he said. There was no uncertainty in his voice. In fact, there was an imperious quality he had never had in the old days. "The question was: Would they breed true? Was the Pith effect only temporary?"

"Was it?"

"No. It persisted. I had to know if they were regressing or evolving, and they remained the same in subsequent generations, save for natural selection, and there isn't much of that."

Jase watched Lori, her stubby fingers untangling mats in her fur. Her huge brown eyes were alive and vital. She was a lovely creature, he decided. "Doc, what are the children?"

"What do you think?"

"You know what I think. An alien species wants our worlds. In a hundred years they'll land and take them. What they'll do with the children is anybody's guess. I—" He couldn't bring himself to look at Eve. "I wish you'd sterilized them, Doc."

"Maybe you do, Jase. But, you see, I don't believe in your aliens."

Jase's breath froze in his throat.

"They might want our world," said Doc, "but why would they want our life forms? Everything but Man is spreading like a plague of locusts. If someone wants Ridgeback, why haven't they done something about it? By the time they land, terrestrial life will have an unstoppable foothold. Look at all the thousands of years we've been trying to stamp out just one life form, the influenza viruses.

"No, I've got another idea. Do you know what a locust is?"

"I know what they are. I've never seen one."

"As individuals they're something like a short grasshopper. As individuals, they hide or sleep in the daytime and come out at night. In open country you can hear them chirping after dusk, but otherwise nobody notices them. But they're out there, eating and breeding and breeding and eating, getting more numerous over a period of years, until one day there are too many for the environment to produce enough food.

"Then comes the change. On Earth it hasn't happened in a long time because they aren't allowed to get that numerous. But it used to be that when there were enough of them, they'd grow bigger and darker and more aggressive. They'd eat everything in sight, and when all the food was gone, and when there were enough of them, they'd suddenly take off all at once.

"That's when you'd get your plague of locusts. They'd drop from the air in a cloud thick enough and broad enough to darken the sky, and when they landed in a farmer's field he could kiss his crops goodbye. They'd raze it to the soil, then take off again, leaving nothing."

Jase took off his glasses and wiped them. "I don't see what it is you're getting at."

"Why do they do it? Why were locusts built that way?"

"Evolution, I guess. After the big flight they'd be spread over a lot of territory. I'd say they'd have a much bigger potential food supply."

"Right. Now consider this. Take a biped that's man shaped, enough so to use a tool, but without intelligence. Plant him on a world and watch him grow. Say he's adaptable; say he eventually spread over most of the fertile land masses of the planet. Now what?

"Now an actual physical change takes place. The brain expands. The body hair drops away. Evolution had adapted him to his climate, but that was when he had hair. Now he's got to use his intelligence to keep from freezing to death. He'll discover fire. He'll move out into areas he couldn't live in before. Eventually he'll cover the whole planet, and he'll build spacecraft and head for the stars."

Jase shook his head. *"But why would they change back,* Doc?"

"Something in the genes, maybe. Something that didn't mutate."

"Not *how* Doc. We know it's possible. *Why*?"

"We're going back to being grasshoppers. Maybe we've reached our evolutionary peak. Natural selection stops when we start protecting the weak ones, instead of allowing those with defective genes to die a natural death."

He paused, smiling. "I mean, look at us, Jase. You walk with a cane now. I haven't been able to read for five years, my eyes have weakened so. And we were the best Earth had to offer; the best minds, the finest bodies. Chris only squeeked by with his glasses because he was such a damn good meteorologist."

Jase's face held a flash of long-forgotten pain. "And I guess they still didn't choose carefully enough."

"No," Doc agreed soberly. "They didn't. On Earth we protected the sick, allowed them to breed, instead of letting them die . . . with pacemakers, with insulin, artificial kidneys and plastic hip joints and trusses. The mentally ill and retarded fought in the courts for the right to reproduce. Okay, it's humane. Nature isn't humane. The infirm will do their job by dying, and no morality or humane court rulings or medical advances will change the natural course of things for a long, long time."

"How long?"

"I don't know how stable they are. It could be millions of years, or . . . ?" Doc shrugged. "We've changed the course of our own development. Perhaps a simpler creature is needed to colonize a world. Something that has no choice but to change or die. Jase, remember the Cold War?"

"I read about it."

"And the Belt Embargo? Remember diseromide, and smog, and the spray-can thing, and the day the fusion seawater distillery at San Francisco went up and took the Bay area with it, and four states had to have their water flown in for a month?"

"So?"

"A dozen times we could have wiped out all life on Earth. As soon as we've used our intelligence to build spacecraft and seed another world, intelligence becomes a liability. Some old anthropologist even had a theory that a species needs abstract intelligence before it can prey on its own kind. The development of fire gave Man time to sit back and dream up ways to take things he hadn't earned. You know how gentle the children are, and you can remember how the carefully chosen citizens of Ridgeback acted the night we voted on the children's right to reproduce."

"So you gave that to them, Doc. They are reproducing. And when we're gone they'll spread all over the world. But are they *human*?"

Doc pondered, wondering what to say. For many years he had talked only to the children. The children never interrupted, never disagreed . . . "I had to know that too. Yes. They're human."

Jase looked closely at the man he had called friend so many years ago. Doc was so sure. He didn't discuss; he lectured. Jase felt an alienness in him that was deeper than the mere passage of time.

"Are you going to stay here now?"

"I don't know. The children don't need me anymore, though they've treated me like a god. I can't pass anything on to them. I think our culture has to die before theirs can grow."

Jase fidgited, uncomfortable. "Doc. Something I've got to tell you. I haven't told anyone. It's thirty years now, and nobody knows but me."

Doc frowned. "Go on."

"Remember the day Roy died? Something in the Orion blew all the motors at once? Well, he talked to Cynnie first. And she talked to me, before *she* disappeared. Doc, he got a laser message from Earth, and he knew he couldn't ever send it down. It would have destroyed us. So he blew the motors."

Doc waited, listening intently.

"It seems that every child being born on Earth nowadays bears an uncanny resemblance to Pithicanthropus erectus. They were begging us to make the Ridgeback colony work. Because Earth is doomed."

"I'm glad nobody knew that."

Jase nodded. "If intelligence is bad for us, it's bad for Earth. They've fired their starships. Now they're ready for another cycle."

"Most of them'll die. They're too crowded."

"Some will survive. If not there, then, thanks to you, here." He smiled. A touch of the old Jase in his eyes. "They'll *have* to become men, you know."

"Why do you put it like that?"

"Because Jill uncrated the wolves, to help thin out the herds."

"They'll cull the children, too," Doc nodded. "I couldn't help them become men, but I think that will do it. They will have to band together, and find tools, and fire." His voice took on a dreamy quality. "Eventually, the wolves will come out of the darkness to join them at their campfires, and Man will have dogs again." He smiled. "I hope they don't overbreed them like we did on Earth. I doubt if chihuahuas have ever forgotten us for what we did to them."

"Doc," Jase said, urgently, "will you trust me? Will you wait for a minute while I leave? I . . . I want to try something. If you decide to go there may never be another chance."

Doc looked at him, mystified. "Alright, I'll wait."

Jase limped out of the door. Doc sat, watching his charges, proud of their alertness and flexibility, their potential for growth in the new land.

There was a creaking as the door swung open.

The woman's hair had been blond, once. Now it was white, heavy wrinkles around her eyes and mouth, years of hardship and disappointment souring what had once been beauty.

She blinked, at first seeing only Doc.

"Hello, Nat," he said to her.

She frowned. "What . . . ?" Then she saw Eve.

Their eyes locked, and Nat would have drawn back save for Jase's insistent hand at her back.

Eve drew close, peering into her mother's face as if trying to remember her.

The old woman stuttered, then said, "Eve?" The Pith cocked her head and came closer, touching her mother's hand. Nat pulled it back, eyes wide.

Eve cooed, smiling, holding her baby out to Nat.

At first she flinched, then looked at the child, so much like Eve had been, so much . . . and slowly, without words or visible emotion, she took the child from Eve and cradled it, held it, and began to tremble. Her hand stretched out helplessly, and Eve came closer, took her mother's hand and the three of them, mother, child and grandchild, children of different worlds, held each other. Nat cried for the pain that had driven them apart, the love that had brought them together.

Doc stood at the edge of the woods, looking back at the colonists who waved to them, asking for a swift return.

Perhaps so. Perhaps they could, now. Enough time had passed that understanding was a thing to be sought rather than avoided. And he missed the company of his own kind.

No, he corrected himself, the children *were* his kind. As he had told Jase, without explaining, he knew that they were human. He had tested it the only way he could, by the only means available.

Eve walked beside him, her hand seeking his. "Doc," she cooed, her birdlike singsong voice loving. He gently took their child from her arms, kissing it.

At over sixty years of age, it felt odd to be a new father, but if his lover had her way, as she usually did, his strange family might grow larger still.

Together, the five of them headed into the forest, and home.

THE THAW

by Tanith Lee

Cryogenics, or the art of cold-storage for the wealthy half-dead in hope that some future generation will be foolish enough to defrost them, caught the public attention a number of years ago. Since then it has receded into the limbo of other ten-day wonders, but it is not entirely forgotten. There still exist organizations that are trying to make it effective, endeavoring to work out ways of reviving the frigid semi-cadavers. Tanith Lee, who is achieving a high reputation for her amazing variety of imaginative creations, takes on the cryogenic problem with a twist that may never have occurred to the would-be immortals laboring amid the icepacks.

Ladies first, they said.

That was O.K. Then they put a histotrace on the lady in question, and called me.

"No thanks," I said.

"Listen," they said, "you're a generative blood-line descendant of Carla Brice. Aren't you interested, for God's sake? This is a unique moment, a unique experience. She's going to need support, understanding. A contact. Come on. Don't be frigid about it."

"I guess Carla is more frigid than I'm ever likely to be."

They laughed, to keep up the informalities. Then they

mentioned the Institute grant I'd receive, just for hanging around and being supportive. To a quasi-unemployed artist, that was temptation and a half. They also reminded me that on this initial bout there wouldn't be much publicity, so later, if I wanted to capitalize as an eyewitness, and providing good old Carla was willing—I had a sudden vision of getting very rich, very quick, and with the minimum of effort, and I succumbed ungracefully.

Which accurately demonstrates my three strongest qualities: laziness, optimism, and blind stupidity. Which in turn sums up the whole story, more or less. And that's probably why I was told to write it down for the archives of the human race. I can't think of a better way to depress and wreck the hopes of frenzied, shackled, bleating humanity.

But to return to Carla. She was, I believe, my great-great-great-great-great grandmother. Give or take a great. Absolute accuracy isn't one of my talents, either. The relevant part is, however, that at thiry-three, Carla had developed the rare heart complaint valu—val—well, she'd developed it. She had a few months, or less, and so she opted, along with seventy other people that year, to undergo Cryogenic Suspension till a cure could be found. Cry Sus had been getting progressively more popular, ever since the 1980s. Remember? It's the freezing method of holding a body in refrigerated stasis, indefinitely preserving thereby flesh, bones, organs and the rest, perfect and pristine, in a frosty crystal box. (Just stick a tray of water in the freezer and see for yourself.) It may not strike you as cozy anymore, but that's hardly surprising. In 1993, seventy-one persons, of whom four-or-five-or-six-great granny Carla was one, saw it as the only feasible alternative to death. In the following two hundred years, four thousand others copied their example. They froze their malignancies, their unreliable hearts, and their corroding tissues, and as the light faded from their snowed-over eyes, they must have dreamed of waking up in the fabulous future.

Funny thing about the future. Each next second is the future. And now it's the present. And now it's the past.

Those all-together four thousand and ninety-one who deposited their physiognomies in the cold-storage compartments of the world were looking forward to the future. And here it was. And we were it.

And smack in the middle of this future, which I naively called Now, was I, Tacey Brice, a rotten little unskilled artist, painting gimcrack flying saucers for the spacines. There was a big flying saucer sighting boom that year of 2193. Either you recollect that, or you don't. Nearly as big as the historic boom between the 1930s and '90s. Psychologists had told us it was our human inadequacy, searching all over for a father-mother figure to replace God. Besides, we were getting desperate. We'd penetrated our solar system to a limited extent, but without meeting anybody on the way.

That's another weird thing. When you read the speculativia of the 1900s, you can see just how much they expected of us. It was going to be all or nothing. Either the world would become a miracle of rare device with plastisteel igloos balanced on the stratosphere and metal giblets, or we'd have gone out in a blast of radiation. Neither of which had happened. We'd had problems, of course. Over two hundred years, problems occur. There had been the Fission Tragedy, and the World Flood of '14. There'd been the huge pollution clear-ups complete with the rationing that entailed, and one pretty nasty pandemic. They had set us back, that's obvious. But not halted us. So we reached 2193 mostly unscathed, with a whizz-bang technology not quite as whizz, or bang, as prophesied. A place where doors opened when they saw who you were, and with a colony on Mars, but where they hadn't solved the unemployment problem or the geriatric problem. Up in the ether there were about six hundred buzz-whuzzes headed out into nowhere, bleeping information about earth. But we hadn't landed on Alpha Centauri yet. And if the waste-disposal jammed, brother, it jammed. What I'm trying to say (superfluously, because you're ahead of me), is that their future, those four thousand and ninety-one, their future which was our present, wasn't as spectacular as they'd trusted or feared. Excepting the Salenic Vena-derivative drugs, which had rendered most of the diseases of the 1900s and the 2000s obsolete.

And suddenly, one day, someone had a notion.

"Hey, guys," this someone suggested, "you recall all those sealed frosty boxes the medic centers have? You know, with the on-ice carcinomas and valu-diddums in 'em? Well, don't you think it'd be grand to defrost the lot of them and pump 'em full of health?"

"Crazy," said everybody else, and wet themselves with enthusiasm.

After that, they got the thing organized on a global scale. And first off, not wanting to chance any public mishaps, they intended to unfreeze a single frost box, in relative privacy.

Perhaps they put all the names in a hat. Whatever, they picked Carla Brice, or Brr-Ice, if you liked that Newsies' tablotape pun.

And since Carla Brr-Ice might feel a touch extra chilly, coming back to life two hundred years after she's cryonised out of it, they dredged up a blood-line descendant to hold her cold old thirty-three-year hand. And that was Tacey Brr-Ice. Me.

The room below was pink, but the cold pink of strawberry ice cream. There were forty doctors of every gender prowling about in it and round the crystal slab. It put me in mind of a pack of wolves with a carcass they couldn't quite decide when to eat. But then, I was having a nervous attack, up on the spectator gallery where they'd sat me. The countdown had begun two days ago, and I'd been ushered in at noon today. For an hour now, the crystal had been clear. I could see a sort of blob in it, which gradually resolved into a naked woman. Straight off, even with her lying there stiff as a board and utterly defenseless, I could tell she was the sort of lady who scared me dizzy. She was large and well-shaped, with a mane of dark red hair. She was the type that goes outdoor swimming at all seasons, skis, shoots rapids in a canoe, becomes the co-ordinator of a moon colony. The type that bites. Valu-diddums had got her, but nothing else could have done. Not child, beast, nor man. Certainly not another woman. Oh my. And this was my multiple-great granny that I was about to offer the hand of reassurance.

Another hour, and some dial and click mechanisms down in the strawberry ice room started to dicker. The wolves flew in for the kill. A dead lioness, that was Carla. Then the box rattled and there was a yell. I couldn't see for scrabbling medics.

"What happened?"

The young medic detailed to sit on the spec gallery with me sighed.

"I'd say she's opened her eyes."

The young medic was black as space and beautiful as the stars therein. But he didn't give a damn about me. You could see he was in love with Carla the lioness. I was simply a pain he had to put up with for two or three hours, while he stared at the goddess beneath.

But now the medics had drawn off. I thought of the Sleeping Beauty story, and Snow White. Her eyes were open indeed. Coppery brown to tone with the mane. She didn't appear dazed. She appeared contemptuous. Precisely as I'd anticipated. Then the crystal box lid began to rise.

"Jesus," I said.

"Strange you should say that," said the black medic. His own wonderful eyes fixed on Carla, he'd waxed profound and enigmatic. "The manner in which we all still use these outdated religious expletives: *God, Christ, Hell,* long after we've ceased to credit their religious basis as such. The successful completion of this experiment in life-suspense and restoration has a bearing on the same matter," he murmured, his inch-long lashes brushing the plastase pane. "You've read of the controversy regarding this process? It was seen at one era as an infringement of religious faith."

"Oh, yes?"

I kept on staring at him. Infinitely preferable to Carla, with her open eyes, and the solitary bending medic with the supadermic.

"The idea of the soul," said the medic on the gallery. "The immortal part which survives death. But what befalls a soul trapped for years, centuries, in a living yet statically frozen body? In a physical limbo, a living death. You see the problem this would pose for the religious?"

"I—uh—"

"But, of course, today . . ." he spread his hands. "There is no such barrier to lucid thought. The life force, we now know, resides purely in the brain, and thereafter in the motor nerves, the spinal cord, and attendant reflexive centres. There is no *soul.*"

Then he shut up and nearly swooned away, and I realized Carla had met his eye.

I looked, and she was sitting, part reclined against some medic's arm. The medic was telling her where she was and what year it was and how, by this evening, the valu-diddums would be no more than a bad dream, and then she could go out into the amazing new world with her loving descendant, who she could observe up there on the gallery.

She did spare a glance for me. It lasted about .09 of a mini-instant. I tried to unglue my mouth and flash her a warming welcoming grin, but before I could manage it, she was back to studying the black medic.

At that moment somebody came and whipped me away for celebratory alcohol, and two hours later, when I'd celebrated rather too much, they took me up a plushy corridor to meet Carla, skin to skin.

Actually, she was dressed on this occasion. She'd had a shower and a couple of post-defrosting tests and some shots and the anti-valu-diddums stuff. Her hair was smouldering like a fire in a forest. She wore the shiny smock medical centers insisted that you wore, but on her it was like a design original. She'd even had a tan frozen in with her, or maybe it was my dazzled eyes that made her seem all bronzed and glowing. Nobody could look that good, that *healthy*, after two hundred years on ice. And if they did, they shouldn't. Her room was crammed with flowers and bottles of scent and exotic light paintings, courtesy of the Institute. And then they trundled me in.

Not astoundingly, she gazed at me with bored amusement. Like she'd come to the dregs at the bottom of the wine.

"This is Tacey," somebody said, making free with my forename.

Carla spoke, in a voice of maroon velvet.

"Hallo, er, Tacey." Patently, my cognomen was a big mistake. Never mind, she'd overlook it for now. "I gather we are related."

I was drunk, but it wasn't helping.

"I'm your gr—yes, we are, but—" I intelligently blurted. The "but" was going to be a prologue to some nauseating, placatory, crawler's drivel about her gorgeousness and youth. It wasn't necessary, not even to let her know how scared I was. She could tell that easily, plus how I'd shrunk to a shadow in her high-voltage glare. Before I could complete my hiccupping sycophancy, anyway, the medic in charge said: "Tacey is your link, Mz Brice, with civilization as it currently is."

Carla couldn't resist it. She raised one manicured eyebrow, frozen exquisite for two centuries. If Tacey was the link, civilization could take a walk.

"My apartment," I went on blurting, "it's medium, but—"

What was I going to say now? About how all my grant from the Institute I would willingly spend on gowns and perfumes and skis and automatic rifles, or whatever Carla wanted. How I'd move out and she could have the apartment to herself. (She wouldn't like the spacine murals on the walls).

"It's just a bri— a bridge," I managed. "Till you get acclimatosed—atised."

She watched me as I made a fool of myself, or rather, displayed my true foolishness. Finally I comprehended the message in her copper eyes: Don't bother. That was all: Don't bother. You're a failure, Carla's copper irises informed me, as if I didn't know. Don't make excuses. You can alter nothing. I expect nothing from you. I will stay while I must in your ineffectual vicinity, and you may fly round me and scorch your wings if you like. When I am ready, I shall leave immediately, soaring over your sky like a meteor. You can offer no aid, no interest, no grain I cannot garner for myself.

"How kind of Tacey," Carla's voice said. "Come, darling, and let me kiss you."

Somehow, I'd imagined her still as very cold from the frosty box, but she was blood heat. Ashamed, I let her brush my cheek with her meteoric lips. Perhaps I'd burn.

"I'd say this calls for a toast," said the medic in charge. "But just rose-juice for Mz Brice, I'm afraid, at present."

Carla smiled at him, and I hallucinated a rose-bush, thorns too, eviscerated by her teeth. Lions drink blood, not roses.

I got home paralyzed and floundered about trying to change things. In the middle of attempting to re-spray-paint over a wall, I sank on a pillow and slept. Next day I was angry, the way you can only be angry over something against which you are powerless. So damn it. Let her arrive and see space-shuttles, mother-ships, and whirly bug-eyed monsters all across the plastase. And don't pull the ready-cook out of the alcove to clean the feed-pipes behind it that I hadn't seen for three years. Or dig the plant out of the cooled-water dispenser. Or buy any new garments, blinds, rugs, sheets. And don't conceal the Wage-Increment cheques when they skitter down the chute. Or prop up the better spacines I'd illustrated, on the table where she won't miss them.

I visited her one more time during the month she stayed at the Institute. I didn't have the courage not to take her anything, although I knew that whatever I offered would be wrong. Actually, I had an impulse to blow my first grant cheque and my W-I together and buy her a little antique stiletto of Toledo steel. It was blantantly meant to commit murder with, and as I handed it to her I'd bow and say, "For you, Carla. I just know you can find a use for it." But naturally I didn't have the bravura. I bought her a flagon of expensive scent she didn't need and was rewarded by seeing her put it on a shelf with three other identically packaged flagons, each twice the size of mine. She was wearing a reclinerobe of amber silk, and I almost reached for sunglasses. We didn't say much. I tottered from her room, sunburned and peeling. And that night I painted another flying saucer on the wall.

The day she left the Institute, they sent a mobile for me. I was supposed to collect and ride to the apartment with Carla, to make her feel homey. I felt sick.

Before I met her, though, the medic in charge wafted me into his office.

"We're lucky," he said. "Mz Brice is a most independent lady. Her readjustment has been, in fact, remarkable. None of the traumas or rebuttals we've been anxious about. I doubt if most of the other subjects to be revived from Cryogenesis will demonstrate the equivalent rate of success."

"They're really reviving them, then?" I inquired lamely. I was glad to be in here, putting off my fourth congress with inadequacy.

"A month from today. Dependent on the ultimately positive results of our post-resuscitation analysis of Mz Brice. But, as I intimated, I hardly predict any hitch there."

"And how long," I swallowed, "how long do you think Carla will want to stay with me?"

"Well, she seems to have formed quite an attachment for you, Tacey. It's a great compliment, you know, from a woman like that. A proud, volatile spirit. But she needs an anchor for a while. We all need our anchors. Probably, her proximity will benefit you, in return. Don't you agree?"

I didn't answer, and he concluded I was overwhelmed. He started to describe to me that glorious scheduled event, the global link-up, when every single cryogone was to be revived, as simultaneously with each other as they could arrange it. The process would be going out on five channels of the Spatials, visible to us all. Technology triumphant yet again, bringing us a minute or two of transcendental catharsis. I thought about the beautiful black medic and his words on religion. And this is how we replaced it, presumably (when we weren't saucer-sighting), shedding tears sentimentally over four thousand and ninety idiots fumbling out of the deep-freeze.

"One last, small warning," the medic in charge added. "You may notice—or you may not, I can't be positive—the occasional lapse in the behavioural patterns of Mz Brice."

There was a fantasy for me. Carla, *lapsed.*

"In what way?" I asked, miserably enjoying the unlikelihood.

"Mere items. A mood, an aberration—a brief disorientation even. These are to be expected in a woman reclaimed by life after two hundred years, and in a world she is no longer familiar with. As I explained, I looked for much worse and far greater quantity. The odd personality slip is inevitable. You musn't be alarmed. At such moments the most steadying influence on Mz Brice will be a non-Institutional normalcy of surroundings. And the presence of yourself."

I nearly laughed.

I would have, if the door hadn't opened, and if Carla, in mock red-lynx fur, hadn't stalked into the room.

I didn't even try to create chatter. Alone in the mobile, with the auto driving us along the cool concrete highways, there wasn't any requirement to pretend for the benefit of others. Carla reckoned I was a schmoil, and I duly schmoiled. Mind you, now and again, she put out a silk paw and gave me a playful tap. Like when she asked me where I got my hair *done*. But I just told her about the ready-set parlours and she quit. Then again, she asked a couple of less abstract questions. Did libraries still exist, that was one. The second one was if I slept well.

I went along with everything in a dank stupor. I think I was half kidding myself it was going to be over soon. Then the mobile drove into the auto-lift of my apartment block, the gates gaped and we got out. As my door recognized me and split wide, it abruptly hit me that Carla and I were going to be hand in glove for some while. A month at least, while the Institute computed its final tests. Maybe more, if Carla had my lazy streak somewhere in her bronze and permasteel frame.

She strode into my apartment and stood flaming among the flying saucers and the wine-ringed furniture. The fake-fur looked as if she'd shot it herself. She was a head taller than I was ever going to be. And then she startled me, about the only way she could right then.

"I'm tired, Tacey," said Carla.

No wise-cracks, no vitriol, no stare from Olympus.

She glided to the bedroom. O.K. I'd allocated the bed as hers, the couch as mine. She paused, gold digit on the panel that I'd pre-set to respond to her finger.

"Will you forgive me?" she wondered aloud.

Her voice was soporific. I yawned.

"Sure, Carla."

She stayed behind the closed panels for hours. The day reddened over the city, colours as usual heightened by the weather control that operates a quarter of a mile up. I slumped here and there, unable to eat or rest or read or doodle. I was finding out what it was going to be like, having an apartment and knowing it wasn't mine anymore. Even through a door, Carla dominated.

Around 19, I knocked. No reply.

Intimidated, I slunk off. I wouldn't play the septophones, even with the ear-pieces only, even with the volume way down. Might wake Granny. You see, if you could wake her from two hundred years in the freezer, you could certainly wake her after eight hours on a dormadais.

At twenty-four midnight, she still hadn't come out.

Coward, I knocked again, and feebly called: "Night, Carla. See you tomorrow."

On the couch I had nightmares, or nightcarlas to be explicit. Some were very realistic, like the one where the trust bonds Carla's estate had left for her hadn't accumulated after all and she was destitute, and going to remain with me for ever and ever. Or there were the comic-strip ones where the fake red-lynx got under the cover and bit me. Or the surreal ones where Carla came floating towards me, clad only in her smouldering hair, and everything caught fire from it, and I kept saying, "Please, Carla, don't set the rug alight. Please, Carla, don't set the couch alight." In the end there was merely a dream where Carla bent over me, hissing something like an anaconda—if they do hiss. She wanted me to stay asleep, apparently, and for some reason I was fighting her, though I was almost comatose. The strange thing in this dream was that Carla's eyes had altered from copper to a brilliant topaz yellow, like the lynx's.

It must have been about four in the morning that I woke up. I think it was the washer unit that woke me. Or it could have been the septophones. Or the waste-disposal. Or the drier. Or any of the several gadgets a modern apartment was equipped with. Because they were all on. It sounded like a madhouse. Looked like one. All the lights were on, too. In the middle of chaos: Carla. She was quite naked, the way I'd seen her at the first, but she had the sort of nakedness that seems like clothes, clean-cut, firm and flawless. The sort that makes me want to hide inside a stone. She was reminiscent of a sorceress in the midst of her sorcery, the erupting mechanisms sprawling round her in the fierce light. I had a silly thought: *Carla's going nova.* Then she turned and saw me. My mouth felt as if it had been security-sealed, but I got out, "You O.K., Carla?"

"I am, darling. Go back to sleep now."

That's the last thing I remember till 10 A.M. the next day.

I wondered initially if Carla and the gadgets had been an additional dream. But when I checked the energy-meter I discovered they hadn't. I was plodding to the ready-cook when Carla emerged from the bedroom in her amber reclinerobe.

She didn't say a word. She just relaxed at the counter and let me be her slave. I got ready to prepare her the large breakfast she outlined. Then I ran her bath. When the water-meter shut off half through, Carla suggested I put in the extra tags to ensure the tub was filled right up.

As she bathed, I sat at the counter and had another nervous attack.

Of course, Carla was predictably curious. Back in 1993, many of our gadgets hadn't been invented, or at least not developed to their present standard. Why not get up in the night and turn everything on? Why did it have to seem sinister? Maybe my sleeping through it practically non-stop was the thing that troubled me. All right. So Carla was a hypnotist. Come to consider, should I run a histotrace myself, in an attempt to learn what Carla was—had been?

But let's face it, what really upset me was the low on the energy-meter, the water-meter taking a third of my week's water tags in one morning. And Carla luxuriously wallowing, leaving me to foot the bill.

Could I say anything? No. I knew she'd immobilize me before I'd begun.

When she came from the bathroom, I asked her did she want to go out. She said no, but I could visit the library, if I would, and pick up this book and tape list she'd called through to them. I checked the call-meter. That was down, too.

"I intend to act the hermit for a while, Tacey," Carla murmured behind me as I guiltily flinched away from the meter. "I don't want to get involved in a furor of publicity. I gather the news of my successful revival will have been leaked today. The tablotapes will be sporting it. But I understand, by the news publishing codes of the '80s, that unless I approach the Newsies voluntarily, they are not permitted to approach me."

"Yes, that's right." I gazed pleadingly into the air. "I guess you wouldn't ever reconsider that, Carla? It could mean a lot of money. That is, not for you to contact the Newsies. But if you'd all—allow me to on your beh—half."

She chuckled like a lioness with her throat full of gazelle. The hair rose on my neck as she slunk closer. When her big, warm, elegant hand curved over my skull, I shuddered.

"No, Tacey. I don't think I'd care for that. I don't need the cash. My estate investments, I hear, are flourishing."

"I was thinking of m— I was thinking of me, Carla. I cou—could use the tags."

The hand slid from my head and batted me lightly. Somehow, I was glad I hadn't given her the Toledo knife after all.

"No, I don't think so. I think it will do you much more good to continue as you are. Now, run along to the library, darling."

I went mainly because I was glad to get away from her. To utter the spineless whining I had had drained entirely my thin reserves of courage. I was shaking when I reached the autolift. I had a wild plan of leaving town, and leaving my apartment with Carla in it, and going to ground. It was more than just inadequacy now. Hunter and hunted. And as I crept through the long grass, her fiery breath was on my heels.

I collected the twenty books and the fifty tapes and paid for the loan. I took them back to the apartment and laid them before my astonishing amber granny. I was too scared even to hide. Much too scared to disobey.

I sat on the sun-patio, though it was the weather control day for rain. Through the plastase panels I heard the tapes educating Carla on every aspect of contemporary life; social, political, economic, geographical, and carnal.

When she summoned me, I fixed lunch. Later, drinks and supper.

Then I was too nervous to go to sleep. I passed out in the bathroom, sitting in the shower cubicle. Had nightcarlas Carla eating salad. Didn't wake up till 10 A.M. Checked. All meters down again.

When I trod on smashed plastase I thought it was sugar. Then I saw the cooled-water dispenser was in ninety-five bits. Where the plant had been, there was only soil and condensation and trailing roots.

I looked, and everywhere beheld torn-off leaves and tiny clots of earth. There was a leaf by Carla's bedroom. I knocked and my heart knocked to keep my hand company.

But Carla wasn't interested in breakfast, wasn't hungry.

I knew why not. She'd eaten my plant.

You can take a bet I meant to call up the Institute right away. Somehow, I didn't. For one thing, I didn't want to call from the apartment and risk Carla catching me at it. For another, I didn't want to go out and leave her, in case she did something worse. Then again, I was terrified to linger in her vicinity. A *lapse*, the medic in charge had postulated. It was certainly that. Had she done anything like it at the Institute? Somehow I had the idea she hadn't. She'd saved it for me. Out of playful malice.

I dithered for an hour, till I panicked, pressed the call button and spoke the digits. I never heard the door open. She seemed to know exactly when to—*strike;* yes that *is* the word I want. I sensed her there. She didn't even touch me. I let go the call button.

"Who were you calling?" Carla asked.

"Just a guy I used to pair with," I said, but it came out husky and gulped and quivering.

"Well, go ahead. Don't mind me."

Her maroon voice, bored and amused and indifferent to anything I might do, held me like a steel claw. And I discovered I had to turn around and face her. I had to stare into her eyes.

The scorn in them was killing. I wanted to shrivel and roll under the rug, but I couldn't look away.

"But if you're not going to call anyone, run my bath, darling," Carla said.

I ran her bath.

It was that easy. Of course.

She was magnetic. Irresistible.

I couldn't—

I could *not*—

Partly, it had all become incredible. I couldn't picture myself accusing Carla of house-plant-eating to the medics at the Institute. Who'd believe it? It was nuts. I mean, too nuts even for them. And presently, I left off quite believing it myself.

Nevertheless, somewhere in my brain I kept on replaying those sentences of the medic in charge: *the occasional lapse in the behavioural patterns . . . a mood, an aberration . . .* And against that, point counter-point, there kept on playing that phrase the beautiful black medic had reeled off enigmatically as a cultural jest: *But what befalls a soul trapped for years, centuries, in a living yet statically frozen body?*

Meanwhile, by sheer will, by the force of her persona,

she'd stopped me calling. And that same thing stopped me talking about her to anybody on the street, sent me tongue-tied to fetch groceries, sent me grovelling to conjure meals. It was almost as if it also shoved me asleep when she wanted and brought me awake ditto.

Doesn't time fly when you're having fun?

Twenty days, each more or less resembling each, hurried by. Carla didn't do anything else particularly weird, at least not that I saw or detected. But then, I never woke up nights anymore. And I had an insane theory that the meters had been fiddled, because they weren't low, but they felt as if they should be. I hadn't got any more plants. I missed some packaged paper lingerie, but it turned up under Carla's bed, where I'd kicked it when the bed was mine. Twenty days, twenty-five. The month of Carla's post-resuscitation tests was nearly through. One morning, I was stumbling about like a zombie, cleaning the apartment because the dustease had jammed and Carla had spent five minutes in silent comment on the dust. I was moving in that combined sludge of terror, mindlessness and masochistic cringing she'd taught me, when the door signal went.

When I opened the door, there stood the black medic with a slim case of file-tapes. I felt transparent, and that was how he treated me. He gazed straight through me to the empty room where he had hoped my granny would be.

"I'm afraid your call doesn't seem to be working," he said. (Why had I the notion Carla had done something to the call?) "I'd be grateful to see Mz Brice, if she can spare me a few minutes. Just something we'd like to check for the files."

That instant, splendid on her cue, Carla manifested from the bathroom. The medic had seen her naked in the frosty box, but not a naked that was vaguely and fluently sheathed in a damp towel. It had the predictable effect. As he paused transfixed, Carla bestowed her most gracious smile.

"Sit down," she said. "What check is this? Tacey, darling, why not arrange some fresh coffee?"

Tacey darling went to the coffee cone. Over its bubbling, I heard him say to her, "It's simply that Doctor Something was a little worried by a possible amnesia. Certainly, none of the memory areas seem physically impaired. But you see, here and there on the tape—"

"Give me an example, please," drawled Carla.

The black medic lowered his lashes as if to sweep the tablotape.

"Some confusion over places, and names. Your second husband, Francis, for instance, who you named as Frederick. And there, the red mark—Doctor Something-Else mentioned the satellite disaster of '91, and it seems you did not recall—"

"You're referring to the malfunction of the Ixion 11, which broke up and crashed in the midwest, taking three hundred lives," said Carla. She sounded like a purring textbook. She leaned forward, and I could watch him tremble all the way across from the coffee cone. "Doctor Something and Doctor Something-Else," said Carla, "will have to make allowances for my excitement at rebirth. Now, I can't have you driving out this way for nothing. How about you come to dinner, the night before the great day. Tacey doesn't see nearly enough people her own age. As for me, let's say you'll make a two-hundred-year old lady very happy."

The air between them was electric enough to form sparks. By the "Great day" she meant, patently, the five-channel Spatial event when her four thousand and ninety confrères got liberated from the sub-zero. But he plainly didn't care so much about defrosting anymore.

The coffee cone boiled over. I noticed with a shock I was crying. Nobody else did.

What I wanted to do was program the ready-cook for the meal, get in some wine, and get the hell out of the apartment and leave the two of them alone. I'd pass the night at one of the all-night Populars, and creep in around 10 A.M. the next morning. That's the state I frankly acknowledged she had reduced me to. I'd have been honestly grateful to have done that. But Carla wouldn't let me.

"Out?" she inquired. "But this whole party is for you, darling."

There was nobody about. She didn't have to pretend. She and I knew I was the slave. She and I knew her long-refrigerated soul, returning in fire, had scalded me into a melty on the ground. So it could only be cruelty, this. She seemed to be experimenting, even, as she had with the gadgets. The psychological dissection of an inferior inhabitant of the future.

What I had to do therefore, was to visit the ready-set hair parlour, and buy a dress with my bi-monthly second W-I cheque. Carla, though naturally she didn't go with me, somehow instigated and oversaw these ventures. Choosing the dress, she was oddly at my elbow. *That* one, her detached and omnipresent aura instructed me. It was expensive, and it was scarlet and gold. It would have looked wonderful on somebody else. But not me. That dress just sucked the little life I've got right out of me.

Come the big night (before the big day, for which the countdown must already have, in fact, begun), there I was, done up like a New Year parcel, and with my own problematical soul wizened within me. The door signal went, and the slave accordingly opened the door, and the dark angel entered, politely thanking me as he nearly walked straight through me.

He looked so marvellous, I practically bolted. But still the aura of Carla, and Carla's wishes, which were beginning to seem to be communicating themselves telepathically, held me put.

Then Carla appeared. I hadn't seen her before, that evening. The dress was lionskin, and it looked real, despite the anti-game-hunting laws. Her hair was a smooth auburn waterfall that left bare an ear with a gold star dependent from it. I just went into the cooking area and uncorked a bottle and drank most of it straight off.

They both had good appetites, though hers was better than his. She'd eaten a vast amount since she'd been with me, presumably ravenous after that long fast. I was the waitress, so I waited on them. When I reached my plate, the food had congealed because the warmer in the table on my side was faulty. Anyway, I wasn't hungry. There were two types of wine. I drank the cheap type. I was on the second bottle now, and sufficiently sad I could have howled, but I'd also grown uninvolved, viewing my sadness from a great height.

They danced together to the septophones. I drank some more wine. I was going to be very, very ill tomorrow. But that was tomorrow. Verily. When I looked up, they'd danced themselves into the bedroom and the panels were shut. Carla's cruelty had had its run and I wasn't prepared for any additions, such as ecstatic moans from the interior, to augment my frustration. Accordingly, garbed in my New Year parcel frock, hair in curlicues, and another bottle in my hand, I staggered forth into the night.

I might have met a thug, a rapist, a murderer, or even one of the numerous polipatrols that roam the city to prevent the activities of such. But I didn't meet anyone who took note of me. Nobody cared. Nobody was interested. Nobody wanted to be my friend, rob me, abuse me, give me a job or a goal, or make me happy, or make love to me. So if you thought I was a Judas, just you remember that. If one of you slobs had taken any notice of me that night—

I didn't have to wait for morning to be ill. There was a handsome washroom on Avenue East. I'll never forget it. I was there quite a while.

When the glamourous weather-control dawn irradiated the city, I was past the worst. And by 10 A.M. I was trudging home, queasy, embittered, hard-done-by, but sober. I was even able to register the tabloes everywhere and the holoid neons, telling us all that the great day was here. The day of the four thousand and ninety. Thawday. I wondered dimly if Carla and the Prince of Darkness were still celebrating it in my bed. She should have been cold. Joke. All right. It isn't.

The door to my apartment let me in. The place was as I'd abandoned it. The window-blinds were down, the table strewn with plates and glasses. The bedroom door firmly shut.

I pressed the switch to raise the blinds, and nothing happened, which didn't surprise me. That in itself should have proved to me how far the influence had gone and how there was no retreat. But I only had this random desultory urge to see what the apartment door would do now. What it did was not react. Not even when I put my hand on the panel, which method was generally reserved for guests. It had admitted me, but wouldn't let me out again. Carla had done something to it. As she had to the call, the meters, and to me. But how—personal power? Ridiculous. I was a spineless dope, that was why she'd been able to negate me. Yet—forty-one medics, with a bevy of tests and questions, some of which, apparently, she hadn't got right, ate from her hand. And maybe her psychic ability had increased. Practice makes perfect.

. . . *What befalls a soul trapped for years, centuries, in a living, yet statically frozen body?*

It was dark in the room, with the blinds irreversibly staying down and the lights irreversibly off.

Then the bedroom door slid wide, and Carla slid out. Naked again, and glowing in the dark. She smiled at me, pityingly.

"Tacey, darling, now you've gotten over your sulks, there's something in here I'd like you to clear up for me."

Dichotomy once more. I wanted to take root where I was, but she had me walking to the bedroom. She truly was glowing. As if she'd lightly sprayed herself over with something mildly luminous. I guessed what would be in the bedroom, and I'd begun retching, but, already despoiled of filling, that didn't matter. Soon I was in the doorway and she said, "Stop that, Tacey." And I stopped retching and stood and looked at what remained of the beautiful black medic, wrapped up in the bloodstained lionskin.

Lions drink blood, not roses.

Something loosened inside me then. It was probably the final submission, the final surrender of the fight. Presumably I'd been fighting her subconsciously from the start, or I wouldn't have gained the ragged half-freedoms I had. But now I was limp and sodden, so I could ask humbly: "The plant was salad. But a man—what was he?"

"You don't quite get it, darling, do you?" Carla said. She stroked my hair friendlily. I didn't shudder anymore. Cowed dog, I was relaxed under the contemptuous affection of my mistress. "One was green and vegetable. One was black, male, and meat. Different forms. Local dishes. I had no inclination to sample you, you comprehend, since you were approximate to my own appearance. But of course, others who find themselves to be black and male, may wish to sample pale-skinned females. Don't worry, Tacey. You'll be safe. You entertain me. You're mine. Protected species."

"Still don't understand, Carla," I whispered meekly.

"Well, just clear up for me, and I'll explain."

I don't have to apologize to you for what I did then, because, of course, you know all about it, the will-less indifference of the absolute slave. I bundled up the relics of Carla's lover-breakfast, and dumped them in the waste-disposal, which dealt with them pretty efficiently.

Then I cleaned the bedroom, and had a shower, and fixed Carla some coffee and biscuits. It was almost noon, the hour when the four thousand and ninety were going to be roused, and to step from their frost boxes in front of seven-eighths of the world's Spatial-viewers. Carla wanted to see it too, so I switched on my set, minus the sound. Next Carla told me I might sit, and I sat on a pillow, and she explained.

For some reason, I don't remember her actual words. Perhaps she put it in a technical way and I got the gist but not the sentences. I'll put it in my own words here, despite the fact that a lot of you know now anyway. After all, under supervision, we still have babies sometimes. When they grow up they'll need to know. Know why they haven't got a chance, and why we hadn't. And, to level with you, know why I'm not a Judas, and that I didn't betray us, because I didn't have a chance either.

Laziness, optimism, and blind stupidity.

I suppose optimism more than anything.

Four thousand and ninety-one persons lying down in frozen stasis, aware they didn't have souls and couldn't otherwise survive, dreaming of a future of cures, and of a reawakening in that future. And the earth dreaming of benevolent visitors from other worlds, father-mother figures to guide and help us. Sending them buzz-whuzzes to bleep, over and over, *Here* we are. *Here. Here.*

I guess we do have souls. Or we have something that has nothing to do with the brain, or the nerve centers, or the spinal cord. Perhaps that dies too, when we die. Or perhaps it escapes. Whatever happens, that's the one thing you can't retain in Cryogenic Suspension. The body, all its valves and ducts and organs, lies pristine in limbo, and when you wake it up with the correct drugs, impulses, stimuli, it's live again, can be cured of its diseases, becoming a flawless vessel of—nothing. It's like an empty room, a vacant lot. The tenant's skipped.

Somewhere out in the starry night of space, one of the bleeping buzz-whuzzes was intercepted. Not by pater-mater figures, but by a predatory, bellicose alien race. It was simple to get to us—hadn't we given comprehensive directions? But on arrival they perceived a world totally unsuited to their fiery, gaseous, incorporeal forms. That was a blow, that was. But they didn't give up hope. Along with their superior technology they developed a process whereby they reckoned they could transfer inside of human bodies, and thereafter live off the fat of the Terrain. However, said process wouldn't work. Why not? The human consciouness (soul?) was too strong to overcome, it wouldn't let them through. Even asleep, they couldn't oust us. Dormant, the consciousness (soul?) is still present, or at least linked. As for dead bodies, no go. A man who had expired of old age, or with a mobile on top of him was no use. The body had to be a whole one, or there was no point. Up in their saucers, which were periodically spotted, they spat and swore. They gazed at the earth and drooled, pondering mastery of a globe, and entire races of slaves at their disposal. But there was no way they could acheive their aims until—until they learned of all those Cryogenic Suspensions in their frost boxes, all those soulless lumps of ice, waiting on the day when science would release and cure them and bring them forth healthy and *void*.

If you haven't got a tenant, advertize for a new tenant. We had. And they'd come.

Carla was the first. As her eyes opened under the crystal, something looked out of them. Not Carla Brice. Not anymore. But something.

Curious, cruel, powerful, indomitable, alien, deadly.

Alone, she could handle hundreds of us humans, for her influence ascended virtually minute by minute. Soon there were going to be four thousand and ninety of her kind, opening their eyes, smiling their scornful thank-yous through the Spatials at the world they had come to conquer. The world they did conquer.

We gave them beautiful, healthy, moveable houses to live in, and billions to serve them and be toyed with by them, and provide them with extra bodies to be frozen and made fit to house any leftover colleagues of theirs. And our green depolluted meadows wherein to rejoice.

As for Carla, she'd kept quiet and careful as long as she had to. Long enough for the tests to go through and for her to communicate back, telepathically, to her people, all the data they might require on earth, prior to their arrival.

And now she sat and considered me, meteoric fiery Carla-who-wasn't-Carla, her eyes, in the dark, gleaming topaz yellow through their copper irises, revealing her basic inflammable nature within the veil of a dead woman's living flesh.

They can make me do whatever they want, and they made me write this. Nothing utterly bad has been done to me, and maybe it never will. So I've been lucky there.

To them, I'm historically interesting, as Carla had been historically interesting to us, as a first. I'm the first Slave. Possibly, I can stay alive on the strength of that and not be killed for a whim.

Which, in a way, I suppose, means I'm a sort of a success, after all.

OUT THERE WHERE THE BIG SHIPS GO

by Richard Cowper

Though from its title this sounds like an interstellar epic, it is not. This is a different evaluation of the possible future of humanity after encounter with other species and non-Terrestrially derived cultures. It takes place on Earth in a time not very remote from the present. It may be a sort of utopian era, though that is not precisely stated; still this unusual British writer projects a preoccupation for the restless human mind that may signify a coming epoch of contemplative peace. Zen, anyone?

It was at breakfast on the second day that Roger first noticed the grey-haired man with the beard. He was sitting a the far corner table, partly shadowed by the filmy swag of the gathered gauze curtain. It was the ideal vantage point from which to observe what ever might be going on outside the long vista-window or to survey the guests as they came into the hotel dining room. But the bearded man was doing neither. He was just sitting, staring straight ahead of him, as though he could see right through the partition wall which divided the dining room from the hotel bar, and on out across the town and the azure bay to where the giant clippers unfurled their glittering metal sails and reached up to grasp the Northeast Trades.

"Don't stare, Roger. It's rude."

The boy flushed and made a play of unfolding his napkin and arranging it on his lap. "I wasn't staring," he muttered. "Just looking."

A young waiter with a sickle-shaped scar above his left eyebrow moved across from the buffet and stood deferentially at the shoulder of Roger's mother. He winked down at Roger, who smiled back at him shyly.

"You go on cruise today maybe, Senor? See *Los dedos de Dios*, hey?"

Roger shook his head.

Mrs. Herzheim looked up from the menu. "Is the fish real *fresh?*"

"*Si*, they bring him in this morning."

"We'll have that then. And grapefruits for starters. And coffee."

"*Si*, Senora." The young waiter flapped his napkin at Roger, winked again and hurried away.

Mrs. Herzheim tilted her head to one side and made a minuscule adjustment to one of her pearl eardrops. "What're your plans, honey?" she enquired lazily.

"I don't know, Mom. I thought maybe I'd—"

"Yoo-hoo, Susie! Over here!"

"Hi, Babs, Hi, Roger. Have you ordered, hon?"

"Yeah. We're having the fish. Where's Harry?"

"Collecting his paper."

The dining room was beginning to fill up, the waiters scurrying back and forth with laden trays, the air redolent with the aroma of fresh coffee and hot bread rolls. A slim girl with a lemon-yellow cardigan draped across her shoulders came in from the bar entrance. She was wearing tinted glasses, and her glossy, shoulder-length hair was the color of a freshly husked chestnut. She passed behind Roger's chair, threading her way among the tables until she had reached the corner where the bearded man was sitting. She pulled out a chair and sat down beside him so that her profile was towards the other guests and she was directly facing the window.

Roger watched the pair covertly. He saw the man lean forward and murmur something to the girl. She nodded. He then raised a finger, beckoned, and as though he had been hovering in readiness just for this, a waiter hurried over to their table. While they were giving their breakfast order, Roger's waiter reappeared with the grapefruits, a pot of coffee and a basket of rolls. As he was distributing them about the table, Susie Fogel signed to him.

He bent towards her attentively.

She twitched her snub nose in the direction of the corner table. "Is that who I think it is?" she murmured.

The waiter glanced swiftly round. "At the corner table? *Si, Senora*, that is him."

"Ah," Susie let out her breath in a quiet sigh.

"When did he arrive?"

"Late last night, Senora."

The waiter took her order and retreated in the direction of the kitchens. Mrs. Herzheim poured out a cup of coffee and handed it to Roger. As he was reaching for it, Harry Fogel appeared. He wished Roger and his mother a genial good morning and took the seat opposite his wife.

Susie lost no time in passing on her news.

Harry turned his head and scanned the couple in the corner. "Well, well," he said. "That must mean Guilio's around too. How's *that* for a turn-up?"

Roger said, "Who is he, Mr. Fogel?"

Harry Fogel's round face transformed itself into a parody of wide-eyed incredulity. *"Oi vai,"* he sighed. "Don't they teach you kids *any* history these days?"

Roger flushed and buried his nose in his grapefruit.

"Aw, come on, son," protested Harry. "Help an old man to preserve his illusions. Sure even a twelve-year-old's heard of *The Icarus?*"

Roger nodded, acutely conscious that his ears were burning.

"Well, there you are then. That's Mr. Icarus in person. The one and only. Come to add luster to our little tourney. Very big deal, eh, Babs?"

Roger's mother nodded, reached out for the sugar bowl and sprinkled more calories that she could reasonably afford over her grapefruit.

Roger risked another glance at the corner table. To his acute consternation the bearded man now appeared to be gazing directly across at him. For a moment their eyes met, and then, in the very act of glancing away, Roger thought he saw the old man lower his left eyelid ever so slightly.

At ten o'clock, Roger accompanied his mother to the youth salon. It was a trip he had been making in innumerable resorts for almost as long as he could remember. Hitherto, it had not occurred to him to resent it any more than it would have occurred to the poodles and chihuahuas to resent their diamante studded leashes. Had anyone thought to ask him, he would probably have admitted that he genuinely enjoyed the warm, familiar femininity of the salons with their quiet carpets, their scents of aromatic waxes and lacquers, their whispered confessions which came creeping into his ears like exotic tendrils from beneath the anonymous helmets of the driers while, mouselike and unobserved, he turned the pages of the picture magazines. But today, when they reached the portico of the salon he suddenly announced: "I think I'll go on down to the harbor and take a look at the clippers, Mom."

Mrs. Herzheim frowned doubtfully. "All on your *own* honey? Are you *sure?* I mean it's—well. . . ."

Roger smiled. "I'll be fine. You don't have to worry about me."

"But we can go together this afternoon," she countered. "I'm looking forward to seeing those clippers too, honey."

Roger's smile remained inflexible, and suddenly it dawned upon his mother that the only way she would get him inside that salon would be to drag him in by main force. The realization shocked her profoundly. She gnawed at her bottom lip as she eyed askance her twelve-year-old son, who had chosen this moment to challenge, gently, her absolute authority over him. She consulted her Cartier wristwatch and sighed audibly. "Well, all right then," she conceded. "But you're to be right back here on this very spot at noon sharp. You hear that? Promise me, now."

Roger nodded. "Sure, Mom."

Mrs. Herzheim unclipped her handbag, took out a currency bill and passed it over. Roger folded it carefully, unzipped the money pouch on his belt and stuffed the note inside. "Thanks," he said.

They stood for a moment, eying each other thoughtfully; then Mrs. Herzheim leant forward and kissed him lightly on the forehead. "You're going to tell me all about it over lunch," she said. "I'm counting on it."

Roger grinned and nodded as he watched her turn and vanish through the swing doors of the salon; then he too turned lightly on his heel and began skipping down the cobbled street towards the harbor. After a few seconds he broke into a trot which gradually accelerated into a sort of wild, leaping dance which lasted until he hurtled out, breathless, through the shadow of an ancient arched gateway and found himself on the quayside.

He clutched at a stone stanchion while he got his breath back. Then he blinked his eyes and looked about him. The sunshine striking off the ripples was flinging a shifting web of light across the hulls of the fishing boats. The very air seemed to swirl like the seabirds as they circled and swooped and dived for floating fragments of fishgut. Dark-eyed women in gaudy shawls, brass combs winking in their black hair, shouted to one another across the water from the ornate iron balconies of the waterside tenements. Donkey carts rattled up and down the slabbed causeway. Huge swarthy men, sheathed in leather aprons, their bare arms a-shimmer with fish scales, trotted past crowned with swaying pagodas of baskets and flashed white teeth at him in gleaming grins. A posse of mongrels queued up to cock their legs against a shell-fish stall only to scatter, yelping, as the outraged owner swore and hurled an empty box at them. Roger laughed, relinquished his stanchion, and began dodging among the fishermen and the sightseers, heading past the dim and echoing warehouses towards the light tower on the inner harbor mole.

When he reached his goal he sat down and drew a deep breath of pure delight. On a rock ledge some ten meters beneath him, two boys of about his own age were fishing. He watched them for a moment, then raised his eyes and looked up at the dark volcanic hills. He noted the scattering of solar "sunflower" generators; the distant globe of the observatory; the tumbling, trade-driven clouds; the lime-washed houses clambering on each other's shoulders up the steep hillside; the great hotels squatting smugly high above. By screwing up his eyes he just managed to make out in one of them the shuttered windows of the rooms which, for the next fortnight, were to be his and his mother's.

Suddenly, for no particular reason, he found himself remembering the old man and the girl with auburn hair. He tried to recall what he had read about *The Icarus*, but apart from the fact that she had been the last of the starships, he could not recall very much. As Mr. Fogel had said, that was history, and history had never been his favorite subject. But there was something about that grey-haired, bearded man which would not let his mind alone. And suddenly he knew what it was! "He just wasn't *seeing* us," he said aloud. "He didn't *care!*"

Hearing his voice, the two boys below glanced up *"Cigarillo, Senor?"* one called hopefully.

Roger smiled and shook his head apologetically.

The boys looked at one another, laughed, shouted something he could not understand, and returned to their fishing.

Far out to sea, sunlight twinkled from the dipping topsails of an eight-masted clipper. Roger thrust out his little finger at the full stretch of his arm and tried to estimate her speed, counting silently to mark off the seconds it took her to flicker out of his sight and back again. Twenty-four. And an eight-master meant a least 200 meters overall. Two hundred in twenty-four seconds would be one hundred in twelve would be . . . five hundred in a minute. Multiply 500 by 60 and you got . . . 30 kilometers an hour. Just about average for the Northeast Trade route. But, even so, six days from now she would be rounding Barbados and sniffing for the Gulf. Very quietly he began to hum the theme of *Trade Winds,* the universal hit of a year or two back, following the great ship with his dreaming eyes as she dipped and soared over the distant swells and vowing that one day he too would be in command of such a vessel, plunging silver-winged along the immemorial trade routes of the world.

He sat gazing out to sea long after the great ship had slipped down out of sight below the horizon. Then with a sigh he climbed to his feet and began making his way back along the harbor, dimly conscious that some part of him was still out there on the ocean but not yet sufficiently self-aware to know which part it was.

A clock in a church tower halfway up the hillside sent its noonday chimes fluttering out over the roofs of the town like a flock of silver birds. Roger suddenly remembered his promise to his mother and broke into a run.

Mrs. Herzheim discovered that the youth salon had given her a headache. So after lunch she retired to her bedroom leaving Roger to spend the afternoon by the hotel pool. He had it to himself; most of the other guests having opted for one or another of the organized excursions to the local beauty spots, or, like Roger's mother, chosen to rest up prior to the ardors of the night's session.

Roger swam the eight lengths he had set himself, then climbed out and padded across to the loafer where he had left his towel and his micomicon. Who was it to be? He sat down, gave a cursory scrub to his wet hair, then flipped open the back of the cabinet and ran his eye down the familiar index. Nelson, Camelot, Kennedy, Pasteur, Alan Quartermain, Huck Finn, Tarzan, Frodo, Titus Groan—his finger hovered and a voice seemed to whisper deep inside his head *"each flint a cold blue stanza of delight, each feather, terrible. . . .* He shivered and was on the point of uncoiling the agate earplugs when he heard a splash behind him. He glanced round in time to see the head of the girl who had shared the old man's breakfast table emerging from the water. A slim brown hand came up, palmed the wet hair from her eyes; then she turned over on her back and began threshing the water to a glittering froth, forging down the length of the pool towards him.

Five meters out, she stopped kicking and came gliding in to the edge under her own impetus. She reached up, caught hold of the tiled trough, and turned over. Her head and the tops of her shoulders appeared above the rim of the pool. She regarded Roger thoughtfully for a moment then smiled. "Hello there."

"Hi," said Roger.

"Not exactly crowded, is it?"

"They're all out on excursions," he said, noting that she had violet eyes. "Or taking a siesta."

"All except us."

"Yes," he said. "Except us."

"What's your name?"

"Roger Herzheim."

"Mine's Anne. Anne Henderson."

"I saw you at breakfast this morning," he said. "You were with. . . ."

She wrinkled her nose like a rabbit. "My husband. We saw you too."

Roger glanced swiftly round. "Is—is he coming for a swim too?"

"Pete? No, he's up at the observatory."

Roger nodded. "Are you here on holiday?"

She flicked him a quick, appraising glance. "Well, sort of. And you?"

"Mom's playing in the tourney. She's partnering Mr. Fogel."

"And what do *you* do, Roger?"

"Oh, I come along for the trips. In the vacations, that is."

"Don't you get bored?"

"Bored?" he repeated. "No."

The girl paddled herself along to the steps and climbed out. She was wearing a minute token costume of gold beeswing, and the sunlight seemed to drip from her. She skipped across and squatted down beside him. "May I see?" she asked, pointing to the micomicon.

"Sure," said Roger amicably. "I guess they'll seem a pretty old-fashioned bunch to you."

She peered at the spool index and suddenly said, "Hey! You've got one of mine there!"

"Yours?"

"Sure. I played Lady Fuchsia in *Titus* for Universal."

Roger stared at her with the sort of absorbed attention a connoisseur might have given to a rare piece of Dresden. "You," he repeated tonelessly. "You're Lady Fuchsia?"

"I *was,*" she laughed. "For nine solid months. Seven years ago. It was my first big part. Gail Ferguson. You'll find me among the credits."

"I wiped those off," he said. "I always do."

She glanced up at him sideways. "How old are you, Roger?"

"Twelve and a half."

"You like *Titus,* do you?"

"It's my favorite. Easily."

"And Fuchsia?"

He looked away from her out to where the distant aluminized dishes of the solar generators, having turned past the zenith, were now tracking the sun downhill towards the west. "I wish . . ." he murmured and then stopped.

"What do you wish?"

"Nothing," he said.

"Go on. You can tell me."

He turned his head and looked at her again. "I don't know how to say it," he muttered awkwardly. "Not without seeming rude, I mean."

Her smile dimmed a little. "Oh, go on," she said. "I can take it."

"Well, I just wish you hadn't told me, that's all. About you being Fuchsia, I mean."

"Ah," she said and nodded. There was a long pause, then: "You know, Roger, I think that's about the nicest compliment anyone's ever paid me."

Roger blinked. "Compliment?" he repeated.

"Really?"

"Really. You're saying I made Fuchsia come alive for you. Isn't that it?"

He nodded. "I guess so."

"Here. Close your eyes a minute," she said. "Listen." Her voice changed, not a lot, but enough, became a little dry and husky. *Sunflower,* she murmured sadly, *Sunflower who's broken, I found you, so drink some water up, and then you won't die—not so quickly anyway. If you do I'll bury you anyway. I'll dig a long grave and bury you. Pentecost will give me a spade. If you don't die you can stay. . . .*"

She watched his face closely. "There," she said, in her own voice. "You see? Fuchsia exists in me and apart from me: in you and apart from you. Outside of time. She won't grow older like the rest of us."

Roger opened his eyes. "You speak about her as if she was real," he said wonderingly.

"*Real!*" There was a sudden, surprising bitterness in the girl's voice. "I don't know what the word means. Do you?"

"Why, yes," he said, puzzled by the change in her tone. "You're real. So am I. And this"—he waved a hand towards the pool and the hotel—"that's real."

"What makes you so sure?"

He suspected that she was laughing at him. "Well, because I can touch it," he said.

"And that makes it real?"

"Sure."

She lifted her arm and held it out to him. "Touch me, Roger."

He grinned and laid his right hand lightly on the sun-warmed flesh of her forearm. "You're real, all right."

"That's very reassuring," she said. "No, I mean it. Some days I don't feel real at all." She laughed. "I should have you around more often, shouldn't I?"

She stood up, walked to the edge of the pool, flexed her coral-tipped toes and plunged in, neatly and without fuss.

Roger watched her slender body flickering, liquid and golden against the tiled floor. Then he snapped shut the micomicon, sprinted across the paved surround, and dived to join her.

The tourney was due to start at eight o'clock. Mrs. Herzheim was all a-flutter because she had just learnt that she and Harry Fogel were drawn against the co-favorites in her section for the first round. "Do you think it's a good omen, Roger?" she asked. "Be honest now."

"Sure, Mom. A block conversion at the very least."

"Wouldn't that be marvelous? Certain sure Harry would muff it though. Like that time in Reykjavik, remember? I could've *died!*" She leant close to the dressing table mirror and caressed her eyelashes with her mascara brush. "You going to watch So-Vi, honey?"

"I expect so."

Mrs. Herzheim eyed her reflection critically and then sighed. "That's the best you'll do, girl. Can't turn mutton into lamb. How do I look, baby?"

"You look great."

"That's my pet." She restored the mascara brush to its holder and zipped up her toilet case. "Well, all you can do for me now is to wish me luck, honey."

"Good luck, Mom."

She walked over to the bed where her son was lying, bent over and kissed him, but lightly so as to avoid smearing her lips. "I'll mouse in so's not to wake you," she said.

He smiled and nodded and she went out, wafting him a final fingertip kiss from the doorway.

Roger lay there for a few minutes, his fingers laced behind his head, and gazed up at the ceiling. Then he got up from his mother's bed and walked through into his own room. From the drawer of the bedside cabinet he took out his recorder, ran it back for a while and listened to the letter to his father which he had started taping the previous evening. He added a description of his visit to the harbor and was about to move on to his meeting with Anne Henderson when he suddenly changed his mind. He switched off the recorder, went back into his mother's room and retrieved his micomicon. Having slotted home the *Titus* cartridge, he uncoiled the earphones and screwed the plugs into his ears. Then he lay on the bed, reached down, pushed the button which activated the mechanism, and, finally, dragged the goggles down over his eyes.

At once the familiar magic began to work. The wraiths of milk-white mist parted on either side; gnarled specters of ancient trees emerged and lolloped past to the slow pacing of his horse; he heard the bridle jingle and the whispering waterdrops pattering down upon the drifts of dead and decaying leaves. At any moment now he would emerge upon the escarpment and, gazing down, behold by the sickly light of a racing moon, the enormous crouching beast of stone that was the castle of Gormenghast. Then, swooping like some huge and silent night bird down over the airy emptiness and up again towards the tiny pinprick of light high up in the ivied bastion wall, he would gaze in through the latticed, candlelit window of Fuchsia's room. He heard the telltale rattle of the pebble dislodged, and the mist veils thinned abruptly to a filmy gauze. He had reached the forest's edge. His horse moved forward one more hesitant pace and stood still, awaiting his command. He leant forward and was about to peer down into The Valley That Never Was when the vision dimmed abruptly and, a second later, had flickered into total darkness.

Roger swore, dragged off the goggles and hoisted the machine up from the floor beside the bed. The ruby telltale was glowing like a wind-fanned spark. He pushed the OFF button, and the light vanished. He stared glumly at the all-but-invisible thread, then activated the rewind mechanism and plucked the slender cartridge from its slot. Perhaps he would be able to find a repair depot in the town somewhere. It did not seem likely. He unfastened the earplugs, restored them to their foam-molded cache beside the goggles and closed up the insepction panel. Then he let himself out into the corridor and rode the elevator down to the reception hall.

His spirits revived a little when the desk clerk informed him that there was indeed a Universal Elektronix shop in the town. He added regretfully that, so far as he knew, it ran no all-night service. Roger thanked him and was about to head for the So-Vi lounge when an impulse persuaded him to change his mind and he walked out on to the terrace instead.

The sun had set a quarter of an hour past, but the western horizon was still faintly fringed with a pale violet glow that deepened precipitately to indigo. Directly overhead, the equatorial stars were trembling like raindrops on the twigs of an invisible tree. Roger walked slowly to the edge of the pool and gazed down at the quivering reflections of unfamiliar constellations. The air was soft and warm, balmy with the scent of spice blossom. From somewhere on the dark hillside below him he could hear the sound of a guitar playing and a girl's voice singing. He listened, entranced, and suddenly, unaccountably, he was struggling in the grip of an overwhelming sadness, an emotion all the more poignant because he could ascribe it to no specific cause. He felt the unaccustomed pricking of tears behind his eyelids and he stumbled away towards the dark sanctuary of the parapet which divided the pool area from the steeply terraced flower gardens.

There was a flight of steps, carpeted with some small creeping plant, which he remembered led down to a stone bench where earlier he had seen a small green lizard sunning itself. He scuttled down into the comforting shadows, skirted a jasmine bush and, with eyes not yet fully adjusted to the deeper darkness, felt his cautious way forward. The bench was occupied.

The shock of this discovery froze the sob in his throat. His heart gave a great painful leap and he stared, open-mouthed, at the suddenly glowing end of a cigar. There was a faint chuckle from the shadows, and a deep voice said, "Well, hello there. Roger, isn't it?"

Roger swallowed. "I'm sorry, sir," he gulped. "I didn't know. . . ."

"Sure you didn't. Why should you? So help yourself to a seat, son. And mind the bottle."

Roger hesitated for a moment, then edged carefully forward and sat down on the very far end of the bench.

"Saw you at breakfast, didn't I?" said the voice, and added, parenthetically: "The name's Henderson, by the way."

"Yes, sir," said Roger. "I know. You're The Master."

"Ah," said the voice thoughtfully. There was a long pause, then: "So, tell me, what brings you out roaming in the gloaming?"

Roger said nothing.

"Me, I come to look at the stars," said the old man. "That sound crazy to you?"

"No, sir."

The cigar flower bloomed bright scarlet and slowly faded. "Well, it does to a lot of people," said the deep voice, once more disembodied.

"Not to me," said Roger, surprised to hear how firm his own voice sounded.

There was a clink of glass against glass, followed by a brisk gurgle. "Care for a mouthful of wine?"

"No, thank you, sir."

There was a moment of silence and then the sound of a glass being set down again. "I gather you met Anne this afternoon."

"Yes, sir."

"You like her?"

"Yes, sir," Roger affirmed fervently.

"Beautiful, isn't she?"

Roger said nothing, partly because he could think of nothing to say, partly because he had just realized that his recollection of touching Anne's sun-warmed arm had been a primal cause of his sudden loneliness.

"Well, she is," said The Master. "And let me assure you, Roger, I know what I'm talking about."

"Yes, she's lovely," murmured Roger, and wondered where she was now.

"Beauty isn't just *shape,* boy. It's spirit too. A sweet harmony. Did you know that?"

"I—I'm not sure I know what you mean, sir."

"Well, take The Game. What grade are you, Roger?"

"Thirty-second Junior, sir."

"Ever make a clear center star?"

"I did nearly. About a year ago."

"How'd it feel?"

"I don't really know, sir. It just sort of happened. I wasn't even thinking about it."

"Of course not. It's a sort of natural flow. You lose yourself in it. That's the secret of The Game, boy. Losing yourself." The cigar tip described a rosy, fragrant arabesque in the air and ended up pointing toward the heavens. "Out there beyond Eridanus. That's where I found that out. Might just as well have stayed at home, hey?" Again the glass clinked. "How old are you, son?"

Roger told him.

"Know how old I am?"

"No, sir."

"Take a guess."

Roger groped. "Sixty."

The Master gave a brusque snort of laughter and said, "Well, I'm surely flattered to hear you say so, Roger. Tell me, do the names Armstrong and Aldrin mean anything to you?"

"No, sir."

The Master sighed. "And why should they, indeed? But when I was your age, they were just about the two most famous names on this whole planet. '68 that was—the year all the kids in our neighborhood grew ten feet tall overnight!" He gave another little mirthless snort. "We were the ones who bought the dream, Roger, the whole goddamn, stardream package, lock, stock and barrel. And in the end one or two of us even got there. The chosen few. Hand-picked.

Know what they called us? Knights of the Grail!" He spat out into the darkness, and a moment later the tiny furnace of the cigar glowed bright and angry as he dragged hard at the invisible teat.

"Like Sir Lancelot and Sir Gawain?" suggested Roger timidly.

"Maybe," said The Master. "All I know is they told us we'd been privileged to live out man's eternal dream on his behalf. And we believed them! Thirty-nine years old I was, boy, and I still swallowed that sort of crud! Can you credit it?"

Some small creature rustled dryly in the jasmine bush and was silent again. Down below in the scarf of shadow that lay draped across the shoulder of the hill between the hotel and the twinkling lights of the town, the sound of the girl's voice came again, singing sweetly and sadly to the accompaniment of the plucked strings.

Roger said, "What was it *really* like out there, sir?"

There was a pause so long that Roger was beginning to wonder whether the old man had heard his question, then: "There comes a moment, boy, when for the life of you you can't pick out the sun from all the rest of them. That's when the thread snaps and you slip right through the fingers of God. There's nothing left for you to relate to. But if you've been well-trained, or you're as thick as two planks, or maybe just plain lucky, you come through that and out on the other side. But something's happened to you. You don't know what's *real* anymore. You get to wondering about the nature of Time and how old you *really* are. You question everything. But *everything*. And in the end, if you're like me, the dime finally drops and you realize you've been conned. And that's the second moment of truth."

"Conned?"

"That's right, son. Conned. Cheated. Hood-winked. Look." He took the cigar from between his lips and blew upon the smoldering cone of ash until it glowed bright red. "Now what color would you say that was?"

"Why, red, of course."

"No. I'm telling you you're wrong. That's blue. Bright blue."

"Not *really*," said Roger.

"Yes, really," said The Master. "You only say it's red because you've been told that's what red is. For you blue is something else again. But get enough people to say that's blue, and it *is* blue. Right?"

"But it's still red, really," said Roger, and gave a nervous little hiccup of laughter.

"It's what it is," said The Master somberly. "Not what anyone *says* it is. That's what I discovered out there. Sometimes I think it's all I did discover."

Roger shifted uneasily on the stone bench. "But you said. . . ." he began and then hesitated. "I mean when you said before about spirit . . . about its being beautiful. . . ."

"That too," admitted The Master. "But it's the same thing."

Was it? Roger had no means of knowing.

"Spirit's just another way of saying "quality"—something everyone recognizes and no one's ever defined. You can recognize quality, can't you, Roger?"

"I—I'm not sure, sir."

"Sure you're sure. You recognized it in Anne, didn't you?"

"Oh, yes."

"I suspect it's what you were out looking for down by the harbor this morning. It's what brought you out here tonight when you could have been sitting there snug and pie-eyed in front of the So-Vi with all the rest of the morons."

"My micomicon broke," said Roger truthfully.

The Master chuckled. "You win, son," he said.

"Did you know that Anne was Lady Fuchsia in *Titus Groan?*"

"She was?"

"Yes. She told me this afternoon. I was going to see if it seemed any different now I know."

"Ah," said The Master. "And was it?"

"I don't know. The spool broke before I got to her."

"That's life, son," said The Master, and again gave vent to one of his explosive snorts of laughter. "Just one long series of broken spools. You're here for the tourney, are you?"

"Mom is."

"And your father?"

"He's in Europe—Brussels. He's a World Commodity Surveyor. He and mom are separated."

"Ah." The sound was a verbal nod of understanding.

"I get to go on vacation with him twice a year. We have some great times together. He gave me the micomicon. He's fixing a clipper trip for us next spring."

"You're looking forward to that, are you?"

Roger sighed ecstatically, seeing yet again in his mind's eye the silver-winged sea-bird dipping and soaring over the tumbling, trade-piled Atlantic hills, wreathed in spraybows.

"You like the sea?"

"More than anything," avowed Roger. "One day I'm going to be master of my own clipper."

The cigar glowed and a pennant of aromatic smoke wavered hesitantly in the vague direction of far-off Eridanus. "That's your ambition, is it?"

"Yes, sir," said Roger simply.

"And how about The Game?"

Before Roger could come up with an answer, a voice called down from the terrace above them: "Hey! Isn't it time you were getting robed-up, Pete?"

"I guess it must be, if you say so," responded The Master.

"Guilio's in the hall already. Who's that down there with you?"

"A fan of yours, I gather."

"Roger?"

"Hello," said Roger.

With a faint groan The Master rose from the bench, dropped his cigar butt on the stone-slabbed parterre and screwed it out beneath the sole of his shoe. Then he picked up his glass and the almost empty wine bottle. With eyes now fully accustomed to the gloom, Roger saw that the old man was bowing gravely towards him. "I must beg you to excuse me, Roger," he said, "but as you will have realized, duty calls. I have greatly enjoyed our conversation. We shall meet again. Perhaps tomorrow, heh?"

"Thank you, sir. Good luck."

"Luck?" The Master appeared to consider the implications of the courtesy for a moment. He smiled. "It's a long, long time since anybody wished me that, Roger. But thank you, nontheless."

Mercifully the darkness hid the bright flush of mortification on the boy's cheeks.

The Master and his challenger, Guilio Romano Amato, sat facing each other on a raised dais at one end of the tourney hall, separated from the other players by a wide swath of crimson carpet and the token barrier of a thick, gilded cord. On the wall above their heads a huge electronic scoreboard replicated the moves in this, the third session of the Thirty-Third World Kalire Championship.

Besides the two contestants seven other people shared the dais: the Supreme Arbitrator, The Master's two Seconds, Amato's Seconds, and the two Official Scorekeepers, one of whom was Anne. They all sat cross-legged on cushions at a discreet distance from the two principals. If they were conscious that their every movement, every facial expression, was being relayed by satellite to a million Kalire temples around the world, they evidenced no sign of it. They dwelt apart, isolated, enthralled by the timeless mystery and wonder of The Game of Games, the Gift from Beyond the Stars.

Into those silent, fathomless, interstellar reaches, the mere contemplation of which had once so terrified Pascal, Man in the person of The Master had dared to dip his arm. Two full centuries later, long after he had been given up for dead, he had returned to Earth, bearing with him the inconceivable Grail he had gone to seek.

He had emerged to find a world exhausted and ravaged almost beyond his recognition—a world in which the fabulous mission of *The Icarus* had dwindled to little more than an uneasy folk memory of what was surely the purest and most grandiloquent of all the acts of folly ever perpetrated in the whole crazy history of the human race.

When the great starship, scorched and scarred from its fantastic odyssey, had finally dropped flaming out of the skies to settle as gently as a seed of thistledown upon its original launching site on the shore of Lake Okeechobee, few who witnessed its arrival could bring themselves wholly to believe the evidence that was so manifestly there before them. The huge, tarnished, silver pillar standing there among the rusting debris and the crumbling gantries whispered to them of those days, long since past, when their forefathers still had the capacity to hope.

A hastily convened reception committee had driven out to welcome the wanderers home. Grouped in a self-conscious semicircle on the fissured and weed-ribbed concrete of the ancient launch pad, the delegation stood waiting for the port to open and the Argonauts to descend.

At last the moment came. The hatch inched open, slowly cranking itself back to reveal a solitary figure standing framed in the portal and gazing down upon them.

"Who is it?" They whispered to one another. "Dalgleish? Martin? No, I'll swear that's Henderson himself. God, he hardly looks a day older than the pictures, does he? Are you *sure* it's him? Yeah, that's Henderson all right. Christ, it doesn't seem possible, does it?"

And then someone had started to clap. In a moment everyone had joined in, beating the palms of their hands together in the dry, indifferent air.

Thirty feet above them, Peter Henderson, Commander of *The Icarus,* heard the strange, uncoordinated pattering of their applause and slowly raised his left hand in hesitant acknowledgement. It was then that some sharp-eyed observer noted that beneath his right arm he was carrying what appeared to be an oblong wooden box.

At first practically nobody took Henderson seriously, and who could blame them? Yet the memory banks of *The Icarus* appeared to confirm much of what he said. The gist of it was that out there, beyond Eridanus, on a planet they had called "Dectire III," they had finally discovered that which they had gone forth to seek. The form it took was that of a fabulous city which they called "Eidothea," a city which, if Henderson was to be believed, was nothing less than all things to all men. It was inhabited by a race of gentle, doe-eyed creatures who differed from themselves only in being androgynous and in possessing an extra finger upon each hand. They were also, by human standards, practically immortal. The Eidotheans were the professed devotees of an hermaphrodite deity they called Kalirinos, who, they maintained, held sway over one half of the existing universe. The other half was the ordained territory of her counterpart (some said her identical twin) Arimanos. Kalirinos and Arimanos were locked in an eternal game of Kalire (The Game) whose counters were nothing less than the galaxies, the stars and the planets of the entire cosmos. By reaching Eidothea, humanity, in the persons of the crew of *The Icarus,* had supplied the evidence that their species was ready to join The Game and, by so doing, to take another step up the evolutionary ladder.

There had followed a period of roughly six months devoted to their initiation and instruction in the rudiments of Kalire, at the end of which Henderson alone had gained admission to the very lowest Eidothean rank of proficiency in The Game—a grade approximately equivalent by our own standards to the First Year Primary Division. After his victory he had been summoned before the High Council, presented with his robe of initiation, with the board marked out in the one hundred and forty-four squares, each of which has its own name and ideogram, and with the box containing the one hundred and forty-three sacred counters, colored red on one side and blue on the other, which alone constitute the pure notes from which the divine harmonies of The Game of Games are derived. "And now you shall return to your own world," they had told him, "and become the teacher of your people. Soon, if we have judged correctly, your world will be ready to take its place in the timeless federation, and Kalirinos will smile upon you."

Henderson had protested passionately that he was wholly unworthy of such an honor, but the truth was that he could not bear the thought of having to tear himself away from the exquisite delights of Kalire, which, like those of the fabled lotus, once they have been enjoyed, must claim the soul forever. However, the Eidotheans had seemingly been prepared for this. The commander was placed in a mild hypnotic trance, carried aboard *The Icarus,* and the ship's robot brain was instructed to ferry him back to his own planet. The rest of the crew were graciously permitted to remain behind in Paradise.

Within the terms of the eternal symbolic struggle between Kalirinos and Arimanos (and certainly against all the odds), the conversion of the Earth was accomplished with a swiftness roughly commensurate to the reversal of a single counter upon the Divine Board. Within twenty-four hours of his setting foot once more upon his native soil, Commander Henderson had been interviewed upon International So-Vi. There, before the astonished eyes of about a billion skeptical viewers, he had unfolded his board, set down his four opening counters in the prescribed pattern, and had given an incredulous world its very first lesson in Kalire.

The Japanese, with their long tradition of Zen and Go, were the first to become enmeshed in the infinite subtleties of The Game, and within a matter of weeks the great toy factories of Kobe and Nagoya were churning out Kalire sets by the million. The Russians and Chinese were quick to follow. And then—almost overnight it seemed—the whole world had gone Kalire-crazy. It leapt across all barriers of language and politics, demanding nothing, offering everything. Before it armies were powerless, creeds useless. Time-hallowed mercenary values, ancient prejudices, long-entrenched attitudes of mind—all these were suddenly revealed as the insubstantial shadows of a childhood nightmare. Kalire was all. But was it a religion, or a philosophy, or just a perpetual diversion? The answer surely is that it was all these things and more besides. The deeper one studied it, the more subtle and complex it became. Layer upon layer upon layer of revelation awaited the devotee, and yet there was always the knowledge that however profoundly he delved he would never uncover the ultimate penetralia of the mystery.

Soon international tourneys were being organized, and the champions started to emerge. They too competed among themselves for the honor of challenging Peter Henderson. The first contender so to arise was the Go Master, Subi Katumo. He played six games with Henderson and lost them all. From that point on Henderson was known simply as "The Master." He traveled the world over playing exhibition games and giving lectures to rapt audiences. He also founded the Kalirinos Academy at Pasadena, where he instructed his disciples in those fundamental spiritual disciplines so vital to the mastery of the art of Kalire and into which he himself had been initiated by the Eidotheans. He wrote a book which he called *The Game of Games* and prefaced it with a quotation taken from "The Paradoxes of the Negative Way" by St. John of the Cross—

In order to become that which thou are not,
Thou must go by a way which thou knowest not. . . .

The *Game of Games* became a world best-seller even before it had reached the bookshops, and within six months of publication had been translated into every language spoken on Earth.

And so Henderson grew old. Now, in the thirty-fourth year of his return, at the physical age of seventy-eight, he was defending his title yet again. His challenger, Guilio Amato, the twenty-eight-year-old Neapolitan, was the premier graduate from the Kalirinos Academy. In his pupil's play The Master had detected for the first time a hint of that ineffable inner luminosity which others ascribe to genius but which he himself recognized as supreme quality. Having recognized it, he dared to permit himself the luxury of hoping that his long vigil might at last be drawing to its close.

So far, they had played two games of the ordained six: one in Moscow and one in Rome. The Master had won both. But in each, in order to ensure victory, he had had to reach deeper than ever before into his innermost resources for a key to unlock his pupil's strategy. Now the third game had reached its critical third quarter. If The Master won (and who could doubt that he would?), the title would remain his. Even if, by some miracle, Amato managed to win the three remaining games, the resulting draw would still count as a victory for the title holder. To state the matter in a way wholly foreign to the spirit of the contest—let alone of Kalire itself—to keep his chances alive, Amato had to win this third game.

Such was the situation when The Master, having entered the hall, bowed to the Supreme Arbitrator, sat down, touched hands formally across the board with his challenger and then accepted the envelope containing Amato's sealed move. He opened it, scanned the paper, nodded to his pupil, and permitted himself the ghost of a smile. It was exactly the move he had expected. He leant forward and placed a blue counter upon the designated square. On the display board above their heads a blue light winked on and off. A faint sigh went up from the main body of the hall. The struggle was rejoined.

Immediately after breakfast the following morning, Roger took his micomicon down to the depot in the town and left it for the broken spool to be repaired. Having been assured that it would be ready for him to collect within the hour, he elected to retrace his path of the previous day, wandering out along the stone-flagged quay to where the mole jutted out across the harbor mouth.

The morning sun was shining just as brilliantly upon the flanks of the volcanic hills and scooping up its shimmering reflections from the restlessly looping wavelets in the inner basin; the brightly shawled women were still crying out to each other in their strange parrot-patios from their ornate balconies; the gulls were still shrieking and swirling as they dived for the scraps; ostensibly it was all just as it had been the day before. And yet the boy was conscious that, in some not quite definable way, things were subtly different. Something had changed. Frowning, he scanned the horizon for signs of clippers plying the trade route but could see nothing. Then, moved by a sudden impulse, he clambered over the parapet and scrambled down the rocks to the ledge where he had last seen the two boys fishing.

There were dried fish scales glinting like chips of mica on the rocks, and he picked one or two of them off with his fingernail. Having examined them, he flipped them into the green, rocking waters below him. Then he squatted down, cupped his chin in his hands and stared down at the flickering shadows of the little fish as they came darting to the surface attracted by the glittering morsels.

He thought of Anne finning her golden way across the bottom of the sunlit pool, and from there his memory winged on to the curious conversation he had had with the old man. As he started to recall it, he began to realize that it was his recollection of their meeting in the darkness which had contrived to insinuate itself between him and the brilliant scene about him. "It's what it *is,* not what anyone *says* it is." What was that supposed to mean? And how could red *be* blue? Even if everyone *called* it blue, it would still *be* red. Or would it? A sharp splinter of sunlight struck dazzling off a wave straight into his eyes. He covered them with his hands, and suddenly, bright as an opal on his retina, he seemed to see again the glowing spark of The Master's cigar and above it the shape of the bearded lips blowing it brighter. Yet, even as he followed the point of light, its color began to change, becoming first mauve, then purple, and finally a brilliant aquamarine. And yet, indisputably, it was still the original spark.

He opened his eyes wide, blinked, and gazed about him. As he did so, he heard a voice calling down to him from above. He looked up and saw the silhouette of a head against the arching blue backdrop of the morning sky. He screwed up his eyes, smiled, and shook his head.

The man's voice came again, and Roger guessed it must be one of the waiters from the hotel. He spread his hands helplessly. *"No habla Espanol,* senor," he tried. *"Scusi. Estoy Americano."*

The man laughed. "I was only asking what it was like down there," he said in perfect English.

Roger shrugged. "Well, it's OK. I guess," he said. "If you like sitting on rocks, that is."

"Nothing I like better. Mind if I join you?"

"Sure. Come on down."

The man stepped over the low parapet and descended, sure-footed, to the ledge. Once there, he glanced about him, selected a smoothish rock and sat down, letting his long legs dangle over the waters. He drew a deep breath and let it out in a luxurious sigh. "That's great," he murmured. "Just great."

Roger scrutinized him out of the tail of his eye. He was dark-haired, his face was tanned, and he had pale smile creases at the corners of his eyes and mouth. Roger placed him as being in his middle twenties. "Are you here for the tourney?" he asked.

"That's right."

"I thought you must be."

"How so? I speak a pretty fair Espanol, don't I?"

"Yes. I guess so. But you're not Spanish, are you?"

"No."

"Where are you from?"

"California mostly."

Roger poked his little finger up his nose and scratched around thoughtfully for a moment. Then he glanced sideways at the newcomer, removed his finger and said, "Would you mind if I asked you a question?"

"Well, that all depends, doesn't it? I mean there are questions and questions."

"Oh, it's not personal," said Roger hastily.

"Then I'd say there's just that much less chance of my being able to answer it. But go ahead anyway."

Roger pointed across the inner harbor to where a woman in a flame-colored shawl was leaning over a fisherman on the water below her. "Do you see that woman in the red dress?" he asked.

The man followed his pointing finger. "I see her," he said.

"If I said she was wearing a *blue* dress, would I be right or wrong?"

The man glanced at him, and his brown eyes widened in fractional astonishment. "Would you mind repeating that?"

Roger did so.

"Yes, I thought that's what you said." The dark head turned and he stared again at the woman. "A *blue* dress?" he repeated. "What kind of a crazy question is that, for Godsake?"

"I don't know," Roger confessed. "But last night The Master told me that if enough people said red was blue, then it *was* blue."

The young man turned and stared at him. "Come again. *Who* said it?"

"The Master. I was talking to him out in the hotel garden after supper last night. But what I'm wondering is, if there's only *two* people and one says a thing's red and the other says its blue—well, what *is* it?"

The young man lifted his right hand and drew it slowly across his mouth. "He said red *was* blue?"

"Well, not exactly. He said it's what it is. He said it's not *really* red or blue or anything—except itself."

The young man's eyes had taken on a curiously opaque expression, and though Roger knew he was looking *at* him, he also knew he wasn't really seeing him. "I guess it's a pretty dumb sort of question," he said at last. "But, I don't know, somehow it's been bothering me."

"How's that?"

"It's just been bugging me, that's all."

"Yes, I can see that." The young man nodded. "So. What kind of an answer are you hoping for?"

"I don't know."

"What's your name, son?"

"Roger. Roger Herzheim."

"Well, Roger, I don't know that I can help. But how's this for a start? Let's say there are *things* and there are the *names* of those things. Right? Well, it's from the names we derive our *ideas* of the things. D'you follow?"

Roger nodded.

"OK. Now if we play around with the *ideas* for long enough, then, sure as hell, we'll get to believing that the ideas *are* the things. But they're not. Not really. The things are the things themselves. They always have been and, I guess, they always will be. It's a pretty profound truth really. At least that's what I think he was saying. But, hell, Roger, I could be *way* out."

Roger nodded rather doubtfully, and as he did so, his attention was caught by a sudden silver flickering far out on the eastern horizon. "Hey! Look!" he cried. "That's the first today! Just look at her *go!*"

The young man grinned broadly as he turned and gazed out to sea. "Yep, she's a real beauty," he said. "*Leviathan* class, I'd guess."

"*Leviathan?*" echoed Roger scornfully. "With five t'gallants? Why sure she's an *Aeolian*. And on the Barbados run too. Do you know that bird can *average* thirty knots?"

"Thirty knots, eh?" repeated the young man reverently. "You don't say so? Incredible!"

Half an hour later they strolled back into town to collect Roger's micomicon. As they were walking up the main street, Roger heard someone cry out: "Guilio! Where the helluv you *been*, man? I've been scouring the whole goddamn *town* for you! Tuomati's done a depth analysis of the whole Mardonian sector and he reckons he's found us some real counter chances."

"That's great, Harry," said the young man, with what seemed to Roger rather tepid enthusiasm. "Well, *ciao,* Roger. I'm really glad to have met you. I surely won't ever again mistake a *Leviathan* for an *Aeolian.*"

Roger smiled and waved his hand shyly, but Guilio Romano Amato was already striding away up the hill deep in conversation with his Second.

Roger spent the afternoon beside the pool hoping that Anne would reappear. She never did. Nor did she show up in the hotel dining room for the evening meal. Roger accompanied his mother up to their bedroom and, in response to her query as to how he intended to spend his evening, told her that he thought maybe he'd look in at the Spectators' Gallery for a while.

"I'm truly flattered to hear it, honey. But isn't *Clippers* on So-Vi tonight?"

"Sure it is. But not till ten. So I thought I'd finish off my letter to dad first, then take in a bit of the tourney. You've drawn 58, haven't you?"

"That's right, pet. Board 58, Section 7. I'll give you a wave."

It was not until his mother had wafted him her ritual kiss and left the apartment that it occurred to the boy to wonder why he had not told her of either of his meetings with the two champions.

At nine o'clock he rode the elevator down to the first floor and followed the indicators to the Spectators' Gallery. The sign STANDING ROOM ONLY was up, but Roger contrived to squeeze his way in and found a place to squat down on one of the steep gangways. The general tourney had already been in session for over an hour, but The Master and his challenger had only just taken their seats on the dais, and the red light which marked The Master's sealed move was still winking on the display board. There was an almost palpable atmosphere of tension in the hall as Amato surveyed the field before him.

Roger glanced across at one of the monitor screens and saw a huge close-up of the young man's face. It could almost have been a death mask, so total was its stillness. Then the picture flicked over to the board itself and showed Amato's hand dipping into his bowl of counters. The whole vast hall had become as silent as though everyone had been buried beneath a thick, invisible blanket of snow.

Beneath Guilio's slim fingers the counter slowly turned and turned again. Red, blue; red, blue; red, blue; and then he had reached out and laid it quietly on the board. The tip of the index finger of his right hand lingered upon it for a long, thoughtful moment and then withdrew.

As the blue light sprang out on the display, there came a sound which was part whisper, part sigh, as the spectators let out their pent breath. And then, from somewhere down below out of Roger's view, in the section of the tourney which held the players of the Premier Grade, there came the shocking sound of someone clapping. In a moment it had caught hold like a brush fire, and it was at least a minute before the controller's impassioned pleas for silence could make themselves heard above the unprecedented hubbub.

"What is it?" Roger demanded, shaking the arm of the person beside him. "What's he done?"

"I don't know, son. Frankly it seems crazy to me. But I guess it must be something pretty special to earn that sort of hand from the Premiers."

Roger turned to the monitor screen for enlightenment and was treated to a close-up of The Master's face. He was smiling the sort of smile that might have wreathed the face of a conquistador as he emerged from some high Andean jungle to find himself gazing down upon El Dorado. He leant across the board and murmured something to the impassive Amato. The concealed microphones picked up his voice instantly, and around the world was relayed one single vibrant word, the supreme accolade: *"Beautiful!"*

As he was fully entitled to do under the rules, The Master requested a statutory thirty-minute recess, which the Arbitrator immediately granted. The clocks were stopped; the two contestants touched hands; and The Master rose from his cushion, beckoned to Anne, and vanished with her through the curtained exit at the back of the dais.

The microphones picked up the whisper of conversation between Amato and his Seconds. As the cameras zoomed in on them, Roger saw that the two men were gazing at Guilio with what can only be described as awe. The young man simply shook his head and shrugged as if to signify that what they were saying scarcely concerned him. He was right.

That single move of Amato's has justly earned the title of "The Immortal," though, by today's standards, one must admit that it does have a distinctly old-fashioned air. The fact is that after an interval of close on thirty years, it is all but impossible to convey just how exceptional it was at the time it was first played. To appreciate it fully, one would have to re-create the whole electric atmosphere of that tourney and the seemingly impregnable position that The Master had established for himself in the match. It has been claimed with some substance that Amato's ninety-second move in the third game of the Thirty-Third World Series marked mankind's coming of age. But probably Amato himself came closer to the truth when he remarked to a reporter at the conclusion of the match: "Hell, man, it was just a matter of realizing that you can walk backwards through a door marked PUSH."

Twelve years later, in the preface to his monumental work *One Thousand Great Games,* Guilio elaborated upon this as follows: "I realized at that moment why The Master had chosen that particular paradox from St. John of the Cross as prefix to his *Game of Games.* Up to that instant in time, my whole approach to Kalire had been based upon the overwhelming desire to win. In order to become that which I was not (in my case, at that time, the winner of that vital third game), I had to go by a way which I did not know. There was only one such way available to me. I had to desire not defeat (that seemed inevitable anyway) but the achievement of a state of mind in which winning or losing ceased to have meaning for me. In other words, I had to gain access to the viewpoint from which Kalirinos and Arimanos are perceived to be one and the same being. In the timeless moment during which I turned that counter over between my fingers, I understood the significance of The Master's casual observation which I had heard for the first time that very morning: 'There is neither red nor blue, there is only the thing itself.' The thing itself was nothing less than the pure quintessence of The Game—an eternal harmonic beauty which obeys its own code of laws and whose sublime and infinite subtlety we are fortunate to glimpse perhaps once or twice in a lifetime. Let us call it simply 'the Truth of the Game.' At that moment I recognized it, and I laid my counter where I did for no other reason that my overwhelming desire to preserve the pattern forever in my own mind's eye."

So the shapes dissolve and reassemble in the swirl of Time. Everything changes; everything remains the same. We know now what we are, and some of us believe we have an inkling of what we may become.

Thirty-four years have passed since Guilio Romano Amato dethroned The Master and became The Master in his turn. He held the title for seven years, lost it to Li Chang, and then regained it two years later in the epic encounter of '57. In '62 the Universal Grade of Grand Master was established, and The Game moved into its present phase.

It only remains to outline briefly the subsequent histories of those persons who have been sketched in this little memoir.

First, The Master himself. He died peacefully at his home in Pasadena three years after relinquishing his title. At the time of his death his age by calendar computation was 273 years; by physical measurement, 81 years. Despite his insistence that he wished for no ostentatious ceremonial of any kind, his funeral was marked by a full week of mourning throughout the capitals of the world, and the memorial service at the academy was attended by the ambassadors from more than two hundred nations.

Guilio Amato retired from active play in '61 and since then has devoted his energies to supervising the work of the academy, of which he had been principal since The Master's death. His best known work—apart from the *Thousand Great Games* already mentioned—is undoubtedly his variorum edition of The Master's own *Championship Games*, which in itself probably constitutes the best standard world history of Kalire.

After The Master's death Anne Henderson returned to the theater, where she enjoyed a successful career up until her second marriage in '59. She now lives in Italy with her family. Her delightful *Memories of The Master* was published in '64.

Roger Herzheim never did become a clipper captain. At the age of fifteen he sat for a scholarship to the academy and soon proved that he had an outstanding talent for The Game. At 21 he won his first major tournament, emerging a clear four points ahead of all the other contestants. By 25 he was an acknowledged Master and acted as Second to Guilio Amato in his final Championship match. He gained his own Grand Master's Robe in '67 and was unsuccessful challenger for the World Title two years later. He won the Title conclusively in '71 and has held it ever since. But his days too are surely numbered. *Sic itur ad astra.*

(This fragment of autobiography was found among the papers of the ex-World Master, Roger Herzheim. He died on March 23, 2182, aged 68 years.)

CAN THESE BONES LIVE?

by Ted Reynolds

There have been several pieces in this collection dealing with the ethical and moral problems of a human society adrift in an infinite multi-world universe. This story sums it all up with one final smasher of a question on which hangs the entire argument for the existence of the intelligent species homo sapiens terrestris.

She spins in space, a mere point of view, and far away the stars wheel slowly about her. Curiosity builds, and with gathering intensity she strives to see, to pierce through those uncaring flares of silence. With effort comes strain, comes pain, mounting in linked agony with her struggle. The stars begin to shimmer and melt, the blackness coating the universe beyond them to ripple, thin, transluce . . . and then the pain mounts past endurance, she gives over in defeat; victorious night rolls back, a ponderous black drop framing meaningless lights. The pain wanders off somewhere, leaving her limp with exhaustion, and for ages she hangs bodiless in nothing, the stars sliding steadily past her vision, until once more she will be ready to try to see *through* . . .

She woke.

She lay on the soft slope of a swelling which rose gently in the middle of a wooded noplace. Sun beat down warmly on bare shoulders. She lay a while, blinking her eyes, the dream fading away as consciousness grew that something was wrong, unexpected.

Finally she sat up and looked at herself. In sudden panic reflex she whipped herself over and burrowed belly down, as best she could in the short grass. She lay there, breathing rapidly, as minutes passed with no sound but quiet wind and distant bird, no movement but that of a small industrious ant a few inches from her eyes.

Slowly raising her head, she scanned the horizon cautiously. Mellow dips and swells. Shrubs in flower, a few drifting cirrus high, high up. A bird flitted twittering across the sky. No one in sight.

Thank God. And she lying here in the open, stark naked . . .

Squirming on her stomach like a celluloid Indian, she negotiated her way to the nearest bush, where she squatted for a longer look around. Not a soul anywhere. How did she ever get herself into *this*! Well, first things first. Times enough to think of reasons after she'd found herself something to wear.

She reached the top of the rise; the world spread about her lovely, lonely, bare as herself. No house; no road. An opossum curled under a bush, ignoring her. She sat there in bewilderment, and gradually another thought grew in upon her, something else that didn't make sense, that wasn't quite right.

She had died. She clearly remembered her death.

By late afternoon, fear that someone would see her was being supplemented by fear that no one would. Still unclothed, but bearing a large portion of bush before her, she moved down the slope of a hill towards the rivers, lying beneath her in leisurely looping swaths which gleamed in the sunlight.

Anywhere in her part of the world, she thought, there would be some sort of town at the confluence of two rivers of this size. Here was nothing but the grassy slopes, studded with isolated groves of slender trees, slurring off along the river borders into marshes and mudflats where waterbirds splashed and fed. No river traffic; no jet trails; no.

It was now clear she was heading west, at least if the sun kept to the old path . . . if that *were* the old sun. At this point, she wasn't laying any odds.

When the moon rose, its familiar face told her she was on Earth after all. But wasn't it a shade too large? No, don't think about *that* one! It's just the right size.

Perhaps, she thought vaguely, she was Eve? Was Adam around the next bend? No, far more likely she was around the bend.

That night she huddled beside a fallen trunk; not for warmth, (she discovered for the first time, *emotionally*, that trees are not warm-blooded) but for the rough contact with something solidly actual. Staring blankly up into the featureless night, she retreated into her memories, recalling the tubes and needles and pains, the fading lights and voices and her dying. The last things she could recall were those instants of observing the operation from outside of her own body, and realizing even then this was only her mind's final defense mechanism to soften the inevitable annihilation—and she had *known* it was for keeps. So why hadn't it been? Why was she here? And why wasn't anybody else?

I can't hold a Jehoshaphat, she thought, all by myself, can I?

The night was warm, the trees stoically silent. The largest animal she had seen all day was a badgery or woodchuckish thing looking out of a hole in a clay bank. That kind of fear didn't touch her now. Just the one cry filled her mind as she fell asleep. How am I here at all; why aren't I still dead?

She didn't really expect a reply. She got one.

She was standing on the slope where she had first awakened, and was looking out across the world when the Roanei appeared, quite abruptly, as their habit always and everywhere is. She watched them as they debarked themselves and spread out for picnicking, and she understood them, as one will in a dream, and at the same time knew that neither the way they had arrived nor the way they looked would make the least bit of sense to her when she awoke. She couldn't even be sure if the Roanei were many, or was one.

One of them, or part of it, appeared at her side. A truly lovely little world, it indicated somehow, and, oh, my, it went on in exaggerated surprise as if an adult condescending to a child's make-believe, what have we here? It signified the ground at her feet where a minute gleam sparked the soil. It uncovered the gleam and withdrew a shining bone. The Roanei totality flowed around the spot to contemplate the discovery.

The one turned to her and waved the bone gently. So there was once a species of some accomplishment on this world, it rendered cheerfully, and now there are no more of it. How interesting. Reconstruction is in order. It tossed the bone on the earth, where it lay as the Roanei resurrected it, in that unique way of theirs, which they make appear so simple, and which perhaps really is simple, only they never let on how it's done. In a gradual, perhaps mildly obscene process the bone became her own unclad unconscious form.

One aspect of the Roanei turned to her dream portion and conveyed, you know we are nothing like this, but it will serve you well enough as symbol, all of this is metaphor, it chanted,

is metaphor,
is metaphor,
all of this is metaphor
for a somewhat complex reality.

It touched her forehead. Your questions will be answered, it remarked. Forever farewell. And they were gone.

At least that was as near as she could reconstruct the dream when she woke by the fallen log.

The dream stayed solidly with her as she wandered down the way of the river. It had been very real, had spoken with authority, not as one of the scribes. Either it was a message, a real answer to the question she had fallen asleep with, or her dreaming self now had resources of imagination she'd certainly never had her first time through life. She would rather have dreamed of frustrating cocktail parties and ominous taxicabs the way she'd used to.

An *authentic* dream? She wished there were some people around (among other reasons) to ask whether this fell within *their* range of experience. It might well be one of those numerous everybody-else-knows-it-happens-but-nobody-thought-to-tell-*me* phenomona.

She went on, and the further she went, the more people she didn't find, nor their leftovers. She found and munched berries, drank from the river, and didn't die a second time on the spot, though the diet hardly excited her. She went to some lengths to find *something* to wear at first, with the dogged persistence of an Edison trying electric light filaments. Eventually she found a kind of tree, from which the bark came off in fairly large slices, and lashed herself up in some of it with creepers. She called the tree 'birch' provisionally, and thought there might never be anyone to tell her if she had guessed right.

The vestments were rather unpleasant to wear, and already seemed a waste of time and modesty. She could no longer really believe there was anyone left to see or to know or to care.

It appeared a beautiful world, if one cared about such things. Summer, she supposed, nature at its most prodigal expansiveness. Nothing hovering here of Man, not even a dwindling fond memory. I wonder, she wondered, how they finally managed to do us all in, but she soon found she'd rather not think about that.

For several nights she carefully kept that, and all other questions, out of her mind as she composed herself to sleep. She wasn't ready for any more answers just yet.

Sometime during the second week of her second life she gave up on her leggings completely. They seemed quite superfluous. She decided to carve a diary on the bark instead.

She scratched with the sharp end of a stick.

"Dear Diary:

"In order to preserve my sanity, in case I've still got it, I shall write what occurs in proper order. Or in case, in my lonely senile years, I forget the earlier days of this second fleshy incarceration. Or rather, that I may inscribe the relevant facts within which lie the clues I may be someday able to decipher, as to the reason for my improbable situation. Or maybe for the hell of it. Anyway, I write.

"Item: what we used to call humanity is gone, extinct, obliterated. There's just me, alone, at a time seemingly long after the close of man's gory story. I have found some suspicious mounds, but within them, as deep as I've cared to dig, no paper, wood, or metal, nor plastic nor ceramic. A couple of bones. But for all I know, not even human bones.

"So I linger on, long after the multitudes have passed from off the stage of life. This, then, is a posthumanous diary.

"Ouch. That wasn't very successful.

"Hell, one tries to write pretty, even to a private diary, in the vague feeling that someone sometime will read the words. Even when I was a girl, locking my personal diary in my desk, screaming in wrath if my brother entered while I was writing, somehow I wrote for everybody, for posterity maybe. I winced at a grammatical lapse, an awkward phrase . . .

"What does it matter now? I'm everybody else's posterity, and they've left nothing for me to read.

"But I do seem to have strayed from the subject . . ."

Thus far took many hours, and endless pieces of bark. She realized she couldn't lug all that bark around with her. She also found she couldn't even make out a lot of what she'd just written. She gave up her diary.

A little later, threading through breast-high wild grasses down a shallow valley, her dream recurred to her, bound up somehow with trappings of guilt. She tried half-heartedly to dismiss it. So what if she couldn't remember dreams with such authentic auras from her earlier existence? Hadn't she been absolutely convinced by other auras, that afterwards, to her sorrow, had proved quite meretricious?

Still, she couldn't pass it off as just another dream. For one thing, if it was more than a dream, if it somehow embodied honest-to-God's-sake truth, then it was probably very important.

She sat down where she was amid the grasses and tried to work it out. If one quite impossible thing had happened—she *had* come back to life—then why not think of other impossible things? Like maybe the whole human race could be brought back.

If me, she thought, why not anybody else? Why not everybody else?

And then there would be plenty of people to read my diary. Isn't *that* worth something?

She lay on her back where she was. It was a moist day, and she stared up past the long stalks gratefully condensing droplets from the hazy air, to the heavy blade tips far above her, and thought hard. She thought all the afternoon, and finally fell asleep in the same spot with a single question, cut and hewed and placed upright in the forecourts of her mind.

"Can *everybody* be brought back to life the way I've been?"

And answer came, of a sort.

She stands on the Moon, on the harsh dead lunar soil, and watches the Earth in the sky, so beautifully smeared in its streaky whites, blues, browns, greens that her throat throbs with longing. It hangs up there in the black, unmoving, unwinking, and she watches it in the cold and the silence.

A speck of red, tiny but fluid, appears at the rim of the sphere, out of tune, oddly malignant. It grows, flings out ex-

tended filaments across the globe, which coalesce, puddle together, as the Earth slowly becomes tinged with crawling, hideous with roiling, bloated with loathsome red, until the last touch of green is extinguished; and at that moment the whole creeping cancerous red Earth . . . opens up . . . into a . . . perfect white blossom floating serene and still and beautiful on the face of darkness . . .

Do you really want it back the way it was, ask the lunar rocks in their barren silent idiom.

It's not clear why you'd want the whole race back, blazes the sun, shining down eternally, up top left center, but you can always ask; *not promising any reply.*

Ask once only, *that is, tinkle the constellations, strewn endlessly across forever. It is tedious to consider invalid requests. One individual per species is usually* quite *sufficient.*

And the Earth, silent blossom, silently whispers, be very sure before you ask. Cannot unwish wishes once wished. Remember . . .

And just before she wakes, one very brief glimpse of a withered hag, creeping under the weight of a string of sausages firmly welded to the tip of her nose.

That last touch might account for the intense irritation with which she awoke. It seemed to be rubbing it in a little *too* much!

She had been around long enough that the season seemed to be changing. With an abrupt memory of what winter would mean without civilized amenities, she headed south.

A few months of utter solitude, and she was about ready to take the Roanei up on their offer, or challenge, and ask for the return of humanity. But the terms in which the matter had been couched had somehow kept her up till now from requesting a total species regeneration. She hadn't been able to bring herself, quite, to fall asleep with that demand in the forefront of her thoughts.

She headed south, wondering if she were on the North American continent, or if that geographical distinction didn't mean anything any longer. She had no idea how long it had been since the Age of Man. Some animals and constellations were quite familiar to her, others she felt she should surely have been aware of it they'd existed before. But maybe not. There were no large animals, predatory or otherwise; she ate randomly, things bland but sustaining; she never grew ill. She passed various flora, fauna, and geography, and paid little attention, existing most often by choice in the world of her own thoughts. She played there-are-other-people-somewhere games till it hurt too much.

She wished she were a logical thinker, a scientist or something, rather than an ordinary nobody-special. Here they brought back one person, and perhaps the future existence of the whole race hung on the person's decisions, and it was only her. It didn't, somehow, seem very fair. She wasn't all that bright, why didn't they bring back Einstein or von Neumann or somebody, who could figure out what to do in these really rather unprecedented circumstances? I mean, she thought, if I've virtually got to decide whether to ask for the resurrection of the whole human race, hadn't I ought to be a better representative of the species? Why couldn't they have snagged Gandhi or Schweitzer?

She knew what she should do, she thought—ask them for the whole human race back. Then she wandered off into wondering if that included the ancient Romans and Egyptians, or just the last generation that went defunct. There'd be population problems again. She wondered if she'd be allowed to pick and choose . . . "no Albanians or Victorians, please" . . . and realized she was off the track again.

Why *not* ask for the race back? What countervailing factors were there? They said she could *ask*.

Not, she had to admit to herself, that she'd ever been a true mankind enthusiast. She'd liked some people, sure. But she'd never reached the point, never lived long enough, maybe never *would* have lived long enough, to accept the existence of others with that wholehearted acceptance with which she accepted her own.

Of course she felt very strongly the responsibility, (if her dreams weren't just dreams,) of being the one who *could* decide, any night now, whether humanity should be brought to life again. But humanity had never turned her on. Of course she would like someone, almost anyone, to talk to, to write a diary for, to show things to, to sleep with . . . that was not meant, that was to be censored, please ignore . . . surely, you understand what goes through the mind, through the body, when one is *alone*. Forgive . . .

Who was there to understand? Who to forgive?

She eventually came to a conclusion, and with it, came back to awareness of her surroundings. She had attained different types of foliage than she was used to, less stark and noble, more entwined and languorous; her images of the south, bayou and magnolia and mangrove, seemed to be closer. South, she thought, how much further?

She found some hammocky roots and made herself comfortable, determined to do this thing right. The onus had fallen on her, for whyever, and she would pick it up and get it over with. She must be cunning and clever, pit herself against the Roanei for the lives of her own unreborn species. These Roanei will have their price. For sufficient reason, they'll resurrect. Find the price, persuade them, convince them . . .

Sleepline, to be held into the night shadows. "What must we pay you for the rebirth of mankind? We'll pay you anything. Name the price."

And slept. And dreamed.

It crouches towering against the stars on a pinnacle ridge, far above her, black against the sky. Its clutching talons curve among the rocks, its hawk features jut proudly upwards against the cold sparks of fire. It is utterly awesome and arrogant.

She knows, in her dream that she sees the last, the resurrected specimen of the Mnestepoi. He is making his great pitch to the Roanei, and is he laying it on strong! Power he offers, in all four hands, and knowledge unimagined, and riches untold. It is a bit hard to follow, because it is full of concepts she can't quite get her mind around, but the idea that the Mnestepoi hold the riches of all yearning, the knowledge of all ages, the powers of the universe, comes through loud and clear. And all these will be for the Roanei alone, if they'll only bring the rest of the Mnestepoi back to life. The Roanei can rule the universe forever, cries out that thing on the crag, they will have the cosmic mastership the Mnestepoi had planned for themselves and almost attained, would have attained but for one little unforeseen accident which had erased them. All will be for the Roanei, the Mnestepoi will be their humble servants, if only they can live. If a few of them can live. If a single mate can live . . .

And from among the stars, from that distant wherever the Roanei have got to, comes the answer.

"What would we want with power, you call it, with riches, with knowledge? These mean nothing to us. We do not comprehend the value you put on these things, nor do we care. The answer to your request is no."

And with a shriek of despairing rage, the last of the Mnestepoi hurls himself with ravening fury at the sky, hangs clawing against the stars, and plunges to sickening destruction on the cliffs beneath.

It shook her up a bit, that dream. She felt at the time that that creature could actually deliver what he promised. If ever she had felt the cold beat of power, it was in the looks and the speech of that monster. She had to admit she was sort of glad that the Roanei didn't take him up on the proposal. Maybe she was being provincial, and the Mnestepoi were just grand folks when you got to know them, but still . . .

And she never thought again that the Roanei might be bribable—not with anything man had to offer . . .

She had stopped going south. She had run out of things she knew were good to eat, and had to face learning all over again, or staying up where things were more familiar. It had come to her with a sort of unpleasant realization that there wasn't a thing known to be poison that wasn't found out by a lot of people dying rather unpleasantly. As the last human being, there was need to be more careful of her existence. She'd have to accept a few cool nights.

So much for her half-planned scheme of getting across to Africa where her memory told her the Atlantic was narrower, (if she *was* in America, and if the continents hadn't drifted) and seeing if any traces of the pyramids or the Great Wall of China could still be traced. She'd stay around here, wherever that was, and try to make friends with the animals that looked like rabbits but acted like squirrels; they looked the most tamable. She'd never been much for pets before, but circumstances alter cases.

She couldn't forget her responsibility completely. It came creeping back into her mind in subtle ways, alternately making her curse herself, the Roanei, or the rest of humanity. Another day arrived when she realized she'd have to try again. She couldn't let her own hang-ups keep her from seeing if she could bring back humanity. It didn't matter what she thought of people, whether she liked them or not. It was a trust, like when her mother had given her money to buy something at the grocery, and she'd had to get what Mama wanted, even if she'd rather have had bubble gum instead. Anyway, if mankind can be brought back, she thought, it will have to include some psychoanalyst who can make me feel better about it all.

Man must be brought back; the Roanei have to be convinced we're worth saving. Why? Why indeed?

She walked to the top of a hill to sleep. She gazed out to where a shallow sea drowsed on the horizon. The climate was definitely softer this life, yes, and healthier. She never felt the need of constructed shelter. She lay down under the deepening evening blue and pondered her approach.

She planned her dream query, etched her question with all her subtlety, and the selective memory of an arts major the first time around. She ran over in her mind all that man had made of wonder and beauty, for it was all part of the question. She let her mind, dimming toward sleep, dip and soar over the finest she knew of man's creations; the spacious perspectives of the Taj Mahal, and the clumped hallelujah of Manhattan, Raphael's wistful Madonnas and the bleak clarity of Hokusai's ink line. She ran trippingly over Dante and Milton and Goethe, dipped into Keats, dabbled in Shelley, flirted with Swinburne, hovered over Blake, soaking in from each only the beauty, the feeling of joy she had received when she had first met them. In her preplanned tour she conjures up what she knows or imagines of Babylon and Athens and Samarkand, Louis XIV's Versailles and Charles II's London, Shakespeare and Michelangelo, Dostoevski and Klee and Melville and Miro and Bartok and Pynchon, and as she feels herself slipping into the nightly oblivion she rolls it all up in a single ball of ultimate question, a cry of the heart, "Can you let all this die? Don't you care to bring back all this creation, this searching for beauty and truth and loveliness . . . this *humanness* back?"

And she falls asleep. The hard thing in this case being to *avoid* certain humannesses.

And she dreams.

They are the Coronolee. What they look like is irrelevant. It is what they touch that matters. They stroke the rocks and the trees till they respond in joy and beauty. They build mild cities that fondle the seas and skies, plant gardens that woo the earth; and grow in skill and art and scope with the ages, till all they handle becomes a wonder and a delight. All that see the works of the Coronolee exclaim "Ahhh, yes!"

They soften their suns to mellow hues that gentle all they fall upon. They form worlds from which one would willingly never part, where momentary existence is a flowing environmental caress. They meet other races and speak to them and touch them and somehow, species with hard edges and callous beginnings and mean needs begin to warm and soften and flow in beauty.

And of a mere moment, as the universe plunges through time, the Coronolee are gone. Something had happened to them or been done to them or . . . anyway, it was so ugly, such *bad art, that they went quietly.*

And—how long after, who knows—the Roanei arrive and hear of the extinct Coronolee, still somewhat of an epic in that part of space at that time. And so, as they always do, the Roanei resurrect one member of that species, and leave it alone on the barren remains of one of the Coronol worlds, amid the relics and wreckage of departed splendour, and depart—leaving, of course, a dream-channel link. And the last of the Coronolee lives a short space, as their livespan goes, puttering about the shards of beauty, trying to set things to rights, and then asks from the depth of its heart and the height of its soul that its people might be brought back from nothingness to correct this ugliness. The Roanei hear immediately from the far places they were then in, and answer:

No. What value is there in the things your people have done? None of them matter to us at all.

And the dream link is broken forever. And the last Coronal dies, in shame and chagrin, at the ugliness of the world. And no one ever lives there again.

That was her dream. It was quite discouraging. In the face of what the Coronolee had achieved, even what she could rescue clinging to from the wrack of dream, what man ever did seemed not a little childish. If she'd ever loved anything human, it was the arts, but compared to what *they* were capable of, even Mozart and Seami looked like the triflings of a child that may amount to something someday if he ever grows up and doesn't get too snotty.

And *they* didn't impress the Roanei one smidgeon.

She had lost, she knew, another round.

She lived pleasantly enough under the trees, that might be oaks or beeches, or banyans for all she knew, surrounded by her squirabbits, and on the whole content. Time passed, usually without her noticing or being bothered by its passing, but once in a while she was reminded by something or other of time passing and duty undone, and went through a heavy guilt session.

It was really a bit chilling to think that she hadn't yet actually *asked* for humanity to be brought back yet. She did have some symptoms of growing older, and someday she might drop dead of an aneurysm or something, and there's the last chance gone for everybody that ever was. Even if *she* didn't much believe it's a chance, shouldn't she at least *try* it? Think of all the people who are dead forever, and just maybe her mere asking could bring them back.

Sometimes, now she could never bring herself to say it out loud but she thought it . . . sometimes she thought she just didn't want to bring anybody back. Did she really want any of them? Had they ever been at all important to her? Had she once been better off or more contented in the old human days?

On the other hand, she supposed she'd be very important to them, a sort of goddess at least, if she could have them all brought back . . . *if* they ever believed what she told them, that it was her that brought them back. She imagined all sorts of people would be quick to claim all kinds of things once they were brought back.

Finally, on the eve of a rare day of rolling thunder and rain, she looked out at the last fugitive wisps of sun through angry clouds, the first she'd seen of its light all day, and thought she had the answer. She dreaded using the dream channel again, but she would have to. She hoped it would be the last time.

She spent the evening thinking over the good and just and decent things men had (sometimes) done. She poured into a common pool her ideal portraits of Jesus and Buddha and Thomas Assisi and Florence Nightingale and little dutch boys at dikes and men in newspaper writeups who die saving children from burning buildings and her cousin Martha who broke an elbow getting a kitten out of a well. She wished she could add something of her own, but she well knew that she had never lived for anybody or died for anybody but herself. Maybe now she could make up for that. Alone on the wet earth, naked to the chill breeze, no human eye to see, she slept her question.

"I challenge you, Roanei. These are things men have done. Are you worse than man was? Can you do less for man than man, at his best, could do for his fellow man?"

She learned the answer.

It was early enough in the history of the cosmos that the

galaxies were not far strewn as yet, and blazed in the sky as thick as stars.

She dreamt the ancient story of the Toomeer, or so the Roanei termed them. They were already of age when the Roanei were young, and they guided the Roanei and taught and aided and nurtured them, as they did so many of the races that first came into being on the earlier worlds of the earliest suns. They gave unstintingly of their time and their energy and their sustenance, and yet never seemed to call guilt into existence, as if they were rewarded simply by being permitted to give.

And the Roanei, young and precipitous race, found itself abruptly on the rim of annihilation, despite their unique talent of resurrection, or rather because of it. For the races of a galaxy rose against the arrogance and the parsimony of the Roanei in the use of their gift, and descended upon them to erase them totally.

And at the point of doom, unexpectedly, the Toomeer were there, interposing themselves between the furious attackers and the fleeing Roanei. This race is young and foolish, said the Toomeer, but let it live. We should all be for life together, not death. If you must slay, we are here . . . slay us.

And the attacking races did. In their fury and hate for the Roanei, they destroyed the intervening Toomeer to the last member of the species. But by the time the path to the Roanei lay clear again, the bloodlust had died, and they were aghast at what they had done, and at the virtue of the race they had destroyed. And they slunk back to their various home-worlds and what became of them is instructive, but not part of the dream in question.

*But the Roanei followed their customary procedure. They resurrected one of the Toomeer, and told him he could re*quest *the resurrection of his species if he chose. Perhaps he never asked; certainly the Roanei never acted. They did not understand why the Toomeer had behaved in that suicidal manner, but presumably they had their own satisfactions in so doing. So the Roanei reasoned. The values of the Toomeer were as meaningless to them as those of the Mnestepoi or the Coronolee or Man. Of gratitude, they showed not a trace. The Toomeer have been extinct for many billion years.*

The next day was a mental seething. She sat or paced for hours, gnashing, weeping, boiling over. Those Toomeer were teachers and parents and *friends* to the Roanei, and if they were allowed to rot forever, after they had died for the Roanei, she figured she wasn't going to get far with an appeal to altruism.

In fact, she figured she'd give up.

No, wait. She could still *ask* them anyway.

Who was she trying to kid? The Roanei weren't just giving out life for the asking, that was clear. And she had never forgotten that she could ask only once; she kept remembering the sausages on the nose. She'd better hold off on that ultimate request a little longer. Once she'd pulled that, there'd be nothing left.

That night, still with fury smouldering in her breast, and an icier determination than she'd ever known in either of her lives, she stood a while, sniffing the scents she had come to know, feeling the rough bark of the trees, tasting fear and anger in the back of her throat. She did not know the answer, but she would find out. She lay down. Sleep was long in coming as she worried her question into place.

"Show me those races who *have* been granted rebirth. Why were *they* resurrected?"

It was a sleep profoundly empty of dream.

The dreamlessness had the authoritative aura of the dreams. She knew that itself was the answer.

There were no such cases. There never had been one.

She was somewhat hindered in the comments she wished to make to the Roanei by a lack of adequate knowledge of their progenitive processes or their personal antipathies. But she requested them quite strongly to be so kind as to attempt to reproduce themselves in liaison with that lifeform most unbearably repugnant to them.

She would be damned if she'd give such moral monsters the satisfaction of seeing her cringe. She'd been long taken for a sucker, but that was over. Now she'd just have to forget it.

She was sorry for the rest of mankind, but now she knew that nothing she could have done would have brought them back anyway.

Sadists!!!

Years passed over her head, long in the passing, short in looking back on them. She was getting old.

At times the thought flirted with her mind . . . should she not at least try? There is always a first time, people used to say, and perhaps the Roanei might make their first exception in favor of man.

She wouldn't care to bet on that, though.

She had traveled long, and then settled long, developed a spot that was particularly hers in a world that was all hers in general, showed elderly crotchets to her line of squirabbits, forgot at times who and where she was.

A night came at last when, sitting on the shore of her own peculiar lake, she was in terror of death.

It had almost had her that day and was still waiting, invisibly final, in the shadows. She could no longer promise herself the whole night.

She felt she saw herself as she truly was—a lonely, selfish old woman. She never had cared for her fellow men. They could not have had a more indifferent advocate than herself.

She would not live forever. She felt an aura that told her she would not live out the next sleep. Let her at least go knowing she had done what she could. Let her pray for man to the Roanei.

The stars wheeled overhead. She could not do it. She *could not*! She was terrified to sleep without, and yet she could not. All her life, both her lives, spun about her, and all the other lives waiting for her to speak out for them, and she could not. What kind of abominable thing, then, she thought, must I be?

The east paled, she supposed it was the east, though it was only its paling that had ever told her so, and soon the sun would rise again. She could stay awake no longer, but at last she had brought her soul to a balance she could live or die with.

Lying on the shore of the lake, she wearily closed her eyes.

She did not think the Roanei ever granted wishes.

But if she could get only one wish, she would wish big.

She would wish alive something the universe needed badly, something the Roanei could not comprehend. She would wish for humanity; but not for Man.

She thought, her withered cheeks wet with her last tears, "Roanei, I wish for the rebirth of the Toomeer, they who gave themselves to death that you yourselves might live."

For the last time she moved in the landscapes of responsive dream, where human symbols clothed alien reply.

Wearily she struggled across the floor of the barren valley. The hummocks were strewn with countless bones, and they were white, and they were very dry. At a turning in the path she came across a dwarf. It squatted among the bones and stared up at her.

"Good evening," the dwarf said quietly.

"Good evening."

"You are quite certain of your wish?" it asked. "This is forever, you know. You wish for the rebirth of a race you do not know, rather than your own?"

She nodded mutely.

The dwarf's face puckered oddly. "This is very hard to understand. Did you hate your own kind so?"

"I didn't hate," she said, "but I never learned to love. I didn't have the Toomeer to teach me," she added with a touch of bitterness.

"Do you hate us, *then?" asked the dwarf.*

"I am trying not to hate anything for a few minutes more, and then it won't matter," she said.

The dwarf looked down at its gnarled palms, spat into them and wiped them on its thighs.

"The universe is full of creatures," it said slowly, "and all live their separate lives and crave their varied wants and hold their distinct values, and little do we comprehend or sympathize with any of them. One thing we find always and everywhere. When an individual is brought back to brief existence, and permitted to request racial rebirth, it invariably wishes the return of its own species. Each being appreciates the existence of its own kind, shares their particular values. We never grant such requests. We are rather . . . amused."

It looked at her, its eyes almost pleading. "But you . . . you have shamed us."

It was silent awhile, rocking back and forth on its haunches, considering.

"If you ask for rebirth," it said at last, "not for your own kind, but for another, we can only assume that, however little we can appreciate the reasons for such requests, there is something in that other race of higher and more universal value than the contingent preference of a single species. We feel we must grant such a request. For what is higher, should be."

The dwarf tightened its lips. "We can restore life when we choose. But the cost to us is high. High not in your concepts of money, or time, or energy, but in terms you could not grasp, though to us they are of highest importance. But somehow at this moment, although we feel the costs, we shall ignore them. Your request is granted, then. The race of the Toomeer shall live again, as they did when we were young."

She bowed her head. "Thank you," she said softly.

And the heavens darkened with a crash as a sheet of lightning caromed from end to end of the heavens above them, and out of the darkness and the lightning a voice spoke in rolling thunder.

"WE HAVE NO WISH NOR NEED TO RETURN," boomed out the voice, awesome beyond belief and yet more human than she had ever heard from the lips of men. "FOR CYCLES WE HAVE BEEN CONTENT TO REMAIN FAR BEYOND YOUR VIEW. EVER SINCE THE EVENT YOU PRESUMED OUR ANNIHILATION WE FOUND THAT THE VALUES WE HAD HELD FOR THEIR OWN SAKE WERE NOT AS EPHEMERAL AS WE HAD FEARED, FOR THEY ARE CHERISHED IN A REALITY YOU HAVE NOT YET GLIMPSED. WE OURSELVES WERE SURPRISED."

The thunder softened to an organ richness.

"WE HAVE LONG WISHED YOU TO JOIN US, ROANEI, BUT UNTIL YOU RECOGNIZED THE NEED, WE COULD NEITHER REACH NOR INSTRUCT YOU. WHAT YOU HAVE THIS DAY FOUND LACKING WITHIN YOU, WE CAN TEACH YOU TO POSSESS. WE CALL YOU TO US. WILL YOU COME?"

As the dwarf nodded, tears funneled the gnomish face.

"AND BRING BACK THIS RACE," continued the words on the wind. "WE ARE GRATEFUL TO IT. GIVE IT YOUR POWERS AS WELL. PERHAPS THEY MAY DO SOMEWHAT WITH THEM."

The dwarf stared into the sky. "Will they do better than we? They were a race riddled with weakness and folly beyond imagining."

"THAT IS TRUE. AND WITH STRENGTH AND UNDERSTANDING. PERHAPS MAN WILL BECOME THE LATTER-DAY ROANEI OR MNESTEPOI. BUT PERHAPS IT WILL BE A NEW CORONOLEE OR TOOMEER. THE RACE HAS THE SEED, THE POTENTIAL FOR ALL THINGS. THE UNIVERSE IS A TEST-

ING GROUND, AND WE MUST NOT PREJUDGE WHAT THEY MAY BECOME.

"BUT FOR YOU, ROANEI, WE HAVE BEEN LONG WAITING. COME, CHILDREN."

There was a long silence. Through the air a shaft of brighter sunlight struck down and bathed the dwarf. Finally he sighed deeply, rose to his feet, stretched his arms towards the heavens. He stood there, winds whipping his hair, tears drying on his craggy face; and as she watched, his form dwindled, dissolved, was gone.

She stood alone on the bare plain, the bones scattered far about her, white and bare and dry, to the furthest horizon. As she watched, they began to stir.

"And he said unto me, Son of man, can these bones live? And I answered, O Lord God, thou knowest."

HOMAGE TO JULES VERNE

The year 1978 marked the one hundred and fiftieth anniversary of the birth of Jules Verne. In European circles this did not go unnoticed. Jules Verne is still revered and read, honored for his Voyages Extraordinaires *which include, for the most part, classics which have remained the foundation stones of science fiction the world over.*

In France there were a number of works produced about Jules Verne: biographic, bibliographic, special editions of magazines, a set of commemorative dishes, and several coffee-table albums reprinting photographs, reviews, and illustrations from the 19th Century. A series of beautiful facsimile editions of his complete works are in production, recreating even the elaborate gold-embossed covers of the finer volumes of his lifetime. In Italy, in Holland and Belgium, in other countries, similar works have appeared. Even in Britain at least one commemorative volume, edited by Peter Haining, was produced.

In the United States the event went unnoticed. No magazine devoted itself to Verne, no fan gathering paid attention, nothing appeared in print—with one exception. In 1978 Joanna Russ wrote a fine story, in the Verne style, against a typical French background with which Verne himself would have been familiar. The story appeared in a 1979 issue of Fantasy & Science Fiction, *with Ms. Russ's dedicational line:* Hommage à Jules Verne.

We are pleased to reprint this delightful tale as the eleventh story of this year's "best ten" in belated homage to the greatest name in the science fiction galaxy.

THE EXTRAORDINARY VOYAGES OF AMÉLIE BERTRAND

by Joanna Russ

In the summer of 192- there occurred to me the most extraordinary event of my life.

I was traveling on business and was in the French countryside, not far from Lyons, waiting for my train on a small railway platform on the outskirts of a town I shall call Beaulieu-sur-le-Pont. (This is not its name.) The weather was cool, although it was already June, and I shared the platform with only one other passenger: a plump woman of at least forty, by no means pretty but respectably dressed, the true type of our provincial *bonne bourgeoise,* who sat on the bench provided for the comfort of passengers and knitted away at some indeterminate garment.

The station at Beaulieu, like so many of our railway stops in small towns, is provided with a central train station of red brick through which runs an arch of passageway, also of red brick, which thus divides the edifice of the station into a ticket counter and waiting room on one side and a small café on the other. Thus, having attended one's train on the wrong side of the station (for there are railroad tracks on both sides of the edifice), one may occasionally find oneself making the traversal of the station in order to catch one's train, usually at the last minute.

So it occurred with me. I heard the approach of my train, drew out my watch, and found that the mild spring weather had caused me to indulge in a reverie not only lengthy but at a distance from my desired track; the two-fifty-one for Lyons was about to enter Beaulieu, but I was wrongly situated to place myself on board; were I not quick, no entrainment would take place.

Blessing the good fathers of Beaulieu-sur-le-Pont for their foresight in so dividing thoir train depot, I walked briskly but with no excessive haste towards the passage. I had not the slightest doubt of catching my train. I even had leisure to reflect on the bridge which figures so largely in the name of the town and to recall that, according to my knowledge, this bridge had been destroyed in the time of Caractacus; then I stepped between the buildings. I noticed that my footsteps echoed from the walls of the tunnel, a phenomenon one may observe upon entering any confined space. To the right of me and to the left were walls of red brick. The air was invigoratingly fresh, the weather sunny and clear, and ahead was the wooden platform, the well trimmed bushes, and the potted geraniums of the other side of the Beaulieu train station.

Nothing could have been more ordinary.

Then, out of the corner of my eye, I noticed that the lady I had seen knitting on the platform was herself entering the passage at a decorous distance behind me. We were, it seems, to become fellow passengers. I turned and raised my hat to her, intending to continue. I could not see the Lyons train, but to judge by the faculty of hearing, it was rounding the bend outside the station. I placed my hat back upon my head, reached the center of the tunnel, or rather, a point midway along its major diameter—

Will you believe me? Probably. You are English; the fogs and literature of your unfortunate climate predispose you to marvels. Your winters cause you to read much; your authors reflect to you from their pages the romantic imagination of a *refugé* from the damp and cold, to whom anything may happen if only it does so outside his windows! I am the product of another soil; I am logical, I am positive, I am French. Like my famous compatriot, I cry, "Where is this marvel? Let him produce it!" I myself do not believe what happened to me. I believe it no more than I believe that Phileas Fogg circumnavigated the globe in 187- and still lives today in London with the lady he rescued from a funeral pyre in Benares.

Nonetheless I will attempt to describe what happened.

The first sensation was a retardation of time. It seemed to

me that I had been in the passage at Beaulieu for a very long time, and the passage itself seemed suddenly to become double its length, or even triple. Then my body became heavy, as in a dream; there was also a disturbance of balance as though the tunnel sloped *down* towards its farther end and some increase in gravity were pulling me in that direction. A phenomenon even more disturbing was the peculiar *haziness* that suddenly obscured the forward end of the Beaulieu tunnel, as if Beaulieu-sur-le-Pont, far from enjoying the temperate warmth of an excellent June day, were actually melting in the heat—yes, heat!—a terrible warmth like that of a furnace, and yet humid, entirely unknown to our moderate climate even in the depths of summer. In a moment my summer clothing was soaked, and I wondered with horror whether I dared offend customary politeness by opening my collar. The noise of the Lyons train, far from disappearing, now surrounded me on all sides as if a dozen trains, and not merely one, were converging upon Beaulieu-sur-le-Pont, or as if a strong wind (which was pushing me forward) were blowing. I attempted to peer into the mistiness ahead of me but could see nothing. A single step farther and the mist swirled aside; there seemed to be a vast spray of greenery beyond—indeed, I could distinctly make out the branches of a large palm tree upon which intense sunlight was beating—and then, directly crossing it, a long, thick, sinuous, gray serpent which appeared to writhe from side to side, and which then fixed itself around the trunk of the palm, bringing into view a gray side as large as the opening of the tunnel itself, four gray columns beneath, and two long ivory tusks.

It was an elephant.

It was the roar of the elephant which brought me to my senses. Before this I had proceeded as in an astonished dream; now I turned and attempted to retrace my steps but found that I could hardly move *up* the steep tunnel against the furious wind which assailed me. I was aware of the cool, fresh, familiar spring of Beaulieu, very small and precious, appearing like a photograph or a scene observed through the diminishing, not the magnifying end, of an opera glass, and of the impossibility of ever attaining it. Then a strong arm seized mine, and I was back on the platform from which I had ventured—it seemed now so long ago!—sitting on the wooden bench while the good bourgeoise in the decent dark dress inquired after my health.

I cried, "But the palm tree—the tropical air—the elephant!"

She said in the calmest way in the world, "Do not distress yourself, monsieur. It was merely Uganda."

I may mention here that Madame Bertrand, although not in her first youth, is a woman whose dark eyes sparkle with extraordinary charm. One must be an imbecile not to notice this. Her concern is sincere, her manner *séduisante*, and we had not been in conversation five minutes before she abandoned the barriers of reserve and explained to me not only the nature of the experience I had undergone, but (in the café of the train station at Beaulicu, over a lemon ice) her own extraordinary history.

"Shortly after the termination of the Great War" (said Madame Bertrand) "I began a habit which I have continued to this day: whenever my husband, Aloysius Bertrand, is away from Beaulieu-sur-le-Pont on business, as often happens, I visit my sister-in-law in Lyons, leaving Beaulieu on one day in the middle of the week and returning on the next. At first my visits were uneventful. Then, one fateful day only two years ago, I happened to depart from the wrong side of the train station after purchasing my ticket, and so found myself seeking to approach my train through that archway or passage where you, Monsieur, so recently ventured. There were the same effects, but I attributed them to an attack of faintness and continued, expecting my hour's ride to Lyons, my sister-in-law's company, the cinema, the restaurant, and the usual journey back the next day.

"Imagine my amazement—no, my stupefaction—when I found myself instead on a rough wooden platform surrounded on three sides by the massive rocks and lead-colored waters of a place entirely unfamiliar to me! I made inquiries and discovered, to my unbounded astonishment, that I was on the last railway stop or terminus of Tierra del Fuego, the southernmost tip of the South American continent, and that I had engaged myself to sail as supercargo on a whaling vessel contracted to cruise the waters of Antarctica for the next two years. The sun was low, the clouds massing above, and behind me (continuing the curve of the rock-infested bay) was a jungle of squat pine trees, expressing by the irregularity of their trunks the violence of the climate.

"What could I do? My clothing was Victorian, the ship ready to sail, the six months' night almost upon us. The next train was not due until spring.

"To make a long story short, I sailed.

"You might expect that a lady, placed in such a situation, would suffer much that was disagreeable and discommoding. So it was. But there is also a somber charm to the far south which only those who have traveled there can know: the stars glittering on the ice fields, the low sun, the penguins, the icebergs, the whales. And then there were the sailors, children of the wilderness, young, ardent, sincere, especially one, a veritable Apollo with a broad forehead and golden mustachios. To be frank, I did not remain aloof; we became acquainted, one thing led to another, and *enfin* I learned to love the smell of whale oil. Two years later, alighting from the railway train I had taken to Nome, Alaska, where I had gone to purchase my *trousseau* (for having made telegraphic inquiries about Beaulieu-sur-le-Pont, I found that no Monsieur Bertrand existed therein and so considered myself a widow) I found myself, not in my Victorian dress in the bustling and frigid city of Nome, that commercial capital of the North with its outlaws, dogs, and Esquimaux in furs carrying loads of other furs upon their sleds, but in my old, familiar visiting-dress (in which I had started from Beaulieu so long before) on the platform at Lyons, with my sister-in-law waiting for me. Not only that, but in the more than two years I had remained away, no more time had passed in what I am forced to call the real world than the hour required for the train ride from Beaulieu to Lyons! I had expected Garance to fall upon my neck with cries of astonishment at my absence and the strangeness of my dress; instead she inquired after my health, and not waiting for an answer, began to describe in the most ordinary manner and at very great length the roast of veal which she had purchased that afternoon for dinner.

"At first, so confused and grief-stricken was I, that I thought I had somehow missed the train for Nome, and that returning at once from Lyons to Beaulieu would enable me to reach Alaska. I almost cut my visit to Lyons short on the plea of ill-health. But I soon realized the absurdity of imagining that a railway could cross several thousand miles of ocean, and since my sister-in-law was already suspicious (I could not help myself during the visit and often burst out with a '*Mon cher Jack!*') I controlled myself and gave vent to my feelings only on the return trip to Beaulieu—which, far from ending in Nome, Alaska, ended at the Beaulieu train station and at exactly the time predicted by the railway timetable.

"I decided that my two-years' holiday had been only what the men of psychological science would entitle an unusually complete and detailed dream. The ancient Chinese were, I believe, famous for such vivid dreams; one of their poets is said to have experienced an entire lifetime of love, fear, and adventure while washing his feet. This was my case exactly. Here was I not a day—nay not an hour—older, and no one knew what had passed in the Antarctic save I myself.

"It was a reasonable explanation, but it had one grave defect, which rendered it totally useless.

"It was false.

"Since that time, Monsieur, I have gone on my peculiar voyages, my holidays, *mes vacances,* as I call them, not once but dozens of times. My magic carpet is the railway station at Beaulieu, or to be more precise, the passageway between the ticket office and the café at precisely ten minutes before three in the afternoon. A traversal of the passage at any other time brings me merely to the other side of the station, but a traversal of the passage at this particular time brings me to some far, exotic corner of the globe. Perhaps it is Ceylon with its crowds of variegated hue, its scent of incense, its pagodas and rickshaws. Or the deserts of Al-Iqah, with the crowds of Bedawi, dressed in flowing white and armed with rifles, many of whom whirl round about one another on horseback. Or I will find myself on the languid islands of Tahiti, with the graceful and dusky inhabitants bringing me bowls of *poi* and garlands of flowers whose beauty is unmatched anywhere else in the tropical portion of the globe. Nor have my holidays been entirely confined to the terrestrial regions. Last February I stepped through the passage to find myself on the sands of a primitive beach under a stormy, gray sky; in the distance one could perceive the roarings of saurians and above me were the giant saw-toothed, purple leaves of some palmaceous plant, one (as it turned out) entirely unknown to botanical science.

"No, monsieur, it was not Ceylon; it was Venus. It is true that I prefer a less overcast climate, but still one can hardly complain. To lie in the darkness of the Venerian night, on the silky volcanic sands, under the starry leaves of the *laradh,* while imbibing the million perfumes of the night-blooming flowers and listening to the music of the *karakh*—really, one does not miss the blue sky. Although only a few weeks ago I was in a place that also pleased me: imagine a huge, whitish-blue sky, a desert with giant mountains on the horizon, and the lean, hard-bitten water-prospectors with their dowsing rods, their high-heeled boots, and their large hats, worn to protect faces already tanned and wrinkled from the intense sunlight.

"No, not Mars, Texas. They are marvelous people, those American pioneers, the men handsome and laconic, the women sturdy and efficient. And then one day I entrained to Lyons only to find myself on a railway platform that resembled a fishbowl made of tinted glass, while around me rose mountains fantastically slender into a black sky where the stars shone like hard marbles, scarcely twinkling at all. I was wearing a glass helmet and clothes that resembled a diver's. I had no idea where I was until I rose, and then to my edified surprise, instead of rising in the usual manner, I positively bounded into the air!

"I was on the Moon.

"Yes, monsieur, the Moon, although some distance in the future, the year two thousand eighty and nine, to be precise. At that date human beings will have established a colony on the Moon. My carriage swiftly shot down beneath one of the Selenic craters to land in their principal city, a fairy palace of slender towers and domes of glass, for they use as building material a glass made from the native silicate gravel. It was on the Moon that I gathered whatever theory I now have concerning my peculiar experiences with the railway passage at Beaulieu-sur-le-Pont, for I made the acquaintance there of the principal mathematician of the twenty-first century, a most elegant lady, and put the problem to her. You must understand that on the Moon *les nègres, les juifs* even *les femmes* may obtain high positions and much influence; it is a true republic. This lady introduced me to her colleague, a black physicist of more-than-normal happenings, or *le paraphysique* as they call it, and the two debated the matter during an entire day (not a Selenic day, of course, since that would have amounted to a time equal to twenty-eight days of our own). They could not agree, but in brief, as they told me, either the railway tunnel at Beaulieu-sur-le-Pont has achieved infinite connectivity or it is haunted. To be perfectly sincere, I regretted leaving the Moon. But one has one's obligations. Just as my magic carpet here at Beaulieu is of the nature of a railway tunnel, and just as I always find myself in *mes vacances* at first situated on a railway platform, thus my return must also be effected by that so poetically termed road of iron; I placed myself into the railway that connects two of the principal Selenic craters, and behold!—I alight at the platform at Lyons, not a day older.

"Indeed, monsieur" (and here Madame Bertrand coughed delicately) "as we are both people of the world, I may mention that certain other of the biological processes also suspend themselves, a fact not altogether to my liking, since my dear Aloysius and myself are entirely without family. Yet this suspension has its advantages; if I had aged as I have lived, it would be a woman of seventy who speaks to you now. In truth, how can one age in worlds that are, to speak frankly, not quite real? Though perhaps if I had remained permanently in one of these worlds, I too would have begun to age along with the other inhabitants. That would be a pleasure on the Moon, for my mathematical friend was age two hundred when I met her, and her acquaintance, the professor of *le paraphysique*, two hundred and five."

Here Madame Bertrand, to whose recital I had been listening with breathless attention, suddenly ceased speaking. Her lemon ice stood untouched upon the table. So full was I of projects to make the world acquainted with this amazing history that I did not at first notice the change in Madame Bertrand's expression, and so I burst forth:

"The National Institute—the Académie—no, the universities, and the newspapers also—"

But the charming lady, with a look of horror, had risen from the table, crying, "Mon dieu! My train! What will Garance think? What will she say? Monsieur, not a word to anyone!"

Imagine my consternation when Madame Bertrand here precipitously departed from the café and began to cross the station towards that ominous passageway. I could only postulate, "But madame, consider! Ceylon! Texas! Mars!"

"No, it is too late," said she. "Only at the former time in the train schedule. Monsieur, remember, please, not a word to anyone!"

Following her, I cried, "But if you do not return—" and she again favored me with her delightful smile, saying rapidly, "Do not distress yourself, monsieur. By now I have developed certain sensations—a *frisson* of the neck and shoulder blades—which warns me of the condition of the passageway The later hour is always safe. But my train—!"

And so Madame Bertrand left me. Amazing woman! A

traveler not only to the far regions of the earth but to those of imagination, and yet perfectly respectable, gladly fulfilling the duties of family life, and punctually (except for this one time) meeting her sister-in-law, Mademoiselle Garance Bertrand, on the train platform at Lyons.

Is that the end of my story? No, for I was fated to meet Amélie Bertrand once again.

My business, which I have mentioned to you, took me back to Beaulieu-sur-le-Pont at the end of that same summer. I must confess that I hoped to encounter Madame Bertrand, for I had made it my intention to notify at least several of our great national institutions of the extraordinary powers possessed by the railway passage at Beaulieu, and yet I certainly could not do so without Madame Bertrand's consent. Again it was shortly before three in the afternoon; again the station platform was deserted. I saw a figure which I took to be that of Madame Bertrand seated upon the bench reserved for passengers and hastened to it with a glad cry—

But it was not Amélie Bertrand. Rather it was a thin and elderly female, entirely dressed in the dullest of black and completely without the charm I had expected to find in my fellow passenger. The next moment I heard my name pronounced and was delighted to perceive, issuing from the ticket office, Madame Bertrand herself, wearing a light-colored summer dress.

But where was the gaiety, the charm, the pleasant atmosphere of June? Madame Bertrand's face was closed, her eyes watchful, her expression determined. I would immediately have opened to her my immense projects, but with a shake of her head the lady silenced me, indicating the figure I have already mentioned.

"My sister-in-law, Mademoiselle Garance," she said. I confess that I nervously expected that Aloysius Bertrand himself would now appear. But we were alone on the platform. Madame Bertrand continued: "Garance, this is the gentleman who was the unfortunate cause of my missing my train last June."

Mademoiselle Garance, as if to belie the reputation for loquacity I had heard applied to her earlier in the summer, said nothing, but merely clutched to her meager bosom a small train case.

Madame Bertrand said to me, "I have explained to Garance the occasion of your illness last June and the manner in which the officials of the station detained me. I am glad to see you looking so well."

This was a clear hint that Mademoiselle Garance was to know nothing of her sister-in-law's history; thus I merely bowed and nodded. I wished to have the opportunity of conversing with Madame Bertrand more freely, but I could say nothing in the presence of her sister-in-law. Desperately I began: "You are taking the train today—"

"For the sake of nostalgia," said Madame Bertrand. "After today I shall never set foot in a railway carriage. Garance may if she likes, but I will not. Aeroplanes, motor cars, and ships will be good enough for me. Perhaps like the famous American, Madame Earhart, I shall learn to fly. This morning Aloysius told me the good news: a change in his business arrangements has enabled us to move to Lyons, which we are to do at the end of the month."

"And in the intervening weeks—?" said I.

Madame Bertrand replied composedly, "There will be none. They are tearing down the station."

What a blow! And there sat the old maid, Mademoiselle Garance, entirely unconscious of the impending loss to science! I stammered something—I know not what—but my good angel came to my rescue; with an infinitesimal movement of the fingers, she said:

"Oh, monsieur, my conscious pains me too much! Garance, would you believe that I told this gentleman the most preposterous stories? I actually told him—seriously, now—that the passageway of this train station was the gateway to another world! No, many worlds, and that I had been to all of them. Can you believe it of me?" She turned to me. "Oh, monsieur," she said, "you were a good listener. You only pretended to believe. Surely you cannot imagine that a respectable woman like myself would leave her husband by means of a railway passage which has achieved infinite connectivity?"

Here Madame Bertrand looked at me in a searching manner, but I was at a loss to understand her intention in so doing and said nothing.

She went on, with a little shake of the head. "I must confess it; I am addicted to storytelling. Whenever my dear Aloysius left home on his business trips, he would say to me, '*Occupe-toi, occupe-toi, Amélie!*' and, alas, I have occupied myself only too well. I thought my romance might divert your mind from your ill-health and so presumed to tell you an unlikely tale of extraordinary voyages. Can you forgive me?"

I said something polite, something I do not now recall. I was, you understand, still reeling from the blow. All that merely a fable! Yet with what detail, what plausible circumstance Madame Bertrand had told her story. I could only feel relieved I had not actually written to the National Institute. I was about to press both ladies to take some refreshment with me, when Madame Bertrand (suddenly putting her hand to her heart in a gesture that seemed to me excessive) cried, "Our train!" and turning to me, remarked, "Will you accompany us down the passage?"

Something made me hesitate; I know not what.

"Think, monsieur," said Madame Bertrand, with her hand still pressed to her heart, "where will it be this time? A London of the future, perhaps, enclosed against the weather and built entirely of glass? Or perhaps the majestic, high plains of Colorado? Or will we find ourselves in one of the underground cities of the moons of Jupiter, in whose awesome skies the mighty planet rises and sets with a visual diameter more than that of the terrestrial Alps?"

She smiled with humor at Mademoiselle Garance, remarking, "Such are the stories I told this gentleman, dear Garance; they were a veritable novel," and I saw that she was gently teasing her sister-in-law, who naturally did not know what any of this was about.

Mademoiselle Garance ventured to say timidly that she "liked to read novels."

I bowed.

Suddenly I heard the sound of the train outside Beaulieu-sur-le-Pont. Madame Bertrand cried in an utterly prosaic voice, "Our train! Garance, we shall miss our train!" and again she asked, "Monsieur, will you accompany us?"

I bowed, but remained where I was. Accompanied by the thin, stooped figure of her sister-in-law, Madame Bertrand walked quickly down the passageway which divides the ticket room of the Beaulieu-sur-le-Pont station from the tiny café. I confess that when the two ladies reached the mid-point of the longitudinal axis of the passageway, I involuntarily closed my eyes, and when I opened them, the passage was empty.

What moved me then I do not know, but I found myself quickly traversing the passageway, seeing in my mind's eye Madame Bertrand boarding the Lyons train with her sister-in-law, Mademoiselle Garance. One could certainly hear the train; the sound of its engine filled the whole station. I believe I told myself that I wished to exchange one last polite word. I reached the other side of the station—

And there was no Lyons train there.

There were no ladies on the platform.

There is, indeed, no two-fifty-one train to Lyons whatsoever, not on the schedule of any line!

Imagine my sensations, my dear friend, upon learning that Madame Bertrand's story was true, all of it! It is true, all too true, all of it is true, and my Amélie is gone forever!

"My" Amélie I call her; yet she still belongs (in law) to Aloysius Bertrand, who will, no doubt, after the necessary statutory period of waiting is over, marry again, and thus become a respectable and unwitting bigamist.

That animal could never have understood her!

Even now (if I may be permitted that phrase) Amélie Bertrand may be drifting down one of the great Venerian rivers on a gondola, listening to the music of the *karakh;* even now she may perform acts of heroism on Airstrip One or chat with her mathematical friend on a balcony that overlooks the airy towers and flower-filled plazas of the Selenic capitol. I have no doubt that if you were to attempt to find the places Madame Bertrand mentioned by looking in the Encyclopedia or a similar work of reference, you would not succeed. As she herself mentioned, they are "not quite real." There are strange discrepancies.

Alas, my friend, condole with me; by now all such concern is academic, for the train station at Beaulieu-sur-le-Pont is gone, replaced by a vast erection swarming with workmen, a giant *hangar* (I learned the name from one of them), or edifice for the housing of aeroplanes. I am told that large numbers of these machines will soon fly from *hangar* to *hangar* across the country.

But think: these aeroplanes, will they not in time be used for ordinary business travel, for scheduled visits to resorts and other places? In short, are they not even now the railways of the new age? Is it not possible that the same condition, whether of infinite connectivity or of hauntedness, may again obtain, perhaps in the same place where the journeys of my vanished angel have established a precedent or predisposition?

My friend, collude with me. The *hangar* at Beaulieu will soon be finished, or so I read in the newspapers. I shall go down into the country and establish myself near this *hangar;*

I shall purchase a ticket for a ride in one of the new machines, and then we shall see. Perhaps I will enjoy only a pleasant ascension into the air and a similar descent. Perhaps I will instead feel that *frisson* of the neck and shoulder blades of which Madame Bertrand spoke; well, no matter: my children are grown, my wife has a generous income, the *frisson* will not dismay me. I shall walk down the corridor or passageway in or around the *hangar* at precisely nine minutes before three and into the space between the worlds; I shall again feel the strange retardation of time, I shall feel the heaviness of the body, I shall see the haziness at the other end of the tunnel, and then through the lashing wind, through the mistiness which envelops me, with the rushing and roaring of an invisible aeroplane in my ears, I shall proceed. Madame Bertrand was kind enough to delay her own holiday to conduct me back from Uganda; she was generous enough to offer to share the traversal of the passage with me a second time. Surely such kindness and generosity must have its effect! This third time I will proceed. Away from my profession, my daily newspaper, my chess games, my *digestif*—in short, away from all those habits which, it is understood, are given us to take the place of happiness. Away from the petty annoyances of life I shall proceed, away from a dull old age, away from the confusions and terrors of a Europe grown increasingly turbulent, to—

—*What?*

The above copy of a letter was found in a volume of the Encyclopedia (U-Z) in the Bibliothèque National. *It is believed from the evidence that the writer disappeared at a certain provincial town (called "Beaulieu-sur-le-Pont" in the manuscript) shortly after purchasing a ticket for a flight in an aeroplane at the flying field there, a pastime popular among holiday makers.*

He has never been seen again.

DAW PRESENTS MARION ZIMMER BRADLEY

"A writer of absolute competency . . ."—Theodore Sturgeon

☐ **THE FORBIDDEN TOWER**
"Blood feuds, medieval pageantry, treachery, tyranny, and true love combine to make another colorful swatch in the compelling continuing tapestry of Darkover."—**Publishers Weekly.** (#UJ1323—$1.95)

☐ **THE HERITAGE OF HASTUR**
"A rich and highly colorful tale of politics and magic, courage and pressure . . . Topflight adventure in every way."—**Analog.** "May well be Bradley's masterpiece."—**Newsday.** "It is a triumph."—**Science Fiction Review.** (#UJ1307—$1.95)

☐ **DARKOVER LANDFALL**
"Both literate and exciting, with much of that searching fable quality that made **Lord of the Flies** so provocative." —**New York Times.** The novel of Darkover's origin. (#UW1447—$1.50)

☐ **THE SHATTERED CHAIN**
"Primarily concerned with the role of women in the Darkover society . . . Bradley's gift is provocative, a top-notch blend of sword-and-sorcery and the finest speculative fiction."—**Wilson Library Bulletin.** (#UJ1327—$1.95)

☐ **THE SPELL SWORD**
Goes deeper into the problem of the matrix and the conflict with one of Darkover's non-human races gifted with similar powers. A first-class adventure. (#UW1440—$1.50)

☐ **STORMQUEEN!**
"A novel of the planet Darkover set in the Ages of Chaos . . . this is richly textured, well-thought-out and involving." —**Publishers Weekly.** (#UJ1381—$1.95)

☐ **HUNTERS OF THE RED MOON**
"May be even more a treat for devoted MZB fans than her excellent Darkover series . . . sf adventure in the grand tradition."—**Luna.** (#UE1568—$1.75)

If you wish to order these titles,
please see the coupon in
the back of this book.

FLYAWAY VACATION SWEEPSTAKES

OFFICIAL ENTRY COUPON

This entry must be received by: SEPTEMBER 30, 1995
This month's winner will be notified by: OCTOBER 15, 1995
Trip must be taken between: NOVEMBER 30, 1995-NOVEMBER 30, 1996

YES, I want to win the vacation for two to Orlando, Florida. I understand the prize includes round-trip airfare, first-class hotel and $500.00 spending money. Please let me know if I'm the winner!

Name______________________________

Address ____________________ Apt. __________

City State/Prov. Zip/Postal Code

Account # ______________________________

Return entry with invoice in reply envelope.

 COR KAL

FLYAWAY VACATION SWEEPSTAKES

OFFICIAL ENTRY COUPON

This entry must be received by: SEPTEMBER 30, 1995
This month's winner will be notified by: OCTOBER 15, 1995
Trip must be taken between: NOVEMBER 30, 1995-NOVEMBER 30, 1996

YES, I want to win the vacation for two to Orlando, Florida. I understand the prize includes round-trip airfare, first-class hotel and $500.00 spending money. Please let me know if I'm the winner!

Name______________________________

Address ____________________ Apt. __________

City State/Prov. Zip/Postal Code

Account # ______________________________

Return entry with invoice in reply envelope.

© 1995 HARLEQUIN ENTERPRISES LTD. COR KAL

"I asked why you're here, Luke."

Rebecca moved clear of him, survival instincts finally coming to the fore.

Luke mirrored her stance, thinking it was such a simple question. Up until five minutes ago, he was sure he knew exactly why he was here—to see her, talk to her, and yes, convince himself that she was merely one of many women he'd known.

Trouble was, five minutes ago he hadn't seen her, hadn't touched her, hadn't looked into those liquid blue eyes of hers, the ones that were making his breathing a little unsteady.

Faster than ice dissolves when touched by a flame, his reasons vanished, and he told her honestly, "I came to see you."

"Why?" she asked, and instantly regretted the question. It didn't matter why—or did it?

"I came because—" his voice dropped to a husky timbre "—because I couldn't stay away any longer. . . ."

Dear Reader,

When Susan Amarillas's novel *Snow Angel* was featured in our 1993 March Madness promotion for first-time authors, it was received with great enthusiasm. *Rendezvous* claimed, "If you like western stories, this one has everything...." Ever since then, Ms. Amarillas has been delighting readers with her western tales of love and laughter. This month, we are very pleased to bring you her newest book, *Scanlin's Law*, the story of a jaded U.S. Marshal and the woman who's waited eight years for him to return. We hope you enjoy it.

Also this month, gifted author Deborah Simmons returns to Medieval times with her new book, *Taming the Wolf*, the amusing tale of a baron who is determined to fulfill his duty and return an heiress to her legal guardian, until the young lady convinces him that to do so would put her in the gravest danger.

For those of you who like adventure with your romance, look for *Desert Rogue*, by the writing team of Erin Yorke. It's the story of an English socialite and the rough-hewn American soldier of fortune who rescues her. And from contemporary author Liz Ireland comes her debut historical, *Cecilia and the Stranger*. This month's WOMEN OF THE WEST selection is the charming tale of a schoolteacher who is not all he seems, and the rancher's daughter who is bent on finding out just who he really is.

Whatever your taste in historical reading, we hope you'll keep a lookout for all four titles, available wherever Harlequin Historicals are sold.

Sincerely,

Tracy Farrell

Senior Editor

SUSAN
AMARILLAS

SCANLIN'S LAW

Harlequin Books

TORONTO • NEW YORK • LONDON
AMSTERDAM • PARIS • SYDNEY • HAMBURG
STOCKHOLM • ATHENS • TOKYO • MILAN
MADRID • WARSAW • BUDAPEST • AUCKLAND

ISBN 0-373-28883-2

SCANLIN'S LAW

This edition published by arrangement with Harlequin Books S.A.

Printed in U.S.A.

Books by Susan Amarillas

Harlequin Historicals

Snow Angel #165
Silver and Steel #233
Scanlin's Law #283

SUSAN AMARILLAS

was born and raised in Maryland and moved to California when she married. She quickly discovered her love of the high desert country—she says it was as if she were "coming home." When she's not writing, she and her husband love to travel the back roads of the West, visiting ghost towns and little museums, and always coming home with an armload of books.

To Barbara Musumeci, a dearest friend who is far away but close to my heart. This one's for you. There's nary a horse in sight.

Chapter One

San Francisco
October 1880

What the hell was he doing here?

Luke Scanlin swung down off his chestnut gelding and looped the reins through the smooth metal ring of the hitching post. Storm clouds, black and threatening, billowed overhead. Rain spattered against the side of his face. It caught on his eyelashes and plastered his hair to his neck. He shivered, more from reflex than from cold.

Three days. He had been in town three days. It had been raining when he finally stepped off the train from Cheyenne, and it was raining now. Aw, hell, he figured it was destined to rain forever.

Fifty feet away, the house, *her* house, stood like some medieval fortress. It was gray, and as intimidating as any castle. Three floors high, it was as impressive as the other Nob Hill mansions that lined both sides of California Street.

A wry smile played at the corners of his mouth. A princess needs a castle, he thought. But if she was a princess, then what was he? Certainly Luke Scanlin was nobody's idea of a prince.

That blasted rain increased, trickling off his drooping hat brim and running straight down his neck. "Damn," he muttered as he flipped up the collar of his mud-stained slicker. He was cold and wet and generally a mess, and still he stood there, staring up at the house.

His hand rested on the hitching post, two fingers on the cold iron, three fingers curled around the smooth leather reins. He ought to mount up and ride away, logic coaxed for about the hundredth time in the past hour. His muscles tensed, and he actually made a half turn, then stopped.

This was pathetic. Here he stood like some schoolboy, afraid to go in there and see *her.*

Well, *she* wasn't just anyone.

When he rode away that day eight years ago, he'd been so certain he was right.

The breeze carried the scent of salt water up from the bay, and the rain intensified, soaking the black wool of his trousers where they brushed against the tops of his mud-spattered black boots. Oak trees rustled in the breeze, sending the last of their golden leaves skittering along the street.

Beside him, the gelding nickered, his bridle rattling as he shook his head in protest at being out in the storm.

"Quiet, Scoundrel." Luke soothed the animal with a pat and stared up at the house once more.

Well, what's it going to be? You going to stand here all day?

He sighed. What was he going to say to her after all these years? Pure and simple, this was flat-out asking for trouble. *Leave well enough alone.*

But trouble was something Luke had never shied away from. A smile tugged at one corner of his mouth. In fact, he and trouble were old friends.

He started toward the house.

Rebecca Parker Tinsdale strode into the parlor of her home shortly past nine in the morning. The distant rumble of thunder accompanied her arrival. The storm-shrouded sunlight gave the white walls a grayish tinge, and the rich rococo-style mahogany furnishings only added to the dark and ominous feeling of the day. A pastoral painting by Constable hung over the fireplace, but the scene—a picnic on a bright summer day—seemed inappropriate, given the ominous dread that permeated the house.

She managed to keep her expression calm. Inside, fear was eating her alive. Her hands shook, and she buried them in the folds of her dark blue dress. The faille was smooth against her fingers.

In four carefully measured steps, Rebecca crossed the room to where Captain Amos Brody, chief of the San Francisco police, waited near the pale rose settee.

"Have you found Andrew?" She spoke slowly, struggling to hold the fear in check. Even as she asked, she could tell the answer by his grim expression.

If anything happened to Andrew . . . If he was hurt or . . .

Steady. Don't fall apart. Andrew needs you.

"Well, Mrs. Tinsdale . . ." Brody began, his rotund body straining at the double row of brass buttons that marched down the front of his dark blue uniform,

"I've had two men searching all night. They've looked everywhere, and I'm sorry to say there's no sign of the boy."

"Keep looking, Captain."

"Oh, you can rely on us," Brody returned in an indulgent tone. "I'll personally tell the men on the beat to keep an eye out."

Rebecca stiffened. She and Brody made no secret of their mutual dislike. That series of articles she'd been running in the *Daily Times* on police corruption was leading a path straight to Brody and half of his department. Still, he was in charge and, like it or not, she had to deal with him.

"Captain, I expect you to do more than keep an eye out. This isn't a lost kitten you can dismiss and hope it eventually finds its way home. This—" she emphasized the words, as though to drive them into his thick balding skull "—this is my *son.* And you *will* help me find him."

She saw him bristle—saw his Adam's apple work up and down in his throat.

They faced each other, the refined lady and the harsh man, each appraising the other. Rebecca had wealth, and she published a small newspaper. That gave her power. A mother's fear gave her determination. She knew Brody was the one who ultimately made the assignments, determined how and when and where things were done. It galled her to have to ask the man for help. If Brody chose to make only a half-hearted effort because of their feud, she might not know until it was too late for her—for her only child.

Outside, the rain spattered against the lace-curtained front window, drawing Rebecca's attention. Silvery streaks of water cascaded down the glass.

Andrew was out there somewhere, cold and afraid. He was only seven, so small, and so fragile since his illness last year. Terror, stark and real, swept through her, and she advanced on Brody. "Whatever it takes, Captain. Send more men, ten men, a hundred—"

"I'd like to do that, Mrs. Tinsdale, but I can't." Brody punctuated his statement with a nonchalant shrug that pushed her rapidly rising temper up another notch. "Finding one boy is small compared to the job of protecting this city. With less than two hundred men on the force, well, I have an obligation to *all* the citizens of this fair community," he finished, in a pious tone that would have made her laugh at any other time. "As it is, I've taken men from other areas to search, and—"

"I don't care about other areas." Condescending bastard, she thought as she paced away from him, her rage too great for her to remain still. She talked over her shoulder. "I don't care about other citizens." She turned back, her hands balled into tight fists, feeling the perspiration on her palms. "I don't care about anything or anyone but finding my son. I've been out there all night myself. Dammit, Captain, I expect you to do the same."

Brody nodded and held up his hand in a placating gesture that only aggravated her dangerously short temper.

"Mrs. Tinsdale, I know you're upset and all, but I've handled this sort of thing before and I know what I'm doing."

Rebecca closed on him, contemplating serious bodily injury. "Captain Brody, either you do your job or I'll ask the mayor to find someone who can." It was a hollow threat since the mayor was a strong supporter of Brody's, but she made it just the same.

"Now look here, lady," he sputtered. "I know you're upset, but don't tell me how to do my job. Before you start ordering me around, you might as well face facts. The boy's probably run off, is all. It's only been since last night." Maliciousness sparked in his blue eyes. "Sooner or later he'll get tired and hungry, then turn tail and head for home..." He paused thoughtfully. "Unless someone's taken him. Then, of course, it's another matter."

Her blood turned to ice. It was that thought that had circled in her mind all night, the way a wolf circles in the shadows of a camp. In a voice that was barely audible, she spoke the terrifying words. "Someone has taken my son?"

Brody gave a one-shoulder shrug, then picked up his cap, as though he were about to leave. "It's possible." He turned the dark blue hat absently in his pudgy hand. "I'll do the best I can, but you gotta remember this is a big city. It can be a mean city, too, and people, including children, disappear here all the time. Ships go in and out of this harbor with all kinds of cargo, if you get my meaning."

She did. God help her, she understood his meaning all too well. Her knees buckled, and she sank down in a chair. Brody was wrong. He *had* to be wrong. Andrew was lost. He'd gotten too far from home and become confused. Yes, that was it. That *had* to be it. To think otherwise... To think of some depraved person with her son, scaring him, hurting him, kil— No!

With sheer force of will, she refused to think that and, looking up, saw that Brody was still talking.

"—figure out who the boy is, what he's worth." She saw him glance around the elegant room, as if to confirm his appraisal. "Maybe they'll make a try for ransom, otherwise th—"

Brody broke off in midword, and she saw that his gaze was focused on the doorway behind her. Still seated, she turned.

An eerie silence fell as Rebecca and Brody stared at the powerful man standing two feet inside the parlor. He looked every inch the outlaw, dressed as he was in range clothes and a slicker. For a breathless moment, Rebecca thought Brody's prediction had come true.

The man was tall, with broad shoulders, and his dark countenance seemed in stark contrast to the refinements of a San Francisco drawing room.

She was about to demand his identity when her gaze flicked to his face and she looked straight into dark eyes, bottomless eyes, familiar eyes.

Her hand fluttered to her throat. "Oh, no..." The words were a thready whisper. She felt the blood drain from her face.

Speechless, Rebecca stared at him. Luke Scanlin. His mere presence emanated a power that surged through the room faster than lightning.

So he's finally here. The odd thought flashed in her mind.

"Hello, Princess," he said, in a husky tone that sent unwelcome and definitely unexpected shivers skittering up her spine.

What in God's name was Luke doing here? Not once in nearly eight years had she seen or heard from him, and now he strolled in here as though it were the most natural thing in the world.

Well, it wasn't the most natural thing, not in her world. Never mind those delicious shivers. He was firmly and irrevocably in her past.

Out of the corner of her eye she saw Brody take a menacing step in Luke's direction. "Mister, just who are you, and how did you get in here?" he demanded with an appraising stare. "Do you know something about this?"

"Name's Scanlin," Luke returned, with an impudent Texas drawl. He walked slowly into the room, his steps muffled by the thick flowered carpet. "I saw you through the window. When no one answered the door, I let myself in."

Luke never let a little thing like a closed door stop him from getting what he was after. What he was after right now was perched on the edge of a chair about five feet away.

Absently he sized the other man up and quickly dismissed him, keeping his gaze focused on the object of his visit.

Becky.

She was more beautiful than he remembered, and he remembered very, very well. A little thinner, perhaps, and obviously upset. He'd only caught the tail end of the conversation. "What's going on?"

"Scanlin?" Brody rubbed his chin thoughtfully and ignored the question. "You by any chance Luke Scanlin, the one who brought in Conklin?"

"Yeah, that's me."

"I've heard of you. Thought you were with the Rangers down around . . . San Antonio, wasn't it?"

"Amarillo," he replied. "I'm not with the Rangers anymore."

Luke closed on Rebecca, stopping in front of her. Dark smudges shadowed her blue eyes, and her skin was winter white. Her hair was the same, though, golden, and done up softly, tiny wisps framing the fine bones of her face. He'd remembered her hair down and loose around her shoulders, remembered it gliding like silk over his bare chest while he—

He gulped in a lungful of air and stilled the direction of his thoughts. Damn. He didn't know what he'd expected, but this wasn't it.

Rebecca stared at him as he dropped down on one knee in front of her. Absently she noted that his slicker left a smudge of dirt on the carpet.

"Becky? Princess? What's happened?" he asked, in a tender voice that was nearly her undoing. *Oh, Luke don't do this to me. Not now.*

All her defensive instincts were screaming that she should move, get up, walk away. She didn't. His face filled her line of vision.

He looked at her, his eyes as black as sable and just as soft, and her heart took on a funny little flutter. She had to stop herself from reaching out and brushing his cheek.

The years had been kind to him, she thought. He was as handsome as ever, maybe more so. His chiseled face was all high ridges and curved valleys, the sternness softened by the tiny lines around his eyes and mouth that showed he was a man who liked to smile. She remembered that smile, roguish and charming enough to melt granite. The other thing she remembered was that way he had of looking at her, lover-soft. The way he was looking at her now.

"Rebecca?" he said, his tone coaxing.

"Hello, Luke," she managed to say, surprised that her voice sounded so steady. "What... what are you doing here?"

Purposefully Luke plopped his rain-soaked hat beside him on the carpet and raked one hand through his hair. She looked so forlorn, like a lost kitten, and it was the most natural thing to want to wrap her in his embrace and protect her from whatever the hell was wrong. All things considered—things like his timing, and the fact that they weren't alone—he reluctantly decided on a more formal approach.

"My apologies for dropping by unannounced, but I—"

He fired a glance at the police officer, who was watching them with open interest, then back to Rebecca's worried face. Concern won out over formality, and he cut to the point.

"Somebody want to tell me what the devil is going on? I heard something about a boy being missing."

"That's correct," the policeman replied, in a tone tinged with an arrogance that rankled Luke. Arms folded across his chest, the man leaned one shoulder against the white marble mantel.

Luke reined in his infamously short temper and said, "And the boy is..."

"My son," Rebecca supplied, so softly he might not have heard if he hadn't been looking straight at her.

Holy sh—

Luke sank back on his heels, his slicker pouching out around his knees. Becky had a child, a son. All these years he'd never thought of her having a child. He'd known she had married. He'd also learned her husband had died last year. That was part of the reason he'd taken this assignment.

"Aw, hell, Becky, I'm sorry," he said, with real sincerity. And that need to protect prompted him to cover her hands with his, his thumb rubbing intimately over her knuckles. Her skin was ice-cold, and he felt her tremble. "Is the boy your only child?" he asked, as much from curiosity as from concern.

Rebecca's heart seemed to still in her chest, then took off like a frightened bird. A surprising reaction. She was not given to flights of fancy, and Luke Scanlin was definitely a fantasy—a young girl's fantasy. "Don't, Luke." She slipped her hands free and stood. "Yes, Andrew is my only child." She moved clear of him, survival instincts finally coming to the fore. "What are you doing here?"

He mirrored her stance, thinking it was such a simple question. Up until five minutes ago he'd been sure he knew exactly why he was here—to see her, talk to her and, yes, convince himself that she was merely one of many women he'd known.

Trouble was, five minutes ago he hadn't seen her, hadn't touched her, hadn't looked into those liquid blue eyes of hers, the ones that were making his breathing a little unsteady.

Faster than ice dissolves when touched by a flame, his reasons vanished, and he told her honestly, "I came to see you."

"Why?" she asked, and instantly regretted the question. It didn't matter why—or did it?

"I came because—" his voice dropped to a husky timbre "—because I couldn't stay away any longer."

His voice, his closeness, it was all too much, and she felt cornered. Moreover, she didn't like the feeling, not one bit. In fact, she resented Luke for making her feel this way. She feigned thoughtfulness as she took refuge behind the settee. "I have no time, Luke. My son's missing, and I have business with Captain Brody here. So another time, perhaps."

He recognized the dismissal. Oh, it was formal and polite, but it was a dismissal all the same. Luke wasn't buying. He was here and he was going to stay, though he still wasn't quite sure why. Missing children were hardly his line of work, not unless they held up a bank along the way. Maybe it was his lawman's curiosity. Maybe it was that the policeman annoyed the royal hell out of him. Maybe it was that he wanted to see her smile, once, for him. Whatever it was, he said simply, "I prefer now." He unfastened the buttons on his slicker and tossed it on the floor near his hat.

Brody spoke up. "Mrs. Tinsdale, would you like me to show him out?"

Luke straightened. A slow smile, one that didn't reach his eyes, pulled up one corner of his mouth. "Captain, you couldn't if you tried."

Brody shifted away from the mantel and took a threatening half step in Luke's direction. Luke did likewise. Who the hell did this son of a bitch think he was?

"Stop it!" Rebecca ordered hotly. "I won't have this in my house!"

Luke turned on her. Anger flashed in his black eyes. That short temper of his had shot up faster than a bullet, and he wasn't used to backing down. But this was her house, and—

"All right," Luke muttered, with a slight shake of his head to dispel the anger.

Brody, too, gave a curt nod and retreated to his place by the hearth.

Luke dropped down on the settee, making clear his intention to stay, in case there was still some doubt in someone's mind. "Okay, someone tell me what happened."

He was arrogant and self-involved as ever, Rebecca thought, her own temper moving up a notch. Looking at him sitting casually on her sofa, for the briefest moment she was tempted to recant and let Brody escort Luke out.

Who did she think she was kidding? Brody throw Luke out? Not hardly. Not without a scene. There was only one way to make him budge, and that was to give him what he wanted.

"My son disappeared yesterday," she told him flatly. *And it's all my fault.* She wasn't sure how, but she knew it must be. Her guilt added to her anguish.

"What time?" Luke leaned forward, resting his elbows on his knees.

Her mind wandered back to the terrible moment when she'd realized he was really gone. Disbelief had turned to shock, then fear. It was the fear that was twisting noose-tight in her stomach as the minutes slipped past. "What? Oh..." She began to pace again, her hem brushing the carpet as she walked. "Luke, I've already gone over this with Captain Brody." She nodded in Brody's direction, and he responded with a smug sort of nod.

"Well, tell me, then we'll all know," he said, his tone a mix of sarcasm and demand.

She was so astounded by his firm tone that she was more surprised than angry. And maybe that was the best thing. People made mistakes, said things better left unsaid, when they were angry. She needed all her wits about her when dealing with Luke.

She halted by the grand piano and looked out through the lace-curtained window. Rain sheeted on the glass, the lawn and the street beyond, casting blurred shadows, dark and menacing as the vivid fears she had for her son.

With sightless eyes, she continued to stare out as she spoke. "It was about four in the afternoon. I'd let him play in on the porch until dinner was ready. When I went to check on him, he was gone."

"Any sign of a struggle, of any . . . injury?"

She turned sharply. "What do you mean, injury?"

"Blood?"

"Dear God, no!"

"Could he have run off?" he countered quickly, not wanting to upset her more than necessary. "Maybe he's gone somewhere he isn't supposed to go? Boys have a way of doing that sort of thing. Maybe he's afraid to come home."

"No." She shook her head adamantly. "Andrew's not afraid of me. He knows, no matter what, I love him. Besides, I've checked with his friends, and no one has seen him. The only family we have is my mother-in-law, Ruth. She lives with us. She's out there now searching . . . like I should be, would be if—"

He held up a placating hand. "Just a couple more questions."

Luke stood and faced Brody directly. So the boy had been missing all night. He was beginning to get a bad feeling about this. Still, there was no sense jumping to conclusions. "All right, Captain, what have you done to find the child . . . Andrew?"

"Listen, Scanlin, this is none of your business," Brody flung back at him, obviously still smarting from the earlier challenge.

Luke didn't give a damn. "Becky's child is missing. I'm making it my business."

Brody slapped his cap on his head and made as if to leave.

Luke blocked his path.

"I asked you a question, mister, and I want an answer. What have you done to find this child?"

Brody took a couple of steps back and looked up at Luke. Rage colored his blue eyes. "Look, Scanlin, you don't have authority here, and I—" he thumbed his chest, near his badge "—don't answer to you. I'm handling this just fine."

"Sorry to disappoint you," Luke said, without an ounce of remorse in his voice, "but I do have authority here." With thumb and forefinger, he peeled back the edge of his gray wool vest to reveal a small silver badge. "U.S. marshal for this region, as of last Monday."

Brody puffed up like an overstuffed bullfrog. "So?" he sputtered. "This ain't a federal crime. This is local, and that means it's my jurisdiction."

"I wouldn't let a little thing like a technicality get in the way. Becky's in trouble. Her son's in trouble, and that's all the authority I need. This is personal." And it was, he realized with a start—very personal.

Brody's gaze flicked from Luke to Rebecca and back again. "Personal, huh? You and 'Becky' old friends?" he said smugly, in a way that implied something illicit. It implied something that could ruin a lady's reputation.

Luke grabbed a fistful of blue uniform and yanked the man up close, so close their faces were only inches apart. "I don't think I like your tone...Captain." He spit the words out harshly. "The lady and I *are* friends. You wanna make something more out of it?"

Brody covered Luke's hand with his own, trying to pry it loose. His pudgy fingers cut into Luke's knuckles. Luke responded by giving the man a shake. "Now either watch what you say, or you and I can step outside and discuss this more vigorously."

"Luke, for heaven's sake," Rebecca cut in. Luke ignored her this time. No way was he letting this bastard make a remark, start some gossip. He didn't know much about society, but he knew firsthand how hurtful gossip could be.

Brody's cheeks were mottled with red. His eyes literally bulged in his face. Through clenched teeth, Luke continued, "Well, what's it gonna be?" He saw Brody's gaze dart around the room, as though he were looking for help or an escape.

Luke's mouth pulled up in a crooked smile that held no warmth, a smile that said there was no escape.

Helplessly Brody bobbed his head up and down like a puppet on a string. "You and her—"

"Who?" Luke demanded.

"Mrs. Tinsdale! You and Mrs. Tinsdale are friends."

"Damned straight," Luke snarled. "If I hear anything to the contrary, you and I are gonna tangle, Brody." Luke released his hold so suddenly the man stumbled back a couple of steps before regaining either his balance or his composure. "Now, answer my question. What have you done to find the boy?"

This time Brody did answer, though to say it was curt would have been an understatement. Luke listened to Brody's half hearted excuse for a search plan. The man couldn't find his hat in a room full of spurs.

Good thing Luke had spent the past three days looking over the files in the office, the map of the city, police rosters and the like. It was always his habit to familiarize himself with a town. Luke had never thought he'd need his knowledge so quickly, or for such an unhappy reason.

Without hesitation, he said, "Pull the patrolmen from the residential areas. Those are low-risk and can spare the men. Leave the business districts and the, ah . . . entertainment areas down by the docks at full staff. If there's any trouble, it'll be there first. Have the men here within an hour."

Brody smoothed his rumpled uniform over his belly. "Who the hell do you think you are, coming in here—"

"I think I'm the man who's gonna find that boy." If it wasn't too late, he thought but didn't say. Becky looked upset enough, without him adding to it, especially if it wasn't necessary.

Brody made a derisive sound in the back of his throat. "The men won't like being pulled off duty to search for some kid who's probably holed up somewhere, laughing his head off at all the excitement."

Rebecca spoke up. "Andrew would never—"

Luke cut across her words. "I don't want to hear your opinions, Brody. Do what I'm telling you, and do it now, dammit!"

Brody slapped his cap on his head and stormed toward the front door. "I'll see the mayor about this, Scanlin." He disappeared around the doorway.

"Yeah, well, tell him to wire President Hayes if he's got any complaints," Luke snarled. There were some advantages to being a U.S. marshal. Being a presidential appointee was one of them.

Quickly he called out, "Right here, one hour—or I'll come looking for you."

The door slammed with glass-rattling force. With an anger he didn't mean to take out on Rebecca, Luke whirled and said, "I'll need a room."

"What?" she muttered. She was still trying to assimilate the fact that Luke was a U.S. marshal. Of all the places in this country that needed a marshal, why did he have to be here—now?

Suddenly his demand penetrated her thoughts. "What do you mean, you want a room? Don't marshals get offices and quarters?"

"Offices yes, quarters no—"

"Well, you *can't* stay here." she said, meaning more than in this house and more than this minute. She wanted him gone.

"Becky, my room is way the other side of town. The search area is here. I need to be close to the trouble."

He obviously wasn't going to go quietly. "Look, I appreciate you helping me with Captain Brody, and I appreciate you wanting to help with the search, but I hardly think you need to stay *here.*"

She started for the hallway. Luke followed, not bothering to bring along his hat and slicker.

She could be just as determined as he was. Lifting her coat from the mirrored hall tree, she pulled it on. The black wool was expensive and cashmere-soft against the side of her neck.

Luke positioned himself between her and the doorway. "Are you deliberately trying to make this difficult?"

"I'm not." It was already more difficult than anything should be. With both hands, she pulled her hood up to cover her hair. "Staying here isn't—"

"Do you want the boy—"

"Andrew."

"Andrew," he said with a nod. "Do you want him back or not?" He ran both hands through his hair, leaving furrows in the inky blackness.

"Of course, but—"

"I'm telling you, I need to be *here*. I need to coordinate with the police, and I can't do that if I'm running back and forth most of the time. Look, if it's so troublesome, I'll camp in the damned front yard. It wouldn't be the first time I've been cold and dirty."

She looked up then, saw the determination and the concern mirrored in his grim expression. Was there some plan to make her life as difficult as possible? She desperately needed help, had prayed for help, but not from Luke Scanlin. Anyone but Luke Scanlin.

Logic warred with fear—fear of herself and him and the sudden flare of pleasure she'd felt when he first walked in here. What kind of a woman was she to have even the barest trembling of desire when her son was missing?

Without thinking, she took a retreating step back. "Why are you doing this?"

"Because you need me."

"I don't need you," she countered emphatically.

"Well, you need someone, 'cause even I can see that Brody's not getting the job done. I do this for a living, and I'm damned good at it."

That she had no doubt about. It was the needing-him part that was grating on her already raw nerves. She needed Luke Scanlin like she needed to be trampled in a stampede, but it all came down to this: Brody was next to useless. Luke had managed to get more from the man in the past few minutes than she'd managed since last night. Andrew was out there, and if it would help her get her son back, she'd dance with the devil himself. Looking at Luke's hypnotic black eyes, she had a sinking feeling that the dance was about to begin.

"There's a guest room at the top of the stairs." She gestured with her head. "I'll have the maid show you."

"I can track down a guest room." He smiled, and this time he touched her shoulder, very lightly.

It was the second time he'd touched her. The second time those familiar shivers had skittered up her spine. No! She wouldn't give in to him. Not this time. Not ever again. Needing distance, she moved away. "Third door on the left." She fumbled with the ebony buttons on her coat. "The bed's made, and I'll have towels brought in when I return. The housekeeper's been sick. She'll be back tomorrow. My mother-in-law will be here tonight."

Luke smiled. It was a lopsided smile, filled with enough roguish charm to melt the coldest heart. If she stood here looking at that smile much longer, her knees were going to melt, that was for certain.

"I'll be back later." She was reaching for the shiny brass doorknob when his hand on her shoulder turned her to face him again. His dark brows were drawn together in a frown.

"Back? What do you mean, back? *Where* are you going?"

"Out." She made a show of tugging on her kidskin gloves while she slipped free of his touch. Darn those goose bumps.

Luke's expression drew down. "Out? Why, for heaven's sake? The police will be here in an hour, and then—"

"I'm going now." She turned the knob and pulled the door partially open. The rain dripped from the roof and made noisy *plick-plops* on the wooden planks of the porch. The sudden draft felt blessedly cold against the side of her face.

"Look," he started to say with a nod—a gesture Rebecca suspected was meant to pacify rather than to indicate agreement. He grasped the edge of the open door, holding it firmly, and looked at her in a way that was all too familiar, a way that brought better-forgotten memories rushing to the surface faster than lava in a volcano, and just as hot.

"This is crazy. We're gonna cover the same ground in an hour." He pushed on the door.

Rebecca held fast, as though this were a test of wills between them. Accepting help was one thing, surrender was another. This felt like giving in. "I'm going." She pulled, and he released his hold on the door.

She slipped out and pulled the heavy oak door closed behind her. She knew he was watching her through the clear etched glass. Until thirty minutes ago, she had thought she'd closed the door on Luke Scanlin just as easily. It seemed she was wrong.

Chapter Two

Rebecca took the front steps in five firm strides. She was angry, and it wasn't until the rain splattered against her cheeks that she realized she'd forgotten to take an umbrella. Clenched-jawed and angry, she kept going. She'd drown before she'd go back in there. She'd had enough of him for now. She'd had enough of him for good.

Raindrops clung to her eyelashes, and she swiped them away with the back of her gloved hand, then yanked her hood farther forward—not that it did much good. It was raining like hell. By the time she turned through the gate, her coat was soaked and the wet had penetrated through to her dress. Goose bumps were prickling across her shoulders, and a shiver was inching down her spine.

She made a sharp left turn that would have been the envy of any military cadet. Thunder rumbled, but failed to silence the steady *click-clack* of her heels on the concrete sidewalk. Her coat flopped open with each step, further drenching her dress. Nothing and no one was cooperating—not the police, not the weather, and not even the good Lord, it seemed. She cast her eyes upward. "How could you do this to me? Luke? You sent me Luke?"

With a sigh of resignation, she increased her pace, and promptly stepped in an ankle-deep puddle for her trouble.

"Thanks," she muttered, and kept going.

She passed the Johnson mansion, four colors of clapboard and geegaws in the latest style. *Circus tent* was the thought that flashed in her mind as she paused long enough to scan the yard and porch for the third time since Andrew had disappeared. The Hogans', next door, was more sedate—plain, white siding and blue trim, the usually pale green roof shingles now forest-dark from the rain.

A delivery wagon rumbled past, splashing her with more water. "Hey!" she hollered, but the driver kept going. So did she, scanning the yard yet again.

All the while, she kept thinking that Andrew was out here and Luke was back there. She wished it was the other way around. She wished Luke was gone—back to Texas or Wyoming or Timbuktu, anywhere but here. Part of her wanted to deny it, pretend it wasn't true, pretend that Luke Scanlin, the man who had changed her life forever, the one man who unknowingly had the power to ruin her life, wasn't sitting in her parlor.

She stopped still. He'd be there tonight. He'd be sleeping down the hall. He'd talk to Ruth. Oh, no! Oh, no, this wasn't going to happen. She wasn't going to take this kind of risk, not again.

When she got home, she was going to send him packing. That was all there was to it. She didn't have to explain or justify herself to him. In fact, the more she thought on it, the more she thought she didn't even *need* him.

Brody's going to find Andrew, right?

Sure. "I'll have the men keep an eye out," he had said. Yes, that would go a long way toward finding Andrew, she thought, her heart sinking as she faced reality.

Okay, so Brody was unreliable. Luke's take-charge attitude obviously was going to get the job done, she admitted—only to herself, and only because she was alone.

Since she was admitting things, she'd also admit she should have stayed at the house, should have waited for the search parties he was organizing. And yes, dammit, she was grateful for his help.

A smile tickled her lips. It had been something to see, watching Luke put that pompous Brody in his place. One side of her mouth actually curved upward in a sort of smile—not a real one, though. She wouldn't give Luke that much.

Water splashed and soaked up her stockings as she stepped off the curb and crossed the street. *What are you getting all worked up about?* she asked herself. *You can handle Luke Scanlin. You're not affected by him anymore, remember?*

Not affected by Luke Scanlin anymore? Yes, she remembered. That first year, she'd said it to herself more often than a nun would say the rosary.

She was entirely different from the way she had been at eighteen, a young girl whose head was full of adventure and romance. A young girl waiting for her knight in shining armor to whisk her away to his castle.

There were darned few knights in San Francisco, but a real Texas cowboy had come awfully close. She'd met Luke Scanlin at a party. He'd been a guest of Lucy Pemberton's brother, Tom. The rumor had quickly circulated that Luke was a war hero, on his way to join the Texas Rangers.

He had been tall, dark and handsome—*and* forbidden. At least by her mother, who had reminded her that he didn't have any social position, any name. In short, he wasn't *somebody.*

Luke hadn't seemed to know or care about such things, and that had made him all the more exciting. He'd been the stuff of Miss Pennybrook's romantic novels—the ones respectable young ladies were not supposed to read.

Never mind that she had been practically engaged to Nathan Tinsdale. Never mind that she had been expected to marry and settle down to a respectable life that had been all planned out for her since the day she was born.

Nathan had been older than she by nearly twenty years, a man who had chosen to forgo marriage in order to pursue business. He hadn't been nearly so appealing to a young girl as a cowboy who enticed her with word and touch until she surrendered to him.

Her hands shook, and it was from the memory, not the cold rain. She stopped still as feelings that were both deep and delicious washed over her. She remembered being in his arms. Her fingers brushed her lips as she remembered the sensation of his mouth on hers.

Excitement exploded in her like a shot. Despite the rain, her mouth was desert-dry. Her eyes fluttered closed.

Luke.

As quickly as the feelings had come, they were gone, replaced by guilt, gut-wrenching guilt. Dear God, what was the matter with her? How . . . how could she even think of anyone or anything else when her son, her baby, was missing?

She shook her head to clear away the cobwebs, send the ghosts back to their graves. What she and Luke had shared had been over a long time ago. Nathan was gone, but she had Andrew, and that was all she needed, would ever need.

It had been a fearful thing when she learned she was expecting. But somehow things had worked out, and from the first moment she set eyes on her baby, she'd thanked the good Lord for giving her this child. Andrew was a joy in her life, sometimes the only joy. Her world was built around him. Without him, there was a giant emptiness where her heart should be.

You'll find him. You'll get him back.

With a great sigh, she started walking again, startling a blackbird perched on a nearby picket fence. She watched as the bird took flight, and wished she could fly away from her troubles as easily.

Light gray clouds warred with darker ones, and it didn't take an expert to know this storm wouldn't be letting up anytime soon. She skirted a parked carriage whose shiny blue wheels were dulled by mud and crossed the street, turning left on Taylor.

She scanned the area, but she already knew Andrew wasn't there. She had covered this whole section twice yesterday. Still, she called out. "Andrew! Andrew, are you there?"

No answer.

She focused on the narrow houses that lined the street like ornately painted dollhouses. Straining to look between them, she clung to the faint glimmer of hope. Perhaps . . .

A mother's instinct told her that he wasn't here. He wasn't anywhere she'd searched already. Brody's admonition about Andrew being kidnapped circled in the shadows of her mind, and she held it off with the bright light of hope.

They needed a methodical search of the area, not some ragtag hit-or-miss stroll through the neighborhoods. And yes, Luke was right.

He'd been here less than an hour and already he was taking over. Luke had a way of taking over, she thought, remembering how it had been with them.

He'd taken over her life back then. She'd wanted to be with him every minute, and when she wasn't she'd been thinking about him, planning how to slip away to be with him. Then, two days after they made love, Luke Scanlin had gotten on his horse and ridden away. Just like that. A brief note saying he was off to Texas. He hadn't even come by in person to tell her.

Her heart lurched as she remember the devastation, the hurt. She'd feigned illness and locked herself in her room for a day. It had seemed that most of that time she spent crying, or cursing his name, or praying it was a mistake and he'd return for her.

A month later, she'd given up on that idea. She'd known the truth then, about Luke, about trusting him.

Well, she thought, her chin coming up a notch in a defiant gesture, she'd done a lot of growing up that month, and she'd made some difficult choices.

Thunder rumbled, and a single bolt of lightning slashed across the sky, seeming to dive into the bay.

It had rained the day she married Nathan. What a dear, sweet man he'd been. Even if theirs had not been a marriage of passion, it had been a good marriage. She'd cared for and respected Nathan. She was eternally grateful to him.

She could still remember how frightened she'd been when she told him...everything. He'd been so understanding, telling her that he was not so free of sin that he could judge her. At that moment, Rebecca had felt her life was beginning anew, and she'd been grateful to Nathan for giving her that chance.

They had spent their honeymoon in Europe, and it had been a wonderful time, spent visiting wondrous museums in England, dining at romantic sidewalk cafés in Paris, going to the opera in Italy. Then they'd returned to San Francisco, and she'd moved into the home he shared with his mother, Ruth. A warmth came over her at the thought of Ruth. She was the dearest person Rebecca had ever known. She'd welcomed Rebecca to the family with a love and affection that had never failed through all the years since.

Then a slick street, a steep hill, a horse that lost its footing, and Nathan's carriage had turned over, killing Nathan, the driver, and two pedestrians. It had been an awful, tragic time. This only a year after her father's death. When it seemed things couldn't get worse, her mother, too, had passed away, only six months later.

It had been more than she could bear. Confused, overwhelmed by it all, she'd withdrawn into herself, refusing to leave her room, refusing to see anyone, refusing to eat or sleep.

It had been Ruth who had stood by her, forced her to eat, sat with her while she slept, cared for Andrew when Rebecca wasn't up to the task. It had been Ruth who gave her hope and love and slowly brought her back and, yes, it had even been Ruth who insisted that Rebecca keep and run the small newspaper that was part of Nathan's estate.

Somehow Ruth had known that working would give Rebecca the focus, the purpose, she needed. With that purpose, she'd recovered, devoting her life to Andrew and Ruth and the paper.

They were her world, and they'd been there for her through it all, good and bad.

She owed Ruth her life, and the debt was more than she could ever repay.

She pushed a lock of water-soaked hair back from her face and stopped, staring hard at the dark silhouette of a woman standing near the corner on the opposite side of the street. Dressed in a black coat and holding an equally black umbrella, she was a dark form against the gray-black sky. Rebecca took another step and saw the woman sway, then clutch an oak tree for support.

"Ruth!" she yelled. Hitching up her skirt, Rebecca ran flat out to help. Jumping over the rivulet of water near the curb, she grabbed Ruth by both arms. "Are you all right?"

Ruth looked up. She was cold, soaked to the skin, and her whole body seemed to be shaking with the force of a small earthquake. It was the painful, frantic beating of her heart that was scaring the devil out of her. At seventy, a body had to expect such things, she supposed. At least that was what that quack Doc Tilson kept telling her. Trouble was, she kept forgetting that she was old. In her mind, she was still twenty, and she had a lot to live for, like her grandson and Rebecca.

So, gulping in a couple of deep breaths, she forced a shaky smile and said, "I'm fine. Just a little winded."

"Sure you are!" Rebecca obviously didn't believe her for a minute. "Stay here. I'm getting the buggy."

Rain trickled down from the oak tree, spattering on the walk.

"No." Ruth shook her head. "I'm fine, or I will be. I need a minute to catch my breath." She straightened to prove her point, and was rewarded with a sharp pain that started in the center of her chest and shot down her left arm, making her fingers tingle. She clenched her teeth, refusing to reveal the pain. Rebecca had enough to worry about.

"Come on," she said firmly, reaching out. "I'll just take your arm."

"No chance. I'm getting that buggy, then we're calling the doctor." She made a half turn to leave.

"I'm not helpless." Ruth started walking. Her steps were slow and measured, but she was determined to keep going. Rebecca had no choice but to snatch up the umbrella and fall in step with her.

"At least let me help you," she chided gently. "You're more hardheaded than . . . than . . ."

"A mule," Ruth put in with a smile that was forced. She took Rebecca's offered arm.

"Than a mule," Rebecca returned. Holding up the umbrella, she managed to give them both a little protection from the steady downpour. They stepped off the curb and crossed Taylor Street. "If anything happened to you, I—"

"Nothing's going to happen to me," Ruth told her, knowing what Rebecca was going through. She loved Rebecca like a daughter. Rebecca had been exactly the right one for Nathan. She'd been patient and kind and loving to Ruth's only son. Since Nathan had died, they'd been through a lot together. "Believe me. Nothing is going to happen to me. I'm too old and too cantankerous to die."

"You shouldn't be out here," Rebecca chided gently. Wet leaves, stirred by the breeze, clung to their shoes and the hems of their dresses. "You know the doctor said you should rest and—"

"Dr. Tilson's an old worrywart." She didn't have the strength to smile this time. "Besides, you can't think I'd sit at home when Andrew is—" pain clenched in her chest like a vise, and her step faltered, but she recovered and continued on "—out here lost." She gulped some air. That pain was increasing. Maybe she really had overdone it this time.

They turned onto California Street, and the house came blessedly into view.

Only half a block. Only half a block.

Ruth said the words over and over, counting the steps in her mind. Pretending she knew how many it was to the house made her feel better. All she needed was to sit down for a few minutes, maybe a cup of strong tea, and she'd be right as rain.

Poor choice of words, she thought, glancing up and getting a faceful of water for her trouble. Her dress was wet from the hem up and the shoulders down, the only dryness somewhere in the middle. She was cold clear through, and she clenched her teeth to keep them from chattering.

Rebecca paused. "Slow down, there's no hurry."

But there was. Ruth was afraid that if she stopped she might not get started again. All she wanted was to get home. Funny how home was the ultimate remedy.

And yet, with the house in sight, she was anxious. "Let's keep going. This rain is getting worse." She pressed on. One foot in front of the other. The pain was a constant now. "Tell . . . me about . . . Andrew," she managed, a little breathless.

"The police didn't find anything."

Ruth nodded her understanding. "We'll find him." She ground out the words firmly, needing to believe them as much as she needed Rebecca to believe them.

Rain cascaded off the tips of the umbrella in delicate rivulets. Rebecca covered Ruth's hand with her own in a reassuring gesture. They turned through the gate and up the walk. Ruth took the stairs slowly, one step, then the next, then the last. It hurt to breathe.

"I think. . . I'll lie down for a little while," Ruth said as Rebecca tossed the umbrella aside and started helping her with her coat. "If you'll help me up the stairs."

At the sound of the door, Luke glanced up from the large hand-drawn map he had spread across one end of the long, narrow dining room table. He wasn't alone. Three policemen had arrived about five minutes ago, with a less than friendly attitude, which he was ignoring. He'd also rounded up several of the neighbors, who were more than willing to help and had brought as many of their household staff with them as possible. All in all, there were nine of them.

Keeping an eye on the doorway, he said, "Now, gentlemen, what I want is a complete and thorough search of these areas." He pointed to the map, his fingers tracing the outline of an area approximately ten blocks square.

The policemen glared. "We covered that area," one of them snapped.

In a voice filled with concern, Luke said, "Did you cover it as though it was *your* son out there?"

The policemen all looked sheepish.

Luke turned to the others. "I want a complete search, under every porch, inside every stable loft, behind every outhouse. Look in chicken coops, doghouses and tree houses. Look anywhere big enough for a boy to hide. Remember, he could be hurt, could be unconscious and unable to call out. It's up to us to find him."

Everyone, including the policemen, nodded, and Luke felt confident that he'd get a thorough search this time.

They were finishing, and he kept expecting to see Rebecca appear in the doorway. He was still angry—well, annoyed, anyway—that she'd gone out, but he figured that now that she was back, she'd want in on this discussion. When she didn't come in, he said, "Excuse me a moment," and, edging sideways between the police and the mahogany table, he strode for the hallway, his footsteps muffled by the carpet.

One hand resting on the door frame, he paused to see Rebecca and another woman. Obviously someone she knew. The woman was short, barely over five feet, he guessed. Her black dress made her seem more so. Her white hair was pulled back in a knot at the base of her neck. She looked pale and shaky.

"Becky? Everything all right?"

Her head snapped around. "Luke, help me." She was struggling to help the woman out of her drenched coat. "Ruth isn't feeling well, and—"

"I'm—" Ruth swayed slightly, then collapsed like a rag doll.

"Ruth!" Rebecca screamed, making a grab for her.

Luke was there instantly and caught her. He lifted her limp body in his arms. At the sound of Rebecca's scream, the other men came thundering into the tiny hallway.

"What's happened?"

"What's wrong?"

Luke was already moving toward the steep staircase. "Where's her room?" he demanded.

"Top of the stairs, first door on the left." Rebecca hitched up her skirt to follow, but she hesitated long enough to address the neighbor standing closest. "Mr. Neville, please send someone for Dr. Tilson."

"Of course. Is Mrs. Tinsdale—"

"I'll let you know. Please hurry." She turned and took the stairs as fast as her confining skirt would let her.

Careering through the doorway, she skidded to a halt as Luke put Ruth's motionless body on the four-poster bed.

"I've sent for the doctor." She started unbuttoning the tiny buttons down the front of Ruth's high-necked dress. The foulard was wet and clingy, making the work difficult. "We've got to get her out of these wet things."

He was already slipping one of Ruth's shoes off. "Stockings?" he questioned.

She nodded and, lifting Ruth's skirt slightly, he pulled off her silk stockings, then helped Rebecca remove Ruth's dress and petticoats and corset. The woman was ill. This was no time to stand on formality. "What happened?"

"Bad heart." She pulled up the coverlet and glanced frantically at the door. "Where's that doctor?" It was a rhetorical question, born of desperation. She took

Ruth's hand in hers. "Ruth..." Rebecca rubbed her cold hand, trying to bring some warmth back. "Ruth? Can you hear me? Oh, Luke, she's like ice. If anything happens to her, too..." She rubbed her other hand. "She isn't moving." Her voice rose. Wild-eyed, she turned on him. "Why isn't she moving?" Terror welled up in her. "Oh, God! She isn't—"

Luke touched the woman's face, then checked for a pulse. "No, honey, she isn't dead."

Muscles relaxing, Rebecca swayed into him. "Thank God." He held her, and she leaned into him, feeling the warmth of his body, feeling the hard muscles, feeling secure. "She can't die," she murmured, and felt his fingers tighten on her shoulder.

"She'll be all right, honey," he said, with such confidence that she believed him.

She angled him a look, seeing the sincerity of his expression, and she was tempted to stay here in his partial embrace. It felt so good, too good. It would be too easy to give in to it.

She couldn't. She couldn't trust him, or herself, evidently. Dragging in a couple of lungfuls of air, she straightened slightly, and he released his hold, leaving her feeling strangely alone.

"Okay?" he asked softly.

She forced her chin up a notch, shoved the wet hair back from her face and said, "Thank you."

"Anytime," he said, and headed for the warming stove near the window. He made quick work of starting a fire.

Rebecca tucked the comforter more securely around Ruth and dragged a Windsor chair over to the bed.

"You oughta get out of those wet clothes yourself," Luke said as he closed the stove door with a bang.

"As soon as the doctor comes."

"You'll catch your— You'll catch a cold."

"Soon," she murmured, holding Ruth's hand. "Where the devil is that doctor?"

Luke crossed back to stand at the foot of the bed. "I take it this isn't a new problem."

"It's her heart. She's had trouble the last couple of years, but nothing like this." She craned toward the doorway. "Why doesn't she open her eyes?"

"Well, I'm no doctor, but I do believe that the Almighty has a way of taking care of things. As long as she's asleep, she's not moving around and she's not in pain."

Rebecca nodded her understanding. "This is awful. I feel so responsible. She hasn't slept since Andrew disappeared, and—"

"Neither have you I'll wager, and you *aren't* responsible for her, or for whatever has happened to Andrew," he said firmly.

She was only half listening, her gaze focused on Ruth. "I should never have let her go out there. I should have insisted."

"You take on a lot of responsibility. Seems to me the lady had something to say about things. You didn't push her out the door, you know."

She sighed. "I know you're right, but..."

The crackle and pop of the fire seemed to warm the room as much as the actual burning log. The sweet scent of pine saturated the damp air.

"Where's the extra blankets?" Luke broke the silence.

"Cedar chest."

Luke retrieved a heavy blue quilt and covered Ruth with it.

Rebecca kept staring at her mother-in-law, rubbing first one hand, then the other. "Ruth. You'll be fine." She said it like an order, or perhaps a prayer.

Luke watched from the foot of the four-poster bed, one hand wrapped around the smooth, cool mahogany. "This is your mother-in-law, right?"

Rebecca nodded. "It was too much for her." She turned to him with soulful eyes. "It's Andrew. She loves him so. He's her only grandson. They're very close—best friends, I guess."

Luke closed on her, rubbing her shoulder in a familiar way. "Don't give up on her."

"Never," she said firmly, glancing up at his downturned face. "She's *my* best friend, too." Her voice cracked, and she swiped at the tear that suddenly slipped down her cheek. "I feel so helpless."

"I know, honey. Why don't you come over here and get warm, at least?" He gently led her the few steps to the stove.

The pale green drapes were pulled back, and she could see the storm continuing in all its fury outside. Lightning flashed across the morning sky, followed by a clap of thunder so loud it made her jump.

Her gaze swung back to Ruth, who didn't move. "Does it look like her color is coming back?" she asked cautiously.

"A little," he agreed.

She dragged in another deep breath, as though she hadn't breathed at all since they'd walked into the house.

The warmth of the stove reached her skin through the water-stained fabric of her dress. She instinctively turned and rubbed her hands together, letting the warmth inch up her arms. When she glanced up, he was staring at her.

Their gazes locked. His was dark and knowing, as though he could see inside her mind, as though he could touch her soul. Feeling awkward, she asked, "Why are you here, Luke?"

"I told you. I came to see you."

Absently she rubbed her hands together, this time refusing to look at him. "Why now?"

He seemed to consider her question, then said, "Truth?"

She stilled. "Truth."

"Because I had to know if the reality was as good as the dream."

"What dream?" She slanted him a look, not trusting herself to do more.

He crooked one finger under her chin and turned her face fully toward his. She looked into his eyes, eyes that were bottomless, soft, inviting. He brushed a wisp of hair back from her face, and her skin tingled from his touch. He was so close. Her control seemed to be slipping away.

His gaze rested on her lips. His voice was a husky whisper. "You, Princess. You haunt my dreams."

His words were explicit. Tiny sparks of electricity skittered across her skin, warm, exciting, stirring a familiar longing much too quickly.

Stop this—now! The words ricocheted in her brain, but her body refused to move, somehow refusing to give up the nearness of him. The air was ripe with sudden anticipation.

His mouth pulled up in a slow, lazy smile. "I've missed you."

Rebecca didn't move, held as she was by his hypnotic gaze. Her breathing got a little ragged. At least she thought she was breathing. She wasn't actually sure. He was too handsome, too charming, too dangerous. Oh, yes, he was very, very dangerous.

It was the danger that sparked her to say, "I haven't missed you."

If he took offense, he didn't show it. In fact, he seemed amused.

"Never play poker, honey. You can't bluff worth a darn."

The man was too arrogant for words. But she was about to try anyway, when there was a knock at the door. Almost in the same instant, a voice, a male voice, called, "Mrs. Tinsdale?"

Her chin came up a notch and, with a little smile of her own, she turned and called, "Yes, Doctor, in here." She went to meet him.

Luke introduced himself to the doctor and quickly left. She didn't even bother to glance up. If he thought she was at all bothered by him, well, he was wrong.

Never mind that she was distracted enough that she had to ask the doctor to repeat a couple of questions. What was wrong with her? Guilt twisted knife-sharp in her stomach. Ruth was lying in a sickbed, and here she was thinking about Luke.

No, she wasn't thinking about Luke. She was wishing he'd go to—well, to wherever it was marshals went to.

In the meantime, she had to get her mind back on the people who mattered.

Twenty minutes later, the doctor was ready to leave. He had prescribed bed rest, and laudanum for pain—which Ruth, who had awakened shortly after his arrival, adamantly refused to take.

"All right," she finally said, in a tone that reminded Rebecca of Andrew when he had to take a bath. It was good to see her awake and snapping at the doctor. It was good to have her back.

Feeling much relieved, she walked the doctor to the door.

"Now try to keep her in bed," he admonished quietly.

"I heard that," Ruth called, and they both smiled. "She's gonna be all right, Mrs. Tinsdale," the doctor said, with a reassuring grin and a pat on the shoulder. "She's gonna be fine."

"Thank you, Doctor." Rebecca grinned. "Do you mind letting yourself out?"

"Not at all. Not at all."

Still smiling, Rebecca turned to find Ruth sitting—not lying—in the bed. "Just what do you think you're doing?" She crossed the room, pausing long enough to get Ruth's nightdress from the closet.

"I'm getting up, of course."

"You'll do no such thing," Rebecca countered, with an emphatic shake of her index finger. "We're going to finish getting you undressed and then get you back into bed."

Ruth screwed up her face in protest, but she did put on the flannel nightdress. "What about finding Andrew?" She fumbled with the bone buttons, and Rebecca helped her.

"I've got help." She pulled back the covers and coaxed Ruth to lie down.

"What help? You mean Brody? Bah!" She fussed with her pillows until she was propped up.

"No, not Brody." Rebecca smoothed the covers. "Someone—"

"Can I come in?" a decidedly male voice said from behind her. She didn't have to turn to know Luke was there, in the doorway. She sucked in a breath and mustered her best formal pose. She needed all her composure when it came to Luke.

"Come in, Marshal Scanlin."

Rebecca was sitting in the Windsor chair and holding Ruth's hand. She was still wearing her navy dress, and Luke could see that she was drier now, though he figured that she was soaked to the skin underneath.

She should have changed, but she was stubborn to the end.

"Why, thank you, Becky." He used her familiar name, disregarding her formality. He saw the irritation flash in her eyes, and he had to fight the smile that tugged at his lips.

He stopped at the foot of the bed. "Ma'am," he said politely. "I'm glad to see you are feeling better. I saw the doc downstairs, and he said you were doing better, so I thought it would be okay for me to stop by."

For a long moment, Ruth didn't speak, didn't even move. She just stared at Luke. Feeling uncomfortable, he shifted his stance and raked one hand through his hair. "Ma'am, is something wrong?"

Ruth blinked, then blinked again. "No...Marshal, is it?"

"Yes, ma'am. Luke Scanlin. I'm the marshal for this region." He gave her his best smile.

"Have we met before, Marshal?" She kept on studying him. "You look like someone..." She shook her head, and Rebecca stilled.

Luke arched one brow in question. "Who?" He shoved one hand through his hair again.

Ruth's face drew up in a puzzled expression. "I..." Slowly her eyes widened. "So it's you..." Her gaze shot to Rebecca, then back to Luke. The color drained from her face.

Rebecca surged from her chair. "Ruth? Are you all right? Shall I send for the doctor?"

Luke made a half turn, as if to do just that.

"No." Ruth's voice cracked. "No," she repeated, holding up one hand. "I'm all right."

"Maybe I'd better go," Luke said.

"No, Marshall, stay," Ruth countered, more firmly. She adjusted her position on the propped-up pillows behind her back. Rebecca helped her.

"So it's me what, ma'am?" Luke asked.

"What? Oh, so, it's you who helped me to my room," Ruth answered quietly.

"Yes, ma'am."

"The marshal is new in town," Rebecca said, smoothing the covers before sitting down again.

"Well, that explains a great deal." Ruth's tone was thoughtful. "Under the circumstances, Marshal, I think you know me well enough to call me Ruth. 'Ma'am' sounds so old, and—"

"And old is twenty years older than you are...Ruth," he filled in, grinning.

"Marshal, I think I like you. I always did have a weakness for charmers."

"Not me. I'm telling the truth," he teased innocently.

Ruth laughed. "So this must be the help you said you had."

"Yes" was all Rebecca said.

"Well, Marshal, we are thankful for all the assistance we can get. Aren't we, Rebecca?"

"Grateful. Yes."

Luke came around to stand close to Rebecca. "I'm sorry we're meeting under these circumstances. I hope I can help find Becky's boy. Actually, one of the reasons I came up here was to tell you that the search parties have gone out and I'm going myself, right now." He touched her shoulder lightly in a familiar gesture. "They'll come back here as soon as they've covered their assigned areas."

Rebecca spared him a look that didn't last as long as a heartbeat. "Thank you."

He headed for the door.

Ruth's voice stopped him. "Marshal Scanlin."

"Yes." He didn't turn, only looked back over his left shoulder, one hand braced on the edge of the door frame.

Her expression and tone had turned serious. "It's very important that you find Andrew."

"Yes, ma'am. I know."

"I wonder if you do," Ruth said gently.

Chapter Three

The Barbary Coast was only a few short blocks from Nob Hill, but it might as well have been the other side of the earth. The Coast was several square blocks of the seediest, raunchiest real estate anywhere. It was the reason San Francisco was the most dangerous city in America.

Sin was for sale on the Barbary Coast. A man could name his pleasure and be certain to find it. He could lose his money in the gambling halls and saloons, lose his virtue in the brothels, or lose his life in the opium dens along Pacific Street. All in all, there were over five hundred concert saloons serving alcohol, and anything else, to the unsuspecting.

The good people of San Francisco gave the Barbary Coast a wide berth. The trouble was, so did the law. "Enter at your own risk," said some. "Let 'em kill each other, and good riddance," said others.

So it was only natural that when a man wanted something done that was, well, less than lawful, he'd come to the Barbary Coast.

That was exactly what Frank Handley had done last week, and tonight he was back, seated at a table near the back wall of Fat Daugherty's.

It wasn't much of a saloon, he thought, taking in the long, narrow room. The ornate mahogany bar took up all of one wall, and the mirror behind the bar had a couple of cracks as big as earthquake fissures. A bartender with a handlebar moustache and greasy hair was serving rotgut that the patrons didn't seem to mind consuming.

Cigarette smoke grayed the air, and the planked floor was sticky from too many spilled drinks and too much tobacco juice.

The place was doing a brisk business, though, he noted with a bit of surprise. Nearly two-thirds of the tables were taken, by groups of sailors—whalers, most likely—and wide-eyed farmers and cowboys in town to "see the elephant" before going home flat broke, if the cardsharps had their way. They usually did. Hell, Will and Finck were actually putting out a catalog of devices for the professional gambler who didn't mind using a little sleight of hand to ensure that he won. Yup, cheating was an industry, he thought, somewhat amused.

A man dressed in denim pants and a buckskin shirt edged past on his way to the bar, bumping into Frank with a thud, then glaring at Frank as though he were the one doing the bumping.

"Sorry," Frank muttered.

"Yeah," the man growled, and blessedly continued on his way.

Frank released the breath he'd been holding. He felt as out of place as a rabbit at a wolf convention. But he was here now, and he had business, so he leaned back in his chair and tried to look calm and composed.

The chair wobbled pretty much like Frank's confidence. One of the back legs was shorter than the others, so he leaned forward again, forearms on the edge of the table. His finely tailored gray suit was in sharp contrast to the stained and gouged surface of the square table.

He was waiting for the Riggs brothers, who were late. Where were they? All he wanted was to say his say and get the hell out of here. This was not his sort of place, after all. Frank had finer tastes. He preferred saloons like the one on Montgomery Street—slate billiard tables, gilt-framed paintings and glittering chandeliers.

If it weren't for his job, he wouldn't spend five seconds in a place like this.

Music started up from the out-of-tune piano. An argument broke out at the table next to him. A man shouting at another about fixed dice in a game of high-low-jack. The two lunged for each other, and Frank shrank back against the wall, praying he wouldn't get involved, or hurt.

The bartender scrambled over the bar, wielding an ax handle, and effectively and efficiently ended the dispute with a resounding blow across the shoulders of one man. Frank winced as the man sagged to the floor.

"I ain't puttin' up with no fightin' in here," he snarled, the saloon suddenly quiet. He waved the ax handle in the air to punctuate his order. Grabbing the unconscious man by the shirt collar, he dragged him toward the door. His boot heels left trails on the filthy floor. For the span of two heartbeats, no one moved. Then, as if nothing had happened, everyone went back to doing what they had been before.

Heart pounding, Frank slid back into his wobbly chair. If the Riggs brothers didn't show up soon, he was leaving. Instinctively he patted the envelope that was making a small bulge in his jacket pocket. Damn. He couldn't leave.

But, hell, he was a lawyer, not some street ruffian. Oh, sure, there were some who'd put his profession close to a criminal's, but they'd be wrong, emphatically wrong.

Lawyers were hired by someone to do a job that that same someone didn't want to do, or couldn't do themselves. And that was exactly what Frank was doing. Okay, so maybe it wasn't exactly legal, or ethical, but it paid well, very well, and no one got hurt. Frank had his code, too. It was simple. In business, everything was fair as long as no one got hurt—physically hurt, that is. Financially, well, that was another story.

Frank nodded to himself, pleased with his code of ethics. Across the saloon, a ruddy-faced man in a lopsided top hat kept pounding out music on the badly tuned piano. One of the saloon girls, dressed in nothing but white pantaloons, black stockings and a bright yellow corset, decided to sing along. The sound was reminiscent of fingernails on a chalkboard, and made his skin prickle and his ears ache.

He craned his neck, searching the room. God, where were they? He scanned the crowd again and flinched as the singer hit a particularly painful note that didn't exist on any known musical scale.

It was reflex that made him pour a glass of whiskey from the bottle he'd ordered when he came in. Good sense stopped him from drinking it. The liquid was the color of a polluted stream and smelled like the contents of a chamber pot. He grimaced.

He'd take Irish whiskey any day. Still, he toyed with the glass, hoping he looked at home. Where the hell were the Riggses? Five minutes. He'd give them five minutes, and boss or no boss, he'd—

"Evenin'," a male voice said, and Frank jumped at the sound, it was so close.

"We scare you?" Bill Riggs chuckled as he and his brother Jack circled around each side of him in a flanking maneuver. They dragged up chairs opposite him and sat down.

"You're late," Frank told them, feeling more than a little intimidated by the two hard-looking men.

"Sorry. I was—" Bill glanced at his brother, then back to Frank "—detained." He lounged back. "Upstairs."

Frank grimaced. "Take care of that stuff on your own time. Did you finish the job I hired you to do?"

"Sure." Bill smoothed the lapel of his rumpled brown suit. His white shirt was open at the neck and had no collar.

Jack leaned forward, his lean face grim, his blue eyes hard as winter. "You got the money?"

With a furtive glance at the nearest table, Frank discreetly slipped the envelope from his pocket and placed it squarely in front of him, his fingers resting lightly on the edges.

"This is half of the money. You get the rest *after* the exchange is made."

He pushed the envelope toward them. The white paper seemed to gleam against the dark pine table.

Bill pried the envelope partway open and ran his thumb across the stack of greenbacks before carefully slipping it in his jacket pocket. He looked up with a broken-toothed grin. "We're right pleased to do business with you, Mr. Handley." Elbows on the edge of the table, he looked at Frank Handley with a ferret-eyed gaze. "Just how'd you choose us for this job, anyway?"

Frank toyed with the full shot glass in front of him. Whiskey spilled over the top onto his fingers, making them sticky. "I needed someone who wasn't... squeamish about such things, and you boys—" he looked first at one, then at the other "—you have that reputation."

This time both men grinned, as though they'd just been congratulated for perfect attendance at Sunday school, instead of for being immoral thieves and worse.

"Nice to know a man's reputation is worth somethin' these days," Jack told him, then elbowed his grinning brother. "We're always lookin' for a little work... of one kind or another."

Yeah, Frank thought, he knew all about the brothers and their reputation. He'd asked around for someone who'd ask no questions and whose scruples declined in direct proportion to the amount of money paid. Everyone he'd talked with had mentioned the brothers, and they'd been right.

At the mention of kidnapping, they hadn't blinked an eye, just asked when and how much.

"So..." Jack reached across to help himself to the untouched glass of whiskey. Tossing back the brown liquid in one gulp, he wiped his mouth with the back of his hand. "What next? You want us to get rid of the kid? 'Cause that would be easier, and—"

"No!" Frank quickly glanced around to see if anyone else had heard his sudden outburst.

"No," he repeated, more softly, but just as firmly. He drew the line at murder. "No harm is to come to the boy. He'll be exchanged for the money tomorrow night."

"Why not tonight?"

"Because we want to give the mother a chance to worry a little. That way, she'll have to—" Frank broke off, then started again. "Just make the exchange tomorrow night. Nine o'clock, in the alley on Kearney, behind the So Different. I'll make arrangements for the ransom note to be delivered."

The brothers eyes him intently, and Frank could practically see them calculating, trying to figure how to make more out of this than he'd allowed for.

"And just how much money is the woman putting up for her brat?"

Frank frowned. "Don't get any ideas." His fingers trembled slightly, and he carefully hid them under the table. "Just do the job."

"Sure. Sure."

"I'll be across the street, at the Bella Union. Bring me the bag, and you'll be paid the balance owed you."

"Yeah. Yeah," said Bill, with a casual wave of his grimy hand. "We understand." He cleared his throat and winked at his brother. "Don't we understand, Jack?"

There was a smugness to his tone that made Frank's stomach clench nervously.

"Sure, Mr. Handley. We understand," Jack said.

The two men stood, almost in unison. "By the way, are you expectin' any trouble makin' the exchange?"

"Trouble?" Frank mirrored their stance, already eyeing the door. "What kind of trouble?"

Jack shrugged. "You know—law, for one, or them decidin' not to pay, that sort of thing."

Frank shook his head. "No, there should be no trouble. I'm certain she'll pay. She may come herself, or send a messenger. Either way, take the bag and turn over the boy, and no one is to get hurt."

"Okay. Okay. We've got it. Don't worry."

He started past Frank, then stopped when Frank said, "Don't mess this up. If you do, if you get caught somehow, you're on your own. If you tell anyone that I'm involved, I'll swear on a stack of Bibles that I've never seen you before in my life."

The two men didn't seem to take offense, and they certainly didn't seem concerned. "Don't you worry, Mr. Handley. We're not gonna get caught, and nothin's gonna go wrong."

Chapter Four

The sun was nothing but an orange glow in a gray sky when Luke got back to the house. That damnable rain had moved on about twenty minutes ago, and the clouds actually showed signs of breaking up.

He took his horse to the stable. It was white clapboard outside, dark stained pine inside. The place was fancier than half the hotels he'd stayed in, and this just for a horse.

"Well, boy," he said with a chuckle, "enjoy it, but don't get used to it."

Four stalls lined each side. The familiar scent of hay and the acrid scent of horses greeted him. A pair of chestnut carriage horses peered at him over the wooden stall gates. A couple of saddle horses also poked their heads out to check out the visitor.

A young stable hand of about fifteen hurried to meet him. "I'll put him away for you, sir," he said, his sandy hair falling across his left eye. He shoved it back.

"No thanks. I always take care of my horse." Spotting an empty stall, he asked, "This one okay?"

"Fine. Help yourself to whatever you want. Oats is there—" he pointed, "—and water's over there. I'll be in the back, working on some harness. You need anything, sing out."

"Will do."

With that, the boy turned and ambled away.

Luke stretched, trying to ease the tension out of tired muscles and joints. He shrugged off his slicker and tossed it over the gate.

It had been a hell of a day, and it wasn't over yet, he thought as he unsaddled his horse and hefted the saddle over the partition. The stirrup banged into the wood, and he actually checked to see if he'd scratched it.

"Hell of a place to keep a horse," he muttered.

Becky was waiting for him up at the house. He was stalling for time. He picked up a curry brush and set to work, but all the while he kept thinking about her.

It wasn't the first time. Now there was an understatement. Since the day he'd ridden out all those years ago, hardly a day, or night, had passed when he didn't think about her or dream about her or curse himself for leaving her. For a while there, he'd tried to convince himself she was just another woman, nothing more and nothing less than the others he had known.

It didn't work. Knowing other women didn't work. Nothing worked. It was always Becky.

Becky of the luminous want-to-drown-in-them eyes. Becky of the throaty voice that brushed his skin and his nerves like warm velvet. Vivid memories merged with lush fantasies, and all of them had to do with her naked in his arms.

He stopped dead, letting the sudden desire wash over him, enjoying the feeling.

Yeah, Scanlin, you've got it bad. There's a name for "it," you know.

Lust. That was it. Lust.

Sure, Scanlin. Sure.

His mouth pulled down in a frown. He went back to work, making long downward strokes with the brush. The horse shivered and sidestepped.

"Hold still, will ya?" Luke snapped, and ducked under the horse's neck to rub down the other side.

Being with Becky was getting more complicated by the minute. First off, he'd never figured on her having a child. Second, he'd never figured on her son being in trouble. And no way had he counted on the sudden intense feelings, the fierce need to comfort her, the drive to protect her, and the desire—oh, Lord, the desire that heated and swirled in him every time she got within ten feet of him.

He stilled, remembering her today. She'd been so proud, so controlled, this morning. Most women—hell, most men—would have fallen apart under the strain of a missing child.

She hadn't. She was strong, and he admired her strength. It was tough enough raising a child these days. Raising a child alone, a son, without a father to help her—that must be real tough.

The lady had courage.

But did she have enough courage to hear what he had to tell her?

He *could* tell her he hadn't found the boy, apologize, then turn it over to the local authorities again. He'd be out from under.

Scared, Scanlin? Gonna run out on her again?

Jaw clenched, he curled his hands into fists. He was here, and he was staying. She needed him. This was his chance to convince her. This was his chance to assuage some of his guilt.

You looking for absolution, Scanlin?

Perhaps.

Or perhaps forgiveness had nothing to do with why he was staying.

Thirty minutes later, he knew he couldn't stall any longer. He swung his worn saddlebags over his left shoulder. Slicker, bedroll and rifle clutched in his other hand, he headed for the house—and Becky.

His boots made watery puddles in the grass. The last of the rain dripped from the corners of the house. A blackbird, perched on the edge of the roof, watched his progress intently.

The evening air was as fresh and clean as it can be only after a rain, and it looked as though a fog bank was building over the bay. The street in front of the house was quiet, and as he rounded the corner he saw a light go on in the parlor.

Okay, Scanlin, what are you going to tell her?

Dragging in a couple of gulps of air, he reviewed the possibilities in his mind. Regrettably, there weren't many.

If kids wandered off, they were usually found within a couple of hours, playing somewhere they weren't supposed to be or with someone they weren't suppose to be with. Becky had said they'd checked. There was one more possibility. The boy could be dead—accidentally or not. That *would* explain why there'd been no trace of him.

That very unpleasant thought didn't sit well. Seeing a dead child—gunned down in a cross fire, killed in a Comanche raid—that was one thing he never got used to.

Besides, this was a city. Gunfights and Indian raids were pretty remote, especially in this neighborhood.

He glanced at the mansion. In his work, he knew people did things like this only for money or revenge. He discounted revenge. For the life of him, he couldn't imagine Rebecca doing anything so terrible that someone would want to take it out on her son.

His brows drew down thoughtfully. That left money. The lady certainly appeared to have more than enough of that, and there was always someone who figured he was entitled to a share—without doing any work for it, of course.

It was a hell of a thing to have to tell someone, someone special, that her only child had been kidnapped. He'd rather face down all four of the Daltons than have to do this.

Maybe someone else found him.

After two days? Sure. And maybe cows could fly.

He clenched his jaw so hard the pain radiated down his neck. Well, there was nothing for it but to go in there.

Inside the entryway, he hung his water-stained hat and damp slicker on the hall tree. Water puddled on the polished plank floor, and he would have cleaned it up, but where the hell would a person find a cleaning rag around this place? He tossed his saddlebags down with a thud—caused by his spare .45—and dropped his bedroll and rifle right beside them. He'd take them upstairs later.

The house was quiet, still and lifeless. Any fleeting hope that someone else had found the boy disappeared in the funereal silence.

He saw Rebecca step through the double doorway of the dining room. Her hair was down, all golden silk, tied back at her neck with a blue ribbon in a way that made her look young, that made him remember her that way.

She'd changed into dry clothes since he'd left. She was wearing a high-necked long-sleeved blouse that was pale blue, with enough starch to effectively hide the gentle swell of her breasts, and at least a hundred tiny buttons that would take a man an hour to get undone. Her skirt was straight and black, and it drew flat across her belly, provocatively outlining her hips in a way that Luke couldn't help appreciating.

She was head-turning beautiful, even in this tragic time.

She didn't speak, just stared at him with those haunting blue eyes of hers. The ones he'd seen every night in his dreams—only then they'd been filled with excitement and passion. Now they were filled with so much sadness he had to look away from the intensity of it.

He tried to say something, something encouraging, something promising. God, he wished he had come home with the boy. He saw her straighten, as though bracing for a blow, and he delivered it with the barest shake of his head.

For a full ten seconds, she stood there motionless, and he wondered if perhaps she needed him to tell her.

"I—" The words wouldn't come.

His hands drew up in a fist against the rage that filled him, that made his breathing a little harsh and his muscles tense. At that moment, he felt the loss as surely as if it were his child, and, without thinking, he crossed to her.

"Becky. Honey."

Rebecca jumped, not having realized he was so close. "I'm all right." It was a lie. Luke was her last hope, her certain hope. "All day, as the search parties returned . . . nothing. I kept thinking that you would—" She closed her eyes and turned away.

"I know," he said softly. "Becky, answer me one question. Is there anyone who would have something against you? Anyone who would want to hurt you?"

Her eyes flew open, sparked with astonishment. "No. No one."

"You're certain?"

She shook her head. "No one. Why?"

"Then, since the boy hasn't been found, all my experience is telling me that he's been kidnapped."

She didn't move. Deep down, she'd known all along that was the truth; she'd simply refused to acknowledge it until now. She rubbed her eyes against the tears that threatened. "Why?" she murmured, her voice thick with emotion. "Why is this happening?"

"I don't know, darlin'." His tone was soft and easy.

Fresh tears slipped down her cheeks. Dear God, hadn't she cried enough? Rage and fear mixed and mingled until she started to shake, and the tears continued.

"I can't—" Tears clogged her throat.

Wanting privacy, she started past Luke, but he blocked her way. He caught her face in his work-roughened hands and looked at her in that way that was uniquely Luke's, and much too familiar.

He had the softest eyes she'd ever seen, and a way of looking at her that made the world spin away. She could drown in those eyes and not care. She felt her defenses dissolving, releasing the pain and fear she'd stored there since Andrew's disappearance.

"Tell me what you're thinking." His voice caressed her like the summer sun. "You need someone. You're trying to carry the weight of the world on those slender shoulders of yours." His hands traced the line of her shoulders. Her skin warmed to his touch. "Everyone needs someone. I'm here for you." She didn't resist when he pulled her into the fold of his arms and kissed the top of her head, resting his cheek there. "Tell me your fear." He kissed the top of her head again. "It isn't half so bad when you put a little light to it."

That fear that had been circling in her mind grew fiercer, more intense. She slipped her arms around his narrow waist and pressed her cheek against the hard wall of his chest. He smelled like rain and leather. He felt like sanctuary.

Luke.

He was here, and she needed him.

"I—"

"Yes, honey?"

"I'm afraid Andrew is dead."

With the words came a great sob, and all the horror she'd held in check came rushing forth, threatening to carry her away if not for Luke's strong arms around her. Desperately she clung to him, her hands splayed against the soft cotton of his shirt, feeling the work-hardened muscles beneath.

"It's all right, honey. You go on and cry. You cry all you want."

And she did cry. Tears washed down her cheeks and stained the front of his shirt. She sobbed and cried, and he let her. Never once did he try to stop her.

"I'm here, honey. I won't let you go." He tightened his grip with one hand and rubbed her back with the other.

It felt so good to cry. It felt so good to be in his arms. When at last her crying slowed, she looked up at him.

"I shouldn't—"

He covered her lips with the tips of two fingers. "Shh. Don't." He leaned back and brushed the tears from her cheeks with his thumbs. "Of course you should. Aren't you allowed to have feelings? Aren't you allowed to break down sometimes?" He cupped her face in his hands. "Hold on to me."

And she did. Standing there in the entryway, she continued to cling to him, letting the strength of his touch and the slow, steady rhythm of his heart soothe her raw, aching nerves. All her earlier threats to send him packing were forgotten as she held on to him for dear life.

They stood like that for a moment or an eternity, she wasn't certain. It didn't matter. All she knew was that she felt safe and warm and protected. For the first time in two days, she felt good, and the fact that Luke Scanlin was the one who gave her that— Well, so be it.

He angled backward, and she craned her neck to look up at him.

"Luke, I can't..." She started to pull away. He tenderly tightened his hold and smiled down at her. There was a lazy lifting of his mouth, a gentleness in his eyes that made her sigh. She made a halfhearted attempt to return the smile, grateful for his comfort and his concern.

He surprised her when he reached up with the pad of one finger and traced her bottom lip, then pulled the ribbon from her hair, arranging it over her shoulders. A shiver of anticipation fluttered through her. Her heart rate moved up ever so slightly.

Their gazes met and held for the span of two heartbeats, and then his slid down to her lips and lingered. She opened her mouth to speak, but no words came forth. The world seemed strangely still, as though it were holding its breath in anticipation. She knew she wasn't breathing. How could she? All the oxygen in the room had disappeared. He was going to kiss her, she was certain of that. She was also certain that she was going to let him.

Slowly his smile faded. He was very aware of the woman in his arms—every curve, every flat plane seemed custom-made for him, only him. "Becky. Darling Becky." He dipped his head.

"Luke, don't," she ordered, and it stopped him for the span of one heartbeat. Hers.

His breath was warm on her cheek and lips, and she saw his eyes flutter closed an instant before his lips touched hers, lightly, lingering there only to lift away. It was a sensual invitation, one her body remembered even as her mind refused.

He waited to see if she'd object, if she'd move away. She didn't.

"It's been such a long time, Becky," he said, cupping her face lightly between his hands. "It's been much too long."

This time, when he lowered his head, he saw her lips part an instant before his mouth took hers in a demanding kiss that gave no quarter and accepted no retreat. She set off a hunger in him that plunged through his blood, heating, exciting. He leaned into her, wanting to feel her body against his, wanting to feel her, length to length.

His mouth slanted one way, then the other, and he felt her fingers digging into the fabric of his shirt and the flesh beneath.

He groaned deep down inside at the longing that was consuming him. He wanted her. He wanted her naked, and he wanted her now.

Rebecca was lost in a world of desire. She leaned into him, feeling his chest pressed hard against her breasts, her nipples pulled into tight, aching nubs. She twisted against him, trying to assuage the ache there. She felt his hand curving around the side of her neck, his thumb hooked under her chin as though to prevent her escape.

She didn't want to escape. She wanted exactly what he was offering. Longing, familiar as yesterday, unfurled within her, warm and pulsing, spiraling outward, touching every part of her, rekindling a fire she'd banked years ago.

It felt so good, so right, as though they'd never been apart. Her body awakened to his touch, nerves coming slowly to life with each passing moment, with each strong, steady beat of his heart and hers.

She made a small animal-like sound deep in her throat, and it was enough to send Luke's control spinning. His arm curved around her slender waist, his fingers digging into the boning of her corset. Damn, he hated corsets, hated all the cumbersome layers of clothes women wore.

She was like flame-warmed brandy, the kind that flowed smoothly down inside to set a man on fire, inch by delicious inch. And he was on fire. Lord help him. Rebecca was the spark that ignited his passion.

His body tensed with urgency, and his mind flashed on images of her naked in his arms, her wild mane of hair loose and falling around both of them, her soft breasts pressed against his bare chest, her long legs, bare and silky-soft to his touch, curved around his waist.

Urgency and primal need overcame judgment. His hand drifted lower, past her bustle, to the gentle curve of her bottom, and he groaned, wanting her more than he'd ever thought possible.

"Woman, you're setting me on fire. Do you know what you are doing to me?"

Maybe it was the momentary absence of his mouth on hers. Maybe it was the bluntness of his words. Whatever it was, warning bells went off in Rebecca's head, loud and clear.

Stop this! the faint voice of reason called, as though from a great distance. *Are you out of your mind?*

She pushed at his chest. It was like pushing on a stone wall, she thought, and panic fueled her sudden alarm. She tried again, tearing her mouth from his.

"No, Luke! Stop!"

Luke lifted his head. His eyes were glazed with passion, his breathing was ragged and unsteady, and it took a full five seconds for her order to register.

Disbelief replaced the passion in his eyes. "Becky, I didn't—"

"No." She shook her head adamantly, her loose hair spilling across her shoulders. "Whatever it is. No. No!" She shook her head again. Her breathing was unsteady and labored. No one had ever kissed her like that, no one except Luke.

She kept her hands braced on his chest while she fought to regain control and to shake off the delicious feelings that saturated every fiber of her being.

What was wrong with her? What kind of a woman was she? Her son was missing, and here she stood kissing Luke Scanlin, the one man in the whole world she'd loved and trusted, the one man who had betrayed her in ways she'd sworn never to reveal, never to forget.

This could not be happening. She refused to let it happen. "I am not the same schoolgirl you knew all those years ago."

"I can see that," he said, and ran his tongue along his bottom lip in a provocative gesture.

She took a purposeful step back. "Don't you *ever* do that again—" Her voice cracked, and anger sparked in her eyes. "You took advantage of me, Luke. It's not the first time." She hitched up her skirt and strode purposefully for the staircase. "You won't do it again. Not *ever* again."

With that, she turned her back and marched, military-straight, up the stairs.

Still breathing hard, Luke braced one hand on the smooth mahogany railing and watched her go.

He hadn't meant to kiss her, and he sure as hell hadn't meant to kiss her like that.

Like what? Like some cowhand who's been six months on the trail?

Heart racing, breathing shallow, he stood there for a moment. She was something, really something.

Spotting her hair ribbon on the floor, he picked it up. It slid across his palm and curled around his fingers. He could smell the scent of her rose perfume on the soft satin. He folded it carefully and tucked it in his shirt pocket.

Woman, I think you protest too much.

* * *

It was late. Nearly midnight, according to the clock on the wall of the guest room. He was stretched out on the bed.

Hell of a thing, a damned feather bed, he thought with a quirk of a smile. He'd heard about feather beds, but he'd never actually seen one, let alone slept on one.

He ran his hand lightly over the smooth white cotton covering. Feather beds were the best there were, like everything else in the room.

A lot different from the last place he'd slept before coming to San Francisco. That room over the Red Dog Saloon in Auburn had a rope-strung bed frame and a straw-filled mattress. The bureau had more gouges in it than a strip mine.

This bed was big. Big enough for two, and almost long enough for him to stretch his six-foot-two-inch frame out completely.

Abruptly he snatched up the two pillows and jammed them between his back and the walnut headboard. If he wasn't going to sleep, he might as well sit up. The bed creaked with the shifting of his weight.

Wearing just his black wool trousers, he crossed his bare feet at the ankle, his toes brushing against the smooth footboard.

Any other time, all he had to do was lay his head down and he was asleep. He never lost sleep worrying. Tonight was different. Tonight he couldn't get Rebecca and that kiss out his mind.

What the devil had he been thinking? Aw, hell, he hadn't been thinking. How could a man think when she was looking at him with those luminous blue eyes of hers?

It wasn't entirely his fault—the kiss. She could have stopped him. He'd expected her to. Instead, she'd kissed him back, and not some little tight-mouthed kiss. No, she kissed him as though she were coming apart in his arms, as though she'd been waiting for him, as though she were welcoming him home.

She had sent desire racing through him, faster than a prairie fire in July. All he'd known was that while she was in his arms, he wanted her, never wanted to let her go. Thoughts, images, lush and erotic, had flashed in his mind and sent his heart rate soaring. He'd wanted to give and take and please until they both went up in flames.

He dragged in a deep breath, and another. It didn't help. When had it gotten so hot in here? Swinging his legs over the side of the bed, he made to stand, but her hair ribbon, lying on the night table, caught his eye. He picked it up, letting the satin glide over his callused palm. Instantly he remembered pulling it from her hair, the cool smoothness of her hair entwined around his fingers.

No matter what she said, she'd liked that kiss, liked it as much as he did. He might not understand a lot of things, but he understood when a woman wanted him, and she did. She absolutely did.

But there were a few small obstacles; she'd made it clear she wasn't about to cooperate, and, of course, she was distraught over her son's disappearance. Then there was the little matter of their past history.

Okay, Scanlin. What are you going to do about it?

"How the hell do I know?" he muttered to the empty room.

She had money, position, power. He had the horse he rode, about five hundred dollars in the bank, and no more clothes than he could stuff in a couple of saddlebags. Not exactly the sort of man she was used to, he thought with a rueful glance around the tastefully furnished room. He squirmed; the damned feather bed was starting to make him uncomfortable.

He'd been a loner most of his life. Being with Becky, he was having thoughts about things like settling down, having a son. Yeah, a son. He'd like that. He'd like it even more if it was Becky's son. He'd be a good father, too, not like his old man.

He'd been fourteen when his mother died on that dirt-poor ranch they had down in Amarillo. A week later, his father had stopped coming home. Not that Luke had minded much, considering his old man had spent most of his time either drinking or beating on Luke. So Luke had waited two days, and when he asked in town, the bartender had said Luke's father had taken the afternoon stage for Lubbock with one of the girls from the Gilded Garter. He had never seen or heard from his father again.

Ain't fatherly love wonderful?

His muscles tensed abruptly, and he felt suddenly edgy. Standing, he crossed over to the white porcelain warming stove tucked neatly in the corner of the room, near the window. The carpet was green as grass and just as smooth against his bare feet.

There was already a fire going in the stove—the maid, he figured. There was a maid, an upstairs maid, he'd learned. There was also a cook, and a housekeeper, who was down with a cold, which was why no one had answered the door this morning.

He'd felt a little disconcerted at finding his bed turned down when he walked in tonight. It was all very foreign, the thought of having people actually wait on him, except maybe in a saloon.

He rubbed his bare arms against the chill, turning his back for a little extra warming. He had to admit this was a pleasant luxury. He'd spent a lot of time cold and dirty, and there sure hadn't even been anyone to light a stove for him or turn down his bed. Maybe that was why he'd barged in when he heard the boy was missing. If that kid was out there—and he was determinedly hanging on to that notion—then the little guy must be scared to death. Becky had said he was only seven. Poor little guy.

Whoever had him had better be taking real good care of the lad. Yeah, real good, he thought fiercely. If they hurt him...well, Luke wouldn't take too kindly to that.

He knew firsthand about being alone and so scared that he cried himself to sleep, curled up in the back of some stable.

That first year after his old man ran off, Luke had scrambled for work. He'd swamped out saloons, mucked stables and even dug outhouses, anything for food and a place to sleep.

And scared—he'd never known a person could be so scared. Then, one day, it had been as though he just couldn't be scared anymore. Pride had welled up inside him. He might be digging outhouses, but he wouldn't take the cursing or the snide remarks anymore.

He'd decided he was never going to be put down again, by anyone. He gave an honest day's work for an honest day's wage, and he expected to be treated with respect, same as anyone else.

But respect, he'd quickly discovered, came faster when he could demand it—and a six-gun was a great equalizer. Luke was a natural with a gun, men said. Fast, others added.

As he got older, he'd done a little scouting for the army, but he hadn't liked all the rules. He'd done some bounty hunting later, and he'd been better at that—no rules and being on his own, he guessed.

He'd met Tom Pemberton in a saloon in Dallas. Tom had been having a little trouble with a gambler—apparently Tom had called the gambler a cheat, and the man had pulled a .32 out of his coat. Not liking gamblers much, and feeling sorry for the greenhorn who was about to have his head blown off, Luke had stepped in and laid his .45 upside the gambler's head.

Tom had been grateful and persuasive, and when he went back to California, Luke had gone along. He'd never seen San Francisco or the Pacific Ocean. He'd figured he would stick around a few weeks, then head on back to Texas to meet a friend who was joining up with the Texas Rangers. Luke had thought he might give it a try, too.

He hadn't known a man's world could be turned upside down in a month.

He'd met Rebecca at a party. They'd danced, and talked, and danced again. Tom had told Luke she was practically engaged. But Luke had been young—okay, arrogant—and he hadn't cared about rules, he admitted to himself now. She hadn't been married and that was all that had mattered. Apparently it was all that had mattered to her, also, because she had come out to meet him every day during the next week.

He'd never known anyone like her. She'd been so beautiful—not as beautiful as she was now, but beautiful. She had been smart, and funny, and so alive. Everything had been an adventure with her. The most ordinary things had been exciting when he was with her. All he had known was that he couldn't get enough of her, so it was no wonder that eventually he'd made love to her.

Seduced her, you mean, his conscience chided, none too gently.

Okay. Maybe. Anyhow, that was when everything had changed. Being with Rebecca hadn't been just having sex, satisfying a physical need. No, with Rebecca he'd wanted to please her more than himself, to give more than he took. Feelings so new, so intensely powerful, had rocked him to the very core of his being, and he'd panicked.

Yeah, Scanlin, you son of a bitch, you ran off in the middle of the night like a skulking dog.

But it seemed there was no peace and no escape from those feelings.

His eyes fluttered closed, and instantly the memory of their kiss flashed in his mind and ricocheted through his body like a shot.

It felt as though he'd been doing penance for the past seven years. Deep down, he'd figured he deserved every long, guilt-ridden, stupidity-cursing moment of it.

But along the way he must have done something right, because the Lord was giving him a second chance. A chance to free himself, he'd thought when he walked in here. Obviously he'd been wrong.

He glanced over at the well-worn Bible lying on the round walnut table near the bed. The cover was creased, and one corner was torn off. It was his mother's Bible. It was all he had of her. He'd taken solace in that book many a long, cold night by a campfire.

He chuckled and said aloud, "Never thought you'd get me to read it, did you, Ma?"

He could almost hear her laugh.

She'd had a nice laugh and a warm smile. The kind that made you want to laugh even if you didn't know why.

Rebecca had that kind of smile—not that she had anything to smile about these days.

He started pacing. A vision of Rebecca filled his mind...the biggest, bluest eyes he'd ever seen in a woman, and hair the color of sunshine.

Well, Scanlin, you gonna get it right this time?

Edward Pollard arrived shortly after eight that evening. It was really too late for a proper call, but he was confident that under these distressing circumstances allowances would be made.

He rang the bell twice and shifted anxiously from one foot to the other as he waited for the housekeeper to answer the door.

"Rebecca," he said, his eyes widening at the pleasant surprise, "where's Mrs. Wheeler?"

"Hello, Edward. She's down with a cold," she told him, stepping aside. Edward breezed past her. Oddly, her first thought wasn't that she was glad to see him, but that he was wearing another new suit, gray gabardine with a matching vest. Edward was always the very picture of the well-dressed gentleman. "I've just heard the terrible, terrible news about your son." He put his hat and gloves on the hall table. "I'm in shock. If only I'd been in town when this happened."

She allowed him to lightly kiss her cheek. "Thank you, Edward. I appreciate your concern."

"Is there any new information?"

"None," she said, preferring not to discuss speculations with him. She led the way into the parlor.

Edward was a frequent visitor, and so made himself at home. "You poor dear." He spoke as he walked to the liquor table by the hearth. "Let me get you something. Sherry, perhaps?"

"Yes, sherry," she agreed, thinking a drink was just what she needed after the day she'd had.

Rebecca's hand was surprisingly steady as she accepted the delicate crystal glass. She drank the thimbleful that Edward had poured her in one large swallow and handed him the glass. "Pour me another, please, Edward. Considerably more this time." She held up her thumb and forefinger to indicate how much.

He looked surprised, but he obliged, returning a moment later. "Now sip that slowly. We don't want it going to your head."

"Edward, liquor doesn't 'go to my head.'" She wasn't much of a drinker, but she never got that fuzzy feeling that people so often spoke of. Tonight, though, she thought she'd like to be fuzzy, or foggy, or anything else that would keep her from thinking of the man who was no doubt asleep in her guest room.

She leaned back against the fine rose silk of the settee, but she wasn't relaxed. They sat in companionable silence for a long moment, and she absently adjusted the folds of her black skirt, making creases with her fingers where there shouldn't be any.

Outside, the night was still. A few brave crickets made a halfhearted attempt at chirping. It was too late for them. Was it too late for her, as well?

Out of the corner of her eye she saw Edward take another swallow of her best bourbon. He had delicate hands, she thought, watching the way his fingers curled around the glass. And he had delicate features.

She vowed she wouldn't make comparisons and, ten seconds later, she did just that.

Edward was blond, neat, and always the height of fashion. He was polite and courteous to a fault. Luke was dark and handsome and provocative as sin. His hair was overly long, and his clothes were those of a cowboy, entirely out of place here. Yet when he walked into a room he had a commanding presence that made people turn and stare. She knew that first-hand.

She took another swallow of sherry to soothe her suddenly jumpy nerves.

Edward was everything a lady wanted in a man. Half the mothers in San Francisco were trying to tempt him with their daughters. Edward was considered quite a catch, and she understood that perfectly.

Oh, not that Rebecca thought of him that way, as a catch. She wasn't interested in anyone. She had her life all nice and neat, and she liked it just fine. As soon as Andrew was home, they—

She finished off the sherry in one long swallow, putting her glass on the side table with a delicate clink.

"How did it happen?" Edward's voice broke into her musings.

"I don't honestly know. He was playing on the porch, and then he was gone."

"I'm so sorry." His expression was serious, grave.

"Thank you, Edward. I appreciate your concern, and your coming here at this late hour."

"Anything for you, Rebecca." He faced her fully. "You know that, don't you?"

"You are a good friend, Edward."

She'd known Edward ever since she'd married Nathan. He had been an occasional investor with Nathan, and had always been their friend. Why, it was Edward who had held the first party for them after they returned from their honeymoon.

Oh, she knew that since Nathan's death Edward had wanted them to be more than friends. That was very apparent. He'd taken her to parties, the theater, anywhere she wanted to go, really.

She liked that. Edward was always the perfect gentleman. Unlike *someone* she could think of.

Unfortunately, thinking of that nameless someone made her fingers tremble and goose bumps skitter up her spine with a deliciously pleasant sensation. And the fact that it was so delicious annoyed her and, yes, frightened her a bit.

So she smiled, twisted in her seat and focused on her company. "I'm glad you're here," she told him, and was rewarded with a smile that had absolutely no effect on her pulse.

"Now, my dear, tell me everything that happened."

They had known each other long enough that he'd taken to using an affectionate term occasionally, in private only.

Rebecca related the entire story—her search for Andrew, how she'd sent for the police, their efforts. Then she said, "Captain Brody is a difficult man, and

I don't think he would have helped me much if Marshal Scanlin hadn't arrived."

Edward paused, his drink halfway to his mouth. "Who?"

"Marshal Scanlin," she repeated nonchalantly, not bothering to mention that he was sleeping upstairs, in the room next to hers.

"I assume you mean a U.S. marshal?" Edward said casually, and sipped his drink.

She nodded.

"What's a marshal got to do with this? I mean, isn't this Captain Brody's jurisdiction?"

He took a large swallow of whiskey, draining the glass.

"True, but Edward, you know Brody. The man's hostile, argumentative and, well, perhaps worse."

"No, *my dear,*" he said in that patronizing tone that he used sometimes, the one that made the hair on the back of her neck prickle. "You've got Amos all wrong. He's been police captain quite a while, and he does a good job. He's just not very good with people, especially ladies, is all. I'm sure he's competent."

Rebecca stared at him in open surprise. "I know you and Brody are old friends, but surely you realize that we've been at odds for months. I've told you that there is every indication that he's taking bribes, looking the other way for gambling and...and women and who knows what else!" She made an impatient gesture.

"Rebecca, I don't know how you can say that." He shook his head adamantly. "You're treading on dangerous ground. It's a miracle you haven't been sued, or worse, with all these thinly veiled accusations in your paper. Fortunately, I've been able to persuade people that it's all harmless, and that you'll soon lose interest and move on."

"I will not move on, as you put it. Crime is up, and anyone with half a brain can figure out why. And I don't need you to defend me. I take care of myself."

"Of course you can, dearest. Of course you can. It's just that you're so obsessed with this Barbary Coast business. Surely there are more important matters to write about than who was in a fight in some saloon."

"Edward, how can you say that? This isn't the *Police Gazette* I'm running, this is a respected newspaper," she said proudly, "and it's my job to expose crime and corruption wherever I find it."

"What are you going to do, go down to the Barbary Coast and ask if anyone's been giving money to Captain Brody?" he retorted sharply.

"Maybe I will," she told him, ignoring his sarcasm.

"Rebecca!" His thin brows shot up. "I absolutely won't allow it! You can't possibly mean—"

"Oh, honestly, Edward. Don't be such a...a... banker. Don't carry on so." She wisely decided against being too pointed and telling him his worrying was beginning to annoy her greatly.

He toyed with the gold charm that sparkled on his watch chain. She was braced for another lecture when he surprised her. "Now, Rebecca, your determination to find a story is admirable, of course. And I'm certain you think you're doing good, but—"

He broke off and strolled to the piano, putting his empty glass down on the gleaming surface. "I'm sorry, my dear. This is neither the time nor the place to discuss this. I'm only upsetting you. Please forgive my thoughtlessness. Come. Walk me to the door."

As he picked up his hat, he said, "Is there anything I can do to help? Anything at all?"

"No, nothing. Thank you, Edward." She offered her hand, which he took. "Marshal Scanlin's helping, and the police, too. There's really nothing for you to do."

She was reaching to open the door when, without a word, Edward kissed her—and not on the cheek this time.

Surprise flashed in her eyes. "Edward, what's come over you?"

"I detest leaving you," he said, and squeezed her hand. "If we were married, dearest Rebecca, I'd be here for you all the time. You wouldn't have to go through this, or anything else, alone again."

"Edward, surely you can't expect me to think about marriage *now?*"

He pressed her hand against his heart in a gesture that was more dramatic than effective. "Why not? If we were married, I could hold you in my arms all through the night...."

"Edward! Please, remember yourself!" She pulled free of his grasp.

"You care for me, I know you do—"

"Yes, but—"

He tried to pull her to him again, and she braced both hands against his chest in denial, her fingers digging into smooth gabardine. "Edward, we've been friends for years."

"Liking each other is important, don't you think?"

"Well, yes, but...what about love?"

His blue eyes softened. "You know that I love you."

She sighed. "Yes, but I don't feel...I don't think—"

"You will come to love me, in time, I'm certain," he said. "We have the same interests, the same goals. It's so much more than most have, starting out."

"Edward," she said firmly, easily pulling free of his touch and stepping out of his reach. "I can't think now... not about this."

"All right, Rebecca. I understand." His tone contradicted his words. "It's just that seeing you reminds me how wonderful it could be. Think of what we could do together, with you at my side. The Tinsdale name linked with mine. I'm certain to be the next mayor." He shrugged and smiled. "All you have to say is yes."

Rebecca touched his arm affectionately, yet with regret, too. "You are the dearest man I know. You were my friend when Nathan died and I was so lost. Without you and Ruth, I couldn't have managed. And I do care for you, but not—"

"Let's put this conversation aside, and we'll take it up later, after Andrew is home and everything is back to normal," he interrupted. "You'll see. Andrew *will* be home safely, and we *will* be together."

With a light brush of his lips on her cheek, he left, closing the door with a gentle snap.

For a long moment, she stood there, staring at the smooth wood, wondering what the devil was wrong with her. Edward was dear. He was right when he said they were good together. And she was certain that Edward would follow his dream—perhaps even to the governor's mansion and beyond.

What woman in her right mind wouldn't dream of accompanying a man on such an exciting journey? She should be thrilled. Perhaps she should even love him. Trouble was, she didn't.

She started up the stairs, then stopped abruptly. "How long have you been standing there?"

Luke stood on the landing. He leaned forward, resting his forearms on the banister as if he owned the place, and her. He had an infuriatingly arrogant grin on his face. "So that's the competition."

He straightened. It was then that she realized he wasn't wearing a shirt. The man was half-naked, and heart-stoppingly gorgeous. It gave her heart a lurch. A warm blush popped out on her cheeks, like two rosebuds. She was staring right at his chest, and at the provocative curve of black hair that arched over each nipple, then plunged down his chest and disappeared into his waistband.

Her gaze flicked to his face. He had a wicked look in his eyes—hot enough to boil water.

Rebecca tore her gaze away, but stayed firmly rooted to the bottom stair. She wasn't going up there now. Not now! And she wasn't going to let him know that looking at him was turning her knees to oatmeal.

So, with as much firmness as she could muster, she said, "*You* don't have any competition."

His grin was immediate and devastating. "You're right about that, Princess. I don't, and thanks for the reassurance."

Her temper shot up. Before she could object, Luke turned sharply on his heel and strode down the hallway. Still smiling, he went to bed, and this time he knew he'd sleep.

Chapter Five

Rebecca didn't sleep well. In fact, she couldn't remember when she'd last slept. Oh, she was sure she had dozed once or twice—the nightmares were proof of that. Even now, if she closed her eyes, the terrifying dreams would return—Andrew frightened, cowering, crying for her, while she struggled in vain to get to him.

With a sudden intake of breath, she surged to her feet and left her bedroom. Heart pounding, she marched down the hallway. With each firm step, she willed her fears under control.

Stay calm. Andrew needs you. He'll be all right. Luke said so.

She stopped still, one hand steady against the smooth surface of the plastered wall near the closed door to his room. Abruptly she jerked her hand away.

His room. *His* promises. *His* plans.

What the devil was happening to her? Since when did Luke Scanlin matter so much to her? Since when did she need his word to make things right?

Since the moment he walked in here and looked at you with those devil black eyes of his.

No! You're not doing this to me. Not again.

Curling her hand into a fist, she prepared to knock on his door.

She stopped.

What was she going to say? Don't look at me in that way that makes my body pulse? Don't talk to me in that low, caressing way that soothes and excites me at the same time? Don't be so damnably tempting that for breathtaking moments I forget everything, including my son?

Guilt overcame fear, and she let her hand fall to her side, took an unsteady half step backward, then turned.

If he was right, and Andrew, her darling Andrew, had been kidnapped, then she was going to need him even more. She knew Brody wouldn't do more than "keep an eye out," which was as good as doing nothing at all. While she didn't trust Luke with her heart, in some strange way she trusted him to do the job he'd set out to do. After all, he was a U.S. marshal.

She was trapped. To send Luke away could put Andrew's life at risk. To let him stay could put all their lives at even greater risk.

One thing at a time, she told herself. Get Andrew back first, then deal with other...matters. She'd kept her secret from everyone, all this time. She would keep it forever. Feeling a little more confident, she went to check on Ruth.

"Are you awake?" she said softly as she peeked around the edge of the door.

"Come on in." Ruth was propped up in the bed and had a breakfast tray balanced on her lap. She fussed with the ruffle on her bright yellow nightdress, then twisted her gray hair up into a bun.

"You're looking better," Rebecca said as she crossed the room to stop at her mother-in-law's bedside. "There's a little color in your cheeks. I was awfully worried yesterday."

"I know, honey, and I am sorry." Ruth shifted to a more comfortable position in the bed.

"Any pain today?"

"None," she replied happily. "Did you get any sleep at all last night?"

"A little," Rebecca muttered, and sat on the edge of the bed, holding the tray to prevent spilling.

"Very little, would be my guess. Am I going to have to send for the doctor again?" Ruth's tone was loving. "We're a fine pair, aren't we?"

"Yes. I think we are." Rebecca smiled and covered Ruth's hand with her own, her fingers tightening in a way that expressed the love and reassurance she felt. "When Andrew's home, I'll sleep."

Ruth tossed back the coverlet and scooted toward the edge of the bed.

"Where do you think you're going?" Rebecca asked sternly.

"Lying around here isn't going to find Andrew, and I—"

"Oh, no, you don't." Rebecca yanked the covers free and gently nudged her back into bed. "There'll be no repeats of yesterday. Besides..." She made a show of smoothing the quilt. "Luke—Marshal Scanlin—thinks that Brody is right. That Andrew has been kidnapped."

Ruth stilled, surprise and fear reflected in her eyes. "What do you think?"

"I think . . . it's true," Rebecca returned in a barely heard whisper, and blinked hard against the tears that threatened.

Ruth squeezed Rebecca's hand. "You know, in some strange way I actually feel better knowing—thinking—that. I mean, if all someone wants is money, then they can have it. They can have it all. I just want my only grandson back."

"I know." Rebecca sighed inwardly. She, too, hoped that Luke and Brody were right, that it was a kidnapping, that all someone wanted was money. It was a strange, perverted kind of hope, but it was all she had, and she clung to it. Because if that was true, then it meant that Andrew wasn't dead. And Andrew couldn't be dead. The pain would be too much to survive.

Glancing up, she saw Ruth watching her, her mother-in-law's big brown eyes filled with concern. She forced a smile. "Why don't I take that tray down and let you get a little more sleep?"

"Rebecca, we'll get him back. At least you've got Marshal Scanlin."

Rebecca's eyes widened in surprise. "What do you mean, I've got Marshal Scanlin?" Feeling suddenly edgy, she released Ruth's hand and stood.

"Why, nothing, dear. I mean you've got someone you can count on to help you, to help us both."

"Help us . . . yes." She strolled over to the walnut dresser and fussed with the doily there.

"He seems a very passionate man. . . about his work, I mean."

"Passionate" was an understatement, Rebecca thought. It was heaven in his arms, she remembered with a sudden racing of her heart. She needed to keep her feet firmly anchored to the ground. With as much nonchalance as she could muster, she said, "I suppose so. This is the first time I've seen him in a long time."

"How long?"

"A little over seven years," she returned vaguely. "Why?"

"Oh, just wondering." Ruth gave a casual shrug. "I never knew any of your friends from before you married Nathan. Was the marshal a beau?"

"Certainly not!" Rebecca snapped quickly—maybe a little too quickly.

"I see." Ruth looked into the distance. "He's very handsome. There's something about his eyes . . . I can certainly see how a woman would be attracted to him."

"What woman?" Sudden apprehension inched up Rebecca's spine.

"Oh, any woman." Ruth's tone was innocent. "I mean, he's strong and dark, and much too charming. Oh, and exciting. After all, he earns his living in a dangerous profession. Almost like a knight, don't you think?"

"No, I most certainly don't think. He's selfish and arrogant, and he acts like he—" Like he has a right to make love to me, she almost said. A lush feeling moved through her, low and warm, making her knees tremble a bit.

Good Lord, he'd been here a day, and it was as if all the years had not intervened. Well, she wasn't going to give in to him. She wasn't going to let him shatter her life again.

Her chin came up in a determined gesture, and it was then that she realized that Ruth was staring at her with unconcealed surprise.

"Marshal Scanlin is only here to help find Andrew. Then he's leaving." Rebecca's tone was firm, as much for herself as for Ruth.

"I see," Ruth muttered again, in a way that was making Rebecca both anxious and annoyed. Her temper was short after her confrontation with Luke last night, and she wasn't looking forward to seeing him over the breakfast table this morning. She'd almost asked for a tray in her room, but that had felt too much like retreat, and that she refused to do.

Wanting to end this conversation, Rebecca crossed to the bed and picked up the tray. "I think I'll take this down and get a cup of coffee for myself." She was halfway to the door as she spoke. "Do you want anything else?"

"Why, no, dear. I think you've given me all I needed."

Rebecca arched one brow questioningly, but decided not to press the issue. "You just rest. I need you to get better. When Andrew comes home, I'll never be able to manage without you. That boy has enough energy for an entire company of cavalry."

Ruth chuckled. "That's true. Why do you think I taught him how to play checkers? It was the only way I could get him to sit still for a while."

They shared a smile, remembering the little boy they loved and the times they had shared.

"It'll be all right," Ruth added. "Andrew is coming home. I feel it."

Rebecca dragged in a steadying breath. "I keep telling myself that, but—"

"No buts."

"Okay," Rebecca agreed with a firm nod. "Now you get some more rest. And I need you and Andrew." Her voice was unsteady. "Don't you worry, Ruth. No one is going to take away your grandson."

With that, she headed for the kitchen.

There was a place set on the dining room table—crystal, silver, and sparkling white china. A dark blue napkin, folded in a triangle, accentuated the paleness of the blue linen tablecloth.

Rebecca paused near the mahogany sideboard. One place setting—obviously for her. Where was Luke?

She went into the kitchen.

"Good morning," Rebecca said to her housekeeper, Mrs. Wheeler, who was drying a plate near the sink. The smell of cooked ham and fresh-baked biscuits gave the large, square room a warm, comfortable feeling.

"Ma'am," the cook said by way of greeting. "Your egg will be ready in a minute."

"That's fine. Thank you, Emily."

Mrs. Wheeler promptly sneezed, then gently blew her nose in a lacy white handkerchief, which she kept tucked in the cuff of her stiff black uniform. Her slender cheeks were flushed a bright pink, and her pale blue eyes looked a little watery.

"Mrs. Wheeler, are you certain you're feeling all right?"

"Oh, yes..." She sniffed. "Fine."

It was Rebecca's habit not to stand on ceremony and, as she'd done every morning since she'd married Nathan, she went to the stove and helped herself to a steaming cup of coffee. More than any other room, she liked the kitchen. There was something homey, almost comforting, about the room. Since Nathan's death, sometimes she would slip down here late at night to make a cup of sassafras tea and reflect on her past, and her future—which didn't include a dark-eyed devil, no matter how handsome.

"Mrs. Tinsdale?"

The housekeeper's voice roused her from her thoughts. Snatching back her shaky emotions, she took a sip of coffee, smiled and said, "Sorry. What were you saying?"

"I was saying how sad I am . . ." She glanced at the cook, and back to Rebecca again. "How sad we *both* are to hear about Master Andrew."

"Thank you both."

"Is there anything we can do?"

Rebecca tried to sound optimistic. "No, nothing. The police are working on it, and Marshal Scanlin . . . By the way have you seen—"

"Oh, yes, the marshal," Mrs. Wheeler said, and grinned. A small breeze fluttered the bright yellow curtain at the window behind her. "He was here this morning."

"Really?" Rebecca kept her tone nonchalant as she strolled over to the kitchen table. She dragged out a ladder-back chair and perched sideways on its edge, coffee cup still in hand. "And do you know where the marshal is now?" she asked, as though she'd just asked when the milk would be delivered, revealing none of the excitement that he'd stirred in her when he kissed her.

Sunlight poured through the open window above the sink and glinted off the silver, laid out on the table, obviously ready for polishing.

Mrs. Wheeler sniffed, then coughed, then sniffed again. She dabbed at her red nose with her hanky. "He said he had to leave."

"Leave?" Abruptly Rebecca put the cup and saucer down on the scarred pine surface of the table. "Luke's gone?" she asked softly, not bothering with formality.

"Yes, ma'am," the housekeeper continued, edging sideways, away from the stove and the spattering butter. "He was here when I came down at six." She tucked an errant lock of graying hair back into her topknot. "I was surprised to see a man in the kitchen. He introduced himself, and he already had coffee going and was about to cook some eggs." She walked over to the table, her leather heels drumming on the flooring. "Seems like a nice man." She started to inspect the silver and continued talking. "You know, he offered to make eggs for me." She chuckled. "Can you imagine? Of course, I told him—"

"Where—" Rebecca's stomach clenched. Disappointment warred with desire. "Where has he gone? Did he say?"

"No, ma'am, he didn't say. Oh," she said, arching one brow, "I think he mentioned something about important business."

"Did he say when—if—he was coming back?"

"No, ma'am, I don't believe he did."

"I see," she mumbled, and reached for her coffee again in an attempt to be casual. All the while she felt like screaming. Damn the man. This was so typical of him—to breeze in here, try to seduce her and leave when she refused him.

She took too large a gulp of coffee, and burned her tongue.

Thank goodness she was smart enough to hold him off. And so what if he was gone? She didn't need him anymore. If he was right about Andrew being kidnapped—and she was more and more certain he was—then all she had to do was try to remain sane until the ransom note arrived. She'd pay the money and get her son back.

She sipped her coffee, more cautiously this time. No, she didn't need Luke. In fact, the less he was around, the better for everyone.

"Mrs. Tinsdale, your breakfast is ready." The cook's voice startled her, and she looked up.

"Why, thank you, Emily," she said, and stood and carried her cup toward the dining room doorway.

Luke paced back and forth in the governor's elegant suite in the Palace Hotel. His booted footsteps were muffled by the patterned carpet. He'd spent part of the morning at the police station, trying to find out if there had been any other kidnappings in the area in the past year or so.

The police were about as friendly as a pack of coyotes. Luke didn't mind much. He knew how to deal with varmints. So, after a few minutes of getting acquainted, which, in this case, meant pushing and threatening a little, he'd gotten the information he wanted.

There had been no kidnappings in the past year or so. They had no suspects. They had not heard any rumors, and they didn't know where to begin to look.

Disgusted, Luke had made a quick swing through the Barbary Coast, just to get the lay of the land. He was planning to go back later, maybe tonight, do a little looking, ask a few questions.

The governor was late. The only thing Luke hated more than damned meetings was damned meetings with politicians. Since he'd become a U.S. marshal, he'd had to learn to live with both.

He ran both hands through his hair in an agitated gesture, then paced the length of the room. Six long strides. The walls were painted a pale yellow, and the furniture was all dark wood and royal blue satin. There was a leather folder on the center table and some other files lay on the carved mahogany desk in the corner.

There was only one way in, a door, and there were three ways out, if you counted the two windows, which he did. *Always watch your back, and never get cornered.* Force of habit made him brush the worn handle of his .45, where it pouched out under his black wool jacket.

He paused by the desk. The surface was so highly polished, he could see himself in the dark wood. Some poor maid must have a hell of a time keeping this place up, he mused.

It didn't take an expert to see that the upholstered side chairs matched the settee and the tables. He squinted. What the heck were those carvings along the wood trim, anyway? He took a closer look. Little roses, or leaves, or both, he thought, running his hand lightly over the surface. The wood felt smooth and cold against his callused fingers.

He took another glance around and shook his head. Fancy. Real fancy. Must be the latest fashion. Of course, except for the names, Luke didn't know Chippendale from rococo, and he didn't really care. All he knew about style was that chairs were for sitting and tables were a place to prop your boots at the end of the day.

He chuckled. These spindly things were just like the ones at Becky's house. He could imagine himself propping these size-twelve boots of his on one of Rebecca's tables. Even if the thing didn't collapse under the weight, he was certain she'd give him hell anyway.

One corner of his mouth lifted in a smug sort of smile. He liked seeing her all riled up, seeing her guard slip away. That was the real Becky, the one she'd tried so hard to deny. Why? Last night she'd kissed him as though there were no tomorrow. It had left him breathless at the fierce wonder of it. She'd drugged his senses so fast, he'd nearly lost all control.

Desire stirred within him, and he shifted uncomfortably.

The click of the door opening brought him out of his musings. The governor walked into the room, closing the solid pine door firmly behind him. Tall and thin, wearing a well-tailored brown suit, he crossed the room, his hand already extended in greeting.

"You must be Marshal Scanlin," he said, smiling.

"Yes, sir," Luke returned, accepting the offered handshake.

"Please." The governor gestured toward the side chair, and Luke sat down.

"I'm not going to keep you long."

"All right."

The governor dropped down on the settee opposite Luke and flipped open a leather file on the table. Several newspaper clippings fluttered in the stirred air before settling randomly on the tabletop. "Have you seen these?"

"No." Luke tipped his head and quickly spotted the *Daily Times* banner above a headline that read Gambling runs rampant as officials refuse to act. With the tips of two fingers, he nudged the clippings aside, reading similar headlines on each.

"Looks like the *Times* is on a campaign to clean up the city." He straightened. "I can't fault them for that."

"Nor can I," the governor told him. "In fact, it's because of these articles that you're here."

Luke settled back in his chair, one booted foot resting on the opposite knee. "I'm listening."

"In recent months," the governor began, "I've become aware of an effort—a plan, shall we say—to form a new political machine in this state." The governor lounged back against the settee, his arm draped along its back. His suit pulled tight across his chest, and he unbuttoned his jacket.

"There's nothing new," Luke interjected, "or illegal about groups forming with their own political agenda.

"Ah—" the governor nodded in agreement "—but my sources tell me this one is different. This one is funded by the same men who control the crime in this city."

"There are those who'd say it wasn't the first time a politician had taken money from less than reputable sources," Luke said carefully. "Besides, politics aren't usually the concern of the U.S. marshal's office, unless there's a federal crime involved."

The governor's thin face drew up in thoughtful appraisal before he spoke. "As I told the president, this is a little different."

Luke didn't miss the less-than-subtle way the governor mentioned the president. It was no secret that Luke was here on direct orders from the president. "Go on."

Leaning forward, the governor continued. "What I'm talking about is not just a little questionable money being slipped into someone's campaign fund. This is an organized group based on corruption . . . at all levels . . . whose ultimate goal is to have their own men in the city government, perhaps eventually the state, too. You're here, Marshal Scanlin, because I needed someone from the outside. Someone I knew wasn't involved, wasn't on the take." He looked at Luke directly. "You come highly recommended. The president personally vouched for you."

"I appreciate his confidence."

The governor stood and paced to the window. "San Francisco—" he lifted the lace curtain and peered out through the glass as he spoke "—has become a center for crime. Gambling, prostitution, opium dens, sailors shanghaied off the streets in broad daylight. Why, there are even reports of men dealing in the white-slave trade. The crime is getting worse, and none of this can happen unless officials, highly placed officials, are willing to turn their heads."

Sitting straighter, Luke said, "Let me make sure I understand. You're saying there's a move by the criminal element of this city to take over the government through a system of bribes, and eventually put their own men in office?"

"Exactly." The governor let the curtain fall back into place as he turned to face Luke across the room. "This is serious. These people will stop at nothing, if the rumors I've been hearing in Sacramento the last few months are correct . . . and I believe they are."

Luke's brows drew down as he absorbed this news. Thoughtfully he said, "What about kidnapping?"

"What about it?"

"Did you know that Rebecca Tinsdale's son is missing?"

"When? Has there been a search? Maybe he's just run off." Concern was clear in the governor's voice and manner.

Luke took a long, deep breath and let it out slowly. "That's what I thought, but we've searched, and the boy's nowhere to be found. My hunch is, someone has him for ransom. You know, taking a child is easy, and the money's a sure thing, but now I'm wondering . . ." He shook his head.

"I'd say your hunch is right, considering that Mrs. Tinsdale owns the *Times*."

Luke's head came up with a start. "What?"

"Didn't you know? No, of course, you just got here. How would you know?"

The governor gestured toward the newspaper clippings. "Mrs. Tinsdale is the one who's been writing the articles on the corruption. It's her stories that have confirmed all the rumors and—" he gave an obviously grudging smile "—she's stirred up no end of controversy, I can tell you that."

"Dammit, why didn't she tell me?" Luke said, to himself as much as to the governor.

"You know Mrs. Tinsdale?" The governor arched one brow.

"Oh, yes," Luke snapped. "I know her. But obviously not as well as I thought."

"I want you to investigate this, Marshal." He pointed to the newspaper articles. "I want to have names and, most importantly, who's heading up this little scheme. Get me hard evidence, and I'll see to it that arrests are made, no matter who's involved."

"You mean like Captain Brody." Luke didn't bother to mince any words.

This time, the governor made a derisive sound in his throat, or a chuckle, Luke wasn't certain. "I gather this means you've met the illustrious chief of police?"

"We've crossed paths."

"Well, your suspicions are well-founded. I'm fairly certain Brody's involved, but the man's not smart enough to be putting something this well organized together. No, someone else is behind this, and that's who I want."

"The mayor, perhaps?"

"Maybe. I'm just not sure. In the meantime, you're new here. Your face isn't known, and the president tells me you are experienced in undercover work . . . a range war and some labor-union troubles, I believe, are the incidents he cited."

"Yeah." Luke nodded. "I've done a little undercover." He snatched up his hat and the leather folder before heading for the door. "I'll do my best, Governor."

"Get me names, Marshal. Hard evidence. I'll see to it arrests are made. If we can't arrest them, there are ways of exposing people and plans that will effectively stop their schemes dead in their tracks."

Luke nodded again and pulled open the door.

"Stay in touch," the governor added, with a final handshake. "I'll be leaving on Friday for the capital, so see me before then."

"Friday," Luke repeated, and strode from the room.

He skimmed over the articles on the carriage ride back to her house. The more he read, the angrier he got. The woman was stirring up trouble, and then she wondered what had happened to her son? No wonder even Brody figured it was a kidnapping. Hell, if the governor was right, Brody could be in on the whole thing.

He'd asked her point-blank if she had any enemies. "No," she'd said. Like hell. What did she think these were?

What on earth was wrong with her?

Damned if he knew, but he was going to find out. This whole thing had just gotten a lot more complicated, and a lot more dangerous.

Luke stormed into the house. He flung the leather folder down so hard on the hall table that it slid across the waxed surface and he had to make a grab for it to keep it from sliding off the other side.

Thirty seconds, and he was out of his jacket and had tossed down his hat.

Where the hell was everyone?

Most importantly, where was Rebecca? He was primed for battle, but it took two and so far he was the only one.

The house was still, and for a moment he had the uneasy feeling that something had happened in the time he'd been gone.

Had there been some news? Had the boy been found? Was he dead? It was a real possibility, and it was getting more real with every passing hour. No. He quickly discarded that notion. If the boy was back there'd be a celebration going on. If he was dead, well, there'd be the unmistakable sound of crying and the hushed tones of friends offering consolations.

If Luke had his way, it'd eventually be the former. And if she'd deigned to tell him about these damned articles and all the trouble they'd created, he might have had a better chance of getting the boy back.

He went upstairs. The door to Ruth's room was closed, and there was the barest hint of snoring, which confirmed that she was asleep.

All the other doors appeared closed, and he was about to go back downstairs when he noticed a ray of sunlight slicing across the carpet near the end of the hallway.

Striding in that direction, he found a door partially ajar and, pushing it open a little farther, he saw Rebecca seated at a small drop-front desk. Her back was toward him, and she appeared intent on some papers she had spread out in front of her. The room was small and square, and three walls were covered with floor-to-ceiling walnut bookcases. There were leather-bound volumes in neat lines, intermixed with scraggly stacks of papers. One good shake and they would slide to the floor. Her desk was between the two windows. Through the white lace curtains, he could see the front lawn and the street beyond.

So this was the lady's inner sanctum. The place where she worked. It wasn't what he'd expected, but then, there were a great many things he hadn't expected, it seemed.

With more harshness than he'd intended, he said, "Why the hell didn't you tell me you owned the *Times?*"

She jumped at the sound of his voice, surging to her feet and clutching her chest all at once. She wore a dark green dress with tiny white stripes. The neck was high and the skirt full, and Luke momentarily wondered why she was so intent on disguising her God-given attributes.

"You scared me," she said, a little breathless.

"Why didn't you tell me about the paper and about the articles?"

For the span of three heartbeats, Rebecca didn't move. She looked at him, filling her doorway like a dark specter, like the ghost who'd lived in the shadows of her life all these years.

Each time she saw him, it was as though she were seeing him for the first time. And each time she was overcome by the intensely masculine appeal of him. The way his white shirt pulled tight against the work-hardened muscles of his chest and shoulders, the provocative way his black wool trousers hugged his narrow hips and legs.

Their eyes met; his were focused fully on her, while hers drifted to his mouth, and she remembered the delicious passion of his kiss.

A shiver prickled down her spine, and she blinked against the sudden sensation. "I don't answer to you." She dropped down in her chair and pretended to go back to her work. "Besides, I thought you left."

"Why should I leave? I live here, remember?" He walked into the room, his boots making hollow thuds on the bare floor before he stepped on the square carpet in the center.

"You don't *live* here," she fired back as she struggled to ignore the suddenly vivid memories of being in his arms. "You're a guest—until Andrew is returned. That's all. And stop swearing at me!"

"I'll damned well swear if I want."

"Not at me, you won't. Get out and leave me alone. I'm busy."

"I know all about your work, sweetheart, and I'm staying."

"Do you want to test that?" She regarded him with casual disdain.

He arched one black brow in surprise, then said, "Okay, then, I'm staying until I get the boy back."

"Well, you weren't here this morning," she returned, shuffling the article she was working on until the pages were a scrambled mishmash. "If something had happened, you'd have been off doing whatever suited your fancy, I suppose."

He took another step in her direction, but she refused to be intimidated by him, not this time.

"I was not suiting my fancy, as you put it. I went by the police station, and then I had a meeting." He stood so close she could see the steady rise and fall of his chest. "It was important."

"More important than me?" The instant the words were out, she regretted them, regretted even more that after seven years, his leaving still affected her. He was too disturbing to her senses. Too dangerous to her plans. She squared her shoulders and steadied herself. "I *mean*—" she dragged out the last word "—your meeting was more important than *helping* me?"

His gaze sought hers, and as quick as that, his mood changed, softened. She could see it in his eyes. The man was more quixotic than anyone she'd ever known. Maybe that was why she was more intrigued than angry.

"Nothing—" he let the word linger between them before he finished "—is more important than you."

"Than *helping* me, you mean."

His mouth curved up in a lazy sort of smile that pushed her heart rate up about three levels.

"Whatever you say."

There was something in the huskiness of his tone that made her nervous, kind of skittish, like a sparrow eye to eye with the hawk. Feeling cornered and not liking the feeling, she skirted around him and strolled to the window. The wood made a scraping sound as she lifted the sash. The air was fresh and clean. The distinctive sound of a ship's bell carried up from the harbor.

"Now what were you asking when you barged in here... uninvited?" She never looked at him, only stared out the window as she struggled to maintain an aloofness she didn't feel. "I asked," Luke repeated in a much gentler tone, "why you didn't tell me you owned the *Times*."

She was quite breathtaking, Luke thought, watching the way the sunlight caught her upswept hair, the way her silhouette was outlined by the light. Yes, very, very beautiful. And he wanted her.

"I already told you that I don't answer to you. A great many things can change in nearly eight years. I can hardly tell you everything."

Luke dropped down in her swivel desk chair, making its gears squeak. He glanced at the papers on her desk. "Much as I'd like to know *everything*, let's stay with this, shall we?"

She spared him a look, seeing his hand resting lightly on the column she'd been working on, or at least trying to when she wasn't thinking about Andrew or Luke. "It's my next article on city corruption."

"I figured as much. Why?"

"Why what?"

He shook his head resolutely. "Why would you go stir up a mess like this? Why didn't you take it to the authorities? You had to know there'd be retaliation."

She turned sharply on her heel and walked to the desk. Her hands curved, white-knuckle tight, over the edge. "What do you mean, retaliation? There's no retaliation, and there weren't any authorities to take it to. None that I could trust, anyway. Besides, I put two years of my life into this paper. Do you think I'd give away a story this big? Circulation is up twenty percent."

"What's the big deal? Didn't you inherit the paper?"

"Of course," she returned, with a negligent wave of her hand. "But it was small, operating in the red, and about to close. Nathan had gotten it as part of a larger business deal. He was never interested in it, and just let it be. After he died, I decided to keep it, to see if I could make it into something."

"Why, for heaven's sake? You certainly don't need the money. Couldn't you have sold it?" He was astonished that she'd take on a job like this.

"I could have. As a matter of fact, I have an offer on my desk right now." She was thoughtful for a moment. "Why should I discuss this with you?"

"Why not? Is it a secret?"

"I have no secrets," she snapped, then abruptly walked over to the bookcase and scanned the shelves, apparently looking for something.

"Come on, Becky. I honestly want to know. Why would you want to run a newspaper?"

She glanced back, as though considering his question, then said softly, "Because it was mine. For the first time in my life, I had something that was all mine, with which to succeed or fail." She closed the book and returned it to the shelf. Surely you must understand the feeling of taking on a task, a seemingly insurmountable task, and succeeding."

"Well, sure. But I'm a man, and—"

Impatience flashed in her eyes. "And I'm every bit as smart and capable as you."

"No one said you weren't," he said sincerely, knowing it was true. He had great respect for any woman who could run a home and family single-handedly, and add to that a complicated business like a newspaper... "But men don't have choices about these things. We're expected to..."

"To what?"

"I was going to say that men are expected to provide, to take care of our families."

"And I," she returned, speaking slowly, as if to make certain he understood, "I am taking care of myself and providing for my child."

"You mean you *have* to work?"

"I mean, I like it. No, I love it—every decision, every obstacle, every failure, every success. It doesn't matter. It's mine. Someday it will be Andrew's."

He didn't miss the possessiveness in her voice. And then he understood. It was her pride, her self-respect, that she'd built. He couldn't fault her for that. Wasn't that exactly what he'd spent his life doing?

"And I gather the paper is making an impact?" He already knew the answer, if the governor's reaction to her articles was any indication.

"Yes." She favored him with a smug smile. "And two months ago we moved into the black."

Luke knew pride was all well and good, but sometimes there was such a thing as discretion. "It seems that while you were building this newspaper, you managed to stir up no small amount of trouble."

Rebecca shook her head and sighed. "It's the primary function of a newspaper to inform the public. If there's trouble, then so be it."

He lounged back, the chair tipping and squeaking as he did. "From what I hear, these articles of yours have tongues wagging all the way to Sacramento. People are nervous."

"Good," she said adamantly. "That's exactly what I want."

"When criminals get nervous, they tend to take revenge. Dammit, Becky. I asked you if you had any enemies."

"I don't," she retorted. "I haven't done anything except point out the obvious—that there is no way the crime can flourish in this city without someone being paid off. The Barbary Coast is going twenty-four hours a day, and it's expanding. Someone is letting that happen. It's obvious who."

"You're dealing with—hell, you don't even know who you're dealing with."

"Of course I do. I suspect the mayor and Chief Brody, for starters. Probably some lower officials, clerks, policemen, and so forth."

"Suspect? Don't tell me you don't have any hard proof."

She blanched, but didn't back down. "Not yet. Nothing in writing."

Lord, she really was in over her head. "Has it occurred to you that someone might have taken your child, might have *harmed* your child, to get back at you for these stories? To stop you from finding hard proof?"

She paled, and a trembling hand fluttered to her throat. "No one would do such a thing! Only the lowest form of human life would do that!"

"Well, someone sure as hell did." He paced away from her. "Wake up, woman. These little articles of yours have rattled someone's cage, and they don't like it."

"If you're right—and I'm not saying you are—what would someone hope to gain?"

That was still a bit of a puzzle, but Luke figured things might clear up when the ransom note arrived. "I'm guessing they're letting you know they can get to you anytime they want. They can hurt you anytime. If they make a demand, you'd damn well better do it, is what they're telling you."

She stared at him for the longest moment, then slowly shook her head in denial. "No. I don't believe it. As much as I believe the mayor and the chief are involved in city corruption, I don't believe either one of them would do this, would take my child as part of some dastardly scheme to get even with me." She shook her head more emphatically.

"I'm telling you this paper is the cause of all your trouble."

"Not true. Why, only two years ago John Woodson's wife was dragged right out of her carriage in broad daylight. The perpetrators demanded money, and she was released, and neither she or her husband had anything to do with newspapers."

"I'm telling you you're wrong, sweetheart."

"I don't agree, and don't call me sweetheart. I'm not your sweetheart, or anyone else's."

"Really? That's gonna come as a big surprise to the joker who was trying to play kissy-face with you last night."

"How dare you mention such a thing!" Rebecca set her balled fists on her waist. "If you were any kind of a gentleman, you would have made your presence known or returned to your room until *Edward—*" she emphasized his name "—had left."

He chuckled. "Well, if I was any kind of a gentleman, I guess you'd be right. I must have missed school the day they were teaching drawing room manners."

"No, Luke, no one could accuse you of being anything but what you are—arrogant, presumptuous..." She faced him head-on. "As far as I'm concerned, you barged in here yesterday morning, started giving orders to everyone—including the chief of police—took over without asking or being asked, and eavesdropped on a private conversation with my guest." She paced back to the window. "I acknowledge your abilities as a lawman, and for that I am grateful, but as you can plainly see, we have nothing in common, and I do not have the time or inclination to reminisce about a brief...encounter that we are both better off forgetting about."

If he was insulted by her tirade, he showed no signs of it. In fact, she thought she heard him laugh, but she wouldn't give him the satisfaction of looking at him, so she couldn't be certain.

"Princess," she heard him say, "that was a fine speech. Trouble is, I don't see it quite that way. When I walked in here yesterday you were in trouble, and we both know it. Brody had you over a barrel, and there wasn't a thing you could do. You needed me then, and you need me now. If that's arrogant, then so be it. I did the right thing, whether you admit it or not."

"So you're always right."

"No, not always. Sometimes it takes me a while to admit a mistake." His voice took on a strange, husky quality that seemed to caress her already raw nerves. "Sometimes it takes years—eight years, to be exact."

Before she knew what he was about, he pulled her to him and kissed her, fully, intensely, possessively. About the time her knees liquefied, he tore his mouth from hers and in a fierce tone said, "You can't dismiss me. You can't dismiss the sparks that fly whenever we're together. You want me as much as I want you, whether you're willing to admit it or not. I'm a patient man. I can wait. I've waited eight years. I'll wait another eight, or eight hundred, but you're going to be mine, make no mistake about it."

Then, releasing her, he left the room.

Chapter Six

Rebecca quietly but oh-so-firmly closed the door. Her hand twisted around the brass knob as though she were wringing a chicken's neck. Lord knew she wanted to wring someone's neck.

She counted to a hundred. Her heart was still pounding like a Gatling gun. She clamped her jaw down so hard her teeth ached. She counted to a hundred again—this time in French—just for good measure.

She wanted to hit something or someone. Definitely someone—a specific someone, with the sable-soft eyes of the devil himself.

Damn the man. Damn his arrogance. In one fluid motion, she grabbed the white porcelain vase from the bookshelf and hurled it against the closed door. The distinct sound of breaking porcelain only momentarily eased her temper.

It was that momentary relief that sent her searching for something else to throw, something else to destroy the way he destroyed her carefully built defenses.

"Who do you think you are, Luke Scanlin?" She shook her fist in the air. "What kind of woman do you think I am?" she ranted to the empty room.

She kicked at her chair, sending it lurching across the room to slam into the wall with a hollow thud that made a sizable chink in the plaster.

She inspected the damage. "This is your fault, too!"

Everything was his fault. Every disaster, every heartache, every minute of lost sleep...it had all started the day Luke Scanlin walked into her life.

She stormed to the bookshelves, then back to her desk and back to the bookshelves again. The air stirred by her quick movements made the loose papers flutter in the breeze of her wake, like so many fingers shaking to rebuke her for her foolish actions. With narrow-eyed determination, she retaliated by flinging them off the shelf to float and tumble until they settled onto the floor.

She would show them. And she would show him. She would show everyone!

She hadn't needed him then, and she most certainly didn't need him now.

The man had a colossal nerve. How dare he think he could say he wanted her and she'd just swoon into his arms in gratitude!

You did swoon, her conscience reminded her.

"I was seduced," she countered through clenched teeth. "Then and now."

Call it anything you like, but he's right. You do want him.

She froze. The truth hit her like cold water on a hot day. She sagged down in her chair, her head lolling back against the smooth, cool plaster.

Like it or not, this was reality. Luke, the one man she'd thought she would never see again in her life, was here, and he'd made his desires very clear to her.

Oh, yes, very clear. Her pulse fluttered at the memory of his explicit words.

Dammit. She snatched back the thoughts, and the feelings. Well, the thoughts, at least. Having Luke rip through her life had nearly been her undoing once.

Her eyes fluttered closed, and in her mind she could see her mother's stern countenance as she admonished her to give up her flights of fancy, to stop romanticizing, to do her duty to herself and her family. None of which included a certain cowboy, no matter how handsome he was.

Yes, she thought ruefully, her mother had warned her, and she'd been so right. If only she'd listened. But all her life her mother had been the strict one, the demanding one, the disciplinarian, and, after a while, Rebecca had simply stopped listening.

Oh, it hadn't really been Mama's fault that she was so strict, so determined, so rigid. After all, she had been one of *the* Stanleys of Virginia—first family, and all that.

But the Stanleys had fallen on hard times, and what little was left had been finished by the war. Analise had been raised to be a spoiled belle, only with no money and no society left in the South, well, there had been no one to spoil her—except Papa. What little money he had, he spent on her.

So, they'd married. What a pair they had made—the underpaid college professor and the society belle. Mama was constantly after Papa to work harder, demand raises, demand promotions, and Papa, so engrossed in his books and his research he'd never even noticed that other, younger men were passing him by.

It was no wonder, then, that Mama had gotten more than a little desperate. One day she'd simply announced that she'd decided they were moving to California. There was gold in California. Not that she expected Papa to go prospecting. Heavens, no, that would be beneath them. No, she expected Papa to get a position in some nice school, and she expected Rebecca to attend one of those same nice schools, but for an entirely different reason.

You see, there was no society in California, at least not anything like in Virginia, where families had been on the same land for generations. No, in California, things were new, rules were... flexible, and the daughter of a schoolteacher and a disadvantaged Southern aristocrat had as much chance as anyone to marry up, to marry into society.

Yes, that was the life Analise Stanley Parker had aspired to. That was the life Rebecca had been trained for, educated for and told in no uncertain terms would be her destiny.

As far back as Rebecca could remember, she'd been taught the *important* things—how to arrange flowers, serve a formal tea or a formal dinner, play the piano and dance the latest dances. She'd been required to be well versed in the latest fashions, theater, gossip. Oh, yes, gossip was most important. One had to know who was in—and who was out—in this newly forming society. It wouldn't do to be seen associating with the wrong person, Mama would admonish her.

Rebecca lifted her head away from the wall and sat up straighter. What it had all boiled down to was how to fawn and simper over some man—the right man—until he offered for her.

It was planned, pretentious and preposterous. She had hated every minute of it, but she had loved her mother, so she had tried. But when she couldn't stand one more minute of fine embroidery, she would slip off to her father's study and its book-lined walls—just like these, she thought with a ghost of a smile.

Standing, she strolled over to the bookcases on the far wall. Sunlight filtered through the curtains and caught the smooth surface of each leather spine. Lightly, lovingly, she ran the tips of her fingers along the row. Her father's books. He'd left them to her when he died. It was all she had of him. That and a few faded tintypes.

Her hand paused on a volume of Plato's Dialogues. How Papa had loved to discuss philosophy. How she had loved her father, and now these books. Each one was like an old friend. Each one, a special memory of a time shared with her father.

Many had been the night they had stayed up well past midnight. Ensconced in his tiny study, they had explored the world through the pages of these books. They had shared views on education and women's rights and argued politics. He'd taught her all she knew about ethics and honor, about caring and loving.

Perhaps it was naive, but she had thought all men held the same high codes and principles. Perhaps that was why she had risked so much with Luke, or perhaps it was as simple as rebelling against a lifetime of rules and plans. Whatever it was, it was a mistake, she thought with stomach-clenching certainty.

A mistake that seemed certain to engulf her and drag her down, down the way a tidal wave engulfs an otherwise safe harbor.

Oh, in the endlessly long hours after Luke left, after she realized what had happened, the logical part of her mind had said that Luke hadn't made any promises. And it was true.

But certain things had been implied, even if they had remained unspoken. Hadn't they? A woman didn't give herself to a man unless she loved him. Luke had to have known that. He had to.

And if she believed that—and she did—then he had betrayed her at the most intimate level.

So now what? He was here. Right in the middle of her worst nightmare. She could send him packing, but she knew she needed him. Andrew needed him.

A cold chill raced down her spine at the thought.

Abruptly she stooped and started to gather the papers scattered across the floor. The white pages were smooth and cool against her fingers. She glanced up in time to see a hummingbird pause briefly near the open window, then dart away.

Rebecca wished she could leave her troubles behind as easily and as quickly.

But, like before, she had to face it through. Luke would not stay. She was certain of that. So all she had to do was keep him at a distance, and pray that Andrew was returned soon.

Once Luke realized that this time he couldn't get what he wanted, what she'd given so freely, so trustingly, before, he'd move on.

She gathered the last of the papers and tapped the stack lightly on the floor to even them in her hands.

She sat back on her haunches, her skirt flowing around her legs as she stared at the grouping of photographs on the top of her desk. One, in particular, in a small silver frame.

Luke Scanlin would never know of her heartbreak—or anything else. That was a vow she would not break.

Chapter Seven

Another man might have been angry. Another man might have taken her little speech to heart. Not this man. No, Luke was smiling as he stepped off the porch and headed for the stable. The sun was shining. Songbirds chirped in a nearby oak tree.

The lady was something. Her words said one thing, but her kisses, the way she melted into him every time he pulled her into his arms, told an entirely different story. He was right this time. She did want him. Lord knew he wanted her. It was only a matter of time.

Lady, there's no escape. You've met your match.

A smile lingered on his lips as he saddled his horse and rode out. He was headed for the Barbary Coast.

He was becoming more and more convinced that the kidnapping and the corruption were connected. How, he didn't know—yet. But he was going to find out. He was going to get that boy back. He was going to get the woman, too.

While you're at it, why don't you bring in the James gang. That seemed about as easy as the tasks he'd set for himself.

Twenty minutes and he was on "Terrific Pacific" Street. Gin mills, dance halls and bordellos greeted him.

It was late afternoon, and already the narrow streets were filled with milling people—men, mostly. The Coast was hardly a place for ladies—except certain kinds of ladies, he amended, spotting a woman dressed in nothing but pantalets, black stockings and a corset as she lounged near a saloon entrance across the street. His mouth curved upward in an appreciative smile. Hey, he was a man after all. He could look.

Get your mind on business, Scanlin. Time to do a little of that undercover work you've been recruited to do.

His hand rested naturally on the worn handle of his .45 as he pushed open the rickety doors of the Midway Plaisance and walked in. The place was large and square. It had been a long time since the floor had seen the business end of a mop. The scents of tobacco, whiskey and unwashed bodies made his nose crinkle. God, how many of these kinds of places had he been in the past few years? *Too many* came the reply.

A roulette wheel clattered an invitation, which he ignored. Nearby, a dark-haired man dressed in black dealt faro to a table of miners.

Luke shook his head. They had a better chance of striking the mother lode than they did of winning. Too bad they were too drunk to know it.

Edging between the tables, he headed for the mahogany bar that ran the length of one wall. It was scarred and worn, and the brass footrail hadn't been polished since the day it was delivered.

Wedging in between a cowboy and a sailor, he caught the eye of the greasy-haired bartender. "Whiskey."

The man quickly complied.

Luke tossed a two-fifty gold piece on the scarred surface. "Busy place," Luke commented absently to the man as he sipped the rotgut.

"First time?" the bartender commented. He spit in a glass, then wiped it clean with a bar towel that was as black as a witch's heart.

"Yeah." Luke thumbed his hat back and surveyed the room. "Couldn't come to town and not partake of a little... sin." He laughed, and the potbellied barkeep joined him.

"Well, if'n it's sin you're lookin' for, this here is the place, all right. You name it, we got it. If'n we don't, wait ten minutes—someone'll get it for you."

They laughed together. Luke helped himself to another drink. It burned like lit kerosene.

A bald-headed man was pounding out a melody on a piano so out of tune it made him want to grind his teeth. Luke guessed that was what the whiskey was for. A couple more of these, and he wouldn't even notice. Sure as hell looked like no one else minded.

The tables were crowded, and getting more so every minute. Cardsharps and working girls seemed to be appearing in proportion to the increase in the crowd. They must have a sixth sense about these things, he mused, turning to lean back, his elbows on the bar. He lingered for a few more minutes, long enough to get a feel of the place, before he decided to move on. There were a lot of saloons and brothels, not to mention opium dens. Those he planned to stay far away from.

He strolled casually down the sidewalk, pausing to glance in a window or two. He wandered down a couple of alleys, getting the lay of the land, so to speak.

After three more saloons and more rotgut than he wanted, he wandered into the Fat Daugherty's. It was pretty much like the others, a little squarer, a little fancier, in a run-down sort of way. There was still a bar along one wall. This one had a mirror behind it, adorned with a crack big enough to put your fingers in. On the wall opposite, there was a painting of a woman, generously endowed, and naked as the day she was born.

Located conspicuously under the painting was a roulette wheel, next to a table for dice. A bunch of slick operators were dealing cards at other tables scattered nearby.

Luke strolled over to the bar. He cringed, forced a smile and said, "Whiskey." A man should never switch horses in midstream, but next time he was going to ask for buttermilk!

A ferret-faced bartender served up the murky-looking liquid. "Thanks," Luke said casually, and plunked down a silver dollar.

He'd been making the rounds all afternoon. He wasn't exactly sure what he was looking for, but he'd know it when he saw it. How's that for vague? he thought.

But that was what police work was. He couldn't just walk up to someone and say, "Pardon me, do you know anyone who kidnaps children or bribes officials?"

No, he just hung around, chatting occasionally, drinking as little as possible and watching. In the past few hours, he'd seen more faces from wanted posters than he had in three years. Obviously he'd been wasting his time down in Texas. All the scum of the world was here.

Speaking of scum, there were a couple of men at a corner table that he'd been watching in the mirror for several minutes. They were dark, and unwashed, judging by their greasy hair, and they looked like they had slept in their clothes.

These two he didn't recognize. Yet something about them pricked his lawman's instincts. There was enough of a resemblance that he thought they might be related, but what had caught his attention was that, unlike everyone else in the place, they weren't gambling or cursing or playing cards. They had consumed an incredible amount of liquor, judging by the two empty whiskey bottles on the table and the one they were working their way through now.

Even with that, these two had their heads together like they were planning to rob the Central Pacific and they didn't want any one else to know. Now, he realized that this was a modern day Sodom, and the two could be discussing anything from drugs to whores, but still, they intrigued him.

And since he was in no hurry, he settled down at a table in the shadows at the end of the bar.

Shortly before dark, the bartender lit the gas lamps along the opposite wall, keeping the flame low enough to hide the faded pattern on the wallpaper. Why the devil would anyone put wallpaper in a saloon? Luke mused, taking another sip of his drink.

About that time, a woman with hair in a shade of red God never made sidled up to him. Having known a few whores in his day, Luke figured she was twenty-five going on forty.

"Hi, honey," she said, dragging out a chair to straddle, which left absolutely no question about her intentions. Not that he'd had any, anyway. She was wearing a dress that was above her knees and nearly below her nipples. She had enough rouge on her cheeks to make a rose jealous.

She was looking at him with what he guessed was her come-hither stare. "Buy a girl a drink, cowboy?"

Luke wasn't interested in whores. But he knew what kind of a life these women lived, and though he knew it was their choice, he also knew most women didn't *have* a lot of choices.

Become a whore or get married to some dirt farmer. The result wasn't much different. They still aged ten years in one and died way before they should. It was more sympathy than interest that made him say, "Sure." He signaled the bartender for another glass.

The woman leaned forward, pressing her breasts against the back of the chair in a blatant invitation, which Luke ignored. Okay, sort of ignored.

He sipped his drink. She downed hers in one swallow and wiggled her glass for another. He obliged.

Around them the crowd was getting thicker and noisier. Someone was yelling for another drink at the bar, and the bartender was threatening to cut off a vital part of his anatomy if he didn't shut up.

A sailor, too young to know what a razor was for, wandered over to fondle the girl.

"C'mon..." he managed to slur. He half fell across her shoulder, and she gingerly pushed him back.

"Not now," she told him sharply. "Can't you see I'm engaged?" She grinned at Luke.

The sailor stared, bleary-eyed, from the girl to Luke and back to the girl again. With an unsteady shrug, he wandered off in search of new sport.

"Business is good, I see," Luke said, half teasing.

"Not bad," she returned, emptying her glass again. "Could be better, though. If you get my drift," she added, her hand gliding up his thigh toward his crotch.

Smiling, Luke covered her hand with his, stopping her. "Thanks," he said softly, "but I'm not really interested. No offense."

"What's the matter, handsome?" she said, with a lilting tone to her voice. "If there's a problem with the..." Her hand inched closer to his crotch. He stopped her again. "Millie is just the one who can cure you."

Luke laughed. "Darlin', believe me, there's nothing wrong." Hell, every time he kissed Rebecca, he was painfully aware there was absolutely nothing wrong.

"How about you just keeping me company?" he asked, knowing that whores and bartenders knew everything that was going on. He also knew a whore's time was money, so he shoved a ten-dollar gold piece in her direction. "Just so your time's not wasted."

She looked genuinely surprised, and this time, when she smiled, he could tell she really meant it. She helped herself to another whiskey.

"So what brings you to town?" she said amid the din.

"Oh, nothing much. Just a cowboy up from Texas. Only been in town a couple of days, and thought I'd check things out."

She raked him with an appraising stare. "Honey, if you're what Texas cowboys look like, I think I might have to head south."

Luke chuckled at the flattery. "Thanks." He poured her another drink. "So tell me, is the Barbary Coast as bad as everyone says?"

She toyed with the drink. "Worse. You name it, it happens here. Shootings, gambling, opium, women..." She sliced a glance at him. "Boys, if that's your interest."

"Not mine," Luke assured her.

She seemed relieved.

"How's it all keep going on?" he inquired casually. "I mean, down in Texas, about the time things are getting to be fun, some upstanding citizen complains, next thing you know there's women's betterment leagues campaigning for temperance and such." He shook his head in disgust.

She laughed. It was a harsh, tinny sound. "Ain't it the truth? Everybody knows a man has to have a place to... let off a little steam. Too much... steam is bad, don't you think?" Her hand found his thigh again.

"Exactly."

Luke poured her another drink, then lounged back casually. "You know, I was riding around today. I noticed some mighty fine-looking houses not too far from here."

"Ain't that a sight? Them big mansions, not ten blocks from here." She shifted and fussed with a lock of hair that had come loose from her combs. Her arms were raised to give him an ample view of her full breasts, straining dangerously near the top of her dress. "Used to be Fern Hill, before them swells built up there. Lately folks have taken to calling it Nob Hill. Oughta be Snob Hill, if you ask me."

If she moved another inch, Luke was certain, she was coming out of that dress. Not that he'd mind entirely. All things considered, he figured she wouldn't mind.

Business, remember.

Taking a big slug of rotgut, he winced and said, "So don't they get pissed, looking down here and seeing all that's happening?" He screwed his face up in a frown. "Please, tell me there's no women's betterment league. I'd hate to see a fine place like this disappear."

She laughed. "Ain't no chance of that, honey."

"Why?" he asked nonchalantly, turning his empty glass in his fingers. "If there's some secret, I'd sure like to know, so I can tell the boys what we're doing wrong...when I get home." He gave her his best smile, all dimples and charm.

The woman swilled her whiskey and leaned closer. In a conspiratorial tone, she said, "You gotta know who to pay, is the secret."

Luke's eyes widened in mock surprise. "You mean like government fellas and such?"

In a hushed voice she said, "Exactly. But don't ask me who, 'cause that I don't know. I only know a piece of everything I earn, everything the house makes, everything everybody makes, goes so we can keep in business."

"Pretty slick," Luke said in a tone of admiration. "I'll bet there's a lot of money goes through here in a week."

She nodded again. "But it's worth it. Everybody pays, and everybody's happy. Lord knows it's the first place I worked where I ain't worried about getting arrested all the time."

He saw her glance around, as though checking the crowd for prospective clients. He didn't want to lose her. So he pressed the conversation to keep her interested.

"So how do they know who to pay? I mean, anyone could show up with his hand out."

She eyed him suspiciously. "Say, how come you wanna know so much?"

"Oh, just naturally curious, I guess." He gave a one-shoulder shrug. "Besides, like I said, when I get back to Texas I wanna explain this to a couple of boys I know who are running a saloon in Amarillo."

She seemed to consider this.

Damn. He'd pushed too hard, and now he'd lost her. What the hell was he thinking about?

She shifted in her chair. "I like you, honey," she told him, resting her chin on the curved back of the chair.

"Well, thanks. I like you, too." *Take it slower.*

Another waitress sashayed past, running her hand provocatively along Luke's shoulder as she did. He smiled.

"Yup," he mused out loud. "I think a man could get to like being in the saloon business."

The woman seated across from him chuckled. "Yeah, I hear it gets mighty cold down your way in the winter."

Luke nodded. "That's why a couple of us was thinking about doing something...different. You think we could make some money at it?"

"Sure, honey. If you do, send me a letter and I—" She stopped abruptly, her gaze focused on someone or something across the room.

Luke followed her line of sight and realized she was looking straight at one of the two men he'd been watching earlier.

"Someone you know?"

"Yeah," she said, in a quiet tone that seemed more fearful than anything else. "My, ah... gentleman friend. He doesn't like me spending too much time with one man. Leastways not down here." She snatched up the gold piece and dropped it in her cleavage. "I gotta go." She lurched to her feet.

She hesitated long enough to say, "Thanks, cowboy. It's nice to talk to someone for a change without being... Thanks."

Luke watched her make her way through the crowd. When she reached the man, he grabbed her hard by the wrist and pulled her down on her knees next to him. Luke couldn't hear the words, but he could see the fear in her face and the rage on the man's.

Whores weren't known to keep the best company, he told himself. It wasn't any of his concern. Without thinking, he polished off his drink and stood to leave. He spared the girl one last glance. It was then that he saw the man hit her.

Her scream was hardly noticed by those in the saloon. Luke noticed, though. Damn. He kept moving toward the door, but then he saw the man drag her to her feet and hit her again.

Son of a bitch. He didn't care if she was a whore—he didn't stand for men brutalizing women. He'd seen enough of that at home. Before he realized what he was doing, Luke shouldered through the crowd.

"Hey!" he snarled. "Let go of the lady!"

The man cut him a glance. "Ain't no lady here." He gave an ugly sort of laugh and turned back to the woman, giving her a teeth-rattling shake as he did. "Next time I tell you to do something, maybe you'll remember." With that, he made to strike her again.

"Don't." Luke grabbed the man's wrist. "Not if you want to see morning."

All eyes suddenly focused on the two men. No one moved. The place was quiet as a church on Sunday.

The saloon girl gazed up at Luke. Blood pooled at the corner of her mouth. "It's . . . it's all right, mister. Really," she added tearfully.

Luke ignored her plea. "I'm not going to repeat myself." His voice was deadly cold.

The man continued to hold her, predator-tight. His free hand drifted conspicuously near the Colt tied to his wool-clad thigh.

"Back off, you two!" the bartender hollered. "I ain't havin' no trouble!"

"No trouble," the man repeated loudly, in a threatening tone.

"You son of a bitch," Luke said, in an equally threatening tone, "you're buying more trouble than you ever thought existed."

The saloon girl squirmed, trying to free herself. She clawed at the man's hand. "Please, honey, let me go."

"Shut up, Millie," the man returned, with a sharp shake to make his point.

Luke narrowed his gaze. "Well, it's up to you." Luke's tone was calm, more annoyed than worried.

That seemed to give the man pause. He looked around for his friends, as if needing reassurance that they were there to back him up.

Luke stood alone. His hand steady near his .45, he knew his only trouble would be the man in front of him, or the other one, who was trying to edge into the shadows.

"Stand still," he said flatly.

Startled, the man obeyed.

Finally the one holding on to the girl said, "Mister, just *who the hell are you?*"

"I'm the last man you're going to see if you don't let go of the woman—now!"

The man's eyes widened, and slowly he released his hold. The girl snapped free and ran toward the wall.

"A wise decision," he said. With his gaze still locked on the man, Luke said, "Lady, why don't you take a walk for a while, until things cool down or sober up?"

She made a beeline for the front doors.

"What's this to you?" the man asked, more puzzled than afraid now that he'd released the girl.

Luke grabbed a fistful of jacket and dragged the man halfway across the table. "I don't like bullies or cur dogs. You, you mangy son of a bitch, are both. Don't you ever let me see you hit a woman again."

Luke released his hold so abruptly the man sprawled on the table with a groan.

Luke backed away, then turned and went out the door.

He swung up in the saddle, and was about to turn away when a small voice stopped him. "Cowboy."

He turned to see the woman, her face already turning blue on one side. His hand curled into a fist, tightening on the rein enough to make the horse shy.

"You okay?" he asked, even though the answer was obvious.

She nodded.

He'd have liked to help her more, but he knew she'd probably go right back in there. There were a lot of things he didn't understand about women, and this was sure one of them.

With a cautious glance around, she came closer. Her hand resting lightly on his knee, she craned up to look at him. "Thanks. No one's ever done anything like that for me before. If I can ever repay—"

"You're welcome. Take care of yourself, Millie."

Her smile turned into a grimace, and she touched her cut lip. "Thanks, cowboy."

He touched two fingers to the brim of his hat, then reined over and rode for home.

Chapter Eight

Rebecca tried to convince Ruth to have dinner in her room. She was willing, even eager, to dine alone with her mother-in-law. It had nothing to do with avoiding a certain handsome marshal. No, she was merely trying to be thoughtful, considerate.

Unfortunately, Ruth had other ideas.

"Rebecca," she said, obviously surprised, "I appreciate what you're saying, but I've been cooped up in this room for two days, and it's about all I can stand. Besides," she continued as she pulled her wrapper from the wardrobe, "it wouldn't be polite to leave Marshal Scanlin alone."

"I'm certain the marshal wouldn't mind. I mean, he'd understand," Rebecca went on smoothly.

"Nope." Ruth was already slipping on her brown-and-white-striped wrapper. She did up the two dozen large bone buttons down the front and tied the sash. "I may not be up to wearing corsets, but I'm looking forward to getting out of this room." She adjusted the wrapper's high collar and long sleeves, then started for the door. "You coming?" It was a rhetorical question, and she disappeared out the door as she spoke.

With a sigh of resignation, Rebecca hurried out, and they entered the dining room together. The room was cast in early-evening shadows of blue and purple. On the sideboard candles flickered, reflected in the polished silver holders. Three places were perfectly set at the far end of the table, white china and fine crystal on blue linen.

But Rebecca wasn't appreciating the Wedgwood. No, her gaze went instantly to Luke. She hadn't seen him since that little scene this morning, which had been fine by her. She didn't have another vase to offer up to the god of bad temper.

Luke was by the window, seemingly unaware of their presence. His dark outline was perfectly silhouetted against the white lace curtains.

His forest green shirt was pulled tightly across his broad shoulders, and his denim trousers fit snugly down the length of his legs. She saw him run one hand through his hair, in a gesture of thoughtfulness, or perhaps annoyance—she wasn't certain which.

What was he thinking about? Was he thinking about the kiss they'd shared, about them being in each other's arms? Her pulse moved up a peg, and a delicious shiver prickled the flesh on the backs of her legs.

Stop it! she cried inwardly. *What difference does it make?*

None, she told herself, her chin coming up in a defiant gesture. Whatever Luke thought or wanted or expected didn't matter, not one whit. *She* was in charge. This was her house. Her life. And she was smart enough to never, ever, make the same mistake twice. He was not to be trusted. Besides, to let him get too close was to risk a great deal more than her heart.

"Good evening." Ruth's voice broke the silence, and Luke turned.

His smile was immediate, and devastating to her aching nerves. Discreetly, she dragged in a calming breath.

"Good evening to you, ladies," he said, helping Ruth with her chair. "Nice to see you up and around. I guess this means you're feeling better."

"I am." Ruth scooted her chair in and craned her neck to look around at him.

Rebecca eyed him suspiciously as he helped her with her chair. Where had he been all day? she wondered, then chided herself for wondering.

A shadow of beard grazed his chin, and his eyes were a little red. When she turned slightly, there was the distinctive aroma of...whiskey. Her eyes widened. Whiskey and... She crinkled her nose, testing. Whiskey and cheap perfume.

Why, that—

Anger stirred. Here she'd been fretting and fuming and worried about seeing him again, and all the while he'd been out getting drunk and who knew what else.

It was the "what else" that made her straighten, made her lips pull back into a thin line.

Her temper, the one she'd thought she'd banished, returned to a full boil. The man had the morals of an alley cat. Not that she cared. She most certainly did not care. It was outrage, not jealousy, that made her stomach clench. Obviously, when he said he wanted her, he'd meant immediately. When she didn't acquiesce, he'd gone out and found someone else to satisfy him.

Just like before. He would get what he wanted, then move on—or, in this case, move on when he didn't get what he wanted.

Well, there was a certain satisfaction in that, anyway, she added rather smugly.

If he noticed her staring, he didn't acknowledge it.

Ruth continued speaking. "Thank you for your concern, Marshal. And thank you for your able... assistance. Up the stairs, I mean. Rebecca told me it was you who gallantly came to my assistance."

"Why, ma'am—" he chuckled as he joined them at the table "—having a lovely lady in my arms is always a pleasure." His grin was roguish, full of boyish charm that, judging by the sudden pink blush on her cheeks, Ruth wasn't immune to.

Damn the man. He'd been here less than two days, and already he'd charmed every woman in the place. Well, not every woman. Not her. Not Rebecca Tinsdale. No. She was immune to his charms.

With a sharp snap, Rebecca opened her napkin and plopped it down on her skirt. The blue linen blended with the darker blue of her skirt. Let's get this over with, she thought sharply, and rang the dinner bell so hard it was a wonder the fine crystal didn't crack.

Right on cue, Mrs. Wheeler appeared with a platter of roast pork ringed with oven-browned potatoes that smelled every bit as good as it looked.

"I made extra," she said, with a little smile very much directed at Luke. "It's nice to have a man to cook for again."

"Mrs. Wheeler," Rebecca said flatly, more than a little disgusted, "you may finish serving."

"What?" Mrs. Wheeler looked a little flustered. "Oh, right away, ma'am." With a sniff and a cough that sounded more like a choking puppy, she hurried into the kitchen and promptly returned with a basket of biscuits and a bowl of green beans cooked with fat back.

The food smelled wonderful, but Rebecca didn't have an appetite. Wordlessly she passed the platter to Luke. Their fingers brushed, and for the barest of moments their gazes met and his lingered, amusement dancing in his dark eyes, as though he knew of that little scene in her office after he left.

"So, Marshal," Ruth began as she put her napkin on her lap and accepted the bowl Rebecca passed to her, "what news do you have about my grandson?" She passed the bowl without taking any green beans.

"Nothing yet." His expression was grim, serious. "I don't know if Becky has told you, but with certain new information—" he shot her an exasperated glance but didn't mention their little discussion "—I'm convinced that someone *has* taken the boy—kidnapped him." Softly, sincerely, he continued. "I'm sorry to be blunt, but there's no sense trying to hide the truth. If I'm right, and my gut tells me that I am, then all we can do is wait."

Ruth nodded, seemed to consider what he'd said. "There must be something more we can do."

Rebecca looked up hopefully.

Luke shook his head. "I suspect we'll be getting some sort of ransom demand. I've checked at the police station for similar crimes, men with histories of kidnapping or—" Child murder, he was about to say, but thought better of it. "Anyone who might seem a logical suspect."

"And?" Ruth asked.

Luke shook his head again, raking one hand through his hair as he did. "And nothing, I'm sorry to say. I spent the afternoon on the Barbary Coast, looking around." He didn't mention that he now believed that Rebecca was right about the corruption. "It's a waiting game."

"A game," Rebecca snapped, days of fear and anger over her son's disappearance merging with fear and anger over her unwanted attraction to Luke. The feelings were too intense, too great, to be contained, and she needed to lash out at someone. "Is that what this is to you? Some kind of game? We're going insane here, trying to get through the hours, scared that every passing minute means Andrew is—" Tears pooled in her eyes and slid down her cheeks. She swiped them back with the heels of her hands. "We're terrified, and you . . . *you* are out drinking and . . . and whoring." She surged to her feet and threw her napkin down on the table.

Luke mirrored her stance. "I was not out whor—"

"Don't deny it!" She raked him with a disdainful stare. "You can't deny it. Damn you, Luke." She swiped at her tears again. "Damn you for doing this . . . again."

Anger clenched and unclenched in her stomach until she thought she would scream if she'd didn't get out of there. Her gaze flicked to Ruth. "I'm sorry." Her voice cracked. "I can't—"

She strode from the room.

Luke watched her go, then turned an entreating stare on Ruth, who was watching him intently.

"I have not been out drinking and whor— Sorry. But I haven't." He dropped down in the chair, the wood creaking from the sudden weight. "Dammit," he muttered, more to himself than to Ruth. "I've been on the Barbary Coast trying to gather information. I found out that she's right. It looks like there are bribes being paid to officials. Now I just have to find out who and when and how much. I have a real strong feeling that the bribery and the articles in the paper and the kidnapping are connected."

Ruth leaned forward, her arms on the edge of the table. "Are you certain?" She tilted her head to one side. "How?"

But Luke was only half listening. Jaw clenched, he had his gaze fixed on the doorway. Dollars to door-knobs this was about that kiss, both those kisses. This was about her and him. But what the hell was she so angry about?

She liked the kisses. And just about the time things were getting intense, she'd haul off and pull away, like she was scared, or like she was hiding something, something she was afraid of revealing if her guard was down. But what?

He decided to find out.

"Marshal?" Ruth's voice stopped him halfway out of his chair. "How long have you and Rebecca known each other?"

The question came out of the blue, and he was momentarily taken aback. "What? Oh, I knew her... We knew..." A little too biblical, he thought, and started again. "We were friends, oh, going on eight years ago now, I guess."

"You know, Andrew has a birthday coming up in a couple of months." Her tone was completely nonchalant, and she reached for a biscuit as she spoke. "He'll be eight."

"Really? A December baby, huh?" He smiled. "I know you're worried sick about him, and I can't blame you a bit." His gaze flicked to the doorway again. "You know if there was something more to do, I'd do it."

"I know, Marshal," she told him sincerely. "And so does Rebecca. It's just that things have been difficult for her, especially since Nathan died."

"I'm sorry about your son's death, ma'am," he said softly, with great sincerity. "I know what it's like to lose someone you love."

"Do you, Marshal?"

"Yes, ma'am. My mother died when I was a boy."

"Then you do understand, Marshal. Maybe you can also understand what it's been like for Rebecca, her folks dying so close together, then Nathan—all within a couple of years."

Luke was startled. "I didn't know...about her folks, I mean. She never said."

"No, I don't suppose she would. She's like that—strong. Never asks for help. Never likes to admit she's in trouble."

Luke made a small chuckle. "Yeah, I have noticed that about her."

"I thought you might have. But don't give up on her. She needs you, whether she says so or not."

"Needs me?" Luke repeated cautiously, wishing it was true, wishing she did need him, and not just until Andrew was home again.

"Oh, yes. You have to help us get our boy back."

"Oh," he said, a little crestfallen. "Sure. I see."

"Do you, Marshal? I wondered," Ruth muttered.

"What, ma'am?" Luke cocked his head questioningly.

"Nothing. Maybe you should go and check on her, just in case."

Luke's head came up sharply. "You think?"

"Yes. Please."

He skirted around the table, his black wool trousers catching on the linen tablecloth, and he paused to put it back in place.

"Oh, Marshal..." Her voice stopped him at the doorway.

He glanced back.

"I'm glad you're here." She smiled, and he returned the gesture.

Luke headed for the parlor and found Rebecca seated at the piano. She wasn't playing, only sitting there running her fingers noiselessly over the yellowed ivory keys.

"Becky."

She looked up, jumped, really, as though she'd come back from some great distance, and he wondered briefly why she'd been so lost in thought.

He didn't like the tears on her cheeks, or the way her skin was funereally pale. Damn. Had he done that?

"Becky, honey, please don't cry. I didn't—"

He started toward her, wanting to explain, to soothe, to hold her and make it all better.

"No more, Luke." She shook her head and held up one hand. "No more."

He stopped near the settee, one hand curving over the smooth wood trim. "About today...what I said—"

"It doesn't matter."

"Of course it matters." At least it mattered to him, and he wanted it to matter to her. "Becky, I wasn't doing what you think I was doing. I was trying to get a lead on Andrew's kidnappers."

"Of course you were," she said, in a tone that belied her words.

He ran his hands through his hair, leaving deep furrows in the inky blackness. "Dammit. Becky, I'm telling you the truth."

"Luke, you came in here smelling like a saloon..." She lightly tapped one piano key. The deep bass tone seemed to vibrate through the room. "You've been gone most of the day, for some meeting that was so important you had to go, but not so important that you remembered to tell me." She struck the next note. "Then you expect me to believe whatever you say?"

"Yes." His tone was adamant.

She craned her neck to look at him. "Why? Why should I believe you? I believed you once before, and look what happened."

"What?" He arched one brow in question and took another half step toward her. The air in the room seemed suddenly charged. "What are you talking about?"

"I'm talking about eight years ago." She closed the piano case with infinite slowness. "I'm talking about a young girl who believed that you loved her. I'm talking about a young girl who loved you enough to give you everything she had, and then you left."

Her words, her truth, hit him like a fence post in the chest. And just as though he'd been struck, he dragged in a lungful of air, then another, letting the words penetrate his mind as the oxygen did his body. "Oh, God, Becky. I didn't know. I *swear,* I didn't know." This time he did close on her, and, taking her shoulders in his hands, he lifted and turned her to face him. She refused to look at him, and that was the worst hurt of all.

She twisted away easily. "How could you not know? Did you think I was in the habit of having sex with every man I knew?"

"Becky, don't." His expression was grim. Of all the things he'd expected—accusations, threats, denial—he hadn't expected this, and he wasn't quite certain how to deal with it. Was this the reason she pulled away every time he got close?

He cursed himself for every kind of a selfish fool. She had loved him.

You had it all, Scanlin, and you walked away. Now it's too late.

The hell it was, came the resounding answer. If he'd had her love once, then he would win it again.

With all the tenderness and honesty he possessed, he said, "I was barely twenty. I'd been on my own since I was fourteen. I didn't know anything about love, about how it was between a man and a woman who cared for each other. All I'd ever known were whores, and—"

"And still do, I see." Sarcasm dripped from her voice, and his temper overcame his good sense.

He grabbed her by the shoulders and turned her to face him. "Look at me!"

She did, and the hurt and distrust in her eyes was like a living entity. It was enough to make him pull her into his embrace. "I'm sorry, honey. I'm sorry for a great many things," he said against the top of her head. Her hair was silky on his cheek, and the scent of her rose perfume tantalized his nostrils.

Gently he put her away from him, never releasing his hold completely. She was limp in his arms.

"I was not with another woman today. Not the way you mean. Yes, I was in a saloon. Actually I was in several. Yes, I talked to a woman. I did not, *did not,* make love to her."

For a full ten seconds, she studied him, and he held her gaze, refusing to look away, wanting her to know, to understand, the truth of his words.

Then, just when he thought perhaps she did, she looked away, and he felt his heart sink. "I believed you once. I can't, I won't, risk it again." She dropped down onto the piano stool, lifted the cover and began to play a sad, melodic tune. He didn't know its name, but the tone was clear. She was giving up on him. But he damned well wasn't giving up on her, or them.

"No, you don't, woman. You're going to believe me if I have to—"

The hollow thud of bare knuckles on wood caught their attention. Rebecca hurried to the front door, Luke close on her heels.

A young boy, not more than ten, stood there. His face was smudged, his dirty blond hair unkempt. His blue shirt was about two sizes too big, and his brown britches were riding a little high at the ankles.

"Yes?" Luke snarled. He wanted to finish his conversation with Rebecca. "What do you want?"

"I want the lady," the boy said firmly.

"What lady?"

"That one." He gestured with fingers that hadn't seen a washbowl in days.

Ruth joined them. "What's going on?"

"That's what we're trying to find out," Luke returned, exasperated.

The boy pulled a wadded-up piece of paper out of his pocket and offered it to Rebecca.

Her heart stilled, then took on a frantic beat. She knew this was it, this was what she'd been waiting for, praying for, yet she couldn't seem to take the note.

When she didn't, Luke did.

One eye on the boy, he scanned the note.

Bring ten thousand dollars at 9 tonight to the alley behind the So Different saloon, or the boy will be killed.

"Who gave you this, boy?" Luke demanded.

"A man down on Broadway. He gave me a silver dollar to fetch it up here to you."

"And I'll give you five more if you'll tell me the man's name." Luke fished in his pocket and snapped the greenback temptingly in front of the boy's face.

The boy's eyes widened. "Ain't nobody givin' names down there, mister."

"Have you ever seen him before?"

Even as Luke spoke, the boy was shaking his head and inching backward toward the open door. Luke caught him by one small shoulder. "Tell me what the man looked like."

The boy's brown eyes widened in fear, and he struggled to twist loose from Luke's grip. "Let me go, mister. I ain't done nothin'."

Luke held firm, but he did drop down on one knee to look the lad in the eye. "Look, a boy, a little younger than you, is in trouble. We're trying to help him. Do you understand?"

The boy stilled and nodded.

Cautiously Luke released his grip. "Please—tell us what the man looked like."

"Honest, mister. I'd help you if I could. The man come up to me and says to take the note here and he gives me the dollar." The boy produced the shiny coin, as if to validate his statement.

"But you must have seen him."

The boy shoved the coin back in his pocket. "He was tall... like you. I ain't never seen him before. Honest." He held up his hand in a pledge. "He was wearin' a hat and a black coat, kinda fancy-like. I couldn't see his face, 'cause it's dark out, and—" He took an instinctive step backward again.

"Okay." Luke fished in his pocket and produced a two-fifty gold piece, which he tossed the boy. "If you see the man again, come and tell me, and there's another one of these for your trouble."

The boy beamed. "Yes, sir, Mr.—"

"Marshal Scanlin."

"Marshal Scanlin," the boy happily repeated before he turned and ran off into the night.

Rebecca turned to Luke. "Is Andrew alive?" Her voice was a tremulous whisper.

"Yes," he said adamantly. He handed her the note and watched as she read and reread it. She kept staring at the crumpled yellow paper until finally he slipped it from her fingers.

To no one in particular, she said, "They want money, a lot of money, or they are going to... kill Andrew." Her voice broke. The world seemed to tilt on its axis. She dragged in some air and told herself in no uncertain terms that she was going to get him back.

Then reality hit her. "It's Saturday night. The banks are closed," she mumbled. She turned a terrified gaze on Ruth, who was looking as pale as winter snow. Rebecca continued, "I don't have that kind of cash in the house." Or anywhere else, she suddenly realized.

"Where am I going to get the money?"

Chapter Nine

She needed money, and she had three hours to get it.

"What about the bank?" Luke prompted.

"The bank is closed." She paced away toward the bottom of the stairs and back.

"They'd open for you," Luke suggested. He wished like hell *he* had the money. He didn't. He had about forty bucks in his pocket, and another fifty in his saddlebags. Hardly a drop in the bucket.

"Open the bank," she repeated numbly.

"Yes. Of course. I mean, they do that kind of thing for—" for rich people, he meant to say, but couldn't.

"There isn't that much cash." She turned to him, her eyes wide as a frightened doe's. "Everything is tied up in stocks, bonds, annuities, mortgages. Why would they wait until the banks were closed, until I didn't have a chance to borrow—" Her expression lit up. "Borrow," she repeated. "Yes, that's it!" Grabbing her coat, she charged for the door.

Luke was so startled, it took him a couple of seconds to react. When he did, he snatched his hat and jacket from the mirrored hall tree and raced after her. "Where are you going?" he demanded, keeping pace with her as she went to the stable.

She ignored him, ordering the stable boy to hitch the buggy.

Luke circled around in front of her. "Where are you going?"

"Edward." She paced back and forth like a caged tigress, straw crunching under her shoes and clinging to her hem. "Edward can give me the money." Then, to the stable boy, she said, "Hurry, John. Hurry."

"You mean that pompous—" He ground his jaw shut to keep from finishing the statement. She was in trouble, and now was not the time to evaluate her...friend. It stuck in his gut like a lump of dried mush, this helpless feeling. Needing to keep busy, he helped the stable boy finish the hitching.

As he snapped the last ring, she was already climbing up onto the black leather seat.

"I'm coming with you," Luke said in a no-nonsense tone, and swung up beside her as the stable boy ran and opened the double doors.

She gave him the briefest of looks, as though to say, "Are you sure?" or "Thanks"—he wasn't certain which. He only knew that there was no way in hell he was letting her go alone.

With a sharp snap, he slapped the leather reins on the horse's rump, and they lurched out of the stable.

"Which way?" he shouted as they cleared the gate.

"Left!" She grabbed the edge of the seat as they made the turn at breakneck speed. The horse's hooves beat a tattoo on the pavement as they careened through residential neighborhoods. Rebecca shouted directions at every turn, praying that Edward was at home and not out at some meeting or social fund-raiser for his upcoming campaign.

They turned on Jackson, then Leavenworth, the oak trees whizzing past like silent sentinels. The only light was from the moon and the lights that shone in the windows of houses.

"There!" She pointed. "The pale blue one near the corner!"

Luke reined up sharply, the horse skidding so hard he nearly sat down in the harness.

She was out of the buggy and up the sidewalk before he could help her.

Luke stayed in the buggy. He might have driven her here, but he didn't have to watch. He hated that she had to do this, hated it even more that she was going to another man for help.

Rebecca pounded on the door, her heart in frantic rhythm with her urgent knocking.

"Edward! Come on. Come on." She shifted from one foot to the other, the wood planks creaking and giving with each motion. Why didn't they answer the door? This was taking too long, and—

The door swung open. She pushed past a uniformed butler with gray hair and a gaping expression. "Ma'am?"

"Edward," she demanded, already handing the butler her coat. "Mr. Pollard. Where is he?"

"Ma'am, I—"

Edward stepped out of the dining room, a dinner napkin in his hand. His white shirt was in stark contrast to his midnight blue suit. "Rebecca, what a pleasant surprise!" He dabbed at his mouth. "Won't you join me for—"

"Edward, thank goodness you're home!" Heart pounding in her chest, she rushed toward him. Her hair came down from her pins, and she blew it back. "You've got to help me." Her tone was desperate.

"Certainly." His fine blond brows drew down in concern. "Rebecca. What's happened?"

She allowed him to wrap her in the curve of his arm and escort her into the parlor. She could feel the warmth of his hand through the fabric of her blouse. Oddly, his touch was not comforting, and she stepped free and circled around a burgundy settee.

The room was dungeon-dark, paneled as it was in walnut. Not at all to her taste. The furniture was equally dark, burgundy brocade. Matching crystal gas lamps on either side of the mantel provided the only illumination. The drapes were open, as were the French doors.

Night air and the first traces of fog wafted into the room, like mist in a graveyard. She snatched back the direction of her thoughts.

"Edward, please. I need money. A great deal of money. I need it now!"

"Is it Andrew?"

"Oh, Edward..." Gut-wrenching fear consumed her until she thought she would surely collapse from the pain. "I've received a ransom note."

"Oh, no." He sank down on the settee.

"They want ten thousand dollars. *Tonight.*"

He visibly stilled. "Do you have that much cash?"

"No." She paced to the double doors. The camel-back mantel clock tick-tocked, losing pace with her increasing urgency, and she turned back to Edward.

"You know I'll help you any way I can." He stood and went purposefully to his desk. "I have some cash here, and I could write a check—" As he produced the dark blue checkbook, he looked up in sudden realization. "That won't help, will it?"

"No." She shook her head again. "They want *cash*, or they are going to kill Andrew." She clenched and unclenched her fists until her hands ached. "Please, Edward. You've got to go to the bank and get the money."

Their gazes met, but then he looked away. Eyes downcast, he lowered himself into his chair. "You know I'd do anything for you, but—"

She raced to the desk. "It's a loan, Edward. You know I'm good for it."

"Rebecca . . ." he began already shaking his head. "That's a great deal of money. The bank is closed until Monday."

"Yes, I know that," she snapped, impatiently wondering if he was being deliberately dense. "I wouldn't be here otherwise. You are a vice president of the bank. Surely you can—"

"But that's just it. I don't own it. The board of directors would have to make such a decision, and they're...well..." Frowning he absently fingered some papers there. "I don't know if they can be reached." Even in this dim light, he refused to meet her eyes. "I know Mr. Wilson left town yesterday for his daughter's wedding in Los Angeles, and I think Mr. Rubens was planning to accompany him. Without them . . ." He made a helpless gesture.

"Edward, please." She braced her hands on opposite sides of the desk. "This is my son."

"I know. I know." He reached in his desk and produced a small metal box, flipping open the lid to reveal cash. "I'll give you all that I have on hand—about eight hundred dollars."

"Not enough." She slammed her hand on the smooth walnut surface of his desk for emphasis.

"I'd help you if I could, you know that. I mean—"

"I've got to have that money!" she raged.

"Isn't there some other way? Something you could sell, perhaps?"

"Sell? What would I sell at this time of night? My house? My jewels? My— Of course!" She turned on her heel and rushed from the room. Snatching her coat from the hall tree, she didn't bother to put it on as she practically ran up the walk toward Luke.

It struck her then that she was somehow glad he was there waiting for her, strong and tall and steady. It felt reassuring to see him there.

Luke saw her bolt out of the house and tear down the steps. Moonlight filtered through the oak trees, casting the ground in moving shadows, and he strained to see her expression. That damned bastard had better have given her the money, or else he—

One close look at her face, and he knew the answer.

"What happened?" he asked, his voice deadly quiet.

"Edward can't give me the money without the board of directors' approval, and they're unavailable." She struggled into her coat and shoved her disheveled hair back from her face.

"Why, that son of a bitch..." He started toward the house. He'd get that money for her, one way or another. "I'll tell him about approval," he snarled. She stopped him with a touch.

"No, Luke, there isn't time."

He helped her into the buggy. He'd remember this night and that bastard, and sooner or later their paths would cross again.

He swung up on the buggy seat. "Don't worry, honey. I'll figure out something. Hell, just say the word and I'll rob that damned bank for you."

"This is no time for jokes. I—"

"I'm not joking. I've never been more serious. You need money, and I'll get it for you." His expression was as hard as granite. "Whatever it takes to get the boy back."

"I believe you're serious," she said into the sudden quiet.

"Damn straight. Hell, I'm half outlaw anyway. Gotta be, in my line of work."

She believed him. Believed he'd rob a bank for her if she asked him. Not because she asked him, because he was determined to help her and Andrew, with no thought for himself.

In that instant, everything changed. Fears faded and were replaced with a new emotion, familiar yet vague. But there was no time to examine it more closely now.

She touched him on the arm, feeling the soft cotton of his shirt and the hard tendons of the work-toughened muscles beneath. "Thank you for your offer," she said softly, sincerely. "It's not necessary. Just get me home."

"All right." Luke slammed back into the seat, slapped the reins hard on the horse's rump, and they took off. The wheels made a high-pitched whine that was the melody to the pounding staccato of the horse's hooves as they retraced their path.

All the while, the clock was running out. "Okay, how about this?" he said, making the turn onto Pine

Street. "I'll go to the meeting place. I'll pretend to have the money. Then, when they hand over the boy, I'll—"

"No! I'm not taking any chances. I can get the money."

"How?"

They pulled into the stable, and Rebecca jumped down the instant the buggy stopped. The horse pawed the straw-covered floor, seeming to sense the tension. "Leave him," she instructed the stable boy and, hitching up her skirt, she ran full out for the house. Luke followed.

He caught up to her in her office. She was rummaging through papers.

"What are you doing?"

She didn't even look up. Papers scattered like leaves until she found the one she was looking for. She held it high like a trophy. "This." She waved the paper. "It's an offer to buy the paper. I've had it for several weeks. It's exactly enough money, and they said the offer was good indefinitely."

Luke eyed the proposal suspiciously. "How's that help?"

"Because they offered cash. Some eastern group who want to branch out. See?" She waved the papers under his nose, her finger tapping the pages. "If they want it, they can have it, but they've got to give me the money *tonight.*"

She scrawled her name on the document in the required places. "Let's go." She breezed past him, and he fell in step behind her.

"Where to?"

"The lawyer's office."

Ruth was halfway up the stairs when they started down. "Did you see Edward? Did you—" She turned as Rebecca and Luke charged past.

"No," Rebecca called over her shoulder as she headed for the door.

"No?" Ruth shouted from her place on the stairs. "What do you mean, no?"

Rebecca stopped long enough to give Ruth the barest details. "Edward can't help without the board of directors' approval."

"What are we going to do? I've got some cash upstairs. Maybe they'll take less, or—"

"I'm selling the paper." She waved the documents in verification of her statement.

"No, Rebecca, you can't! That paper is every—"

"It's nothing if I lose Andrew. We're on our way to the lawyer's house. They offered cash, and if he's got it, then we're set."

"And if not?"

Rebecca stood very still. For a full ten seconds, she didn't speak, didn't move. Then she said simply, "He must."

With Luke at her side, they drove out of the yard.

She gave instructions, and Luke followed them. Occasionally he stole a quick glance in her direction. Her delicate face was bathed in moonlight. Her chin was set, rigid, actually, and she kept her eyes focused straight ahead.

He could only begin to imagine what was going on in her mind. Perhaps the realization that she could have her son back in a few hours if, and only if, she could raise the money.

Damn, he wished he could do this for her. He wished he'd found the boy days ago, but it was a big city, and looking for one small boy was like looking for the proverbial needle in a haystack.

It galled him that he was so helpless in this, that he could only drive her around and wait while she begged for help, for money. A fierce protectiveness welled up in him—not that it did much good.

There wasn't anything he could do except stand by and wait, and waiting was not something he did well. No, Luke Scanlin was not known for his patience, nor was he known for his willingness to forgive and forget. He wouldn't forget this night, or that bastard, Edward, who wouldn't help her.

There were only two things that mattered in her life, and now she'd have to sell one to save the other.

This goddamned lawyer better have the money.

Fifteen minutes later, they pulled up at the lawyer's home—white clapboard with dark green gingerbread trim.

This time, when she bolted from the buggy, Luke jumped down and went along. This time, they were getting the money. There'd be no taking advantage of her—not now. It was the least he could do.

Ten long steps up the front walk to the wooden porch. A hideous little gargoyle stood guard outside the door. Luke knocked on the door. He could see lights on through the stained-glass panels.

The door swung wide. A portly man of about forty, with thinning brown hair, answered the knock.

"Mrs. Tinsdale. What a pleasant surprise. I wasn't expecting you. Please come in." Smiling, he stepped aside.

"Mr. Handley." Rebecca walked past him into the small, square entryway. "I apologize for the late hour but I've come to see you about that offer to buy the *Times.*"

He shot Luke a questioning glance. "I don't believe we've met, sir. Frank Handley." He offered his hand.

"Luke Scanlin. U.S. marshal for this region." Luke wasn't one for titles, but under the circumstances, he thought this was a good time to use his. Just to let the man know there'd be no deceptions—not tonight, not with Becky.

His handshake stopped in midmotion, and his gaze flew to Luke's face. "Marshal? Did you say marshal?"

"That's right. Is there a problem?"

"What? Oh, no." He released Luke's hand abruptly. "I was just startled, is all. Maybe I should ask you the same thing?"

"Everything's fine... so far," Luke returned politely, but didn't bother to smile.

"Good. Well, please, since this is business, let's go into the office."

He led the way down the narrow, carpeted hall beside the stairs, to a room near the back of the house. The gas wall sconces were barely a flicker, and he turned them up, the gas flame hissing in response.

The office was barely ten by ten, just enough room for a small mahogany desk, one matching file cabinet and two Windsor chairs.

"Have a seat, won't you?"

Rebecca took the chair by the warming stove.

"I'll stand," Luke said at the lawyer's questioning glance.

"Suit yourself."

"I always do."

Luke folded his arms across his chest and leaned one shoulder against the smooth doorframe, effectively blocking the doorway.

The lawyer hardly hesitated. He was good, Luke thought with grudging admiration, and he should know. He'd seen enough of them over the years, what with trials and all.

Rebecca broke in. "Mr. Handley, about the sale."

Frank Handley circled around his desk and sat down, his swivel chair squeaking as he twisted.

"I've brought the papers, signed." She balanced them on her lap. "You had said cash. Is that right?"

"Yes, that's right."

"Here. Now," Luke clarified from his place in the doorway.

"Yes. I have the cash in the safe."

Rebecca straightened, and Luke could see her sigh. There was even the barest hint of a smile. "Fine. Then we have a deal."

She stood and offered him the papers, which he accepted. He glanced at the signature, then went to a safe hidden behind a painting—so obvious an idiot could have spotted it.

Thirty seconds, and the small door swung open with a squeak. He produced a tan envelope bulging with cash, which he handed to Rebecca.

"You're welcome to count it, if you like."

She clutched the envelope to her as though her life depended on it. In a way, it did. It *would* save her life, for God knew that if she lost Andrew, her life wouldn't be worth living.

"No, that's all right, Mr. Handley. I trust you."

She started for the door. Luke blocked her path. They exchanged a glance. His gaze quickly flicked to the lawyer, the one who was Cheshire-cat pleased with himself. Something about the man bothered Luke. Maybe it was that there had been no haggling, no discussing, no questions. Maybe it was that the money had just been sitting there waiting, as though they'd known she'd sell.

Oh, hell, it was more likely that his suspicious nature was getting the better of him. After all, the offer had been made weeks ago, and, she hadn't turned them down, so why shouldn't the money be sitting here waiting?

Still, his male pride, pride that was all tied up in knots because he couldn't reach in his pocket and produce the needed money, made him say, "You sure about this?" His tone was executioner-quiet.

"I am."

He saw tears pool in her eyes, and that helpless feeling inside him quickly turned to rage.

He let her pass, though it felt more as if he were letting her go. Somehow he was going to make this up to her. Somehow he was going to make her see that even though he didn't have thousands in the bank, he was still the one she needed.

The ride back to the house was somber. She had the money, but the cost he knew had been terribly high. The paper was her heart. Andrew was her soul.

"I'm sorry this is happening, Becky."

She nodded, clutching the envelope to her breasts. "I have the money, that's all that matters. Andrew is all that matters."

The horse's hooves click-clacking on the street and the hum of the buggy wheels irritated her already throbbing nerves. Houses, lights blazing, passed like soldiers in review, while oak trees stood shadowy sentry duty. There was no breeze, just the light gray misting of the incoming fog.

"You know, I can't help wondering why that lawyer had the money on hand, instead of in a bank." Luke shifted the reins to one hand.

"The offer said cash," Rebecca explained. "It was supposed to be an incentive. No lengthy paperwork, no financing."

"But cash? I mean, most people, when they say cash, they mean in a bank, write a check, that kind of cash."

"I don't know, and I don't care. All I know is, I've got *exactly* the amount of money I need. What time is it?"

He fished his watch out of his pocket and clicked open the cover, twisting it to catch enough moonlight to read it. "Eight. We've got an hour."

He let her off in front of the house, and watched her hurry up the walk before he drove the buggy around to the stable.

"Put it away," he told the boy. He saddled his horse and led him around to the front. There was at least one thing he could do. He could deliver the ransom. Walking into dark alleys was something he was all too familiar with. If someone was going to get hurt, it wasn't going to be her.

The entryway was empty when he walked in. He went upstairs and found Ruth with Rebecca, in her bedroom.

The room was large, square, and conspicuously feminine. All soft shades of blue and green. There was lace at the windows and lace trim on the bed coverings. The furniture was cherry, polished to a gleaming shine. It looked just the way he would have imagined Becky's room.

"You okay?" he asked, knowing she was far from it, but needing to say something, needing to let her know he was there for her.

"Yes." Her back was to him. She was rummaging in her wardrobe cabinet. "I'll be ready in a few minutes."

"Ready?" He arched one brow suspiciously. "Ready for what?"

Her head snapped around. "Why, to go, of course." She pulled out a black riding skirt and a dark print blouse.

"Just where is it you think you're going? I'm taking the money."

"I thought you'd say that."

"So?"

"I'm going with you." She dropped down in a chair and hitched her skirt to her knees, then started undoing the buttons on her shoes as if he weren't standing ten feet away, gaping at her stocking-clad ankle.

His mouth dropped open. He snapped it shut. The woman was more brazen, more stubborn, than most men.

He shot a help-me glance at Ruth, who shrugged helplessly.

Okay, then, he'd handle this himself. Taking a firm step into the room, feet braced, he gave her his sternest look. The one that had made Johnny Jenks think twice, then decide surrender was better than dying. "I—" he emphasized the singular word "—am making the delivery. *You* are not coming along."

That fierce look of his failed miserably. The woman didn't even hesitate. "Yes." She tossed her shoes aside and pulled her blouse free of her waistband, shooting him an impatient look. "I am."

"No," he countered, as though he were talking to a headstrong child. "You aren't. You don't know what we're dealing with here. I do this for a living, remember?"

With cold determination in her eyes, she advanced on him. He held his ground, though he'd seen kinder looks in the eyes of warring Comanches.

Ruth spoke up from her place near the foot of the bed. "I tried to tell her it was too dangerous."

"Thank you," he said, in a smug confirmation that didn't slow Rebecca's advance one iota.

"Now, you listen to me." She jabbed the tips of two fingers in his chest, and he flinched in surprise. "I'm going. That's *my* son. It's *my* money, and—"

"I know it's *your* money, dammit. I just drove you all over town to get it," he snapped, still smarting from the frustration and the blow to his pride.

"Either you take me, or I go alone. But make no mistake, Scanlin—I'm going. Now..." She jabbed him again, and this time he retreated a half step. Comanches could take lessons from her. "You coming with me or not?"

"Dammit, Becky, you can't—"

"Yes or no, Scanlin. Those are the only words I want to hear."

"This is wrong. It's dangerous as hell."

"Yes or no."

He didn't doubt for one second that she was bullheaded enough to do exactly what she said. Trouble was, she'd probably get herself, and maybe that boy, killed in the process.

Every instinct he had was screaming that this was a big, big mistake.

He was cornered.

"All right!"

"What?" she countered, with a smugness that rankled his dangerously short temper.

"Yes, I'm coming with you."

"Fine." She turned away, already beginning to unbutton her blouse. "Now get out of here so I can change."

Ten minutes later, Luke was still fuming.

He paced the length of the entryway. He'd had a Missouri mule once with a gentler disposition than her. He clenched his jaw so hard, pain inched down his neck and up behind his eyes.

Yeah. Okay. He knew she was worried about the boy. So was he. He knew she'd been frantic. He would be, also, if it were his son.

He kept pacing, his boots making hollow thuds on the polished planks.

Yeah, he also understood that sitting around doing nothing, waiting, wasn't his style—or hers, obviously.

But this was dangerous, more dangerous than she could begin to understand, and he didn't have time to explain the fine points of the outlaw mentality. How they were about as trustworthy and honorable as rabid wolves. Make that hungry, rabid wolves.

He should have been in that alley an hour ago. He should have gotten there first so that there would be no chance of a trap, no chance of being surprised. As it was, with all this running around trying to get the ransom, they'd make the deadline with only minutes to spare. That triggered a warning bell in his mind. He didn't have time to think about it now, but later, after everyone was home, then . . . He nodded thoughtfully to himself.

For about the tenth time in as many minutes, he checked his .45, the one he had tied low on his right thigh. He hefted the gun, testing the cylinder, the weight and feel, as though he were shaking hands with an old friend. Yeah, he mused, slipping the weapon smoothly into the worn holster, sometimes this was his only friend. Tonight he also had a .32 in a shoulder holster under his jacket. Just in case.

He paced away again, this time to stand in the open doorway. The sky was filled with stars, like diamonds on a jeweler's black velvet cloth. The moon was half-full, the other half faintly visible, like a shadow. It was hard to believe that something so terrible was happening on such a beautiful night. It was a night for lovers, just enough chill in the air for a man to put his arm around his girl under the pretense of keeping her warm.

Yeah, a night for lovers. Too bad he and Becky weren't going out somewhere, maybe to a restaurant or a theater. He'd like that.

Instead, he was taking her into an alley on the Barbary Coast. If it weren't so awful, it would be appropriately funny. They were about as opposite as the Barbary Coast and Nob Hill, he mused, not for the first time.

He sucked in a slow breath to calm his nerves. His heart pounded heavily in his chest, and his fingers curled and uncurled in a nervous gesture. Yes, he was nervous. The famous Luke Scanlin was downright scared.

He'd faced outlaws and Indians, robbers and range wars, but this was different. All those other times, nothing had mattered. He'd had nothing to lose but his life, which he'd always figured wasn't worth much anyway. He'd had no family who'd miss him or mourn. Hell, he'd barely had enough money to get himself buried, whenever that necessity arose.

He leaned one shoulder against the doorjamb and settled his battered old Stetson a little lower on his forehead.

All evening he'd hardly been able to keep his thoughts on the business at hand. His mind had been on that revelation of hers. She'd said she had loved him. All those years ago, Rebecca had loved him.

He shook his head in disbelief. He could have had it all. This could have been his.

He made a derisive sound in the back of his throat. Not this, he thought, glancing over his shoulder at the mansion spread out behind him. But he could have had Rebecca. Maybe they would have had a child, a son.

Becky's child. That thought settled gently in his mind. He'd like that—like that a lot.

He wanted her. He had realized after that first kiss that he had always wanted her, had come back to claim her. But was it too late?

Abruptly he lifted away from the doorframe. He had work to do, a child to bring home, and a woman—his woman—to protect.

His arm brushed against the gun securely tucked in the shoulder holster under his jacket. He adjusted it to a more comfortable position.

A glance at the clock on the mantel in the parlor showed it was twenty to nine. He'd already been to the stables and had another horse saddled for her. He stopped pacing at the bottom of the stairs.

"Becky—"

He broke off when he spotted her on the top step. She was dressed in a black split skirt that brushed the tops of her riding boots. The ebony buttons down the front were unfastened, revealing the split in the skirt. She wore another of those high-necked blouses, this one in a navy blue print. Her hair was down, tied back with a ribbon.

She looked a little pale, dark smudges obvious under her eyes. Her usually sensuous mouth was drawn into a thin line. She was tired, and more than a little afraid, he knew, and he remembered her tremulous voice when she'd admitted that weakness to him.

He wanted to pull her into his arms, to hold her, to tell her that he would bring her son home. She could trust him. She could believe in him. Sadly, he knew now that he'd destroyed her trust once before. But times had changed, and so had he. He was going to regain her trust, and then her love.

First, he was going to get that boy back.

Ruth was hot on Rebecca's heels. "Now be careful. Don't take any chances." She shook her finger in admonition.

"I won't." Rebecca pulled on her black kid gloves.

Ruth was still talking as they joined Luke near the door.

He picked up the shotgun he had propped beside the mirrored hall tree.

"Get Andrew and get the blazes out of there."

"I will," Rebecca said.

She raked Luke with an appraising stare that focused mostly on the arsenal he had with him. "Is that necessary?"

"Yes, and *this* isn't up for discussion."

She shook her head and gave Ruth a quick kiss on the cheek.

"Rebecca," Ruth said as they started out the door, "bring our boy back. I—" She broke off and swiped briskly at the tears in her eyes. "When you see him, tell him I love him."

They hugged again. Then, abruptly, Rebecca pulled back. "I know, Ruth. I'll tell him. No one is going to take your grandson away from you." She turned and went out the front door.

Luke followed and motioned toward the waiting horses. "More manageable, less conspicuous," he said at her questioning glance.

"All right."

He gave her a leg up.

"Sidesaddles." He said it like a curse, then swung up onto his horse. The gelding pawed and pranced sideways, seeming to sense the tensions of his rider.

The night was oddly still and empty. No traffic, no pedestrians. A quiet residential neighborhood.

On the Barbary Coast, however, it was the shank of the evening, and things were just heating up, so to speak.

Rebecca stared in obvious amazement at the gaudy buildings that lined both sides of Pacific Street. Men gathered on street corners to drink openly, leer, and make comments that were lewd enough to make her blush.

Half-naked women leaned out of second-story windows, yoo-hooing to Luke and any other man who'd give them notice. In the bay beyond, two dozen ships, sails rolled and tied, bobbed in the harbor, while moonlight glistened on the moving water, making it look silver-bright.

The distinct smell of salt water and cheap whiskey irritated her nostrils. Somewhere close, there was an alley where she'd hand over money and ride home with her son.

She tried to focus on the street ahead, though she watched Luke out of the corner of her eye. He looked dark and powerful and more like an outlaw than a marshal. She saw a muscle flex in his jaw and knew he was tense, nervous about this exchange.

But she was confident. Yes, she understood there was the potential for danger. After all, those involved were ruthless enough to take her child. Still, they had asked for money, which she'd brought. They wanted the money, and she wanted her child.

It'll be fine. She said the words over and over in her mind, like a litany. Needing to hold on to the thought and the promise.

"We're almost there," Luke's voice startled her, and she jumped, instinctively tightening her grip on the reins. The horse sidestepped in response, and she steadied the mare with a pat.

A drunk staggered into their path and, frightened, she reined in sharply. The cowboy wandered away, seemingly not even realizing they were there.

It was with a shaky smile of relief that she cut a glance in Luke's direction. But he wasn't looking at her. His expression was cold, harder than granite, and his hand rested conspicuously on his gun.

Just as quickly, she saw him relax, saw his hand move down to rest lightly on his wool-clad thigh.

"Here." He gestured with his head, never looking at her.

Luke nudged his horse in front of her, and both horses stopped at the gnarled hitching rail in front of the So Different gambling hall. Men milled around on the boardwalk, and the sound of distinctly feminine laughter carried outside over the sound of a reed organ.

Tying his horse, he came around to help Rebecca. His hands closed around her waist, and he felt the stiff bone stays of her corset beneath her blouse. As he lifted her down, her hands naturally rested on the tops of his shoulders, and he could feel the tightening of her fingers for that instant she was suspended in the air.

Instinctively their gazes sought each other. Black eyes locked with royal blue as she slid down the front of him. It was a simple motion, not uncommon, yet for them it was highly provocative, and each of them tensed with sudden awareness.

Lost in the sensation, the closeness, Luke hesitated, his hands tightening perceptibly at the longing that surged through him.

As though she sensed his awareness, her lips parted, the words she'd meant to say unspoken as she lost herself in the depths of his bottomless black eyes. Her breath came in shallow gulps, and she thought she saw his head dip when—

"Hey, lady!"

That quickly, the spell was broken, and Luke released her, stepping back. Rebecca fussed with straightening her blouse.

"Hey, lady!" a young sailor carefully enunciated from his place near the batwing saloon doors. His face mottled red, his blond hair sticking out in haphazard directions, he staggered toward them, catching himself on the porch post with an elbow. "You wanna dwink?" He waved a half-full bottle of Kendall's whiskey in her direction.

Luke was making a show of tying up the horses. Not because they needed to be tied, but because he was trying to get his breathing back to something close to normal. So he only spared the man a quick appraisal. "Drunk and working on being disorderly," he told Rebecca, then told the sailor, "No, she doesn't."

Rebecca didn't feel quite as confident as Luke about dealing with an inebriated man and, though he did seem frightfully young and was unarmed, she edged a little closer to Luke.

Luke wasn't worried about the sailor as much as what was waiting for them in that alley about twenty feet away. "He's just feeling his oats."

Luke took the money from the saddlebags, where he'd put it earlier. It was hard to believe that ten thousand dollars could make such a small package. Men worked their whole lives for this much money, and here it was all tied up in a nice little parcel.

"Let's go. The alley is over here." He remembered the locale from his trip earlier today, and was glad now that he'd done a little scouting around, even if it had cost him yet another argument with Becky.

Giving the sailor a wide berth, he escorted Rebecca onto the walkway. But the sailor was evidently determined not to take no for an answer. He cut across their path, waving the bottle under Rebecca's nose this time.

"Come on, 'oney," he slurred, taking a long swallow of the caramel-colored liquid, a small trickle dribbling down his chin. He grinned, then wiped the top of the bottle on his blue woolen sleeve with an unsteady flourish.

"'ave a taste." He shoved the bottle in her direction, his hand slamming into her breast.

"No!" she screamed, more disgusted than fearful.

Faster than she could blink, Luke grabbed two fistfuls of the man's shirt and, in one motion, slammed him up against the wall. The bottle crashed to the ground, the glass breaking with a sharp clink and the remaining liquid running between the cracks in the walkway.

That was when she realized Luke's gun was jammed tight under the sailor's chin. Good Lord, she hadn't even seen him draw. The look on his face was hangman-cold, and sent an icy shiver up her spine.

"'ey," the sailor mumbled, trying to move and seeming confused about why he couldn't.

When the man touched Becky, rage had exploded red-hot in Luke's brain, and he took it out on this unwary victim.

"The lady is with me." Luke shook the man, whose reddened eyes widened in surprise. "Don't touch her. No one touches her."

The sailor's head bobbed up and down like a rag doll's.

"Luke," Rebecca begged, pulling uselessly on his arm, "don't hurt him. He didn't mean anything. He just scared me."

Luke's eyes were sharp with fury. "Don't you think I know he scared you?" He shook the man again. "Did he hurt you?" He slammed the squirming sailor against the wall with a head-banging thud that made him groan.

A crowd had gathered. Miners, cowboys, saloon girls, all staring at her, at them. Embarrassment replaced fear in Rebecca.

Someone offered three-to-one odds on the "cowboy"—Luke, she supposed. Oh, God, this was awful.

"Luke." She tugged on his elbow, harder this time. "I'm fine."

Brows knitted in anger, he glared at the sailor, then back to her again. He studied her through narrowed eyes, seemingly unaware of the crowd. Then, without a word and in one motion, he released the sailor, turned, took her by the arm and escorted her away, as though he hadn't nearly killed the man.

A chill ran down her spine as she stepped out to keep pace with him. Her boot heels scraped on the uneven boardwalk.

"Luke, you almost killed him."

"If he hurt you—if anyone hurt you—I *would* kill them." This close she could see that his breathing was rapid and his eyes were hard as obsidian, and she knew, without a doubt, that he meant every word he said.

Luke Scanlin was a man capable of great tenderness, and now she knew he was a man capable of equally great rage. A man capable of making his own law. Scanlin's law.

That frightened her more than anything, for what would he do if he knew the whole truth?

Taking a step, freeing herself from his grasp, she forced herself to be calm, as calm as possible when everything and everyone she cared about was at stake.

When he halted, she said, "Is this the alley?"

"Yes." He eyed her sternly. "I wish you'd change your mind and let me do this. It's not too late to—"

She shook her head. "I'm going."

He thumbed back his hat. "Okay." Luke glanced around. Satisfied that no one was paying them any mind, he said, "I want you to do everything I say." He pulled her out of the way of a group of cowboys who were strolling by.

"Agreed," she said firmly, determined to get on with this, determined not to let the terror that was fast pushing her heart rate to something equal to a stampede, get the best of her.

"Stay close and stay behind me. Do you understand?"

She nodded.

"If there's any trouble—" he bent to look her straight in the eye "—any trouble," he repeated, as though to force the words into her mind, "then I want you to run like hell. Don't worry about me. Don't worry about Andrew. Just run. Do you understand me?"

"Trouble? What kind of trouble?" She shook her head in denial. "I've done as they demanded. They'll be satisfied to take the money and leave, won't they?"

"I don't know." He glanced toward the alley, which resembled the opening of some monster's mouth in a yawn. "I'm going to do my best to get him back, but you've got to know that anyone who would take a child isn't . . . well . . . It's not like we're dealing with honorable men here."

Her stomach drew in tight. She didn't like the direction of his thoughts. "But they said—"

He cut in, obviously annoyed. "I know what they said. I'm telling you to let me handle this. Do everything I say, when I say—and not before—and maybe we'll all get out of this alive."

"This has to work." Rebecca's voice cracked. "I have to get Andrew back. He's so small, and he'll be so afraid without me."

This time Luke didn't hesitate to pull her into his comforting embrace, and he was pleased when she let him. He felt her body tremble, and he rubbed his hand up and down her back in what he hoped was a soothing gesture. Then, putting her away from him slightly, he gave her a little smile. "It'll probably go fine. I tend to worry too much," he lied, smoothly trying to calm her, and praying that she'd remember his instructions.

She looked so forlorn, so vulnerable, that he couldn't help brushing her cheek with his knuckles. He lightly kissed her forehead, some small part of him thinking it might be for the last time. "You ready?"

She nodded and said a silent prayer. *Please, God, help us save Andrew.*

"Remember what I said." It was an order, gently given.

They stepped off the walk and turned into the alley.

Chapter Ten

Rebecca squinted, trying to make her eyes focus in the sudden darkness. Shapes and shadows mingled and merged, making all indiscernible. The only light was the moon, partially obscured by the rooftops.

Anxiety sent her heart pounding in her chest, so loud she was certain Luke could hear it. Her breath came in shallow gulps.

Andrew was out there somewhere. Desperately she scanned the long, narrow confines of the alley, searching for the familiar silhouette of a small boy—her boy. Wishing, hoping, that she'd see him, hold him in her arms again as she silently pledged to ask his forgiveness for somehow failing to keep him safe, and promised that she'd never ever let go of him again.

But she didn't see Andrew, or anyone else, and dread coiled inside, snaking up her spine. Instinctively her hand sought Luke's, touching his back, feeling the smooth cotton of his shirt. He seemed to know what she needed, and he reached back without a word, his work-roughened fingers closing around hers in a blessedly reassuring gesture.

Behind his back, Luke transferred her hand to his other one, freeing his gun hand. He was prepared for trouble.

He moved ahead slowly, each step carefully measured, testing the trash-littered ground before putting his weight fully on his foot.

They were out there somewhere. Waiting. He could feel it, prickling over his skin like electricity before a storm. One sound, one misplaced step, could reveal his position—and Rebecca's.

No matter what happened, he'd protect her—with his life, if necessary. Muscles tensed along the tops of his shoulders and down his back. His eyes strained to peer into the shifting shadows created by the buildings and the debris stacked along the raw wood walls. He listened for every sound. Eight years of survival had taught him well. He hoped like hell it was enough.

The alley was still. This guy, whoever he was, had known exactly which one to choose. The muffled sound of a piano carried through the plank walls of the Boar's Head.

Rebecca stumbled slightly, and he tightened his grip on her hand. She responded in kind, as a way of letting him know that she was all right. He felt her close, felt the heels of his boots brush against the hem of her skirt. That was fine. The closer the better. Less chance of someone singling her out.

One step. Then another. Then another. He walked Indian-soft on the hard-packed earth, feeling it slippery beneath his feet, though from what he didn't want to know. The smell was stale whiskey and rotting garbage and the acrid scent of an outhouse.

Just the kind of place vermin like this would choose. He stayed shoulder-rubbing close to the wall, inching along. His free hand slid on the raw wood. Splinters caught and plowed into his finger tips.

He ignored them. Every fiber of his being was focused on the job, the task at hand. His heart pounded erratically in his chest. It was a new sensation for him. Lord knew this wasn't the first time he'd walked into some trap or ambush. Somewhere along the way he'd made peace with the inevitable realization that one of these times he wouldn't make it out. What did it matter?

But this time it mattered a great deal, because *this* time he wasn't alone.

Without turning, he laced his fingers through Rebecca's.

Rebecca was glad for the tightening of Luke's hand on hers. She was glad he was here. No matter what had happened before, she was very glad he was here now. For reasons she didn't fully understand, she trusted him to get Andrew back, to get them both safely out of here and home.

Something small and fast brushed across Rebecca's feet. "Oh!"

"Rats," Luke whispered through clenched teeth.

She gulped down a sudden rise of bile and steeled herself to continue.

Another small, cautious step, and then another. It was like walking on eggshells, she felt the need to be so quiet, so cautious.

Where was Andrew? Why didn't they show themselves? They hadn't changed their minds, had they? No!

"Luke, I—"

"Shh..."

Luke stopped abruptly, making her come up short. Her hand slammed into his back, and she felt the muscles wire-tight there. He nudged her behind him, trapping her against the rough wood surface of the saloon wall.

"What?" she whispered, pushing lightly on the hard plane of his back. Heart racing furiously, she peered around his shoulder into the blue-black darkness.

Luke didn't answer.

"Is it Andrew?" she said softly, remembering his admonition to be careful and do as he said.

He didn't answer her, didn't even glance her way. She could see that he was staring hard into the blackness near a stack of wooden crates. Packing straw spilled over the top and onto the dirt.

When Luke finally spoke, his voice was so hard, so cold, it didn't seem to come from him at all.

"You gonna stand in those shadows all night, or are you coming out?"

Her heart pounding like a runaway locomotive, she lifted herself on tiptoe and tried to peer around him again. This time he purposely inched in front of her, blocking her view. She sank back, annoyed. "Let me see."

He didn't.

For a full ten seconds, nothing moved. Just when she was about to ask him who he was talking to, a scratchy male voice that seemed to come from nowhere and everywhere said, "Hey, mister, you got the money?"

"Depends on who's asking." Luke sounded as though he were negotiating a deal for a two-dollar saddle instead of paying a ransom.

How could he be so calm? Rebecca wondered briefly. This time she did inch free of him. "It's Andrew, isn't it? Can you see him? Move so I can see him!" She pushed at Luke. She might as well have been pushing on a slab of granite, for all the good it did her.

About that time, Luke pulled his hand free of hers. She felt his elbow brush against her ribs as his hand moved closer to the gun tied to his thigh.

Her earlier joy was instantly replaced by alarm. "Please, Luke, tell me—is it Andrew?" she begged him, desperate to see her son.

Fear tied a knot in her stomach as large as a hangman's noose. "Luke, give him the money." She shoved the small cloth bag into his hand.

He didn't move, didn't acknowledge that he'd felt the bag in his hand.

That was when she heard the scratchy voice again. The man was still unseen, at least by her. "Who you got with you, mister?"

"Where's the boy?" Luke said flatly, ignoring the question.

"Like I said. Money first."

A shadow moved in the darkness and slowly emerged enough that Luke could make out the distinct outline of a man. One man.

His first thought was for Becky and her safety, and, for a second, he cursed himself for allowing himself to be bullied into bringing her. But there was no time for self-recriminations now.

He shifted, bracing his feet, making certain that Becky was behind him and hoping she remembered his instructions to run if things went wrong.

"Gimme the money," the man said harshly.

"Boy first," Luke replied. Son of a bitch, there was no kid, and the odds were the boy was already dead, he thought with heart-sinking sadness. But if there was even one chance in a million, he'd play out the hand.

"You do what I'm tellin' you or we'll kill that kid," the man threatened. "Now gimme the goddamn money."

The odds had just gotten a little better. Maybe they really did have the boy as insurance and were planning to do away with him later. "How do I know you've got the boy? How do I know you're the ones?"

He felt Rebecca's fingers curl and dig into the muscles of his upper arm, and knew what she was thinking. It was the same thing he was thinking. This would tell it all.

"Little kid, about eight, black hair, black eyes, wearing brown pants and a white shirt."

"Yes," Rebecca said, softly enough that only Luke heard. He also heard the terror in her voice.

"So where is he?" Luke pressed, convinced now that the boy was alive. And there was no way he was turning over the money without the boy.

"The kid's safe. That's all you have to know."

"When do we get to see him?"

"After we get the money, dammit."

Luke felt Rebecca's hand on his back. "Luke, give him the money." She slid out from behind him before he realized what she was doing.

"Here," she announced, waving the parcel in front of her. "Here's the money."

"Becky!" Luke grabbed her arm and jerked her hard against the wall. The packet fell to the ground at his feet. "Stay put," he growled, in a fierce voice that made her hesitate long enough for him to say, "Okay, mister. You want the money, here it is." With the toe of his boot, he nudged it forward into a small spot of yellow moonlight.

"Luke," Rebecca said, and squirmed behind him, making it difficult for him to concentrate. "Where's Andrew?" She squirmed again. "Did he take the money? Where's Andrew?"

Luke spared her a glance. "Wait," he growled quietly.

"But—"

Out of the corner of his eye, Luke saw the man inch forward, like a rat going for the bait. Come on, he silently coaxed. Come on. If he could get this guy, then he could make him talk.

The man, clad in dark clothes, crept into the light. Recognition hit Luke about five seconds before the man looked up.

"You," the man snarled, staring at Luke with ferret eyes.

"Small world," Luke answered. "You still beating up women?" Dread was moving fast through him, tensing his muscles, turning his blood to ice. This was the same man he'd had the run-in with at the saloon. He should have known any man who'd beat a woman wouldn't be above stealing a child. Trouble was, this kind wouldn't mind killing one, either.

"Mister, you know a man could get hisself killed, poking around where he ain't got no concern."

"Now, you know, I agree, except I do have a concern here. I want that boy. It's that simple. Turn him over and you can have the money...all ten thousand—"

The man's head came up with a start at the mention of the amount. It was almost as though he hadn't known how much was there, which was odd, unless... unless someone else had sent the note. A boss perhaps?

The man inched farther into the light and, bending, reached for the money.

"Don't," Luke said, and edged his hand closer to his gun. The unmistakable click of a gun's hammer being pulled back stopped him cold. Another man, one Luke also recognized from before, stepped out of the shadows. Damn. He should have known.

The first man picked up the money and regarded Luke smugly. "I sure do appreciate you comin' all the way down here to bring us this—" he tossed the packet in the air once and caught it "—money."

The kidnapper drew his gun as his cohort joined him.

This was going from bad to worse. Luke knew exactly what was about to happen, and he wasn't going to let it. They were both silhouetted by the light, and Luke was at least partially concealed in the shadows. He figured he could get one for sure, and maybe the other. Anyway, he'd keep them busy long enough for Becky to get away.

In a hushed tone, he said, "When I tell you, make a run for it." Discreetly he moved his hand toward the .32 concealed under his jacket.

"No!" she shouted, and bolted out in front of him. "Where's my son?"

Panicked, Luke grabbed for her. "Becky, no!"

"My son!" Becky shouted, and lunged at the two men. It was all the distraction Luke needed. In one motion, he shoved Becky hard away from him, drew his gun and fired twice.

He heard her groan as she slammed into a stack of wooden crates. He'd ask her forgiveness later. Right now, he was trying to keep them both alive.

One man doubled over and crumpled to the ground, dead in a pool of his own blood. The other man took off, firing as he ran. Luke dodged for cover. "Stay down!" he ordered Becky as he scrambled to his feet.

"Luke!" Becky's scream echoed through the alley.

"Stay down!" he ordered again. Gun drawn, he ran flat out after the other man. Down the alley, he saw the man duck into the back door of a saloon. If the boy was alive, he wouldn't be for long—not if that guy got to him first.

Luke hated leaving Becky in the alley, but he didn't have any choice. He kept going, and momentum propelled him into the closed door with a force that rattled his teeth. He hammered on the door with his fist. The knob turned when he tried it, but the door refused to open.

"Son of a bitch! Open the damned door!"

Heart racing, he hurled his shoulder into the door. Once. The wood creaked. The vibration ricocheted through him with bone-jarring force. Twice. The distinct sound of wood tearing spurred him on.

"Dammit, come on! Give!" he ordered the solid door, slamming into the pine with all his strength.

The wood shattered and split. Half stumbling, he fell through the door into a small, cramped storeroom.

He was scrambling to his feet when he heard Rebecca calling his name. Seconds later, she grabbed his arm. Her skin was deathly pale in the dim light of the storeroom, her eyes were bright with terror, and her clothes were covered with dirt. "I'm coming with you," she said, clutching the money in her left hand.

"No," he snapped, in a tone that brooked no argument. "This time we do it my way." In one quick motion, he concealed her in an alcove of boxes. He shoved the gun from his shoulder holster into her hand. "Don't move. Do you understand me? Don't move from this spot. If anyone tries anything, comes near you, kill 'em."

She stared blankly at the gun in her hand. "I can't. I—"

He shook her—hard. "Do it." A little softer, he said, "Stay put, and trust me."

Luke didn't have time to argue with her. That bastard had a head start, and it only took a second to pull a trigger. Luke spun on his heel and disappeared out the other door.

Rebecca stood in the cramped storage room, surrounded by crates labeled Whiskey and Beer. She stared down at the gun Luke had shoved in her hand, feeling the smooth wood of the handle against her palm and the cold metal against her finger, where it curled naturally around the trigger.

It had all gone so wrong. How? How had it happened? Luke had been right—all along he'd been right about tonight. If he hadn't been here, they would surely have killed her and taken the money.

Fury beyond anything she'd ever known consumed her. These men had taken her son. One was dead, lying in a pool of blood with all the other garbage. She felt no sympathy for him, no remorse. Her grip tightened on the gun. Amazing how something so small could take a life, she thought.

She glanced up at the closed door. How long had Luke been gone?

The sounds of voices mixed with piano music, each drowning out the other until there was nothing but an unpleasant din. She paced to the door and back, the gun in one hand, the money in the other. She'd been willing to comply with their request, to give them all she had for her son.

Now it was as if a clock were running in her head, the minutes ticking past with every beat of her heart. Time was running out. If Luke didn't find Andrew... If Andrew was already dead...

She glanced down at the gun in her hand. For the first time in her life, she understood blood lust, the desire to kill another human being.

The saloon was packed tighter than a stockyard feeder lot, and smelled about the same, from the unwashed bodies and unwashed clothes. Men stood four deep at the bar, and every table in the place was full.

Luke made his way around the room, his gaze searching every whiskered, red-eyed face.

All right, where are you?

The roulette wheel was going full out, and the click-click of the little ball grated on his nerves. A gray-haired man was dealing faro at a table near the bar.

A scantily clad woman was dealing blackjack, and winning easily, since the men seemed more interested in her endowments than in her hole card.

Luke scanned the room again. Maybe the man wasn't even in here. Now that gave him pause. Maybe he'd just ducked through here and headed out the double doors. Damn, if that was true, then he'd never find him.

Tobacco smoke was thick as fog, and the smell of cheap rotgut made his stomach turn. He kept one eye on the staircase that led upstairs. There were rooms up there, the girls' rooms, but they offered a place to hide or a place from which to take aim. This guy wouldn't hesitate to shoot into a crowd if he thought it would help him.

Luke kept moving, scanning faces, drunken faces, puffy faces. Searching. Searching. Moving in the direction of the stairs.

When he got close to the bar, he grabbed the narrow-faced bartender by the front of his stained white shirt and dragged him up close. "You see a man come in here, maybe bleeding?"

The man shook his head frantically.

"Listen, you, I want that man." Luke shook him hard. Everyone gave them a wide berth, and no one tried to interfere. "Where is he?"

"I—" The barkeeper swallowed hard, his brown eyes bulging in his head. "I ain't seen no one."

Furious, Luke let go. Damn.

Time was running out. The frantic pounding of his heart told him he'd lost that scum, and most likely the boy.

How could he have been so stupid? He should never have let this happen. What kind of a lawman was he? He should have known. Ah, hell, he did know better than to walk into an alley like that—and with Becky. He should have locked her in her room and done the job he'd spent the last eight years of his life perfecting. The one time she counted on him, he failed. *No, make that two times, Scanlin.*

"Hello, sweetie," a saloon girl purred.

"Not interested," he said shortly, and kept working his way through the crowd. He was headed for the stairs.

Six doors faced the balcony and the saloon beyond. One was as good as another. Gun drawn, he turned the brass knob and shoved the door open with a bang.

A half-naked whore looked up, startled. "What the—" she muttered. The naked man she was draped on top of looked embarrassed.

He yanked the door closed.

Two steps, and he twisted open the knob on the next door. Empty.

Moving fast, he tried the next door. Locked. Not for long. One good kick, and the door flew open, banging into the wall and nearly slamming shut again.

A woman screamed. Luke took in the scene in the blink of an eye, then flattened himself against the wall beside the partially opened door.

"Give it up," Luke ordered. "This is the U.S. marshal."

Gun drawn, he pulled back the hammer. He sucked in a deep breath, like a man about to dive underwater. With steely determination, he hurled himself around the doorway.

The kidnapper was slumped on the end of the bed. Bloodstained and pale, he was packing bandages against his wounded side. "Hold it right there, you son of a bitch!" Luke yelled.

As though by magic, a gun appeared in the kidnapper's hand. He fired three, four shots. The woman screamed again.

A bullet whizzed past Luke's head like a saw blade and buried itself in the plaster wall. Luke dived for the bed, his shoulder bouncing off the iron footrail, and slammed into the floor with a thud that made him see stars.

It was all the time the man needed to jump through the open window. Momentarily dazed, Luke staggered to his feet and raced to the window to peer out into the darkness. The man was gone. He had escaped down the back staircase.

Angrier than he'd ever have thought possible, Luke turned back to see the woman he'd helped earlier, pale and shaking, hugging the wall for all she was worth.

She didn't move, didn't give any sign she even knew he was there. "Millie! Where'd he go?"

When she didn't respond, he grabbed her shoulders and began to shake her.

"Millie. Come on. Where'd he go?" She thrashed her head, her red hair falling down to cover half her face.

"You know what he's been up to, don't you? Don't you?"

She gave a shaky, dazed sort of nod.

"He's gonna kill that child if I don't get to him first."

Luke knew the instant that recognition dawned in her eyes. "He . . . can't." She swallowed hard, as if gulping down the horrible realization.

"He can, and he will. That boy is a witness."

Panic pounded in his blood and his brain. Like a drowning man, he made one last desperate attempt to survive. "In the name of God, Millie, if you know where that boy is, tell me!"

Chapter Eleven

"He's here."

If she'd announced she was about to join a convent, he couldn't have been any more surprised or disbelieving. "Here? What do you mean, here?"

He scanned the room in one swift motion. Ten by ten, a rumpled, bloodstained bed, a scarred table and a broken kerosene lamp, a well-used camelback trunk behind the door.

"What do you—"

Millie opened the trunk. A wardrobe of gaudy dresses burst out. It was as if she'd opened a can of worms.

"Boy," she said softly, "you all right?"

Nothing happened. Nothing moved.

Then a small voice said, "Yes." A second later, an equally small face, dirty and tear-stained, peeked out from the mix of faded satin and frayed lace.

Rebecca paced the confines of the storeroom. Four steps to the broken door, and four steps to the one Luke had disappeared through.

Luke was out there somewhere, and so, God help her, was her son. Where was he? Why hadn't he come back? Had he found Andrew? Was he in time?

Not knowing was driving her insane. What ever happened, she had to know. So she stuffed the money into the inside pocket of her skirt. Concealing the gun in the folds of the black velvet riding skirt, she reached for the door and went out into the saloon.

"Andrew?" Luke said in cautious disbelief.

"Yes, sir" came the polite reply. He didn't move out of the trunk.

A Christmas-morning grin slashed across Luke's face. Good Lord, there must really be such things as guardian angels, because someone was sure watching over this boy.

Anger was forgotten, and fear was replaced by elation. "Andrew, are you all right?" Luke dropped down on the bare planks, hard against one knee. He snapped his gun back into the holster. "Are you hurt?"

"No, sir."

Luke let out the breath he'd been holding. "You can come out now." The boy was a welcome sight after all the grim visions that had fluttered through Luke's mind the past twenty-four hours.

Staring into the child's sable black eyes, eyes that were wide with uncertainty, Luke felt his heart melt. The kid was all right. The feeling of relief wrapped around him like a warm blanket in winter.

Thank you, he said silently, with a quick glance upward.

"Who are you?" the boy inquired, his voice shaky. Luke saw his chin quiver, and smiled when he also saw that the boy was struggling not to cry.

"I'm a friend of your mother."

At the mention of his mother, a grin flashed across the boy's face. All charm and dimples, Luke thought. He'd be one to get his way with that smile.

"Will you come here to me, Andrew?" He knew the boy was frightened, and he didn't want to snatch him up and scare him further. But he had to strain not to, because Becky was down there, and he couldn't wait to see her, to see the look on her face when he walked in with this miracle in his arms.

"Where's my mother?" the boy inquired, shifting in the trunk, pushing a red satin dress to one side.

"She's downstairs. I'll take you to her."

The boy seemed to consider this. Then, slowly, he climbed out of the trunk. While he did, Luke glanced up at Millie.

"How?" he asked directly.

She gave a small shrug. "Jack brung him back the other day. He locked him in the toolshed behind the old stables." She patted Andrew's head affectionately. "I took him food, and we talked. I felt *real* bad. I mean, taking a boy from his folks ain't right. I tried to tell Jack to take him home, but he wouldn't hear none of it." She touched her bruised face and forced a little smile. "You know how Jack is. I brung him up here tonight figuring maybe I could sneak him back to his mama.

"But why didn't you tell me today, when I was here?"

"Why should I?" Her expression was puzzled. "I don't know you from Adam. Still don't for that matter, but you helped me out today, and I think you're all right." Her hand rested lightly on Andrew's shoulder, and he leaned against her leg. It was obvious that if Millie hadn't intervened, the boy would have died, if not from a bullet, then from not being found. Kids died quick without food or water.

"Lady, you saved his life and, in a way, mine." He knew he wouldn't have cared much about living if he'd had to face Becky with the horrible alternative. His grip tightened on the small boy in his arms. "Just so you know, I'm the U.S. marshal for this district. Luke Scanlin." He produced his badge as proof. "I owe you, Millie."

Millie smiled, her eyes crinkling. "I knew you was too good to be an *ordinary* cowboy."

"Pretty ordinary," he told her. "You might wanna consider leaving town for a while, all things considered."

"I was thinking along them same lines myself. Texas seems to be on my mind a whole bunch of late." She winked.

Luke chuckled and shook his head. "You and Texas will get along fine."

He turned his attention to the boy, who was watching him intently from four feet away. "Andrew, what say you and I go find your mother?"

"Yes!" Andrew squealed, with all the joyful enthusiasm of a seven-year-old. And Luke understood perfectly. He was feeling pretty joyful himself.

Luke scooped the boy up in his arms. "It's a little crowded downstairs right now, so I think it's better if I carry you."

Luke looked at the boy in his arms. His black eyes were bright with excitement, his black hair was short and rumpled, and his face was the same heart shape as Rebecca's.

The strangest sensation came over Luke, like nothing he'd known before. It was a feeling akin to the possessiveness he felt for Rebecca, yet different. He narrowed his eyes and studied the boy. There was something... He shook his head. Probably relief at finding the boy, he mused. He smiled again.

"Sir," Andrew inquired, looping his small arms around Luke's neck, "are you really a marshal?"

"I am. No one is going to hurt you now, Andrew, and I'm going to make sure no one scares you or tries to hurt you again."

Luke saw the boy's chin quiver again, saw him swallow fast, and knew he was trying to keep from crying. It was one of those things boys seemed to know at birth. Never cry. No matter what, never cry. But if ever a boy had a right to, it was this one.

Luke felt like crying a little himself, he was so happy. So he pressed the boy's face to his shoulder in a gesture of understanding and an offer of privacy. His little body shook, and a small damp spot soaked through the cotton of Luke's shirt. But nary a sound came out of the boy's mouth to reveal this breach of male resolve.

Something instinctive made Luke kiss the top of the boy's head and cradle his hand against the back of his neck, feeling the smoothness of his coal black hair above his little shirt collar.

"Come on, cowboy. We're going home." And he was. He was going to get Becky, and the three of them were going to do just that.

Chapter Twelve

She'd never been in a saloon before. Gas lamps blazed bright against dirt-smudged mirrors. Too many tables were crowded into the square room.

"Hiya, honey," a drunk slurred. His breath was strong enough to knock down a mule.

This time, Rebecca didn't panic, didn't scream. With a cold look, she elbowed past him and pushed deeper into the crowd. Luke had come this way, though where he was now was anyone's guess. All she knew was that her son was somewhere out here—maybe in the saloon, maybe not—and she couldn't just stand here and wait.

She edged between the tables, but nonetheless, dressed in her riding shirt, she stood out from the other women present, who seemed to have forgotten to put their dresses over their pantalets and corsets. Any other time, she might have been offended, but tonight, after what she'd been through already, nothing could faze her.

The talking, shouting, piano playing, all blended together in an ear-deafening roar. Briefly she thought, *So this is what men call enjoyment.*

She didn't see Luke anywhere. She decided to work her way toward the front door. If she didn't see Luke in here, then she'd head outside, and if he wasn't there, then she'd go from saloon to saloon, if that was what it took.

She kept scanning the crowd, looking for Luke's familiar frame, looking for his dark head, his broad shoulders.

She was ten feet from the double doors when she happened to glance behind her. That was when she saw them.

Against a backdrop of peeling paint and bawdy saloon misfits, Luke was holding Andrew in his arms, as though it were the most natural thing in the world.

"Oh, God." Her heart stopped beating in her chest. She was certain she wasn't even breathing. The sight of them together would be forever imprinted on her brain.

As though he knew she was there, he looked straight at her, and she saw him smile. That was all—he just smiled. His eyes sparkled with joy and tenderness and understanding.

And there was the briefest hesitation on her part, at seeing them together, seeing Andrew's small arms clinging to Luke's neck. With a mother's desperation, she rushed in their direction, pushing, shoving, clawing her way between men who were totally unaware of the scene around them.

All she cared about was that Andrew was alive and safe. Everything else would take its course. Andrew was all that mattered to her, and she was heartbreakingly frantic to hold him again.

"Mama! Mama!" Andrew yelled at the top of his lungs. His small voice was so out of place in this den of iniquity that everyone present turned to stare.

The piano player stopped playing, the room became strangely quiet, and men, suddenly aware, parted to let Rebecca through. Their gazes moved from the beautiful woman to the dangerous-looking man standing on the stairs.

Luke's gaze had followed her through the crowd. And as she reached for her son, he gave her a smile. Its effect was devastating, and suggestive enough to make her falter for the barest second.

"Madame," Luke said with great formality, his eyes sparked with happiness, "I give you your son." With that, he let the boy slip into her waiting arms as she handed him the gun she'd been holding.

Tears streamed unchecked down her cheeks, and she hugged her son tightly, her fingers wrapped around his rib cage and legs. A cry of relief broke from her lips. "Andrew! Thank God, Andrew!"

Andrew is all right. She hugged him and kissed him and hugged him some more, and the joyful words resounded in her head and heart.

Holding him in her arms, she knew this wasn't a dream. It was real. They had done it. No, told herself, Luke—Luke had done this wonderful deed.

Risking his own life, Luke had given her back her son. Joy greater than any she'd ever known bubbled in her laugh and shone in her eyes as she cast her gaze up to meet his.

With her son cradled in her arms, she said simply, "I don't... Oh, Luke, thank you."

"You're welcome," he returned, in a voice soft with emotion.

It was then that she realized a crowd had gathered around them, staring openly.

Luke moved in closer. Without even asking, he hoisted Andrew into his arms. "Come on," he ordered gently with a firm hand on Rebecca's elbow. "Let's get out of here."

He pushed through the crowd and out the double doors onto the sidewalk. It was instinct that made him glance around; there was, after all, a kidnapper still at large. The quicker he got them out of here and home, the better he'd feel.

"I think it would be easier if Andrew rode with me, considering sidesaddles and all."

Reluctantly she agreed, not because she didn't trust Luke, but because she hated to let go of Andrew even for a second.

"Up you go, cowboy," Luke said as he swung Andrew up on his gelding's back. "Hang on to the horn," he told him. Going around, he gave Rebecca a leg up, then paused, his hand resting dangerously near her thigh. "Becky?"

She looked down into his upturned face. "Are you all right? I mean, did I hurt you...earlier, when I pushed you? I didn't mean to—"

Without thinking, she brushed his cheek with the tips of her fingers, feeling the warmth of his skin against hers, the prickle of whiskers. "I'm all right."

She saw his eyes flutter closed. His hand covered hers, and he turned his face into her palm, lingering there, reveling in her touch. When he looked up again, his eyes brimmed with tenderness and a knowing passion that held her a willing prisoner. His touch, his closeness, made long-denied feelings warm and stir.

As though sensing the electric tension, her horse stamped and shifted, breaking the spell. They exchanged timid smiles.

"All right, then," he said loudly, swinging up on his horse and settling Andrew securely in front of him. "Let's go home."

As they rode, those words haunted Luke. *Go home,* he'd said. Too bad it wasn't true. Too bad it wasn't his home, his wife, his son.

A sadness replaced his joy as he watched Rebecca, beaming at Andrew and telling him how much she'd missed him and how much his grandmother was missing him, too.

He felt very much the outsider.

Perhaps that was why, when they stopped at the house and Luke hoisted Andrew down, then helped Rebecca, he didn't follow them inside.

But Rebecca stopped walking and turned back to him. "Aren't you coming in?"

He glanced toward the porch, smiling when he saw Andrew catapult himself into Ruth's waiting arms. Luke's sadness got a touch deeper.

"Naw," he said quietly. "You go on and enjoy your reunion."

Absently he toyed with the reins of the two horses, slapping the ends against his palm.

"You have to come in. Ruth will want to thank you, and—"

"Thanks aren't necessary. Just doing my job."

Rebecca stepped up directly in front of him. "It was more than your job." She touched his chest lightly with the palm of her hand, and he sucked in a steadying breath. "You...you aren't leaving? Tonight, I mean? Are you?"

"I thought in the morning, if it's okay with you?"

He could feel her hand, warm and delicate over the area of his heart, and he didn't move, didn't want to.

"I wish you'd come in." Her voice was as warm and tempting as whiskey. "We'll be up half the night, I'm sure, and—"

He nodded, taking off his hat and hooking it over the saddle horn. "I'm going to the police station to take care of...unfinished business." Like a body in an alley and a kidnapper who was still on the loose.

He'd been so scared, for her, for the boy, for them, and now it was over. Though he was glad, really glad, there was a sense of finality, of ending, that he hadn't quite expected.

He had no more reason to stay, no more reason to see her, except that he didn't think he could be anywhere within a million miles of her and not see her, not touch her.

"I'm happy for you, Princess," he began, uncertain what he was trying to say.

She smiled—it was a slow, lush smile—and her hand, the one that was on his chest, glided provocatively up to curve over his shoulder. Then she did something he was totally unprepared for. She lifted up on her toes and kissed him. Not a big kiss, but not some little cousin-type kiss, either.

"Thank you," she said on a throaty whisper, which brushed across his nerves like a summer wind.

As though in slow motion, Rebecca stepped back, her gaze never leaving his. She let her hand drop to her side, and was unprepared for the sense of loss that came when she did.

The moment was tense with anticipation. The cool night air did little to soothe her heated flesh. He made a motion as though to reach for her. Instantly, her body flared to life, and she became more aware of the effort it took to breathe.

"Princess," he murmured, his voice husky. His face was bathed in moonlight. His strong features held a sensuality that was nearly irresistible. Nearly.

The voice of reason was annoying but insistent. *He's not for you.* There was more at stake here than her heart, a great deal more, now that Andrew was back.

With more strength than she'd thought she had left, she took a faltering step backward. "I can never repay what you have done this evening," she said honestly, wanting him to know that no matter what else, she understood the risks he'd taken and was sincerely grateful.

He was silent for so long she thought he wouldn't answer, but, as she turned toward the house, he said, "I'd do anything for you, Princess."

On the front stairs, one foot resting on the step above, she hesitated and, without turning, glanced back over her shoulder. He was there, watching, a violet shadow against a black-velvet sky.

Dressed as he was in range clothes, he was a man in contrast to this time and place. He was everything she disdained in a man, rough, violent, and yet he exuded an intensity that was as riveting and compelling as the lure of Satan himself.

Without a word, without a touch, he stirred the promise of pleasure that she'd long ago assured herself she'd overcome. Determinedly she went into the house, closing the door quietly on the man and his enticing invitation. She stood there, unmoving, for a long minute, while pulse points throbbed and heated the sensuous centers of her body.

What was this ability he had to stir the flame of desire so easily in her?

"Oh, Luke," she murmured, very, very softly. "What have you done to me?"

Rebecca spent the next hour telling Ruth all that had happened. They plied Andrew with a lifetime's supply of cold milk and oven-fresh cookies—it seemed Ruth had needed something to do while she waited for their return. Rebecca, sensing that Andrew was still upset from his ordeal, was more than happy to give in to him.

Seated at the kitchen table, Andrew reached for his fourth molasses cookie, and Ruth, in a conspiratorial way, dragged the plate more fully within his reach.

Rebecca poured another cup of coffee and briefly related the events of the ransom delivery and Andrew's subsequent rescue. She mentioned that she had retained the money, which she would put in the safe later. She carefully did not mention that she—that they—had almost died in that disgusting alley. She was adamant, though, in telling her that Luke had risked his life and had saved them both. To which Andrew enthusiastically agreed.

Ruth listened to Rebecca's narration, but she was more intent on her expression, the way her eyes lit up whenever she mentioned the marshal's name, the way her cheeks flushed. And when Rebecca was finished, Ruth said, "Marshal Scanlin is a good man. I hope he comes to visit often."

"Me, too," Andrew piped up, his mouth full of cookie, which he promptly washed down with a cheek-bulging gulp of milk that left a snow-white mustache on his upper lip.

Rebecca laughed—really laughed. It was the first time she'd laughed in days. It felt good, and she knew Luke had done that for her, too, for without Andrew there could be no happiness in her life.

The next two hours were spent talking, playing four games of checkers, which Andrew won, and eating more cookies. Somewhere around midnight, an exhausted Andrew climbed onto Rebecca's lap and promptly fell asleep, snuggled against her shoulder.

It didn't take much to put him to bed. He roused when she washed his face and hands and slid his nightshirt on—the one with the blue stripes not the solid green one. He climbed in his bed and was asleep instantly.

"I think I'll do the same," Ruth said from her place near the partially opened window. The night fog seeped in, falling over the windowsill in a gray mist that pooled on the floor before disappearing in the warmer inside air.

"Close that window, will you?" Rebecca asked, and Ruth obliged.

"Good night," Ruth said, stifling a yawn. "He looks fine, doesn't he?" She smiled and lingered beside Rebecca.

"Yes. He doesn't appear to be hurt. I checked when I changed his clothes."

"That's good."

"I'm trying not to remind him of it too much. If he wants to talk about it, fine, but now that I have him home and he's unhurt, well, I don't see any reason to keep reliving it, do you?"

"None. Let's try to get on with our lives, and, as you said, be here for him if he needs us. Lots of love and keeping him close for a while is probably all we can do." She gave Rebecca's shoulder an affectionate squeeze.

Rebecca patted her hand in reply. "Thanks." She fussed with smoothing the linen sheets. "I think I'll just sit here awhile."

Ruth nodded, a few wisps of hair coming loose from the bun at the back of her neck. "I'll see you in the morning. Maybe we can all sleep in."

Rebecca chuckled and glanced at her sleeping son. "I wouldn't count on it."

Ruth grinned. "Good night, dear, and thanks for all you did. I'm so thankful that you're all right and Andrew is back. We owe the marshal a great deal, don't we?"

"Yes," Rebecca said softly. "I owe him more than you know."

With a confirming nod, Ruth went to her room.

Rebecca moved to the rocker. Loosening her collar and removing her boots, she lounged back in the chair to watch her son sleep. She smiled at the little sound he made on each expelled breath, more like humming than snoring.

A pain in her back was the first indication that she'd fallen asleep in the chair. A quick glance reassured her that Andrew was, in fact, sleeping peacefully in his bed.

Flexing her shoulders and back, she stretched, yawned and stood, only to flex again. Bed, she thought, and, leaving the door to his room partially open, she headed for her room.

Luke was alone in his room—correction, Rebecca's guest room. Yeah, that was him, a guest. He'd be leaving at first light. No sense prolonging the inevitable.

He thought about packing. Why bother? Packing for him was getting dressed and throwing a couple of shirts in his saddlebags. That took a whopping two minutes. Goodness knew, he was in no hurry to get back to his rooms over on Washington. Oh, they were nice enough, better than most, but they were just rooms.

Sitting on the edge of the bed, he stripped out of his shirt and kicked off his boots. The warming stove was working overtime, competing with the chill from the half-open window. The night air was damp and heavy. Goose bumps prickled the bare flesh of his back.

Everyone must be asleep by now. A smile teased his lips. That little guy was probably out like a light.

If Luke lived to be a hundred and ten, he'd always remember the look on the kid's face as he emerged from that trunk, his ebony eyes wide with surprise and fear, his black hair all tousled.

A strange feeling moved through him, a lightness in his chest. It was a new feeling, yet not unpleasant, and he narrowed his eyes in puzzlement. That was the second time he'd felt that way. The first had been when he saw the boy for the first time.

He shrugged off the feeling and strolled over to the window. Pulling back the curtain, he peered out into the night, watching the stars twinkle and blink in the cloudless sky.

Shoulder against the window frame, he let his eyes drift closed and his mind wander. As always, his thoughts went to Becky. Tonight, in that alley, she'd been courageous and determined. He'd been damned proud of her. She was one to cross the river with, as the drovers said. Then, later, there by the front walk, when she hauled off and kissed him, he'd just stood there, 'cause he was afraid he'd drag her into his arms and kiss her back and never stop. Yeah, he'd like that, kissing Becky and touching her, feeling her exposed flesh slid against his as they—

His eyes snapped open, and he shifted uncomfortably at the sudden swelling in his loins.

Abruptly he straightened, letting the curtain fall back into place. It was a good thing he was leaving tomorrow, he told himself firmly as he crossed the room. Yeah, a real good thing, because she'd made it clear that she had no more feelings for him. That kiss tonight had been merely a thank-you, nothing more.

He grimaced at the truth, his hand unconsciously curling into a fist. "Ouch."

Glancing down, he saw a half-dozen splinters embedded in the fingertips of his right hand. Souvenirs, he thought wryly.

Fishing in his saddlebag, he found his small sewing kit. Sliding a needle free of its paper holder, he sank down on the bed near the side table and turned up the lamp.

"Ouch," he muttered again, digging at the offending sliver.

The first splinter poked its head up enough for him to grab it with his teeth and spit it out. A drop of blood glistened ruby red on his fingertip, and he wiped it on his pant leg.

Next.

"Ouch," he muttered again, a little more intensely this time. Working with his left hand was about as awkward as trying to pick up eggs with a snow shovel.

"May I help?" a softly feminine voice said, and he knew without looking that it was Rebecca. There was no other voice that caressed his senses quite so easily.

His heart lurched, then took on a slow, heavy rhythm. Turning his head, he let his gaze travel across the carpeted floor to where she stood in the partially opened doorway.

Her black riding skirt was badly wrinkled and its hem caked with dirt, and her usually stiff-fronted blouse was opened at the collar and her sleeves were rolled up. Her cheeks were flushed and her hair was tousled, loose tendrils curving provocatively around her face. She looked like a woman who'd just roused from sleep, or just made love. His heart slammed against his ribs.

Erotic images flashed unbidden in his mind, those same images he'd banished not ten minutes ago. His throat convulsed and, for a full five seconds, he stared at her, willing the images and the sudden hot reflexes of his body to still.

He wasn't having much success.

"Please, come in," he finally returned, when he was certain his voice would work.

Rebecca didn't move. About the same instant she spoke, she'd realized he was sitting there half-naked. She saw his tight, corded muscles flex and stretch as he moved slightly. She should look away. She should *go* away.

She stared right at his chest, at the black hair that arched over each nipple, then plunged down his chest to disappear into his waistband. It was uniquely male, and provocative beyond reason.

Her gaze flicked to his face, chiseled and heart-stoppingly handsome, with a wicked look in devil-black eyes.

She should never have come to his room. But she had seen his light on, and she'd wanted to thank him, that was all, she told herself—not quite as convincingly as she would have wished.

Caught up as she was in the nearness of him, the voice of reason was faint, but it was insistent, screaming *Run for your life.*

She didn't. Closing the door, she crossed to him and sat down beside him on the bed, sinking a little into the feather mattress. It was madness, this attraction to him. Insanity, to give in to the sudden surge of longing. But then he smiled at her in that knowing way of his, and the first tremors of desire stirred deep inside, warm and inviting. She could no more leave than she could stop breathing.

Not trusting her voice, she simply took his hand in hers. He had nice hands, she thought, long, graceful fingers. She remembered those same fingers touching her, brushing seductively across her cheek, caressing her neck. In another time, those hands had stroked her body, heating her flesh . . .

"Is the boy asleep," he asked, startling her.

She swallowed hard. "Yes."

"Is he all right? I mean *really* all right?"

"Thanks to you."

He lifted his hand free of hers to cup her chin, and he looked at her with eyes as black as midnight fire. "You scared the hell out of me, running out in front of me like that." It was the kindest of rebukes.

"I'm sorry. I didn't mean to."

"I know," he told her with a half smile. "I'm sorry, too. Sorry you had to go through that, and especially sorry you had to see me . . . kill a man."

She heard the sudden sadness in his voice, saw the regret in his eyes. It surprised her, this remorse. He'd seemed so calm that she'd thought he was unaffected. She could see now that she'd been wrong, and the need to console him made her say, "You had no choice. He would have killed us both if you hadn't—" Her voice broke as the reality tore at her insides.

"Shh, honey. It's all right." He kissed her cheek, ever so lightly, and brushed the hair back from her face.

It felt nice, his kiss, the way his lips caressed her skin. Tears pooled in the corners of her eyes. The fears she'd controlled all evening would no longer be denied. "I thought they were leaving," she told him through a muffled sob.

"I know." His gaze never left hers as he lifted her hand and kissed her palm. It was a provocative gesture that soothed and excited her at the same time.

"When...when they didn't bring Andrew, I thought he was—"

He stopped her words with the touch of two fingers to her lips. "Don't." His eyes brimmed with tenderness and passion.

"What about tomorrow, and the next day, and the next? What about sending him off to school, or out to play? Can I be with him every minute, every second? I want to keep him locked safely in his room until he's twenty-five, maybe longer."

Luke chuckled. "Princess, I wish life were that easy." He kissed her palm again, leaving her flesh warm and moist, making her heart rate increase by half.

"All you can do is take precautions, warn him to be careful, and then—then you have to let him go. You have to trust."

For reasons both obvious and vague, she trusted Luke. At least for tonight, this moment in time, she trusted him completely. Knowing that, feeling that, she leaned her head into the curve of his shoulder, taking solace from the warm smoothness of his bare skin against her cheek. His strong arm wrapped around her shoulder, pulling her tight against him.

It was wrong, she thought in the dim recesses of her mind. Wrong to be here with him. Wrong to touch him and be touched. Wrong to linger. He was dangerous, more dangerous than even he knew, and yet she could not deprive herself of his comforting strength.

She stayed that way for several seconds, letting his steady heartbeat drum away the fears and rage of the past few days, and perhaps even longer.

"A year from now—" she felt his breath caress the edge of her ear, tiny shivers of delight raced down her neck "—this will seem like a bad dream. As though it never happened. You will have forgotten all about it...and me."

There was note of sadness in his husky voice that touched her heart, and, without thinking, she said, "You're not an easy man to forget."

She felt, more than heard, him chuckle. "Why, thank you, Princess." He kissed the top of her head in a familiar way that made her crane her neck and press her face into the side of his neck. He smelled like leather and musk and felt like salvation to a lost soul.

She let her eyes drift closed, lost in the enticing nearness of him and the soothing effect his touch had on her exhausted nerves. At last, she looked up. He was watching her with a slow, easy smile that she understood all too well.

"Becky," he whispered, his fingers tightening perceptibly on her shoulder. She was so beautiful, so close. If only she'd stop looking at him with those luminous blue eyes of hers, he might, *might,* have a chance of not kissing her.

Being here, with her in his arms, was too intimate, too seductive. The door was closed, the night was still, and a parade of erotic fantasies was flashing in his mind, hotter than a lightning strike.

He hated what she'd been through, hated that he hadn't been able to do more for her. He wanted her to know this. "I'll always be here for you, Becky. You know that, don't you?"

Rebecca was lost in the depths of his soft, knowing gaze. Her heart fluttered in her chest like the wings of a frightened butterfly, yet she was not frightened. No, she had never felt as alive as she did right now. Nerves that had been frayed with exhaustion now pulsed with anticipation. A forgotten longing stirred deep within her, heating, swirling, reaching out to enfold every part of her.

She knew he was going to kiss her. She could see it in the passion that sparked in the depths of his eyes. So it was no surprise when his hand moved around to cradle the back of her neck.

The world stilled, as though poised in expectation. There was no sound except the uneven pounding of her heart.

Her eyes fluttered closed an instant before his lips touched hers. It was the barest of kisses, a tasting, a testing. He lifted his head. His gaze traveled over her face and searched her eyes, as though he were seeking an answer to an unspoken question.

Her lips parted, perhaps in reply, perhaps in surrender—she'd never know, because he covered her mouth again, fully this time, completely. It was not a gentle kiss, it was harsh and fierce, as though he were claiming what was rightfully his.

She should have been outraged. She should have denied his claim. But her body flared to life like a skyrocket, white-hot and riveting.

There was nothing but the lush sensation of his mouth on hers. His arms drifted down to her waist, pulling her tighter against him. Her hands glided up his arms and slid around his neck, her fingers dug into the firm flesh of his back, and she clung to him, giving herself up to the rapidly increasing desire.

At the first touch of her lips on his, desire exploded in Luke like a gunshot. Everywhere their bodies touched was on fire. He was acutely aware of her fingers curling, nail-sharp, into the top of his shoulder. Tendrils of her hair caressed his face, like a temptress's touch, which heated his blood. He turned toward her. His fingers dug into the fabric of her blouse, feeling the stiff bones of her corset. God, how he hated corsets and clothes and anything else that kept him from having her. And he did want her. He wanted her so much that, with expert ease, he pulled her blouse from her waistband. Swiftly his hand moved toward the row of buttons that held the blouse closed.

Is this it, Scanlin? You gonna seduce her? You gonna take advantage? Her earlier accusation came back to haunt him.

With steely determination, he tore his mouth from hers. Every muscle in his body screamed in protest. He still held her in his arms, unable to release her completely.

He looked at her, her eyes dilated, her cheeks flushed, her sensual lips parted in a provocative way that was making this magnanimous gesture of his damned difficult, maybe impossible.

On a husky whisper, raw with emotion, he said, "You take my breath away."

The logic that had guided Rebecca's life was strong. *Stop this! Stop this now!* Swallowing hard, she cleared her throat. "I should go," she said, but her muscles refused to work.

Uncertainty flashed in his eyes, but then his mouth curved up in a tantalizing smile that sent her pulse rate higher than a kite on a summer wind. "I like seeing you like this," he said. He tucked a loose strand of hair behind her ear, his finger sensually tracing the rim before gliding, feather-light, along her jaw.

Delicious shivers prickled down her neck. Her eyes drifted closed as she reveled in the sensation of his touch and the heat that was building in the core of her. "Like what?" she murmured, only half-aware of what she was saying.

"Like this," he repeated in a hushed tone, touching her open collar. He let his hand linger there while his fingers slid inside to brush the sensitive, swelling mound of her breast.

Her breath caught on a rapid intake of air and, though her heart was pounding a frantic rhythm, her body went absolutely still, poised, waiting for him.

He didn't disappoint her. Through the cotton of her blouse, he brushed his thumb over the peak of her breast. Once. Only once.

Her nipples pulled up into marble-hard peaks, and delicious heat radiated outward to coil tightly in the junction of her legs.

Luke's voice was rich, and lover-soft. "I was thinking about you before you came in."

"Were you?"

"Oh, yes." He cupped one side of her face with his hand. "You do that to me, you know. Make me think about you...make me want you."

She looked alarmed, as though he'd just revealed some great secret. Perhaps he had. His passionate gaze never wavered as he reached around her and removed the remaining pins from her hair. His fingers combed through the tumbling silken threads. "I always think of you with your hair down...like this...like the last time." That quickly the memory, lush and primitive, of her naked and wild assailed his senses. The sudden swelling between his legs was strong and potent.

He hovered close, overtaking her with the sheer male power of him. His thumb teased her bottom lip, but he didn't move. It was as though he were waiting for something, she thought, perhaps giving her a chance to change her mind, to flee this madness.

She didn't want to flee. God help her, she wanted this. She wanted him.

Sensing her surrender, Luke gracefully dipped his head toward hers. "Rebecca..." was all he said an instant before his lips brushed hers. Desire, long denied, surged to the surface with electric clarity.

"Luke, please..." she managed to say, though uncertain what she was asking for.

His breath mingled with hers. "I want you, Becky." His voice was quiet, yet tinged with urgency.

With the pads of two fingers, he turned her face up to his. "If you stay here, I'm going to make love to you. You must stop me now, or..."

His hand dropped away but his gaze sought hers and held her as surely as if he were touching her. He waited, willing her to know, to understand, that he was giving her this chance. Prepared to let her go, he wondered if a man could die of wanting a woman.

She smiled then; it was the barest curving of her lips, but all the encouragement he needed.

With infinite slowness, as though still uncertain he'd read her correctly, he lowered his head. When she made no effort to stop him, he covered her mouth with his.

The sensation of Luke's lips on hers was startling in its intensity. His lips, warm, gentle and exploring, offered her an invitation to carnal delights. He cupped her face between his hands, the tips of his fingers threading into her hair.

With each beat of her heart, his kiss deepened, becoming more and more demanding. For Rebecca, there was no thought of resistance. There was no thought at all. She reached up to meet him, opening to him, welcoming him.

His tongue grazed her bottom lip, tracing its curve, teasing the corners of her mouth in a way that sent waves of desire pulsing through her. When his tongue demanded entrance, she eagerly obliged, feeling him lave at the tender flesh inside her lower lip.

A rhythm as old as time pulsed low in her body, and she let her tongue glide into his mouth, feeling his groan. He tensed, and, taking her firmly by the shoulders, he turned her fully toward him and pulled her against the hard plane of his bare chest.

Desire, raw and savage, exploded within her. She clung to him, her hands curving over his broad shoulders, her fingers clawing at his flesh.

Luke kissed her lips, her cheeks, her brows. He blazed a fiery path of moist kisses along her jaw, pausing to nip and lick the sensitive flesh behind her ear. Pleasure shot through him when she moaned in response.

His mouth caressed her throat and, greedily, she arched back to give him better access. His breath fanned her moistened skin, inciting her desire to greater heights, as though she'd been waiting for him all these years. Perhaps she had.

Luke knew the instant she gave in to him. The instant her muscles relaxed, the instant her body swayed toward him. He heard her moan. It was the barest of sounds, but enough to send his heart racing faster.

Sitting side by side was awkward, so he stood, pulling her up to him, desperate to feel her full length against his.

Deftly he managed to unbutton her blouse and slip it from her shoulders. His mouth quirked up in an appreciative smile. She was wearing black. Black corset. Black camisole. It was fine lace, and sheer as gauze, and he could see the crest of her hardened nipples straining at the translucent material.

"You are a temptress," he murmured against her lips.

His mouth blazed a moist path down her throat, his teeth nipping at her flesh, then kissing away any hurt.

She shivered, trembled, and felt the coil of heat beginning to swirl and spiral inside her.

"I don't mind being tempted," he added, his hands already reaching for the straps of her camisole. He slid them down, returning to tug the fine material low enough to free her firm, ripe breasts above the stiff corset edge.

The cool air was like ice to her heated flesh, which made her skin prickle, her nipples pull even tighter.

"Oh, Luke . . . what . . . are you . . ."

"Exactly what I said. I'm making love to you," he told her, his voice raw with emotion. Slowly, he drew the tip of her nipple into the wet, warm interior of his mouth. With tongue and teeth, he teased and enticed, until Rebecca was certain she would die of the enchantment.

He paused to move to the other breast. "Don't stop," she pleaded. Her hands threaded hard into his hair as she held him to her.

"Don't worry, honey. I have no intention of stopping."

She was dimly aware of his hands around her waist, of him lifting her and settling her on his lap. Her riding skirt bunched up around her knees and covered his wool-clad thighs.

Having her seated in front of him gave Luke better access to her mouth, her shoulders and her delicious breasts. Those dusty-rose peaks begged to be kissed.

His hands splayed over her back, he held her to him, taking his fill of her. As his tongue licked and curled around each nipple, he heard her groaning in pleasure.

His blood turned to fire as he felt her move on his lap, felt her press and squirm against his throbbing manhood, straining against the wool of his trousers.

Blindly he fumbled with the laces of her corset, cursing the double knots until they came loose. His fingers actually shook as he worked the laces free, one after the other.

She never moved, never tried to stop him. Slowly, so slowly, he pulled the laces through the eyelets. As the corset loosened, her breasts eased down, looking fuller, rounder and more even more enticing, if that was possible.

When he reached for her constricting waistband, he said, "Stand up."

Passion-driven, she complied. Her knees wobbled a bit, and he hooked his arm around her for support.

His fingers moved to her waistband, unfastening the buttons and pushing the skirt down to pool around her stocking-clad ankles.

Blood pounded in his ears and neck as he looked at her, in her camisole and pantalets. She was all long legs and bright eyes, and the insistent throbbing of his arousal made him wonder if he could wait much longer.

With urgent hands, he cupped the contours of her buttocks and hauled her to him, wanting to feel the length of her against the length of him. She was lush and luscious and she was inflaming his desire faster than a storm moving over the wild Texas prairie.

She molded herself to him. All heated flesh and soft, throaty purring. He groaned as he captured her mouth once more, feeling his desire cresting and knowing he had to have her soon.

He pulled the tie on her pantalets and felt it ease down between them.

Rebecca felt his fingers intimately touching her like fire on her skin. The flimsy material of her camisole pulled erotically against her hard, cresting nipples, her flesh aching for his touch, his mouth.

He found the edge of the camisole and began to lift it, shirtlike, over her head. The thin lace caught on the fullness of her breasts. But Luke was not daunted. He wanted her naked. Taking her lush breasts in his hand, he lifted them and slid the material over her nipples with his other hand. He tossed it aside.

She stood naked before him, dressed only in her stockings, the smooth black silk a lush contrast to her paler skin.

Reverently, as if in prayer, he knelt before her. With exquisite slowness, his hands encircled her thigh. She gasped. Her body weak from the sensation, she clutched at his shoulders. His touch a heated caress, he rolled the silk languidly down her shapely leg. Lifting her foot, he slid the stocking off, brushing a finger across the length of her sensitive insole, making her shudder. He guided her foot to the carpet.

Thinking she could stand no more, she swayed, her nails digging into his flesh as he lifted her other foot and repeated the sensual gesture.

Her legs shaky, her muscles turned the consistency of sweet, sun-warmed honey. She swayed again. He caught her in his powerful embrace and settled her gently on the bed, apricot flesh against stark white cotton. She was an erotic vision. It would be a dream come true for him as soon as he was deep within her. He shed his trousers and joined her on the bed.

Rebecca felt his weight for an instant before he shifted upward, supporting his upper body on his elbows. The feather bed bunched up around them, shutting out everything in the room but the two of them.

Stop this now! Rebecca's voice of reason called, as though from a great distance.

But her body was consumed by desire, and the voice was silenced by the demands of her body.

Luke's mouth devoured hers. Breathing was nearly impossible. Surely she didn't need to breathe. All she needed, all she wanted, was to feel. And she did. Her body was alive with feelings so raw, so intense, so powerful, that there was no room for thought.

The mat of hair on his chest prickled the sensitized flesh of her breasts and nipples and ribs. Everywhere he touched, she was on fire.

She clutched at his shoulders, feeling the fine sheen of perspiration against her fingers. She exulted in him, every touch, every movement, stoking the flame of desire to new intensity.

Fearlessly, driven by a force more powerful than any she'd ever known, she began to move beneath him, her body too inflamed to remain still.

Her hand played down his back, touching, tracing, the corded muscles pulled wire-tight as he levered above her.

"Luke..." She clawed at him. "Luke, please..."

"I will, darlin'. I will."

There was no more thought, no more hesitation. His mouth found her nipples once more, rougher now, and he took his pleasure in hearing her moan, feeling her buck and writhe beneath him.

His hand wedged between them, seeking the juncture of her legs. Wanting to touch her, to stoke the fire of passion, to make her ready for him.

"Open your legs," he ordered, his voice gentle yet demanding.

She hesitated.

But his fingers stroked her body from hip to breasts and back again in a rhythmic way, his hand always pausing to caress her aching nipples, to make her moan and strain toward him, and make the tight core of longing between her legs throb and pulse ever stronger.

He nuzzled her jaw and licked the inside of her ear. This time, when she felt his hand slip between her legs, she eagerly opened them to accept his touch.

Luke's fingers glided expertly to the center of her, feeling the slick moistness gathered there. Levered on one elbow, his leg firmly between hers, he slid two fingers into the folds of her womanhood.

Instantly she bucked and grabbed for his wrist, but he stroked her again, and she groaned in pleasure, her hand dropping back to her side, her legs opening wider.

Lightly he ran his fingers over the sweet wetness of her, watching the play of emotions on her face, watching passion draw her mouth down.

"Is it better there?" he whispered next to her ear. "Or. . . there?"

She whimpered her answer.

"Ah," he murmured, and stroked the spot, deeper and more fully. "There."

"Oh, yes," she told him through clenched teeth. "There. Please. There."

She bucked and twisted and clutched handfuls of the bedding as he teased her relentlessly, his own passion increasing with every touch.

She moved against his hand, pressing hard against his skilled fingers. He knew the release her body was seeking. His arousal was hard and pulsing and pressed hard against her hip as his own body begged for release.

He felt her movements increase, and knew she was close. He needed to be inside her when she reached her orgasm, needed to feel her convulse around him.

In one motion, he slid his hand free and moved between her legs.

His throbbing erection was poised at the entrance to her heated core, the wetness clinging to his aching tip. She moved then, straining up toward him, her hands at his hips, pulling him to her.

He thrust into her, feeling her sticky wetness surround him as he glided fully into her. He withdrew and thrust again, testing, coaxing, wanting her to match him in need and pleasure.

She was wild beneath him, arching her back to take more of him inside her. Her hardened nipples brushed against the plane of his chest, her hands roamed his back from shoulder to buttocks and back again.

With each touch, each movement, the flame inside him grew until it was like a prairie fire, hot and impossible to stop.

His mouth took hers roughly, twisting, slanting, demanding, and she met him, biting at his lip, sucking at his invading tongue.

Too many days, and far too many nights, had fueled his desire. He could wait no longer.

His thrusts became bold, full, reaching for the depths of her. Again and again he pounded into her, and she rose up to meet him each time.

Her breathing was ragged. His was nearly nonexistent. She took all he offered, and demanded more. She touched and kissed and nipped at his shoulder. She was feverish and wild, and he felt the first tiny tremors of her orgasm. He knew it would be only seconds. He withdrew fully and plunged into her with a slow, deliberate thrust that made her cry out her pleasure.

He covered her mouth with a silencing kiss, letting himself give in to the desire that threatened to carry him over the brink of all control.

He felt her orgasm a second before he poured himself into her.

The world around them dissolved. There was only the two of them and this bliss, this rapture they found in each other's arms.

Chapter Thirteen

The first rays of sunlight were cutting through the partially opened window when Luke awoke. There was a fog-laced dampness in the air that felt soft and good against his bare torso, the part that wasn't covered by the quilt.

He stretched, flexing the muscles in his shoulders and back, and rolled over onto his side. His head cushioned on the down pillow, he caressed the empty place next to him. She was gone. She'd slipped silently from the bed as the morning doves cooed their wake-up call. He'd roused from his blissful sleep in time to see her closing the door.

They didn't need to speak. They'd said it all last night. With touch and taste and words whispered in flame-hot passion, they'd said and done it all.

Well, maybe not all, he thought with a smile that didn't come close to expressing his feelings. There were no words for this bliss, this contentment. He felt good, really good. He felt alive and right, as if he could conquer the world single-handed. He sure as hell was willing to try.

That smile turned into an all-out grin, and he chuckled to himself. He was in love. No ifs, ands or buts about it. Luke Scanlin was head over heels a goner. He didn't mind at all. Nope. He liked the notion. Liked it a lot.

He turned, putting his head on her pillow. The barest trace of her rose scent lingered there, stirring lush, heated memories of their wild lovemaking last night. His heart eased down into a slow, steady rhythm, and he let the feeling, new and exciting, wash over him. Love. From the minute he'd walked in here two days ago, from the second he'd kissed her that night in the entryway, this had been inevitable. It was as sure and certain as his next breath—no, more so, he decided with a gentle smile. He could stop breathing more easily than he could stop loving her.

Luke pushed down the covers—the cotton was soft and smooth against his fingers—and swung his bare legs over the side of the bed, his body making the shifting feather bed sink. The house was quiet. It was barely sunup, and way too early for the family to be up and around. They'd be sleeping in, he figured, and Lord knew they deserved it. No one had had a minute's sleep since this kidnapping mess started.

Sunlight caught his eye. He squinted, then rubbed the sleep from his face. He stood, relishing the way the cool air made goose bumps prickle over his body. He figured he'd get dressed and head on down to the kitchen, maybe get some coffee and wait for her.

He ambled over to the blue porcelain washbasin on the stand near the window and splashed some cold water on his face.

"Argh," he muttered as the water trickled down his neck, and he grabbed for the white linen towel. Another ten minutes and he was shaved and his hair was brushed. He fished his best shirt out of the bureau, frowning at the wrinkles in the white cotton. Someday he had to learn how to fold things.

He tried hand-pressing it. The hand-pressing—cowboy for laying it on the bed and pushing it flat with his hand—wasn't working any better now than it had any of the other times he'd made this same futile effort. Aw, hell, he thought, snatching up the shirt and putting it on anyway. He wanted to look good, special. Frowning, he pushed at the wrinkles where the shirt draped down his chest. He was behaving like some schoolboy on his first date.

He chuckled. They were long past the courting stage. Ah, yes, he thought with a sudden warming in his blood. He stilled the direction of his thoughts and made to button his shirt. Good Lord, his hands were actually trembling. He held his hand up. This was what she'd done to him. He'd faced the entire Johnson gang, all four of them, with steadier hands than these.

He really did have it bad. Ah, he thought, pulling on his black wool trousers and stuffing his shirt into the waistband, he didn't mind being all hot and bothered, because after last night, he knew she was, too.

Yeah, she had come to him. He had given her a chance to leave, and she'd stayed. He'd told her in explicit detail what he was going to do to her, to every inch of her, if she stayed, and she had. Wild and wet and passionate beyond anything he ever imagined, she'd stayed with him until the early morning. They'd made love and dozed in each other's arms, only to wake and make love again. She was insatiable, and he was exhausted, but blissfully content. He dragged in a long, slow breath and released it just as slowly.

Nothing could be any better than this. Okay, well, one thing. Waking up leisurely with her curled and naked in his arms.

With a confident smile, he headed for the kitchen.

Lost in thought, Rebecca sat in the window seat in her bedroom, watching pink and yellow streaks of sunlight chase away the night. The cooing of mourning doves caught her attention, and she pushed back the lace curtain to look out more easily.

The world looked perfectly normal, the way it did every morning. Except it wasn't normal. Nothing was as it had been. Nothing would ever be the same again.

Fear fluttered through her, and she drew up her legs, her chin resting lightly on her knees. Her silk dressing gown fell away, and she tucked it securely around her body. Beneath it, she was still naked from a night of lovemaking.

Two hours. Two hours she'd been sitting here. At least she thought it was two hours. The time, like the night spent with Luke, was a blur in her mind.

She remembered quite clearly seeing the light on in his room, remembered going in with the intention of thanking him for saving her son. That was the polite, reasonable thing to do, wasn't it?

He'd looked so helpless there, trying to pull those splinters from his fingers. More like a little boy than the harsh, cold man who had accompanied her into that alley. Maybe it was his helplessness that had gotten past her wall of defenses. Maybe it was simply exhaustion from the days and nights of worrying. Whatever it was, it had seemed that one moment she was sitting on the edge of the bed, helping him with the splinters that laced the tips of his fingers, and then . . . then she was in his arms. He was kissing her with a passion that inflamed her senses; holding her with a strength she was powerless to overcome; touching her with an intimacy that ignited an all-consuming desire.

Oh, God, how could this have happened? Heat and guilt and shame washed over her like a tidal wave, leaving her breathless and frightened. This *could not* have happened. It was too awful, too terrifying, even to contemplate. A shaking started inside, the subtle beginnings of an earthquake. Her muscles cramped.

Rebecca Tinsdale did not—repeat, did not—give herself wantonly to men, and certainly not to this man . . . never to this man.

Her arms encircled her knees, pulling them tighter against her, and her head lolled back against the smooth, cool plaster wall, trapping her hair tightly behind her. Annoyed, she shifted and pulled it over one shoulder.

As she glanced down at her hair where it covered one breast, she remembered Luke arranging her hair in just such a way, his knuckles brushing enticingly over her breast, and her nipples puckering into hard, aching nubs.

She swallowed hard against the sudden memories.

This was awful, and getting worse by the second. It had seemed so innocent when she went to his room. A simple conversation, nothing more, had been intended. An expression of thanks, and a goodbye—most importantly, a goodbye. How could it have gotten so out of control? How could *she* have gotten so out of control?

All she had to do was close her eyes, and the images of them together flashed hot and erotic in her mind, making her pulse quicken. Like a series of mind-searing photographs, they flashed one after another; naked and writhing under him, her legs wrapped around his waist, his mouth sucking on her nipples, while she moaned and pleaded and demanded more.

Heat seared her mind and body. Her breathing got a little more intense, a little more unsteady. Oh, this was worse than she'd thought.

In all the years of her marriage to Nathan, their times together had been nothing, *nothing,* like this. There had been quick kisses, an occasional coupling under the covers in the dark. Over the years she'd convinced herself that that was married life, that her memories of lovemaking with Luke were merely exaggerated daydreams.

Now...oh, now she knew, with a heart-pounding certainty, that they were real—wonderfully, deliciously, luxuriously real. Last night he had done things, said things, made her feel things that, in her most vivid dreams, she'd never imagined. How could she? How could she possibly know that a man and woman could give and take and please each other in ways such as that?

It was wrong. It had to be wrong. Everything about it was wrong, and yet...yet it felt so right. She'd never felt so alive in her life.

That earthquake inside was racing toward her soul, threatening to destroy her in the process.

How would she face her family, her friends? They would know what a wanton she had been. Surely no one could do the things she'd done with this man and survive intact.

Abruptly she stood and paced toward the closet, pausing to gauge her reflection in the mirror. Could it be? She looked exactly the same. There was no scarlet brand, no mark to indicate what she'd done. Perhaps it would be all right. She would simply go on as before, she thought with a confident tilt of her chin.

The terror inside her began to subside—for about thirty seconds, until she realized that this was not over. She would have to see him, at least, this morning. Maybe not. Maybe she'd take her breakfast in her room and hope that he would be gone by the time she went downstairs.

She sighed at the absurdity of that idea. She was going to have to face him sooner or later. The question was, what was she going to say?

Ah, so now we're down to it, Rebecca. How do you feel? What do you want?

How did she feel? She felt glorious. What did she want? She wanted him to leave, to go away and never, ever come back, because he was too tempting, too dangerous, and she had responsibilities to others that had to supersede all her personal feelings, no matter how heavenly.

She frowned. Logic and guilt merged in her mind, and her joy was replaced by hostility. It galled her, how willingly she had surrendered to him, despite all her fine words and pledges.

Well, all was most certainly not lost, not yet—and she intended to keep it that way. There would be no repeat of eight years ago.

She was not the naive girl of eighteen he had seduced and left shattered and disillusioned. No, dammit! She was a woman now, assured and in control of her life and her emotions, she told herself fiercely.

After all, she had made the choice to stay with him last night. She conveniently ignored her guilt-ridden thoughts of moments ago.

Feeling more confident, she strode for the wardrobe cabinet. She yanked open the door and grabbed a blouse, forest green, and a skirt, straight and black, to suit her ever-darkening mood.

She shrugged out of her dressing gown and washed up in the basin next to the wardrobe, scrubbing her face and arms hard, wishing she could wash him out of her mind as easily.

She put on her undergarments and reached for the corset she'd worn the night before. As she picked it up, the laces slipped to the floor, and she snatched them up. She started the arduous task of threading the laces through the dozen or so sets of eyelets, her resentment building.

A shiver passed through her as she remembered his expert fingers loosening the laces with exquisite slowness, freeing her breasts and body to his masterful touch, his mouth teasing the valley between her breasts.

Her eyes slammed shut against the sensual images.

"No," she said out loud to the empty bedroom. "No," she repeated more firmly, her hands curling into fists.

Would it always be like this? Whenever she saw him, would she remember every touch as though it were happening again?

With every speck of will she had, she would resist the temptation of Luke Scanlin, and all that he stirred within her. Not just for herself, but for the others, and for the secrets she guarded. Oh, yes, for those secrets most of all.

What was done was done. The past could not be changed, but the present could.

She would face Luke straight on, the same way she'd faced most things in her life. She would handle this calmly, firmly, and with dispatch. Now that she'd given herself to him, there was nothing to keep him here...once again, she thought with a tinge of sadness, he would go. She was certain. Only this time it was the best thing—the only thing for all their sakes.

The distinctive aroma of fresh-brewed coffee greeted Rebecca as she pushed through the kitchen door. It was too early for the staff to be up, she was thinking, when she heard, "Good morning, darlin'."

Luke. His tone was cheerful. He was perched on the edge of the kitchen table, acting like he owned the place. "I made coffee." He gestured with his cup. "Want some?" He wore a white shirt and black wool trousers, and his hair was damp and finger-combed back from his face. It ought to be illegal for a man to be that handsome this early.

For the span of two heartbeats, all she could do was look at him.

His smile was warmer than sunshine, and his eyes were soft and familiar; his expression was like an unspoken invitation. She fought the impulse to walk to him, to touch him, to ask him to take her in his arms again.

Her gaze flicked to his hand, curved around the white porcelain cup, and she remembered that same hand curved over the sensitive flesh of her breast. She was flooded with memories, and she couldn't speak or tear her gaze away.

Erotic thoughts, flashes of their naked bodies writhing and moving together, the moaning sounds of pleasure, the pleading demands, all seemed to engulf her in an instant. Swift and crystal-clear, they heated her body with anticipation and flushed her cheeks with shame.

It was the shame and fear that she hung on to like a lifeline, in a desperate attempt to strengthen her crumbling resolve.

Pulling herself up to her full height, she faced him squarely. "I expected you to be gone this morning."

He stilled, his coffee cup stopped in midmotion. His eyes widened in open surprise, and she saw him straighten slightly. He raked her with an assessing stare. It took every bit of willpower she had to stand there and not flinch. She was braced for an argument.

Evidently he wasn't. "Not exactly the greeting I was expecting. Most people are at least civil to their lover the next morning." He put his cup down and advanced toward her. "Have you forgotten already? Maybe you like to be kissed first thing in the morning? You have to tell me these things."

He was dark and powerful, and his intentions would have been clear even to a cloistered nun. She was not as immune to him as she had thought. As she watched him close in on her, her throat went dry and, God help her, she actually felt her body sway toward him, as though reaching for the enchantment that logic demanded she refuse.

Teeth-gnashing willpower kept her anchored to the spot. It didn't keep him from touching her, though. If only he wouldn't touch her. If only he weren't so heart-stoppingly handsome.

Though it felt like a retreat, self-preservation made her take a firm step backward. "Don't touch me!"

Alarm was obvious in her voice, and it gave him pause. His hand dropped away. "What?" His tone was incredulous.

"I said, don't touch me."

Luke stare at her intently. "That's not what you said last night."

She spun away and walked to the cupboard near the sink. Reaching up, she helped herself to a coffee cup. "I don't know what you're talking about," she said, pleased her voice sounded so casual, so calm. She didn't turn around to face him.

"I'm talking about us making love last night—until just a few hours ago, actually," he added, his tone firm.

Discreetly she gripped the edge of the counter, needing support. "We... I... Last night was a mistake." She straightened and turned to face him, though her hands still sought the support of the counter.

"I don't think so."

"Well, I do. Furthermore, I will not discuss it, now or ever again. It will *not* happen again. And if you bring it up or mention it to me or anyone, I will continue to deny it."

Here in the middle of this kitchen, on a bright October day, her announcement could not have surprised him more than if he'd been struck by lightning.

Was this some kind of a joke? It was a joke—right? Okay, her expression was grim, but she had to be joking.

His mind was working overtime. What the hell was going on? Could she have been that wild, that willing, and not care anything for him? Could he have been that wrong?

Not moving, he sought her gaze. That was when he knew. She was serious. He could see it in the hard glint of her eyes, as clearly as he'd seen the unbridled passion in them last night. It wasn't anger or even shame. No, what he saw there was fear, stark and raw. He knew it, had seen it in men's eyes before they made a deadly miscalculation.

But there was no miscalculation here, no reason to flee. Was there? Their lovemaking had been beautiful, passionate, endless.

His head came up with a start. Was that it? Was she afraid of the passion he'd ignited in her, afraid of her wild abandon?

Being with her, making love to her, had been more than he'd remembered, more than he'd imagined. What they had shared was soul-searing in its power. But her eyes held only fear and regret. It was perhaps the regret, most of all, that ate at him.

His desire faded under her cold stare. What had been blissfully beautiful dissolved, transformed into something quite different, something dark and ugly and cold.

An hour ago, he would have bet his life on her, on them—he'd been that certain. When she walked in here ten minutes ago, he'd been ready to reveal his feelings, tell her he loved her, tell her she'd given him all he ever wanted from this life.

Instead, here she stood, telling him that she wished last night had never happened. It hurt.

Though his expression was hard, Rebecca saw the emotions cloud his eyes. He raked both hands through his hair, his mouth pulled down in a hard line.

"Let me see if I have this right. You're telling me that what happened— Sorry," he said sarcastically, "that *nothing* happened. Is that it, sweetheart?" His face was stiff. A muscle played back and forth in his cheek. "If it wasn't you who left bloody claw marks on my back, then who the hell was it? Tell me, and I'll thank her for a mighty fine fu—"

"Go to hell, you arrogant bastard!" she snarled at him.

His eyes narrowed and his face went stone-hard. Rebecca inched backward, suddenly afraid, knowing firsthand the fury he was capable of.

But he never moved. In a voice that was tinged with barely controlled rage, he said, "I don't care what you say or what you do or how you lie, it won't change things. We *did* make love, and dammit, it was good, really good." His voice softened. "You enjoyed every breathless minute of it as much as I did. You can lie to yourself and you can lie to me, but I'm in your blood, sweetheart, and God help me, you're in mine."

Rebecca cringed, hating herself for hurting him, hating him for being right. She had enjoyed it, but the risk was too great. If her secrets were revealed, lives would be in jeopardy. There was no way she could explain without revealing the very thing she was guarding so fiercely. If she stayed with him, let him stay with her, it was only a matter of time until he guessed. No, she had to end this, had to send him away. It was her only choice, her only hope.

"It's over. Please leave."

"You're dismissing me? What's the matter... I'm not good enough for you, Princess? Afraid of what people would think if you were consorting with a common cowboy, instead of some high-class banker?"

"That has nothing to do with it, and you know it."

He shrugged. "It appears I don't know anything, sweetheart," he offered smoothly, glancing around the room with a disdainful look before focusing on her again. "Except you, of course. I know *you* quite well."

Heat flushed her cheeks, and she drew in a sharp breath, the air fueling the rage inside her. "Please accept my sincere thanks for your assistance in returning my son," she replied, her words cold and flat. "If any remuneration is required, I'll have the bank send you a check."

"Payment is not mine to accept," he said, with equally cold politeness. He started for the door, his boots drumming on the polished plank floor. "It was you who came to my room, remember, so if anyone is due payment..."

He tossed a gold piece on the counter. It landed with a piercing clink. He walked out of the room. For a long moment, she stood there, trembling with rage.

Damn the man. She grabbed hold of the counter edge, her fingers white-knuckle tight. She clenched her jaw so hard pain shot down her neck, then ricocheted up to give her a pounding headache. She wanted to shoot him. How dare he say such a thing to her—no matter what they'd shared, what she'd done, how she'd hurt him!

She rubbed at her temples, hard enough to make the headache worse instead of better. How she could have been attracted to him for even one instant was beyond her. She dragged in a couple of cleansing breaths, trying to still the anger that his remarks had evoked. She never wanted to see him again, she never wanted to hear his husky voice or see his sable-soft eyes or feel his provocative touch.

She dispelled the image of him by pounding her small fist on the smooth pine of the countertop. Yes, she thought with satisfaction, she'd made her feelings perfectly clear.

Luke Scanlin was gone from her life for good.

Chapter Fourteen

He was there before breakfast the next morning. Rebecca stood in the shadows inside the back door.

Every single member of her household, including all the servants, was in the backyard. They were laughing and shouting and throwing a ball in ways that made no sense to her.

"Here. Throw it to me, Luke," Andrew shouted. His small foot was braced on a five-pound sack of cornmeal that was leaking badly, apparently from being kicked.

"Run, Jack," Mrs. Wheeler called to the stable boy, who was racing between the other sacks of cornmeal and headed right at Andrew.

Luke tossed the leather-covered sphere to Andrew, and it sailed right past him. He took off after it while Jack slammed into the sack Andrew had just vacated.

There was more shouting and cheering, and Andrew was hollering something about the game not being over. Everyone was laughing and having a good time.

Mrs. Wheeler picked up a large stick and rested it on her shoulder, seemingly heedless of the dirt mark it left on her navy blue uniform. The usually perfect bun at the nape of her neck was loose and half-down.

Her cheeks flushed as she took a couple of swings with the stick. "Okay, Marshal, pitch it," she said with a fierce determination that was undermined by her ear-to-ear grin.

It was at that exact moment that Rebecca stepped out into the sunlight of the porch.

"What the devil's going on?" she demanded more harshly than she'd intended.

Everyone turned to see her standing there. In a glance, Luke took her in. Her black skirt, curve-hugging tight in front, with yards of fine muslin gathered over the bustle in back. Another of those high-necked blouses, this one in royal blue, tucked securely into her narrow waist. Her hair was done up in a style that was prim and proper, accenting her neck, all smooth and warm and soft. Beautiful as always, he thought with a sudden flash of familiar desire that he mildly resented.

"Mama!" Andrew exclaimed, his high voice breaking into Luke's thoughts. "Look! Luke's here! Isn't that great? He's teaching us to play baseball!"

"Great, dear," she muttered as she took in the scene in a heartbeat. Every face was bathed in a radiant smile that bespoke relief from the anguish and fear that had stalked them. Songbirds, finches and doves, sang merrily from the oak trees that bordered the yard. Even the sky was bright and clear and blue—not all that common in San Francisco.

It was good to see Andrew so happy, so excited—a miracle actually, considering the ordeal he'd been through. Now here he was, playing in a childish reverie. That was terrific. Trouble was, it was Luke who had brought the color back to his cheeks and the spark of excitement to his eyes. Why did it have to be Luke? Hot resentment flooded through her. *He can't be here. He can't!* her consciousness screamed in denial. This wasn't supposed to be happening. She'd thought she'd seen the last of him. Hadn't she made her feelings clear? With a sigh, she realized that now was not the time or the place to confront him.

Whatever his reason for being here, it was obvious that Andrew was thrilled. The two had taken an instant liking to each other. If there had been any doubt in her mind, Andrew had dispelled that yesterday. From the moment he got up and found Luke gone, he'd done nothing but talk about him. Luke was brave. Luke was strong. Luke was a marshal who'd saved him from the bad men. Luke. Luke. Luke! Until finally, in a fit of temper, she'd said, "He's gone and he won't be back, and I don't wish to discuss him any further."

Ruth had looked startled at the vehemence in her tone. Andrew had looked genuinely hurt. Rebecca had been instantly contrite. After all, it wasn't Andrew's fault that she was in this state of emotional turmoil. It was Luke's.

No wonder, then, that she was furious to see him. *Besides,* her rapidly elevating temper coaxed, *just look at the man.* He was dressed in faded denim, which molded provocatively to his legs like it was put on wet, and his midnight blue shirt was loose and opened at the collar. He wasn't even wearing a tie—not that he ever had, but it would be nice to see him conform, once in a while, she thought ruefully. His hair was too long, his hat was too old, and his black jacket barely concealed the gun he had tied to his right thigh.

Gun. The word and the reality slammed together in her mind. Good Lord, he was wearing a gun! Yes, she'd seen him wear one before, but not with her child so close. Not while he was in *her* backyard, playing with *her* son.

"Good morning," Luke called, with a smile that was warmer than sunshine. He waved, as though yesterday hadn't happened. "We were beginning to think you were never getting up."

"Oh, Mama likes to sleep late on Sundays," Andrew supplied, rushing up to stand next to Luke and cling to his hand.

Rebecca bristled. "Why are you here?" she demanded bluntly. "I mean, it's early." She stepped farther out onto the porch, squinting in the harsh sunlight. "We usually don't *receive*—" she emphasized the word "—until late afternoon."

If he noticed her rebuke, he gave no indication of it.

Luke's hand rested affectionately on Andrew's shoulder in a way that made her uneasy. "Is it early? I didn't realize," he drawled smoothly. "I didn't know. I haven't been to bed yet."

I'll just bet, she fumed inwardly, remembering his affection for cheap perfume and cheaper whiskey. "Come on, Andrew." She motioned to him with her hand. "We have to go in now." She made a half turn, certain he would comply. To her great surprise, he didn't.

Andrew's eyes widened in puzzlement. "Aw, Ma, I don't—" His gaze immediately flicked to Ruth, who turned a questioning stare on Rebecca, as if to say, "Why?"

Rebecca ignored the unspoken question. She didn't want to say, *Because Luke Scanlin is here and he heats my blood and makes me want him.* Her pulse fluttered unsteadily.

"Andrew!" Rebecca repeated in a no-nonsense tone.

Andrew merely inched closer to Luke. Luke's hand moved more fully around the boy's shoulder in a gesture of noncompliance, which fueled that quickly rising temper of hers. Andrew pushed protectively against Luke's denim-clad hip, his back nestled against the holstered gun.

Alarm made her shout, "Andrew! Get away from him, right now!"

Luke's black eyes glowed with an anger that his expression did not betray. He cocked his head slightly to one side in thoughtful consideration. "Why?" His tone was calm, and there seemed to be a slight nodding of heads, affirming that the same question was on everyone's mind.

"The gun! He's—" She pointed.

"What?" Startled, he glanced down, relieved to see the weapon still securely hooked in his holster. His gaze flicked sharply back to her. "He's safe," he told her, folding his arms across his chest in what felt like a challenge. "He'll always be safe with me. Won't you, cowboy?" he added affectionately.

"Yup." A beaming Andrew craned his neck to look up at Luke's face. Even from this distance, Rebecca could see the adoration on her son's face, adoration that had always been reserved for her alone. Until Luke. Tears glistened in her eyes. He'd obviously won over her entire staff, and Ruth, and now even Andrew. Damn the man. Was there no limit to his charm? Was no one immune?

She was, she told herself firmly and, as though needing to prove it, she stepped down off the porch and took a step, one step, in his direction. "Guns, Marshal, are dangerous, and I prefer *not* to take chances."

"So I've noticed." His words were innocent, but charged with a smoldering intent that sent a shiver down her spine. "You needn't worry, Becky. I wear a gun for protection, mine and other people's." Moving his gun hand, he ruffled Andrew's hair playfully.

The implication of his words was lost on Andrew, but she understood. Oh, yes, she understood, with gut-twisting reality. He was here for Andrew, to protect Andrew. One of the men who had taken her child was still out there. Andrew was a witness. No matter what had happened between them, Luke had not forgotten that her son could still be in danger.

And here she'd been thinking only of herself, assuming that he was here because of her, when all the time he'd come to protect Andrew. Oh, God, how could she have been so foolish? She felt about two inches high. She wanted to apologize. She wanted to thank him. Pride wouldn't let her do either.

"Andrew, I think all this activity is too much for you," she said in a more subdued tone. "I don't want you to get overtired." She turned to her mother-in-law. "Ruth, do you think *you* are up to all this?" It was a gentle rebuke.

"Lord, yes," Ruth replied with a negligent wave of her hand. "You think I'd miss a chance to play baseball with my only grandson?" She winked broadly at Andrew. "Besides, I'm not doing anything. I'm the . . . the . . ." She shot Luke a questioning look.

"Umpire."

"Ah, yes," Ruth repeated with a smile. "I'm the umpire." She thumbed her chest.

"Oh, really?" Rebecca replied absently. "That's very nice, but why don't we all go in and—"

"Nooo, Mama," Andrew whined. "The game's not over."

Luke ruffled Andrew's hair again, making him grin and laugh before he raked it back with his stubby fingers.

"Why don't you join us? You like games, don't you?" Luke added, in a deep, husky tone that made Rebecca take a faltering step backward. With a pat on Andrew's shoulder, he said, "Go get your mother."

"Oh, yes, Mama." Andrew raced across the grassy yard to fetch her. Tugging firmly on her hand, his voice shrill with excitement, he said, "You can do it, Mama. Don't be afraid. Luke will teach you. Won't you, Luke?"

He was already pulling her reluctantly toward the place where Ruth and Mrs. Wheeler were standing, about ten feet from Luke.

"Of course," Luke said. "It would be my pleasure to teach you...everything I know." The words were innocent, the tone was not. Nor were the erotic images that flashed, hot and luscious, in her mind.

Was he deliberately trying to...to... *What? Inflame your senses?* If he was, then he was doing a really fine job of it—not that she'd tell him so, of course. Mostly what she felt was trapped and, judging by the smug way he was regarding her, he knew exactly what he was doing. Moreover, he was enjoying every minute of it.

So the trap tightened, as if she were a rabbit in a snare. The more she struggled the tighter it got.

Her trap was emotional, not physical. Luke was a danger to her safe, orderly life, to her peace of mind, to her secrets, yet he was protection for her son. At least for Andrew's physical safety. The rest . . .

She wanted him far away from her, but close to her son. How could she have one without the other? How would she survive his constant nearness?

There had to be a way. There had to be a middle ground, but right this minute she didn't have the vaguest idea what that would be. For sanity's sake, her only hope was that the police found the kidnapper soon.

In the meantime, Luke was here, and she had to grin and bear it. There was no point in arguing. Sending him away would mean putting Andrew at risk. This was his job, after all, and, grudgingly, she decided to let him do it.

"All right," she said cautiously. "I'll play along . . . for a while." She meant more than the game.

Relief flashed in Luke's eyes. A smile threatened the corners of his mouth, but he restrained himself. So, she understood his meaning, and more than just the part about protecting Andrew. He was here for that, certainly. He liked the little guy—liked him a lot. She wouldn't send him away now. It was a start, anyway. Shifting his weight to one leg, he watched while the others surrounded Rebecca and tried to explain the game to her.

He'd like to explain a few things, too, but they had nothing to do with baseball. No, he had indoor sports in mind, very private indoor sports. Standing away from the others, he let his mind wander while he half listened. Ruth and Andrew were both talking at once, each telling Rebecca the rules of the game.

"Luke will throw the ball..." Andrew was explaining.

Luke smiled at the boy's enthusiasm. He sure could have used some of his energy yesterday. Goodness knew he'd needed something, and that bottle of whiskey he bought had only given him a headache. And it hadn't been cheap, either. It had been good single-malt whiskey from Kentucky. He'd sat in his room all night, drinking and reflecting about her and about that scene in the kitchen.

The more he'd thought about it, the angrier he'd gotten. At one point, he'd actually made up his mind to say the hell with the whole thing. It was a little vague what the whole thing was, but it was certainly anything that had to do with that woman. Yeah, even through a whiskey haze, he'd been sure of that.

But giving up didn't sit well with him. He was a man who was used to getting what he wanted. He wanted Rebecca. Trouble was, the lady didn't seem inclined to cooperate. So he'd forced himself to sit there, and the whiskey haze had made sure he did just that. At first he'd been angry, angrier than he'd ever been. Half a bottle of whiskey had dulled the anger to a manageable level.

"Then you hit the ball..." he heard Ruth saying. He was watching Rebecca, and the hurt he'd felt yesterday curled cold inside him. If she'd reached in and wrenched his heart out of his living chest, it couldn't have hurt more. He'd been so euphoric, so elated, so certain and so damned wrong. Luke had thought he knew women. At least, he'd thought he knew this woman. Evidently, he hadn't.

Looking at her now, he figured he should have known what the outcome would be. She was a lady, a woman with a position in San Francisco society, and he was a cowboy—sure a U.S. marshal, but mostly a common cowboy.

Well, dammit, this cowboy loved her. And no matter what she said, she cared for him. No woman could give herself so completely to a man and not care for him. Could she? He was damned if he knew, but he was gonna find out.

"... run really fast," he heard Ruth say. The sound of her voice jolted him out of his musings. He looked up in time to see her pointing to the bags of cornmeal.

Rebecca was nodding, her sensuous mouth drawn down in determined concentration. He knew that look, had seen it often enough. The anger he'd shrugged off circled near the edges of his mind. Abruptly he straightened, not willing to give it credence. "Okay, let's get going." He cleared his throat and tossed the ball lightly a couple of times. "The championship of the backyard is about to be decided."

Andrew returned to his place against the fence. He paced back and forth, his small face drawn in a frown that made Luke chuckle.

Ruth turned to Rebecca. "Now, I don't want to pressure you—" amusement danced in her eyes "—but the honor of women everywhere is at stake here, so if you don't hit the ball, we'll never hear the end of it." She shook her head in mock despair.

A grinning Mrs. Wheeler nodded in agreement.

"Fine." Rebecca hefted the stick to her shoulder. "Let's get this over with."

"Come on, Luke!" Andrew shouted through cupped hands. "Mama can't hit!"

"Really?" He smirked. "Glad to hear it."

"Hit it, Mrs. Tinsdale," the housekeeper called encouragingly.

Rebecca braced her feet in the soft grass. She focused on Luke, saw him pull back and release the ball. It whizzed past her head faster than a crazed hummingbird.

"Hey," she muttered, her gaze darting to Jack, who'd caught the ball and tossed it back to Luke. "Try that again, mister." Her competitive spirit rose to the surface. She wasn't about to let him win.

Again the leather sphere sailed past. She swung and missed. The action took some of the wind out of her and made a lock of hair come loose from her comb and bob up and down over her left eye. She blew it back.

"Strike two," Ruth said, apologetically.

"One more and we got 'em!" Andrew called jubilantly from his place near the back fence.

Rebecca didn't understand the rules exactly, but she knew one more wasn't good, so when she saw Luke prepare to throw, she braced her feet and . . .

"Swing!" Ruth yelled, obviously forgetting her impartiality.

Rebecca swung with all her might. The stick and the ball collided hard enough to make her teeth rattle. The ball flew past Luke's head and dropped inside the fence, about twenty feet from where a startled Andrew was racing to retrieve it.

"Run!" Ruth and Mrs. Wheeler shouted simultaneously. "Run and touch the sacks with your foot!"

Dazed, Rebecca hitched her skirt up above her knees and took off as if she were being chased by hornets.

"Get the ball," Luke called to Andrew.

"Keep going!" Ruth hollered, jumping up and down as if she had wagon springs on the soles of her shoes. "Run faster!"

Andrew scooped up the ball and threw it, but it fell far short of its destination, so he had to rush forward and repeat the process.

"Throw the ball, Andrew!" Luke shouted, laughing, as he ran toward home base.

Rebecca touched the second sack, then the third, and saw Mrs. Wheeler waving her on to the starting point.

Halfway to Ruth, she saw Luke step between her and the coveted home base.

"Here!" Luke shouted, arms held high, while he effectively blocked her path.

"Faster, Rebecca! Run!" Ruth shrieked, hopping up and down.

Rebecca put her head down and charged for home. A pain stitched her side. Her breath was short. She kept going, determined to win. She was moving so fast, she couldn't have stopped if she wanted to. Full force, she slammed into what felt like a brick wall. It was Luke's chest.

Together, they went down. Luke cushioned her fall, and Rebecca sprawled full length on top of him. His legs tangled with her skirts. His arms wrapped around her waist. When she looked down, he was laughing, really laughing. Tears glistened in his eyes, he was laughing so hard, and soon so was she.

The group converged on the spot, yelling and shouting, but mostly laughing.

"She's safe! We won!"

"She's out! We won!"

Luke sobered, and with genuine concern said, "Are you all right?"

"Fine," she replied, embarrassingly aware of their position, though no one else seemed the least concerned.

She squirmed to get up, but his grip around her waist tightened enough to give her a moment's pause. Then, in one motion, he rolled them over and stood, pulling Rebecca up with him. The group surrounded Luke and Rebecca, everyone arguing about who was the winner.

Brushing himself off, Luke said, "It was a nice try, Becky, but you were out by a mile."

"She was safe, Luke, and you know it," Ruth countered.

"Absolutely!" affirmed Mrs. Wheeler.

"Positively not!" Jack, the stable boy, put in, then looked startled that he'd been so outspoken with his employer.

"Safe!" Luke groaned in a playful tone. "How could she be safe? Didn't you see me catch that ball?" He was brushing dirt off his sleeve.

"Yeah," Andrew chimed in, taking Luke's side. "Didn't you see?"

Ruth and Mrs. Wheeler both gave Luke rather smug looks that said the decision was made. Both women hugged Rebecca. "You were wonderful."

Luke raked both hands through his hair, then settled his hat on his head. "Okay. I give up. You win."

"Naturally," Ruth said, amusement sparking in her eyes.

"Well," Luke added, "if I've got to lose, this was a rather pleasant way to do it. I'll have to remember the benefits of having ladies play." There was a wicked gleam in his eyes that made Mrs. Wheeler chuckle and Rebecca blush.

"Come on, Luke," Andrew argued, "you can't let 'em win like that. She was out, and—"

Luke swung Andrew up on his shoulders. "It's okay, cowboy. A man's got to be a good loser... sometimes. You've got to choose your fights, and then, when it's really important...never give up." He looked at Rebecca, the double meaning of his words obvious. Feeling awkward, she broke eye contact first.

With a knowing smile, Luke started for the house, Andrew balanced on his shoulders.

"Lemonade! Can we have lemonade?" Andrew called out to Mrs. Wheeler.

"Coming right up," the housekeeper agreed, and hurried to oblige.

"Wait for me," Ruth called after her. "You never put in enough sugar."

"Sure I do."

The two were still discussing how much sugar was enough as they disappeared inside.

Rebecca stood in the center of the yard. The breeze off the bay gently rustled the hem of her skirt against her ankles. Lord, look at me, she thought with irritation. There were grass stains on the front of her muslin skirt, and there was dirt, brown dirt, on her elbows and front. She looked like she'd been in a brawl and come out the loser.

That stray lock of hair bobbed in front of her face again, annoying her. She blew it back. It plopped down again with a vengeance.

She should be angry. She should be really angry, she told herself as she made a futile effort to brush away those grass stains. Instead, she chuckled. Then she laughed. She was a mess, but she'd had a good time. It had been fun, she realized. For all the dirt and stains, she'd had a really good time. Running around the yard like a kid. What would the fine ladies of San Francisco society say if they had seen her? Probably have apoplexy. She chuckled again, and, still brushing at her sleeve, headed for the house.

Shoving back that errant lock of hair back, she secured it with a comb. She spotted Luke near the porch, Andrew still balanced effortlessly on his broad shoulders.

It was a sight that brought her up short. The two men in her life; one who was everything she cared about, the other who had the power to destroy it. There they were, chatting together, clearly unaware of the torment this scene caused her.

They were engrossed in conversation, Andrew nodding solemnly at whatever Luke was saying. They were so natural together, so easy, as if they'd known each other forever. In a way, they had.

She hurried in their direction, fear outweighing all other emotions. Luke gave her a mischievous grin that sent tiny sparks skittering across her skin.

"Lemonade!" Mrs. Wheeler called from the porch with a wave. Luke plopped his hat on Andrew's head and gave him an affectionate swat on his bottom. Giggling, Andrew took off at a run.

"Come on, Luke," the boy called over his shoulder, the hat down around his ears.

Luke waved, but didn't follow. He waited for Rebecca. She stopped directly in front of him. His expression was unreadable and, for a second, she tensed, worried about what he would say to her.

The breeze ruffled his hair. He combed it back with his fingers. His eyes assessed her boldly. "It was a lonely night."

She had been prepared for any of a dozen different remarks. She had not been prepared for that simple statement. Nor was she prepared for the sudden tingling in the pit of her stomach.

Unsteady, she tried to change the conversation. "That was nice." She gestured with her head toward the playing area behind her. "I liked that."

"That's two things I now know you enjoy." His voice was soft, and disturbing to her already sensitive nerves. She felt a blush warm her, then travel up her neck. "Is the game a new one?"

His smile was immediate, and rich as sun-warmed honey. "Ah, no, Princess, it's as old as time."

Her stomach did that funny flip-flop again. "I was talking about baseball." She glowered, refusing to respond to his seductive charm.

"I wasn't." His words were blunt. His tone was lush.

"Hey, you two," Ruth called from the porch, blessedly breaking the spell he was weaving much too easily around her. "Lemonade's ready. Come on. We've got ice melting in here." With a wave, she went back inside.

Luke took a measured half step in Rebecca's direction. Towering over her, he said softly, "We've got ice melting out here, too." He pretended to brush a lock of hair back from her cheek.

She shivered in response, then stiffened, steeling herself against his sensual caress.

"Don't."

"Don't what? Don't touch you? Don't want you? Don't care?"

"Yes."

"I can't do that."

"You have no choice."

"Neither do you."

She shook her head emphatically. "That's where you're wrong. There are always choices, and I—"

"Rebecca, dearest," a male voice called. Startled, they both looked up, to see Edward striding across the yard toward them.

Chapter Fifteen

Instantly the mood changed.

"What the hell?" Luke muttered.

Rebecca, desperate for any interruption, skirted around Luke and greeted Edward warmly.

Luke watched the two of them. They were both all smiles. It didn't make a bit of sense. How the hell could she do that, greet him like that, after the way he'd wormed his way out of helping her? Now, if she'd asked him to shoot the man on the spot, that would have made sense.

It's none of your business, he warned himself.

The hell it isn't, he thought with a rush of possessiveness that made his hands curl into fists. He had to resist the urge to strike the man.

"Rebecca." Edward's brows drew down as he appraised her appearance critically. "What on earth has happened?"

"We were playing."

His gaze shot to Luke, then back to Rebecca. "Playing?" he repeated cautiously.

Rebecca understood his meaning, and resentment flared. He had no right to question her. But Luke was watching them too intently and, feeling that Edward was the safer of the two, she forced a smile and said, "Baseball, Edward. We were playing baseball with Andrew and Ruth."

"Oh, I see," he confirmed, in a way that said he didn't see at all. And that rankled her even more.

Edward straightened, adjusting the sleeves of his perfectly tailored blue suit.

"Morning, Ed," Luke said, with a nod but no trace of a smile. "A bit early for calling, isn't it? I mean, Becky and I haven't even had breakfast yet."

Edward's brows drew down. "Sir, I believe you have the advantage." His tone was polite, and if he was surprised, he hid it well. The man was too smooth, too slick, and Luke took an instant dislike to him.

"Name's Scanlin," Luke said, not bothering to offer his hand. "And yes—" he glanced over at Rebecca, then back to Edward "—I believe I do have the advantage."

Edward's gaze turned razor-sharp. "Just what—"

Rebecca stepped between them, her color high. Anger sparked in her eyes.

"Edward..." she said warmly, her hand resting lightly on his sleeve. She offered her cheek for a kiss, then cut Luke a quick glance to make sure he noticed. He did.

"Marshal, I believe you said you were leaving."

Luke didn't move.

There was an awkward silence before Edward said, "Ah, Marshal, Rebecca was telling me last night over dinner—" he let the implication sink in "—that you were instrumental in the return of Andrew."

"Yes, that's correct. And I understand that you were not."

Edward's head came up with a snap. His eyes sharp with unconcealed anger, he took a half step in Luke's direction. Luke held his ground.

"Wait, you two." Rebecca demanded. "I won't have any trouble here." She flashed them each an angry look. "Luke, maybe you'd better go."

She saw him stiffen, saw a muscle flex in his cheek, and she thought for a moment he would refuse. Thankfully, he didn't.

Without a word, he strode for the porch and disappeared inside.

Rebecca let out the breath she'd been holding. Forcing a smile she didn't feel, she slipped her arm through Edward's, and they strolled toward the big oak near the back fence. She didn't think now was a good time to go into the house, because Luke might decide to linger awhile.

"Rebecca, is that man still staying here? You told me he left yesterday."

"He did," she answered, not liking this cross-examination. "He came back this morning."

"To stay?" His tone was sharp.

"Of course not. I told you he was here to see Andrew. We were playing baseball." She angled him a look. "I made a home run."

"Is that so?"

The significance was plainly lost on Edward. Even so, a little feigned enthusiasm would have been appreciated.

She sighed. "Why are you here, Edward?"

"What? Oh, I'm sorry to call so early, but I wanted to come by before you made any plans. The governor is in town, and I was hoping you would come for luncheon. You know how much he likes you."

She stopped. "Edward, I can't possibly. I mean, Andrew—"

"Of course, we'll take the boy, too, if you like, though I suspect it would be quite boring for him—political talk and all."

There was something in the way he always referred to Andrew as "the boy" that was unpleasant. She pushed the feeling aside.

"Edward, surely you can understand that under the circumstances I can't possibly go to luncheon today."

He looked genuinely puzzled. "Why, dearest? Andrew is home safe. Surely you can spare a few hours for something important to me."

Two days ago she'd begged him to help her save her son, and he'd failed her miserably. Now he was here asking her to put aside her plans and her feelings to do something as trivial as going to luncheon?

Anger nuzzled the edges of her mind. She'd thought she'd gotten past this. They'd had dinner last night, and Edward had explained his situation, offered his apologies and pleaded for her forgiveness until finally she acquiesced.

Yet now she was unable to restrain herself from making comparisons. Luke hadn't hesitated, hadn't pleaded rules and restrictions and fear of recriminations. He'd gone with her, stayed with her, put his life on the line, all for her.

Suddenly Edward came up lacking. But they had been friends, good friends, for a long time. It was difficult not to at least *try* to be understanding.

Again, Rebecca forced a smile she didn't feel. "I would like to help, Edward. But I won't leave Andrew. Not now."

"You aren't worried something will happen, are you?" He touched her arm. "I'm absolutely certain there will be no more trouble."

"I'm not so certain. Marshal Scanlin has reminded me that there is another kidnapper at large. Besides, Andrew is still frightened. You must understand."

"But, dearest, Ruth is here, and the servants..."

"I'm not leaving Andrew."

"But, Rebecca, to give up an opportunity to meet with the governor... His support could make all the difference to my campaign in the upcoming city election."

So that was it, Rebecca thought with a mix of disappointment and frustration. Edward saw Andrew's safe return much as he would any business deal. Transaction complete. Next.

"I'm sorry, Edward. I'm not interested in the governor or...anyone else at the moment. I nearly lost my son, and through a miracle—" a dark-eyed cowboy of a miracle, she thought but didn't say "—I have him back. As I told you last night, since I no longer have the paper, I intend to spend more time with my son."

"Rebecca, dearest, of course you want to be with your son." His tone was contrite. "I was being a rude and selfish bore. Please forgive me."

"Of course, Edward," she replied, out of courtesy, not sincerity.

He looked doubtful but didn't press the point. "I am sorry about the paper, but you'll find that you won't miss it." He brightened. "I intend to count on you heavily for your guidance and support in the upcoming campaign. Why, I'll venture to say that we'll be so busy you won't have any time for regrets."

"We'll see," Rebecca murmured, and started for the house. Edward fell in alongside her.

"Rebecca."

"Yes."

"About the marshal..."

"What about him?"

"You are certain he's no longer staying here?"

"I told you so, didn't I?" she snapped.

"Yes. Yes. It's just that people will talk, and—"

"I really don't care what *people* think, Edward. It's none of their business."

"Now, dearest, don't get upset. I know you've been under quite a strain, and you haven't been thinking as clearly as you normally would."

"I am thinking quite clearly, thank you very much. I'll have anyone I like stay here or not, and I don't give a da—"

"Rebecca!"

She sighed. "For heaven's sake, Edward. My son was kidnapped, Ruth was ill... The man is an old friend, and a professional lawman. He was the one who risked his life to get Andrew back."

Edward looked serious. "I never meant to imply anything wrong. It's just that Andrew is home now, and the man is still here."

"He's not here. How many times do I have to say it?"

"Yes, dear. I'm only looking out for your own good."

There was that paternal tone again and, right on cue, her temper edged up. She knew he was right. She had run the risk of gossip having a stranger—a single, handsome, unmarried stranger—stay with her. Having him there had been an even greater risk, one that the good people of San Francisco would never suspect.

They climbed the three porch steps and went into the back entryway and down the hall to the front of the house. She avoided the kitchen, fearing that Luke was there. She didn't want another scene.

"It's very thoughtful of you to worry about me and my reputation, Edward." She couldn't keep a tinge of sarcasm out of her voice. "Please don't. I scandalized this town when I kept the paper, and they managed to get over it. I think everyone will get over this, too."

"This isn't a matter for joking, Rebecca."

"What makes you think I am?" She pulled open the front door. "Now, you'll have to excuse me. I want to spend the rest of the day with my son."

"I'll give the governor your regrets."

"Please do." She closed the door softly behind him and headed for the kitchen.

"What do you mean they aren't here?" She addressed Ruth, who was finishing a glass of lemonade, the ice cubes clinking against the side of the crystal.

Ruth peered at her over the rim of the glass. "Well, a policeman came, saying they needed more information on the kidnapping. The marshal said he'd take Andrew and bring him back."

"And you just let them go?"

"Well, yes. I mean, Andrew is safe with the marshal." Her brows drew down. "He said they'd be back in a couple of hours."

"How could you do that without asking me?"

"What was there to ask? The marshal needed Andrew to help relate the whole story to the police."

"But Andrew—"

"Was more than happy to go along. I saw you were with Edward, and I thought you might be talking business or some such, and I didn't want to disturb you. If it had been anyone but the marshal, of course, I would have said no, but under the circumstances, Andrew can't be with anyone better."

"Or anyone worse," Rebecca muttered.

Chapter Sixteen

Luke kept Andrew wedged securely in front of him as they rode double. They were headed for police headquarters, on California Street. Saddle leather creaked as Andrew shifted and squirmed in thc saddlc.

"We coulda won, you know, Luke," Andrew pronounced, twisting his small body to look back at Luke.

"Next time, partner," Luke countered. He adjusted his hat lower against the midmorning sun. "There's always next time."

Andrew's face screwed up in serious consideration, and Luke chuckled. He hadn't realized that kids took things so seriously. Of course, his experience with children was virtually nonexistent, so this was a learn-as-you-go proposition.

"You wanna hold the reins?" he asked.

"Can I?" Andrew craned around, his black eyes sparkling with anticipation, then bounced up and down.

"Sure. Sit very still." Luke threaded the reins through Andrew's fingers. The thick leather was so wide he could barely hold them. Luke knew the gelding had a soft mouth, and so he cautioned, "Now don't pull back, okay? You don't want to hurt him."

"I'll be real careful" came the solemn reply.

Luke kept his hands resting lightly on his thighs, letting the boy get the feel of the horse. "Do you know how to ride?" he asked after a minute or so.

"Well, no. My papa was gonna teach me, but he went to heaven before he could."

Luke felt a tug of sadness for the boy, knowing what it was like growing up without a father. "What about your mother?"

"She said she's gonna . . . soon. Real soon."

"You think she'd mind if I gave you a lesson?"

"Oh, no, sir." The eagerness in his voice was unmistakable.

So Luke spent the next couple of minutes explaining the fine points of riding in the Western fashion. He didn't know the first thing about those tiny little saddles the dudes seemed to prefer. As they continued, he realized he was enjoying this—a great deal. There was something about being with Andrew that felt, well, familiar, which was silly. They'd only just met. Still, it was a feeling he'd had from the first. It was a nice feeling, and he gave in to it.

He showed Andrew how to neck-rein as they turned onto Stockton Street. He'd decided to take the long way around. Carriages rolled past them, their wheels humming harshly against the hard street.

The horse was well trained, and moved along at a steady pace. "Now give him a pat," Luke told Andrew. The boy did, and the horse shivered in response, making them both laugh.

Down the street they rode, past the small shops—a tailor's, a butcher's, and a hat shop with a flashy red hat in the window that Luke instantly thought would look perfect on Rebecca.

He frowned. He should have asked her before—well, at least told her they were leaving. But dammit, it galled him the way she'd just forgiven that weasel and welcomed him into her home again. Damned if he was going back out there and interrupt their intimate little chat.

How could she do that? he wondered with jaw-clenching anger. How could she stand there and talk to the pasty-faced little weasel? Hell, she treated that bastard better than she treated him, and he, *he,* was the one who'd stood by her. What the devil was wrong with her?

He steeled himself against the sudden rage and got his mind back on immediate business. He had to get this child to the police station and see what they could do about motivating the officers to get up off their duffs long enough to find that other kidnapper.

Turning onto Sacramento, they made their way past an odd mix of houses and stores, and cut up Kearney so that Andrew could see the fire station. The doors were open and the firemen were outside, washing the fire wagon. Its bright red paint glistened in the sun. A dalmatian barked happily at a freight wagon that lumbered past.

"What's her name?"

"Whose? The dog?"

"No. Your horse."

"Oh." He chuckled. "*His* name is Scoundrel."

"What's a . . . a . . . scoundrel?"

"It's something you don't want to be, cowboy. Believe me."

"Are you?"

"Depends on who you ask, I guess." Now, Becky might have a real strong opinion on that one, he mused.

Andrew was busy tugging on the reins, making the horse chew on the bit, shaking his head and making his bridle rattle.

"Here, let me help you." Luke gently reached around to guide his hands, easing the reins. "Remember, this is a living, breathing animal, sort of like you and me. You have to treat him kindly, not like a toy."

Andrew nodded his head, banging into Luke's chest with the movement.

"Okay, now you try," Luke told him.

Andrew did, and his eyes were wide when the horse obeyed each command. "Look, Luke, I did it! He likes me, I think."

"Sure he likes you." And so did he, Luke realized. The boy was smart and eager, and all he needed was someone to show him. Luke thought he wouldn't mind being that someone. As they rode, the boy cradled in the curve of his arm, an easy feeling curled, warm and comfortable, in Luke's heart.

It was a real surprise. A man could get to like this real quick.

Of course, Andrew was a special kid. Luke had known that right off. The way he'd hung on, refusing to cry, while all hell was breaking loose around him. A hell of a special kid. Becky had done a good job with him. Must have been tough, what with her husband dying and all. Good thing she had Ruth. Anyone with eyes could see she thought the sun rose and set in this boy. And it was just as obvious that the boy felt the same way. Lucky kid. Things might have gone a little easier for Luke when he was a kid if there'd been a grandmother to care for him.

You did all right anyway, Scanlin.

Yeah, but it had been tough, damned tough. Nothing that he'd wish on anyone else.

Hey, where'd all this melancholy come from all of a sudden? he asked himself. *Get back to work.*

He spotted the city hall and, lifting the reins from Andrew's fingers, stopped the horse.

Luke slid down and then helped Andrew dismount.

"Where are we goin'?" Andrew asked cautiously.

Luke dropped down on one knee and took Andrew's shoulders in his large hands, feeling sun-warmed cotton smooth against his touch. He pushed back Andrew's breeze-tousled hair.

"Now, we're going in here, because we have to make a report of everything that happened to you."

Andrew went pale. He didn't move.

Two uniformed policemen strolled past and went inside.

"Andrew?" He lifted the boy's chin with his thumb. "It's all right. There's no one in there who's going to hurt you. They need to know if the men said anything to you, told you anything that might help the police find the bad men and put him in jail. Do you understand?"

Andrew nodded, but his expression was grim. "I don't wanna talk about it. Can't we go home?" He made a half turn, and Luke turned him around.

He rubbed the boy's shoulders, feeling them tremble beneath his hands. Poor kid, he was scared to death, and with good reason. The kid put up a brave front, though. This morning at the house, no one would ever have known anything had happened.

"Andrew, you're not alone," he said, very softly. "I know you were scared when those men took you. I know you were even more scared when no one came for you."

Andrew nodded again. His chin quivered, and he stared hard at the toe of his shoe. "It's all right to be scared. I'm scared a lot of times."

Andrew lifted his head cautiously, and Luke saw the tears glistening in his black eyes. "You are?"

"Sure." He gave a little smile.

"But you're a marshal, and you have a gun..."

"Guns don't always help. Sometimes the things that scare you the most are things you can't fight with a gun. Things like being alone in the dark."

"Are you afraid of the dark?"

"In a way," he said, thinking that the dark he was afraid of was the empty place in his heart.

"Will you trust me, Andrew? Will you believe I wouldn't let you do anything that would hurt you?"

A tear pooled in the corner of Andrew's eye and trickled down the side of his nose. Luke pulled off his neckerchief and swiped at the tear. Then he looped the neckerchief around Andrew's neck and made a show of placing it just so.

Andrew studied the knot as if he were considering the fate of the nation. Then, slowly, he looked into Luke's face again and said, "Okay."

Standing, Luke took the boy by the hand and led him inside. The police were on the first floor. A series of offices surrounded an open central area with a large front desk, which was manned by an enormous sergeant. Dust motes floated in the sunlight pouring through the large window behind the desk.

"Scanlin," Luke said, by way of introduction. "Here to see Captain Brody."

He squeezed Andrew's hand in reassurance.

Brody's office was large, square and surprisingly neat. File cabinets and bookshelves lined one wall.

Brody greeted them from behind his desk and, though he didn't offer Luke a handshake, he was particularly kind to Andrew, letting him sit in his swivel chair while he perched on the corner of the desk, asking questions.

It took the better part of an hour to fill out the necessary forms, make notes and answer questions. Luke hovered like a lion over a cub while Brody and one of his assistants asked questions of Andrew—descriptions of the men, where he was kept, if he'd heard the men say anything about where they were going.

Andrew bravely told everything he knew. Occasionally his chin would quiver and his gaze seek Luke out. Luke would answer with a smile or a wink of encouragement, and that seemed to be enough. Brave kid, Luke thought with admiration.

When they finished, Luke spoke to Brody out of Andrew's hearing.

"Did you find the body?"

"Yeah, we found it. Bartender in the saloon said he was Jack Riggs. He had a brother named Bill. It was probably him that got away."

"Well, if you know who you're looking for, then you shouldn't have any trouble finding him."

Brody made a derisive sound in the back of his throat. "Come on, Scanlin. You know it's not that easy."

"Yeah," he reluctantly agreed.

"Besides, who says he hasn't ridden outa here by now?"

"Not in the condition he's in. I'm sure I winged him. How bad, I don't know, though."

"We'll keep checking. In the meantime, the boy's back and Mrs. Tinsdale should *finally* be happy."

Luke bristled, remembering Brody's earlier snide remark about Becky and knowing now about the articles on police corruption. "Yeah, she's happy, no thanks to you." He turned sharply, took Andrew by the hand and walked out.

"You were very brave," Luke said, lifting Andrew up onto Scoundrel's back. The boy was still pale and quiet, and it gnawed at Luke to see the little fellow so unhappy. Since he was the one who'd brought the boy down here, put him through this, he felt, well, responsible.

"You know, Andrew, I was just thinking about ice cream." He feigned a frown. "I don't suppose you like ice cream . . . do you?"

"Ice cream. Sure I do. Strawberry!"

"Strawberry? Really?" He grinned. "Why that's my favorite, too." Gathering the reins, he swung up behind Andrew, settling him comfortably on the tops of his legs. He handed him the reins, helping him a little. "What do you say we go find us some ice cream?"

"Yes!" He bounced up and down in excitement.

With a shift of his weight and a nudge of his spur, the horse turned left and headed down Kearney Street. It seemed that what wasn't a bank or a hotel was a market or a bakery. They passed the post office, the customhouse, several cigar stores and a couple of harness makers.

San Francisco was a thriving metropolis, that was for sure. And you'd think in such a city there'd be at least one ice cream parlor.

He stopped to ask a merchant who was sweeping the walk in front of his restaurant.

"Clayton's, over on Montgomery. It's a family place. They don't serve no liquor, just ices and sweets."

"Thanks." Luke touched two fingers to the brim of his hat. Out of the corner of his eye, he saw Andrew do likewise in a way that made him feel pleased.

Fifteen minutes later, they were seated in one of the swankier places in town. Not exactly your run-of-the-mill ice cream parlor, Luke thought, taking in the cut-crystal chandeliers, antique mirrors and European paintings.

"Two dishes of strawberry ice cream," Luke told the uniformed waiter, who returned a few minutes later with two heaping dishes of a fluffy pink confection.

Andrew made quick work of his, spilling a little on his shirt and leaving a little more on his chin. Luke ordered another round. A boy could never get enough ice cream.

"Tell me, Andrew, what do you like to do for fun?" Luke said in between bites.

"Well, sometimes Grandma and me play checkers. I like that. Grandma's not very good," he said, shaking his head sadly, "so I win most times, but she's fun. She tells me stories, too."

Luke nodded, and took another spoonful of ice cream. "Do you like school?"

Andrew seemed to consider this for a moment. "Sometimes. I like arithmetic and reading. I don't like spelling." He shoveled in another mouthful. "Too many letters. Numbers are easier, 'cause there are only ten and I can remember those."

"Ah," Luke returned with great seriousness, while struggling not to laugh. "What do you like to read?"

"In school they make us read McGuffy's reader." He screwed up his face. "It's about dogs and cats and people just walking around and stuff like that. But Grandma Ruth helps me read the good books."

"Good books?" Luke was intrigued.

Andrew took another bit of rapidly melting ice cream and ignored his napkin to wipe his mouth on his sleeve. "The ones about Deadwood Dick and Jesse James."

"Ah," Luke said knowingly, "you mean the dime novels, the adventure stories."

"Oh, yes, they're fun. Did you read the one about the Comanche raiders? I liked that one the best so far, I think. About a hundred Indians stole some horses and killed the rancher, and one Texas ranger had to go get 'em back and there was a big fight and the ranger killed all the Indians and took back the horses to the rancher's wife and she was real glad." He said it all in one breath.

"My goodness, Andrew, are you sure there were a hundred Indians and only one ranger? I mean, I was a ranger, and we—"

"You were a ranger!" Andrew shouted, making everyone in the shop turn and stare.

Luke grinned. "Well, yeah, before I was a marshal I was a ranger."

"A ranger . . ." Andrew repeated, in a reverent tone that actually made Luke blush. He couldn't remember the last time that had happened.

"Well, it's not all like they write in the books. Mostly you're alone all the time, and it can be dangerous."

Andrew's small mouth drew down in a frown. "I know. I told Mama once I was gonna be a ranger, and she got all funny and sad like and said she didn't want me to go away. Was your mama sad when you went away?"

"My mother died when I was a few years older than you."

"Oh," Andrew returned, his voice suddenly small. "My father died, too."

For a moment they were both silent, the man and the boy, so much alike in so many ways.

The sound of music carried in through the open windows, and it was getting louder, as though the music were moving closer. People around them began to crane their necks or stand, trying to see out the glass windows that bordered the street.

Luke twisted in his chair, the cane creaking as he shifted his weight. That's when he saw the wagon go past. It was big and enclosed and painted in bright, garish colors, red and yellow and green.

"What the—" He went to the door. Andrew dogged his steps.

People crowded around the windows, peering out. Luke stepped out onto the sidewalk as a second wagon rolled past.

"A circus," he said, grinning at a white-faced clown doing a handstand. He glanced back to see Andrew hanging back near the doorway.

"Come on, cowboy. Look. It's a circus." He held out one hand, and Andrew rushed forward, slipping a hand into his.

The music was louder now, a pump organ with pipes sticking up through the roof of one of the wagon. The noise was ear-piercingly loud.

More clowns romped and skipped past, distributing hand bills that announced that the Dubin Circus had arrived in San Francisco and would be setting up in Golden Gate Park.

Glancing down, Luke thought he would forever remember the wide-eyed wonder on this child's face. It was obviously a first for him.

It didn't look like much of a circus to Luke. It seemed a little old, a little worn, not at all like the one he'd seen in St. Louis one year. But seeing it with Andrew made it look fresh and new and exciting.

The red wagons lumbered past, stacked high with rolls of brightly striped canvas and long poles bobbing up and down while they extended beyond the wagon beds. A woman dressed in pink tights was riding bareback on a white horse.

She stopped long enough to say, "Circus tomorrow, handsome."

Luke smiled. "Thanks."

"Bring your son!" she added as the white horse pranced and pawed the ground. "He's gonna be a looker like his father." She winked and nudged the horse, who pranced away.

"He's not—"

She was out of hearing distance. What the devil made her think they were related? He glanced down to see that Andrew was mesmerized by the spectacle. There was a clown, and a trained bear that rolled and tumbled down the street. There was a rather scrawny-looking mountain lion in a cage that snarled and lunged at the iron bars. Andrew jumped and squeezed Luke's hand. Luke squeezed back.

He was about to suggest that they head for home when he spotted the elephant. What the devil they were doing with an elephant was anyone's guess, but they had one.

When the elephant lumbered past his trunk moved, snakelike, in Andrew's direction, brushing across the boy's chest—in search of food, no doubt. Finding none, it quickly retreated.

"Did you see?" Andrew asked, a little breathless. "The elephant touched me...here," he explained, running his hand lightly over his chest, now smudged with dirt, as well as strawberry ice cream.

"I did see."

"I never saw an elephant before, except in a picture book at school. Do they really eat through their nose?"

Luke chuckled. "It's called a trunk, and no, they use it like a hand and pick things up, then put them in their mouths."

"An elephant... And the pretty lady. Did you see the lady all dressed in pink? I never saw Mama dressed like that."

Luke laughed. "No, I don't suppose you ever will." *Though I wouldn't mind,* he thought.

The boy was so excited, and Luke was enjoying being with him. It was impulse that made him say, "Do you want to go watch while they set up?"

"Oh, could we?" It was a plea, not a question.

"Sure, let's go."

The word of Andrew's rescue and of the shooting spread quickly through San Francisco's social elite.

People began calling shortly after noon. Neighbors, friends, business associates, all with congratulations on Andrew's safe return, many wanting to meet the man who had saved Rebecca's son.

She tried to focus on serving tea, offering sandwiches and cakes and making conversation. Yes, she was very grateful for the marshal's help. Yes, Andrew was unhurt. No, she didn't miss the paper. It seemed she answered the same questions over and over, until she finally had a pounding headache.

The last of the guests lingered interminably long. Rebecca was seriously considering making up some excuse about an appointment or some such thing in an effort to induce them to leave. The words were forming on her lips when Andrew, looking more like a ragamuffin than the well-dressed young man who'd left here this morning, barreled through the double doors and skidded to a halt in front of her.

Any concern she had had about Andrew being at the police station disappeared. There was not the slightest indication that anything traumatic had been suffered. In fact, he looked inordinately happy, she thought grudgingly.

"Hi, Mama. We had ice cream, and we went—"

"So I see." She touched the pink smudge on the front of his shirt. "Is that where you've been...all this time?"

"Oh, no, we—"

She cut across his words. "We have company, dear. You can tell me later."

Luke strolled in, looking tall and dark and head-turning handsome, just like always. And, just like always, those same darned goose bumps scampered up her legs.

Evidently Mrs. Hillebrand and her teenage daughter were not unaffected. They stared openmouthed at Luke, and Rebecca was tempted to caution Ariel not to drool in polite society.

She made introductions.

"Mrs. Hillebrand and Ariel, may I present Marshal Scanlin?" Her voice was flat, and she kept her anger barely under control. They'd been gone for hours and hours without a word, and now Luke strolled in here calm as you please, without any apologies, any explanations.

"Ladies," he said, tossing his hat down on the pale silk side chair. He acted as though he were coming home, which he wasn't, she thought petulantly. He took each woman's hand in turn. His smile was radiant, boyish and charming. "I'm always pleased to meet two such lovely ladies."

Mrs. Hillebrand blushed. Ariel giggled. Rebecca seethed.

Devilment sparked in Luke's eyes as he settled comfortably on the settee. Andrew squirmed into the vee of his legs, and Luke pulled him fully onto his lap.

"Marshal," Mrs. Hillebrand began, "everyone is talking about what a hero you are."

"Not at all," he said as Andrew lounged back against Luke's chest.

"Of course you are. I'm certain Mrs. Tinsdale agrees. Don't you?"

"Oh, yes," she said, tight-lipped.

"Just doing my job." His chin was resting on Andrew's dark, tousled hair in a pose that would have seemed casual to most, but made her pulse race. She curled her hands around the arms of the chair, as if the smooth wood could steady her nerves.

Mrs. Hillebrand was still talking. "My goodness, facing desperadoes all alone like that, saving Andrew from the clutches of those awful people. Why, it's wonderful!" Her chubby face lit up in a smile.

"Yes, wonderful," Ariel agreed with a sigh.

"There's even talk that you should run for mayor."

Luke grinned and chuckled. "I'm not a politician, ma'am. But thanks."

Mrs. Hillebrand reached for her tea, the cup rattling in the saucer as she lifted it from the serving tray. "Well, Marshal, we've had politicians, and my husband, for one, says it's time for someone else, someone who's not a politico to run this city."

Rebecca couldn't believe her ears. Good Lord, people were talking about running him for office. What office? Police chief? Mayor? King? It wasn't that she didn't think he could do a good job. She did. He was honest and dedicated, to give the devil his due—so to speak. But was there no end to this? Why couldn't he leave? Go back to his marshal's job? Better yet, go somewhere else and be marshal?

"It's very flattering," she heard him saying politely, with a smile that was making young Ariel blush again. "Please thank your husband for me, and—" his smile widened "—thank you ladies, too." In one motion, he stood, lifting a giggling Andrew with him. "I think it's time to get Andrew cleaned up." He peered at the boy tucked under his arm like a sack of potatoes. "What do you say, cowboy? Time to wash up for dinner?"

"Okay, Luke."

Luke put him down, and he ran to Rebecca and gave her a big hug. "Oh, Mama, I had the best time ever. Luke showed me how to ride his horse, and then we had ice cream, and then we went to watch the circus men put the tent up, and—"

"All right, Andrew." Rebecca silenced him with a gentle look. "Later, remember?"

"Oh. Sorry," he muttered, more to his shoes than to anyone in particular.

Mrs. Hillebrand stood, as did Ariel. "Well, we have to be going. Very nice to meet you, Marshal. I'm sure we'll see you again. I understand you're staying with Mrs. Tinsdale."

She said it so casually that if a person wasn't paying close attention, he might not realize the importance of what she was asking. It was provocative, to say the least.

Normally, Rebecca took this kind of question in stride; it was part of life, especially in San Francisco. Tonight, however, all things considered, she was aching for a fight, and if these two busybodies wanted one, they'd come to the right place.

"I really don't think—"

"May I?" Luke cut in smoothly. "Mrs. Tinsdale was kind enough to let me *use* a room as my headquarters while we searched. I have my own quarters, at the Halifax on Washington Street. Perhaps you know it?"

Mrs. Hillebrand never faltered. "Why, yes, I believe I do."

"Well, if you ladies will excuse me?"

"Of course."

His back to the others, he winked at Rebecca. Then, grinning, he said, "All right, Andrew, race you to the stairs."

Andrew took off as if he'd been shot out of a cannon, and Luke followed at a more respectable pace.

Rebecca escorted the ladies to the door.

After closing the door, she turned and sank back against it. She stood like that for several minutes. Luke had come to her defense, she realized. She was startled by the act, and by the fact that he'd done so with such grace that the ladies hadn't even hesitated to believe him.

Her earlier feelings of fear and anxiety quieted. If he didn't suspect anything by now, surely he never would. But her heart still fluttered frantically in her chest, and she thought that it was as much the instant attraction she felt each and every time she looked at him as it was her fear that he would discover her secret. He lingered in her mind, inflaming her senses. She allowed herself to acknowledge the feelings, though she refused to surrender to them, just as she refused to surrender to the man.

Mrs. Wheeler roused her from her musings. "Dinner will be ready in twenty minutes, Mrs. Tinsdale. Shall I wake Mrs. Tinsdale?"

"No, that's all right, I'm going up anyway. I'll call her." She started up the stairs.

Luke was washing the last of the soap from Andrew's face with a yellow washcloth. Andrew, with the smoothest bit of pleading ever seen outside a courtroom, had convinced Luke that a complete bath wasn't necessary. In one of those man-to-man things, Luke had agreed—but only after swearing Andrew to secrecy.

Stretching, Luke dragged the towel from the rack beside the bed and tossed it to Andrew.

"Okay, where do you keep your clean shirts?"

"There," Andrew said, and pointed. "Top drawer." Andrew was busy finger-combing his damp hair. It looked more smashed than combed, Luke thought, chuckling. Two persistent cowlicks were giving him fits. "I hate to tell you, but we're gonna have to comb it, cowboy."

"Aw, Luke. It's good enough." Andrew smashed at a particularly ornery cowlick, licked his fingers and tried again.

"No sense doing that," Luke explained. "I know. I've tried. Why do you think I keep mine long?" He ran his hand through his hair to illustrate the point.

Andrew's chin came up in determination. "Then I'll grow mine, too."

"Ah, well, we'll see what your mother has to say about that."

Luke was grinning as he walked the three steps to the walnut dresser, his boots cushioned by the royal blue carpet. The top of the dresser was covered with a white lace doily. He glanced at the collection of tin soldiers lined up military-straight on one side, and the two silver frames with photographs on the other side.

"Did you say top drawer?"

"Uh-huh."

The drawer slid out with a scraping sound to reveal a half-dozen or so shirts, all starched, ironed, folded and arranged neatly in two stacks. Since Luke was doing the choosing, he chose his favorite color—blue, like Becky's eyes.

Seemed everything he did made him think of her.

As he thought of Becky, his eyes naturally flicked to the photographs. Nudging the drawer closed with his hip, he picked one up for a closer look. The silver frame was cool and smooth against his fingers.

The faces staring back at him were smiling, happy. A much younger Andrew, about two, Luke guessed. Cute face... He looked like someone...

His eyes narrowed as he stared at the fuzzy photograph. He angled it slightly, catching the fading light through the lace curtain covering the window. A thought stirred in the back of his mind, a feeling that he couldn't quite get ahold of. He decided to stop trying. These things had a way of coming along in their own good time.

He let his eyes wander to Rebecca. She was wearing a dress—dark, full skirt, high neck, of course. She was smiling. Her hand was resting lightly on the sleeve of the man beside her.

"This your father?"

"Yes."

Luke glanced over to make sure he hadn't upset the boy. It appeared he hadn't, so Luke moved a little closer to the window and pushed back the curtain with one hand to get more light.

He'd never seen Rebecca's husband, and he was curious. What kind of a man would she marry? He had his answer. He was tall like Luke, but that was where any resemblance ended. Where Luke was dark, he was fair. Where Luke was cowboy, he was society gentleman.

He had a nice face, though, kind, Luke decided grudgingly. He could see the family resemblance to Ruth—same eyes, same mouth. His gaze flickered to Andrew, who was still working on the cowlick.

Andrew looked like...who? Rebecca, he guessed. He sure didn't look like his father.

He glanced at the photograph again, for an instant imagining himself there, imagining what it would be like to have a family, a son.

Suddenly a sadness washed over him. Regrets and mistakes came to mind, making him feel the loss intensely. He tensed and put the photograph down with a clunk. He had enough trouble dealing with the present; there was no sense dredging up the past.

"How's this one?" He held up the shirt.

"Good. Mama likes that one. Blue is her favorite color."

"What's yours?" Luke asked, unfastening the small buttons and helping Andrew slip it on.

"I like red...and green," Andrew said, firmly glancing up from the last of his buttoning.

"Red, huh? You mean like the fire wagons?"

"Oh, yes. I like the fire wagons. Mama got me a toy one last year for my birthday. Wanna see it?"

"Sure."

Wearing only his shirt, Andrew charged out of the room. Luke could hear his bare feet thudding on the plank flooring. A door slammed. Andrew barreled into the room, hefting a fire wagon with a double team of snowy white horses attached to the wagon's tongue.

Luke held up the toy for a careful inspection. "That's a beauty. Looks like the one we saw today, doesn't it?"

"I know. It's my favorite toy. I got it for my birthday last year. You can play with it sometimes, too, though, if you want."

"Why, thanks, cowboy. Next time I get some free time, I'll take you up on that, okay?"

"Okay."

Luke helped him with his trousers, then socks and shoes. He reached for the comb. "What are you getting this year... for your birthday?"

"Ouch," he groaned when the comb caught in a tangle.

"Sorry." Luke started again.

"I don't know what I'm getting this year?" He brightened. "Maybe I'll ask for a pony, now that I know how to ride and all."

"Well, you might need a little more practice."

"Would you help me?"

"Sure," Luke agreed, happy to spend time with the boy. That niggling thought got closer to the surface of his mind. There was something he'd forgotten... or something...

He shrugged. "Say, when is your birthday? Do you know?"

"Sure I do." Andrew seemed indignant. "It's December tenth."

"December. That's right. I remember your grandmother telling me. Do you mind having your birthday so near Christmas?"

"Naw. Mama always makes a big party. It's like having Christmas two times."

Luke was still chuckling when he dropped down on one knee to help Andrew tuck his shirt into the waist of his brown wool trousers. Andrew's stared up at him, black eyes staring back at equally black eyes. A strange feeling moved through Luke, a sudden lightness that made his breathing shallow. A thought flashed crystal-clear in his mind. All the air rushed out of his lungs.

He did some fast arithmetic. He'd left Rebecca in March—seven years and nine months. Dear God, could it be true?

He searched the boy's face as though he were photographing it, as though he were seeing him for the first time. In a way, he was. "Are you certain, Andrew? You aren't guessing?" There was an urgency to his voice.

"No," Andrew said, somewhat indignantly. "I know my birthday and my address, and I can write them down. You wanna see?"

"No." Luke brushed the hair back from the boy's face. Without standing, he took Andrew by the shoulders and turned him to face the mirror. Almost shoulder to shoulder, the two looked into the glass. The reflection that stared back sent an icy chill down Luke's spine.

"Luke, we've got the same color eyes. Isn't that great? We've even got the same cowlick. Look! See, mine's here and yours is..."

"Here," Luke said very softly. Suspicion became reality, soul-shattering reality. Luke sank back on his heels, his hands still resting on Andrew's...on his son's shoulders. Oh, Lord, he had a son. A son. The word turned into a soft, gentle feeling that wrapped itself forever around his heart.

He glanced away long enough to look at the photograph on the bureau. The fair-haired couple and the child, a boy with raven black hair and equally black eyes, just like the eyes that looked back at him every time he looked in the mirror.

His fingers tightened slightly, possessively, on Andrew's small shoulders, and tears welled up in his eyes and slid unchecked down his cheeks.

Luke knew Rebecca was there even before he looked to the doorway. "Why didn't you tell me?" His voice was soft with emotions too new to name, and he thought at this moment that no man could be happier than he was. The woman he loved had given him a son. He didn't care about the rest, about having to find out himself, about the lost years. He was overjoyed to know. He would forgive her the rest.

Rebecca's voice was very calm when she spoke. "Andrew, why don't you go on down to dinner? Grandma is there already, and she'll be lonely. Tell her we'll be along shortly."

Andrew slipped free of Luke's light touch. "Okay."

"See you later, Luke."

"See you later, son," he couldn't resist saying, testing the word and the feeling.

Andrew didn't understand the double meaning of Luke's remark, but Rebecca did. She saw the tears on his cheeks. It tugged at her heart, her guilt and regret and anger. There was one more feeling that overwhelmed the others—the sense of duty. She had a duty to the people she loved, Andrew and Ruth. She owed them security and love and protection. She would protect them, even at her own expense. Rebecca stepped into the room and closed the door softly, leaning back against it, effectively blocking it, as though she could keep the secret locked up as easily.

Luke stood and started for her, wanting to take her in his arms, to hold her and tell her that he forgave her for keeping the secret.

She stopped him with an upraised hand. "Just what is it you think you know?"

"I know that Andrew is my son."

"I say he's not."

Luke hesitated. He walked to the photograph and held it up for her. The dark-haired boy and the fair-haired couple. No, Andrew had Luke's eyes and hair and coloring. The imprint of his features was true and unmistakable. He glanced back at Rebecca. "Like hell he isn't. I should have seen it from the first. He's my son."

"Try and prove it."

The silence in the room was overpowering in its intensity. It took a full thirty seconds for the reality of her words to penetrate his brain.

In a voice that was hard and cold and ripe with menace, he said, "Goddamn you, Rebecca. All this time, and you never told me. You took what we shared and turned it into something dark and immoral. You hate me so much that you would keep my son from me."

"I thought you were too busy chasing fame and excitement. Once you got me in the hay, you used me and left." She said it plainly; it only took a few words to explain a mountain of anger and distrust.

"Sure I left, I—"

"Don't give me that story about being young, because I'm not buying it."

"I don't *have* to explain my life to you. If you'll remember, sweetheart, no one forced you into the hay with me. You went willingly...both times." With that, he leveled the mountain.

"Yes, Luke, I did." Her voice was ripe with sarcasm and regret. "I absolve you of all responsibility. There. Are you happy? It's not your fault. None of it. You can leave with a clear conscience."

"I've tried to explain to you."

"A little late, isn't it?" She advanced on him this time. "About a lifetime too late."

"You got married." He said it like an accusation.

"Yes." Her tone was defiant. "I got married. Thank goodness Nathan was *willing* to marry me, knowing I was pregnant with another man's child."

"You could have written, wired. I would have come back."

"Oh, certainly. A letter addressed to Luke Scanlin, Somewhere, Texas. Yes, that would have been a perfect choice. In the meantime, I could have gotten bigger and bigger, disgraced my family, risked my son's name, all in the faint hope that the man who thought so little of me as to take my virginity and then ride off would want to come back and get married."

"Dammit to hell, Rebecca. If I'd known, I'd never have left. I'm not that much of a—"

"*Bastard,* I think, is the word you're looking for."

He started for the door. "It didn't have to be like this."

She blocked his way. "What are you going to do? Tell him? Are you going to go down there and shatter his life? If one word of this gets out, the scandal will be unrecoverable. Andrew's name will be forever ruined in this town."

"Then we'll go to another town."

"This is my home, and Andrew's, and Ruth's. Have you forgotten that Ruth thinks Andrew is her grandson, her *only* grandson? They love each other dearly. Are you going to take that away from them, too?"

"Damn you!" he said finally, feeling trapped. "He's my son and I want him."

"He's *my* son, and you can't have him."

"Watch me."

He stormed from the room. Rebecca raced after him. She caught up with him at the bottom of the stairs. He stood in the doorway of the dining room and, for a frantic moment, she thought he was about to say the words that would change her life and lives of those she loved forever.

"Luke," she entreated. "You can't."

He looked at her with eyes as hard as granite, then turned on his heel and slammed out the front door.

Ruth turned to Rebecca. "What's come over him?"

Chapter Seventeen

He needed a drink, and he needed it now. If ever a man deserved to get drunk, this, he fumed, slamming out the front door, was the time. He headed for his horse, tied at the hitching post.

He snatched up the reins and the gelding shied and shook his head.

"No one cares what you think," Luke snapped, swinging up without bothering with the stirrups. Yeah, a drink. A hell of a lot of drinks. After all, a man was entitled to celebrate when he became a father—even if it was eight years too late, he thought bitterly.

He reined over so hard the gelding reared and shook his head in defiance. Luke held on easily, and instead of softening his touch, he yanked harder, spurred the horse in the sides and took off down the street.

Ten seconds, and he reined up as hard as before. The horse skidded and pranced and pawed the ground. What the hell was he doing, racing through the city streets like this?

What's wrong with you, Scanlin. You wanta hurt someone?

The answer was a resounding yes. He wanted to hurt someone the way he'd been hurt. That, however, was impossible. The kind of hurt he was feeling went deep, to the very core of him.

She'd lied to him. The woman he had come back to, the woman he knew he loved, the woman... *that* woman... had lied to him.

All through the nightmare of the kidnapping, she'd never said a word. All the time that had been *his* son out there. The child might have died, and he would never have known. When had she been planning to tell him—when they lowered the coffin into the ground? Had she been planning on telling him at all?

He knew the answer. His hand curled tight around the reins, and the leather cut into his fingers. Muscles tensed along the tops of his shoulders and down his spine. He urged the horse into a lope as he headed for the waterfront. That was a good place to get drunk and get into a fight. Right now, that was exactly what he wanted.

He turned onto Pacific Street. The sun was already down. The street was crowded. A patchwork quilt of miners, sailors and businessmen mingled on the sidewalk as they made their way along. They were looking for entertainment, for fun.

Fun was the last thing on his mind. He was sulking, brooding, and a man needed a dark place to do that. So he passed up the fancier places, the Palace and the Golden Lady.

He spotted the Purple Crescent at the end of the street. It was all peeling paint and raw wood. The glass windows hadn't seen a soap-filled sponge since they'd been put up. The lettering announcing beer at twenty-five cents was so faded as to be more smudge than paint.

He tied up at the gnarled hitching post and pushed through the batwing doors. A couple dozen tables cluttered the dirt-caked floor. The scent of burning tobacco and unwashed bodies overpowered the brisk saltiness of the night air. There was a painting of a voluptuous woman, buck naked, hanging over the bar.

The place was crowded. Most of the men were standing around the faro table or over at the roulette wheel. Luke shouldered his way through to the bar.

"Bottle" was all he said to the bartender. He tossed some coins on the scarred surface of the bar. "Let me know when that's gone."

The barman nodded, gathered the coins with one hand and set down the bottle and a glass with his other hand.

Luke took both, then moved toward an empty table near the back staircase. It was as close to a dark hole as he could get.

It was habit that made him sit with his back to the wall. Out of the corner of his eye, he could watch the comings and goings on the staircase. There seemed to be a lot of those—grinning men with scantily dressed women.

Just his kind of place, he mused, tossing back a drink and feeling the rotgut burn a path to his stomach. Yeah, this was the kind of place he was used to. It was the kind of place Rebecca had accused him of taking full advantage of.

Well, dammit, he hadn't before, but he was here now and—he tossed back another drink—maybe he'd just go on up those stairs. Might as well, since she'd accused him of the act.

She'd accused him of a lot of things tonight, of using her, of not caring, of leaving her. Well, she was wrong! He tossed back another drink. The alcohol was beginning to work—he felt the first signs, muscles uncoiling, a fuzziness in his brain.

Lifting his hat, he raked one hand through his hair and settled it back in place.

"Hello, cowboy," a female voice said from close by.

His gaze traveled up the trim navy skirt, past the pale yellow blouse opened at the neck, to a familiar face.

"Millie?" He took in the traveling costume and the washed face. She looked like a kid—all blue eyes and freckles, except for that red hair, of course, that was a dead giveaway.

"Yeah." She grinned and made an awkward attempt at a curtsy. "It's me."

He managed a trace of a smile. "I hardly recognized you in your...out of your working..." He dragged out a chair. "What are you doing here? This isn't your place."

"I come by to collect some money from Sally—" she motioned with her head toward the upstairs "—before I catch the night train for Salt Lake. What about you? What are you doing here?" She settled in, her elbows on the gouged surface of the table.

"I'm on my way to getting drunk," he said flatly, and poured another drink. "You want one?"

"Sure." She signaled the bartender, who brought another glass. She helped herself to the liquor. "Is the boy all right?" She sipped at the drink.

"Yeah, the boy is fine. He's more than fine." He glanced at her. "He's great."

"I'm glad." She smiled a broken-toothed grin. "I'm real sorry for what happened. Is there any news of Jack?"

"None that I know of. The police are supposed to be looking. My guess is, he left town."

She nodded. "I hope so. Anyways, I ain't taking no chances. I'm heading out, like you suggested."

"Good."

Millie emptied her glass and poured another.

"So if everything's okay, how come you're here—" she hefted the half-empty bottle "—soon to be drunk?" She glanced around and, quietly, for his ears only, said, "This ain't a good place for marshals, especially if they're a little fuzzy...if you get my drift."

"I'm not fuzzy, as you put it. Though God knows I'd like to be."

"How come?"

"How come, she asks," he muttered to no one in particular. "Well, Millie," he said with great ceremony, "it seems I'm celebrating."

"Celebrating?"

"Yeah." He filled her glass to the brim. "Today, I became a father." He toasted her with his drink before he emptied the glass.

Her blue eyes flashed in surprise. "What?"

"Yeah. It's something, isn't it? Turns out the boy, Andrew, is my son."

Millie let out a low whistle. "And you didn't know?"

"Hell, no, I didn't know," he snapped. "That damned woman never told me. All these years I had a son, a child, and I didn't know."

"Oh, my." Millie seemed to be considering this for a long moment. She turned her half-full glass slowly between her fingers. Looking at the glass, she said, "So how come you didn't know?"

"I told you, his mother didn't tell me." He shifted in the rickety chair, and the wood creaked in protest.

"It's usually pretty obvious when a woman's pregnant. Kinda hard not to notice." She still didn't look at him.

"Dammit, Millie, I wasn't here. I was in Texas. All she had to do was write me, and I woulda come back. I woulda married her, for chrissakes. She knew that."

Millie sank back in her wooden chair. One hand holding the drink, the other in her lap. She raked him with an appraising stare that was tinged with enough surprise and contempt as to make him shift uncomfortably.

"What the hell's wrong with you?" Luke didn't like being the object of her scrutiny.

"I figured, from the kid and all, his mama is some society lady, right?"

"Society," Luke repeated with disdain.

"So you're tellin' me you got some society lady pregnant, then you rode off and left her like she was..." She straightened. "Nobody."

"No," he retorted. "It wasn't like that."

Millie arched one brow questioningly.

"It wasn't like that," Luke repeated, more vehemently. "All she had to do was tell me. I woulda come back. I woulda married her, if that's what she wanted."

"Aren't you the hero?" Millie tossed back her drink. The noise of the saloon filled their silence. The constant click-click of the roulette wheel grated on

Luke's nerves. He reached for the quarter-full bottle, wondering why the whiskey wasn't helping to blot out the anger.

He signaled for another bottle, and the bartender obliged.

"That ain't gonna help a guilty conscience, you know," Millie said as he pulled the cork and tossed it aside.

"What guilty conscience? I'm not the one who did anything wrong here. She's the one who didn't tell me, remember?"

"Sounds to me like you're the one who left, *remember?*" she flung back at him.

"Say, what's this to you, anyway? Why are you taking her side in this?"

"I ain't taking her side. I don't even know her. But if I was some rich society lady and I let some cowboy get me in a family way and then he rode off and left me, I'd be plenty scared. I know I wouldn't have too many choices."

"Choices? Sure she had choices. She coulda told me."

"Did she know where you where?"

"How many times have I gotta tell you, I was in Texas?"

"Ah..." She nodded. "Texas, according to all you boys, is mighty big. Did she know where you was?"

It was a full ten seconds before he answered. "No."

Millie gave a knowing nod. "She musta loved you a lot, to take a chance like she done."

"Loved me! Now there's a laugh." He rocked his chair back on two legs, his head resting against the smooth plaster of the wall. "She loved me so much she didn't tell me I had a son for nearly eight years. If I hadn't guessed I never would have known."

"What else would you figure would make her risk everything to have your baby? She sure as hell didn't have to."

Luke went very still. He slowly lowered the chair to the floor. In a voice that was so soft she had to lean in to hear him over the noise, he said, "What do you mean, she didn't have to?"

Still leaning in, Millie replied, "There are ways to take care of... unwanted babies." She sat back, her face grim. "Believe me, I know." The was a hint of sadness in her voice.

The truth of her words hit him like cold water on a hot day. Rebecca hadn't had to have the child. He knew that, had heard about treatments, elixirs, even certain women who knew how to end an unwanted, embarrassing pregnancy.

"She didn't, did she?" he muttered. "But—"

"No buts about it. She took a hell of a chance. I mean, I've heard them rich folks don't take kindly to this sorta thing. Daughters get sent away, or—what do they call it? Oh, yeah, disowned, for rolling in the hay with the wrong man."

"Yeah," Luke put in. "I'm the wrong man, all right."

"It doesn't appear so. She had your baby, didn't she?"

The words tumbled around in his brain like thunder.

She didn't have to...

Could have ended...

Took a risk...

Must have loved you...

Slowly, reality dawned on Luke. She had spent the past eight years guarding this secret. She had protected their child from scandal and harm.

She'd been afraid, of everyone, and especially of him. He'd been the one who could guess, he'd been the one who, with one word, could destroy her life and Andrew's.

So she'd guarded her secret, protected the child, right down to, and including, lying. He should have seen, should have realized.

But like an arrogant bastard, he'd accused her, threatened her, when what he should have done was take her in his arms and hold her until she stopped being afraid.

When he looked up, Millie was watching him closely. "Thanks, Millie." He reached over and covered her hand with his in a gesture of sincere gratitude.

"What are you gonna do?"

Luke stood. "First, I'm going to put you safely on that train. Then I'm gonna go claim what's mine."

Two men met in the elegant private room of Barry and Patten's saloon. Downstairs, the crowd was heavy, busy with the business of sin. It was easy for the men to slip in and out without anyone giving them the least bit of notice.

The room was perched on the balcony overlooking the stage, where, in thirty or so minutes, the latest songbird from New York would be entrancing the customers.

The burgundy drapes were drawn against prying eyes, and the two men seated themselves at the linen-covered table. One candle flickered in the glass globe in the center. A gas wall sconce glowed dimly, giving the room an almost romantic feel, and Frank Handley thought that more than once this room had probably been used for an illicit meeting.

He pulled out a chair—red satin and gilt trim. Elegant, with a touch of the wicked.

"We'll have whiskey," Frank told the uniformed waiter. "Make sure it's Irish."

His boss sat opposite him. His slender face was hidden in the shadows, but Frank didn't have to see his face to know he was displeased.

The music of the reed organ carried upstairs. An energetic version of "Camptown Races," if he wasn't mistaken. Silently he hummed along in his head.

The waiter returned with the whiskey, served in cut-crystal glasses imported from Ireland.

"Anything else, gentlemen?" he asked with a slight bow.

"Nothing," Frank returned, already reaching for the bottle. "See that we aren't disturbed."

The waiter nodded, gave another small bow and left.

The bottle clinked against the glasses as Frank poured the drinks. He shoved one toward the other man, the glass leaving a track in the white linen cloth.

"All right, Frank," the man said softly, holding his glass up to study the contents against the flickering candle on the table. "What the hell happened?"

"I don't know." Frank took a sip of the liquor, needing to feel the calming effects of alcohol on his nerves.

"I pay you to take care of things. You were supposed to have it all set. Nothing was supposed to go wrong. Now we have a dead kidnapper, and another one running loose somewhere—" he took another swallow of whiskey "—and I'm out ten thousand dollars, I might add."

"I had it all set." Frank knew this wasn't a man to cross. "All they had to do was turn over the kid. I'd pay them off and send them out of town for a while. How was I suppose to know they'd get greedy?"

"All right, Frank," the other man said softly. "I'll make it work, though I wish to hell I had that money. I need it for..." He lifted his eyes negligently. "I need it. At least the newspaper is mine. She doesn't know, does she?"

"No." Frank smiled. "She doesn't suspect a thing. She thinks it's an eastern syndicate."

"Good. Let's keep it that way. It's only a matter of time until she comes to me." He lounged back, and a smile tugged at one corner of his mouth. "In the meantime, I want you to put the word out, discreetly—" he sliced a glance in Frank's direction "—that Jack Riggs has money, and if anyone finds him and wants to take the money away, well, you would be grateful."

"They'll kill him for that kind of money," Frank said on a sudden intake of breath.

The other man gave a one-shoulder shrug. "Just put the word out. The wolves will hunt him down if he's in town, and what they do then, well, it's out of our control."

A chill snaked up Frank's spine at the cold way the man could order someone's death. "But murder—"

"Not murder," the other man snarled. Then, more gently, "I told you, it's out of our hands. Besides, if they'd followed orders, no one would have been hurt, now would they?"

Frank shook his head.

"So, there, you see. It's not our doing. They brought it on themselves. If Jack is arrested and talks, it's you he'll name, Frank, and if anyone looked really hard, they might find the connection between you and me. I'm only looking out for your best interests."

"I understand." Frank drained his glass.

The man chuckled. "Don't look so worried, Frank. It'll be all right. I'll take care of you."

The man stood, tossed some money on the table and left.

Frank lingered awhile over his whiskey. He'd never bargained on murder.

Chapter Eighteen

Luke didn't go to Rebecca's that night. He didn't go the next morning. Oh, he wanted to. He just didn't know what to say. And even if he had he doubted she'd give him more than two seconds before she slammed the damned door in his face. Let's face it, they hadn't parted the best of friends. That was a polite way of saying they'd argued. Okay, they'd fought. Hell, they always fought, except when they were making love.

If fighting with her was hell, then having her in his arms was heaven, pure and simple. Holding her was magic, like holding a flame in the palm of his hand—too hot to hold and too exciting to release. It was a fire he was more than happy to be consumed by.

He dragged in a deep breath and held on to it, letting the oxygen fuel the fire that flared inside him. His eyes slammed shut. Dear God, how he wanted her.

But she didn't want him. At least she'd made it clear that she was determined *not* to want him. Now that was an entirely different matter, he thought, intrigued by the notion. He didn't believe her, didn't care what she wanted. He wanted her and his son, and he damned well was going to have them.

She, on the other hand, was convinced that to love him was to expose Andrew to scandal and to deprive Ruth of her only grandson—who, unfortunately, wasn't her grandson, at least not by blood.

He didn't want to hurt anyone, but, dammit, there had to be a way.

So he sat here in his office, feet propped on the corner of his desk, trying to come up with a plan. Trouble was, he didn't have a plan, not even a remote glimmer of a plan.

With unfocused eyes, he stared at the white plaster wall opposite his desk. He kept thinking, turning the problem over and over in his mind.

Sunlight poured through the dirty windows, and he idly watched the dust motes floating in the air. His gaze flicked from one white plaster wall to the other, and he felt confined. He hated offices, hated being cooped up inside. This place was the size of a jail cell, with barely enough room for his desk, a couple of chairs, and a well-used filing cabinet on the back wall, under a faded picture of George Washington.

Why the hell did every government office he'd ever been in have a picture of George Washington? he suddenly wondered, distracted. You'd think there hadn't been another president since.

Dammit, this was getting him nowhere. Sitting up, he let his feet slam to the floor. He toyed with the mail, a month's worth, piled high on his desk. A couple of wanted posters, an official notice of a change in reporting procedures, something that looked suspiciously like an invitation, and a note from the governor.

He slit the white envelope with his pocket knife. The note said the governor had had a change of plans. He was leaving for Los Angeles and would be back next week to attend a social event. He'd want a report then on Luke's progress.

Luke tossed the note down, letting it flutter to a stop on top of the other papers scattered over the smooth walnut surface. He was a lawman, not a paper pusher, he thought irritably. Yeah, that meant he was short on organization and long on action.

Ha! You couldn't prove either, looking at him now.

Well, don't just sit there. Do something.

Yeah, get moving. He always thought better when he was moving, working. *Like maybe a little of the work you were hired to do.*

There was that investigation into city corruption he was suppose to be conducting for the governor, among other things. With a mumbled curse, he set about organizing the office. He took to the files first, straightening, sorting, putting the damned things in alphabetical order. It was menial work that required little brainpower, so he was able to keep trying to come up with a plan to win Rebecca.

He spent the next couple of hours sorting through the reports and such that had mounted up between his predecessor's leaving and Luke's arrival. He made up letters to a half-dozen prospective deputies. He'd never win any awards for penmanship, he thought, glancing at the scrawled names and addresses.

He cleaned out the desk drawers, made lists of things he needed to do and cleared off the top of his desk. By midafternoon, he was finished, and he still didn't have a plan.

He spotted that invitation-looking envelope and thumbed it open. Yup, an invitation, all right. Seemed there was a meeting today at—he glanced at the school clock ticking loudly on the wall over the file cabinet—two o'clock. He was already ten minutes late, *if* he was going to go. A group of business leaders, wanting to talk about the future of the city that they had such a large investment in.

He wasn't much interested in meetings. Right now, he wasn't much interested in anything but Rebecca and his son. A lightness moved through his chest at the thought, making his breathing a little ragged.

It was an incredible feeling to know he had a son. He wasn't a man much given to flights of fancy, but this—this was so incredible he wanted to cry, he wanted to shout every time he thought about it, which was about every other minute.

He reviewed the situation one more time. His goal was very clear. He wanted Rebecca and he wanted his son. They were a package deal, and he absolutely didn't want it any other way.

He walked the two long steps to the window, leaned his shoulder on the smooth wood frame and looked out, only absently aware of Hansen's delivery wagon lumbering up the street toward the corner of Third.

He was thinking. If he tried to take the boy, she'd fight him. He couldn't blame her. What mother would give up her son? Certainly not Rebecca, he realized with more than a little admiration and gratitude.

He ticked off the options. Confrontation, demands, threats? She'd only dig in harder. No, he thought, tapping the invitation on the edge of his hand again. He had to move slowly, carefully. He couldn't afford to make a mistake. A man only got so many chances, and he was well beyond his limit.

Luke glanced down at the invitation he held in his hand and cut a confirming glance at the clock. Two-twenty. Ah, hell, he'd go to the meeting. Maybe by the time it was finished he'd have an idea.

In the past two years, Rebecca Tinsdale had become a power, a force to be reckoned with, in San Francisco politics. With her newspaper, she had been able to shape public awareness and thereby public opinion on candidates and issues, at a time when the other papers in town seemed content to cover national news and ignore the local controversies.

Whether they liked it or not, business leaders and politicians had sought her out, asked for her endorsement or given her little bits of information, in the hope of discrediting their competition.

Rebecca had long since recognized what was happening. While she welcomed these visits, these requests, these bits of gossip, she had always made her own decisions, based on fact and fairness.

It was that trait, perhaps, most of all, that had gained her the respect of so many of San Francisco's community leaders. It was, she suspected, why she'd been invited to this little gathering today, though exactly what the issue was, she wasn't certain.

She was certain that they knew of her son's kidnapping and of his safe return. San Francisco wasn't so big that news didn't travel fast in the right circles.

With Edward at her side, she walked into the grand dining room of the Hotel du Commerce. The men she was there to meet were conspicuously seated around a table for six near a potted palm in a corner.

The rich green carpet cushioned her steps as she and Edward followed the maître d' between tables adorned with white linen and fine silver. She paused twice to speak to people she knew, to accept their good wishes.

The warm afternoon sunlight filtered through the delicate Irish lace curtains that covered the four front windows, opened to coax a breeze. There was none. The room was warm, and she was grateful their table was in a shadowed corner of the room.

"Gentlemen," she said, taking in the three men with one greeting. Edward helped her take off her jacket.

The men stood, almost in unison.

"Mrs. Tinsdale."

"Rebecca."

They were all dark suits and celluloid collars. Except for their ages, they were very much alike, right down to the fashionably short, slicked-down hair.

She allowed Edward to help with her chair.

She sat next to John Riding, with Edward on her left. They chatted amiably while the uniformed waiter took their beverage order, then left, returning shortly with a pot of tea for Rebecca and coffee for the men.

"We'll wait awhile before ordering lunch," Henry Franklin told the waiter, glancing toward the open doorway.

"Expecting someone else?" Rebecca asked as she poured her tea, the rich burgundy liquid filling the translucent white china.

"I had hoped so," Henry muttered.

John Riding spoke up. "Mrs. Tinsdale, we were so sorry to hear about your boy, and relieved when we heard he'd been returned safely."

John was younger than the others. He had inherited money, then and very astutely doubled it. He owned the opera house, and several of the larger stores in town.

"Thank you," Rebecca returned, glancing into his dark brown eyes. She liked John and his wife, and considered them friends.

"It must have been a terrifying experience," Henry Franklin commented. Along with his partner, Logan McCloud, Henry owned the largest fleet in the harbor and controlled most of the city's shipping. He was older than the others, his dark hair already showing signs of gray near his chubby face. His much younger wife had given birth to their first child only a few months ago.

"How is Mrs. Franklin?" Rebecca asked politely. "And the baby?"

"Oh, fine. Fine," he replied with a schoolboy's grin. "Thank you for remembering. And thank you for the lovely gift."

"Of course. Please tell Mrs. Franklin I'll call sometime next week, if she's receiving."

"I'll tell her. I know she'll be glad to—"

Merl Gates cleared his throat, obviously impatient with all this idle chitchat. Rebecca suppressed a small smile. Despite his gruffness, she liked Merl. He was direct to the point of being abrasive, but he was upfront and honest and never reneged on any pledge or promise. "The word around is that the new marshal pulled off a tricky bit of rescuing."

"That's correct," Rebecca returned flatly, not wishing to discuss Luke Scanlin in any way, shape or form. Just the thought of the man, of the power he held over her, made her palms sweat.

"Heard tell there was a shoot-out. One man dead and the other got away. That right?"

"Yes," she said softly, remembering the terror of that night alone in the blackness, with only Luke to help her, to save her. If he hadn't pushed her clear, she might have been killed. If he hadn't risked his life to follow that despicable man, she might never have seen Andrew again.

No wonder her hand shook when she tried to settle her cup back in its delicate saucer.

Edward spoke up for the first time. His slender features were drawn down in concern. "Dearest... Are you all right? All this talk is upsetting you. Perhaps we should go." He made to stand, but hardly got out of his chair before Merl Gates cut in.

"Nonsense. Mrs. Tinsdale is not upset by a little conversation... are you?" It was more an order than a question. She dragged in a couple of breaths and willed her stomach to unclench.

The fear she felt was not so much from what had happened in that alley as from what had come after. She was made more uneasy by the shame and guilt of what had happened later. She had made love to Luke Scanlin. The one thing she'd vowed she'd never do again. He was like a drug in her system. The more she saw him, touched him, heard his voice, the more the addiction grew. And it was a sweet addiction, lush and sensual and carnal.

She had gone to his room, she had sought him out. Somewhere deep in her heart she had known what would happen, had wanted it to happen. And it had. Oh, Lord, it had been more wonderful, more sensual, more erotic, than she'd ever imagined.

Her body pulsed to life, nerves thrumming, and she quelled her rampant emotions. She straightened and squared her shoulders, suddenly afraid these men could sense the erotic path of her thoughts. When she spoke, her voice was shaky even to her own ears, but she toughed it out. "Of course, Mr. Gates. I have nothing to worry about."

Never mind that one word from Luke and her whole life would dissolve faster than snow in the summer. While she didn't think he'd be so cruel as to do it deliberately, he did have a temper, and a word spoken in anger was as destructive as any other.

"What about Brody?" Robert Lister's voice broke into her thoughts, and she glanced up, grateful for this distraction. "Where was he through all this, as if I didn't already know?" He shook his head.

"Captain Brody was..." She sipped her tea and composed her words carefully. After all, Edward was a friend and supporter of Brody's, and she didn't want to have a scene here. "At the marshal's request, he made his men available for a search."

"Ha!" Merl made no secret of his dislike for Brody. "I'll just bet he did. And I'll bet you were glad to see the marshal."

"I—"

"Yes, Becky," a male voice said from very close behind her, making her jump. "Were you glad?"

The sound of his voice went through her like a lightning bolt out of a clear sky. She whirled, her sleeve catching on the tablecloth and making her teacup clatter dangerously in its saucer. Luke stood there, dressed in black trousers and a midnight blue shirt closed at the neck with a string tie. His battered Stetson was in his hand, his black hair ruffled. His eyes were soft, and there was the barest hint of a smile on his lips.

All she could do was stare.

He tore his gaze away and greeted those gathered, then moved around the table, shaking hands.

All the while, he was thinking, *She's here.* Luke had spotted her the minute he walked into the dining room. She was dressed in the latest fashion—he knew that, even if he didn't know the name of the style or the fabric. It was dark green, all flat and fitted in the front. It had a high neck, long sleeves, and a bustle, and so much material in the back that he wondered that she could sit down. As it was, she was perched, sparrowlike, on the edge of the chair.

She wore a saucy little hat—pale silk, he recognized that, with tea roses and ribbons trailing down her back.

She was beautiful—regal, actually. She sure was something. Watching her sitting with these important men, well, it made him proud that Rebecca, his Rebecca, had made such a place for herself with the power men of this town.

And, as he looked at her, an ache welled up in him, from deep in the center of his chest. Had any man ever wanted a woman this much? Had any man ever had as much at stake?

After the introductions, he dragged out the only empty chair, which happened to be opposite her.

"Double bourbon," he told the waiter.

"Little early, isn't it?" she said, before she remembered where she was.

If her rebuke bothered him, he didn't show it. In fact, he smiled—a heart-stopping, lazy smile that made her fingers tremble.

"I'm celebrating," he returned.

Robert spoke up. "Celebrating what?"

Rebecca held her breath.

Luke didn't hesitate. "An addition to my family."

"Congratulations. Your wife have a baby?" Robert replied.

"No" was all he said, and Rebecca released the breath she'd been holding. Was it always going to be like this? Was she going to spend the rest of her life on pins and needles, wondering if he was going to show up, wondering if he was going to say the wrong thing, reveal her indiscretion all those years ago? Was she never to get past that? Was Andrew never to be safe? How long could she live like this?

"Hello there, Ed," Luke said as he accepted his drink from the waiter. He made a slight gesture of salute. "Didn't think I'd be seeing you again so soon."

The other men watched the exchange silently, curiosity apparent in their expressions.

Edward's response was less than friendly. "What are you doing here?"

"I was invited." He sipped his drink, his gaze openly focused on Rebecca. "Sorry to be late. Official business," he lied smoothly. He wasn't about to say he'd been staring out the window for the past several hours trying to figure out a plan to win over the lady sitting four feet away.

Edward's mouth drew into a hard line, and he leaned toward Rebecca in a way that left no doubt he was staking a claim.

Luke hesitated for a fraction of a second, not liking the man's possessiveness.

Merl Gates spoke up. "So you and Mr. Pollard know each other."

"We've met."

The waiter appeared and took their luncheon orders. Rebecca didn't have much of an appetite. She struggled to make small talk over her plate of poached salmon steak and boiled potatoes.

There was a great deal of talk about Luke's part in Andrew's safe return. All those present agreed that Luke was a hero, and quite the topic of conversation these days. There was even the suggestion that he might consider running for political office, that these men would be glad to discuss it further with him.

"I'm not a politician," Luke told them.

"That's exactly why we want you. We're tired of the same handful of men simply moving from one political office to another and back again. Nothing ever changes . . . except for the worst, of course."

Luke shook his head. "Gentlemen, I'm flattered, but—"

"Don't decide now. Think on it, and we'll talk again," Merl said in a no-nonsense tone.

Luke chuckled. "All right, if it'll make you happy, but I don't see any reason why I'll change my mind."

"We'll see," Merl muttered. "We'll see." He forked a bit of chocolate cake into his mouth. "What about it Rebecca? Would the *Times* support the marshal here, if we convinced him to run for some office . . . oh, say, like . . . mayor?" He glanced up, raising his eyebrows.

Before she could answer, Edward cut in. "I hardly think the marshal is interested in being mayor. He's made that quite clear, and I don't think we should force him."

"He's thinking it over," Merl returned, scraping his fork over fine china to get the last bit of frosting.

"You know that I'm running for mayor," Edward said flatly.

Merl feigned surprise. "That's right. I'd forgotten. Well, you haven't declared yet, have you?"

"No."

Merl nodded. "That's why I'd forgotten."

"I had thought I would have your support."

"You'll have the *Times,*" Merl countered.

Rebecca spoke up. "Actually, he doesn't."

Everyone looked surprised. "That is he would, certainly, if... I still owned the *Times*. I don't. I sold it two days ago."

One could have heard a pin drop in the stunned silence.

"But—"

"How? When?"

"Tell 'em why, Becky," Luke said.

"I don't care to explain my reasons. Suffice it to say it's done. The sale is complete."

"Well," Merl muttered. "I had no idea."

Edward cut in. "It's all for the best, dear Rebecca. It's been too much for you for a long time, and you're better off out of it. Why, a woman of your delicate nature in such a harsh business... well, it's just not right."

"Edward, really, I—" she began, then stopped, unwilling to discuss her anger and regret at having to surrender the paper. She would certainly have given all she owned, indeed her very life, to save her son.

"Now, now, dear." He patted her hand. "It's not up to you to save this city. Let Frank Handley and that new syndicate handle things." He cast a smug glance around the table. "They've already promised to support me, and—" he focused his attention on her "—when I'm mayor, you can count on me to see that there are changes made. Of course, as my wife, I'll value your opinion."

Rebecca's head snapped up. "Edward, I—"

"It's all right dear." He patted her hand again. "I know I shouldn't have said anything, but—" he grinned at the others present "—I'm certain I can trust these gentlemen to keep this confidential until we make a formal announcement at the party tomorrow night."

She hadn't promised Edward, and yet, as she looked at Luke, she thought perhaps it was for the best. If she married Edward, quickly, then there would be no discussion. Perhaps Luke would be less inclined to press his paternal rights, perhaps he'd be less likely to come around, perhaps she'd be less likely to ache deep inside every time she saw him. If she gave in to Luke, if she allowed him to tell Andrew that he, not Nathan, was his father, then she would have to tell Ruth that her only grandson, her son's only son, wasn't.

What was to be gained? She would not put her own desire before her son and, yes, even her dear mother-in-law.

No. She would do without Luke. She would marry Edward and be done with it. It would solve a great many problems.

With the thoughts still fresh in her mind, she said, "Yes, it's true. Edward and I are to be married, though no date has been agreed to," she said, as much for Edward as the others, "and we would prefer to make a formal announcement."

"The hell you are," Luke said, his voice menacingly quiet.

The silence was absolute.

The men looked to Rebecca, a look of shock on every face.

Rebecca's head reeled and, before she could speak, Edward spoke up. "Scanlin, how dare you say such a thing! How dare you use such language in front of a lady! You have overstepped yourself, and *we*—" he emphasized the last word "—will not tolerate it." He surged to his feet. With his hand on her elbow, he pulled Rebecca up and grabbed her jacket.

They started away. Rebecca's step faltered ever so slightly. She couldn't help glancing back over her shoulder, willing him to understand, willing him to forgive her, perhaps. She wasn't certain. She only knew that this was the right thing for her to do.

If she hadn't looked back, if she hadn't hesitated, Luke might have believed her. He might have believed that she genuinely cared for the man. But she did look back, and that was enough to tell him that she wasn't certain, that she was remembering all that they had shared—including a son.

And as he watched her walk away, a plan formed in his mind. It was direct. It was forceful. It was seduction—just as lush and carnal and erotic as he could make it.

Because when they were together, when she let her guard down, the fire that flashed between them was hotter than summer lightning, and more dangerous.

"Well, that certainly is a surprise," Merl muttered, meaning more than the announcement. He sank back in his chair.

"Agreed," Robert said, as did John.

Luke sat down again, his gaze still focused on the empty doorway they had disappeared through.

John cleared his throat awkwardly. "I take it, then, Marshal, that you know Mrs. Tinsdale... and don't approve of her plans."

"I know Mrs. Tinsdale very well, and no, I don't approve of her plans."

"Why is that, Marshal? Edward Pollard—"

"Is an egg-sucking—" He broke off, then started again. "He's not the man for her, no matter what she thinks."

John chuckled, and Merl laughed.

"Well, Marshal, I think it's safe to say that we all agree. Mrs. Tinsdale is a fine lady, and Edward is...a royal jackass. He's got political ambitions, you know."

"Yeah, I know. I heard. Did he think Rebecca would use the *Times* to help him?"

"Probably," Robert supplied. "Now that she's sold it... You wouldn't happen to know why she sold it, would you, Marshal?"

"She sold it..." Because I didn't have the ten thousand dollars she needed to save her son, he almost said, but didn't. "Because it was the only way to raise the ransom money in cash in a couple of hours."

"Strange. Why didn't Edward arrange for the money from the bank?"

Luke studied him along the line of his shoulder. "I've been wondering the same thing myself. It's almost as if he wanted her to sell the paper," he mused.

"Well, that's obvious. You heard what he said. A lot of men feel a woman has no place running a business."

"Rebecca isn't just any woman."

"Agreed," John supplied. "She's proven herself to be a capable editor, and her sense of fair play has won her a great deal of respect in this town. When Nathan died, we all thought she'd retire to a quieter life, being a widow and all. We were startled when she took over the *Times*." He lounged back in his chair. "Truthfully, I gave her two months before she packed it in. Damned if she didn't prove me wrong," he added with admiration. "We're going to miss her at the helm of the *Times*. She was doing a lot to bring attention to the corruption in this town."

Robert leaned in. "Well, Edward said some syndicate had taken over. We should talk to them, see how they feel."

Merl shook his head. "Sounds to me like they've already talked to Edward and are prepared to support him."

Luke's brow drew down in a frown. "And you gentlemen aren't?"

"If we could find a better candidate, then, honestly..." Merl lowered his voice so that only those at the table could hear. "We would support someone else."

"Surely there must be someone else in this city to run for mayor," Luke said.

"You know how it is, Marshal. Everyone has an opinion of what's wrong and even what to do about it, but no one wants to give up their precious time to actually do anything about it."

"What about one of you?" Luke asked pointedly.

Merl chuckled. "We are as guilty as everyone else, I'm sorry to admit. We've all got businesses to run, and to be mayor would mean putting those businesses aside for years, if a person was serious about doing a good job. What we need is someone who doesn't have business obligations, someone who's honest, someone who has the best interests of San Francisco in mind." He turned fully toward Luke. "We need someone like you, Marshal."

"Whoa, now, wait a minute there." He held up one hand. "I've got a job, thank you."

"Marshal," Merl returned with a negligent wave of his hand. "You could quit."

Robert piped up. "Yes, why, half the town's talking about the way you saved that boy."

"True," John added eagerly. "Why, Marshal, you're a hero, and heroes make wonderful candidates."

"No thanks," Luke said firmly.

"But, Marshal, we need you. You'd have our full support and...guidance."

"You mean you'd want to tell me what to do," Luke returned bluntly. "When I do a job, gentlemen, I'm my own boss, and—"

Merl cut across his words. "Perfect. Then you'll do it!"

"No. No. And *no,*" Luke said emphatically.

"You said you'd think about it." Merl reminded him. "It would mean settling down. Steady work...for a few years, anyway." He chuckled. "Good salary, house to live in..."

Luke dragged in a long breath and let it out slowly. If he wanted Rebecca, if he wanted his son, he'd need a home and a steady job that didn't mean every time he went out he might not come back. Still, politics?

"Just think about it," John was saying. "Don't make a hasty decision you'll regret later."

Yeah, Luke thought, he knew about hasty decisions.

"Okay," he said. "I'll think on it a couple of days, but I'm not—repeat, not—making any promises."

"Fair enough. We want some serious help with this Barbary Coast situation."

"You're really serious about closing it down."

"Damned straight." Merl helped himself to another cup of coffee from the silver pot on the table. "The Coast is an abomination. We're not so naive as to think that men don't need someplace to let off a little steam. But the Coast is a mess. There's murder going on down there. Prostitution. Men being shanghaied. White slavery. No one's doing anything to stop it. If this city is going to grow and expect the nation to take us seriously, then we've got to clean our own house. We've tried to get the mayor and Brody to listen, but they turn a deaf ear to all our complaints. We're not alone in this. I can list close to thirty civic and community organizations that feel as we do."

"With so much support, why isn't anything happening?"

"Exactly what we're wondering. There's only two things that make any difference—power and money. We decided that with as much money as changes hands down there, money was the key. Short of calling out the vigilantes again like in '56, we decided instead to hire a man to investigate and see what he could come up with. After about two months, he noticed that every Friday night a man appeared and an envelope was exchanged. He followed the man, who seemed to be making rounds. He would go from one place to another, and each time, an envelope was exchanged."

"Who was the man?" Luke's interest was piqued.

"Don't know," John shook his head regretfully. "Our man, Collins, was following the messenger when he was waylaid in an alley and beaten pretty bad. After that, he refused to go back."

"Can't blame him for that," Luke told them.

"Oh, no, we were disappointed, but we understood."

"Did you hire someone else?"

"No. It's difficult to know who to trust. Besides, that was only a week ago, and we haven't had time."

"Collins," Luke repeated thoughtfully.

"Yes. You want his address?"

"Please. I think I'll pay Mr. Collins a visit, and then . . ." He stood, picking up his hat as he did. "I'll think about your suggestion, gentlemen." He took the piece of paper John handed him with Collins's address on it and slid it into his trousers pocket. "I'll be in touch."

With that, he left. Now he had two plans, and they both required some preparation.

Chapter Nineteen

After a jubilant Edward left, Rebecca went into the kitchen and made herself a steaming cup of tea.

"Are you really going to marry him?" Ruth's question was blunt. She joined Rebecca at the kitchen table and helped herself to a cup of tea from the pot.

"Yes, I am."

"Why? You've never seemed interested before. Not in him. Not in anyone."

Rebecca didn't answer for a moment. She looked down into the half-full cup, then up and beyond Ruth, through the kitchen window, to the bare branches of the oak tree outside. "It's time," she said into the cool air.

"One doesn't usually get married on a schedule, or is there a rush of some sort?" They were friends, more than relatives, and they'd shared almost everything since Nathan died. "Is there something you want to tell me?"

She shook her head. "There's nothing to tell. Edward asked, and I said yes."

"He's asked before."

"Yes, I know."

They sat in silence for a long moment before Ruth spoke again. "Of course, all the other times there was no Marshal Scanlin in the picture, so to speak."

"He's not in the picture now."

"Then why the rush? You've turned Edward down at least twice, and then the marshal shows up..." She let the implication hang between them.

"I want to settle down. I want a home for Andrew, with a mother and a... father."

Ruth sipped at her tea. "And you think Edward is the right man for the job?"

Rebecca didn't answer. The silence spoke volumes.

"Does Luke know?" Ruth said very softly.

"Yes. He was at the luncheon today when Edward made the announcement."

Ruth arched one brow. "Did he... say anything?"

"Like what?"

"Oh, I don't know. I thought he might have something to say, some opinion." She toyed with her cup. "He seems to care for you and for Andrew. And Andrew likes him a lot."

"I know."

"I like him, too. He's a good man, Rebecca."

"I thought so, too... once."

"Not now? Why?"

Rebecca pushed the cup and saucer away from her. "I don't know." She looked away. "I knew him a long time ago. We were both different. We were both young and impulsive and—"

"In love," Ruth supplied.

Rebecca's eyes came up slowly to meet Ruth's gaze. "It was a lifetime ago."

"He still loves you, you know. He didn't tell me that, of course, but I've seen the way he looks at you when he thinks no one is watching. He loves you, all right. Take my word for it."

"There've been a lot of mistakes made in the name of love. Promises made and believed, all in the name of love. People get hurt."

"Ah..." Ruth gave a knowing nod. "So you're looking to play it safe, are you?"

"Yes" came her emphatic answer.

"Well, it's up to you, but—" she stood and carried her cup and saucer over to the sink "—I can tell you that anything worth having has a risk attached. I've never seen it otherwise." She put the dishes in the sink and turned back to Rebecca. "I've also never known you to be afraid."

"Maybe you don't know me as well as you think."

"Maybe I know you *better* than you think. As a matter of fact, you'd be surprised at the things I know." She walked out of the kitchen.

Luke was angry when he left the luncheon. He knew exactly what she was trying to do. She was trying to put him off, to put up another barrier between them. She was trying to protect Andrew.

He knew all that, and he was still plain damned angry. No, he wasn't hurt or confused. He was angry—gut-twisting, fist-curling angry. She wasn't going to get away with this. Yes, he knew it would be awkward to tell Andrew the truth. Yes, he knew there were risks, knew there was scandal to be avoided. But this was his son they were talking about, and his woman.

Yes, she was his. He was in love with her, and he damned well wasn't walking away this time. And neither was she. They were going to be together. Luke

Scanlin and Rebecca Parker, the way it should have been.

He made two stops, at the tailor's and the mercantile, before heading for the investigator's office. It took only a few minutes conversation to learn that the pickup man made his rounds every Friday night, late, about one in the morning. The investigator had followed the man as far as Blood Alley, then lost him. That was when the lights had gone out.

Luke got the names of the saloons on the list and a wish for good luck from the man.

Luke sat at a corner table in Fat Daugherty's saloon. He'd been here before, and the bartender seemed to recognize him as a repeat visitor. No one seemed aware of his identity or why he was here.

He played a little poker, coming out only a little the worse for wear after a couple of hours. All the while, he kept his eye on the bar.

By midnight, he relinquished his chair at the poker table and moved to a secluded place in the corner. From there he could watch the doors and the bartender easily.

He was working on beer tonight. This was his fourth mug. It wasn't much better than the rotgut. This looked like horse piss and tasted about the same. But he was less likely to get sick from it or have a hangover tomorrow.

And tomorrow he needed a clear head. Tomorrow he was going to see Rebecca. Only she didn't know it, not yet.

Along about one-fifteen, Luke spotted a man in a black suit striding purposefully to the bar, pushing his way through the crowd as he did. Judging by the bartender's expression, the man wasn't asking for a drink.

The man said something that was impossible to hear over the noise. Grim-faced, the bartender nodded and produced a brown envelope, which he forked over to the man, who tucked it inside his jacket pocket, then turned and left.

Luke got up slowly and made his way through the crowd. By the time he got outside, the man had disappeared. Damn.

Luke scanned the area. Where the hell had he gone so fast? Jesus, a whole night wasted. He was about to step off the sidewalk when a man, the same man, nearly knocked him down as he rode out of the alley and headed north on Grant.

Luke swung up on his horse and took off after him, trying to keep up in the dark streets without getting so close as to be detected. The man zigzagged through residential streets, and twice Luke thought he'd lost him, only to spot him again.

When the man turned onto Broadway, Luke slowed. He saw the man dismounting in front of the only house on the block with lights on. Luke dismounted and, tying his horse, closed the distance on foot.

He recognized the house immediately.

"Son of a bitch," he muttered as he positioned himself in the shadow of a tree across the street.

He watched and waited. Twenty minutes later, the man came out and rode away. Luke crossed the street. The front door was unlocked, and he wasn't inclined to ring the bell.

He let himself in. He knew the way to the office in the back. He walked carefully, noiselessly, stopping in the open doorway.

"Hello, Frank," he said, and the man surged out of his chair.

"What the—" His eyes widened. He took a half step to the right.

"No use, Frank," Luke said, coming into the room and closing the door behind him. "I've seen the money." He took another step closer. "And the man bringing it."

"I don't know what you're talking about. He just owed me some money. There's no law against that."

"Did I forget to mention—" he took another step "—that I know where the man came from, and why he was bringing you the money? I've been following him all night. Let's stop the lying—" he pushed Frank down in his chair "—shall we?" It was an order, not a request. "You and I have some talking to do."

Chapter Twenty

Luke arrived at Rebecca's house about ten Saturday night.

"Mrs. Wheeler," he said as he walked into the entryway. "Nice to see you again."

"And you, too, Marshal," the beaming housekeeper returned. Seeming to know what, or more precisely who, Luke wanted to see, she added, "*Everyone* is in the parlor."

Luke smiled politely.

He took a deep breath and raked his hands through his hair. It was his only outward show of nervousness. All the way over here tonight he'd cautioned himself about propriety, about the need for calm. She would not refuse to talk to him now, not in this crowd, not without making a scene. How would she explain her refusal to talk to the savior of her son?

All he had to do was go up to her and say, "Becky, come with me. We have a few things to discuss." Then they would slip away to another room. A bedroom came quickly to mind, causing the blood in his veins to heat noticeably.

He stood in the doorway a full ten seconds before the whispers started. A handful of the people present knew him, but most did not.

The beautiful women smiled and nodded in a provocative way that a man instinctively understood.

The men he had had lunch with greeted him, bringing with them their wives and others who were anxious to meet San Francisco's newest hero. He politely repeated their names, offered brief answers to their questions or courteous acknowledgment of their praise and compliments as he edged forward.

He scanned the room with interest. And those around him wondered who it was the marshal was searching for so intently.

He hadn't seen Rebecca yet, or Edward, or even Ruth.

The parlor was ablaze with lights, and the carpets had been rolled back, exposing the polished plank floor for those who wished to dance. Those in attendance were bedecked in jewels and satin and evening attire.

A small quartet—harp, cello and two violins—was ensconced near the hearth, playing a demure selection of waltzes. He still hadn't seen Rebecca.

Rebecca saw him, or more precisely sensed his presence, the instant he walked into the parlor. Her first excited thought was that he was wearing evening clothes. It was a major concession on his part.

Wearing all black, with only the white of his high starched collar peeking above his perfectly knotted black tie, he'd never been more handsome, more elegant, she thought. She didn't miss the fact that most of the other women present were noticing the same. Before the thread of jealousy could tighten, she reminded herself that she didn't care if he was the most handsome man in the room. She didn't care that his shoulders were wide and his smile dazzling enough to make her heart take on a shallow, rapid rhythm.

And she especially didn't care why he was here, tonight, now. But he was headed straight for her, and that rapid beating of her heart got faster with each closing step.

Luke's progress was impeded, but not deterred.

"Just part of the job," he said for about the tenth time to another person who offered congratulations on his rescue of Andrew. He spotted Rebecca then, over the heads of the others gathered around.

She was standing with a couple, a tall, dark man and a beautiful blonde. They were chatting, she was smiling up at the man in a way that sparked resentment in Luke, and he didn't even know the man.

If his possessive tenseness showed to those he spoke to, they didn't reveal it. Still, it was several more minutes before he could disengage himself from those wishing to know all the details of what was being referred to as "the great rescue of the decade."

It didn't take long for people to realize that he was a man on a mission and that the object of his quest was the beautiful Rebecca Tinsdale. Most were not surprised. After all, there had been rumors. She had let the man stay in her home—an odd thing for a total stranger, unless they were not strangers, unless they were something . . . more.

Yes, that had been the gossip for days and, judging by the way the marshal was closing in on his prey, it looked very much as if the rumors were correct.

The whispers gathered strength, like a storm cloud building before the first lightning strike. It seemed there was an almost breathless anticipation in the room.

Luke reached her in four more strides. He acknowledged the couple she was with.

The man offered his hand. "Logan McCloud."

"Mr. McCloud," Luke answered, his gaze fixed on Rebecca.

"And my wife, Katherine."

"Ma'am." He spared her a glance. "Rebecca, I want to talk to you." He forced a smile to those present. "Would you excuse us a moment?"

It was a rhetorical question, since he'd already taken her hand in his steely grip and was striding toward the French doors that opened onto the porch and the yard beyond.

Everyone watched them leave, everyone except the one man who might have objected. Edward was in the dining room conducting some campaign business, the old handshake-and-a-promise that was the mark of a politician.

So Luke was able to pull her from the room without confrontation, which was fortunate, some said, for Edward.

White lace curtains fluttered and lapped against his pant leg as he exited keeping her in his tight grip. Outside, he sought the shadows at the farthest end of the porch.

The evening was cool. The breeze off the bay was moist with the threat of fog by morning. Rebecca shivered against the damp chill as the air caressed her bare shoulders and arms.

She was prepared for some demand, some lecture, some order. She was not prepared for him to push her back against the rough cold stone of the house wall and kiss her.

It wasn't a gentle kiss, a sensual invitation to pleasure. No, this was a kiss of possession, one that was fierce and demanding and overpowering.

The fierce relentlessness of his kiss startled her, and she pushed at him, twisting her head as she did, tearing her mouth from his.

"Stop it! What's the matter with you?" she demanded hotly as she continued to shove at the wall of his chest. She expected him to comply, she expected him to realize that they were on her porch, in her home, and that at any moment someone could, and probably would, walk out here and catch them in this compromising position.

He didn't budge. "You, sweetheart. You're what's the matter with me." His voice was a growl, and he leaned into her, trapping her between him and the wall. The instant he saw her, all his caution vanished. He'd been up all night, thinking about her, about her with Edward, about her with any other man. Jealousy overpowered reason and ate at him. His mouth sought hers again.

"I want to go back inside, Luke." She tried to move, but he grabbed her hands and held them outspread against the wall.

His face was a breathless inch from hers. His body pressed hard against hers, so that she felt the stone against her back and the buttons of his vest through the silk bodice of her dress.

"What do you want, Luke?"

"You."

"No!" she snapped, ignoring the fact that she was trapped and powerless to stop him.

His head lifted abruptly, his own anger flashing fire-bright in his eyes. "Tell me, sweetheart, are you and Edward lovers... also?"

It was the "also" that got her, that sent her temper boiling over. She was not willing to give him the satisfaction of knowing that there had been only two men in her life, and only one who haunted her achingly lush dreams. So it was her temper that made her say, "Yes."

It wasn't the answer he wanted, needed. His eyes turned as cold and hard as flint. "You're lying."

"Am I?" she taunted.

"You and that weasel?" he returned in a mocking tone.

"Think what you will," she countered, and tried to twist free of him.

"I think," he started softly, "he doesn't make your heart beat faster. He doesn't caress your skin the way I do, touching all the soft, sensitive places that make you shudder. He doesn't know how to kiss the edge of your ear or the tips of your breasts. He doesn't make you moan in surrender when he's inside you."

"Why, you— How dare you say such vile, disgusting—"

"There's nothing vile or disgusting about it, except in your own frightened little mind. I'm in your blood and you're in mine, and the sooner you admit it the better off we'll both be."

She shook her head in denial. "No." Her voice was shaky. "It's not true."

"Isn't it?" he murmured, and slowly dipped his head and kissed her. Not on the lips, but on the delicate spot behind her ear. His lips were warm and teasing, making her shudder as delicious shivers skipped up the backs of her legs.

When he lifted his head this time, he smiled. It was a slow, lush smile, with a touch of smugness that was more roguish than enraging.

"You and I were meant to be together." His mouth covered hers in a passionate kiss, full of desire and the knowledge that comes from shared intimacy. Her body flared to life like a candle in a dark room. Her fingers trembled with the sudden need to touch him.

He leaned into her, letting her feel the weight of his body against hers while he looped her arms around his neck. Pulling her more fully into his embrace, he deepened the kiss, his mouth slanting one way, then the other, tasting, testing, promising. Willing her to know he loved her. Willing her to admit she loved him, too.

He kissed her cheek and her brow and the slender bridge of her nose. He laved at her ear with the tip of his tongue. It was seduction he was working and, fair or unfair, it was his only hope.

His hands splayed upward, his fingers caressing the smoothness of her bare flesh above the silk edge of her dress. Muscles tensed, and blood drummed hot and hurried in his body.

Rebecca's eyes drifted closed against the magic he was working on her. He slid the lace ruffles from her shoulders, kissing and licking the heated flesh there before his hand brushed, feather-light, over her breasts, where they strained against the confines of her dress.

She stood very still beneath his hands, telling herself that resistance was useless, and hating the fact that her body warmed and opened to him in ways so familiar yet so unnerving.

He cupped her breast through the fabric, his thumbs rubbing with aching gentleness, enticing her nipples to peak. His black eyes were bright with desire.

"Say it, Becky," he murmured as he nipped, then kissed, the exposed skin of her shoulder. "Say you feel the magic."

"No," she managed, her voice shaky.

"No?" he repeated in a gentle tone, then took her mouth in his again, his tongue dipping inside to tease the tender flesh there, to dance and flutter and ignite the ancient pulsing deep within her.

He swayed back and forth against her, letting her feel his arousal, letting her know what being with her did to him.

It was then that she felt the chill of the night air on her legs, and realized with stark terror that he'd hiked up the hem of her dress. She shoved at his chest. He didn't budge. She felt his hand on her thigh, the warmth of his touch penetrating the thin lawn of her pantalets. His hand glided around to cup her buttocks.

Restless, tense, he moved against her, his hand stroking her thigh. She was shamed to realize she was helpless against his sensual onslaught, and she felt his fingers slip between her legs.

Oh, Lord, this couldn't be happening, but it was. She was powerless to stop him, didn't want to stop him. The nearness of him, his touch, aroused her passion and drowned out all logic. Her body heated in eager anticipation of the familiar pleasure he offered. Moisture gathered at the juncture of her legs, and she stood motionless under his hands.

Logic demanded that she resist the building waves of sensation. But the flame of desire was already surging in her blood, skimming over her skin like a fast-moving prairie fire, engulfing all in its path.

He kissed and teased and touched her in all the heated, urgent places, all the places that set the languid need spiraling up in her. She steeled herself against his touch, refusing to acknowledge the rapture his gently stroking fingers caused as they found the opening in her pantalets and slid easily into her wet, aching core. Her breath caught as he touched her deep, deep inside. Pleasure, raw and carnal, uncoiled and shot upward, making her groan, making her dig her fingers into his shoulders for support, crushing the fine wool of his jacket as she did.

"I want you," he groaned against the delicate curve of her ear, his breath warm and wet.

He stilled and glanced at the open doorway nearby. Had he heard voices? Releasing her, he stepped around to protect her, to conceal them both in the shadows.

"Luke, please..." she begged. She had heard the voices also.

"I thought I was, Princess," he murmured, and moved her back a few steps, to the farthest corner of the porch.

She was terrified and aroused and horrified by this wanton desire that overcame all reason, that made her stay here with him in the rich darkness.

"Rebecca..." he groaned as his mouth ate at hers. His hands frantically traveled from shoulder to waist and lower, pulling up her dress again.

"You can't..."

"I am," he countered, already unbuttoning his trousers. Hooking his hands under her arms, he lifted her and, bending slightly, he entered her, his driving need peaking more rapidly than he'd expected. Back and shoulder muscles strained and knotted as he held her securely. He moved in a rhythm their bodies recognized. Desire drove him, drove each deep thrust, each heated stroke.

Voices reached her ears from somewhere nearby. The very real danger only added to the carnal pleasure that he was creating in her.

His mouth closed over hers, his tongue mimicking the rhythm of his body in hers, and suddenly thought was lost, her body craving the release that only he could offer. She clung to him, clawed at him, moved on him, demanding that he fill her completely, while her body melted lushly around the hard, pulsing length of him.

"That's it, Becky. Give in to it. Let it happen."

Encouraged by his words, and the thrusting motion of his body, she pressed in tighter. It seemed natural to wrap her legs around his waist.

Luke slid his hands under her bottom and turned so that he leaned against the wall and supported her full weight in his cupped hands. Their position more secure, he glided into her again, more slowly this time, feeling her pulse and constrict around him in a way that sent his heart rate soaring faster than a comet.

Rebecca whimpered as the pleasure washed over her, as he filled her completely, touching her deep inside and sending shock waves of passion washing over her.

Luke barely breathed, barely moved, his body focused on the luxury of this sensation. Her legs rode high on his hips, and he penetrated her more deeply than ever before.

Though it was sheer madness to cling to him, to give herself over to him, Rebecca was inundated by the extravagant enchantment, the urgent desire, that was melting her reason as fast as it was liquefying her body.

What was it about him that made her risk all for him? But as he kissed and laved at her mouth, as he moved with sure and certain strokes inside her, she knew the answer. She loved him, she realized as the first tiny tremblings of the ultimate bliss convulsed within her. Another heartbeat, another powerful stroke, and she cried out at the peaking desire. Luke quickly covered her mouth with his, absorbing the pleasure-driven cry, and continued the demanding rhythm.

"I love to hear you scream, Princess, but this is not the place. We wouldn't want anyone to come to see what the commotion was."

"There wouldn't be a—" He moved inside her, and she gasped as pulsing need surged through her and the incredible flutters started again. No, she thought, this couldn't be happening. The ache coiled tight inside her, and she knew, God help her, that it was happening.

She struggled against the impending climax, determined to restrain herself, to somehow deprive him of his control. But her body would not still, and tingling nerves and soul-searing passion would not relent.

Aching, tensing, she moved faster and harder, seeking release from this pleasurable pain. Her body reached for the rapture it knew was near. She climaxed in a heart-pounding liquid rush. Feeling her release, responding to her sensual delights, Luke gave in to his own need and slid into her once more. At the same instant, Rebecca kissed him, her mouth soft and inviting against his, and she absorbed his groan as she felt him pour his shuddering release into her throbbing channel.

It was a perfect union, one of pleasure given and taken, lush and erotic and equal.

Minutes later, he was buttoning his trousers and adjusting his shirt and coat. She was straightening the green silk of her dress, pushing at the errant curls that had come loose to drape down her back.

Rebecca stood in ecstatic shock and base anger. Furious at him, and angrier at herself for responding to him so easily, so wantonly.

As she looked at him, she wanted to strike out, to deny what had happened, to rant and scream in indignation, but how could she? There was no turning back this time, no pretense of denial. And so, more ashamed than she'd ever been, she turned away.

His voice stopped her. "Marry me."

She stood there, her back to him. She dragged in a lungful of cool night air. "Eight years ago I would have given anything to hear those words from you."

"And now?"

She refused to face him. "Now, it's too late."

"Why?" He came around to face her. "Why is it too late? We can be married. We can be a family."

She shook her head resolutely.

"I want you." He took her shoulders in his grip. "I want my son."

"How will I explain to Andrew that the man he thinks is his father, isn't?"

"I don't know. We'll find a way."

"How?"

"I don't know. I don't care. All I know is that I want you—both of you."

"But I do care. If I marry you, everyone will know what I did—what we did. They'll know that Andrew is illegitimate."

"He's not illegitimate."

"Only because Nathan married me when he knew I was pregnant."

"Dammit, I know that. I can't change it. I would if I could, God knows, but I can't. I'm grateful to the man. What do you want me to do?"

"I want you to leave me alone. I want you to leave Andrew alone."

"No. You're mine. Both of you belong to me."

"You gave up any claims when you left."

"The hell I did."

"We're not property. We're not some saddle gear you forgot and now have come back for. There are people involved here, scandal to be considered."

"We'll move."

"Oh, move. Just like that. Pack everything up and move. To where?"

"How do I know? Texas, Colorado—I don't much care."

"And that's the trouble, Luke. You don't care about anyone or anything but yourself and what you want. You were selfish enough to walk out eight years ago with never a backward glance, and now you're being just as selfish because you've decided that you want a family."

"Not 'a family.' I want *my* family."

"We don't belong to you, no matter what you think."

"I think I just proved you wrong."

"That was lust."

"The hell it was."

"It was. And I'm not risking my life and Andrew's and Ruth's to satisfy your selfishness *or* my lust.

"What's Ruth got to do with this?"

"She's his grandmother. The only grandmother he's ever had. You want me to tear them apart?"

"She'd understand."

"Would she? Do you want to tell her? Do you want to say, 'Pardon me, your only grandchild isn't your grandchild at all, and we're leaving to avoid the scandal? Hope you'll be fine all alone for the rest of your life?' "

"For chrissakes, Rebecca, I wouldn't be that cold."

"Maybe not, but any way you slice it, it's the same thing. I won't do it. I owe her more than I could ever repay. She was there for me when I had *no one else,* and I won't repay her like this."

"And what am I supposed to do? Pretend I don't have a son?"

"Why not? Until a few days ago, you weren't very interested."

"Until a few days ago, I didn't know."

"But you could have, Luke, if you'd cared about anyone but yourself." She took a step. "Goodbye Luke," she said quietly, and walked away.

He watched her go, and a pain swept over him, a longing, so intense that he had to steel himself or be crushed by it. He thought to call out to her. To tell her that she was right, that he had been selfish, then and now. That he loved her so damned much that he thought the rest of his life would be no more than a shell without her and Andrew to fill it. But at the last second, just before she turned the corner, he stopped and realized he'd said it all, and it wasn't enough.

Hands braced on the porch rail, fingers curled white-knuckle tight against the painted wood, he faced the night, a night as black and bleak as he felt.

It was then that he heard the unmistakable click of a gun hammer being pulled back. In the next second, a raspy male voice snarled, "I've been looking for you, Scanlin."

A soft breeze stirred the bushes beyond the porch. Luke didn't move. He strained to see into the darkness to find the source of the voice.

"Get the hell down here," the voice ordered rough and furious.

Luke straightened, all his senses tuned and focused on the man who stepped out of the bushes. He was dressed in rumpled black, his hair was slicked back, his face was pale.

"Riggs," Luke muttered. "I thought..."

"What? You killed me? Not hardly. But you did kill my brother, you son of a bitch, and I intend to even the score."

As discreetly as possible, Luke edged his hand toward the opening of his coat, and the gun tucked in his shoulder holster.

"Hold it," Riggs snarled, spotting the motion.

Luke froze.

"Don't even try. I'd hate to splatter your brains all over that nice porch. Now take it out and toss it over here. Come on." He gestured with the gun he held.

Reluctantly Luke obliged, all the while watching

the man, waiting for an opening, a chance to do... something other than stand here and be gunned down.

"What now?"

"Now, you and me is gonna take a little walk away from all these witnesses. Like I said, we got us some unfinished business."

Luke glanced toward the open doorway. Rebecca was in there. He hoped to hell she didn't walk out here now.

"Come on. Come on," the gunman said, waving his gun for emphasis again.

"All right, Riggs." Luke started toward the stairs near the doorway.

"Don't try nothin'," the man warned. "I don't wanna hurt nobody else, but I will if you make me."

Luke nodded. The odds were all in the man's favor. If Luke went with him, he was a dead man. The man was advancing, matching Luke step for step. At the top of the porch stairs, Luke stopped still.

There was no way he was going with this guy, and there was no way he could let him get away and possibly come back for Rebecca or Andrew.

A round of sudden laughter erupted from the house. The gunman glanced away for a split second. It was all the time Luke needed. He hurled himself at Riggs, slamming into him, and they hit the ground with a bone-jarring thud. The gun arched through the air and landed a few feet away in the grass.

Luke scrambled to his feet. He started for the gun. Riggs was up, and he grabbed Luke from behind. Luke slammed his elbow into Riggs's ribs. The man cried out, and Luke was able to break free and turn.

"You son of a bitch!" Riggs shouted, loud enough that those inside the house heard and came outside.

"What's going on?" someone said.

Luke was a little too busy to answer. In complete silence, they faced each other. Luke was between Riggs and the gun. He knew that if he tried to turn, Riggs would be on top of him. He also knew that there was no way Riggs could get the gun, not without going through him.

"Give it up, Riggs," Luke told him as the two of them squared off against each other.

Riggs charged at Luke. Head down, he rammed into Luke's midsection. Air whooshed out of Luke's lungs, and he landed on his knees. He grabbed hold of Riggs's legs as he lunged for the gun.

The man sprawled facedown in the grass, his hand outstretched. When he rolled over, there was a gun in his hand.

Luke threw himself on top of Riggs, pinning his body down as he reached for his gun hand. They rolled back and forth, Riggs trying to free himself from Luke's weight, Luke determined to wrench the gun free.

Riggs groaned as he managed to work the gun closer and closer to their bodies, murderous intent in his eyes. Suddenly there was a shot, and then another.

More people rushed out from the party. Men scrambled down the stairs and rushed toward the two men lying still and lifeless on the lawn.

A steady trickle of blood formed a pool against the side of the men.

"Marshal, are you all right?"

Luke felt a hand on his shoulder, then another, felt someone helping him up. His breathing was ragged, and the burning pain in his side hurt like hell.

"I—" He sagged to sit on the ground, and his hand instinctively sought the .45, lying nearby.

"Someone send for the doctor!" a man called. He pulled a handkerchief from his pocket and pushed it against the spreading red stain on Luke's white dress shirt.

It took only a glance to see that Riggs was dead, shot through the heart.

"What happened?" the man nearest was saying.

"One of the... kidnappers..." Luke managed. Every breath hurt, and talking hurt more. "Damn," he muttered as he looked down to check the flow of blood.

"The doctor's on his way," the man said. "Let's get you—"

"Luke!"

It was Rebecca's voice. Rebecca's scream. In an instant she was there, kneeling in the bloodstained dirt beside him.

"Oh, my God!" Frantically she touched his face, his shoulders. She spotted the blood. "Are you all right?"

He looked at her kneeling in the dirt beside him, her face a ghostly white, her hands clutching at him. "I'm all right."

"You're not all right. Oh, God, you could have been killed!" she ranted. Then, in front of everyone, she pulled him into her arms and kissed him.

He didn't move, didn't dare to.

"Becky, honey, you're, uh, getting your dress all messed up."

"I don't give a damn about the dress. Are you all right?"

"I'm okay."

She insisted on helping him to his feet.

"Just took a chunk outa my side, is all, and—"

He was struggling to his feet when suddenly a hand grasped Luke's shoulder and, taken unawares, he was jerked back, releasing Rebecca.

"Get away from her!"

Edward stood there, his face mottled with rage. "What the hell is going on?"

Luke had his arm draped around Rebecca's shoulders and was letting her pretend she was actually holding him up. God, it was pathetic. He was shot and bleeding, and all he could think about was keeping his arm around her, feeling her body next to his.

Edward grabbed Rebecca by the wrist, his grip surprisingly tight, and pulled her away. Rebecca winced as his fingers dug into the tender flesh of her wrist. She managed to twist free.

"Edward," she cried, "for heaven's sake, what's wrong with you? Luke's been hurt, can't you see that? This man was one of the kidnappers, and he tried to..." Tears threatened at the realization that it could be Luke lying there in a pool of blood. "Tried to kill Luke, and—"

"Luke," Edward snarled. "Luke this and Luke that. All I hear these days is Luke Scanlin's name. I'm sick of it, and I'm sick of you, Scanlin. You're interfering in my business."

Luke braced his feet. A couple of men stepped up, as though to help him, but he waved them away. "Well, Ed, you're right about that. I have been interfering in your business, but you see, I'm gonna marry Rebecca—"

"The hell you are!"

Luke smiled, a slow predatory smile. "Who's gonna stop me? You?"

"Edward! Please! He's hurt."

Ruth rushed to Rebecca's side, Andrew hot on her heels. "What going on?" Ruth asked, sizing up the situation in a glance. She held Andrew tightly against her side, trying to cover his face with her skirt to prevent him from seeing such a grisly sight.

Andrew was having none of it. "What happened? Who hurt the marshal? Is that man dead, Grandma?"

"Shh, Andrew," she said gently. "Go back in the house," she told him, but he didn't move.

Edward's eyes glittered with rage. "All right, Scanlin. I don't care if you're a marshal. I don't care if you're God Almighty. I've had enough of your insults."

Rebecca tried again. "Edward, this is hardly the time." Her voice was firm and low as she tried to defuse the situation before someone said the wrong thing.

But Edward wasn't listening. Unbelievably, he took a menacing half step toward Luke, who never moved, just stood there looking calm and relaxed, as though it were the most natural thing in the world for him to be bleeding.

"Don't even try it, Ed. Bad as this hurts, I can kill you and not even think twice about it." The .45 was still in his blood-soaked hand.

No one moved.

Rebecca's hand flew to her throat. "Luke!"

Edward's hand clenched into fists, and he took another step. "You don't scare me, Scanlin." His eyes locked with Luke's as he continued to advance.

Violence, like a strong electrical current, flashed between the two men. Rebecca had never seen Edward behave in such a manner.

Luke's voice was low, and deadly cold. "Well, I oughta scare you, Ed. I oughta scare the hell outa you. You see, I had a nice long chat with your lawyer, Frank Handley, this afternoon."

Edward froze.

Confused, and more than a little angry, Rebecca shouldered into the middle. Eyes blazing, she pushed at one, then the other. "Are you both out of your minds?" Her tone was incredulous. "Stop this at once, do you hear me? Luke, we've got to get you inside."

"Rebecca, stay out of this," Luke ordered hotly. His gaze riveted her. "It's between me and—"

"No!" she shouted.

"Becky, get the hell out of the way! Old Ed here has something in his craw, so let's have at it. Go on, Ed." Luke motioned with his arm, and was rewarded with a stabbing pain through the ribs. Clenching his jaw, he continued, "Tell everyone about what you and Frank have been up to."

Edward straightened. "Don't try to change the subject, Scanlin," he countered smoothly.

Luke didn't miss the furtive way Edward scanned the crowd. *There's no escape this time, Ed.* He kept his pose calm. "I'm not changing the subject, Ed. Go on and tell these folks how Frank's been fronting for you all these months."

"Fronting?" Rebecca questioned quietly.

The other men echoed her.

"Yeah," Luke continued, shifting his weight to his other leg. He could feel the blood oozing down his side, along his leg under his trousers. He knew he was losing a lot of blood, but he'd be damned if he'd pack it in now. Not now!

Gritting his teeth, he said, "I had a nice long talk with Frank. Seems he wasn't ready to go to jail for kidnapping and bribery and falsifying government records, among other things. Seems Frank has been working for Ed here."

Edward took a carefully measured step backward, and several men closed in around him cutting, off any retreat.

"Go on, Marshal," Merl Gates said.

"Well, it seems that Ed here has been extorting money from the saloon and gambling-hall owners down on the Coast, in exchange for protection. He made sure that licenses were granted and renewed, and that new licenses were approved. He even made sure that the police weren't too interested in what happened down there."

Shock and disbelief colored Rebecca's face as she turned to face him. The night was deadly quiet.

"It's a lie," Edward shouted defiantly. "It's all a lie. Scanlin's trying to win you over, Rebecca. Surely you can see that!"

Rebecca didn't say a word.

Luke did. "Shall I have Frank brought around? He's over at the hotel. One of my deputies is keeping him company."

Never taking her eyes from Edward, Rebecca said, "There must be some mistake."

Luke shook his head. "Sorry, Becky. There's no mistake, and I'm afraid it gets worse."

Her eyes flew to Luke. "Worse?" She felt cold inside.

"Frank tells me that it was Edward who was behind Andrew's kidnapping. He did it to get control of the paper—and, I suspect, of you."

"Oh, no. It can't . . . be." She had to grip herself to stop the sudden trembling, to control the sickening feeling deep in the pit of her stomach.

Every man there was silent, watching, waiting.

"It's a lie!" Edward shouted. "There's no proof."

"Well, Ed, I think we'll let a jury decide that. We'll see if they believe you or Frank Handley. I think when we check on who really owns that syndicate that bought the *Times,* we'll find your name."

Edward tried to turn and push through the crowd, but they stopped him cold. The sudden sharp sound of a gun being cocked, stilled his struggle.

Luke's voice cut through the night like a knife. "Mister, you better hope those men hold on to you, 'cause if they don't, then I'll be real happy to blow you in half for what you've done to Rebecca."

The men pushed in. "We've got him, Marshal, don't you worry," someone said.

"And we'll see he gets locked up nice and tight, and not in the city jail, either," Merl added triumphantly as they dragged Edward away.

Luke watched Rebecca. Watched the emotions play over her face. "I'm sorry, Becky. I didn't mean for you to find out like this. I mean, there's no easy way... It's just that . . ." Damn.

"Marshal!" Andrew rushed in, his face pale, his chin quivering. "Are you dying?"

"No, Andrew," Luke assured him. His fist curled against the pain, and he dropped down on one knee to look the child in the eye. He wanted to reassure him.

"Are you hurt bad?" Andrew's voice was quiet.

"Not too bad," Luke told him.

"My mom can make a bandage." His face was solemn. "She's real good at fixing things."

"I don't think she can fix this, Andrew," he said, and Rebecca knew he meant more than his side.

Ruth stepped forward. "Rebecca," she said firmly. "For heaven's sake, you better haul off and marry the man before he up and bleeds to death."

Rebecca didn't move. "I..." Guilt and regret tore at her. She wanted to say something, to explain, but how? Even after all of this, nothing had changed.

Ruth looked at Rebecca, her gentle eyes searching her daughter-in-law's, and she said, "Andrew needs his father."

"Ruth, I..." She actually thought to deny it, her love for Ruth was so great, as was her respect for Nathan, and her gratitude for all he'd done for her.

As though sensing her thoughts, Ruth touched her hand and gave a knowing smile.

"How did you know?" Rebecca asked on a thready whisper, feeling all her defenses dissolve.

Ruth spoke quietly, so that Andrew would not hear. "I've always suspected. When I saw them together, playing baseball..." She cut them a glance. "Well, just look at them."

Rebecca did. The men she loved, together. Her heart slammed hard against her ribs. Joy bubbled up in her. Could this be happening? Could all her fears be so easily dissolved?

What are you waiting for?

She hugged Ruth and then rushed to Luke. He stood and opened his arms to her.

He kissed her. When he looked up, he said gently, "I love you, Becky. I'll never leave you. Marry me."

There. He'd said it all. It was all he had to offer. It was everything he was. He held his breath.

Andrew tugged on his pant leg, and Luke looked down. "Sir, are you gonna be my father?"

Luke glanced at Rebecca, then back to Andrew. "Would you like me to be your father, Andrew?"

"Oh, yes, sir." The boy beamed.

"Then, Andrew—" his tone was rough with emotion "—I am your father." It was enough, Luke realized.

Luke's questioning gaze flicked to Rebecca. "You haven't said yes," he pointed out.

She hesitated long enough to look at Ruth, standing close by. At her confirming nod, she grinned and swiped at the tears streaming down her cheeks. "Yes," she managed, though her voice cracked with the pure joy of loving him.

A wicked glint flashed in his eyes. "Yes, and..."

"I love you," she told him, knowing it was true. She'd always loved him. Luke was her destiny.

He came to her then and pulled her more tightly into his embrace. She loved him. He'd heard the words he'd longed for, prayed for. He wanted to hold her now, and tomorrow, and all the tomorrows that God would give him.

Still in his embrace, he smiled down at her and said, "I think I know where there's a newspaper for sale."

She grinned back. "And I think I know who it will endorse for mayor."

"I love you." He hugged her to him fiercely, then hoisted Andrew up in his arms. "I love you both."

* * * * *

OFFICIAL RULES

FLYAWAY VACATION SWEEPSTAKES 3449

NO PURCHASE OR OBLIGATION NECESSARY

Three Harlequin Reader Service 1995 shipments will contain respectively, coupons for entry into three different prize drawings, one for a trip for two to San Francisco, another for a trip for two to Las Vegas and the third for a trip for two to Orlando, Florida. To enter any drawing using an Entry Coupon, simply complete and mail according to directions.

There is no obligation to continue using the Reader Service to enter and be eligible for any prize drawing. You may also enter any drawing by hand printing the words "Flyaway Vacation," your name and address on a 3"x5" card and the destination of the prize you wish that entry to be considered for (i.e., San Francisco trip, Las Vegas trip or Orlando trip). Send your 3"x5" entries via first-class mail (limit: one entry per envelope) to: Flyaway Vacation Sweepstakes 3449, c/o Prize Destination you wish that entry to be considered for, P.O. Box 1315, Buffalo, NY 14269-1315, USA or P.O. Box 610, Fort Erie, Ontario L2A 5X3, Canada.

To be eligible for the San Francisco trip, entries must be received by 5/30/95; for the Las Vegas trip, 7/30/95; and for the Orlando trip, 9/30/95.

Winners will be determined in random drawings conducted under the supervision of D.L. Blair, Inc., an independent judging organization whose decisions are final, from among all eligible entries received for that drawing. San Francisco trip prize includes round-trip airfare for two, 4-day/3-night weekend accommodations at a first-class hotel, and $500 in cash (trip must be taken between 7/30/95—7/30/96, approximate prize value—$3,500); Las Vegas trip includes round-trip airfare for two, 4-day/3-night weekend accommodations at a first-class hotel, and $500 in cash (trip must be taken between 9/30/95—9/30/96, approximate prize value—$3,500); Orlando trip includes round-trip airfare for two, 4-day/3-night weekend accommodations at a first-class hotel, and $500 in cash (trip must be taken between 11/30/95—11/30/96, approximate prize value—$3,500). All travelers must sign and return a Release of Liability prior to travel. Hotel accommodations and flights are subject to accommodation and schedule availability. Sweepstakes open to residents of the U.S. (except Puerto Rico) and Canada, 18 years of age or older. Employees and immediate family members of Harlequin Enterprises, Ltd., D.L. Blair, Inc., their affiliates, subsidiaries and all other agencies, entities and persons connected with the use, marketing or conduct of this sweepstakes are not eligible. Odds of winning a prize are dependent upon the number of eligible entries received for that drawing. Prize drawing and winner notification for each drawing will occur no later than 15 days after deadline for entry eligibility for that drawing. Limit: one prize to an individual, family or organization. All applicable laws and regulations apply. Sweepstakes offer void wherever prohibited by law. Any litigation within the province of Quebec respecting the conduct and awarding of the prizes in this sweepstakes must be submitted to the Regies des loteries et Courses du Quebec. In order to win a prize, residents of Canada will be required to correctly answer a time-limited arithmetical skill-testing question. Value of prizes are in U.S. currency.

Winners will be obligated to sign and return an Affidavit of Eligibility within 30 days of notification. In the event of noncompliance within this time period, prize may not be awarded. If any prize or prize notification is returned as undeliverable, that prize will not be awarded. By acceptance of a prize, winner consents to use of his/her name, photograph or other likeness for purposes of advertising, trade and promotion on behalf of Harlequin Enterprises, Ltd., without further compensation, unless prohibited by law.

For the names of prizewinners (available after 12/31/95), send a self-addressed, stamped envelope to: Flyaway Vacation Sweepstakes 3449 Winners, P.O. Box 4200, Blair, NE 68009.

RVC KAL